P9-DNO-797

BRIGHTNESS REEF

Book One of a New Uplift Trilogy

David Brin

SPECTRA ™

BANTAM BOOKS
New York   Toronto   London
Sydney   Auckland

BRIGHTNESS REEF
A Bantam Spectra Book

PUBLISHING HISTORY
Bantam hardcover edition / October 1995
Bantam mass market edition / November 1996

SPECTRA and the portrayal of a boxed ''s''
are trademarks of Bantam Books, a division of
Bantam Doubleday Dell Publishing Group, Inc.

ISBN 0-553-57330-6

Published simultaneously in the United States and Canada

Bantam Books are published by Bantam Books, a division of Bantam
Doubleday Dell Publishing Group, Inc. Its trademark, consisting of the
words ''Bantam Books'' and the portrayal of a rooster, is Registered in
U.S. Patent and Trademark Office and in other countries. Marca Regis-
trada. Bantam Books, 1540 Broadway, New York, New York 10036.

PRINTED IN THE UNITED STATES OF AMERICA

OPM   10 9 8 7 6 5 4

to Herbert H. Brin
Poet, journalist, and
lifelong champion of justice

BRIGHTNESS REEF

Asx

I must ask your permission. You, my rings, my diverse selves.

Vote now! Shall i speak for all of us to the outer world? Shall we join, once more, to become Asx?

That is the name used by humans, qheuens, and other beings, when they address this stack of circles. By that name, this coalition of plump, traeki rings was elected a sage of the Commons, respected and revered, sitting in judgment on members of all six exile races.

By that name—Asx—we are called upon to tell tales. Is it agreed?

Then Asx now bears witness . . . to events we endured, and those relayed by others. "I" will tell it, as if this stack were mad enough to face the world with but a single mind.

Asx brews this tale. Stroke its waxy trails. Feel the story-scent swirl.

There is no better one i have to tell.

Prelude

PAIN IS THE STITCHING HOLDING HIM TO-gether . . . or else, like a chewed-up doll or a bro-ken toy, he would have unraveled by now, lain his splintered joins amid the mucky reeds, and vanished into time.

Mud covers him from head to toe, turning pale where sunlight dries a jigsaw of crumbly plates, lighter than his dusky skin. These dress his nakedness more loyally than the charred garments that fell away like soot after his panicky escape from fire. The coating slakes his scalding agony, so the muted torment grows almost companion-able, like a garrulous rider that his body hauls through an endless, sucking marsh.

A kind of music seems to surround him, a troubling ballad of scrapes and burns. An opus of trauma and shock.

Striking a woeful cadenza is the *hole* in the side of his head.

Just once, he put a hand to the gaping wound. Finger-tips, expecting to be stopped by skin and bone, kept going horribly inward, until some faraway instinct made him shudder and withdraw. It was too much to fathom, a loss he could not comprehend.

Loss of *ability* to comprehend . . .

The mud slurps greedily, dragging at every footstep. He has to bend and clamber to get through another blockade of crisscrossing branches, webbed with red or yellow throbbing veins. Caught amid them are bits of glassy brick or pitted metal, stained by age and acid juices. He avoids these spots, recalling dimly that once he had known good reasons to keep away.

Once, he had known lots of things.

Under the oily water, a hidden vine snags his foot, tripping him into the mire. Floundering, he barely manages to keep his head up, coughing and gagging. His body quivers as he struggles back to his feet, then starts slogging forward again, completely drained.

Another fall could mean the end.

While his legs move on by obstinate habit, the accompanying pain recites a many-part fugue, raw and grating, cruel without words. The sole sense that seems intact, after the abuse of plummet, crash, and fire, is *smell*. He has no direction or goal, but the combined stench of boiling fuel and his own singed flesh help drive him on, shambling, stooping, clambering and stumbling forward until the thorn-brake finally thins.

Suddenly, the vines are gone. Instead a swamp sprawls ahead—dotted by strange trees with arching, spiral roots. Dismay clouds his mind as he notes—the water is growing deeper. Soon the endless morass will reach to his armpits, then higher.

Soon he will die.

Even the pain seems to agree. It eases, as if sensing the futility of haranguing a dead man. He straightens from a buckled crouch for the first time since tumbling from the wreckage, writhing and on fire. Shuffling on the slippery muck, he turns a slow circle . . .

. . . and suddenly confronts a pair of *eyes,* watching him from the branches of the nearest tree. Eyes set above a stubby jaw with needle teeth. Like a tiny dolphin, he thinks—a *furry* dolphin, with short, wiry legs . . . and forward-looking eyes . . . and ears. . . .

Well, perhaps a dolphin *was* a bad comparison. He isn't thinking at his best, right now. Still, surprise jars loose an association. Down some remnant pathway spills a relic that becomes almost a word.

"Ty . . . Ty . . ." He tries swallowing. "Ty—Ty—t-t-t—"

The creature tips its head to regard him with interest, edging closer on the branch as he stumbles toward it, arms outstretched—

Abruptly, its concentration breaks. The beast looks up toward a sound.

A liquid splash . . . followed by another, then more, repeating in a purposeful tempo, drawing rhythmically nearer. Swish and splash, swish and splash. The sleek-furred creature squints past him, then grunts a small disappointed sigh. In a blur, it whirls and vanishes into the queer-shaped leaves.

He lifts a hand, urging it to stay. But he cannot find the words. No utterance to proclaim his grief as frail hope crashes into a chasm of abandonment. Once more, he sobs a forlorn groan.

"Ty . . . ! Ty . . . !"

The splashing draws closer. And now another noise intervenes—a low rumble of aspirated air.

The rumble is answered by a flurry of alternating clicks and whistled murmurs.

He recognizes the din of speech, the clamor of sapient beings, without grasping the words. Numb with pain and resignation, he turns—and blinks uncomprehendingly at a *boat,* emerging from the grove of swamp trees.

Boat. The word—one of the first he ever knew—comes to mind slickly, easily, the way countless other words used to do.

A boat. Constructed of many long narrow tubes, cleverly curved and joined. Propelling it are figures working in unison with poles and oars. Figures he knows. He has seen their like before. But never so close together.

Never cooperating.

One shape is a cone of stacked rings or toruses, diminishing with height, girdled by a fringe of lithe tentacles that grasp a long pole, using it to push tree roots away from the hull. Nearby, a pair of broad-shouldered, green-cloaked bipeds paddle the water with great scooplike oars, their long scaly arms gleaming pale in the slanting sunlight. The fourth shape consists of an armored blue hump of a torso, leather-plated, culminating in a squat dome, rimmed by a glistening ribbon eye. Five powerful legs aim outward from the center, as if the creature might at any moment try to run in all directions at once.

He knows these profiles. Knows and fears them. But true despair floods his heart only when he spies a final figure, standing at the stern, holding the boat's tiller, scanning the thicket of vines and corroded stone.

It is a smaller bipedal form, slender, clothed in crude, woven fabric. A familiar outline, all too similar to his own. A stranger, but one sharing his own peculiar heritage, beginning near a certain salty sea, many aeons and galaxies distant from this shoal in space.

It is the last shape he ever wanted to see in such a forlorn place, so far from home.

Resignation fills him as the armored pentapod raises a clawed leg to point his way with a shout. Others rush forward to gape, and he stares back, for it is a sight to behold—all these faces and forms, jabbering to one another in shared astonishment at the spectacle of him— then rushing about, striving together as a team, paddling toward him with *rescue* their clear intent.

He lifts his arms, as if in welcome. Then, on command, both knees fold and turbid water rushes to embrace him.

Even without words, irony flows during those seconds, as he gives up the struggle for life. He has come a long way and been through much. Only a short time ago, *flame* had seemed his final destiny, his doom.

Somehow, this seems a more fitting way to go—by drowning.

I. THE BOOK OF THE SEA

*You who chose this way of life—
to live and breed and die in secret
on this wounded world,
cowering from star-lanes you once
roamed, hiding with other exiles in a
place forbidden by law—what justice
have you any right to claim?*

*The universe is hard.
Its laws are unforgiving.
Even the successful and glorious are
punished by the grinding executioner
called Time. All the worse for you
who are accursed, frightened of the
sky.*

*And yet there are paths that climb,
even out of despair's sorrow.*

*Hide, children of exile!
Cower from the stars!
But watch, heed and listen—
for the coming of a path.*

—The Scroll of Exile

Alvin's Tale

ON THE DAY I GREW UP ENOUGH FOR MY HAIR TO start turning white, my parents summoned all the members of our thronging cluster to the family khuta, for a ceremony giving me my proper name—*IIph-wayuo*.

I guess it's all right, for a hoonish tag. It rolls out from my throat sac easy enough, even if I get embarrassed hearing it sometimes. The handle's supposed to have been in the lineage ever since our sneakship brought the first hoon to Jijo.

The sneakship was utterly gloss! Our ancestors may have been sinners, in coming to breed on this taboo planet, but they flew a mighty star-cruiser, dodging Institute patrols and dangerous Zang and Izmunuti's carbon storms to get here. Sinners or not, they must have been awfully brave and skilled to do all that.

I've read everything I can find about those days, even though it happened hundreds of years before there was paper on Jijo, so all we really have to go on are a few legends about those hoon pioneers, who dropped from the sky to find g'Keks, glavers, and traeki already hiding here on the Slope. Stories that tell how those first hoon sank their sneakship in the deep Midden, so it couldn't be traced, then settled down to build crude wooden rafts, the first to sail Jijo's rivers and seas since the Great Buyur went away.

Since it has to do with the sneakship, I guess my given name can't be too bad.

Still, I really like to be called *Alvin*.

Our teacher, Mister Heinz, wants us upper graders to start journals, though some parents complain paper costs too much here at the southern end of the Slope. I don't care. I'm going to write about the adventures me and my friends have, both helping and heckling the good-natured sailors in the harbor, or exploring twisty lava tubes up near Guenn Volcano, or scouting in our little boat all the way to the long, hatchet-shadow of Terminus Rock.

Maybe someday I'll turn these notes into a book!

And why not? My Anglic is real good. Even grumpy old Heinz says I'm a whiz at languages, memorizing the town copy of *Roget's* by the time I was ten. Anyway, now that Joe Dolenz, the printer, has come set up shop in Wuphon, why should we have to count on the traveling librarian's caravan for new things to read? Maybe Dolenz would even let me set the type myself! That is, if I get around to it before my fingers grow too big to fit around those little backward letters.

Mu-phauwq, my mother, calls it a great idea, though I can tell she's partly humoring a childish obsession, and I wish she wouldn't patronize me that way.

My *dad,* Yowg-wayuo, acts all grumpy, puffing his throat sac and telling me not to be such a human-mimicker. But I'm sure he likes the idea, deep down. Doesn't *he* keep taking borrowed books on his long voyages to the Midden, even though you're not supposed to, because what if the ship sank and maybe the last ancient copy of *Moby Dick* went down with the crew? Wouldn't that be a *real* disaster?

Anyway, didn't he used to read to me almost from the day I was born? Booming all the great Earthling adventure tales like *Treasure Island, Sindbad,* and *Ultraviolet Mars*? So who's *he* to call *me* a humicker!

Nowadays, Dad says I should read the new hoon writers, those trying to go past imitating old-time Earthers, coming up with literature by and for our own kind.

I guess maybe there *should* be more books in languages other than Anglic. But Galactic Two and Galactic Six seem so darn stiff for storytelling. Anyhow, I've tried some of those writers. Honestly. And I've got to say that not one of them can hold a peg to Mark Twain.

Naturally, *Huck* agrees with me about that!

Huck is my best friend. She picked that name even though I kept telling her it's not a right one for a girl. She just twists one eyestalk around another and says she doesn't care, and if I call her "Becky" one more time, she'll catch my leg-fur in her spokes and spin till I scream.

I guess it doesn't matter, since g'Keks get to change sex after their training wheels fall off, and if she wants to stay female, that's her business. As an orphan, Huck's lived with the family next door ever since the Big North-side Avalanche wiped out the weaver clan that used to squat in Buyur ruins up that way. You'd expect her to be a bit strange after living through that and then being raised by hoons. Anyway, she's a great friend and a pretty good sailor, even if she is a g'Kek, and a girl, and doesn't have legs to speak of.

Most times, *Pincer-Tip* also comes on our adventures, specially when we're down by the shore. He didn't need a nickname from some story, since all red qheuens get one the minute they set five claws outside the brooding pen. Pincer's no big reader like Huck and me, mostly because few books can stand the salt and dampness where his clan lives. They're poor, living off wrigglers they find in the mudflats south of town. Dad says the qheuens with red shells used to be servants to the grays and blues, before their sneakship brought all three to hide on Jijo. Even after that, the grays kept bossing the others for a while, so Dad says the reds aren't used to thinking for themselves.

Maybe so, but whenever Pincer-Tip comes along, *he's* usually the one chattering—with all leg-mouths at once—about sea serpents, or lost Buyur treasure, or other things he swears he's seen . . . or else he heard of somebody who knows someone else who might've seen something, just over the horizon. When we get into trouble, it's often on account of something he thought up inside that hard dome where he keeps his brain. Sometimes I wish I had an imagination a dozenth as vivid as his.

I should include *Ur-ronn* in the list, since she comes along sometimes. Ur-ronn's almost as much of a book maniac as Huck and me. Still, she's *urrish,* and there's a limit to how much of a humicker any urs can be, before planting four feet and saying whoa.

They don't take to nicknames, for instance.

Once, when we were reading a mess of old Greek myths, Huck tried calling Ur-ronn "Centaur." I guess you *could* say an urs sort of looks like one of those fabled creatures—if you'd just been conked on the head by a brick and can't see or think too well from the pain. But Ur-ronn disliked the comparison and showed it by swinging her long neck like a whip, nearly taking off one of Huck's eyestalks with a snap of her three-way mouth.

Huck only said "Centaur" just that once.

Ur-ronn is a niece of Uriel, who runs a forge next to fiery lava pools, high up on Mount Guenn. She won a scholarship to 'prentice as a smith instead of staying with the herds and caravans on the grassy plain. Too bad her aunt keeps Ur-ronn busy most of the time and won't *ever* let her go off in the boat with us, on account of urs can't swim.

Ur-ronn used to read a lot, back in that prairie school. Books we never heard of in this hick corner of the Slope. She tells us the stories she can recollect, like all about Crazy Horse and Genghis Khan, and urrish hero-warriors from those big battles they had with the humans, after Earthers came to Jijo but before the Commons got patched together and they started the Great Peace.

It'd be uttergloss if our gang could be a complete Six, like when Drake and Ur-jushen and their comrades went on the Big Quest and were the very first to set eyes on the Holy Egg. But the only traeki in town is the pharmacist, and that *er* is too old to make a new stack of rings we could play with. As for humans, *their* nearest village is several days from here. So I guess we're stuck being just a foursome.

Too bad. Humans are gloss. They brought books to Jijo and speak Anglic better than anybody, except me and maybe Huck. Also, a human kid's shaped kind of like a small hoon, so he could go nearly all the same places I can with my two long legs. Ur-ronn may be able to run fast, but she can't go into water, and Pincer can't wander too far from it, and poor Huck has to stay where the ground is level enough for her wheels.

None of them can climb a tree.

Still, they're my pals. Anyway, there are things they can do that I can't, so I guess it evens out.

It was Huck who said we ought to plan a really burnish adventure for the summer, since it would likely be our last.

School was out. Mister Heinz was on his yearly trip to the great archive at Biblos, then to Gathering Festival. As usual, he took along some older hoon students, including Huck's foster sister, Aph-awn. We envied their long voyage—first by sea, then riverboat to Ur-Tanj town, and finally by donkey-caravan all the way up to that mountain valley where they'd attend games and dramas, visit the Egg, and watch the sages meet in judgment over all six of Jijo's exile races.

Next year we may get our turn to go, but I don't mind saying the prospect of waiting another seventeen months wasn't welcome. What if we didn't have a single thing to do all summer except get caught loafing by our parents, then sent to help pack dross ships, unload fishing boats, and perform a hundred other mindless chores? Even more depressing, there wouldn't be any new books till Mister Heinz got back—that is *if* he didn't lose the list we gave him!

(One time he returned all excited with a big stack of old Earth *poetry* but not a single novel by Conrad,

Coopé, or Coontz. Worse, some grown-ups even claimed to *like* the stuff!)

Anyway, it was Huck who first suggested heading over the Line, and I'm still not sure whether that's giving a friend due credit or passing on blame.

"I know where there's something to read," she said one day, when summer was just getting its early start here in the south.

Yowg-wayuo had already caught us, vegetating under the pier, skipping rocks at dome-bobbers and bored as noors in a cage. Sure enough, he right-prompt sent us up the long access ramp to repair the village camouflage trellis, a job I always hate and I'll be glad when I'm too big to be drafted into doing it anymore. We hoon aren't as fond of heights as those tree-hugging humans and their chimp pets, so let me tell you it can be dizzifying having to crawl atop the wooden lattice arching over all the houses and shops of Wuphon, tending a carpet of greenery that's supposed to hide our town against being seen from space.

I have doubts it'd really work, if *The Day* ever comes that everyone frets about. When sky-gods come to judge us, what good will a canopy of leaves do? Will it spare us punishment?

But I don't want to be called a heretic. Anyway, this ain't the place to talk about that.

So there we were, high over Wuphon, all exposed with the bare sun glaring down, and Huck blurts her remark like a sudden burst of hollow hail.

"I know where there's something to read," she says.

I put down the lath strips I was carrying, laying them across a clump of black iris vines. Below, I made out the pharmacist's house, with its chimney spilling distinct traeki smells. (Do you know that different kinds of plants grow above a traeki's home? It can be hard working there if the pharmacist happens to be making medicine while you're overhead!)

"What're you talking about?" I asked, fighting a wave of wooziness. Huck wheeled over to pick up one of the laths, nimbly bending and slipping it in where the trellis sagged.

"I'm talking about reading something no one on the Slope has ever seen," she answered in her crooning way, when she thinks an idea's gloss. Two eyestalks hovered over her busy hands, while a third twisted to watch me with a glint I know too well. "I'm talking about something *so* ancient, it makes the oldest scroll on Jijo look like Joe Dolenz just printed it, with the ink still wet!"

Huck spun along the beams and joists, making me gulp when she popped a wheelie or swerved past a gaping hole, weaving flexible lath canes like reeds in a basket. We tend to see g'Keks as frail beings, because they prefer smooth paths and hate rocky ground. But those axles and rims are nimble, and what a g'Kek calls a road can be narrow as a plank.

"Don't give me that," I shot back. "Your folk burned and sank their sneakship, same as every race who skulked down to Jijo. All they *had* were scrolls—till humans came."

Huck rocked her torso, imitating a traeki gesture that means, *Maybe you're right, but i/we don't think so.*

"Oh, Alvin, you know even the first exiles found things on Jijo to read."

All right, so I wasn't too swift on the grok. I'm plenty smart in my own way—steady and thorough is the hoonish style—but no one ever accused me of being quick.

I frowned, mimicking a human "thoughtful" expression I once saw in a book, even though it makes my forehead hurt. My throat sac throbbed as I concentrated.

"Hrrrrrm. . . . Now wait just a minute. You don't mean those wall markings sometimes found—"

"On the walls of old Buyur buildings, yes! The few not smashed or eaten by mulc-spiders when the Buyur left, a million years ago. Those same markings."

"But weren't they mostly just street signs and such?"

"True," she agreed with one dipping eyestalk. "But there were really strange ones in the ruins where I first lived. Uncle Lorben was translating some into GalTwo, before the avalanche hit."

I'll never get used to how matter-of-factly she can speak about the disaster that wiped out her family. If anything like it happened to me, I wouldn't talk again for years. Maybe ever.

"Uncle swapped letters with a Biblos scholar about the engravings he found. I was too little to understand much. But clearly there are savants who want to know about Buyur wall writings."

And others who wouldn't like it, I recall thinking. Despite the Great Peace, there are still folk in all six races ready to cry *heresy* and warn of an awful penance, about to fall from the sky.

"Well, it's too bad all the carvings were destroyed when . . . you know."

"When the mountain killed my folks? Yeah. Too bad. Say, Alvin, will you pass a couple more strips over to me? I can't quite reach—"

Huck teetered on one wheel, the other spinning madly. I gulped and passed over the lengths of slivered boo. "Thanks," Huck said, landing back on the beam with a shuddering bounce, damped by her shocks. "Now where was I? Oh yeah. Buyur wall writings. I was going to suggest how we can find some engravings no one's ever seen. At least none of us exile Sixers."

"How could that be?" My throat sac must have fluttered in confusion, making burbly sounds. "Your people came to Jijo two thousand years ago. Mine almost as long. Even *humans* have been here a few hundred. Every inch of the Slope is explored, and each Buyur site poked into, scores of times!"

Huck stretched all four eyes toward me.

"Exactly!"

Floating from her cranial tympanum, the Anglic word seemed stressed with soft accents of excitement. I stared for a long time and finally croaked in surprise.

"You mean to *leave* the Slope? To sneak beyond the Rift?"

I should have known better than to ask.

All it would have taken was a shift in the roll of Ifni's dice, and this would be a very different tale. Things came *that* close to going the way Huck wanted.

She kept badgering me, for one thing. Even after we finished repairing the lattice and went back to loitering near the ships moored under huge, overhanging gingourv trees, she just kept at it with her special combination of g'Kek wit and hoonlike persistence.

"Come on, Alvin. Haven't we sailed to Terminus Rock dozens of times and dared each other to keep on going? We even *did* it, once, and no harm ever came!"

"Just to the middle of the Rift. Then we scurried home again."

"So? Do you want that shame sticking forever? This may be our last chance!"

I rubbed my half-inflated sac, making a hollow, rumbling sound. "Aren't you forgetting, we already *have* a project? We're building a bathy, in order to go diving—"

She cut loose a blat of disgust. "We talked it over last week and you agreed. The bathy reeks."

"I agreed to *think* about it. *Hrm*. After all, Pincer has already built the hull. Chewed it himself from that big garu log. And what about the work the rest of us put in, looking up old Earthling designs, making that compressor pump and cable? Then there are those wheels you salvaged, and Ur-ronn's porthole—"

"Yeah, yeah." She renounced all our labors with a dismissive twirl of two stalks. "Sure, it was fun working on that stuff during winter, when we had to sit indoors anyway. *Especially* when it looked like it'd never actually happen. We had a great game of pretend.

"But things are getting serious! Pincer talks about actually making a deep dive in a month or two. Didn't we agree that's crazy? Didn't we, Alvin?" Huck rolled closer and did something I've never heard another g'Kek do. She rumbled an *umble* at me, mimicking the undertone a young hoon female might use if her big, handsome male was having trouble seeing things her way.

"Now wouldn't you rather come with me to see some

uttergloss writings, so burnish and ancient they were written with *computers* and *lasers* and such? Hr-rm? Doesn't that beat drowning in a stinky dross coffin, half-way to the bottom of the sea?"

Time to switch languages. While I normally find Anglic more buff than smug old star-god tongues, even Mister Heinz agrees that its "human tempos and loose logical structure tend to favor impetuous enthusiasms."

Right then, I needed the opposite, so I shifted to the whistles and pops of Galactic Two.

"Consideration of (punishable) criminality—this has not occurred to thee?"

Unfazed, she countered in GalSeven, the formal tongue most favored by humans.

"We are minors, friend. Besides, the border law is meant to thwart illicit breeding beyond the permitted zone. Our gang has no such intent!"

Then, in a quick flip to Galactic Two—

"—Or hast thee (perverted) designs to attempt (strange, hybrid) procreation experiments with this (virginal female) self?"

What a thought! Plainly she was trying to keep me off balance. I could feel control slip away. Soon I'd find myself vowing to set sail for those dark ruins you can dimly see from Terminus Rock, if you aim an urrish telescope across the Rift's deep waters.

Just then, my eye caught a familiar disturbance under the placid bay. A ruddy shape swarmed up the sandy bank until a dappled crimson carapace burst forth, spraying saltwater. From that compact pentagonal shell, a fleshy dome raised, girdled by a glossy black ring.

"Pincer!" I cried, glad of a distraction from Huck's hot enthusiasm. "Come over and help me talk to this silly—"

But the young qheuen burst ahead, cutting me off even before water stopped burbling from his speech vents.

"M-m-mo-mo-mon—"

Pincer's not as good at Anglic as Huck and me, especially when excited. But he uses it to prove he's as humicking modern as anyone. I held up my hands. "Easy, pal! Take a breath. Take five!"

He exhaled a deep sigh, which emerged as a pair of bubble streams where two spiky legs were still submerged. "I s-s-seen 'em! This time I *really* s-seen 'em!"

"Seen what?" Huck asked, rolling across squishy sand.

The vision band rimming Pincer's dome looked in all directions at once. Still, we could feel our friend's intense regard as he took another deep breath, then sighed a single word.

"Monsters!"

II. THE BOOK OF THE SLOPE

Legends

The better part of a million years has passed since the Buyur departed Jijo, obeying Galactic rules of planetary management when their lease on this world expired. Whatever they could not carry off, or store in lunar caches, the Buyur diligently destroyed, leaving little more than vine-crusted rubble where their mighty cities once towered, gleaming under the sun.

Yet even now, their shadow hangs over us—we cursed and exiled savages—reminding us that gods once ruled on Jijo.

Living here as illegal squatters—as "sooners" who must never dwell beyond this strip between the mountains and the sea—we of the Six Races can only look with superstitious awe at eroded Buyur ruins. Even after books and literacy returned to our Commons, we lacked the tools and skills to analyze the remains or to learn much about Jijo's last lawful tenants. Some recent enthusiasts, styling themselves "archae-ologists," have begun borrowing tech-niques from dusty Earthling texts, but these devotees cannot even tell us what the Buyur looked like, let alone their habits, attitudes, or way of life.

Our best evidence comes from folk-lore.

Though glavers no longer speak— and so are not counted among the Six—we still have some of the tales they used to tell, passed on by the g'Keks, who knew glavers best, before they devolved.

Once, before their sneakship came to Jijo, when glavers roamed the stars as full citizens of the Five Galaxies, it is said that they were on intimate terms with a race called the Tunnuctyur, a great and noble clan. In their youth, these Tunnuctyur had been clients of another species—the patron that up-lifted them, giving the Tunnuctyur mas-tery of speech, tools, and sapiency. Those patrons were called Buyur, and they came from Galaxy Four—from a world with a huge carbon star in its sky.

According to legend, these Buyur were known as clever designers of small living things.

They were also known to possess a rare and dangerous trait—a sense of humor.

—*Mystery of the Buyur*
by Hau-uphtunda, Guild of Freelance
Scholars, Year-of-Exile 1908.

Asx

HEAR, MY RINGS, THE SONG I SING. LET ITS VAPORS rise amid your cores, and sink like dripping wax. It comes in many voices, scents, and strengths of time. It weaves like a g'Kck tapestry, flows like a hoon aria, gallops and swerves in the manner of urrish legend, and yet turns inexorably, as with the pages of a human book.

The story begins in peace.

It was springtime, early in the second lunar cycle of the nineteen hundred and thirtieth year of our exile-and-crime, when the Rothen arrived, manifesting unwelcome in our sky. Shining sunlike in their mastery of air and aether, they rent the veil of our concealment at the worst of all possible times—during the vernal gathering-of-tribes, near the blessed foot of Jijo's Egg.

There we had come, as so often since the Emergence, to hear the great ovoid's music. To seek guidance patterns. To trade the produce of our varied talents. To settle disputes, compete in games, and renew the Commons. Above all, seeking ways to minimize the harm done by our ill-starred presence on this world.

Gathering—a time of excitement for the young, work for the skilled, and farewells for those nearing the end of years. Already there had spread rumors—portents—that this assembly would be momentous. More than a usual quota from each clan had come. Along with sages and roamers, grafters and techies, many simple folk of two legs, four and five—and of wheel and ring—followed

drumbeats along still-frosted mountain tracks to reach
the sacred glades. Among each race, manifold had felt
the tremors—stronger than any since that provident year
when the Egg burst from Jijo's mother soil, shedding hot
birth-dust, then settling to rule our fractious passions
and unite us.

Ah, Gathering.

This latest pilgrimage may not yet have solidified as
waxy memory. But try to recall slowly wending our
now-aged pile of rings aboard ship at Far Wet Sanctuary,
to sail past the glistening Spectral Flow and the Plain of
Sharp Sand.

Did not those familiar wonders seem to pale when we
reached the Great Marsh and found it in bloom? Something seen once in a traeki lifetime? A sea of color—
flowering, fruiting, and already dying gaudily before our
senses. Transferring from boat to barge, we travelers
rowed amid great pungency, under avenues of million-
petalled sylph canopies.

Our companions took this as an omen, did they not,
my rings? The humans in our midst spoke of mysterious
Ifni, the capricious one, whose verdicts are not always
just but are ever-surprising.

Do you recall other sights/experiences? The weaver
villages? The mulc-spiders and hunting camps? And finally that arduous climb, twist by twist of our straining
foot-pads, through the Pass of Long Umbras to reach this
green vale where, four traeki generations ago, geysers
steamed and rainbows danced, celebrating the dark
ovoid's emergence?

Recollect, now, the crunch of volcanic gravel, and
how the normally obedient rewq-beast trembled on our
head-ring, mutinously refusing to lay itself over our eye-
lets, so that we arrived in camp barefaced, unmasked,
while children of all Six Races scurried, shouting, *"Asx!
Asx! Asx, the traeki, has come!"*

Picture the other High Sages—colleagues and
friends—emerging from their tents to walk, slither, roll,
and greet us with this epithet. This label they regard as
permanently attached to "me"—a fiction that i humor.

Do you recall all that, my rings?

Well, patience then. Memories congeal like dripping wax, simmering to coat our inner core. Once there, they can never be forgotten.

On Jijo there is a deep shine in the section of sky farthest from the sun. We are told this is rare on worlds catalogued by the Great Galactics, an effect of carbon grains—the same ones that seed the hollow hail—grains sent by Izmunuti, the glaring star-eye in a constellation humans call Job's Torment. It is said our ancestors studied such traits of their new home before burning and burying their ships.

It is also said that they simply "looked it all up" in a portable branch of the Galactic Library before consigning even that treasure to flames on the day called Never-Go-Back.

There was no hollow hail that spring morning, when the other sages emerged to salute our rings, calling us/ me *Asx*. As we gathered under a pavilion, i learned that our rewq was not the only one grown skittish. Not even the patient hoon could control his translation-helper. So we sages conferred without the little symbionts, fathoming each other by word and gesture alone.

Of all whose ancestors chose hopeless exile on this world, the g'Kek are senior. So to Vubben fell the role—Speaker of Ignition.

"Are we guilty for the failure of rantanoids?" Vubben asked, turning each eye toward a different point of the compass. "The Egg senses pain in the life-field whenever potential is lost."

"Hrrrm. We argue the point endlessly," the hoon sophist, Phwhoon-dau, replied. "Lark and Uthen tell of a *decline*. Rantanoids aren't yet extinct. A small number remain on an Yuqun Isle."

The human sage, Lester Cambel, agreed. "Even if they are past hope, rantanoids are just one of countless species of root-grubbers. No reason to figure they were specially blessed."

Ur-Jah retorted that her own ancestors, long ago and far away, had been *little root-grubbers*.

Lester conceded with a bow. "Still, we aren't responsible for the rise and fall of every species."

"How can you know?" Vubben persisted. "We who lack most tools of science, left to flounder in darkness by our selfish forebears, cannot know what subtle harm we do by stepping on a leaf or voiding our wastes in a pit. None can predict what we'll be held accountable for, when The Day comes. Even *glavers,* in their present state of innocence, will be judged."

That was when our aged qheuenish sage, whom we call Knife-Bright Insight, tilted her blue carapace. Her voice was a soft whisper from one chitin thigh.

"The Egg, our gift in the wilderness, knows answers. Truth is its reward to an open mind."

Chastened by her wisdom, we fell into meditation.

No longer needed, the errant rewq slipped off our brows and gathered in the center, exchanging host-enzymes. We took up a gentle rhythm, each sage adding a line of harmony—of breath and beating hearts.

My rings, do you recall what chose then to occur?

The fabric of our union was ripped by booming *echoes,* cast arrogantly by the Rothen ship, proclaiming its malign power, before it even arrived.

We emerged to stare, dismayed, at the riven sky.

Soon sage and clanfolk alike knew The Day had finally come.

Vengeance is not spared upon the children of the fallen.

The Family of Nelo

THE PAPER-CRAFTER HAD THREE OFFSPRING—A number worthy of his noble calling, like his father, and his father's father. Nelo always supposed the line would go on through his own two sons and daughter.

So he took it hard when his strong-jawed children deserted the water mill, its sluiceways, and wooden gears. None heeded the beckoning rhythm of the pulping hammer, beating cloth scavenged from all six races, or the sweet mist spread by the sifting screens, or the respectful bows of traders, come from afar to buy Nelo's sleek white pages.

Oh, Sara, Lark, and Dwer were happy to *use* paper!

Dwer, the youngest, wrapped it around arrowheads and lures for the hunt. Sometimes he paid his father in piu nodules, or grwon teeth, before fading into the forest again, as he had done since turning nine. Apprenticed to Fallon the Tracker, Dwer soon became a legend across the Slope. Nothing he sought escaped his bow, unless it was shielded by law. And rumors said the fierce-eyed lad with jet-black hair killed and ate whatever he liked, when the law wasn't looking.

As focused as Dwer was wild, *Lark* used paper to plot vast charts on his study wall, some parts almost black with notes and diagrams. Elsewhere, large spaces gaped blank, a waste of Nelo's art.

"It can't be helped, Father," Lark explained near wooden shelves filled with fossils. "We haven't found which species fill those gaps. This world is so complex, I doubt even the Buyur ever fully grasped Jijo's ecosystem."

Nelo recalled thinking that an absurd thing to say. When the Buyur leased Jijo, they had been full citizens of the Community of the Five Galaxies, with access to the fabled Great Library, dwarfing all the paper books in

Biblos! With a word, the Buyur could beckon any answer under the sun. Under a *billion* suns, if tales of the past could be trusted.

At least the sages approved of Lark's work. But what of *Sara*? Always Nelo's favorite, she used to love the smells, rhythms and textures of papermaking—till age fourteen, when she stumbled on a *talent*.

Nelo blamed his late wife, who had entered his life so strangely, long ago, and used to fill the kids' heads with odd tales and ambitions.

Yes, he decided. *It was all Melina's fault—*

A low cough jarred Nelo's drifting resentment. He blinked as a pair of deep brown eyes peered over his pitted desk. Dark fur framed a face so nearly human that unwary traeki sometimes gave *chimpanzees* the courtesy due full members of the Commons.

"Are you still here?" Nelo snapped.

The face winced, then nodded to the left, toward the paper storeroom, where one of Nelo's aides slowly gathered torn sheets from a discard bin.

He cursed. "Not that garbage, Jocko!"

"But Master, you said to fetch waste scraps we can't sell—"

Nelo ducked under the Great Shaft, a rotating horizontal shank of hardwood, carrying power from the village dam to nearby workshops. He shooed Jocko away. "Never mind what I said. Go back to the vats—and tell Caleb to put less water through the millrace! It's four months till rainy season. He'll have us out of business in two!"

Nelo scanned the shelves for himself, finally choosing two reams of slightly flawed sheets, bound in liana vines. They weren't quite rejects. Someone might have paid cash for them. On the other hand, what was there to save for? Didn't the sages warn against investing much pride or care in tomorrow?

For all strivings will be judged, and few will win grace. . . .

Nelo snorted. He wasn't a religious man. He made *paper*. The profession implied some faith in the essential goodness of time.

"These'll do for your mistress, Prity," he told the little chimp, who rounded the desk, holding out both hands. Mute as a rewq, she served Nelo's daughter in ways no other being on Jijo could manage. Ways that few could comprehend. He handed over one of the heavy packages.

"I'll carry the other. It's time I dropped by anyway, to see if Sara's getting enough to eat."

Mute or not, the ape was expressive with rolled eyes. She knew this was just an excuse for Nelo to have a look at Sara's mysterious house-guest.

Nelo growled. "Come along and no dawdling. Some of us work for a living, you know."

A covered walkway linked the dam/factory to the forest, where most villagers dwelled. Fierce sunlight filtered through a canopy of living camouflage. At noon it took an optimist to think the screen would hide the buildings against a resolute scan from space—and among the Six, optimism was viewed as a mild type of heresy.

Alas, it was *not* the type of heresy followed by Nelo's eldest son.

Concealment seemed doubly problematic for the great dam itself. Unlike the ones qheuenish colonists made, bottling small ponds behind barriers that mimicked landslides or piles of logs, this dam spanned half an arrowflight from end to end. False boulders and cascades of melon creepers blurred its outline. Still, many called it the most blatant artifact on the Slope—outside of some ancient Buyur site. Each year, on Denouncement Day, radicals harangued for its destruction.

And now Lark is one of them. Nelo cast a stock complaint toward his dead wife's spirit. *Do you hear, Melina? You brought the boy with you, when you came from the far south. We're taught genes don't matter as much as upbringing, but did* I *raise a son to be a rabble-rousing apostate? Never!*

Instead of camouflage, Nelo put his faith in the promise of the founding ancestors who planted their truant seed on Jijo, claiming there would be *no* determined scan from space. Not for half a million years or so.

He once stressed that point in an argument with Lark. To his surprise, the lad agreed, then said it did not matter.

"I urge drastic measures not because I'm afraid of being caught, but because it's the right thing to do."

Right? Wrong? A cloud of dizzying abstractions. Lark and Sara kept bringing up such fluff—arguing with each other for miduras about fate and destiny. Sometimes Nelo found *Dwer,* the wild boy of the forest, the easiest of his children to understand.

The village carpenter's shop spewed sawdust, making pipe for Jobee, the rotund village plumber, to splice into homes, bringing fresh water and taking away waste to the septic pits. The comforts of a civilized life.

"Deep shade, Nelo," Jobee drawled in a manner that invited a soul to stop and chat a spell.

"Cloudy sky, Jobee," Nelo replied with a polite nod, and kept walking. Not that a few duras' idle banter would hurt. *But if he learns I'm visiting Sara, he'll drop by later with half the town to find out what I learned about her new pet . . . the stranger with the hole in his head.*

Once upon a time, it had been a fallen chipwing with a broken tail rudder, or a wounded toyo pup. Anything sick or hurt used to wind up in his storeroom, where Sara tended it in a box lined with his finest felt. Nelo had figured his adult daughter finally past that phase—till she returned from a routine gleaning trip a few days ago, with a wounded man thrashing on a stretcher.

Once Nelo might have opposed an outsider, even a sick one, lodging in his daughter's treehouse. Now he was glad to see anything draw her from a year's hard work and isolation. One of Sara's guildmasters had written to him recently, complaining that she was shirking a principal duty of a woman of her caste, prompting Nelo to write back, rebuking the fellow's impudence. Still, any interest Sara showed in a man was cause for guarded hope.

From the covered walkway, Nelo spied the town exploser and his young son, inspecting an anchor-pier of the great dam. Forbidding and earnest, with deep-chiseled features, Henrik reached into a recessed hole and withdrew a bulb-ended clay tube. Scrutinizing the charge, the exploser held it for his son to sniff.

Nelo was suddenly acutely aware of the mighty lake, lurking behind the dam, ready to sweep away the locks and factories if ever a signal came for Henrik to do his duty. He also felt a pang of *jealousy* over that knowing tête-à-tête between father and child—the sort that he once had with his own sire. One he hoped to share again, with someone who loved paper as he did.

If only one of the three kids would give me an heir.

I'll have one yet, he vowed. *If I must bribe the sages to command it!*

Henrik slipped the tube back inside, resealing the hole with clay.

A low sigh hissed to Nelo's left, where he saw another person also watching the explosers. *Log Biter,* matriarch of the local qheuenish hive, squatted by a tree stump with all five legs drawn in. Nervous exhalations stirred dust beneath her blue carapace, and she wore a rewq over her vision strip—as if that would tell her much about Henrik and son!

Anyway, what was Log Biter worried about? Surely this was just routine maintenance. Dolo's human villagers would never sacrifice the dam, source of their wealth and prestige. Only a few orthodox fools wanted that.

And Nelo's eldest son.

Everyone's edgy, he thought, turning away. *First an abnormal winter, then Ulkoun's proposition, and Lark's heresy. And now Sara comes home with a mysterious outsider.*

Is it any wonder I have trouble sleeping?

Most villagers' homes lay safe from the glowering sky,

nestled high in the trunks of mighty garu trees, where strains of edible moss flourished on wide branch-top gardens. It seemed a niche made for Earthlings, just as blue qheuens loved lakes, and dry plains suited urrish tribes.

Nelo and Prity had to stop briefly while children herded braying bush-turkeys across the forest loam. A pair of opal-skinned glavers, perturbed while rooting for grubs, lifted their round heads and sniffed haughtily. The children laughed, and the glavers' bulging eyes soon dimmed, the light of anger costing too much effort to maintain.

It was the familiar rhythm of village life, and Nelo would happily go on taking it for granted, but for his eldest son's words before leaving for Gathering, when Lark explained the reason for his heresy.

"Nature is taking hold of this world again, Father, moving beyond the patterns imposed by its former tenants."

Nelo had been doubtful. How could unsapient life change a world in less than a million years? Without a guiding race to tend it, as a farmer manages a garden?

"It's what declaring a world fallow is all about," Lark went on. *"Letting it rest and recover without interference."*

"Without the likes of us, you mean."

"That's right. We aren't supposed to be on Jijo. We do harm simply living here."

It was the moral dilemma of the Six. The ancestors of each race had felt they had strong reasons to come so far in sneakships, planting outlaw seed on a forbidden world. The Scrolls spoke of crime blended with desperate *hope*. But Nelo's son stressed only the felony. Moreover, Lark and his comrades planned finally doing something about it. A grand gesture at this year's Gathering, atoning for generations of guilt with an act of devotion, both holy and terrible.

"What foolishness!" Nelo had protested. *"When civilization finally resettles this galaxy, there'll be no sign our*

kind ever lived here. Not if we live righteously, by Egg and Oath. What you plan will make no difference!"

In any quarrel with *Dwer*, there would have been defiant shouting. But Lark was even more frustrating to talk to, masking his purist heresy behind an obstinate civility he must have inherited from his mother.

"It doesn't matter if our crime is never discovered, Father. What matters is we don't belong here. We simply should not exist."

Villagers saluted their paper-crafter as Nelo and Prity passed by. But today he only glowered, wishing acridly that his offspring wouldn't vex him so—first by neglecting his wishes, then by inflicting the ferment of their disturbing ideas.

Several boats lay berthed at the town dock. Nimble, sleek-furred noor beasts scampered across the masts, tending lines and camouflage shrouds, as their kind had been trained to do for centuries by the tall, long-snouted hoon. The crew of one vessel helped some local men load a cargo of glass and metal, scavenged from a Buyur site upriver, destined for reprocessing by the smiths of Ur-Tanj town, or else bound for the dross pits, far out to sea.

Normally, Nelo might have paused to watch, but Prity tugged his sleeve, urging him upward, into the blue-gray branches of the grove.

As they turned, sudden shouts blared. Men dropped their burdens and hoon sailors crouched, splaying shaggy legs. Creaking tree trunks swayed like the ship masts as lines snapped and ripples stitched the water. A cloud of leaves poured from the forest, filling the air with spinning spiral forms. Nelo recognized the basso rumble of a quake! Spine-tingling fear mixed with a strange *thrill* as he pondered whether to try for open ground.

The tumult passed before he could decide. Branches kept swaying, but the walkway planks ceased vibrating and the watery ripples vanished like dreams. Relieved sailors snorted. Villagers made reverent hand gestures, for Jijo's flexings were sacred omens of the planet's healing force, even when they brought riotous ruin. Once, a century ago, a more violent quake had brought forth the Holy Egg, a blessing worth all the pain that accompanied its birth.

Oh, Mother Jijo, Nelo prayed as the last temblors faded. *Let things go well at Gathering. Let the sages talk Lark and his friends out of their foolish plan.*

And perhaps, he dared add, *let Dwer also meet a girl of good family and settle down?*

He knew better than to ask a third wish. Sara wouldn't want him invoking a deity in her favor. Not unless it were Ifni, the impartially capricious goddess of numbers and fate.

When his pulse steadied, Nelo signaled for Prity to lead. Their route now spiraled up a massive garu, then along branch-tops spanned by rope guideways. Nelo's feet moved by habit and he barely noticed the height, but the bundle of paper grew heavy in his hands.

Sara's treehouse perched so high that daylight spread for hours across one wattle wall. Nelo gripped a guide-rope while crossing the last stretch. The naked sun was so unsettling, he nearly missed noticing a square-sided cage, made of braced rods, that hung from a pulley next to Sara's sky porch.

A lift! Why is a lift attached to my daughter's home? Then he recalled. *It's because of the Stranger.*

Pungent aromas wafted from the house—tart, musty, and sweetly slimy. Peering inside, Nelo made out slanting rays of light, stabbing through louvered blinds. Sara's voice could be heard, muttering unhappily from another room. His hand raised to knock on the jamb, but paused when a pair of shadows loomed from within—one a cone-shaped outline of circular tubes, taller than Nelo's head. Nubby feet propelled the bottommost ring, making squishy sounds as it neared.

Two roller-hoops framed the smaller creature, whose slim torso ended with a pair of graceful arms and four eye-tipped feelers that peered all ways at once. One wheel squeaked as this entity rolled forward, revealing the spotted brain case and droopy eyestalks of an elderly g'Kek.

If any two citizens of Dolo Village could make Nelo feel spry at his age, it was this pair. In all the life-history of their two species, no g'Kek or traeki had ever climbed a tree.

"Cloudy skies, papermaker," the wheeled one said.

"Deep shade, Doctor Lorrek. And to *you,* Pharmacist." Nelo bowed twice. "How goes your patient?"

Lorrek's Anglic was superb after years serving Dolo's mostly human populace.

"Astonishingly, the injured man gains strength, soothed by Pzora's special unguents"— the doctor bent a stalk toward the traeki whose ninth torus looked flushed from hard medicinal labor—"and helped by the care he receives in this clean air."

This *was* a surprise. The Stranger had seemed a goner. "But his wounds! The hole in his head—?"

Shrugging had originally been a human gesture, but no one did it with more poise than a g'Kek.

"A fatal mutilation, I feared. Clearly the outlander owes his life to Pzora's secretions, and your daughter's swift action, hauling him from that foul swamp."

The traeki pharmacist then spoke, turning its jewel-like sense organs, its voice wavering like an untuned metal harp.

"i/we help gladly, though our synthesis rings near-swoon from the effort. Unguents of rare potency were needed. Yet it seems difficult to please."

"How do you mean?"

"Only here, up high where germs are scarce, might the work be done. Miss Sara's abode is ideal, and she will let no other take the patient. Yet she complains so! Aggrieved, she speaks longingly of an end to her work-disruption. Toward getting us all *out of her hair.*"

"It's just a metaphor," Lorrek explained.

"As i/we assumed. Its paradoxical dissonance we/i esteem highly. May her selves understand that."

"I'll see that she does," Nelo told Pzora, smiling.

"Thank you all, excellent Nelos," the young traeki responded, slipping into plural form. "i/we hope for serene work, when we return this evening."

Lorrek wrapped his eyestalks, and Nelo needed no rewq to read the old g'Kek's silent laughter. "Serenity *is* good," he agreed dryly, coughing behind a hand.

He braced the elevator cage, first for the heavy traeki to shuffle aboard. Then Lorrek rolled in, his left wheel wobbling from untreatable degenerative axle disease. Nelo pulled the signal rope, calling an operator far below to start the weight-driven winch.

"Has anything been learned about the Stranger's identity?" Lorrek asked while waiting.

"Not that I heard. Though I'm sure it's just a matter of time."

So far, even merchant traders had failed to recognize the unconscious man, implying he came quite a distance, perhaps from the coast settlements or even The Vale. *No one in Dolo knew Melina, either, when she arrived long ago, with a letter of introduction and a baby on her hip. The Slope is a bigger place than we're used to thinking.*

The g'Kek sighed. "We must resolve soon whether it will better serve the patient to send him on, now that he's stabilized, to be examined in—"

The cage shuddered, then dropped swiftly, cutting Lorrek off midsentence.

Ah well, Nelo thought, watching the car vanish steadily below moss-heavy branches. *That'd explain the shouting. Sara wouldn't want her pet sent to specialists in Tarek Town—even if she does complain about disrupted work.*

Would she ever learn? The last time Sara's nurturing instincts took over—succoring a convalescing bookbinder, in Biblos—it led to a love affair that ended in tragedy, scandal, and alienation from her guild. Nelo hoped the cycle wasn't repeating.

Even now she could win it all back—both her position and marriage to a respected sage. True, I never liked that sour-pussed Taine, but he offers a more secure life than she'd have had with that frail lover of hers.

Anyway, she can still do math while making me some grandkids.

The little chimp plunged into the house first. Sara's voice called from shadows, "Is that you, Prity? It's been nothing but interruptions, but I think I finally whipped that integral. Why don't you look it ov—"

There was a flat sound. A large bundle, landing on a table.

"Ah, the paper. Wonderful. Let's see what the old man sent us this time."

"Whatever *the old man* sends is good enough for one who don't *pay* for it," Nelo groused, shuffling while his eyes adapted. Through the gloom, he saw his daughter rise from a desk covered with notebooks and obscure symbols. Sara's round face spread with a smile *he* always thought beautiful, though it might have helped if she'd taken more after her mother.

My looks and Melina's wild brains. Not a blend I'd wish on a sweet lass.

"Father!" She hurried over to embrace him. "You gave me a start."

Her black hair, cut like a boy's, smelled of pencil dust and Pzora's unguents.

"No doubt." He frowned at the shambles of her quarters, worse now with a mattress by her desk. A jumble of texts, some bearing emblems of the great Biblos trove, lay amid notes on the "new direction" her research had taken, combining mathematics and *linguistics,* of all things.

Prity took one of Sara's papers and perched on a stool. The chimp worked her lower lip, scanning one line of symbols at a time, silent collaborator in an arcane art Nelo would never understand.

He glanced toward the sleeping porch, where sunlight spread across a blanket, outlining two large feet.

"With both of the lads gone, I thought I'd come see how you're doing."

"Well, I'm all right, as you can see." She gestured, as

if the firetrap of a treehouse were a model of home-tending. "And I have Prity to take care of me. Why, I even recall to eat, most days!"

"Well . . ." he muttered. But Sara had taken his arm and was gently maneuvering him toward the door. "I'll come visit tomorrow," she vowed, "when Lorrek and old Stinky want me out of the way. We'll go to Belonna's for a nice meal, hm? I'll even wear a clean gown."

"Well—that'd be fine." He paused. "Just remember, the elders will assign you help, if all this gets to be too much fuss and work."

She nodded. "I know how this looks to you, Father. 'Sara's gone obsessive again,' right? Well don't worry. It's not like that, this time. I just think this place is ideal for preventing infection of those horrid wounds—"

A low moan floated from the back of the house. Sara hesitated, then held up a hand. "I'll be a moment."

Nelo watched her hasten toward the shuttered porch, then he followed, drawn by curiosity.

Prity was wiping the injured stranger's brow, while his dark hands trembled outward, as if warding off something deadly. Livid scars laced the man's arms, and yellow fluid leaked through a gauze dressing near his left ear. The last time Nelo had seen the man, his skin was ashen with a pallor of approaching death. Now the eyes, with near-black irises, seemed to flame with awful passion.

Sara took the wounded man's hands, speaking insistently, trying to soothe the abrupt fit. But the outsider clutched her wrists, clamping down so hard that Sara cried out. Nelo rushed to her side, plucking vainly at the strong fingers gripping his daughter.

"Ge—ge—ge—*dow*!" the stranger stammered, yanking Sara toward the floor.

At that moment, the sky cracked open.

A savage roar blew in the shutters, knocking pottery off kitchen shelves. The entire garu tree *leaned,* as if a great hand shoved it, knocking Nelo off his feet. With ringing ears, father and daughter clutched floor planks as the tree swung over so far, Nelo glimpsed the *ground* through a gaping window. More crockery spilled. Furniture slid toward the open door. Amid a storm of swirling paper, Prity shrieked, and the wide-eyed stranger howled in harmony.

Nelo managed one dumbfounded thought. *Could it be another quake?*

The garu whipped them back and forth like beads in a rattle, for a terrifying interval that felt like eternity—and must have lasted all of a minute.

Amazingly, the house clung to its cleft between two branches. Vibrations thrummed along the tree's abused spine as the wail in Nelo's skull abated at last, trailing to numbed silence. Reluctantly, he let Sara help him rise. Together, they joined the Stranger, who now clutched the windowsill with bone-white knuckles.

The forest was a maelstrom of dust and fluttering leaves. No trees had toppled, much to Nelo's surprise. He sought the great dam and found that it held, thank God. The paper mill appeared intact.

"Look!" Sara gasped, pointing *above* the forest toward the southeast sky.

A thin white trail showed where, high overhead, the air had been riven by something titanic and fast—something that still sparkled in the distance as they glimpsed it streak past the valley's edge, toward the white-tipped peaks of the Rimmer Range. So high and so fleet it seemed—so arrogantly untimid—Nelo did not have to speak his dread aloud. The same fear lay in his daughter's eyes.

The Stranger, still tracking the distant, dwindling glitter, let out a foreboding sigh. He seemed to share their anxiety, but in his weary face there was no hint of surprise.

Asx

DO YOU RECALL, MY RINGS, HOW THE ROTHEN ship circled thrice over the Glade of Gathering, blazing from its hot descent, chased by the roaring protest of a cloven sky? Stroke the wax-of-memory, and recollect how mighty the vessel seemed, halting dramatically, almost overhead.

Even the human tribe—our finest tech-crafters—stared in the round-eyed manner of their kind, as the great cylinder, vast as a glacier, settled down just ninety arrowflights away from the secret sacred hollow of the Holy Egg.

The people of the Six Races came before us, moaning dread.

"Oh, sages, shall we flee? Shall we hide, as the law demands?"

Indeed, the Scrolls so command us.

Conceal your tents, your fields, your works and very selves. For from the sky shall come your judgment and your scourge.

Message-casters asked—"Shall we put out the Call? Shall villages and burghs and herds and hives be told to raze?"

Even before the law was shaped—when our Commons had not yet congealed out of sharp enmities—even then our scattered outcast bands knew where danger lay. We exiles-on-Jijo have cowered when survey probes from the Galactic Institutes made cursory audits from afar, causing our sensor-stones to light with warning fire. At other times, shimmering globe-swarms of *Zang* fell from the starry vault, dipping to the sea, then parting amid clouds of stolen vapor. Even those six times when new bands of misfits settled on this desert shore, they went ungreeted by those already here, until they burned the ships that brought them.

"Shall we try to hide?"

Recall, my rings, the confused braying as folk scattered like chaff before a whirlwind, tearing down the festival pavilions, hauling dross from our encampment toward nearby caves. Yet amid all this, some were calm, resigned. From each race, a few understood. This time there would be no hiding from the stars.

Among the High Sages, Vubben spoke first, turning an eyestalk toward each of us.

"Never before has a ship landed right in our midst. Clearly, we are already seen."

"Perhaps not," Ur-Jah suggested in hopeful Galactic Seven, stamping one hoof. Agitated white fur outlined her flared urrish nostril. *"They may be tracking emanations of the Egg! Perhaps if we hide swiftly . . ."*

Ur-Jah's voice trailed off as Lester, the human, rocked his head—a simple gesture of negation lately fashionable throughout the Commons, among those with heads.

"At this range, our infrared signatures would be unmistakable. Their onboard library will have categorized us down to each subspecies. If they didn't know about us before entering the atmosphere, they surely do by now."

Out of habit, we took his word for such things, about which humans oft know best.

"Perhaps they are refugees like us!" burst forth our qheuenish sage, venting hope from all five leg-vents. But Vubben was not sanguine.

"You saw the manner of their arrival. Was that the style of refugees, treading in fear, hiding from Izmunuti's stare? Did any of *our* ancestors come thus? Screaming brutishly across the sky?"

Lifting his forward eye to regard the crowd, Vubben called for order. "Let no one leave the festival valley, lest their flight be tracked to our scattered clans and holds. But seek all glavers that have come to browse among us, and push those simple ones away, so our guilt won't stain their reclaimed innocence.

"As for those of the Six who are here now, where the ship's dark shadow fell . . . we all must live or die as fate wills."

i/we sensed solidification among the rings of my/our body. Fear merged into noble resignation as the Commons saw truth in Vubben's words.

"Nor shall we scurry uselessly," he went on. "For the Scrolls also say— *When every veil is torn, cower no more. For that day comes your judgment. Stand as you are.*"

So clear was his wisdom, there rose no dissent. We gathered then, tribe by tribe, did we not, my rings? From many, we coalesced as one.

Together our Commons turned toward the ship, to meet our destiny.

Dwer

THE WEIRD NOOR STILL DOGGED HIS HEELS, LEER-ing down at him from tree branches, being an utter pest.

Sometimes the sleek, black-pelted creature vanished for a while, raising Dwer's hopes. Perhaps it finally had tired of dusty alpine air, so far from the swamps where most noor dwelled.

Then it reappeared, a grin splitting its stubby snout, perched on some ledge to watch Dwer hack through thorn-hedges and scramble over upended slabs of ancient pavement, kneeling often to check footprint traces of a runaway glaver.

The scent was already cool when Dwer had first noticed the spoor, just outside the Glade of Gathering. His brother and the other pilgrims had continued toward sounds of gala music, floating from the festival pavilions. But alas for Dwer, it was *his* job to stop glavers who took a strange notion to leave the cozy lowlands and make a break for perilous freedom. Festival would have to wait.

The noor barked high-pitched yelps, pretending to be helpful, its sinuous body streaking along at root level while Dwer had to chop and scramble. Finally, Dwer could tell they were gaining. The glaver's tired footprints lay close together, pressing the heel. When the wind changed, Dwer caught a scent. *About time,* he thought, gauging how little mountain remained before a cleft led to the next watershed—in effect another world.

Why do glavers keep doing this? Their lives aren't so rough on this side, where everyone dotes on them. Beyond the pass, by contrast, lay a poison plain, unfit for all but the hardiest hunters.

Or tourists, he thought, recalling Lena Strong's offer to pay him to lead a trip east. A journey whose sole aim was *sightseeing*—a word Dwer had only heard in tales from Old Earth.

These are crazy times, he thought. Yet the "tour organizers" claimed to have approval from the sages—under certain conditions. Dwer shook his head. He didn't need idiotic ideas clouding his mind right now, with a quarry just ahead.

The noor, too, showed signs of fatigue, though it kept snuffing along the glaver's track, then rising on its hind legs to scan with black, forward-facing eyes. Suddenly, it gave a guttural purr and took off through the montane thicket—and soon Dwer heard a glaver's unmistakable squawl, followed by the thud of running feet.

Great, now he's spooked it!

At last Dwer spilled from the undergrowth onto a stretch of ancient Buyur highway. Sprinting along the broken pavement, he sheathed the machete and drew his compound bow, cranking the string taut.

Sounds of hissing confrontation spilled from a narrow side canyon, forcing Dwer to leave the old road again, dodging amid vine-crusted trees. Finally he saw them, just beyond a screen of shrubs—two creatures, poised in a showdown of sable and iridescent pale.

Cornered in a slit ravine, the glaver was obviously female, possibly pregnant. She had climbed a long way and was pulling deep breaths. Globelike eyes rotated independently, one tracking the dark noor while the other scanned for dangers yet unseen.

Dwer cursed both of them—the glaver for drawing him on a profitless chase when he had been looking forward to festival, and the meddlesome noor for daring to interfere!

Doubly cursed, because now he was in its debt. If the glaver had reached the plains beyond the Rimmer Range, it would have been no end of trouble.

Neither creature seemed to notice Dwer—though he wouldn't bet against the noor's keen senses. *What is the little devil doing up here? What's it trying to prove?*

Dwer had named it Mudfoot, for the brown forepaws marring an ebony pelt, from a flattish tail to whiskers that twitched all around a stubby snout. The black-furred creature kept still, its gaze riveted on the flighty glaver, but Dwer wasn't fooled. *You know I'm watching, show-off.* Of all species left on Jijo when the ancient Buyur departed, Dwer found noor the least fathomable, and fathoming other creatures was a hunter's art.

Quietly, he lowered the bow and unfastened a buck-skin thong, taking up his coiled lariat. Using patient, stealthy care, he edged forward.

Grinning with jagged, angular teeth, Mudfoot reared almost to the glaver's height—roughly as tall as Dwer's thigh. The glaver retreated with a snarl, till her bony back plates brushed rock, causing a rain of pebbles. In her forked tail she brandished a stick—some branchlet or sapling with the twigs removed. A sophisticated tool, given the present state of glaverdom.

Dwer took another step and this time could not avoid crushing some leaves. Behind the noor's pointy ears, gray spines jutted from the fur, waving independently. Mudfoot kept facing the glaver, but something in its stance said—*"Be quiet, fool!"*

Dwer didn't like being told what to do. Especially by a noor. Still, a hunt is judged only by success, and Dwer wanted a clean capture. Shooting the glaver now would be to admit failure.

Her loose skin had lost some opal luster since leaving familiar haunts, scavenging near some village of the Six, as glavers had done for centuries, ever since their innocence was new.

Why do they do this? Why do a few try for the passes, every year?

One might as well guess the motives of a *noor.* Among the Six, only the patient hoon had a knack for working with the puckish, disruptive beasts.

Maybe the Buyur resented having to quit Jijo and left noor as a joke on whoever came next.

A buzzing lion-fly cruised by, under filmy, rotating wings. The panting glaver tracked it with one eye, while the other watched the swaying noor. Hunger gradually prevailed over fear as she realized Mudfoot was too small to murder her. As if to enhance that impression, the noor sat back on its haunches, nonchalantly licking a shoulder.

Very clever, Dwer thought, shifting his weight as the glaver swung both eyes toward the hovering meal.

A jet of sputum shot from her mouth, striking the fly's tail.

In a flash, Mudfoot bounded left. The glaver squealed, struck out with the stick, then whirled to flee the other way. Cursing, Dwer sprang from the undergrowth. Moccasins skidded on spoiled granite, and he tumbled, passing just under the flailing club. Desperately, Dwer cast the lariat—which tautened with a savage yank that slammed his chin to the ground. Though starving and weak, the glaver had enough panicky strength to drag Dwer for a dozen meters, till her will finally gave out.

Shivering, with waves of color coursing under her pale skin, she dropped the makeshift club and sank to all four knees. Dwer got up warily, coiling the rope.

"Easy does it. No one's gonna hurt you."

The glaver scanned him with one dull eye. *"Pain exists. Marginally,"* she crooned, in thickly slurred Galactic Eight.

Dwer rocked back. Only once before had a captured glaver spoken to him. Usually they kept up their unsentient pose to the last. He wet his lips and tried answering in the same obscure dialect.

"Regrettable. Endurance suggested. Better than death."

"Better?" The weary eye squinted as if vaguely puzzled and unsure it mattered.

Dwer shrugged. *"Sorry about the pain."*

The faint light drifted out of focus.

"Not blamed. Dour melody. Now ready to eat."

The flicker of intellect vanished once more under a bolus of animal density.

Both amazed and drained, Dwer tethered the creature to a nearby tree. Only then did he take account of his own wincing cuts and bruises while Mudfoot lay on a rock, basking in the last rays of the setting sun.

The noor couldn't talk. Unlike the glaver, its ancestors had never been given the knack. Still, its open-mouth grin seemed to say—"That was fun. Let's do it again!"

Dwer recovered his bow, started a fire, and spent the day's last half-midura feeding the captive from his meager rations. Tomorrow he'd find it a rotten log to root under for grubs—a favorite, if undignified pastime for members of what had once been a mighty starfaring race.

Mudfoot sidled close when Dwer unwrapped some hard bread and jerky. Dwer sighed and tossed some to the noor, who snatched chunks out of midair and ate with dainty care. Then Mudfoot sniffed at Dwer's gourd canteen.

He had seen the beasts use gourds aboard hoon-crewed riverboats. So after a dubious pause, he pulled the cork stopper and handed it over. The creature used both six-fingered forepaws—nearly as deft as true hands—to adroitly slosh quick dollops over its tongue, smacking loudly.

Then it poured the remainder over its head.

Dwer shot to his feet, cursing. But Mudfoot blithely tossed the empty vessel aside. Rivulets ran down its glossy back, dribbling dark splatters in the dust. The noor chirped happily and began to groom.

Dwer shook the canteen, winning a few drops. "Of all the selfish, ungrateful—"

It was already too late to hike to the nearest stream, down a narrow, treacherous trail. A waterfall growled, close enough to hear but over a midura away by foot. This was no crisis; he'd done without before. Still, the sound would give him dry-mouth, all night long.

Never stop learning, said the sage Ur-Ruhols. Tonight, Dwer had learned one more thing about noor. All told, the price of the lesson was pretty cheap.

He decided to arrange for a wakeup call. For that, he would need a clock teet.

There were good reasons to get an early start. He might still make it back to the yearly Gathering of the Six, before all the unpledged human boys and girls chose partners for jubilee dancing. Then there was his annual report to Danel Ozawa, and Lena Strong's ridiculous "tourism" idea to oppose. Also, if he led the glaver away before dawn, he just might manage to leave Mudfoot snoring by the coals. Noor loved sleep almost as much as upsetting the routines of villagers, and this one had had a long day.

So after supper Dwer brought forth a sheaf of paper folders, his cache of practical things. Many of the wrappers had come from his brother's wastebasket, or Sara's.

Lark's handwriting, graceful and controlled, usually traced some living species on Jijo's complex order of life. Dwer used Lark's castoff notes to store seeds, herbs, and feathers—things useful in the hunt.

Sara's hand was expansive yet tense, as if imagination and order held each other in check. Her discards swarmed with baffling mathematics. (Some failed equations weren't just scratched out but *stabbed* to death in fits of frustration.) Dwer used his sister's work-sheets to hold medicines, condiments, and the powders that made many Jijoan foods edible to humans.

From one folded page he drew six *tobar* seeds—plump, hard, and fragrant—which he spread across a rock some way downwind. Holding his breath, he used his knife to split one open, then fled a rising, pungent cloud. The glaver mewed unhappily, and the noor glared at him until the breeze swept most of the intense aroma away.

Back in his sleeping roll, Dwer waited as the stars came out. Kalunuti was a hot reddish pinpoint, set high on the leering face of Sargon, pitiless enforcer of laws. More starry patterns followed, *eagle, horse, dragon*— and *dolphin*, beloved cousin, grinning with her jaw thrust in a direction some said might lead to Earth.

If we exiles are ever caught, Dwer pondered. *Will the Great Galactic Library make a file about our culture? Our myths? Will aliens read our constellation myths and laugh?*

If all went as planned, no one would ever hear of this lonely colony or recall its tales. *Our descendants, if any, will be like glavers—simple, and innocent as the beasts of the field.*

Fluttering wings grazed the firelight. A squat form landed near the tobar seeds, with wings of grayish plates that slid like overlapping petals. The birdling's yellow beak quickly devoured the nut Dwer had cracked.

Mudfoot sat up, eyes glinting.

Dwer warned the noor, half-dozing—"You bother it, an' I'll have yer hide fer a hat."

Mudfoot sniffed and lay down again. Soon there came a rhythmic tapping as the teet started pecking at the next nut. It would take its time, consuming one kernel each midura—roughly seventy minutes—until the last was gone. Then, with a chattering screech, it would fly off. One didn't need a printout from the Great Library to know what function the Buyur had designed this creature to fill. The living alarm clock still worked as pro-grammed.

Lark is wrong about our place on this world, Dwer thought, lulled by the unvaried tapping. *We do a service. Jijo would be a sad place without people to use its gifts.*

There were dreams. Dwer always had dreams. Shapeless foes lurked beyond sight as he wandered a land covered with *colors,* like a rainbow that had melted, flowed across the ground, then frozen in place. The harsh hues hurt his eyes. Moreover, his throat felt parched, and he was unarmed.

The dream shifted. All of a sudden, he found himself alone in a forest of trees that seemed to stretch up past the moons. For some reason, the trees were even more threatening than the colored landscape. He fled, but could find no exit from the forest as their trunks glowed, burst into flame, then started to *explode.*

The furious intensity of the nightmare yanked him awake, sitting up with a racing heart. Dwer stared wide-eyed, glad to find the *real* woods intact, though dark and threaded by a chill breeze. There was no raging firestorm. He had dreamed the whole thing.

Still, uneasiness gnawed. Something felt *wrong.*

He rubbed his eyes. Different constellations swarmed the sky, fading in the east under a wash of predawn gray. The biggest moon, Loocen, hovered over silhouetted peaks, its sunlit face spangled with bright pinpoints—the domes of long-abandoned cities.

So what's wrong?

It wasn't just intuition. The clock teet had stopped. Something must have disturbed it before the time to chatter its alarm. He checked the area and found the noor snoring on quietly. The glaver tracked Dwer dully with one thoughtless eye, the other still closed.

All at once, he knew the problem.

My bow!

It wasn't where he'd left it, within arm's reach. It was gone.

Stolen!

Anger flooded the predawn dimness with blinding adrenaline outrage. Dozens had spoken enviously of his bow—a masterpiece of laminated wood and bone, fashioned by the qheuenish craftsmen of Ovoom Town. But who . . . ?

Calm down. Think.

Could it be Jeni Shen? She often joked about luring

him into a poker game, with the bow at stake. Or might it be—

Stop!

He took a deep breath, but it was hard disciplining his young body, so full of need to act.

Stop and hear what the world has to say. . . .

First, he must calm the furious spilling of his own unspoken words. Dwer pushed aside all noisy thoughts. Next he made himself ignore the rasping sound of breath and pulse.

The distant, muttering waterfall was by now familiar, easy to cancel out. The wind's rustle, less regular, soon went away, too.

One hovering sound might be the clock teet, cruising in hope of more tobar seeds. Another flutter told of a honey bat—no, a mated pair—which he also disregarded. The noor's snoring he edited, and the soft grind of glaver-molars as the prisoner rechewed her cud.

There! Dwer turned his head. Was that a scrape on gravel? Pebbles rattling down a scree, perhaps. Something, or someone—bipedal? Almost man-size, he guessed, and hurrying away.

Dwer took off after the sound. Gliding ghostlike in his moccasins, he ran some distance before noting that the thief was heading the *wrong direction*. Away from the coast. Away from the Slope. Higher into the Rimmer Range.

Toward the Pass.

Padding up the rocky trail, Dwer's angry flush gave way to the scrupulous cadence of pursuit—a tense, almost ecstatic concentration on each thrust of heel and toe; the efficiency of motion needed for silence; an eager probing beyond his own soft noise to seize any trace of the pursued. His head felt clear, no longer poisoned by fury. Whatever the reason for this chase, he could not help feeling a kind of joy. This was his art, the thing he loved best.

Dwer was near the notch of gray light separating two shadowy peaks, when a problem occurred to him.

Wait a minute!

He slowed to a trot, then down to a walk.

This is stupid. Here I am, chasing off after a sound I'm not even sure I heard—maybe a hangover of a dream— when the answer was there all along!

The noor.

He stopped, beating his fist against his thigh and feeling like an idiot.

It's just what a noor would do—stealing things. Swapping a villager's chipped cup for a treasure, or vice versa.

When he returned, would a pile of ligger turds sit where the bow had lain? Or a diamond wrested from the crown of some long dead Buyur king? Or would they all—noor, bow, and glaver—simply be gone? Mudfoot had been quite an actor, snoozing by the coals. Did the beast cackle when he hightailed off, chasing his own outraged imagination?

Alongside anger, there arose a grudging appreciation.

A good one. He really got me.

Then again, this noor might have a surprise coming. Of all the humans on Jijo, perhaps only Dwer was qualified to *find* the beast and get even.

It would be a difficult chase. Maybe impossible.

Or else the hunt of a lifetime.

Sudden insight filled Dwer with wonder. Was *that* the noor's gift? To offer Dwer—

Ahead of him, in the vague dimness, the corner of a shadow moved.

His unfocused eyes had been open to peripheral vision, habituated to a static scene. A reflex hunter's trick that made one especially sensitive to motion—as when a "boulder" shifted to the left, then moved onward toward the Pass.

Ears snatched distant tickling scrapes, softer than the wind. Dwer's eyebrows knotted as he started forward again, slowly at first, then stealthily faster.

When the blurry shadow stopped, *he* stopped, splaying his arms for balance.

Profiled against predawn gray, the silhouette waited a few duras more, then turned and continued on its way.

Trust your instincts, Fallon the Tracker used to teach. The old man was nobody's fool.

Mudfoot *had* been the obvious suspect. Perhaps that was *why* it didn't occur to Dwer, back at the campsite. He would have wasted valuable time blaming the logical culprit. His first impulse had been right, after all. The initial clue, a true one.

The shadow turned again. Dwer traced a human shape, alarmed now, fleeing with his purloined bow. This time he sprinted, forsaking stealth for speed. Pebbles flew, rattling the pass with echoes. The other swiveled too, leaping away like a striped gusul in flight.

Only three humans on Jijo could outrun Dwer, and none at all in rough terrain.

End game, he thought, bearing down for a final dash.

When his quarry turned, he was ready. When it drew a knife, he knew this was no joke. Dwer launched into a tackling dive, primed to hear shouts of anger and dismay.

Unexpected was the thief's face, looming as he hurtled forward.

Human.

Female.

Terribly young.

Above all—a complete and total stranger.

A~sx~

FATE HAD FALLEN FROM THE SKY.

To Jijo.

To the Slope.

To the Glade of Gathering.

To the nexus of our fears, much sooner than expected.

Across megaparsecs, a ship from the Five Galaxies had come! Such a vast distance . . . the least we poor exiles could do was march a short way to where it landed, and courteously greet it.

Vubben declined the honor of leading. Jijo's gravity so hobbles our dear g'Kek, they must rely solely on wheels, using their stilt-legs for balance only, moving over rough ground almost as slowly as a traeki. So, Vubben and i hobbled along, urging our hoon, qheuenish, human, and urrish counterparts to forge ahead.

Do i/we sense a foul odor of *envy* fuming in our central core? Do some of you, my several selves, resent our awkward slowness compared to those long hoonish legs or nimble urrish feet? Things might have been different had our traeki exile-ship come equipped with the full menagerie of rings our kin were said to own. Legends tell of adroit running limbs—gifts of the mighty Oailie—limbs to make even a heavy stack like ours as speedy as a song jackal. Speedy as a *Jophur*.

But then, would we also have carried Oailie arrogance? Their madness? Would we have fought *wars*, the way qheuens and urs and hoons and men did for centuries here on Jijo, bickering until the Commons grew strong enough for peace? Those traeki who fled to Jijo had reasons to leave some rings behind. Or so we believe.

But again, *digression* thwarts our tale. Discipline, my rings! Give the fumes another spin. Stroke the waxy imprints, and remember—

Recall how we marched, each at ers own pace, toward the side valley where the intruder ship had set down. Along the way, Vubben recited from the Book of Exile, greatest of scrolls, the one least altered by quarrel, heresy, or waves of new arrivals.

"The right to live is tentative," Vubben chanted in a voice that seemed to caress the soul.

"Material things are limited, though the mind is free.

"Of protein, phosphorus, nor even energy is there ever enough to slake all hungers. Therefore, show not affront when diverse beings vie over what physically exists. Only

in thought can there be true generosity. So let thought be the focus of your world."

Vubben's voice had a calming way with our people. The slim-boled welpal trees seemed to resonate his words, tuned as they are to the music of the Egg.

And yet, while Vubben spoke of equanimity, my/our basal segment kept trying to stop, turn its feet around, and carry us away! Dimly, that bottommost ring realized that danger lay ahead, and sensibly voted to flee. Our upper tiers had to apply scent-throbs to urge it onward.

i/we find strange how *fear* functions in non-traeki. They say it infuses all parts of a body, and hence must be fought everywhere at once! Once, i/we asked Lester Cambel how humans keep calm in times of crisis. His answer was that generally they don't!

How strange. Humans always seem so much in control. Is it just a grand act, to fool both others *and* themselves?

Do not digress, Oh Asx. Stroke the wax. Go on. Go on toward the ship.

Sara

HENRIK SEEMED RELUCTANT TO SET OFF HIS charges.

At first this surprised Sara. Wasn't this crisis what an exploser always dreamed of? A chance to make things go boom? To destroy works that others spent their lives building?

In fact, Henrik seemed less avid than many of the citizens crowding the Meeting Tree in panic that night, after witnessing a fireball rattle the forest to its ancient roots. Two gardeners and a worker chimp had fallen from high branches to their deaths, and scores of others had had narrow escapes. The farmers were in a state.

Carved from the spacious heart knot of a grandfather garu, the great hall was crammed with nearly every sapient adult within a rapid day's hike. Like a steaming minnow pie, the room seemed stuffed with perspiring humanity.

A cluster of other folk were also present—hoon sailors mostly, their pale scaly skins and shaggy white leg fur offset by dark green cloaks, cinched with wooden brooches below their puffing throat sacs. Some also wore trembling rewq over their eyes, to help interpret this stew of human emotions.

Near the north entrance, where it was less humid, a few urrish tinkers chafed and stamped, uneasily switching their braided tails. Sara even spied one forlorn g'Kek pilgrim, anxious green sweat dripping from a single eyestalk, while the other three lay curled like socks in a drawer, hiding from the raucous ferment.

Doctor Lorrek had been wise, it seemed, volunteering to spend the evening watching the wounded Stranger.

Pzora, the town pharmacist, had a defense against having ers lower rings trampled. If pressed too closely, the traeki just vented a little pungent steam, and even the most agitated citizen gave er room.

No doubt it was like this wherever folk had seen the dread specter in the sky. Right now *human* visitors were attending qheuen or hoon assemblies and even urrish tribal conclaves, beside roaring fires on the open plains.

The Great Peace is our finest accomplishment, Sara thought. *Maybe it will weigh in our favor, when we're judged. We've come far since the days of war and slaughter.*

Alas, from the rancor of tonight's meeting, the Commons still had a long way to go.

"Minor repairs?"

Chaz Langmur, the master carpenter, protested from the stage, normally used for concerts and theatricals. "We're talking about losing everything below the flood line, and that don't count the dam itself! You ask how many *years* to rebuild, if this turns out to be a false alarm? Let's talk *lifetimes!*"

Merchants and craft workers supported Langmur with shouts but were opposed by cries of "Shame!" from many wearing the gray garb of farmers. Overhead, excited apelike shrieks joined in. Though not voting citizens, tradition let local chimps clamber up the wall tapestries to observe from slit vents high above. How much they understood was debatable. Some screamed lustily for whichever speaker seemed most impassioned, while others were as partisan as Sara's father, who clapped the carpenter's back with encouragement.

It had gone this way for hours. Angry men and women taking turns citing scripture or bemoaning costs, each side waxing ever louder as their fear and irritation grew. Nor were humans the sole partisans. Log Biter, matriarch of the local qheuenish hive, had spoken urgently for preserving Dolo Dam, while her cousin from Logjam Pond proclaimed it a "gaudy monstrosity." Sara feared a mêlée would ensue between two huge armored matrons, until the chief elder, Fru Nestor, interposed her small human form, the rewq on her brow flashing soothing colors until both qheuens finally backed down.

The audience was no better. A woman stepped on Sara's foot. Someone else must not have bathed this week, comparing badly to Pzora's worst secretions. Sara envied Prity, a tiny figure perched high on a windowsill next to several human kids too young to vote. Unlike other chimps, she seemed to find her notebook more engaging than the shouting speakers, tugging at her lower lip while she studied lines of complex mathematics.

Sara envied Prity's escape into abstraction.

One of the tree farmers rose to speak—a dark man named Jop, whose pale yellow hair curled around his ears. He clenched two large hands, knotty with lifelong calluses.

"Penny pinching and farsightedness!" Jop dismissed the carpenter's plea. "What would you preserve? A few workshops and docks? Passing toys like plumbing and paper? Dross! All dross! Some paltry comforts that our sinner ancestors let us poor exiles keep for a while, softening our first steps on the road toward grace. But the Scrolls say *none* of it will last! It's all destined for the sea!"

Jop turned to his partisans, clutching both hands together. "It was planned long ago—what we're sworn to do when starships come. Or else, why've we supported a guild of explosers all this time?"

Sara glanced again at Henrik and son, seated at the back of the dais. The boy, Jomah, betrayed unease with a slow twisting of his cap between nervous young hands. But his pa might have been a statue. Henrik had remained silent throughout, except to report tersely that his charges were ready.

Sara always pictured their craft as a frustrating profession, probably unique to Jijo. After so many years of preparation—performing endless tests in a small canyon in the hills—wouldn't they hanker to see it all finally put to use? *I know I would.*

Long ago, she and Lark and little Dwer used to sit in their attic room, watching moonlight spill over the rumbling water wheel and thrilling each other with lurid tales of what they might see if ever *the* moment came when Henrik lit his fuses. With delicious mock-terror pounding in their chests, they counted down heartbeats until—kablam!

Dwer loved making sound effects, especially the pretend detonation that finished off the dam, accompanied by waving arms and lots of saliva. Sara's younger brother then gleefully described the wall of water tossing proud boats like trifles, smashing Nelo's drying racks, and driving toward their bedroom window like a fist.

Lark took over then, thrilling and terrifying the younger kids as he portrayed their attic being sheared off by a watery blast, sent careening through the garu forest while farmers stared down in pity. Each pretend near-miss made Sara and Dwer cry out till they leaped on their laughing older brother, pummeling to make him stop.

And yet—after Dwer and Lark had done their best to scare her, *they* would toss and turn, while Sara never had nightmares. When she did dream about the dam bursting, she used to picture a great wave simply taking them in the palm of its gentle hand. As froth concealed all of Jijo, it magically transformed into the fluffy, charged substance of a cloud. Always, the fantasy ended with her body lighter than mist, fearless, soaring through a night radiant with stars.

A roar of approval yanked her back to the present. At first she could not tell if it came from the party wanting quick action, or from those resolved not to wreck nine generations' work on the mere evidence of their own eyes.

"We have no idea what it was we saw!" her father declared, combing his beard with gnarled fingers. "Can we be sure it was a spaceship? Perhaps a *meteor* grazed by. That'd explain all the noise and ruckus."

Sneers and foot-stamps greeted this suggestion. Nelo hurried on. "Even if it was a ship, that don't mean we've been discovered! Other vessels have come and gone— Zang globes, for instance, come to siphon water from the sea. Did we wreck everything then? Did the older tribes burn their towns when we *humans* came? How do we know it wasn't another sneakship, bringing a seventh exile race to join our Commons?"

Jop snorted derisively.

"Let me remind the learned papermaker—sneakships *sneak*! They come under the shadow of night an' cloud an' mountain peak. This new vessel made no such effort. It aimed straight at the Glade of the Egg, at a time when the pavilions of Gathering are there, along with the chief sages of the Six."

"Exactly!" Nelo cried. "By now the sages should be well aware of the situation and would have farcast if they felt it necessary to—"

"Farcasting?" Jop interrupted. "Are you serious? The sages remind us over an' over again that it can't be trusted. In a crisis, farcasts may be just the thing to *attract* attention! Or else"—Jop paused meaningfully—"or else there may have been no calls for a more terrible reason."

He let the implication sink in, amid a scatter of gasps. Almost everyone present had a relative or close friend who had taken pilgrimage this year.

Lark and Dwer—are you safe? Sara pondered anxiously. *Will I ever see you again?*

"Tradition leaves it up to each community. Shall we shirk, when our loved ones may've already paid a dearer price than some buildings and a stinkin' dam?"

Cries of outrage from the craft workers were drowned out by support from Jop's followers. "Order!" Fru Nestor squeaked, but her plaint was lost in the chaos. Jop and his allies shouted for a vote.

"Choose the Law! Choose the Law!"

Nestor appealed for order with upraised hands, clearly dreading the dismemberment of her town—its reduction to a mere farming hamlet, rich in reverence but little else. "Does anyone else have something to say?"

Nelo stepped up to try again but wilted under a stream of catcalls. Who had ever seen a *papermaker* treated thus? Sara felt his shame and dishonor, but it would be far worse when his beloved factory was blown to oblivion before an all-destroying flood.

Sara had a strange thought—should she sneak up to her old attic room and wait for the wave? Who had prophesied right? Dwer and Lark? Or those images *she* had foreseen in dreams? It would be a once-in-a-lifetime chance to find out.

Resumed chanting tapered off as someone new moved forward from behind the crowd of pale hoon sailors. It was a centauroid figure with a long sinuous body of mottled suede that branched into a pair of stubby shoulderless arms and a powerful snakelike neck. The narrow-pointed head contained three black eyes, one of them lidless and faceted, all set around a triangular mouth. It was an urrish tinker Sara recognized from past visits to Dolo, buying scraps of glass and metal, selling simple Buyur tools reclaimed from some ruin. The urs stepped daintily, as if worried her hooves might catch in the rough floorboards. She had one arm raised, exposing a glimpse of the bluish brooding pouch underneath, an act that might have different connotations in a meeting of her own kind, but Fru Nestor took it as a request to speak, which she granted with a bow.

Sara heard a human mutter—"*hinney!*"—a rude callback to days when newcomer Earthlings fought ur-rish tribes over land and honor. If the tinker heard the insult, she ignored it, carrying herself well for a youngish urs with just one husband pouch tenanted by a squirming bulge. Among so many humans, the urs could not use a plains dialect of Galactic Two but made do with Anglic, despite the handicap of a cloven upper lip.

"I can ve called Ulgor. I thank you for your courtesy, which is vlessed among the Six. I wish only to ask questions concerning the issues discussed tonight. Ny first question follows—

"Is this not a natter vest decided vy our sages? Why not let those wise ones rule whether the great tine of judgment has arrived?"

With an exaggerated show of mannerly patience, Jop replied, "Learned neighbor, the Scrolls call on all villages to act independently, to erase all signs that might be seen from the sky! The order's simple. No complicated judgment is needed.

"Besides," he concluded. "There's no time to hear from the sages. They're all far away, at Gathering."

"Forgive," Ulgor bowed her forelegs. "*Not* all. A few linger in residence at the Hall o' Vooks, in Vivlos, do they not?"

There was confusion as people looked at one another, then Fru Nestor cried out, "The Hall of *Books,* in *Biblos*! Yes, that's true. But Biblos is still many days away, by boat."

Again Ulgor bent her neck before dissenting. "Yet I have heard that, fron the highest tree in Dolo, one can see across the quicksand narsh to the glass cliffs overlooking Vivlos."

"With a good telescope," Jop acknowledged, wary that this was sapping the crowd's passionate momentum. "I still don't see how it helps—"

"*Fire!*"

Faces turned toward Sara, who had shouted while the thought was still half formed.

"We'd see flames as the library burned!"

Muttering, the crowd stared at her, till she explained. "You all know I used to work at Biblos. They have a contingency plan like everyone else. If the sages command it, the librarians are to carry off what volumes they can, then ignite the rest."

This brought on a somber hush. Wrecking Dolo's dam was one thing, but loss of Biblos would truly signal an ending. No place was more central to human life on Jijo.

"Finally, they are to blow the pillars holding up the roof-of-stone and bring it down on the ashes. Ulgor's right. We could see any change that big, especially with Loocen rising at this hour."

Fru Nestor spoke a terse command. "Send someone aloft to see!"

Several boys leaped up and vanished through the windows, accompanied by a string of hooting chimpanzees. A nervous murmur ensued while the crowd waited. Sara felt uncomfortable under the regard of so many, and lowered her eyes.

That was the sort of thing Lark *would do. Boldly taking over a meeting at the last minute, compelling others to act. Joshu had that impulsiveness, too—till the sickness took him in those final weeks.* . . .

Gnarled fingers grasped hers, halting the bleak gyre of her thoughts. She looked up and saw that Nelo had aged in the last hour. Now the fate of his beloved mill rested on news from above.

As the slow duras passed, the full import of her prediction sank in.

Biblos.

The Hall of Books.

Once already, fire had taken a terrible toll there. Even so, the remaining archive was humanity's greatest contribution to the Commons and a cause of both envy and wonder among the other races.

What will we become, if it's gone? True pastoralists?

Gleaners, living off remnants swiped from ancient Buyur sites? Farmers all?

That was how the other five had seemed, when humans first came. Bickering primitives with their barely functioning commons. Humanity introduced new ways, changed the rules, almost as much as the arrival of the Egg several generations later.

Now shall we slide downslope faster? Losing the few relics that remind us we once roamed galaxies? Shucking our books, tools, clothes, till we're like glavers? Pure, shriven innocents?

According to the Scrolls, that was one path to salvation. Many, like Jop, believed in it.

Sara tried to see hope, even if word came back of flames and dust in the night. At any time, hundreds of books were outside Biblos, on loan to far-flung communities.

But few texts in Sara's specialty ever left their dusty shelves. *Hilbert. Somerfeld. Witten and Tang. Eliahu*—names of great minds she knew intimately across centuries and parsecs. The intimacy of pure, near-perfect thoughts. *They'll burn. The sole copies.* Lately her research had swung to other areas—the chaotic ebb and flow of language—but still she called mathematics home. The voices in those books had always seemed soul-alive. Now she feared learning they were gone.

Then abruptly, another notion occurred to her, completely unexpected, glancing off her grief at a startling angle.

If Galactics really have come, what do a few thousand paper volumes really matter? Sure, they'll judge us for our ancestors' crime. Nothing can prevent that. But meanwhile, aboard their ships . . .

It occurred to Sara that she might get a chance to visit a completely different *kind* of library. One towering over the Biblos cache, the way the noon sun outblazed a candle. *What an opportunity! Even if we're all soon prisoners of the galactic Lords of Migration, destined for some prison world, they can hardly deny us a chance to read!*

In accounts of olden days she had read about "accessing" computer databases, swimming in knowledge like a warm sea, letting it fill your mind, your pores. Swooping through clouds of wisdom.

I could find out if my work is original! Or if it's been done ten million times, during a billion years of Galactic culture.

The thought seemed at once both arrogant and humbling. Her fear of the great starships was undiminished. Her prayer remained that it was all a mistake, or a meteor, or some illusion.

But a rebel corner of her roiling mind felt something new—a wakened hunger.

If only . . .

Her thought broke against an interruption. Suddenly, high overhead, a boy stuck his head through a slit window. Hanging upside down, he cried—*"No fires!"*

He was joined by others, at different openings, all shouting the same thing. Chimps joined in, shrieking excitement across the crowded meeting hall.

"No fires—and the roof-of-stone still stands!"

Old Henrik stood, then spoke two words to the elders before departing with his son. Amid the flustered babble of the throng, Sara read the exploser's expression of resolve and the decisive message of his lips.

"We wait."

Asx

OUR CARAVAN OF RACES MARCHED TOWARD where the alien ship was last seen—a blazing cylinder—descending beyond a low hill. Along the way, Vubben continued chanting from the Scroll of Danger.

Voices cried out ahead. Crowds jostled along a ridgetop, hissing and murmuring. We must nudge past men and hoon to win our way through.

Whereupon, did we not gaze across a *nest*? A new

clearing lined with shattered trees, still smoking from whatever ray had cut them down.

And poised amid this devastation—shimmering from its heat of entry—lay the cause.

Nearby, human and urrish crafters argued in the strange dialect of the engineering caste, disputing whether this nub or that blister might be weaponry or sensors. But which of us on Jijo has the expertise to guess? Our ships long ago went down to join this planet's melting crust. Even the most recent arrivals, humans, are many generations removed from starfarers. No living member of the Commons ever saw anything like this.

It *was* a ship of the Civilization of the Five Galaxies. That much the techies could tell.

Yet where was the rayed spiral? The symbol required to be carried on the forward flank of every sanctioned ship of space?

Our worried lore-masters explain—the spiral is no mere symbol. Silently, it rides. Impartially, it records. Objectively, it bears witness to everything seen and done, wherever the vessel may fly.

We peered and sought, but in the ordained place there lay only a *burnished shine*. It had been rubbed away, smoother than a qheuenish larva.

That was when confusion gave way to understanding. Realization of what this ship represented.

Not the great Institutes, as we first thought.

Nor the righteous, mighty, legalistic star-clans—or the mysterious Zang.

Not even exiles like ourselves.

None of those, but *outlaws*. Felons of an order worse than our own ancestors.

Villains.

Villains had come to Jijo.

III. THE BOOK OF THE SEA

It is a Paradox of Life that all species
breed past mere replacement.
Any paradise of plenty soon fills, to
become paradise no more.
By what right, then, do we exiles
claim a world that was honorably set
aside, to nurture frail young-life in
peace, and be kept safe from hungry
nations?

Exiles, you should fear the law's just
wrath, to find you here,
unsanctioned, not yet redeemed. But
when judgment comes, law will also
be your shield, tempering
righteous wrath with justice.

There is a deeper terror, prowling the
angry sky.
It is a different peril. One that stalks
in utter absence of the law.

—The Scroll of Danger

Alvin's Tale

ALL RIGHT, SO I'M NOT AS QUICK AS SOME. I'LL never think as fast as Huck, who can run verbal circles around me.

It's just as well, I guess. I could've grown up in this little hoon port thinking I was such a clever fellow—as witty and gloss as my literary nicknamesake—just 'cause I can read any Anglic book and fancy myself a writer. Good thing I had this little g'Kek genius living in the khuta next door, to remind me that an above-average hoon is still a hoon. Dull as a brick.

Anyway, there I was, squatting between two of my best friends while they fussed over what we should do with the coming summer, and it never occurred to me that both Huck and Pincer were ring-coring me at more than one level.

Pincer only spent a few duras trying to tell us about his latest "monsters"—grayish shapes he *thought* he glimpsed through the murk, while bored, tending his hive's lobster pens. He's pulled that one on us so many times, we wouldn't listen if he brought us a molar from Moby Dick, with a peg leg jammed like a toothpick on one end. Sighing from all five vents at once, he gave up babbling about his latest sighting, and switched over to defending his *Project Nautilus*.

Pincer was upset to learn that Huck wanted to abandon the scheme. Legs lifted on opposite sides of his hard shell, hissing like tubes on a calliope.

"Look, we already *agreed-deed*. We just *gotta* finish

the bathy, or else what've we been working-king on for a year now-ow!"

"You did most of the carpentry and testing," I pointed out. "Huck and I mostly drew up plans for—"

"Exactly!" Huck interrupted, two eyes bobbing for emphasis. "Sure, we helped with designs and small parts. That was fun. But I never signed on to actually *ride* the dam' thing to the bottom of the sea."

Pincer's blue cupola lifted all the way up, and his slit-of-eyes seemed to spin. "But you *said* it was interesting-ing! You called the idea uttergloss-loss!"

"True," Huck agreed. "In theory, it's totally puff. But there's one problem, friend. It's also jeekee *dangerous*."

Pincer rocked back, as if the thought had never occurred to him. "You . . . never said anything about that before."

I turned to look at Huck. I don't think I ever heard her speak that word till then. *Dangerous*. In all our adventures growing up, *she* always seemed the one ready to take a chance, sometimes daring the rest of us with cutting taunts, the way only a g'Kek can on those rare occasions when they put away politeness and *try* to be nasty. With Huck an orphan, and Ur-ronn and Pincer coming from low-kay races, no one was going to miss them much if they died. So it normally fell on *me* to be the voice of caution—a role I hated.

"Yeah," Huck said. "Well, maybe it's time someone pointed out the difference between taking a calculated risk and committing flat-out *suicide*. Which is what it'd be if we ever took a ride aboard that contraption of yours, Pincer!"

Our poor qheuenish friend looked like someone had stuck him in a leg-vent with a stick. His cupola went all wobbly. "You all know-ow I'd never ask my friends-ends—"

"To go anywhere *you* wouldn't go?" Huck retorted. "Big of you, since you're talking about dragging us around underwater, where *you're* built to be perfectly comfortable."

"Only at first-irst!" Pincer retorted. "After some test

dives, we'll go deeper. And I'll be in there with you, taking all the same chances-ances!"

"Come on, Huck," I put in. "Give the poor guy's shell a buff."

"Anyway-ay," Pincer retaliated, "what about *your* plan? At least the bathy would be lawful and upright. *You* want to break the rules and do *sooner* stuff-uff!"

Now it was Huck's turn to go defensive. "What sooner stuff? None of us can breed with each other, so there's no chance of committing *that* crime while we're over the border. Anyhow, hunters and inspectors go beyond the markers."

"Sure. *With* permission from the sages-ages!"

Huck shrugged two stalks, as if to say she couldn't be bothered with petty legalistic details. "I still prefer a misdemeanor over flat-out suicide."

"You mean you prefer a silly little trip to some brokendown Buyur ruin, just to read boring ol' wall markingsings, over a chance to see the *Midden-idden?* And real live *monsters?*"

Huck groaned and spun a disgusted circle. Earlier, Pincer had told us about a thing he glimpsed that morning, in the shallows south of town. Something with silvery-bright scales swooped by, he swore, flapping what looked in the murky distance like underwater *wings*. After hearing similar stories almost since Pincer's molting day, we didn't give this one a lot of credit.

That was when both of them turned to *me* to decide!

"Remember, Alvin," Huck crooned. "You just promised—"

"You promised *me*, months ago!" Pincer cried, so avid that he didn't stutter.

Right then I felt like a traeki standing between two piles of really ripe mulch. I liked the notion of getting to see the deep Midden, where everything slick and Galactic had gone since the Buyur went away. An undersea adventure like in books by Haller or Verne.

On the other hand, Huck was right about Pincer's plan being Ifni-spit. The risk might seem worth it to a low-kay qheuen, who didn't even know for sure who his mother was, but I know *my* folks would sicken awful if I went off and died without leaving even my heart-spine behind for soul-grinding and vuphyning.

Anyway, Huck offered a prospect almost as gloss—to find writings even more ancient than the books humans brought to Jijo. Real *Buyur* stories, maybe. The idea set off tingles in my sucker pads.

As it turns out, I was spared having to decide. That's because my noor, Huphu, arrived right then, darting under Pincer's legs and Huck's wheels, yapping something about an urgent message from Ur-ronn.

Ur-ronn wanted to see us.

More than that—she had a big surprise to share.

Oh, yes. Huphu needs introducing.

First off, she's not really *my* noor. She hangs around me a lot, and my rumble-umbles seem to work, getting her to do what I want a good part of the time. Still, it's kind of hard to describe the relationship between hoon and noor. The very word—*relationship*—implies a lot of stuff that's just not there. Maybe this is one of those cases where Anglic's flexibility, usually the most utterbuff thing about it, simply falls apart into vagueness.

Anyway, Huphu's no talker-decider. Not a *sapient* being, like us members of the Six. But since she comes along on most of our adventures, I guess she's as much a part of the gang as anyone. Lots of folks say noors are crazy. For sure, they don't seem to care if they live or die, so long as they're seeing something *new*. More have probably perished of curiosity than from liggers on land or sea-starks offshore. So I knew how Huphu would vote in our argument, if she could talk.

Fortunately, even Pincer knows better than to suggest ever letting *her* decide anything.

So there we were, arguing away, when this little noor bounds up the jetty, yipping like mad. Right off we can tell it's a semaphore message she's relaying, on account of it makes sense. Noors can't speak Galactic Two or any other language anyone's ever grokked, but they *can* memorize and repeat any short mirror-flash signal they happen to pick up with their sharp eyes. They can even tell from the opener-tag who a message is for. It's a gloss talent that'd be awfully useful—if only they did it reliably, instead of just when they felt like it.

Huphu sure must've felt like it, 'cause next thing you know she's yelping the upper denotation train of a GalTwo memorandum. (I figure an old Morse code telegraph operator like Mark Twain could've managed GalTwo, if he tried.)

As I said before, the message was from our urrish pal, Ur-ronn, and it said—*WINDOW FINISHED. COME QUICK. OTHER VERY WEIRD STUFF HAPPENING!*

I put an exclamation point at the end 'cause that's how Huphu finished reciting the bulletin she'd seen flash down from Mount Guenn, terminating her report with a bark of ecstatic excitement. I'm sure the phrase "weird stuff" was what had her bounding in circles, biting at her shadow.

"I'll get my water bag," Pincer-Tip said after a short pause.

"I'll fetch my goggles," Huck added.

"I'll grab my cloak and meet you at the tram," I finished. There was no need for discussion. Not after an invitation like *that*.

IV. THE BOOK OF THE SLOPE

Legends

There is a fable told by the g'Kek, one of the oldest handed down since their sneakship came to Jijo, passed on orally for almost two thousand years, until it was finally recorded on paper.

The saga tells of a youth whose "thread skating" prowess was renowned in one of the orbital cities where g'Keks dwelled, after losing their homeworld on a wager.

In this particular city, unhampered by the drag of solid ground, young wheel-lords of a space-born generation fashioned a new game—skimming with flashing rims along the thinnest of colored strands—cables that they strung at angles throughout the vast inner cavity of their artificial world. One skater, the tale says, used to take on dare after dare, relishing risk, hopping among gossamer strands and sometimes even flying free, wheels spinning madly before catching the next cord, swooping in ecstatic abandon.

Then, one day, a defeated opponent taunted the young champion.

"I'll bet you can't skim close enough to wrap a thread round the sun!"

Today's Jijoan scholars find this part of the tale confusing. How could a sun be within reach, inside a hollow, spinning rock? With much of our Space Technologies section destroyed, the Biblos Scholarium is ill-equipped to interpret such clues. Our best guess is that the story became garbled over time, along with most other memories of a godlike past.

The technical details do not matter as much as the moral of the tale—the imprudence of messing with forces beyond your comprehension. A fool doing so can get burned, like the skater in the tale, whose dramatic end ignited a storm of slender, blazing trails, crisscrossing the doomed city's suddenly fiery inner sky.

—Collected Fables of Jijo's Seven,
   Third Edition. Department of Folklore
   and Language, Biblos, Year 1867
   of Exile.

Dwer

SINCE FINISHING HIS APPRENTICESHIP, DWER HAD visited nearly every village and farm in Jijo's settled zone, including the islands and one or two secret places he was sworn never to speak of. He had met a great many settlers from every race, including most of the Slope's human population.

He grew more certain with each passing dura that the new prisoner wasn't one of them.

Surprise flustered Dwer. Irrational guilt made him doubly angry.

"Of all the stupid things to do," he told the girl rubbing her head by the cold campfire, "stealing my bow ranks pretty high. But pulling a *knife* tops all! How was I to know you were just a kid, up there in the dark? I might've broke your neck in self-defense!"

It was the first time either of them had spoken since her skull smacked the ground, leaving her body limp to be slung over a shoulder and lugged back to camp. Never quite losing consciousness, the strange youth had recovered most of her wits by the time he sat her down near the coals. Now she kneaded her bruised head, watched by the glaver and the noor.

"I . . . thought you was . . . a ligger," she stammered at last.

"You stole my bow, ran away, then thought you were being chased by a *ligger*?"

This much could be said in her favor—she was a lousy liar. By dawn's light, her small frame sat bundled in garments of poorly tanned leather, stitched with sinew. Her hair, tied in a chopped-off ponytail, was a wavy reddish brown. Of her face—what could be made out under smudges—the stand-out features were a nose that had once been broken and a nasty burn scar along her left cheek, marring a face that might otherwise have been pretty, after a good scrubbing.

"What's your name?"

She lowered her chin and muttered something.

"What was that? I couldn't hear."

"I said, it's *Rety*!" She met his eyes for the first time, her voice now edged with defiance. "What're you gonna do with me?"

A reasonable question, under the circumstances. Rubbing his chin, Dwer couldn't see where he had much choice. "Guess I'll take you to Gathering. Most of the sages are there. If you're old enough, you've got a grievance to answer, or else your parents will be fetched. By the way, who are they? Where do you live?"

The glowering silence returned. Finally, she muttered—"I'm thirsty."

Both the glaver and the noor had taken turns nuzzling the empty canteen, then scolding him with their eyes. *What am I?* Dwer thought. *Everybody's daddy?*

He sighed. "All right, let's head for water. Rety, you go stand over by the glaver."

Her eyes widened. "Does—does it bite?"

Dwer gaped back at her. "It's a *glaver,* for Ifni's sake!" He took her by the hand. "You'd have reason to fear it if you were a grubworm, or a pile of garbage. Though now that I mention it—"

She yanked back her hand, glaring.

"Okay, sorry. Anyway, you're going to lead, so's I can keep an eye on you. And this will make sure you don't scoot off." He tied the free end of the glaver's tether to her belt, in back where she could only reach it with difficulty. Dwer then hoisted his pack and the bow. "Hear the waterfall? We'll take a break for jerky when we get there."

·   ·   ·   ·   ·

It was a strange trek—the sullen leading the apathetic, followed by the confused, all tailed by the inveterately amused. Whenever Dwer glanced back, Mudfoot's leering grin seemed only a little strained as the noor panted in the bone-dry morning air.

Some folks barred their doors when they heard a noor was nearby. Others put out treats, hoping to entice a change in luck. Dwer sometimes saw wild ones in the marshes, where flame trees flourished on the forested backs of drifting acre-lilies. But his strongest memories were from his father's mill, where young noor came each spring to perform reckless, sometimes fatal dives from the ponderously turning power wheel. As a child, Dwer often scampered alongside, taking the same exhilarating risks, much to his parents' distress. He even tried to bond closer to those childhood playmates, bribing them with food, teaching them tricks, seeking a link like Man once had with his helpmate—*dog*.

Alas, noor were *not* dogs. In time, as his life-path took him farther from the gentle river, Dwer came to realize noor were clever, brave—and also quite dangerous. Silently, he warned Mudfoot, *Just because you weren't the thief, don't think that makes me trust you one bit.*

A steep trail looks and feels different going down than heading up. At times, this one seemed so wild and untamed, Dwer could squint and imagine he was on a *real* frontier, untouched by sapient hands since the world was new. Then they'd pass some decayed Buyur remnant—a cement-aggregate wall, or a stretch of rubbery pavement missed by the roving deconstructors when Jijo was laid fallow—and the illusion vanished. Demolition was never perfect. Countless Buyur traces were visible west of the Rimmers.

Time was the true recycler. Poor Jijo had been assigned enough to restore her eco-web, or so said his brother, Lark. But Dwer rarely thought on such a grand scale. It robbed magic from the Jijo of today—a wounded place, but one filled with wonders.

Rety needed help over some steeper patches, and the glaver often had to be lowered by rope. Once, after wrestling the lugubrious creature down to a stretch of old road, Dwer swiveled to find the girl *gone*.

"Now where did the little—" He exhaled frustration. "Oh, hell."

Rety's affront deserved some penalty, and her mystery shouted to be solved, but fetching stray glavers came first. After delivering this one, perhaps he'd return to pick up the girl's trail, even though it would make him miss most of Gathering—

He rounded a sheer stone corner and almost stumbled over the girl, squatting face to face with Mudfoot. Rety looked up at Dwer.

"It's a *noor,* right?" she asked.

Dwer covered his surprise. "Uh, it's the first you've seen?"

She nodded, bemused by Mudfoot's flirtatious grin.

"Nor ever met a glaver, it seems." Dwer asked—"How far east do you people live?"

The scar on her cheek grew livid as her face flushed. "I don't know what you—"

She stopped as the extent of her slip-up sank in. Her lips pressed in a pale line.

"Don't fret it. I already know all about you," he said, gesturing at her clothes. "No woven cloth. Hides sewn with gut. Good imla and sorrl pelts. Sorrl don't grow that big, west of the Rimmers."

Reading her dismay, he shrugged. "I've been over the mountains myself, several times. Did your folks say it's forbidden? That's true, mostly. But *I* can range anywheres I want, on survey."

She looked down. "So I wouldn't've been safe even if I—"

"Ran faster and made it over the pass? Cross some imaginary line and I'd have to let you go?" Dwer laughed, trying not to sound too unfriendly. "Rety, go easy on yourself. You stole the wrong fella's bow, is all. I'd've chased you beyond the Sunrise Desert if I had to."

That was bluster, of course. Nothing on Jijo was worth

a two-thousand-league trek across volcanoes and burning sands. Still, Rety's eyes widened. He went on.

"I never spotted your tribe in any of my expeditions east, so I'd guess you're from quite a ways *south* of east, beyond the Venom Plain. Is it the Gray Hills? I hear that country's so twisty, it could hide a small tribe, if they're careful."

Her brown eyes filled with a weary pang. "You're wrong. I didn't come from . . . that place."

She trailed off lamely, and Dwer felt sympathy. He knew all about feeling awkward around one's own kind. The loner's life made it hard getting enough experience to overcome his own shyness.

Which is why I have to make it to Gathering! Sara had given him a letter to deliver to Plovov the Analyst. Coincidentally, Plovov's daughter was a beauty, and unbetrothed. With luck, Dwer might get a chance to ask Glory Plovov out for a walk, and maybe tell a story good enough to impress her. Like how he stopped last year's migration of herd-moribul from stampeding over a cliff during a lightning storm. Perhaps he wouldn't stammer this time, making her giggle in a way he didn't like.

Suddenly he was impatient to be off. "Well, no sense worrying about it now." He motioned for Rety to lead the glaver again. "You'll be assigned a junior sage to speak for you, so you won't face the council alone. Anyway, we don't hang sooners anymore. Not unless we have to."

His attempt to catch her eye with a wink failed, so the joke went flat. She studied the ground as he retied the tether, and they resumed moving single file.

A rising humidity turned into mist as they neared the noise of plunging water. Where the trail rounded a switchback, a streamlet fell from above, dropping staccato spatters across an aquamarine pool. From there, water spilled over a sheer edge, resuming its steep journey toward the river far below, and finally the sea.

The way down to the pool looked too treacherous to risk with Rety and the glaver, so he signaled to keep going. They would intersect the brook again, farther along.

But the noor leaped from rock to rock. Soon they heard him splashing joyfully as they plodded on.

Dwer found himself thinking of another waterfall, way up where the Great Northern Glacier reached a towering cliff at the continent's edge. Every other year, he hunted brankur pelts there, during spring thaw. But he really made the journey in order to be on hand when the ice dam finally broke, at the outlet of Lake Desolation.

Huge, translucent sheets would tumble nearly a kilometer, shattering to fill the sky with crystal icebows, bringing the mighty falls back to life with a soul-filling roar.

In his fumbling way, he once tried describing the scene to Lark and Sara—the shouting colors and radiant noise—hoping practice would school his clumsy tongue. Reliably, his sister's eyes lit up over his tales of Jijo's marvels beyond the narrow Slope. But good old cheerful Lark just shook his head and said—*"These fine marvels would do just as well without us."*

But would they? Dwer wondered.

Is there beauty in a forest, if no creature stops and calls it lovely, now and then? Isn't that what "sapience" is for?

Someday, he hoped to take his wife-and-mate to Desolation Falls. If he found someone whose soul could share it the way his did.

The noor caught up a while later, sauntering by with a smug grin, then waiting to shake its sleek back, spraying their knees as they passed. Rety laughed. A short sound, curt and hurried, as if she did not expect any pleasure to last long.

Farther down the trail, Dwer halted where an outcrop overlooked the cascade, a featherlike trickle, dancing along the cliff face. The sight reminded Dwer of how desperately dry he felt. It also tugged a sigh, akin to loneliness.

"Come on, sprig. There's another pool down a ways, easy to get to."

But Rety stood for a time, rooted in place, with a line of moisture on her cheek, though Dwer guessed it might have come from floating mist.

Asx

THEY DO NOT SHOW THEIR FACES. PLANS MIGHT go astray. Some of us might survive to testify. So naturally, they hide their forms.

Our scrolls warn of this possibility. Our destiny seems foredoomed.

Yet when the starship's voice filled the valley, the plain intent was to reassure.

> *"(Simple) scientists, we are.*
> *"Surveys of (local, interesting) lifeforms, we prepare.*
> *"Harmful to anyone, we are not."*

That decree, in the clicks and squeaks of highly formal Galactic Two, was repeated in three other standard languages, and finally—because they saw men and pans among our throng—in the wolfling tongue, Anglic.

> *"Surveying (local, unique) lifeforms, in this we seek your (gracious) help.*
> *"Knowledge of the (local) biosphere, this you (assuredly) have.*
> *"Tools and (useful) arts, these we offer in trade.*
> *"Confidentially, shall we (mutually) exchange?"*

Recall, my rings, how our perplexed peoples looked to one another. Could such vows be trusted? We who dwell on Jijo are already felons in the eyes of vast empires. So are those aboard this ship. Might two such groups have reason for common cause?

Our human sage summed it up with laconic wit. In Anglic, Lester Cambel muttered wisely—

"Confidentially, my hairy ancestors' armpits!"

And he scratched himself in a gesture that was both oracular and pointedly apropos.

Lark

THE NIGHT BEFORE THE FOREIGNERS CAME, A chain of white-robed pilgrims trekked through a pre-dawn mist. There were sixty, ten from each race.

Other groups would come this way during festival, seeking harmony patterns. But this company was different—its mission more grave.

Shapes loomed at them. Gnarled, misgrown trees spread twisted arms, like clutching specters. Oily vapors merged and sublimed. The trail turned sharply to avoid dark cavities, apparently bottomless, echoing mysteriously. Knobs of wind-scoured rock teased form-hungry agents of the mind, stoking the wanderers' nervous anticipation. Would the next twisty switchback, or the next, bring *it* into sight—Jijo's revered Mother Egg?

Whatever organic quirks they inherited, from six worlds in four different galaxies, each traveler felt the same throbbing call toward oneness. Lark paced his footsteps to a rhythm conveyed by the rewq on his brow.

I've been up this path a dozen times. It should be familiar by now. So why can't I respond?

He tried letting the rewq lay its motif of color and sound over the real world. Feet shuffled. Hooves clattered. Ring nubs swiveled and wheels creaked along a dusty trail pounded so smooth by past pilgrims that one might guess this ritual stretched back to the earliest days of exile, not a mere hundred or so years.

Where did earlier folk turn, when they needed hope?

Lark's brother, the renowned hunter, once took him by a secret way up a nearby mountain, where the Egg could be seen *from above,* squatting in its caldera like the brood of a storybook dragon, lain in a sheer-sided nest. From that distant perspective, it might have been some ancient Buyur monument, or a remnant of some *older* denizens of Jijo, aeons earlier—a cryptic sentinel, darkly impervious to time.

With the blink of an eye, it became a grounded *starship*—an oblate lens meant to glide through air and ether. Or a *fortress,* built of some adamantine essence, light-drinking, refractory, denser than a neutron star. Lark even briefly pictured the shell of some titanic being, too patient or proud to rouse itself over the attentions of mayflies.

It had been disturbing, forcing him to rethink his image of the sacred. That epiphany still clung to Lark. Or else it was a case of jitters over the speech he was supposed to give soon to a band of fierce believers. A sermon calling for extreme sacrifice.

The trail turned—and abruptly spilled into a sheer-walled canyon surrounding a giant oval form, a curved shape that reared fantastically before the pilgrims, two arrowflights from end to end. The pebbled surface curved up and over those gathered in awe at its base. Staring upward, Lark knew.

It couldn't be any of those other things I imagined from afar.

Up close, underneath its massive sheltering bulk, anyone could tell the Egg was made of *native stone.*

Marks of Jijo's fiery womb scored its flanks, tracing the story of its birth, starting with a violent conception, far underground. Layered patterns were like muscular cords. Crystal veins wove subtle dendrite paths, branching like nerves.

Travelers filed slowly under the convex overhang, to let the Egg sense their presence, and perhaps grant a blessing. Where the immense monolith pressed into black basalt, the sixty began a circuit. But while Lark's sandals scraped gritty powder, chafing his toes, the

peacefulness and awe of the moment were partly
spoiled by memory.

Once, as an arrogant boy of ten, an idea took root in
his head—to sneak behind the Egg and take a *sample*.

It all began one jubilee year, when Nelo the
Papermaker set out for Gathering to attend a meeting of
his guild, and his wife, Melina the Southerner, insisted
on taking Lark and little Sara along.

*"Before they spend their lives working away at your
paper mill, they should see some of the world."*

How Nelo must have later cursed his consent, for the
trip changed Lark and his sister.

All during the journey, Melina kept opening a book
recently published by the master printers of Tarek Town,
forcing her husband to pause, tapping his cane while
she read aloud in her lilting southern accent, describing
varieties of plant, animal, or mineral they encountered
along the path. At the time, Lark didn't know how many
generations had toiled to create the guidebook, collating
oral lore from every exile race. *Nelo* thought it a fine job
of printing and binding, a good use of paper, or else he
would have forbidden exposing the children to ill-made
goods.

Melina made it a game, associating real things with
their depictions among the ink lithographs. What might
have been a tedious trip for two youngsters became an
adventure outshadowing Gathering itself, so that by the
time they arrived, footsore and tired, Lark was already in
love with the world.

The same book, now yellow, worn, and obsolete
thanks to Lark's own labors, rested like a talisman in one
cloak-sleeve. *The optimistic part of my nature. The part
that thinks it can learn.*

As the file of pilgrims neared the Egg's far side, he
slipped a hand into his robe to touch his other amulet.
The one he never showed even Sara. A stone no larger
than his thumb, wrapped by a leather thong. It always

felt warm, after resting for twenty years next to a beating heart.

My darker side. The part that already knows.

The stone felt *hot* as pilgrims filed by a place Lark recalled too well.

It was at his third Gathering that he finally had screwed up the nerve—a patrician artisan's son who fancied himself a scientist—slinking away from the flapping pavilions, ducking in caves to elude passing pilgrims, then dashing under the curved shelf, where only a child's nimble form might go, drawing back his sampling hammer. . . .

In all the years since, no one ever mentioned the scar, evidence of his sacrilege. It *shouldn't* be noticeable among countless other scratches marring the surface up close. Yet even a drifting mist didn't hide the spot when Lark filed by.

Should he still be embarrassed by a child's offense, after all these years?

Knowing he was forgiven did not erase the shame.

The stone grew cooler, less restive, as the procession moved past.

Could it all be illusion? Some natural phenomenon, familiar to sophisticates of the Five Galaxies? (Though toweringly impressive to primitives hiding on a forbidden world.) Rewq symbionts also came into widespread use a century ago, offering precious insight into the moods of other beings. Had the Egg brought them forth, as some said, to help heal the Six of war and discord? Or were they just another quirky marvel left by Buyur genewizards, from back when this galaxy thronged with countless alien races?

After poring through the Biblos archives, Lark knew his confusion was typical when humans puzzled over the sacred. Even the great Galactics, whose knowledge spanned time and space, were riven by clashing dogmas. If mighty star-gods could be perplexed, what chance had *he* of certainty?

There's one thing both sides of me can agree on.

In both his scientific work and the pangs of his heart, Lark knew one simple truth—

We don't belong here.

That was what he told the pilgrims later, in a rustic amphitheater, where the rising sun surrounded the Egg's oblate bulk with a numinous glow. They gathered in rows, sitting, squatting, or folding their varied torsos in attentive postures. The qheuen apostate, Harullen, spoke first in a poetic dialect, hissing from several leg vents, invoking wisdom to serve this world that was their home, source of all their atoms. Then Harullen tilted his gray carapace to introduce Lark. Most had come a long way to hear his heresy.

"We're told our ancestors were criminals," he began with a strong voice, belying his inner tension. "Their sneakships came to Jijo, one at a time, running the patrols of the great Institutes, evading wary deputy globes of the Zang, hiding their tracks in the flux of mighty Izmunuti, whose carbon wind began masking this world a few thousand years ago. They came seeking a quiet place to perform a selfish felony.

"Each founding crew had excuses. Tales of persecution or neglect. All burned and sank their ships, threw their godlike tools into the Great Midden, and warned their offspring to beware the sky.

"From the sky would come judgment, someday—for the crime of survival."

The sun crept past the Egg's bulk, stabbing a corner of his eye. He escaped by leaning toward his audience.

"Our ancestors invaded a world that was set aside after ages of hard use. A world needing time for its many species, both native and artificial, to find restored balance, from which new wonders might emerge. The civilization of the Five Galaxies has used these rules to protect life since before half of the stars we see came alight.

"So why did our ancestors flout them?"

Each g'Kek pilgrim watched him with two eyestalks

raised far apart and the other two tucked away, a sign of intense interest. The typical urrish listener pointed her narrow head not toward Lark's face but his midriff, to keep his center of mass in view of all three black slits surrounding her narrow snout. Lark's rewq highlighted these signs, and others from hoon, traeki, and qheuen.

They're with me so far, he saw.

"Oh, our ancestors tried to minimize the harm. Our settlements lie in this narrow, geologically violent zone, in hopes that volcanoes will someday cover our works, leaving no evidence behind. The sages choose what we may kill and eat, and where to build, in order to intrude lightly on Jijo's rest.

"Still, who can deny harm *is* done, each hour we live here. Now rantanoids go extinct. Is it our fault? Who knows? I doubt even the Holy Egg can tell."

A murmur from the crowd. Colors flowed in the rewq veil over his eyes. Some literalistic hoon thought he went too far. Others, like the g'Kek, were more comfortable with metaphor.

Let their rewq handle the nuances, Lark thought. *Concentrate on the message itself.*

"Our ancestors passed on excuses, warnings, rules. They spoke of tradeoffs, and the Path of Redemption. But I'm here to say that none of it is any good. It's time to end the farce, to face the truth.

"*Our* generation must choose.

"We must choose to be the last of our kind on Jijo."

The journey back skirted dark caves, exhaling glistening vapors. Now and then, some deep natural detonation sent echoes rolling from one opening, then another, like a rumor that dwindled with each retelling.

Rolling downhill was easier for the g'Keks. But several traeki, built for life in swampy fens, chuffed with exertion as they twisted and turned, striving to keep up. In order to ease the journey, hoonish pilgrims rumbled low atonal music, as they often did at sea. Most pilgrims no longer wore their exhausted rewq. Each mind dwelled alone, in its own thoughts.

Legend says it's different among machine intelligences, or the Zang. Group minds don't bother with persuasion. They just put their heads together, unify, and decide.

It wouldn't be that easy convincing the common citizenry of the Six to go along with the new heresy. Deep instincts drove each race to reproduce as best it could. Ambition for the future was a natural trait for people like his father.

But not here, not on this world.

Lark felt encouraged by this morning's meeting. *We'll convince a few this year. Then more. First we'll be tolerated, later opposed. In the long run, it must be done without violence, by consensus.*

Around noon, a mutter of voices carried up the trail— the day's first regular pilgrims, making an outward show of reverence while still chattering about the pleasures of Gathering. Lark sighted white-robed figures beyond some vapor fumaroles. The leaders called greetings to Lark's group, already returning from devotions, and began shuffling aside to give up right of way.

A crack of thunder struck as the two parties passed alongside, slamming their bodies together and flapping their robes. Hoons crouched, covering their ears, and g'Kek eyestalks recoiled. One poor qheuen skittered over the edge, clutching a gnarled tree with a single, desperate claw.

Lark's first thought was of another gas discharge.

When the ground shook, he pondered an *eruption*.

He would later learn that the noise came not from Jijo, but the sky. It was the sound of fate arriving, and the world he knew coming abruptly to an end, before he ever expected it.

Asx

THOSE WITHIN THE STARSHIP INDUCED A SMALL opening in its gleaming side. Through this portal they sent an emissary, unlike anything the Commons had seen in living memory.

A robot!

my/our ring-of-associations had to access one of its myriad moist storage glands in order to place its contours, recalling an illustration we/i once perused in a human book.

Which book? Ah, thank you my self. *Jane's Survey of Basic Galactic Tools.* One of the rarest surviving fruits of the Great Printing.

Exactly as depicted in that ancient diagram, this floating mechanism was a black, octagonal slab, about the size of a young qheuen, hovering above the ground at about the level of my ring-of-vision, with various gleaming implements projecting above or hanging below. From the moment the hatch closed behind it, the robot ignored every earthly contour, leaving a trail where grass, pebbles, and loam were pressed flat by unseen heaviness.

Wherever it approached, folk quailed back. Just one group of beings kept still, awaiting the creature of not-flesh. We sages. *Responsibility* was our cruel mooring, so adamant that even my basal segment stayed rigid, though it pulsed with craven need to flee. The robot—or its masters in the ship—thus knew who had the right/duty to parlay. It hesitated in front of Vubben, appearing to contemplate our eldest sage for five or six duras, perhaps sensing the reverence we all hold for the wisest of the g'Kek. Then it backed away to confront us all.

i/we watched in mystified awe. After all, this was a *thing,* like a hoonish riverboat or some dead tool left by the vanished Buyur. Only the tools *we* make do not fly, and Buyur remnants show no further interest in doing so.

This thing not only moved, it *spoke,* commencing first
with a repeat of the earlier message.

*"Surveying (local, unique) lifeforms, in this we seek
your (gracious) help.*
*"Knowledge of the (local) biosphere, this you (as-
suredly) have.*
"Tools and (useful) arts, these we offer in trade.
"Confidentiality, shall we (mutually) exchange?"

Our rewq were useless—shriveling away from the intense flux of our distress. We sages nonetheless held
conference. By agreement, Vubben rolled forward, his
roller-wheels squeaking with age. In a show of discipline, all eyestalks turned toward the alien device,
though surely oversurfeited with its frightening stimulus.
"Poor castaways, are we," he commenced reciting, in
the syncopated pops and clicks of formal Galactic Two.
Although our urrish cousins find that language easiest
and use it among themselves, all conceded that Vubben,
the g'Kek, was peerless in his mastery of the grammar.
Especially when it came to telling necessary lies.

"Poor castaways, ignorant and stranded.
"Delighted are we. Ecstatic at this wondrous thing.
"Advent of rescue!"

Sara

SOME DISTANCE BELOW DOLO VILLAGE, THE
river felt its way through a great marsh where even
hoon sailors were known to lose the main channel,
snagging on tree roots or coming aground on shifting
sandbars. Normally, the brawny, patient crew of the

dross-hauler *Hauph-woa* would count on wind and the river's rhythmic rise-and-fall to help them slip free. But these weren't normal times. So they folded their green cloaks—revealing anxious mottles across their lumpy backbone ridges—and pushed the *Hauph-woa* along with poles made of lesser-boo. Even passengers had to assist, now and then, to keep the muddy bottom from seizing the keel and holding them fast. The uneasy mood affected the ship's contingent of flighty noor, who barked nervously, scampering across the masts, missing commands and dropping lines.

Finally, just before nightfall, the captain-pilot guided the *Hauph-woa*'s ornate prow past one last fen of droopy tallgrass to Unity Point, where the river's branches reconverged into an even mightier whole. The garu forest resumed, spreading a welcome sheltering canopy over both banks. After such an arduous day, the air seemed all at once to release passengers and crew from its moist clench. A cool breeze stroked skin, scale, and hide, while sleek noor sprang overboard to splash alongside the gently gliding hull, then clambered the masts and spars to stretch and preen.

Sara thanked Prity when her assistant brought supper in a wooden bowl, then the chimp took her own meal to the side, in order to flick overboard the spicy greens that hoon chefs loved slicing into nearly everything they cooked. A trail of bubbles showed that river creatures, feeding on the scraps, weren't so finicky. Sara didn't mind the tangy taste, though most Earthlings wound up defecating bright colors after too many days of shipboard fare.

When Prity later brought a pair of blankets, Sara chose the plushest to tuck over the Stranger, sleeping near the main hold with its neatly stacked crates of dross. His brow bore a sheen of perspiration, which she wiped with a dry cloth. Since early yesterday, he had shown none of the lucidity so briefly displayed when the ill-omened bolide split the sky.

Sara had misgivings about hauling the wounded man on a hurried, stressful trek. Still, there *was* a good clinic in Tarek Town. And this way she might keep an eye on him while performing her other duty—one rudely dropped in her lap last night, after that frenzied conclave in the Meeting Tree.

Pzora stood nearby, a dark tower, dormant but ever-vigilant over the patient's condition. The pharmacist vented steamy puffs from the specialized ring that routinely performed ad hoc chemistry beyond the understanding of Jijo's best scholars or even the traeki themselves.

Wrapping her shoulders in another soft g'Kek-spun blanket, Sara turned and watched her fellow passengers.

Jomah, the young son of Henrik, the exploser, lay curled nearby, snoring softly after the excitement of leaving home for the first time. Closer to the mast sat Jop, the bristle-cheeked delegate of Dolo's farmers and crofters, peering in the half-light at a leather-bound copy of some Scroll. Over by the starboard rail, Ulgor, the urrish tinker who had spoken at the village meeting, knelt facing a qheuenish woodcarver named Blade, one of many sons of the matriarch, Log Biter. Blade had lived for years among the sophisticated Gray Qheuens of Tarek Town, so his choice as representative of Dolo Hive seemed natural.

From a moss-lined pouch, Ulgor drew a quivering rewq symbiont, of the type suited for lean urrish heads. The trembling membrane crawled over each of her triple eyes, creating the Mask-That-Reveals. Meanwhile, Blade's rewq wrapped itself around the seeing-strip bisecting his melonlike cupola. The qheuen's legs retracted, leaving only the armored claws exposed.

The pair conversed in a bastard dialect of Galactic Two, at best a difficult tongue for humans. Moreover, the breeze carried off the treble whistle-tones, leaving just the lower track of syncopated clicks. Perhaps for those reasons the two travelers seemed unconcerned anyone might listen.

Maybe, as often happened, they underrated the reach of human hearing.

Or else they're counting on something called common

courtesy, she thought ironically. Lately Sara had become quite an eavesdropper, an unlikely habit for a normally shy, private young woman. Her recent fascination with language was the cause. This time though, fatigue overcame curiosity.

Leave them alone. You'll have plenty of chances to study dialects in Tarek Town.

Sara took her blanket over to a spot between two crates marked with Nelo's seal, exuding the homey scents of Dolo's paper mill. There had been little time for rest since that frenetic town meeting. Only a few miduras after adjournment, the village elders had sent a herald to wake Sara with this assignment—to lead a delegation downriver in search of answers and guidance. She was chosen both as one with intimate knowledge of Biblos and also to represent the Dolo craft workers—as Jop would speak for the farmers, and Blade for the upriver qheuens. Other envoys included Ulgor, Pzora, and Fakoon, a g'Kek scriven-dancer. Since each was already billeted aboard the *Hauph-woa,* with business in Tarek Town, they could hardly refuse. Together with the ship's captain, that made at least one representative from all Six exile races. A good omen, the elders hoped.

Sara still wondered about Jomah. Why would Henrik dispatch the boy on a trip that promised danger, even in quiet times?

"He will know what to do," the taciturn explorer had said, putting his son in Sara's nominal care. *"Once you reach Tarek Town."*

If only I could say as much for myself, Sara worried. It had been impossible to turn down this assignment, much as she wanted to.

It's been a year since Joshu died—since shame and grief made a hermit of you. Besides, who is going to care that you made a fool of yourself over a man who could never be yours? That all seems a small matter, now that the world we know is coming to an end.

Alone in the dark, Sara worried.

Are Dwer and Lark safe? Or has something dreadful already happened at Gathering?

She felt Prity curl up alongside in her own blanket, sharing warmth. The hoonish helmsman rumbled a crooning melody, with no words in any language Sara knew, yet conveying a sense of muzzy serenity, endlessly forbearing.

Things work out, the hoonish umble seemed to say.

Sleep finally climbed out of her body's fatigue to claim Sara as she thought—

I . . . sure . . . hope . . . so.

Later, in the middle of the night, a dream yanked her bolt upright, clutching the blanket close. Her eyes stared over the peaceful river, lit by two moons, but Sara's heart pounded as she quailed from an awful nightmare image.

Flames.

Moonlight flickered on the water, and to her eyes it became fire, licking the Biblos roof-of-stone, blackening it with the heat and soot of half a million burning books.

The Stranger

Unconscious, he is helpless to control dark images roiling across the closed universe of his mind.

It is a tight universe—narrow and confined—yet teeming with stars and confusion. With galaxies and remorse. With nebulae and pain.

And water. Always water—from dense black ice fields all the way to space-clouds so diffuse, you might never know they thronged with beings the size of planets. Living things as slow and thin as vapor, swimming through a near-vacuum sea.

Sometimes he thinks water will never leave him alone. Nor will it let him simply die.

He hears it right now, water's insistent music, piercing his delirium. This time it comes to him as a soft lapping sound—the sluicing of wooden boards through gentle liquid, like some vessel bearing him along from a place he can't remember, toward another whose name he'll never learn. It sounds reassuring, this melody, not like the sucking clutch of that awful swamp, where he had thought he was about to drown at last—

—as he so nearly drowned once, long ago, when the Old Ones forced him, screaming, into a crystal globe they then filled with a fluid that dissolved everything it touched.

—or as he once fought for breath on that green-green-green world whose thick air refused to nourish while he stumbled on and on half-blind toward a fearsome glimmering Jophur tower.

—or the time his body and soul felt pummeled,

squeezed, unable even to gasp as he threaded a narrow passage that seemed about to strip him to his spine . . . before abruptly spilling him into a realm where shining light stretched on and on until—

His mind rebels, quailing from brief, incoherent images. Fevered, he has no idea which of them are remembered, which are exaggerated, and which his damaged brain simply invented out of the pitchy stuff of nightmare—

—like a starship's vapor contrail (water!) cleaving a blue sky that reminded him of home.

—or the sight of beings like himself (more water!) living on a world where they clearly don't belong.

Amid the chaos of fevered hallucinations, another impression penetrates. Somehow he knows that it comes from beyond his delusion—from someplace real. It feels like a touch, a stroke of softness on his brow. A brush, accompanied by murmurs in a voice that soothes. He can make no sense of the words, but still he welcomes the sensation, even knowing that it should not be. Not here. Not now.

It is a comfort, that touch, making him feel just a little less alone.

Eventually, it even pushes back the fearsome images—the memories and dreams—and in time he slips from delirium into a quietude of sleep.

V. THE BOOK
OF THE SEA

When judgment comes, you will be
asked about the dead.

What living species, beautiful and
unique, exist no more because you
squatters chose a forbidden place to
live?

And what of your own dead?
Your corpses, cadavers, and remains?
Your tools and cold-made things?
How have you disposed of them?

Be righteous, sooners of Jijo.
Show how hard you tried.
Make small the consequences of your
crime.
(The offense of living.)

Felonies—and their punishment—
can be made smaller, by the simple
fact of doing less harm.

—The Scroll of Advice

Alvin's Tale

THE MOUNT GUENN TRAM CLIMBS A STEEP ROUTE from Wuphon Port all the way up to the workshops of Uriel the Smith. The railway is small and hard to see, even when you're looking for it. Still, it's allowed by the sages only because it's important for getting Uriel's forgings down to market. Also, it uses no artificial power. Water from a hot spring, high up on the mountain, pours into a tank aboard whichever car is waiting at the top station. Meanwhile, the bottom car's tank is emptied, so it's much lighter, even with passengers aboard. When the brake is cut, the heavier car starts down, pulling the cable, which in turn hauls the bottom car *up*.

It sounds gimmicky, but in fact it goes pretty fast and can even get scary for a few seconds in the middle, when the other car seems to be rushing right at you along the same set of slim wooden rails. Then you reach a split section where that car streaks past in a blur. What a thrill!

It's a trip of over forty arrowflights, but the water's still near boiling hot in the first car's tank when it reaches bottom—one reason folks like it when Uriel ships her wares down to port on laundry day.

Ur-ronn says one piece of salvaged Buyur cable is what makes it all possible. A real treasure that can't ever be replaced.

Mount Guenn was behaving itself that day, so there wasn't much ash in the air and I didn't really need my cloak. Huck wore her goggles anyway, one strapped over each eyebulb, and Pincer still had to spray his red cupola as the air got thinner, and Wuphon turned into a toy village under its blanket of camouflage greenery. Thick stands of lowland boo soon gave way to hedge-rows of multitrunked gorreby trees, followed by tufts of feathery shrubs that got sparser as we climbed. This was *not* red-qheuen country. Still, Pincer was excited over the news from Ur-ronn.

"You see? The window's done! The last big piece we needed for the bathy. A little more work an' it'll be ready-eady!"

Huck sniffed disdainfully. She did a good job of it, too, since that's one of those human gestures you read about that we actually get to see pretty often, whenever Mister Heinz, our local schoolmaster, hears an answer he doesn't like.

"Great," Huck remarked. "Whoever rides the thing can *see* whatever's about to eat him."

I had to laugh. "Hrrrm. So now you admit there might be sea monsters after all?"

Huck swiveled three stalks toward me in a look of surprise. It's not often I can catch her like that.

"I'll admit I'd want more than just a slab of urrish glass between me and whatever's down there, twenty thousand leagues under the sea!"

I confess being puzzled by her attitude. This bitterness wasn't like Huck at all. I tried lightening the mood.

"Say, I've always wondered. Has anybody ever figured out exactly how long a league *is*?"

Two of her eyes gazed at each other, then back at me with a glint of whimsy.

"I looked in the dictionary once, but I couldn't *fathom* the answer."

Pincer complained, "Look, are you two about to start—"

I interrupted, "If anyone *does* know the answer, I'd sure like to meter."

"Heh!" Huck made a thrumming sound with her spokes. "That's assuming you could parsec what she says."

"Hrrrm. I don't know if I can take this furlong."

"Oh-oh-oh-oh-oh!" Pincer complained, feigning agony with all five mouths at once.

That's how we passed the time while climbing into chilly badlands bare of life, and I guess it shows my dad's right about us being humickers. But GalTwo and GalSix aren't any fun for word games. You can't pun in them at all! You *can* in GalSeven, but for some reason it just doesn't hurt as much.

The mountainside got even more stark as we neared the top, where steam vents mark Mount Guenn's broad shoulders and mask the hot breath of Uriel's forges. Here some of the old volcanic spills crystallized in special ways that reflect shimmering colors, shifting as your eye moves. Only a short journey from here, the same kind of stuff stretches as far as you can see across a poison plain that's called the Spectral Flow.

That day, my imagination was unhoonly active. I couldn't help pondering all the power bubbling away, deep under the mountain. Nowhere do Jijo's innards churn more intensely than under the region we exiles call the Slope. We're told that's why all the different ancestor-ships planted their seed in the same part of the planet. And nowhere else *on* the Slope do folks live in closer daily contact with that pent-up power than my hometown. No wonder we were never assigned a family of explosers to prepare our village for destruction. I guess everyone figures Wuphon will be blessed by the volcano anyway, inside the next hundred years. A thousand at most. Maybe any day now. So why bother?

We're told it's proper that no trace of our homes will be left after that happens. Still, Jijo can take her own sweet time, as far as I'm concerned.

Despite dozens of tram trips, I still find it kind of surprising whenever the car nears the end of the climb and suddenly a great big cave seems to open out of nowhere, with the rail heading straight for it. Maybe it was all that earlier talk of monsters, but this time I felt a twirl in my heart-spine when that black hollow gaped wide and we plunged toward what looked an awful lot like a hungry *mouth,* set in the face of an angry, impulsive mountain.

The dark stillness inside was suddenly hot and dry as dust. Ur-ronn waited for us when the car came to a jarring halt. She seemed skittish, dancing clip-clop with all four hooves while her stubby work-arms held the door and I helped Huck roll out of the car. Little Huphu rode on Pincer-Tip's back, eyes all aglitter, as if ready for anything.

Maybe the *noor* was ready, but Huck, Pincer, and I were thrown completely off balance by what our urrish friend said at that point. Ur-ronn spoke in GalSix, since it's easier for an urs to speak without lisping.

"I am glad in my pouches that you, my friends, could come so soon. Now swiftly to Uriel's observatory, where she has, for several days, been tracking strange objects in the sky!"

I confess, I was struck dumb. Like the others, I just stared at her for several duras. Finally, we all unfroze at once.

"Hrrrrm, you can't—"

"What do you—"

"Surely you don't mean—"

Ur-ronn stamped her front-left foot. *"I do mean it! Uriel and Gybz claim to have perceived one or more starships, several days ago! Moreover, when last sighted, one or all of them seemed poised to land!"*

VI. THE BOOK OF THE SLOPE

Legends

It seems ironic that most of Jijo's night-time constellations were named by humans, the youngest exile sept. None of the prior six had thought of giving fanciful labels to groups of unrelated stars, associating them with real and mythical beasts.

The quaint habit clearly derives from humanity's unique heritage as an orphaned race—or as self-evolved wolflings—who burst into space without guidance by a patron. Every other sapient species had such a mentor—as the hoon had the Guthatsa and g'Keks had the Drooli—an older, wiser species, ready to teach a younger one the ropes.

But not humans.

This lack scarred Homo sapiens in unique ways.

Countless bizarre notions bloomed among native Terran cultures during humanity's dark lonely climb. Outlandish ideas that would never occur to an uplifted race—one taught nature's laws from the very start. Bizarre concepts like connecting dots in the sky to form fictitious creatures.

When Earthlings first did this on Jijo, the earlier groups reacted with surprise, even suspicion. But soon the practice seemed to rob the stars of some of their terror. The g'Kek, hoon, and urs started coming up with sky-myths of their own, while qheuens and traeki were glad to have tales made up about them.

Since the advent of peace, scholars have disagreed in their assessment of this practice. Some say its very primitiveness helps the Six follow in the footsteps of the glavers. This meets with approval from those who urge that we hurry as quickly as possible down the Path of Redemption.

Others claim it is like the trove of books in Biblos, a distraction from achieving the simple clarity of thought that will help us exiles achieve our goal.

Then there are those who like the practice simply because it feels good, and makes for excellent art.

—*Cultural Patterns of the Slope,* by Ku-Phuhaph Tuo, Ovoom Town Guild of Publishers, Year-of-Exile 1922.

Asx

WHO WOULD HAVE IMAGINED THAT A ROBOT might display *surprise*? Yet did we not discern an unmistakable yank, a twitch, in response to Vubben's manifest lie? An impromptu falsehood, contrived out of sudden necessity by Ur-Jah and Lester, whose quick wits do their hot-blooded tribes proud?

The first scrolls—a mere ten kilowords, engraved on polymer bars by the original g'Kek pioneers—warned of several ways that doom might fall from heaven. New scrolls were added by glaver, hoon, and qheuen settlers, first jealously hoarded, then shared as the Commons slowly formed. Finally came human-sept and its flooding gift of paper books. But even the Great Printing could not cover all potentialities.

Among likely prospects, it was thought the Galactic Institutes charged with enforcing quarantine might someday find us. Or titanic cruisers of the great patron clans would descry our violation, if/when the glaring eye, Izmunuti, ceased spewing its wind of masking needles.

Among other possibilities, we pondered what to do if a great globe-ship of the hydrogen-breathing Zang came to one of our towns, dripping freezing vapors in wrath over our trespass. These and many other contingencies we discussed, did we not, my rings?

But seldom *this* thing which had come to pass—the arrival of *desperados*.

If malefactors ever did come to Jijo, we reasoned, why should they make themselves known to us? With a world to sieve for riches, would they even deign to notice the hovels of a few coarse savages, far devolved from ancient glory, clumped in one small corner of Jijo's expanse?

Yet here they have come into our midst with a boldness that terrifies.

The robot emissary contemplated Vubben's proclamation for ten duras, then responded with a single terse interrogation.

"Your presence on this world, it is a (query) accident?"

Do you recall, my rings, the brief thrill that coursed our linking membranes? The robot's masters were set aback! Against all reason or proportionality of force, the initiative was ours, for a moment.

Vubben crossed two eyestalks in a gesture of polite aloofness.

"Your question, it insinuates doubt.
"More than doubt, it suggests grave assumptions about our nature.
"Those assumptions—might they lay upon our ancestors' necks a shackling suspicion?
"(Query) suspicion of heinous crimes?"

How resilient was Vubben's misdirection. How like the web of a mulc-spider. He denies nothing, tells no explicit lie. Yet how he implies!

"Forgiveness for (unintended) insults, we implore," the machine ratcheted hastily. *"Descendants of castaways, we take you for. An ill-fated vessel, your ancestors' combined ship must have been. Lost on some noble errand, this we scarcely doubt."*

Now *they* were the liars, of that *we* had no doubt at all.

Dwer

EAVING THE CRAGGY RIMMER RANGE, DWER LED
Rety and the others into that region of undulating
hills, gently slanting toward the sea, that was called
the Slope. The domain of the Six.

Dwer tried getting his mysterious young prisoner to
talk about herself. But his first efforts were answered in
morose monosyllables. Clearly, Rety resented the fact
that he could tell so much from her appearance, her
animal-skin clothes, her speech and manner.

*Well, what did you expect? To sneak over the moun-
tains and walk into one of our villages, no questions
asked?*

Her burn scar alone would mark her for attention. Not
that disfigurement was rare on the Slope. Accidents were
common, and even the latest traeki unguents were crude
medicine by Galactic standards. Still, people would notice Rety anywhere she went.

At meals, she gaped covetously at the goods he drew
from his backpack. His cup and plate, the hammered
aluminum skillet, his bedroll of fleecy hurchin down—
things to make life a bit easier for those whose ancestors
long ago forsook the life of star-gods. To Dwer there was
a simple beauty in the woven cloth he wore, in boots
with shape-treated tree sap soles, even the elegant three-
piece urrish fire-starter—all examples of primitive cun-
ning, the sort his wolfling ancestors relied on through
their lonely isolation on old Earth. Most people took
such things for granted on the Slope.

But to a clan of sooners—illegal squatters living jealous and filthy beyond the pale—they might seem marvels, worth any risk to steal.

Dwer wondered, was this the only time? Perhaps Rety
was just the first to get *caught*. Some thefts blamed on
noors might be the fault of other robbers, sneaking over
the mountains from a far-off hermit tribe.

Was that your idea? To swipe the first worthwhile thing you came across and scoot home to your tribe, a hero?

Somehow, he figured more than that must be involved. She kept peering around, as if looking for something in particular. Something that mattered to her.

Dwer watched Rety lead the captive glaver by a rope tied to her waist. The girl's saucy gait seemed meant to defy him, or anyone else who might judge her. Between clumps of grimy hair, he was nauseated to see puckered tracks made by borer bees, a parasite easily warded off with traeki salve. But no traekis lived where she came from.

It forced uncomfortable thoughts. What if his own grandparents had made the same choice as Rety's? To flee the Commons for whatever reason, seeking far reaches to hide in? Nowadays, with war—and war's refugees—a thing of the past, sooners were rather rare. Old Fallon had found only one squatter band in many years roaming across half a continent, and this was Dwer's first encounter.

What would you do if you were raised that way, scraping for a living like animals, knowing a land of wealth and power lay beyond those mountains to the west?

Dwer had never thought of the Slope that way before. Most scrolls and legends emphasized how far the six exile races had already fallen, not how much farther there was yet to go.

That night, Dwer used tobar seeds to call another clock teet, not because he wanted an early wakeup, but to have the steady, tapping rhythm in the background while he slept. When Mudfoot yowled at the burst of aroma, covering his snout, Rety let out a soft giggle and her first smile.

He insisted on examining her feet before bed, and she quietly let him treat two blisters showing early signs of infection. "We'll have healers look you over when we reach Gathering," he told her. Neither of them commented when he kept her moccasins, tucking them under his sleeping roll for the night.

As they lay under a starry canopy, separated by the dim campfire coals, he urged Rety to name a few constellations, and her curt answers helped Dwer eliminate one momentous possibility—that some *new* group of human exiles had landed, destroying their ship and settling to brute existence far from the Slope. Rety couldn't realize the importance of naming a few patterns in the sky, but Dwer erased one more pinprick of worry. The legends were the same.

At dawn Dwer awoke sniffing something in the air—a familiar odor, almost pleasant, but also *nervous*—a sensation Lark once explained mysteriously as "negative ions and water vapor." Dwer shook Rety awake and hurriedly led the glaver under a rocky overhang. Mudfoot followed, moving like an arthritic g'Kek, grumbling hatred of mornings with every step. They all made it to shelter just as a sheet-storm hit—an undulating curtain of continuous rain that crept along the mountainside from left to right, pouring water like a translucent drapery that pummeled everything beneath, soaking the forest, one wavy ribbon at a time. Rety stared wide-eyed as the rainbow-colored tapestry swept by, drenching their campsite and ripping half the leaves off trees. Obviously she had never witnessed one before.

The trek resumed. Perhaps it was a night's restful sleep, or the eye-opening start to the day. But Rety now seemed less sullen, more willing to enjoy sights like a meadow full of bumble flowers—yellow tubes, fringed with black fuzz, which rode the steady west wind, swooping and buzzing at the end of tether-stems. Rety's eyes darted, enthralled by the antic dance of deception and pollination. The species did not exist in the stagnant weather shadow beyond the Rimmers, where a vast plain of poison grass stretched most of the way to the Gray Hills.

Just getting here across all that was an accomplishment, Dwer noted, wondering how she had managed it.

As alpine sheerness gave way to gentler foothills, Rety gave up hiding her fierce curiosity. She began by pointing and asking—"Are those wooden poles holding up your backpack? Don't they make it heavy? I'll bet they're hollow."

Then—"If you're a hunter, where's the rest of your stalking gang? Or do you always hunt alone?"

In rapid succession more questions followed. "Who made your bow? How far can you hit somethin' the size of my hand?

"Did you live in one place the whole time you were little? In a . . . *house?* Did you get to hold on to stuff you wanted to keep, 'stead of leavin' it behind when you moved?

"If you grew up by a river, did you ever see any *hoon?* What're they like? I hear they're tall as a tree, with noses long as your arm.

"Are the *trikki* really tricky? Are they made of tree sap? Do they eat garbage?

"Do noors ever slow down? I wonder why Buyur made 'em that way."

Other than her habit of turning *Buyur* into a singular proper name, Dwer couldn't have phrased the last question any better himself. Mudfoot was a perpetual nuisance, getting underfoot, chasing shrub critters, then lying in ambush somewhere along the path, squeaking in delight when Dwer failed to pick him out of the overhanging foliage.

I could shake you easily, if I didn't have a glaver and a kid in tow, Dwer thought at the grinning noor. Yet he was starting to feel pretty good. They would make quite an entrance at Gathering, sure to be the talk of the festival.

Over lunch, Rety used his cooking knife to prepare a scrub hen he had shot. Dwer could barely follow her whirling hands as the good parts landed in the skillet with a crackling sizzle, while the poison glands flew to the waste pit. She finished, wiping the knife with a flourish, and offered it back to him.

"Keep it," Dwer said, and she responded with a hesitant smile.

With that he ceased being her jailor and became her guide, escorting a prodigal daughter back to the embrace of clan and Commons. Or so he thought, until some time later, during the meal, when she said—"I really ha' seen some of those before."

"Seen some of what?"

Rety pointed at the glaver, placidly chewing under the shade of a stand of swaying lesser-boo.

"You thought I never saw any, 'cause I feared she'd bite. But I seen 'em, from afar. A whole herd. Sneaky devils, hard to catch. Took the guys all day to spear 'un. They taste awful gamey, but the boys liked it fine."

Dwer swallowed hard. "Are you saying your tribe *hunts and eats* glavers?"

Rety looked back with brown eyes full of innocent curiosity. "You don't on this side? I'm not surprised. There's easier prey, an' better eatin'."

He shook his head, nauseated by the news.

Part of him chided—*You were willing to shoot this particular glaver down, stone dead, if it crossed over the pass.*

Yes, but only as a last resort. And I wouldn't eat her!

Dwer knew what people called him—the Wild Man of the Forest, living beyond the law. He even helped nurse the mystique, since it meant his awkward speech was taken for something more manly than shyness. In truth, killing was the part of any hunt he did as capably and swiftly as possible, never with enjoyment. Now, to learn people beyond the mountains were devouring *glavers*? The sages would be appalled!

Ever since surmising that Rety came from a sooner band, Dwer had known his duty would be to guide a militia expedition to round up the errant clan. Ideally, it would be a simple matter of firm but gentle ingathering, resettling lost cousins back into the fold of the Commons. But now, Rety had unknowingly indicted her tribe with another crime. The Scrolls were clear. *That which is rare, you shall not eat. That which is precious, you must protect.* But, above all—*You may not devour what once flew between the stars.*

Irony was ashen in Dwer's mouth. For after the sooners were brought back for trial, his job then would be to collect every glaver living east of the Rimmers—and slaughter those he could not catch.

Ah, but that won't make me a bad person . . . because I won't eat them.

Rety must have sensed his reaction. She turned to stare at the nearby stand of great-boo, its young shoots barely as thick as her waist. The tubelike green shafts swayed in rippling waves, like fur on the belly of the lazy noor, dozing by her foot.

"Are they gonna hang me?" the girl asked quietly. The scar on her face, which was muted when she smiled, now seemed stretched and livid. "Old Clin says you slopies hang sooners when you catch 'em."

"Nonsense. Actually, each race handles its own—"

"The old folks say it's slopie law. Kill anyone who tries to make a free life east o' the Rimmers."

Dwer stammered, suddenly awash in irritation, "If—if you think that, why'd you come all this way? To—to stick your head in a noose?"

Rety's lips pressed. She looked away and murmured low. "You wouldn't believe me."

Dwer repented his own flash of temper. In a gentler tone, he asked—"Why don't you try me? Maybe . . . I might understand better than you think."

But she withdrew once more into a cocoon of brooding silence, unresponsive as a stone.

While Dwer hastily rinsed the cooking gear, Rety tied herself in place ahead of the glaver, even though he had said she could walk free. He found his cooking knife by the smothered coals, where she must have laid it after those sharp words.

The gesture of rejection irked him, and he muttered gruffly, "Let's get out of here."

Asx

WE HAD CHOSEN TO FEIGN A SMALL DISTINCTION between two crimes. At best a slightly lesser felony— that of *accidental* rather than planned colonization.

No one could deny the obvious—that our ancestors had loosed unsanctioned offspring on a fallow world. But Vubben's artful evasion implied an act of culpable carelessness, rather than villainy by design.

The lie would not hold for long. When archaeological traces were sifted, forensic detectives from the Institutes would swiftly perceive our descent from many separate landings, not one mixed crew stranded by mishap on this remote shore. Moreover, there was the presence of our juniormost sept—the human clan. By their own bizarre tale, they are a *wolfling race,* unknown to Galactic culture until just three hundred Jijoan years ago.

Then why even try such a bluff?

Desperation. Plus a frail hope that our "guests" have not the skill or tools for archaeology. Their goal must be to swoop in for a quick sampling of hidden treasures. Then, covering their tracks, they would wish a swift, stealthy departure with a ship's hold full of contraband. To this mercenary quest, our strange, forlorn colony of miscreants offers both opportunity and a threat.

They must know we possess firsthand knowledge of Jijo, valuable to their needs.

Alas, my rings. Are we not also potential witnesses to their villainy?

Sara

NOBODY EXPECTED AN AMBUSH.

It was the perfect place for one. Still, no one aboard the *Hauph-woa* had any idea of danger until it actually happened.

A century of peace had blurred the once-jealously guarded domains of old. Urrish and g'Kek settlers were few, since the former could not raise young near water, and the latter preferred smooth terrain. Still, all types were seen crowding tiny docks when the *Hauph-woa* glided by, eager to share scant news.

Alas, there had been none from downstream since that terrible spectacle crossed the sky.

Mostly, the river folk were reacting constructively, rushing to reinforce their facade screens, cleaning the baffles of their smokestacks, or hauling boats under cover—but one forlorn tribe of traeki marsh-dwellers had gone much further, burning their entire stilt village in a spasm of fear and fealty to the Scrolls. Pzora's topknot shivered at the aroma of woebegone ring-stacks, floundering in the ashes. The *Hauph-woa*'s captain promised to spread word of their plight. Perhaps other traeki would send new basal segments for the locals to wear, making them better suited for evacuation inland. At worst, the swamp traeki could gather rotting matter, settle on top, and shut down higher functions till the world became a less scary place.

The same could not be said for an urrish trade caravan they passed later, stranded with their pack beasts on the desolate west bank, when the panicky citizens of Bing Village blew up their beloved bridge.

The hoonish boat crew back-pedaled with frantic haste, rowing against the current to avoid getting caught in a tangle of broken timbers and mulc-fiber cables, shattered remnants of a beautiful span that had been the chief traverse for an entire region. A marvel of clever camouflage, the bridge used to resemble a jagged snag of jumbled logs. But even that apparently wasn't enough for local orthodox scroll thumpers. *Maybe they were burning it while I had my nightmare last night,* Sara thought, observing charred timbers and recalling images of flame that had torn her sleep.

A crowd of villagers stood on the east bank, beckoning the *Hauph-woa* to draw near.

Blade spoke up. "I would not approach," the blue

qheuen hissed from several leg-vents. He wore a rewq over his vision-ring while peering at the folk on shore.

"And why not?" Jop demanded. "See? They're pointing to a way past the debris. Perhaps they have news, as well."

Sure enough, there did appear to be a channel, near the shore, unobstructed by remnants of the broken bridge.

"I don't know," Blade went on. "I sense that . . . something is wrong."

"You're right avout that," Ulgor added. "I'd like to know why they have done nothing for the stranded caravan. The villagers have voats. The urs could have veen ferried across vy now."

Sara wondered. It certainly would not be fun for any of Ulgor's race to ride a little coracle, with icy water lapping just an arm's breadth away. "The urs may have refused," she suggested. "Perhaps they're not that desperate yet."

The captain made his decision, and the *Hauph-woa* turned toward the village. As they drew near, Sara saw that the only construct still intact was the hamlet's camouflage lattice. Everything else lay in ruins. *They've probably sent their families into the forest,* she thought. There were plenty of garu trees for humans to live in, and qheuenish citizens could join cousins upstream. Still, the toppled village was a depressing sight.

Sara pondered how much worse things might be if Jop ever got his wish. If Dolo Dam blew up, every dock, weir, and cabin they had seen below the flood line would be swept away. Native creatures would also suffer, though perhaps no more than in a natural flood. *Lark says it is species that matter, not individuals. No eco-niches would be threatened by demolishing our small wooden structures. Jijo won't be harmed.*

Still, it seems dubious, all of this burning and wrecking just to persuade some Galactic big shots we're farther along the Path of Redemption than we really are.

Blade sidled alongside, his blue carapace steaming as dew evaporated from the seams of his shell—a sure sign of anxiety. He rocked a complex rhythm among his five chitinous legs.

"Sara, do you have a rewq? Can you put it on and see if I'm mistaken?"

"Sorry. I gave mine up. All those colors and raw emotions get in the way of paying close attention to language." She did not add that it had grown painful to wear the things, ever since she made the mistake of using one at Joshu's funeral. "Why?" she asked. "What's got you worried?"

Blade's cupola trembled, and the rewq that was wrapped around it quivered. "The people onshore—they seem . . . strange somehow."

Sara peered through the morning haze. The Bing Villagers were mostly human, but there were also hoon, traeki, and qheuens in the mix. *Likes attract,* she thought. Orthodox fanaticism crossed racial lines.

As does heresy, Sara noted, recalling that her own brother was part of a movement no less radical than the folk who had brought down this bridge.

Several coracles set forth from tree-shrouded shelters, aiming to intercept the riverboat. "Are they coming to pilot us through?" young Jomah asked.

He got his answer when the first grappling hook whistled, then fell to the deck of the *Hauph-woa*.

Others swiftly followed.

"We mean you no harm!" shouted a thick-armed man in the nearest skiff. *"Come ashore, and we'll take care of you. All we want is your boat."*

That was the wrong thing to say to the proud crew of a river-runner. Every hoon but the helmsman ran to seize and toss overboard the offending hooks. But more grapplers sailed aboard for every one they removed.

Then Jomah pointed downstream. "Look!"

If anyone still wondered what the Bing-ites planned for the *Hauph-woa*, all doubts vanished at the sight of a charred ruin, blackened ribs spearing upward like a huge, half-burned skeleton. It triggered an umble of dismay from the crew, resonating down Sara's spine and sending the noor beasts into frenzied fits of barking.

The hoon redoubled their efforts, tearing frantically at the hooks.

Sara's first instinct was to shield the Stranger. But the wounded man seemed safe, still unconscious under Pzora's protecting bulk.

"Come on," she told Blade. "We better help."

Pirates often used to attack ships this way until the Great Peace. Perhaps the attackers' own ancestors used the technique in deadly earnest, during the bad old days. The grapples, made of pointy Buyur metal, dug deep when the cables tautened. Sara realized in dismay that the cords were mulc fiber, treated by a traeki process that made them damnably hard to cut. Worse, the lines stretched not just to the coracles but all the way to shore, where locals hauled them taut with blocks and tackle. Hoon strength, helped by Blade's great claws, barely sufficed to wrestle the hooks free. Still, Sara tried to help, and even the g'Kek passenger kept lookout with four keen eyes, shouting to warn when another boat drew near. Only Jop leaned against the mast, watching with clear amusement. Sara had no doubt who the orthodox tree farmer was rooting for.

The beach loomed ever closer. If the *Hauph-woa* made it past midpoint, she'd have the river's pull on her side. But even that force might be too little to break the strong cords. When the keel scraped sand, it would spell the end.

In desperation, the crew hit on a new tactic. Taking up axes, they chopped away at planks and rails, wherever a grapple had dug in, tearing out whole wooden chunks to throw overboard, attacking their own vessel with a fury that was dazzling to behold, given normal hoon placidity.

Then, all at once, the deck jerked under Sara's feet as the whole boat suddenly shuddered, slewing, as if the center mast were a pivot.

"They've hooked the rudder!" someone cried.

Sara looked over the stern and saw a massive metal

barb speared through the great hinged paddle the helmsman used to steer the ship. The rudder could not be pulled aboard or chopped loose without crippling the *Hauph-woa,* leaving it adrift and helpless.

Prity bared her teeth and screamed. Though shivering with fear, the little ape started climbing over the rail, till Sara stopped her with a firm hand.

"It's my job," she said tersely, and without pause shrugged out of her tunic and kilt. A sailor handed her a hatchet with a strap-thong through the haft.

Don't everybody speak up all at once to argue me out of doing this, she thought sardonically, knowing no one would.

Some things were simply obvious.

The hatchet hung over one shoulder. It wasn't comforting to feel its metal coolness stroke her left breast as she climbed, even though the cutting edge still bore a leather cover.

Clothes would have been an impediment. Sara needed her toes, especially, to seek footholds on the *Hauph-woa*'s stern. The clinker construction style left overlaps in the boards that helped a bit. Still, she could not prevent shivering, half from the morning chill and partly from stark terror. Sweaty palms made it doubly hard, even though her mouth felt dry as urrish breath.

I haven't done any climbing in years!

To nonhumans, this must look like another day's work for a tree-hugging Earthling. Kind of like expecting *every* urs to be a courier runner, or all traekis to make a good martini. In fact, *Jop* was the logical one for this task, but the captain didn't trust the man, with good reason.

The crew shouted tense encouragement as she clambered down the stern, holding the rudder with one arm. Meanwhile, derisive scorn came from the coracles and those ashore. *Great. More attention than I ever had in my life, and I'm stark naked at the time.*

The mulc-cable groaned with tension as villagers strained on pulleys to haul *Hauph-woa* toward the beach, where several gray qheuens gathered, holding torches that loomed so frighteningly close that Sara imagined she could hear the flames. At last, she reached a place where she could plant her feet and hands— bracing her legs in a way that forever surrendered all illusions of personal modesty. She had to tear the leather cover off the ax with her teeth and got a bitter electrical taste from the reddish metal. It made her shudder—then tense up as she almost lost her grip. The boat's churning wake looked oily and bitter cold.

Jeers swelled as she hacked at the rudder blade, sending chips flying, trying to cut a crescent around the embedded hook. She soon finished gouging away *above* the grapple and was starting on the tougher part below, when something smacked the back of her left hand, sending waves of pain throbbing up her arm. She saw *blood* ooze around a wooden sliver, protruding near the wrist.

A *slingshot* pellet lay buried halfway in the plank nearby.

Another glanced off the rudder, ricocheting from the boat's stern, then skipping across the water.

Someone was *shooting* at her!

Why you jeekee, slucking, devoluted . . .

Sara found an unknown aptitude for cursing, as she went through a wide vocabulary of oaths from five different languages, hacking away with the hatchet more vehemently than ever. A steady drumbeat of pebbles now clattered against the hull, but she ignored them in a blur of heat and fury.

"Otszharsiya, perkiye! Syookai dreesoona!"

She ran out of obscenities in Rossic and was starting to plumb urrish GalTwo when the plank abruptly let out a loud *crack!* The attached cable moaned, yanking hard at the grappling hook—

—and the tortured wood gave way.

The hook snatched the ax out of her hand as it tore free, glittering in the sunlight. Thrown off balance, Sara struggled to hold on, though her hands were slippery from sweat and blood. With a gasp she felt her grip fail and she dropped, sucking in deeply, but the Roney slammed her like an icy hammer, driving air from her startled lungs.

Sara floundered, battling first to reach the surface, then to tread water and sputter a few deep breaths, and finally to keep from getting tangled in all the ropes that lay strewn across the water. A shiny hook passed a frightening hand's width from her face. Moments later, she had to dive down to avoid a snarl of cords that might have trapped her.

The boat's turbulent wake added to her troubles, as the *Hauph-woa* took advantage of its chance to flee.

Her chest ached by the time she hit surface again—to come face-to-face with a lanky young man, leaning on the rim of a coracle, clutching a slingshot in one hand. Surprise rocked him back when their eyes met. Then his gaze dropped to notice her bareness.

He *blushed*. Hurriedly, the young man put aside his weapon and started shrugging out of his jacket. To give to her, no doubt.

"Thanks . . ." Sara gasped. "But I gotta . . . go now."

Her last glimpse of the young villager, as she swam away, showed a crestfallen look of disappointment. *It's too soon yet for him to be a hardened pirate,* Sara thought. *This new, hard world hasn't yet rubbed away the last traces of gallantry.*

But give it time.

Now she had the river's current behind her as she swam, and soon Sara glimpsed the *Hauph-woa* downstream. The crew had the boat turned and were stroking to stay in place, now that they had reached a safe distance from Bing Village. Still, it was a hard pull to reach the hull at last and start up the rope ladder. She only made it halfway before her muscles started to cramp, and the helpful sailors had to haul it in the rest of the way by hand.

I've got to get stronger, if I'm going to make a habit of having adventures, she thought as someone wrapped a blanket around her.

Yet, Sara felt strangely fine while Pzora tended her wound and the cook made her some of his special tea. Sara's hand ached, and her body throbbed, yet she felt also something akin to a *glow*.

I made decisions, and they were right ones. A year ago, it seemed every choice I made was wrong. Now, maybe things have changed.

Clutching her blanket, Sara watched as the *Hauph-woa* labored back upstream along the *west* bank, to a point where they could take aboard the stranded caravan, ferrying the urs and their beasts far enough to have no worries about local fanatics. The calm teamwork of passengers and crew was such an encouraging sight, it boosted her morale about "big" issues, almost as much as the brief fight had lifted something else inside her.

My faith in my own self, she thought. *I didn't think I was up to any of this. But maybe Father's right, after all. I stayed in that damn treehouse long enough.*

Asx

SHORTLY AFTER VUBBEN SPOKE, THE PORTAL RE-opened and there emerged from the ship several more floating machines, growling disconcertingly. Each hesitated on reaching the onlookers lining the valley rim. For several duras, the folk of the Commons held their ground, though trembling in foot, wheel, and ring. Then the robots turned and swept away, toward every point of the compass, leaving cyclones of broken grass in their wake.

"Survey probes—these shall commence their duties," the first messenger explained, buzzing and clicking primly in a formal version of Galactic Two.

"(Preliminary) analyses—these surrogates shall provide.

"Meanwhile, toward a goal of both profit and rescue—let us, face-to-face discussions, commence."

This caused a stir. Did we understand correctly? Our dialects have drifted since our devolution. Did the phrase "face-to-face" mean what it seemed?

Below, the ship's doorway began reopening once more.

"Bad news," Lester Cambel commented gruffly. "If they're willing to let us see them in person, it means—"

"—that they are not worried anyone will be left after they depart, to *tell* whose face was seen," finished Knife-Bright Insight.

Our hoon brother, Phwhoon-dau, shared the gloomy diagnosis. His aged throat sac darkened from somber thought. "Their confidence is blatant, unnerving. *Hrrrhrm.* As is their haste."

Vubben turned an eyestalk toward my/our sensor ring and winked the lid—an efficient, human-derived gesture conveying irony. Among the Six, we traeki and g'Keks hobble like cripples on this heavy world, while hoon stride with graceful power. Yet those dour, pale giants claim to find the rest of us equally frantic and wild.

Something, or rather *two* somethings, stirred within the shadowy airlock. A pair of bipedal forms stepped forward—walkers—slim, stick-jointed, and somewhat tall. Clothed in loosely draped garments that concealed all but their bare hands and heads, they emerged into the afternoon light to peer upward at us.

From the Commons there erupted a low collective sigh of shock and recognition.

Was this a hopeful sign? Out of all the myriad spacefaring races in the Civilization of the Five Galaxies, what impossibly remote chance decreed that our discoverers might turn out to be *cousins*? That the crew of this ship should be cogenetic with one of our Six? Was this the work of our capricious goddess, whose luck favors the anomalous and strange?

"Hyoo-mans-s-s . . ." Ur-Jah, our eldest sage, aspirated in Anglic, the native tongue of our youngest sept.

From Lester Cambel, there escaped a sound i had never heard before, which these rings could not decipher at the time. Only later did we comprehend, and learn its name.

It was despair.

Dwer

RETY LED SINGLE FILE ALONG A TRACK THAT NOW ran atop a broad shelf of bedrock, too hard for greatboo to take root. The slanting, upthrust granite ledge separated two broad fingers of cane forest, which Dwer knew stretched for hundreds of arrowflights in all directions. Although the rocky trail followed a ridgetop, the boo on either side grew so tall that only the highest peaks could be seen above the swaying ocean of giant stems.

The girl kept peering, left and right, as if in search of something. As if she *wanted* something, rather urgently, and did not want to walk past it by mistake. But when Dwer tried to inquire, all she gave back was silence.

You'll have to watch it with this one, he thought. *She's been hurt all her life, till she's prickly as a dartback hare.*

People weren't his specialty, but a forester uses empathy to grasp the simple needs and savage thoughts of wild things.

Wild things can know pain.

Well, in another day or so she won't be my problem. The sages have experts, healers. If I meddle, I may just make things worse.

The stone shelf gradually narrowed until the footpath traced a slender aisle between crowded ranks of towering adult boo, each stem now over twenty meters tall and as thick as several men. The giant green stalks grew so close that even Mudfoot would have trouble getting far into the thicket without squeezing between mighty boles. The strip of sky above pinched gradually tighter becoming a mere ribbon of blue as the trail constricted. At some points, Dwer could spread his arms and touch mighty cylinders on both sides at the same time.

The compressed site played tricks with perspective as he pictured two vast walls, primed to press together at any instant, grinding their tiny group like scraps of cloth under Nelo's pulping hammer.

Funny thing. This stretch of trail hadn't felt nearly so spooky on his way *uphill,* two days ago. Then, the slender avenue had felt like a funnel, channeling him briskly toward his quarry. Now it was a cramped furrow, a pit. Dwer felt a growing tightness in his chest. *What if something's happened up ahead. A landslide blocking the way. Or a fire? What a trap this could be!*

He sniffed suspiciously, picking up only a gummy reek of *greenness* given off by the boo. Of course, anything at all could be going on downwind, and he wouldn't know of it until—

Stop this! Snap out of it. What's gotten into you?

It's her, he realized. *You're feeling bad because she thinks you're a bastard.*

Dwer shook his head.

Well, ain't it so? You let Rety go on thinking she might be hanged, when it would have been easy enough to say—

To say what? A lie? I can't promise it won't happen. The law is fierce because it has to be. The sages can show mercy. It's allowed. But who am I to promise in their name?

He recalled his former master describing the last time a large band of sooners was discovered, back when old Fallon had been an apprentice. The transgressors were found living on a distant archipelago, far to the north. One of the hoon boat-wanderers—whose job it was to patrol at sea the same way human hunters roamed the forests and urrish plainsmen ranged the steppes—came upon a thronging cluster of her kind, dwelling amid ice floes, surviving by seeking the caves of hibernating rouol shamblers and spearing the rotund beasts as they slept. Each summer, the renegade tribe would come ashore and set fires across the tundra plains, panicking herds of shaggy, long-toed gallaiters, sending the frightened ungulates tumbling over cliffs by the hundreds, so that a few might be butchered.

Ghahen, the boat-wanderer, had been drawn by the smoke of one mass killing and soon began dealing with the crime in the manner of her folk. Patient beyond human fathoming, gentle in a way that gave Dwer nightmares to hear of it, she had taken an entire year to winnow the band, one by one, painlessly confiscating from each member its precious life bone, until all that remained was a solitary male elder, whom she seized and brought home to testify, ferrying the dejected captive in a boat piled high with the fifth vertebra of all his kin. After reciting his tale—a crooning lament lasting fourteen days—that final seagoing sooner was executed by the hoon themselves, expiating their shame. All the impounded vertebrae were ground to dust and scattered in a desert, far from any standing water.

The forbidding memory of that story filled Dwer's heart with leaden worry.

Spare me, please, from being asked to do as Ghahen did. I couldn't. Not if all the sages ordered it. Not if Lark said the fate of all Jijo hung in the balance. There's got to be a better way.

Just where the rocky shelf seemed about to narrow down to nothing, letting the divided tracts of boo converge and obliterate the trail, a clearing abruptly opened ahead. A bowl-shaped depression, nearly a thousand meters across, with an algae-crusted lake in its center and a narrow outlet at the far end. A fringe of great-boo lined the crater's outer rim, and spindly tufts of the tenacious plant sprouted from crevices between jagged boulders that lay tumbled across the silent mountain vale. The lake's watery shore was outlined by a dense hedge, appearing at a distance like rank moss, from which radiated countless twisted tendrils, many of them broken stumps. Even where Dwer stood, ropy fibers could be seen half-buried in the dust, some as thick as his leg.

The peaceful quiet was belied by an eerie sense of *lifelessness*. The dust lay undisturbed by footprints, only the scrape of wind and rain. From prior visits, Dwer knew why prudent creatures avoided this place. Still, after the strangling confinement of that tunnel-trail, it felt good to see sky again. Dwer had never much shared the prevailing dread of crossing open ground, even if it meant walking for a short time under the glaring sun.

As they picked their way past the first boulders, the glaver began to mew nervously, creeping alongside Rety to keep in her shadow. The girl's eyes roved avidly. She seemed not to notice drifting off the trail, at an angle that would skirt the fringe of the lake.

Dwer took several long strides to catch up. "Not that way," he said, shaking his head.

"Why not? We're headin' over there, right?" She pointed to the only other gap in the outer wall of boo, where a narrow, scummy stream leaked through the valley's outlet. "Quickest way is past the lake. Looks easier, too, except right by the shore."

Dwer gestured toward a relic webbery of dun strands, draping the nearby jagged boulders. "Those are—" he began.

"I *know* what they are." She made a face. "Buyur didn't only live on the Slope, y'know, even if you westies do think it's simply the best place to be. We got mulc-spiders over the hill, too, eatin' up old Buyur ruins.

"Anyway, what're you so scared of? You don't think this one's still alive, do you?" She kicked one of the desiccated vines, which crumbled to dust.

Dwer controlled himself. *It's that chip on her shoulder talking. Her people must have been awful to her.* Taking a breath, he replied evenly.

"I don't *think* it's alive. I know it is. What's more—this spider's crazy."

Rety's first reaction was to raise both eyebrows in surprised fascination. She leaned toward him and asked in a hushed voice— *"Really?"*

Then she tittered, and Dwer saw she was being sarcastic. "What's it do? Put out sticky lures full o' berrysugar an' sweet gar, to snatch little girls who're bad?"

Taken aback, Dwer finally grunted. "I guess you could say something like that."

Now Rety's eyes widened for real, brimming with curiosity. "Now this I gotta see!"

She gave the rope at her waist a sudden yank. The formidable-looking knot fell apart, and she took off, dashing past several craggy stones. The gaily squeaking noor pursued with excited bounds.

"Wait!" Dwer yelled futilely, knowing it useless to chase her through the boulder maze. Scrambling up a nearby talus slope of rocky debris, he managed to glimpse her ragged ponytail, bobbing as she ran toward where the rocky slabs converged in a tumbled labyrinth rimming the lake shore.

"Rety!" he screamed into the wind. "Don't touch the—"

He stopped wasting breath. The same breeze that pushed the lake's musty pungency against his face stole his words before they could reach her ears. Dwer slid back down to the trail, only to realize—damn! Even the *glaver* was gone!

He finally found it half an arrowflight uphill, shambling back the way they had come, following whatever instinct sometimes drove its kind to wander doggedly east, away from comfort and protection and toward near-certain death. Growling under his breath, Dwer seized the mare's tether and sought something, anything, to tie her to, but the nearest stand of gangly boo lay too far away. Dropping his pack, he whipped out a length of cord. "Sorry about this," he apologized, using his hip to lever the glaver over. Ignoring her rumbling complaint, he proceeded to hobble her rear legs, where he hoped she couldn't reach the rope with her teeth.

"Pain, frustration—both quite tedious are."

"Sorry. I'll be back soon," he answered optimistically, and took off after the sooner child.

Stay uphill and downwind, Dwer thought, angling to

the right of her last heading. *This might just be a trick to let her circle around and head for home.*

A little later, he noticed he had reflexively unlimbered his bow, cranking the string tension for short range, and had loosed the clamp securing the stubby arrows in his thigh quiver.

What good will arrows do, if she makes the spider angry?

Or worse, if she catches its interest?

Toward the valley's rim, many stones retained a semblance to their ancient role, segments of whatever Buyur structure once stood proudly on this site, but as Dwer hurried inward, all likeness to masonry vanished. Ropy strands festooned the boulders. Most appeared quite dead—gray, desiccated, and flaking. However, soon his eye caught a greenish streak here . . . and over there a tendril oozing slime across a stony surface, helping nature slowly erase all vestiges of former scalpel-straight smoothness.

Finally, raising a creepy feeling down his back, Dwer glimpsed tremors of *movement*. A wakening of curling strands, roused from sleep by some recent disturbance. *Rety.*

He dodged through the increasingly dense maze, leaping over some ropy barriers, sliding under others, and twice doubling back with an oath when he reached impassable dead ends. This Buyur site was nowhere near as vast as the one north and east of Dolo Village, where each local citizen dutifully took part in crews gleaning for items missed by the deconstructor spider. Dwer used to go there often, along with Lark or Sara. That spider was more vigorous and alive than this crotchety old thing—yet *far* less dangerous.

The thicket of pale cables soon grew too crowded for an adult to pass, though the girl and noor might have gone on. In frustration, Dwer whirled and slapped a rounded knob of rock.

"Ifni sluck!" He waved his stinging hand. "Of all the bloody damn jeekee . . ."

He slung the bow over one shoulder, freeing both

hands, and started scrambling up the jagged face of a boulder three times his height. It was no climb he would have chosen, given time to work out a better route, but Dwer's racing heart urged him to hurry.

Mini-avalanches of eroded rock spilled over his hair and down his collar, stinging with a dusty redolence of decayed time. Flakey vincs and dried tendrils offered tempting handholds, which he strove to ignore. Rock was stronger, though not always as reliable as it looked.

While his fingers traced one fine crack, he felt the outcrop under his left foot start to crumble and was forced to trust his weight to one of the nearby crisscrossing mulc-cables.

With a crackling ratchet, the vine gave but a moment's warning before slipping. He gasped, suspending his entire weight with just his fingertips. Dwer's torso struck the stone wall, slamming air out of his lungs.

His flailing legs met another strand, thinner than the first, just seconds before his grip would have failed. With no other choice, Dwer used it as a springboard to pivot and launch himself leftward, landing on a slim ledge with his right foot. His hands swarmed along the almost sheer face—and at last found solid holds. Blinking away dust, he inhaled deeply till it felt safe to resume.

The last few meters were less steep but worn slick by countless storms since the boulder had been dragged here, then left in place by the weakening vines. Finally, he was able to get up on his knees and peer ahead, toward the nearby shore.

What had seemed a uniform hedge, lining the lake's perimeter, was now a thick snarl of vines, varying from man-height to several times as tall. This near the water, the cables' gray pallor gave way to streaks of green, yellow, even bloodred. Within the tangle he glimpsed specks of yet other colors, sparkling in shafts of sunlight.

Beyond the thorny barrier, the scummy pond seemed to possess a geometric essence, both liquid and uncannily *corrugated*. Some areas seemed to pulse, as if to a cryptic rhythm—or enduring anger.

One-of-a-Kind, he thought, not really wanting to

evoke the name but unable to resist. He pulled his gaze away, scanning for Rety. *Don't hurt her, One-of-a-Kind. She's only a child.*

He didn't want to converse with the mulc-spider. He hoped it might be dormant, as when the lake was a harmless cranny in the winter snowscape. Or perhaps it was dead, at last. The spider was surely long past due to die. A grisly *hobby* seemed to be all that kept this one alive.

He shivered as a creeping sensation climbed the nape of his neck.

(Hunter. Fellow-seeker. Lonely one. How good of you to greet me. I sensed you pass nearby some days ago, hurrying in chase. Why did you not pause to say hello?

(Have you found what you sought?

(Is it this "child" you speak of?

(Is she different from other humans?

(Is she special in some way?)

Scanning for traces of Rety, Dwer tried to ignore the voice. He had no idea why he sometimes held conversations with a particular corrosive alpine puddle. Though psi talent wasn't unknown among the Six, the Scrolls warned darkly against it. Anyway, most psi involved links among close kin—one reason he never told anyone about this fey channel. Imagine the nicknames, if people learned of it!

I probably imagine it all, anyway. Must be some weird symptom of my solitary life.

The tickling presence returned.

(Is that still your chief image of me? As a figment of your mind? If so, why not test it? Come to me, my unowned treasure. My unique wonder! Come to the one place in the cosmos where you will always be prized!)

Dwer grimaced, resisting the hypnotic draw of the algae patterns, still scanning amid the rocks and tangles for Rety. At least the spider hadn't taken her yet. Or was it cruel enough to lie?

There! Was that a flicker to the left? Dwer peered westward, shading his eyes against the late afternoon sun. Something rustled near the coiled vines, just a dozen or so meters closer to the lake, hidden by the bulk of several stone slabs, but causing a section of hedge to quiver. Squinting, Dwer wished he hadn't been so hasty in dropping his pack, which contained his priceless handmade ocular.

It might be a trap, he thought.

{*Who would trap you, Special One? You suspect me? Say you don't mean it!*}

The wind had died down a bit. Dwer cupped his hands and called, "Rety!"

Queer echoes scattered among the rocks, to be sucked dry by pervasive moss and dust. Dwer looked around for alternatives. He could slip down to ground level and hack his way inward, using the machete sheathed at his back. But that would take forever, and how would One-of-a-Kind react to having its fingers sliced off?

His only real option was to go *over.*

Dwer backed up till his heels hung over empty space, then took a deep breath and sprang forward . . . one, two, three paces, and *leaped*—sailing over a jungle of interlacing tendrils—to land with a jarring thud atop the next slab. This one slanted steeply, so there was no time to recover. He had to scramble fast to reach a long knife-edged ridge. Standing up, he spread his arms and gingerly walked heel-and-toe, teetering for ten paces before reaching a boulder with a flatter top.

Dwer's nostrils filled with sour, caustic odors from the lake. More nearby tendrils throbbed with veins now, flowing acrid tinctures. He skirted puddles of bitter fluid, collecting in cavities of etched stone. When his boot scraped one pool, it left fine trails of ash and a scent of burning leather.

The next time he took a running leap, he landed hard on hands and knees.

"Rety?" he called, crawling to the forward edge.

The shoreline barrier was a dense-woven knot of green, red, and yellow strands, twisted in roiling confusion. Within this contorted mass, Dwer spied *objects*—

each nestled in its own cavity. Each sealed, embedded, within a separate crystal cocoon.

Golden things, silvery things. Things gleaming like burnished copper or steel. Tubes, spheroids, and complex blocky forms. Things shining unnatural hues of pigment or nanodye. Some resembled items Dwer had seen dragged from Buyur sites by reclaimer teams; only those had been decomposed, worn by passing centuries. *These* samples of past glory looked almost new. Like bugs trapped in amber, their cocoons preserved them against the elements, against time. And each item, Dwer knew, was one of a kind.

Not every sample was a Buyur relic. Some had once been alive. Small animals. Insectoids. Anything that strayed too close and caught the mad spider's collecting fancy. It seemed a wonder that a being devoted to destruction—one *designed* to emit razing fluids—could also secrete a substance that conserved. All the more astonishing that it would want to.

The rustling resumed, coming from his left. Dwer slithered that way, dreading to find the girl trapped and suffering. Or else some small creature he would have to put out of misery with his bow.

He edged forward . . . and gasped.

What he saw netted in the profuse tangle, just a few meters ahead, came as a complete surprise.

At first sight it resembled a bird—a Jijoan avian—with the typical clawed stilt for a landing leg, four broad-feathered wings, and a tentacle-tail. But Dwer swiftly saw that it was no species he knew—or any genus listed on his brother's charts. Its wings, flapping desperately against a surrounding net of sticky threads, articulated in ways Dwer thought unnatural. And they beat with a power he found suspicious in any living thing that size.

Feathers had been ripped or burned away in several places. Within those gaps, Dwer glimpsed flashes of glistening metal.

A machine!

Shock made him release the screen on his thoughts, allowing the tickling voice to return.

{Indeed, a machine. Of a type I never before owned. And see, it still operates. It lives!}

"I see that, all right," Dwer muttered.

{And you don't yet know the half of it. Is this my day, or what?}

Dwer hated the way the mulc-spider not only slipped into his mind but somehow used what it found there to produce perfect Anglic sentences, better than *Dwer* could manage, since the spider never stammered or seemed at a loss for words. He found that obnoxious, coming from a being lacking a face to talk back to.

The false bird thrashed in its snare. Along its feathered back gleamed clear, golden droplets that it fought to shake off, flicking most aside before they could harden into a shell of adamant, preserving crystal.

What on Jijo could it be? Dwer wondered.

{I was hoping, now that I have you, to learn the answer.}

Dwer wasn't sure he liked the way One-of-a-Kind put that. Anyway, there wasn't time to bandy words. Dwer pushed aside pity for the trapped creature. Right now he must keep *Rety* from becoming yet another unique specimen in the mulc-spider's collection.

{So, as I suspected. The small human is special!}

Dwer quashed the voice with the best weapon he had—anger.

Get out of my mind!

It worked. The presence vanished, for now. Once more, Dwer lifted his head and shouted. "Rety! Where are you!"

An answer came at once, from surprisingly close by.

"I'm here, fool. Now be quiet, or you'll scare it!"

He swiveled, trying to stare in all directions at once. "Where? I don't see—"

"Right below you, so shut up! I've been followin' this thing for weeks! Now I gotta figure how to get it outta there."

Dwer slid further left to peer into the crisscrossing network just below—and found himself staring straight into the beady black eyes of a grinning noor! Stretched out across a dormant vine as if it were a comfy roost, Mudfoot tilted his head slightly, squinting back at Dwer. Then, without warning, the noor let loose a sudden sneeze.

Dwer rocked back, cursing and wiping his face, while Mudfoot grinned innocently, happily.

"Quiet, you two! I think I see how to get a little closer—"

"No, Rety. You mustn't!" Ignoring the noor, Dwer crept back to the edge and found her at last, close to the ground, perched with a leg on either side of a giant vine, squinting through the gloomy tangle at the mysterious avian.

"Took you long enough to catch up," Rety commented.

"I . . . had some distractions," he replied. "Now just wait a second, will you? There's—some things you ought to know about this—about this here mulc-spider." He motioned at the snarled mesh surrounding them. "It's more, well, *dangerous* than you realize."

"Hey, I been exploring webs since I was little," she replied. "Most are dead, but we got a few big ones in the Hills, still full o' sap and nasty stuff. I know my way around." She swung her leg over the branch and slipped forward.

In a panic, Dwer blurted out—"Did any of those spiders *try* to catch you?"

She stopped, turned to face him again, and smirked.

"Is that what you meant by *crazy?* Oh, hunter. You got some imagination."

Maybe you're right, he pondered. That *could* be why he never heard of anyone else holding conversations with shrubs and lakes.

{What, again? How many times must we speak before you are convinced—}

Shut up and let me think!

The spider's presence backed off again. Dwer bit his lip, trying to come up with something, anything, to keep the girl from venturing deeper into the thicket.

"Look, you've been following that bird-machine for

some time, right? Is that what led you west in the first place?"

She nodded. "One day some o' the boys saw a critter swoop out of a marsh, down by the Rift. Mean ol' Jass winged it, but it got away, leaving a feather behind."

She plucked something out of her leather blouse. Dwer glimpsed a brief metal sparkle before she put it away.

"I swiped it from Jass before I snuck out to go after the bird. Poor thing must've been hurt, 'cause by the time I picked up the trail, it wasn't flyin' so good. Kind of gliding for a stretch, then hoppin' along. I only got one good look. Upslope to the Rimmers it started pullin' ahead. Then I reached the Slope, and it came to me that I risked getting hanged every dura that I stayed."

She shivered, a memory of fear.

"I was about to give up and head back home for a beatin', when I heard a tapping sound in the night. I followed it, and for a minute I thought the clock teet was *my* bird!" She sighed. "That's when I saw you, snorin' away, with that fancy bow of yours lyin' nearby. Figured it'd make Jass an' Bom happy enough to forget knockin' my teeth out for runnin' off."

Dwer had never heard their names before but decided a rope was too good for some sooners.

"That's why you came all this way? To follow that bird-thing?"

Rety answered with a shrug. "I don't spect you'd understand."

On the contrary, he thought. It was what he himself would have done, if something so strange ever crossed his path.

{As would I, were I not rooted to this spot, ensnared by my own limitations. Are we not alike?}

Dwer chased the spider out—and the next instant an idea glimmered, offering a possible way out of this mess, as Rety slid off the branch and began to sidle forward, holding a slim blade that Dwer had never found when he searched her, the day before. It gleamed with razor sharpness.

"Wait. I—think about it, Rety. Shouldn't we work together? Wouldn't we do a better job getting it out?"

She stopped and seemed to consider the idea, looking up through the branches. "I'm listenin'."

Dwer frowned, concentrating on getting the words right. "Look . . . nobody on the Slope has seen an active Buyur machine since—well, long before humans came to Jijo. This is important. I want to get that thing out of there as much as you do."

All of which was true, or would have been if his first concern weren't saving the girl's life and his own. *Stall for time,* Dwer thought. *There's only a midura of daylight left. Get her to retreat till tomorrow. Then you can drag her away by force if you have to.*

"Go on," Rety said. "You want to come down an' chop with your big knife? I bet you'd splatter, hacking at live vines. Lotta pain that way, if the sap goes spraying around." Still, she seemed interested.

"Actually, I know a way that won't bruise a single branch but might spread a hole big enough to get your bird-thing out. We'd use some of the—um, natural resources handy hereabouts."

"Yeah?" She frowned. "The only stuff around here is rock, and dirt, and—"

Her eyes lit. "Boo!"

He nodded. "We'll cut some young shoots, trim them tonight, and return in the morning with bridges and ladders to cross on top of the boulders—and enough pry bars to spread a path through all this"—he waved at the surrounding thicket—"without spilling any acid or gunk on ourselves. We'll get your birdie-thing out long before it's sealed in a crystal egg, and march right up to the sages with a surprise that'll make a hoon's spine pop. How does that sound?"

Dwer saw distrust in her eyes. She was naturally suspicious, and he had never been a very good liar. When she glanced back at the trapped mystery machine, he knew she must be gauging whether it could hold out overnight. "It still looks strong," he told her. "If it lasted in there several days, one more night shouldn't make that much difference."

Rety lowered her head, pondering. "Might even be good if its wings got stickier. Won't be able to fly off when we free it." She nodded. "All right. Let's go cut us some boo."

With one hesitant, longing scan behind her, Rety swung her legs over the thick branch and reached up to begin climbing. She carefully examined each hand or foothold before committing herself, eyeing it for caustic leaks, then testing whether the next vine would bear her weight. Clearly, she was an experienced explorer.

But Rety had never ventured through a spider like this one. When she was about a third of the way through the twisty tangle, she suddenly winced, withdrawing her hand and staring at a single pale-golden droplet, glistening on the back of her wrist. It did not burn, or she would have screamed. For a moment, she seemed more entranced by the color than afraid.

"Quick, shake it off!" Dwer cried.

She complied. The glob flew into the foliage. But instantly there followed two more soft splatting sounds. A drop appeared on her shoulder, and one in her hair. Rety looked up to see where they came from—and took one more in the middle of her forehead. Cursing, she tried wiping it off—but managed only to smear it down her cheek. Rety backed away rapidly.

"Not that way!" Dwer urged. He saw some active vines snake toward her, golden dew oozing from crevices. Rety hissed in dismay, taking more drops in her hair as she scrambled in a new direction.

{Tell her not to fight. There need be no pain.}

Dwer's angry snarl was voiceless, inarticulate, hurling the spider's mind-touch away. He shrugged the bow off of his shoulder, leaving it atop the boulder, and began clambering down to the girl. Vaguely, he was aware that the noor had departed, sensibly fleeing danger. *Unlike some fools I know,* Dwer thought, slipping the machete out of its sheath.

"I'm coming, Rety," he said, testing his weight on a

branch. Dwer saw Rety try to ascend by another route, easily evading the sluggishly pursuing vines.

"Don't bother!" she called. "I'm all right. I don't need your hel—ack!"

The branch she was holding, which had seemed inert moments before, suddenly beaded a line of golden moisture. Rety recoiled, cursing. Several drops adhered to her hand. "Don't rub them!" Dwer urged.

"I'm not an idiot!" she retorted, backing away. Unfortunately, that took her deeper into the morass.

Dwer's machete, an artfully reshaped length of Buyur metal, gleamed as he took a swipe at one of the vines between them. It looked lifeless, but he was ready to leap back in case—

It severed neatly, a crumbling, decaying tube, spilling nothing but cloying dust. A good thing he had decided against using it as a foothold, then. This place wasn't forgiving of mistakes.

He let the machete hang by the pommel loop while he lowered himself one level, to what seemed a stable vine, setting his weight down gingerly; then he sidled along the horizontal span seeking a way downward. The next foothold seemed thinner, less anchored, but he didn't have much choice. At least it didn't gush acid or try to wrap his ankle like a snake. *How did she get this far in the first place?* He wondered, glad that most of the tendrils were dead. The hedge would have been impassable when the mulc-spider was in its prime.

"Dwer!"

He swiveled, wobbling as the ropy strand rocked to and fro. Peering past shadows, he watched Rety climb a chimneylike funnel, offering what seemed a way out. Only now, halfway up the slim gap, she saw something begin twisting into place above. Another clump of living vines . . . moving in to block the promise of escape. Meanwhile, the chimney's base was closing the same way. Her face betrayed rising panic. Flushed, she held out her slim blade, eyes darting for some vital spot to stab her foe. But all she could do was saw at some nearby strand, hoping it would not gush vitriol or golden death.

A short way beyond, Dwer saw the bird-thing, still struggling within its own trap.

Let her go, One-of-a-Kind, Dwer thought as he crouched, then leaped with both hands outstretched for another cable—which fortunately held as he swung across a dark opening to land straddling another almost horizontal branch, as thick as a sapling's trunk. *Let her go, or I'll—*

His mind seemed to strangle on the demand, not knowing how one intimidated a mulc-spider. Could he do more than irritate it with a machete? He might threaten to depart and return with tools to destroy the ancient thing, with flame and explosives, but somehow Dwer knew that would seem too abstract. The spider appeared to have little sense of perspective or cause and effect, only immediacy and *avarice,* combined with enough patience to make a hoon seem like a cranky noor.

Anyway, by the time Dwer could carry out his retribution, Rety would be sealed in a golden cocoon, preserved for all time . . . and dead as a stone.

Let's talk a trade, One-of-a-Kind, he projected as he took up the machete once more. *What will you take in exchange for her?*

There was no answer. Either One-of-a-Kind was too busy pushing vines and fluids around, acting with unaccustomed haste, or else—

The spider's silence felt eerie, predatory. Smug. As if it felt no need for conversation when it had two treasures and seemed about to get a third. Grimacing, Dwer sidled deeper into the quagmire. What else could he do?

He hacked at three more vines. The last sent streams of caustic sap arcing between crisscrossing branches. Smoke curled up from the rubbish-strewn floor below, adding to the acrid stench.

"Dwer, help me!"

Rety was fully hemmed in now, and touchy pride no longer suppressed the normal panic of a frightened child. Seen through a matrix of ensnaring mulc-twine, her hair glistened like an urrish tinker's mane on a dewy morning, coated with a fine dusting of golden droplets. A vine parted under her sawing knife—and two more slithered in to take its place.

"I'm coming!" he promised, splitting two more cables, then dropping to the next stable-looking branch. It sagged, then Dwer's footing went slippery as it seeped a clearish, greasy liquor. He shouted, and his feet slid out from under him.

The same dense tangle he'd been cursing saved him from a broken neck. His windmilling arms caught a vine, wrapping round it desperately as his legs swung in mid-air. But his sigh of relief turned into a gagging gasp. Under his chin, livid veins pulsed with some vile, crimson solution. Blisters formed as corrosive liquid welled beneath the thinnest of membranes. Dwer's eyes stung from escaping vapor.

{No, no. Don't think I would ever harm you so! You are much too precious for that.}

Before Dwer's tear-blurred gaze, the blisters stopped rising—then reddish fluid seemed to drain out of the throbbing arteries.

{That nectar is for plain stone. For you, my unique one, only the gold.}

Dwer grimaced. *Thanks a lot!*

Peering to one side, he found another tangle within reach of his feet. Risking that perch, he pushed away from the loathsome branch that had broken his fall.

{Think nothing of it.}

Dwer was almost at Rety's level now, close enough to see grim determination replace panic in her eyes as she sawed another vine in half. A fine spray rewarded her, gilding the forearm she raised to protect her face. All of a sudden, Dwer realized—*She's cutting in the wrong direction!*

Instead of taking the most direct route toward daylight, she was heading deeper into the morass—toward the mechanical bird-thing!

Of all the times to chase an Ifni-slucking obsession!

Sudden liquid coolness brushed Dwer's wrist. A shimmering meniscus bead lay amid the dark hairs. He moved aside quickly, before another drop could fall from the seep-pore overhead. Dwer shook the droplet off, but even after it was gone, the spot still felt chilled, touched with a not-unpleasant numbness, like when the village dentist spread powdered Nural leaves along a patient's gums, before spinning his hand-cranked drill.

The machete now wore its own streaked coating, already starting to crystallize in places. Certainly it was an artifact worth collecting, a slab of star-god stuff, adapted by a tribe of primitives to new use in a twilight place, between the gritty earth and urbane sky. Grimly, he raised his weapon and set to with a will.

Concentration was vital, so he ignored the stench and grinding dust with a hunter's narrow-minded focus. Sweat beaded his brow, face, and neck, but he dared not wipe. No doubt he already looked like Rety, who now glittered like some fairy confection, dusted with beads of honey. Dwer did not bother shouting for her to turn and head toward him. Given her obstinacy, he might as well save his breath.

Glancing back, he saw his escape route still looked clear—a tunnel lined by chopped branches and dangling severed vines. One-of-a-Kind could marshal more, but the mulc-spider was old, slow. As Dwer neared Rety's cage, he felt sure he could thwart the spider's move, when it came.

Now he called, hoarsely.

"Okay, Rety. No foolin'. Let's get outta here."

The girl was over at the far end of her funnel opening, staring at the bird-thing past the branches that blocked her way. "Hey, it noticed me! It's turning around!"

Dwer wouldn't care if it stood on its head and gave Drake's Farewell Address in Buyur-accented Galactic Three. He sliced another cable and coughed as fumes flowed from both writhing ends. "Rety, we haven't got time!"

When the smoke cleared, he sidled closer and saw that the bird-thing had risen up within its cell, peering skyward and ignoring droplets that settled, mistlike, on its feathered back. Rety, too, seemed to notice its attention shift. She turned to look upward, as Dwer heard a shrill, chittering sound from the same general direction.

It's just the bloody noor.

Beyond the diffracting crisscross of vines, he saw Mudfoot, returned from wherever it had fled. Only now the creature stood on its hind legs, sinuous body upraised, whiskered snout pulled back, snarling at something out of sight, to the south.

Another flicker caught Dwer's eye. Like an epileptic snake, a kinked vine twisted into view, crossing part of the opening Dwer had cut through the hedge. Its jerky fits and starts seemed pathetic, all alone—but that tendril was followed by another, and another still.

"Rety!" He shouted, preparing to slash at the remaining barrier between them. "The trap's closing. It's now or never!"

On her face lay the frustration of coming within arm's reach of her grail, only to have it snatched away by cruel fate. Not waiting for her answer, he lifted the heavy machete with both weary arms and cried out, splitting with three hard strokes the heavy cable blocking his way forward. *Don't throw it away, Rety,* he pleaded inside, knowing it would do no good to say anything more aloud.

With a cry of frustration, Rety whirled around, forsaking her treasure, hurling herself at smaller vines with her tiny blade, then squeezing between others with lithe, squirmy agility. The tight passage smeared gold drops until she resembled a streaked pastry of swirled nut cream. Dwer sliced relentlessly and at last was close enough to stretch one arm into the morass.

Rety's hand clasped his wrist.

Dwer planted his feet and hauled backward, drawing her through a dark, fetid funnel. A low moan accompanied the passage. He could not tell if it came from her, or himself, or both of them at once.

She slid free at last and clung to him with sudden fury, wrapping his torso in quivering arms and legs. Underneath all her macho bravado, Dwer knew she must have been terrified in there.

"We've got to hurry," he said, tugging at one arm.

Rety resisted but a moment, then slithered off. She inhaled. "Okay, let's go."

He gave her a boost with his hands, sending her clambering into the tunnel-chimney he had carved through the hedge.

(Oh, going so soon? Have I been so poor a host?)

"Dry up and burn, One-of-a-Kind," Dwer muttered under ragged breaths as he climbed after Rety, trusting her strong instincts to lead the way.

(Someday I surely will. But by then I'll have preserved a legacy.

(Think on it! When Jijo's fallow age ends, and new tenants possess this world for an aeon of shining glory, they will gaze in wonder at this collection I've gathered. Amid their glittering city towers, they'll cherish my samplings of the interregnum, setting my prize pieces on pedestals for all to see. And paramount among those specimens will be you, my trophy, my treasure. Perhaps the best-conserved exemplar of your by then long-extinct wolfling race.)

Dwer puzzled—how did the spider sink hooks into his brain to draw forth words he didn't recall ever learning, like *exemplar* and *interregnum*? Lark might have used them in his presence sometime, when perhaps they lodged somewhere deep in memory.

You're the one who's going to be extinct, spider! You and your whole damn race.

This time his blistering reply did not shove away the entity's mind-touch.

(By then, certainly. But our type-design is always to be found in the Great Galactic Library, and we are far too useful ever to be forgotten. Whenever a world must be evacuated, tidied up, and allowed to lay fallow once more—whenever the mighty works of some former tenant race must be rubbed down to recycled dust—then we shall always rise again.

(Can your tribe of ignorant monkeys claim such use-

*fulness, my precious? Can you claim any "purpose" at
all? Save a tenacious will to keep on existing?}*

This time Dwer did not answer. He needed to con-
serve his strength. If the earlier descent had been awful,
ascending became pure hell. It was twice as hard cran-
ing backward to hack away at vines overhead as it had
been striking down. In addition to danger from whipping cables and spurting acid, he and Rety had to climb
through a mist of shimmering drops. It was no longer a
matter of shaking them off one by one, but of dodging
the thicker drifts and somehow preventing them from
adhering to their eyes, noses, and ears. Through that
luminous miasma, Dwer saw more creepers twist and
flop into a gathering mesh above, more quickly than he
would have believed possible. Clearly, One-of-a-Kind
had been holding back till now.

*{What did you expect? That I would show you all the
things that I am capable o—*

{. . . that I would show you all the . . .

{. . . that I would show . . .}

When the voice in Dwer's head trailed off, his first
reaction was relief. He had other worries, like an agonizing crick in his neck and a right arm that looked as if it
had been dipped in a jeweler's vat, and that seemed
about to cramp from the repetitive hacking, hacking,
hacking. Now if only the chattering *noor* would shut up
too, with its shrill keening. Mudfoot's piercing chitters
crescendoed, rising in pitch beyond the limit of Dwer's
direct hearing but not past ability to scrape a vexing
runnel under his skull.

Through it all, a nagging worry bothered Dwer.

*I left the glaver all tied up. Will she die of thirst if I
never make it back?*

"Left!" Rety shouted. He quickly obeyed, swinging as
far as possible, trusting her swift reflexes to warn of jets
of yellow sap.

"Okay, clear!" she called.

The machete slipped. Dwer fumbled at the wrist strap
three times before getting a grip to resume chopping the
slender vines filling the chimney overhead, cutting off

the swiftly failing twilight. If they didn't make it out by full nightfall, every advantage would belong to the crazy mulc-spider.

Now a sound he had dismissed as background noise grew too loud to ignore. A low rumbling counterbass overrode the noor's yapping. All around Rety and Dwer, the hedge began vibrating. A number of brittle vines shuddered to dust while others sprouted cracks and dripped fluids—red, orange, and milky—noxious additions to a fog that already stung human eyes. Through that blur, Dwer blinked upward to see Mudfoot, perched nimbly atop the hedge of vines, withdrawing in snarling defiance as something new entered view from the south—something that *hovered* in the air, without any visible means of support!

A machine! A symmetrical, slab-sided form with gleaming flanks that reflected the sunset, drifting to a point just above the shuddering hedge.

Suddenly, its belly blazed forth a bitter light that diffracted past the vines. The slender beam lanced right past Rety and Dwer, as if probing for something deeper. . . .

"It's hunting the bird!" Rety crouched beside Dwer, seizing his arm and pointing.

"Never mind the damn bird!" he cursed. The hedge was shaking worse than ever. Dwer dragged her behind him just as a sundered tube whipped past, spurting caustic fluid, splattering a trail of fizzing agony along his back as he shielded the girl. Purple spots swarmed across his field of vision, and the machete slipped its thong to fall, clattering off branches on its way down.

Now it seemed as if the hedge were alive with stark, fleeing shadows, as the floating machine's searchlight narrowed to a searing needle that scorched anything it touched.

By the same light Dwer glimpsed the bird-thing, trapped inside its cage of ropy mesh and coated with a golden patina, erupting now in a dance of evasion, leaping back and forth as it tried to *dodge* the burning ray of light, its feathers already smoldering in spots. Rety let out a throaty cry of anger, but it was all the two humans could do simply to hold on.

Finally, the bird-thing seemed to give up. It stopped ducking and instead spread its four wings in a pitiful effort to create a shielding canopy, which began to smoke as the blazing shaft struck home and stayed. Only the little bird-machine's head poked out, snaking upward to gape toward the aggressor with one open, staring eye.

Dwer was watching in horrified amazement, mixed with stunned pity, when that dark, jadelike eye abruptly *exploded*.

The blinding flash was the last thing he clearly remembered for a long time to come.

VII. THE BOOK OF THE SEA

*Do not make poisons
that you cannot use.*

*Use all of the poisons
that you make.*

*If others must clean up
after you,
Do not act offended
when they exact a price.*

—The Scroll of Advice

Alvin's Tale

SO THERE WE WERE, JUST ARRIVED AT THE TOP-end tram platform after a long ride from Wuphon Port, and no sooner do Huck, Pincer, and me step off the tram car (with little Huphu riding Pincer's shell for luck) than our urrish pal, Ur-ronn, gallops up all flushed and bothered. Without offering so much as a greeting-preamble, she commences to prancing, snaking her narrow head back and forth, and hissing at us in that awful version of GalTwo she must've picked up back when she was grub-sized, foraging in the grass out on the Warril Plain. You know the dialect I mean—the one that drops every other double-click phrase stop, so at first all I could make out was a bunch of basso tone pulses conveying frenzied excitement.

Worse, a moment later she starts *nipping* at us, like we were a bunch of pack donkeys to be herded down the hall!

"Hrrrrm! Now hold it right there," I insisted. "Nothing ever gets done right by letting yourself get so *igsee* frantic. Whatever you've got to say can surely wait for a proper hello to friends you haven't seen in weeks. After all—*yi-houongwa!*"

Yes, that was a hoonish throat-blat of pain. Huck had rolled one of her main-wheels over my left foot.

"Varnish it, Alvin. You sound just like your father!"

My father? I thought. *How utterly ungloss.*

"Haven't you been *listening* to Ur-ronn?" Huck went on.

My sac panted a few times as I ran back over the last

few duras, piecing together some of what Ur-ronn was nattering about.

It was a wild tale all right, and we've told each other some whoppers.

"Hr-r-r—a *starship?*" I stared at our urrish pal. "You *mean* it this time? It's not just a comet, like you tried fooling us with a year ago?"

Ur-ronn stamped a forefoot, knowing I had her nailed. Switching to Anglic, she swore. "This tine for real! Velieve ne! I heard Uriel and Gyfz talking. They caught it on flates!"

On plates, I translated from the way her cleft upper lip mangles some Anglic consonants. *Photographic plates.* Maybe Ur-ronn wasn't having us on, after all. "Can we see?" I asked.

An urrish moan of frustration. "You jeekee file of scales and fur! That's where I veen trying to take you guys since the tran stoffed!"

"Oh." I bowed with a sweep of one arm. "Well then, what are we waiting around here for? Let's go!"

Years ago, Uriel the Smith inherited the Mount Guenn works from Ur-tanna, who was liege-heir to Ulennku, who got the sprawling underground mill from her own dying master, the great Urnunu, who rebuilt those mighty halls after quakes shook the Slope like a wet noor during the Year of the Egg. Before that, the tale goes back to a misty time before humans brought paper memory to Jijo, when wisdom had to fit in someone's living head or else be lost. Back to days when urrish settlers had to fight and prove themselves more than mere galloping savages, roaming the grassy plains, beholden to high-caste qheuens for everything they owned.

Ur-ronn used to recite the legend during our adventure trips. Even allowing for exaggeration, those must've been brave urs who climbed fuming volcano heights to build the first crude forges near fiery lava springs, toiling through cinders and constant danger to learn the secret of reworking Buyur metal and break the Gray Queens' tool-monopoly forever.

It kind of makes you glad humans didn't come any sooner, 'cause the answers would've been right there in some book—how to make knives and lenses and windows and such. Sure, it would've made it easier for the other exile races to free themselves from dominion by qheuenish woodcarvers. On the other hand, all you have to do is hear Ur-ronn's lisping tale to know what pride her folk won from all that work and sacrifice.

They did it themselves, you see, earning liberty and self-respect. Ask any hoon how *we'd* feel without our swaying ships. Earthling lore has made improvements, but no one *gave* us the sea! Not our far-off Guthatsa patrons, or the Great Galactic Library, or our selfish ancestors who dumped us on Jijo, naive and unready. It's a proud thing to have done it for ourselves.

Pride can be important, when you don't have much else.

Before entering the forge-inferno, Pincer-Tip draped a water-soaked mantle over his soft red carapace. I gathered my cloak around me while Huck checked her goggles and axle-guards. Then Ur-ronn led us past overlapping leather curtains into the Works.

We hurried along a walkway of treated boo, hung between bubbling pools that glowed white with Jijo's blood heat. Cleverly diverted updrafts guided smoldering vapors into stone baffles, venting them outside to look no different than any other smoker on Mount Guenn's flank.

Huge buckets dangled overhead—one filled with reclaimed Buyur scrap and the other with a sandy mix—each waiting to be dipped in that blazing heat, then poured into clay molds. Urrish workers hauled pulleys and ladles. Another twirled a big glob of liquid glass at the end of a tube, spinning it round and round to form a flat whirling disk that turned solid as it thinned and cooled, a *window* destined for homes far away from here.

They were assisted by several gray qheuens who, in

one of Jijo's ironies, turned out to be the other sept well suited to these conditions. The grays may even be happier than when their queens used to dominate the Commons. But I never could read much expression on their stony cupolas. I often wonder how our wild, emotional Pincer could be related to them.

Farther from the heat, half a dozen g'Keks skittered across the smooth floor, handling account ledgers, while a traeki specialist with throbbing synthi rings tasted each mix to certify the mill's products would rust or decay in less than two hundred years, as required by the sages.

Some orthodox scroll-pounders say we shouldn't have smithies at all—that they're vanities, distracting us from salvation through forgetfulness. But I think the place is gloss, even if the smoke frets my throat sac and sets my spine-scales itching.

Ur-ronn led us through more curtains into the Laboratory Grotto, where Uriel studies the secrets of her art—both those hard-won by her ancestors and others delved from human texts. Clever breezes freshened the air, allowing us to loosen our protections. Pincer gratefully doffed his heavy mantle and doused his red carapace at a shower-alcove. Huphu splashed eagerly while I sponged my sac. Ur-ronn kept her distance from the water, preferring a brief roll in some clean dry sand.

Huck skittered down a hallway lined with many doors, peering into various laboratory chambers. "Hsst! Alvin!" she whispered urgently, waving me over with one arm and two eyestalks. "Come look. Care to guess who's here again?"

"Who is it?" Pincer whistled, leaving five wet trails of prints behind him. Ur-ronn daintily avoided the moist tracks with her rattling hooves.

I already had a pretty good idea who Huck was talking about, since no ship passenger enters Wuphon without being known to the harbor master—my mother. She hadn't announced anything, but I knew from overheard snatches that the latest dross ship had brought an important human visitor, one who debarked at night, heading straight to the Mount Guenn tram.

"Hrrrm. I'll bet you a sweetboo cane it's that sage again," I ventured before arriving at the door. "The one from Biblos."

Huck's rear-facing eye looked disappointed, and she groused—"Lucky guess"—while making space for the rest of us.

I knew this room. Many's the previous visit I used to stand at the doorway and stare at the goings-on within. The huge chamber held Uriel's mystery machine—a gimcrackery of gears, cables, and revolving glass that seemed to fill the vaulted cavern with grinding motion like one of those Victorian factories you read about in books by Dickens. Only *this* device didn't make a single blessed thing, as far as any of us could ever tell. Only countless glitters of light as whirling crystal disks spun like hundreds of ghostly little g'Keks, rolling against each other madly, futilely, going noplace the faster they spun.

I glimpsed the human visitor, bent over a trestle table with a precious-looking folio spread open before him, pointing at a diagram, while *Uriel* rocked in a circle, lifting one leg at a time, shaking her pelted head in disagreement. The smith's gray-fringed nostril blew exasperation.

"With all due resfect, Sage Furofsky, you night have gone to Gathering instead of coning all this way. I cannot see how this vook is relevant to our frovlen—to our quandary."

The human wore the black cloak of a lesser sage, the kind who dwell in the sacred halls of Biblos with half a million printed tomes for company, tending wisdom handed down for three hundred years. He was hoonish-handsome, which happens when one of their males gets gray head fleece and lets his facial fur grow long, an effect enhanced by a noble long nose. This worthy jabbed again at the ancient page, so hard I feared he'd hurt the priceless text.

"But I tell you this algorithm is exactly what you need! It can be executed in a tenth the space, with far fewer parts, if you'd just consider—"

I can't write what followed, because it was in that dialect of Anglic called Engineering, and even my hoonish memory won't help me write words I can't understand or spell. The sage must have come to help Uriel in her project. Anyone who knew her could predict Uriel's resistance.

Beyond those two we saw *Urdonnol,* a younger urrish techie, who the Master trusted with general upkeep of this whatever-it-is machine, stretching beyond the farthest reach of the single overhead skylight. Urdonnol peered through the shuddering, squeaking assembly, reaching in to tighten an elastic belt or lubricate a bearing. As senior apprentice, she was two hooves toward being Uriel's heir.

The sole other candidate was *Ur-ronn,* partly because of our pal's school scores, and also because she's the nearest of Uriel's scent-cousins to survive from steppegrub to adult. No doubt Urdonnol worked here—tending the Master's personal project—to improve her chances, though she clearly hated the big machine.

Miniature centaur figures moved amid the whirling disks, making delicate adjustments. Urrish *males,* normally rare to see outside their wives' pouches, tightened belts and gears under Urdonnol's terse direction. Striking a blow for equality, I guess.

I bent and whispered to Huck, "So much for all that talk about—hr-hrrm—*starships!* If they really saw one, they wouldn't be fooling with toy gadgets right now!"

Ur-ronn must've overheard me. She swung her long muzzle, wearing a wounded look. Two out of three eyes narrowed. "I *heard* Uriel and Gyfz," she hissed. "Anyhow, what does a snarty-fants like you know?"

"Enough to know all these whirling glass yo-yos don't have hair on a qheuen's backside to do with visiting spaceships!"

Even if we *hadn't* been snapping at each other, it wasn't easy for a gang like ours to *peer discreetly* into a room, the way you read about humans doing in detective stories. Still, those inside mightn't have noticed us, if Huphu the noor hadn't chosen that moment to go bounding in, yipping at those spinning pulleys and disks. Before we knew it, she leaped onto a leather belt and was running in place like mad, snapping toward a pair of cringing urs husbands.

Urdonnol noticed, waving her arms, displaying the bright glands under both brood pouches.

"This event signifies? It signifies?" the apprentice demanded with slurred interrogative trills. Her agitation grew as the Master snaked a grizzled snout around to peer at the commotion.

Despite stereotypes, a hoon can act quickly if he sees a clear need. I rushed over to snatch Huphu, rumbling my very best umble, and rejoined the others, girding for a group tongue-lashing.

"Behavior that is (astonishingly, horrifyingly) unacceptable," declared Urdonnol in GalTwo. *"Interruption of an important congress by (knavish, microcephalic, unhousebroken)—"*

Uriel cut in, breaking Urdonnol's insult-stream before the fuming, stamping Ur-ronn could be provoked to responding in kind.

"That will do, Urdonnol," the Master commanded in GalSeven. "Kindly take the youngsters to Gybz, who has business of ers own with them, then hurry back. We have several more models to run before we are through for the day."

"It shall be done," Urdonnol replied in the same tongue. Turning to us with an aggressive neck-stretch, the older prentice said—"Come along, you gaggle of jeekee *adventurers.*"

She said it with dripping scorn, which is possible in GalSeven, though not as harsh as Anglic.

"Come swiftly. It's been decided to take you up on your offer.

"Your grand plan.

"Your one-way expedition to Hell."

VIII. THE BOOK OF THE SLOPE

Legends

It is said that glavers are an example to us all. Of the seven races to plant exile colonies on the Slope, they alone have escaped this prison where their ancestors consigned them. They did this by finding, and traveling, the Path of Redemption.

Now they are innocent, no longer criminals, having become one with Jijo. In time, they may even be renewed, winning that blessed rarity—a second chance at the stars.

It is a source of some frustration to Earthlings—the youngest sept to come here—that humans never got to meet glavers as thinking, speaking beings. Even the hoon and urs arrived too late to know them at their prime, when glavers were said to have been mighty intellects, with a talent for deep race memory. Watching their descendants root through our garbage middens, it is hard to picture the race as great starfarers and the patrons of three noble client-lines.

What desperation brought them here, to seek safety in oblivion?

The g'Keks tell us, by oral tradition, that it was the result of financial setbacks.

Once (according to g'Kek lore), glavers were said to be among those rare breeds with a knack for conversing with Zang—the hydrogen-breathing civilization existing aloofly in parallel to the society of races that use oxygen. This aptitude enabled glavers to act as intermediaries, bringing them great wealth and prestige, until a single contractual mistake reversed their fortunes, landing them in terrible debt.

It is said that the great Zang are patient. The debt falls due in several hundred thousand years. Yet so deep is the usury that the glaver race, and all its beloved clients, were hopelessly forfeit.

Glavers had but one thing left to trade, a precious thing they might yet sell, providing they could find the right path.

That thing was themselves.

—Collected Fables of Jijo's Seven, Third Edition.
Department of Folklore and Language, Biblos. Year 1867 of Exile.

A<small>SX</small>

THE PLUNDER SHIP SOON DEPARTED AS IT CAME, amid a storm of whirling fragments of our poor, shattered forest. A tornado leaned in its wake, as if Jijo's own ghostly hand were reaching, clasping, trying to restrain it.

Alas, this departure was no cause for joy, for the crew vowed an early return. Surety of this promise squatted near the steaming scar where the ship had lain—a black *cube*, half an arrowflight wide, featureless save where a ramp led to a gaping hatch.

Nearby, two frail cloth pavilions had been transplanted from Gathering, at the request of star-gods who had stayed behind when their ship departed. One to serve as a place of liaison, and a large tent for "examining specimens." Already a small foray party of star-humans worked under that canopy, feeding dark mysterious machines with samples of Jijoan life.

Shock still throbbed throughout the Commons. Despite unity-entreaties by their sages, the many septs and clans cleaved, each seeking shelter among its own kind. Emissaries darted among these cloistered groups, parleying in hushed secrecy. All save the youngest of the Six, whose envoys were rebuffed.

For the moment no one, not even the traeki, wants to speak to humans.

Sara

AROUND MIDAFTERNOON, THE RIVER SPILLED into canyon country. As if remembering some urgent errand, the water hastened through a terrain of thorny scrub, clinging to eroded slopes. Sara recalled these badlands from childhood fossil-hunting trips with Dwer and Lark. Those had been good times, despite the heat, stale food, and gritty dust. Especially when Melina used to come along, before the final lingering illness that took her away, leaving Nelo an old man.

Their mother's soft accent used to grow stronger, Sara recalled, the farther south they traveled. The open sky never seemed to cause her any dread.

In contrast, the crew of the *Hauph-woa* grew restless with each southward league, especially after the morning's episode of inept piracy, by the shattered bridge. Clearly the hoon sailors would prefer tying up for the rest of the day under some rocky shelter. The captain reminded them, with a farty blat from his violet sac, that this was no leisurely dross run but an urgent mission for the Commons.

A prevailing west wind normally filled the sails of craft climbing upstream. In places where the river's current pushed strongest, trusty hoon operators offered winch tows from cleverly camouflaged windmills—shaped like upright eggbeaters—that tapped the funneled breeze under cliff overhangs. But the first set of lonely vanes swept in and out of sight before anyone could emerge from the attached hut to answer their hails, and half a midura later, the overseer of the next windmill barely finished a rumbling courtesy-preamble before the river hauled the *Hauph-woa* beyond range.

Like the tug of time, Sara thought. *Pulling you into the future before you're ready, leaving behind a wake of regrets.*

If only life let you catch a friendly tow rope now and

then, to climb back into the past, offering a chance to change the flow of your own life-stream.

What would she do, with the last year or two to live over again? Could any amount of foresight have averted the sweet pain of giving her heart where it did not belong? Even with foreknowledge of Joshu's nature, would or could she have rejected in advance all those months of heady joy, when she had pretended in her own mind that he could be hers alone?

Might any amount of prophecy have helped save his *life*?

An image came to her, unbeckoned and unwelcome out of memory. Recollection of the very day she fled Biblos Citadel, clutching her books and charts, rushing home to that treehouse overlooking Dolo Dam, to drown herself in study.

—black banners flapping in a zephyr that blew past the castle's heavy roof-of-stone . . .

—murmur-kites, tugging at their tether strings, moaning their warbling lament during the mulching ceremony for Joshu and the other plague victims . . .

—a tall, fair-skinned woman, newly come by boat from far-off Ovoom Town, standing by Joshu's bier, performing a wife's duty, laying on his brow the wriggling torus that would turn mortal flesh into gleaming, crystal dust . . .

—the poised, cool face of Sage Taine, rimmed by a mane of hair like Buyur steel, approaching to graciously forgive Sara's year-long indiscretion . . . her "fling" with a mere bookbinder . . . renewing his offer of a more seemly union . . .

—her last sight of Biblos, the high walls, the gleaming libraries, with forest-topped stone overhead. A part of her life, coming to an end as surely as if *she* had died.

The past is a bitter place, said the Scrolls. *Only the path of forgetfulness leads ultimately to redemption.*

. . .

A sharp, horrified gasp was followed by a clatter and crash of fallen porcelain.

"Miss Sara!" an aspirated voice called. "Come quickly, please. All of you!"

She hurried from the starboard rail to find Pzora puffing in agitation, ers delicate arms-of-manipulation reaching out imploringly. Sara's heart leaped when she saw the Stranger's pallet *empty,* blankets thrown in disarray.

She spied him, backed between three barrel-caskets of human dross, clutching a jagged pottery shard. The wounded man's eyes gaped, wide and wild, staring at the traeki pharmacist.

He's terrified of Pzora, she realized. *But why?*

"Do not fear," she said soothingly in GalSeven, stepping forward slowly. "Fear is inappropriate at this time."

Eyes showing white above the irises, his gaze swung from her to Pzora, as if unable to picture the two of them in the same frame, the same thought.

Sara switched to Anglic, since some coastal human settlements used it almost exclusively.

"It's all right. It is. Really. You're safe. You've been hurt. Terribly hurt. But you're getting better now. Really. You're safe."

Some words prompted more reaction than others. He seemed to like "safe," so she repeated it while holding out her hand. The Stranger glanced anxiously at Pzora. Sara moved to block his view of the traeki, and some tension diminished. His eyes narrowed, focusing on her face.

Finally, with a resigned sigh, he let the jagged sliver fall from trembling fingers.

"That's good," she told him. "No one's going to harm you."

Though the initial flood of panic was over, the Stranger kept glancing toward the Dolo Village pharmacist, shaking his head with surprise and evident loathing.

"Bedamd . . . bedamd . . . bedamd . . ."

"Now be polite," she chided, while sliding a folded blanket behind his head. "You wouldn't be taking a nice boat trip to Tarek Town without Pzora's unguents. Anyway, why should you be afraid of a traeki? Who ever heard of such a thing?"

He paused, blinked at her twice, then commenced another pathetic attempt to speak.

"A-jo . . . A-joph . . . j-j-jo—joph . . ."

Frustrated, the Stranger abruptly stopped stammering and shut his mouth, squeezing his lips in a tight, flat line. His left hand raised halfway to the side of his head—toward the bandage covering his horrible wound—then stopped just short, as if touching would make his worst fears real. The arm dropped and he sighed, a low, tremulous sound.

Well, he's awake at least, Sara thought, contemplating a miracle. *Alert and no longer feverish.*

The commotion attracted gawkers. Sara called for them to move back. If a *traeki* could set off hysteria in the wounded man, what about the sight of a qheuenish male, with sharp clambering spikes up and down each leg? Even these days, there were humans who disliked having other members of the Six close by.

So the next sound was the last thing Sara expected to hear—

Laughter.

The Stranger sat up, eyeing the gathered passengers and crew. He gaped at Jomah, the exploser's son, who had climbed Blade's broad back, clasping the head-cupola jutting from the qheuen's blue carapace. Blade had always been gentle and popular with the kids of Dolo, so Sara thought little of it. But the Stranger sucked breath, pointed, and guffawed.

He turned and saw a sailor feeding tidbits to a favorite noor, while another hoon patiently let Prity, the chimpanzee, perch on his broad shoulder for a better view. The Stranger let out a dry, disbelieving cackle.

He blinked in puzzled surprise at the sight of the g'Kek scriven-dancer, Fakoon, who had spun over to rest wheels between Pzora and the urrish tinker, Ulgor. Fakoon ogled the injured human with a pair of waving eyestalks, turning the other two toward his neighbors as if to ask—*"What's going on?"*

The Stranger clapped hands like a delighted child, laughing uproariously as tears flowed tributaries down his dark, haggard cheeks.

Asx

IT WAS AS IF A CENTURY'S ENLIGHTENMENT BY OUR Holy Egg—and all the earlier hard work to establish the Commons—were forgotten in the aftermath. Few rewq could be seen anywhere, as suspicion-poisons drove them off our brows to sulk in moss-lined pouches, leaving us to rely on mere words, as we had done in ages past, when mere words often led to war.

my/our own folk brought samples of recent noxious rumors, and i laid our base segment over/upon the vileness, letting its vapors rise up our central core, bringing distasteful understanding of *these* odious thoughts—

—our human neighbors are not trustworthy anymore, if they ever were.

—they will sell us out to their gene-and-clan cousins in the foray party.

—they lied with their colorful tale of being poor, patronless wolflings, scorned among the Five Galaxies.

—they only feigned exile, while spying on us and this world.

Even more bitter was this gossipy slander

—they will depart soon with their cousins, climbing to resume the godlike life our ancestors forsook. Leaving us to molder in this low place, cursed, forgotten, while they roam galaxies.

That was the foulest chattering stench, so repugnant that i/we vented a noisome, melancholy steam.

The humans . . . might they really do that? Might they abandon us?

If/when that happened, night would grow as loathsome as day. For we would ever after have to look up through our darkness and see what they had reclaimed.

The stars.

Lark

THE FORAYER BIOLOGIST MADE HIM NERVOUS. Ling had a way of looking at Lark—one that kept him befuddled, feeling like a savage or a child.

Which he *was,* in comparison, despite being older in duration-years. For one thing, all his lifetime of study wouldn't fill even one of the crystal memory slivers she dropped blithely into the portable console slung over her one-piece green coverall.

The dark woman's exotic, high cheekbones framed large eyes, a startling shade of creamy brown. "Are you ready, Lark?" she asked.

His own pack held four days' rations, so there'd be no need to hunt or forage, but this time he would leave behind his precious microscope. That treasure of urrish artifice now seemed a blurry toy next to the gadgets Ling and her comrades used to inspect organisms down to the level of their constituent molecules. *What could we tell them that they don't already know?* he pondered. *What could they possibly want from us?*

It was a popular question, debated by those friends who would still speak to him, and by those who turned their backs on any human, for being related to invaders.

Yet the sages charged a human—and a heretic at that—to guide one of these thieves through a forest filled with treasure. To begin the dance of negotiating for our lives.

The Six had one thing to offer. Something missing from the official Galactic Library entry on Jijo, collated by the Buyur before they departed. That thing was *recent* data, about how the planet had changed after a million fallow years. On that, Lark was as "expert" as a local savage could be.

"Yes, I'm ready," he told the woman from the starship.

"Good, then let's be off!" She motioned for him to lead.

Lark hoisted his pack and turned to show the way out of the valley of crushed trees, by a route passing far from the cleft of the Egg. Not that anyone expected its existence to stay secret. Robot scouts had been out for days, nosing through the glens, streams, and fumaroles. Still, there was a chance they might mistake the Egg for just another rock formation—that is, until it next started to *sing*.

Lark's chosen path also led away from the canyon where the innocents had been sent—the children, chimpanzees, lorniks, zookirs, and glavers. Perhaps the plunderers' eyes weren't omniscient, after all. Maybe precious things could be hidden.

Lark agreed with the sages' plan. Thus far.

Clots of spectators normally gathered at the valley rim to watch the black cube drink sunlight without reflections or highlights. When the two humans reached those heights, one group of urrish onlookers backed away nervously, hooves clattering like pebbles on hard stone. They were all young unbrooded females with empty mate pouches. Just the sort to have an itch for trouble.

Conical heads bobbed and hissed, lowering toward the humans, displaying triangles of serrated teeth. Lark's shoulders tensed. The rewq in his belt pocket squirmed as it sensed rancor in the air.

"Stop that!" he warned, when Ling started pointing an instrument toward the milling urs. "Just keep walking."

"Why? I only want to take—"

"Of that I'm sure. But now's not a good time."

Lark held her elbow, urging her along. From first contact he could tell she was quite strong.

A rock shot past them from behind and struck the ground ahead. An aspirated shout followed.

"Skirlssss!"

Ling started to turn in curiosity, but Lark kept her moving. Added voices joined in.

"Skirls!"

"Jeekee skirlsss!"

More stones pelted around them. Ling's eyes showed dawning concern. So Lark reassured her, dryly, "Urs don't throw very well. Lousy aim, even after they learned about bows and arrows."

"They are your enemies," she observed, quickening the pace on her own accord.

"That's putting it too strong. Let's just say that humans had to fight a bit for our place here on Jijo, early on."

The urrish rabble followed, easily keeping up, shouting and stoking their nerve—until one of their own kind galloped in from the east, swerving suddenly in front of the throng. Wearing the brassard of a Proctor of Gathering, she spread her arms wide, displaying two full mating pouches and active scent glands. The mob stumbled to a halt as her head bobbed bold, aggressive circles, snapping and shooing them away from the two humans.

Law and order still function, Lark thought, with relief. *Though for how much longer?*

"What were they shouting at us?" Ling asked after marching farther under a canopy of fine-needled vor trees. "It wasn't in GalSix or GalTwo."

"Local dialect." Lark chuckled. *"Jeekee* was originally a hoonish curseword, now in common use. It means smelly—as if those randy little unwed urs should talk!"

"And the other word?"

Lark glanced at her. "Insults are important to urs. Back in pioneer days, they wanted something to call us. Something humans would find both offensive and apropos. So, during an early truce, they very nicely asked our founders to tell 'em the name of an animal familiar to us. One that lived in trees and was known for being silly."

Her eyes, taken straight on, were large and exquisite. Hardly the sort you'd expect on a pirate.

"I don't get it," Ling said.

"To them we're tree-climbers. Just as they must have reminded our ancestors of horses, hinneys, grass-browsers."

"So? I still don't—"

"So we make an effort to act really insulted, when an angry urs calls one of us a *squirrel*. It makes them so happy, you see."

She looked puzzled, as if many parts of his explanation confused her. "You *want* to please your enemies?" she asked.

Lark sighed. "No one on the Slope has enemies anymore. Not on that kind of scale."

That is, not until lately, he added silently.

"Why?" he continued, trying to turn the interrogation around. "Are enemies common where you're from?"

It was her turn to sigh. "The galaxies are dangerous. Humans aren't well-liked by many."

"So said our ancestors. It's because humans are wolflings, right? Because we uplifted ourselves, without the help of a patron?"

Ling laughed. "Oh, *that* old myth!"

Lark stared. "Do you . . . You can't mean . . . ?"

"That we know the truth? Our origin and destiny?" She smiled, an expression of serene knowing. "Goodness, lost child of the past, you people *have* been away a long time. Do you mean that you have never heard of our gracious lords, the Rothen? The beloved patrons of all humankind?"

His foot caught a stone, and Ling grabbed his arm to steady him. "But we can discuss that later. First I want to talk about these—what did you call them—*skirrils?*"

She held out a finger adorned with a bulbous ring Lark guessed must be a recording device. It took an effort of will to switch mental tracks, suppressing his flare of curiosity about galactic issues.

"What? Oh, that's *squirrels*."

"You imply they are arboreal and humanlike. Will we get to see any along the way?"

He blinked at her, then shook his head. "Um, I don't think so. Not this trip."

"Well, what can you tell me about them? For instance, do they show any aptitude for tool use?"

Lark needed neither psi nor rewq to read the mind of his lovely guest. He carried her question toward its unmistakable aim.

Do they show a talent for machinery? For war and commerce? For philosophy and art?

Do they have Potential? The magic essence that it takes to profit from the right kind of help?

Do they have the rare tincture, the promise, that makes a patron's push worthwhile? The stuff to become starfarers someday?

Are they prospects for uplift?

Lark concealed his surprise over her ignorance. "Not to the best of my knowledge," he answered honestly, since the only squirrels he'd seen were in ancient, faded pictures from old Earth. "If we pass near any, you can see for yourself."

Clearly, the star-forayers were here seeking biotreasure. What else might poor Jijo offer that was worth sneaking past the sentries of the Migration Institute, slipping through star-lanes long ceded to the strange, menacing civilization of the Zang, then braving Izmunuti's deadly carbon wind?

What else? Lark pondered. *Except refuge? Ask your own ancestors, boy.*

The newcomers made no pretense, as Lark might have expected, of representing a galactic agency or feigning a legal right to survey Jijo's biosphere. Did they think the exiles had no memory of such things? Or did they simply not care? Their goal—data about changes since the Buyur left—made Lark's lifework more precious than he ever imagined. So much that Lester Cambel had ordered him to leave his notebooks behind, lest they fall into alien hands.

The sages want me to play it close. Try to find out at least as much from her as she learns from me.

A foredoomed plan, of course. The Six were like infants, ignorant of the rules of a deadly game. Still, Lark would do his best, so long as his agenda and the sages' remained the same. Which might not always be the case.

They know that. Surely they've not forgotten I'm a heretic?

Fortunately the forayers had assigned their least intimidating member to accompany him. It might just as easily have been *Rann,* a huge male with close-cropped gray hair, a booming voice, and a wedgelike torso that seemed about to burst from his snug uniform. Of the two others who emerged from the black station, *Kunn* was nearly as masculinely imposing as Rann, with shoulders like a young hoon's, while pale-haired *Besh* was so dramatically female that Lark wondered how she moved so gracefully with a body that prodigiously curved. Compared to her colleagues, Ling seemed almost normal, though she would have caused a stir growing up in any Jijoan town—no doubt provoking many duels among hot-tempered suitors.

Don't forget your vow, Lark reminded himself, puffing in exertion while climbing a steep part of the trail. Perspiration stained the front of Ling's blouse, which clung to her in provocative ways. He forced himself to look away. *You made a choice, to live for a goal greater than yourself. If you wouldn't forsake that aim for an honest woman of Jijo, don't even think about giving it up for a raider, an alien, an enemy of this world.*

Lark found a new way to direct the heat in his veins. Lust can be blocked by other strong emotions. So he turned to anger.

You plan to use us, he mused silently. *But things may turn out different than you think.*

That attitude, in turn, roused an obstinate layer, overcoming his natural curiosity. Earlier, Ling had said something about humans no longer being considered *wolflings,* out among the stars. No longer orphans, without patrons to guide them. From the look in her eye, she had clearly expected this news to cause a stir. No doubt she wanted him to beg for further information.

I'll beg if I must—but I'd rather buy, borrow, or steal it. We'll see. The game's just in its opening rounds.

Soon they passed stands of lesser-boo. Ling took samples of some segmented stems—each no more than ten centimeters across—deftly slicing near-transparent sections into her analyzer.

"I may be a dumb native guide," he commented. "But I'll wager boo doesn't show much sign of pre-sapience."

Her head jerked when he said the word. Thus Lark ended one pretense.

We know why you're here.

Ling's dusky skin did not hide a flush. "Did I suggest any such thing? I just want to track genetic drift since this species was planted by the Buyur. We'll need a benchmark to compare trends in animals. That's all."

So we begin the outright lies, he thought. From fossil evidence, Lark knew that boo already thrived on Jijo long before the Buyur won their lease, twenty million years ago. Perhaps it was imported by a previous tenant. Whole ecosystems had coevolved around the successful vegetal type, and countless animals now relied on it. But things must have been rough for the first aeon or so, as boo pushed native flora out of many watersheds.

Lark knew little about the biochemical level, but from fossils he was sure the genus hadn't changed much in a hundred million years.

Why would she lie about something so unimportant? The Scrolls taught that deceit was not only wrong, but also a fickle, dangerous ally. And habit forming. Once you start lying, it's hard to stop. Eventually it is small, needless lies that get you caught.

"Speaking of pre-sapience," Ling said, folding her sample case, "I can't help wondering where you folks stashed your chimpanzees. I'm sure *they* must have drifted in interesting ways."

It was Lark's turn to give away too much with an involuntary twitch. Denial was useless. *Humans don't need rewq to play this game with each other—reading clues in each other's faces. Lester must know I'll betray as much as I learn.*

"Chimps are like children. Naturally we sent them away from possible danger."

Ling looked left and right. "Do you see any danger?"

Lark almost burst out with sardonic laughter. In Ling's eyes danced a complexity of things he could only guess. But some thoughts were clear without being spoken aloud.

You know that I know. I know that you know that I know. And you know that I know that you know that I know. . . .

There is another emotion that can overcome hormonal lust, or the fury of anger.

Respect.

He nodded to his adversary, meeting her gaze full on.

"I'll let you know if we pass near any chimps, so you can see for yourself."

Ling had extremely sharp vision and proved it frequently by spotting movements Lark would have missed—forest creatures foraging, browsing, hunting, or tending their young. In this, she reminded him of Dwer. But Ling also owned many *tools,* which she brought swiftly to bear on whatever crawling, flitting, or ambling thing caught her attention.

She must really have studied those old Buyur records, for their progress was slowed by frequent sighs of recognition, when she would classify a species of shrub, tree, or four-winged bird, then ask Lark to add whatever quaint name the locals used. Lark gave cautious answers—just enough to support his value as a local expert.

Sometimes Ling would pause and mutter into her ring, as if contemplating what she had learned. Lark realized with a shiver that she must be in contact with her base. This was *speech at a distance,* not like semaphore, farcasting, or even rare psi-telepathy, but the high-tech kind mentioned in books, perfect and reliable. The voice

of the person at the other end could barely be made out
as a whisper. He guessed it must be projected somehow,
compactly, to the region near her ear.

At one point, Ling murmured in a dialect form of Anglic, rather hard to follow.

"Yea, yea. . . . Oright. A'll try to speed ip. But yigotta
chuz—distince er ditail."

The other party must have been persuasive, for Ling
picked up the pace when the march resumed—until the
next excited discovery caused her to forget her promise
and go right back to dawdling over some intriguing detail. Lark found this character flaw—how easily she was
distracted by the sight of living things—the first thing he
honestly liked about her.

Then Ling spoiled it by patronizing him, defining—in
slow, simple words—what "nocturnal" meant. Lark
quashed resentment. He had read enough adventure
novels as a kid to know how a native guide was supposed to act. So he thanked her respectfully. There
might be future advantages to be had in letting her maintain her stereotypes.

For all of Ling's enthusiasm and keen eyesight, she
was no hunter like Dwer. Even to Lark, the surroundings
frothed with signs—footprints and broken stems, feces
and territory marks, wisps of fur, scale, feather, and torg.
Any child of the Six could read such stories, found along
the path. But Ling seemed aware only of what was currently alive.

Thinking about Dwer made Lark smile. *By the time he
gets back from his mundane glaver hunt, I'll be the one
with wild stories to tell, for a change.*

At intervals, Ling unfolded an instrument with twin
"holio screens," one showing a forest scene that rippled
and moved as Lark stared over her shoulder, showing
someplace nearby, he could tell from the foliage. The
other screen displayed charts and figures he found inde-
cipherable—which was humbling. He had read nearly
every biology text in Biblos and figured he should at
least understand the vocabulary.

Maybe the "Yes, bwana" routine isn't such an act. Turns out I may be illiterate, after all.

Ling explained this was data from one of the robot probes, climbing the same path some distance ahead. "Could we move faster now?" she asked eagerly. "The robot has subdued some interesting specimens. I want to reach them before they deteriorate."

She had been the one dawdling. Still, Lark only nodded.

"Whatever you say."

The first specimen was a hapless wuankworm whose burrow had been sliced open with scalpel-smoothness. A web of fibrous stuff defied repeated battering by the worm's bony head, as it fought futilely to escape.

Ling spoke into her ring. "This feral form seems related to ore-gleaners the Buyur imported from Dezni, three aeons ago. Dezni-evolved organisms *should* estivate after injection with clathrate of methane. We'll try a larger dose now."

She aimed a device that sent a slender tube flashing like a resolute predator, piercing a crease between two armor plates. The worm flinched, then slumped, quivering.

"Good. Now let's see if encephalization has changed during the last megayear." She turned to Lark and explained. "That's to see if they have more brain matter."

Now that I knew, he thought, but restrained himself and remarked instead,

"How perfectly amazing."

Lark learned to pass instruments, draw blood, and assist his employer as required. At one point the raspy tongue of an angry longsnout whipped between the strands of its cage and would have torn strips off Ling's arm, if he had not yanked it away in time. After that, Ling seemed to realize her "native guide" had uses beyond toting, carrying, and being impressed whenever she spoke.

Though the robot's specimens were "brainy" types,

living by their wits as hunters or omnivorous gatherers, Lark thought none of them likely prospects for uplift. *Maybe in ten million years, when this galaxy is reopened for legal settlement. By then, longsnouts or leap raptors may be ready, tested by evolution and Ifni's luck, primed for adoption by some kindly elder race.*

Yet, watching her use sorcerous rays and probes to appraise a mangy-looking carrion snorter, Lark could not help but imagine the beast responding by rearing up on its hind legs and reciting an ode to the comradeship of living things. Ling's group clearly thought they might find something precious, emerging on Jijo ahead of schedule. *Once potential is there, all it takes is help from a patron to set a new race on the Upward Path.*

A few texts in Biblos disagreed. A birth does *not* always need a midwife, they claimed.

Lark chose to follow up that idea during the next part of the trek.

"A while back you implied Earthlings aren't known as wolflings anymore."

Ling smiled enigmatically. "Some still believe that old myth. But others have known the truth for quite a while."

"The truth?"

"About where we came from. Who gave humanity the boon of thought and reason. Our true patrons. The Rothen mentors and guides we owe everything we are, and ever will be."

Lark's heart beat faster. A few tomes on the subject had survived the fire that ravaged the Biblos xenology shelves, so he knew the debate was still raging when the sneakship *Tabernacle* left for Jijo, three centuries ago. In those days, some speculated that humanity *had* been helped, in secret by clandestine benefactors, long before the historical era. Others held out for the model of Darwin—that intelligence could evolve all by itself, without outside help, despite the skepticism of Galactic science. Now Ling insisted the debate was settled.

"Who are they?" Lark asked in a hushed voice. "Did some Rothen come to Jijo with you?"

That smile returned, a knowing look, tugging her high cheekbones. "Truth for truth. First *you* tell me the real story. What's a pack of humans doing here on this dreary little world?"

"Uh . . . which pack are you talking about? Yours or mine?"

Her silent smile was his only answer, as if to say—*"Go ahead and be coy, I can wait."*

Ling followed tracers left by the relentless robot, leading from one sedated creature to the next. As the day waned, she picked up the pace until they reached the crest of a long ridge. From there, Lark saw several more plateaus to the north, slanting up toward Rimmer peaks. Instead of the usual covering of native trees, the nearest mesa bore a blanket of darker green, a dense sward of giant boo—stems so huge that individuals could be made out even from where he stood. A few streaks of stone, and one of water, broke the expanse of gently swaying tubes.

Their final specimen was an unfortunate rock-staller, no more than a curled-up ball of spines when they cut away the webbing the robot used to restrain its victims. Ling prodded the creature with a tool that emitted a short, sharp spark, but got no reaction. She repeated, at a higher setting. Lark's stomach turned as he caught a stench from curling smoke.

"It's dead," he diagnosed. "I guess your robot ain't perfect, after all."

Lark dug a latrine ditch and prepared a fire. His meal was leaf-wrapped bread and cheese. Hers bubbled when she broke the foil seals, stinging Lark's nose with unfamiliar, enticing tangs. It wasn't quite dark by the time he gathered her empty packets to be carried back and sealed as dross.

Ling seemed inclined to resume their conversation.

"Your sage, Cambel, says that no one recalls exactly why your ancestors came. Some sooners sneak into fallow worlds as rogue breeding groups. Others are fleeing war or persecution. I'd like to know what your own founders told the races already here, when they arrived."

Among the Six, the term *sooner* applied to small bands who slinked away from the Slope to invade territory forbidden under the sacred Scrolls. *But I guess we're all "sooners" in that sense. Even those living on the Slope.* In his heart, Lark had always known it.

Still, he had been commanded to lie.

"You are mistaken," he said. Deceit tasted foul. "We're castaways. Our combined ship—"

The forayer woman laughed. "Please. That clever trick set us back a day or so. But before our ship left, we knew. The story is impossible."

Lark's lips pressed. No one had expected the bluff to last long. "How do you figure?"

"It's simple. Humans have only been in Galactic space four centuries or so—three hundred and fifty Jijoan cycles. It's quite impossible for Earthlings to have been aboard the same ship that brought g'Keks to this world."

"Why is that?"

"Because, my good rustic cousin, by the time humans entered the galactic scene, there *weren't* any g'Kek to be found."

Lark blinked while she continued.

"When we saw you all there, lining the valley rim, we recognized most of the types. But we had to look up the g'Kek. Imagine our surprise when one word flashed, right at the top.

"The word was—*extinct*."

Lark could only stare.

"Your wheeled friends are rare," Ling concluded. "Those here on Jijo are surely the last of their kind."

And just when I was starting to like you . . .

Lark could swear there was a kind of satisfaction in her eyes, over the shock her news caused.

"So you see," Ling added, "each of us has truths to share. I've just told you one. I hope you'll be as open with me."

He kept his voice even. "You haven't found me helpful so far?"

"Don't get me wrong! Your sages have been so obscure about certain matters. They may not have understood our questions. As you and I converse at greater length, some issues may clarify."

Lark saw what was going on. *Divide and interrogate*. He had not been present when the sky-humans met with the sages. She was sure to catch him in a net of discrepancies if he weren't extremely careful.

"For instance, when Kunn asked about sightings of other spacecraft, since the first sooners came to Jijo, we were told about visits by Zang globes, dipping down to lick the sea, and some distant lights long ago that might have been Institute survey ships. But we're *really* interested in occurrences that might have taken place much more—"

A sharp trill interrupted her. Ling lifted the blue finger-ring.

"Yes?"

Her head tilted, listening to a whisper projected near one ear.

"For *sure?*" she demanded, surprise infecting her voice. Ling's hands flapped at her belt pouch, pulling forth the pocketbook receiver, whose twin screens came alight with forest images, moving ahead through the lowering evening gloom. *Machines don't sleep,* Lark observed.

"Switch view from probe four to probe five," Ling requested. The scene changed abruptly to a blur of static. On the right, all the charts and graphs showed the flat slashes that denoted "zero" in Galactic Six.

"When did it happen?" the forayer woman demanded of her unseen colleague. Lark watched her face, wishing he could hear more of the other end of the conversation than a vague murmur.

"Replay the last ten minutes before the probe failed."

The left-hand screen soon lit with images, showing a narrow green corridor with a ribbon of sky above and a stream of scummy water below. The close walls consisted of closely packed stems of towering great-boo.

"Go to double speed," Ling asked impatiently. The great columns swept by in a blur. Lark leaned closer, finding the scene familiar.

Abruptly, the slim aisle spilled into a shallow crater, a rubble-strewn bowl with a small lake at its center, rimmed by a thorny barricade of looping vines.

Wait a minute. I know this place. . . .

A set of livid cross-hairs crawled across the holio display, converging near the frothy lake shore, while the right-hand screen flashed red symbols in technical Gal-Six. Lark had to labor, but managed to make out certain words—

. . . anomaly . . . unknown source . . . strong digital activity . . .

His stomach churned as the camera-eye sped toward the disturbance, swooping by slabs of ancient Buyur masonry, as crimson symbols clustered toward the central field of view. Everything inside that tunnel of attention grew more vivid, while the periphery dimmed. Seething emblems flashed preparations that Lark read with dismay—the readying of *weapons,* powering up for use.

Dwer always said this mulc-spider was nastier than most and warned people to stay away. But what on Jijo could the robot *have to worry about?*

Another thought struck him.

My God, isn't this the direction Dwer was headed, chasing after that runaway glaver?

The machine decelerated. Lark recognized the thick tangle of an aged mulc-spider, its vines splayed across the remains of some ancient Buyur structure.

The robot's view skimmed past a pale figure, hunched on the ground, and Lark blinked.

Was that a glaver, *lying in the open? Ifni, we went to such trouble hiding them, and this machine shoots past one without noticing.*

Another surprise slipped by the camera's periphery as it slowed. A lean animal, four-footed and wiry, black fur nearly blending with the dark tangle. The white teeth of a *noor* flashed briefly, chattering surprised defiance at the onrushing machine, then vanishing to one side as the robot cruised on, single-mindedly.

A *noor?* Up in the mountains? Without knowing why, Lark tasted bile.

The machine slowed to a crawling hover. Red cross-hairs converged downward toward a point throbbing with rhythms of crimson menace.

. . . *digital cognizance* . . . *level nine or greater* . . . the GalSix symbols throbbed. Little could be made out in the gloomy snarl below, except some vague flut-terings near the center of the cross-hairs. The robot must be targeting with senses other than vision.

. . . *autonomous decision* . . . *terminate threat im-mediately* . . .

Suddenly, the dim scene flashed with brilliance. The central field blazed white as shafts of angry lightning tore into the morass, slicing the mulc-spider's medusa limbs. Boiling juices sprayed from whipping, severed vines while red targeting circles danced back and forth, seeking something that kept dodging randomly within a confined space.

Ling was reading the data-filled right-hand screen, cursing the robot's inability to make a clean kill. So Lark felt sure he alone glimpsed a brief outline at one edge of the holio panel. It flashed just an instant but seemed to sear his optic nerve.

One—no, *two* clusters of arms and legs, intermeshed among the shuddering vines, cowering from the burning fury above.

Static again filled the displays.

"No, I can't head over there right now. It's half a mictaar from here. My guide and I would flounder in the dark. It'll have to wait till—"

Listening again, Ling sighed. "All right, I'll ask him." She lowered her ring and turned.

"Lark, you know this country. Is there a trail—"

She stopped, and stood up quickly, peering left, then right.

"Lark?"

She called into the night, now a velvet blackness dusted with the winking luster of this galaxy's third brightest spiral arm.

"Lark! Where are you?"

Wind stirred branches overhead, brushing the forest silence. There was no way of knowing how long it was since he had left, or in which direction.

With a sigh, Ling lifted her hand and reported the abandonment.

"How should I know?" she replied to a curt query. "Can't blame the nervous monkey for spooking. Never saw a robot's cut-beam at work before. He may be halfway home by now, if he stops before the coast—

"Yes, yes. I know we hadn't decided about that, but it's too late now. Hardly matters, anyway. All he got away with are a few hints and clues. We've got plenty more to bribe the natives with. And there's more where he came from."

A_{sx}

DISSENSION GROWS.

The Commons writhes against itself like a traeki whose rings were cruelly stacked, without nurturing rapport between the married toruses.

Word arrives by galloping urrish courier from settlements downslope, where anxiety and chaos reign like despotic qheuenish empresses of old. Some villages topple their water tanks, their grain silos, solar heaters, and windmills, claiming authority in the sacred Scrolls, overruling the rescript that our sage council sent in haste the day the ship came—a policy urging that all folk wait-and-see.

Meanwhile, others protect their barns and docks and weirs, laboring to pile concealing vegetation—and violently repelling angry neighbors who approach their precious property bearing torches and crowbars.

Should we not do better here at Gathering? Did not the finest of the Six come together here for yearly rites of union? Yet poison also roils in this place.

First discord—foul suspicion of our youngest sept. Might our human neighbors be allied with invaders? With plunderers? If not now, could they grow tempted, in time?

Oh, dire notion! Theirs is the highest grasp of science among the Six. What hope have we, without their aid, ever to pierce the deceits of godlike felons?

So far, some faith has been restored by the noble example of Lester and his deputies, who swear devotion to Jijo and our Holy Egg. Yet do not rumors and odious doubts still fly, like whirling soot, amid these gentle glades?

Dissension *multiplies*. A harvest team returns from one of the deep caves where wild rewq breed, to find the cavern walls deserted, no rewq to be seen. And the ones within our pouches languish. They will not sup our vital fluids, nor help us share the secrets of each other's souls.

Further discord—in each race many are tempted by a siren song. Sweet utterances by our unwelcome guests. Unctuous promises, words of comradeship.

And not merely words.

Do you recall, my rings, when the star-humans spread word they would *heal*?

Under a canopy brought over from the festival grounds—shaded by their dark, cubic outpost—they call forth the lame, sick, and hurt. We sages can but watch, helpless and confused, as queues of our wounded breth-

ren limp inside, then amble out elated, transformed, in
some part cured.

In truth, many seemed palliated only in their pain. But
for some others—miraculous change! Death's door is
transmuted, now a portal to restored youth, vigor, potency.

What can we do, forbid? Impossible. Yet what profuse
samplings do the healers gain! Vials brimming with specimens of our diverse biologies. Whatever gaps once
filled their dossiers, they now know all about our
strengths and weaknesses, our genes and latent natures.

Those returning from the healing, are they well-
greeted? Some call their own sept-mates traitor. Some
perceive defilement, turning away in hatred.

So we divide. In fresh enmity, we *subdivide*.

Are we a gathering any longer? Are we a Commons?

Did not you, my/our own third basal ring—ailing for a
year with the ague known as torus plaque—did you not
attempt to twist this aging pile toward that green pavilion where wonder cures are offered, though not unself-
ishly? If dissension infests this entity which others call
Asx, can a society of individuals cohere any better?

The heavens above have always been our dread. But
disharmony now swarms these very meadows, filling
our frustrated days and nights until Jijo's *soil* now seems
as fearsome as her sky.

Can we hope, my rings?

Tonight we do pilgrimage. The most sage of the Six
shall travail under darkness, arduously, past fuming pits
and misty cliffs, to reach the place of the Holy Egg.

This time, will it answer us? Or shall the fell silence of
recent weeks go on?

Can we still hope?

There is a sensation we traeki have learned to describe only since meeting humans on Jijo. Yet never till
now have i felt this pang so terribly. It is a desolation not
well rendered in Galactic languages, which emphasize
tradition and close relations, subsuming thoughts of self

to those of race and clan. But in Anglic the feeling is central and well known.

Its name is—*alone*.

Dwer

THEY TOOK TURNS RESCUING EACH OTHER.

It wasn't easy. Consciousness kept threatening to drown under surges of pain from his many cuts and burns. To make matters worse, Dwer suspected he was deaf.

Rety kept stumbling, yet she would not use her arms for anything except to clutch her treasure tightly to her breast.

That prize very nearly finished them both off, a while ago, when she plunged screaming back into the maelstrom of fire and acid steam, desperately seeking remnants of her precious "bird" amid smoldering stumps and glowing wreckage of the horrible machine that fell from the burning sky.

Dwer had just about had it by the time he got her out of there a second time.

You go back in again, and you can stay for all I care.

For a distance of two arrowflights, he had carried her with aching lungs and scalded skin, fleeing the burning mulc-spider till the worst stench, heat, and suffocating vapors lay well behind. Finally, he had put her down by the muddy creek at the lake's outlet and plunged his face and arms into the cooling stream. The slaking liquid cut his agony in half, and *that* was almost more shock than his system could bear. Gasping some water into his lungs, he pushed back, gagging and coughing. When his hands slipped, he fell into the muck, floundering weakly. If Rety had not caught his hair and dragged him out, he might have drowned right there.

A hiccup of ironic laughter joined his hacking cough. *After all that . . . what a way to go. . . .*

For some time they lay there, exhausted and shivering side-by-side, stirring only to scoop mud and slather it over each other's seared nakedness. It coated raw nerves and offered some small guard against the deepening night chill. Dwer thought of the warm clothes in his pack, nestled amid the boulders somewhere back there amid the fires.

And my bow, left on a boulder. He suppressed that worry with a silent curse. *Forget the damn bow! Come back for it later. Now just get out of here.*

He tried to gather strength to rise. Rety was pursuing the same goal, with identical results, sagging back with a moan after each effort. Finally, Dwer managed to sit up. The stars swayed as he teetered, pushed by a wintry wind.

Get moving, or you'll freeze.

Insufficient reason. Not enough to overcome shock and fatigue.

The girl then. Get her *moving, or—*

Or what? Dwer somehow doubted even twice this much suffering could kill Rety. Trouble would not spare her yet. Trouble must find her too useful as an ally and friend.

But he was on the right track, Dwer felt sure. There was something else. Another duty. Someone awaiting his return. . . .

The glaver. Dwer's mud-crusted eyelids opened. *I left her hobbled. She'll starve. Or a ligger will get her.*

With quaking limbs, he fought his way up to his knees—and found he could rise no further.

Rety struggled up, too, and sagged against him. They rested, leaning against each other for support. *When folks find our frozen bodies lying together this way, someone's sure to think we must've liked each other.*

That, alone, was good reason to move. But messages to his arms and legs weren't obeyed.

A soft moistness stroked his cheek. . . .

Stop that, Rety.

It repeated. Wet and scratchy.

What's the kid doing now—licking me? Of all the weird . . .

Again a wet tongue—rather long and raspy for a little sooner girl. Dwer managed to turn his head . . . and blinked at the sight of two huge bulging eyes, rotating independently on each side of a broad rounded head. The glaver's mouth opened again. This time the tongue abraded a path right up Dwer's lip and over both nostrils. He flinched, then managed to wheeze—

"H-how . . . how-w . . . ?"

Vaguely, distantly, he heard his own words. So he wasn't completely deaf, after all.

Knowing a better perch when she saw it, Rety transferred her one-armed grip from his neck to the glaver's. The other hand still clenched her prize—a fragment of knobs, lumps, and scorched metal feathers.

Dwer didn't pause to question fortune. He flung himself over the glaver's other side, sucking warmth from her downy hide. Patiently—or apathetically—the creature let both humans hang on, till Dwer finally found the strength to gather his feet and stand.

One of the glaver's hind legs still bore remnants of a rope hobble, chewed off at the knot. Behind her, the cause of this miracle grinned with the other end in its mouth. Mudfoot leered at Dwer, eyes glittering.

Always gotta make sure to get full credit, don't you? Dwer thought, knowing it was ungrateful but thinking it anyway.

Another brilliant explosion sent rays of brightness cutting through black shadows, all centered on the fiery site by the lake. Two more reports followed within a few duras, erasing any thought of going back after his supplies. Flames continued to spread.

He helped Rety up, leaning on the glaver for support. *Come on,* Dwer said, with a slight incline of the head. *Better to die in motion than just lying here.*

· · ·

Even stumbling in the dark, numbed by cold, pain, and weariness, Dwer couldn't help pondering what he'd seen.

One little bird-machine might have been rare but explainable—a surviving relic of Buyur days, somehow preserved into this era, wandering confused across a continent long abandoned by its masters. But the *second* machine—that daunting, floating menace—was no dazed leftover of vanished Jijoan tenants. It had been powerful, resolute.

A new thing in the world.

Together they weaved unsteadily down another avenue between two forests of boo. The channel spared them from the frigid wind, and also from having to make any decisions. Each step took them farther from the lakeside conflagration, which suited Dwer fine.

Where there's one death machine, might there be more?

Could another levitating minifortress come to avenge its brother? With that thought, the narrow, star-canopied aisle ceased seeming a refuge, rather an awful trap.

The boo-lined corridor ended at last, spilling the four of them onto a meadow of knee-high grass swaying before a stiff, icy wind that drained their bodies as they shuffled along. Frost flurries whirled all around. Dwer knew it was just a matter of time before they collapsed.

A grove of scrubby saplings clustered by a small watercourse, some distance from the path. Shivering, he nudged the glaver across the crunching, crackling grass. *We're leaving tracks,* the hunter in him carped. Lessons drilled by old Fallon floated to mind. *Try keeping to bare rock or water. . . . When you're being stalked, head downwind. . . .*

None of which was helpful now. Instinct led him to a rocky ledge, an outcrop shrouded by low bushes. Without his fire-lighter or even a knife or piece of flint, their best hope lay in finding shelter. Dwer yanked Rety off the glaver's neck, pushing till she understood to bend and crawl under the shelf. The glaver shuffled inward on all four knees, Mudfoot hitching a ride on her corrugated back. Dwer yanked some fallen branches where the wind would pile leaves on top. Then he also dropped, slithering to join an interspecies tangle of limbs, fur, skin—and someone's fetid breath not far from his face.

Snowflakes sublimed off flesh as body heat spread through the confined space. *Just our luck to have a late flurry, so far into spring,* he thought. Old Fallon used to say there were just two seasons in the mountains. One was called Winter. The other was *also* winter, with some green stuff growing to trick the unwary.

He told himself the weather wasn't really so bad—or wouldn't be if their clothes hadn't been burned off their bodies, or if they weren't already in shock, or if they had supplies.

After a while, Dwer realized the deafness must be fading. He could hear someone's teeth chattering, then a *murmur* of some sort, coming from behind him. That was followed by a sharp jab on his shoulder.

"I *said* could you *move* jes a bit?" Rety shouted, not far from his ear. "You're lying on my—"

He shifted. Something bony slid from under his ribcage. When he lay back down, his flank scraped icy grit. Dwer sighed.

"Are you all right?"

She squirmed some more. "What'd you say?"

He writhed around to see her blurry outline. "Are you okay?" he shouted.

"Oh, sure. Never better, dimmie. Good question."

Dwer shrugged. If she had energy to be nasty, she was probably far from death's door.

"You got anything to eat?" Rety added.

He shook his head. "We'll find something in the morn. Till then, don't speak 'less you must."

"Why?"

Because robots probably have ears, he almost said. But why worry the kid?

"Save your strength. Now be good and get some sleep."

A slight vibration might have been the girl, mimicking his words sarcastically under her breath. But he couldn't be sure—a blessed side effect to the beating his ears had taken.

With a series of sharp jabs, Mudfoot clambered up his leg to settle in the wedge between his body and Rety's. Dwer squirmed to a position where his head was less sheltered by the glaver's warm flank. A bitter chill greeted his face as he peered back at the trail they had just left—the narrow avenue between two vast stands of boo. As a makeshift hunter's blind, this wasn't bad—if only more snow would fill in the trampled trail they had left in the broken grass.

We got away from you, One-of-a-Kind, he thought, savoring a victory he had not won. Many patches of skin still seemed too numb, too cool for even the glaver's warmth to heat up, tracing where the spider's golden preserving fluid had stuck. No way to clean them right now . . . if the droplets ever *would* come off.

Still, we got away, didn't we?

A faint touch seemed to stroke his mind. Nothing he could pinpoint, but it triggered a tickle of worry. Surely the crazy old mulc-deconstructor couldn't have survived the inferno by the lake?

It's just my imagination. Forget it.

Unfortunately, his imagination also supplied what One-of-a-Kind would surely reply.

Ah, my precious. Is that not what you always say?

Shivering from more than mere cold, Dwer settled for a long watch, eyeing the funnel-avenue for other strange things sneaking over the pass through the Rimmer Range.

A sound roused Dwer from a dream filled with sensations of failure and paralysis. His eyes flinched when he opened them to a chill wind. Listlessly, he tried focusing on what had yanked him awake. But all that came to mind was a preposterous notion that someone had called his *name.*

The Dolphin was up near zenith, its flank shimmering

with blue-white stars, seeming to dive between milky waves.

Clouds. And more snow was falling.

He blinked, trying to stare. Something was moving out there.

Dwer lifted a hand to rub his eye, but the fingers would not uncurl. When they touched his face, they seemed petrified—a sign of shock compounded by frostbite.

Over there. Is that it?

Something *was* moving. Not another robot, wafting on smug pillars of force, but a shambling bipedal figure, hurrying upslope at a pace Dwer found professionally lacking. At that rate, whoever-it-was would tire much faster than necessary. No errand was worth taking such risks in this kind of weather.

Of the Six, only a hoon or human could make it this high in a snowfall, and no hoon would let himself get into that much of a hurry.

Hey, you! Don't go up through the boo! There's danger thataway!

Dwer's voice produced only a croak, barely loud enough to rouse the noor, causing Mudfoot to lift its head.

Hey, fool. Can't you see our trail in the grass and snow? It's like a Buyur highway out there! Are you blind?

The figure plowed right on by, disappearing into the dark cathedral-like aisle between twin walls of vaulting boo. Dwer slumped, hating himself for his weakness. *All I had to do was shout. That's all. Just a little shout.*

Glassy-eyed, he watched more flakes fill the runnel in the grass, slowly erasing all signs leading to this rocky cleft. *Well, you wanted to hide, wasn't that the idea?*

Perhaps the four of them would never be found.

Dwer lacked the strength to feel irony.

Some hunter. Some mighty hunter. . . .

The Stranger

I t will take some getting used to, this curious unlikely voyage, rushing along in a wooden boat that glides down rocky canyons, swooping past high stone walls, giving a sense of incredible speed. Which is odd, since he knows he used to travel much, much faster than this . . . though right now it's hard to recall exactly how.

Then there are his fellow passengers, a mixture of types he finds amazing to behold.

At first, several of them had filled him with raw terror—especially the squishy thing, looking like a stack of phlegmy doughnuts piled up high, venting complex stinks that scrape-tickled his nose and tongue. The mere sight of its corrugated cone wrenched feelings of blank horror—until he realized that something was quite different about this particular Joph—

His mind refuses to bring forth the epithet, the name, even though he trolls and sifts for it.

Words refuse to come easily. Most of the time, they do not come at all.

Worse, he cannot speak or form ideas, or comprehend when others send shaped-sounds toward him. Even names, the simplest of labels, refuse to rest within his grasp but wriggle off like slippery things, too angry or fickle to bear his touch.

· · · ·

No matter.

He resolves to wait, since there is no other choice. He even manages to hold back revulsion when the doughy cone-creature touches him, since healing seems its obvious intent, and since the pain always lessens a bit, each time it wraps oily tendrils round his throbbing head.

In time, the contact becomes oddly pleasant.

Anyway, she *is usually there, speaking to him gently, filling the tunnel-view of his attention with her smile, providing an excuse for frail optimism.*

He doesn't recall much about his former life, but he can dimly remember something about the way he used to live . . . not so much a philosophy as an attitude—

If the universe seems to be trying to destroy you, the best way to fight back is with hope.

IX. THE BOOK OF THE SEA

In order to be blessed,
And to bring redemption,
Forgetfulness cannot come at random.

Aspects of oblivion
Must come in the right order.

First must come detachment from the
driving need
To coerce the material world,
Or to shape other beings to your
needs.

To be shaped is your goal.
First by nature,
And later by hands and minds
Wiser than your own.

—The Scroll of Promise

Alvin's Tale

SO THERE WE WERE, WAY UP IN THE THIN, DRY AIR atop Mount Guenn, surrounded by heat and dust and sulfury smells from Uriel's forge, and what does Gybz the Alchemist want to talk to us about?

The traeki tells us we're being sent to a different *kind* of hell.

But hold on, Alvin. Spin the yarn the way an old-time human storyteller would. Describe the scene, *then* the action.

Gybz concocts recipes for metal and glass in a grimy workshop, quite unlike Uriel's prim, spotless hall of spinning disks. Mineral powders spill across stained wooden shelves and earthenware jars stink with noxious liquids. One slit window overlooks a northern vista stretching all the way down to a splash of painful color that could only be the Spectral Flow, which means the chamber is about as high as you can get without tumbling into Mount Guenn's simmering caldera.

Below the window, flies swarmed over a pile of nicely aged kitchen mulch. I hoped we weren't interrupting Gybz at dinner.

The four of us—Huck, Pincer, Ur-ronn, and me—had come up to the alchemy lab at the command of Uriel, the great blacksmith, ruler of this fortress of industry perched on Jijo's trembling knee. At first I figured she sent us away just to get rid of some irritating youngsters, while she conferred with a human sage over how to improve her beloved mobile of gears, pulleys, and whirling glass. The chief assistant, Urdonnol, muttered disapproval while shepherding us up a long ramp to the traeki's mixing room. Only our pal Ur-ronn seemed cheerful, almost ebullient. Huck and I exchanged a glance, wondering why.

We found out when Gybz shuffled ers mottled, conical bulk around from behind a workbench. Words bubbled from a speaking tube that puckered the third-from-the-top ring.

"Bright youths of four races, be made welcome! Sublime news for you, it is an honor to relate. A decision to approve your expedition, this has occurred. Your endeavor to reach, visit, explore the nearest reaches of the Upper Midden, this you may attempt."

Gybz paused, venting puffs from a purple synthi ring. When the traeki resumed, it was in warbling, uneven Anglic, with a voice that sounded strained.

"The attempt will have . . . the full backing of Mount Guenn Forge. As evidence of this support, behold—your completed window!"

The Master of Mixes gestured with a wraparound tentacle toward a wooden crate near the wall, with its cover removed. Amid drifts of fine sawdust, there gleamed a curved pane of thick glass, flawless to the eye.

Pincer-Tip danced excitedly, his red-clawed feet noisy on the stone floor. "Beautiful-iful!"

Gybz agreed. "It has been treated with proper coatings—for clear vision in the planned environment."

Ur-ronn snaked her long neck around to inspect the bubble-pane.

"This last phase was delicate. Thank you, Gyfz, for the exquisite coatings!"

Ur-ronn turned to explain to Huck and me, "After months of delay, Uriel suddenly agreed just three days ago to allow the casting. And since the results were good on the first try, she will let this count toward a *kun-uru*!"

That was urrish plains dialect for a master work. One qualifying the maker for craftsman status. It would take Ur-ronn a long way toward fulfilling her ambitions.

None of the rest of us have started professions, or even decided what we want to do, I thought, a little jealously.

On the other hand, urs have to hurry. They don't get that much time.

I glanced at Urdonnol, who was Ur-ronn's top rival as Uriel's heir. I didn't need a rewq to read her annoyance with all this fuss over what she called a "childish hobby"—the making of an experimental deep diving craft.

You should know better, I thought, feeling a bit sorry for Urdonnol. *Uriel also has a useless pastime, that room full of spinning disks. Ur-ronn's project shares that just-for-the-hell-of-it quality. It's a similarity between them that goes beyond mere kin-scent.*

To Ur-ronn, then, this had also been a smart career move. I felt happy for our friend.

"The glass was tested to withstand hydrostatic pressures exceeding those at fifty cords depth," she commented with evident satisfaction. "And when you add the lanterns and other gear Uriel is kindly lending us—"

"Us?" Huck cut in, breaking the mood. She spun to face Ur-ronn with three outthrust eyes. "What you mean *us,* honky? You're volunteering to come along, then?"

Ur-ronn's narrow head snapped back, staring at Huck. Then her neck slumped in an S-curve.

"I will . . . if I can."

"Huck!" I chided. It was mean to rub Ur-ronn's nostril in her limitations. I could hear Huck's spokes vibrate with tension.

Gybz interrupted with another venting, this time pungent like rusty metal.

"If possible, an urrish presence will be called for." The traeki seemed short of breath. "But even if that proves impossible, fear not. A member from Mount Guenn shall . . . accompany this bold undertaking . . . to its deepest depths."

I had trouble following Gybz's halting, accented Anglic. Huck and I shared a confused look.

"It is *i/we* . . . who shall part-wise accompany . . . this august group," Gybz explained, wheezing through the topmost ring. With that, the traeki showed us something none of us expected, shuffling around to expose an oozing blister on its far side, halfway up the fleshy stack. It was no normal swelling, where the traeki might be making another tentacle or readying chemicals for the mill. A *crack* split the swollen zone, exposing something slick and wriggly within.

Staring, I realized—the traeki was *vlen-budding* before our eyes!

While the crevice widened, the Master of Mixes seemed to flutter. A complex gurgle of vaguely sickening noises accompanied something that began to *emerge,* slithering through the opening, then sliding down the traeki's sloping flank, trailing loose fibers behind it.

"Gosh-osh-osh-osh-osh . . ." Pincer repeated in turn from each leg-vent, his sensor strip spinning frantically. Urdonnol edged away nervously while Huck rolled back and forth, torn between curiosity and revulsion. I felt sharp, biting sensations as little Huphu, our noor beast mascot, scrambled up my back and onto my shoulder, growling anxiously. Half-consciously I stroked her sleek pelt, rumbling an umble that must have sounded more confident than I felt.

Glistening with slime, the thing landed on the floor with a plopping sound and lay almost still, ripples coursing around its quadruple torus of miniature rings. Meanwhile, realignments quivered under the flaccid skin of the traeki parent.

"Not to . . . be concerned," a somewhat altered voice burbled from the oration peak of the old stack of rings. "i/we adjust . . . reconfigure."

Reassuring words, but everyone knows vlenning is a dangerous time for a traeki, when the unity of the former stack is challenged and sometimes fails. For that reason, most of them reproduce externally, growing new rings singly, in pens, or buying them from expert breeders, exchanging and swapping for the full set of traits they want in an offspring. Still, vlenning has advantages, I hear. Mister Heinz claims to have witnessed several, but I bet he never saw a four-tier bud emerge like this, already stacked and moving on its own!

"This newly detached self may be addressed—for the

time being—as *Ziz*. To that word-phrase it might answer, if engraved training patterns take hold. After performing its function with merit, it may then return for augmentation as a candidate for full life. Meanwhile, it is schooled . . . to serve your quest, coming with traits you may require."

"I don't know." Ur-ronn's head swayed an oval of confusion. "Do you mean—"

Huck muttered, "Gybz, what are we supposed to—"

The traeki cut in.

"i/we no longer answer to that name. Our rings vote among ourselves now. Please do not speak or interfere."

We fell silent, watching in awe as the creature literally wrestled with itself, *within* itself. A rippling seemed to rise from the base segment all the way up, terminating in a belch of yellow vapor. Waves flowed back and forth, crosswise as well as vertical. This went on for many duras, while we feared Gybz was about to tear erself apart.

Finally, the tremors lessened, then faded away. The traeki sensory organs refocused. Words bubbled from the puckered speech mouth, in a voice transformed.

"It is decided.

"Provisionally, you may call us/me *Tyug* and have good odds that this stack will answer."

Another pulse of throbbing.

"That *i* will answer. Please inform Uriel that this thing is done. Furthermore, tell her that my/our major skill cores seem to be intact."

Only then did I realize what had been at risk during the vlenning. The Master of Mixes is a vital member of Uriel's team. If Gybz—if *Tyug*—failed to remember all of its tricks of the trade, Mount Guenn alloys might not shine or cut as well, or decay so completely with the passage of time.

Foolish me. I'd been worried the whole time about the poor traeki's *life*.

Huphu slithered down my back and approached the new-formed traeki half-entity, which was already gathering an array of flipperlike feet under its bottommost segment, waving clumsy tentacles from its stubby top ring. The noor sniffed suspiciously, then settled back with a satisfied trill.

Thus Huphu was first to welcome Ziz—newest member of our band.

Now if only we had a human kid, we'd be a true six.

Omens can be good things, as any sailor knows. Luck is uttergloss. *Fickle,* but a damn sight better than the alternative.

I had a feeling we were going to need all of Ifni's help we could get.

X. THE BOOK OF THE SLOPE

Legends

Among qheuens, it is said that fleeing to Jijo was not as much a matter of survival as of culture.

There is dispute among the legends that have been passed down by the armored ones, since their landing on Jijo over a thousand years ago. Grays, blues, and reds each tell their own versions of events before and after their sneakship came.

Where they agree is that it all began in Galaxy One, where the sept found itself in trouble with its own alliance.

According to our surviving copy of Basic Galactic Socio-Politics, by Smelt, most starfaring races are members of clans—a relationship based on the great chain of uplift. For example, Earthclan is among the smallest and simplest, consisting of humans and their two clients—neo-chimps and neo-dolphins. If the patrons who supposedly raised up Homo sapiens are ever found, it could link Earthlings to a vast "family" stretching back ages, possibly even as far back as the Progenitors, who began the uplift cycle a billion years ago. With membership in such a clan, Earthlings might become much stronger. They might also become liable for countless ancient debts and obligations.

Another, quite separate network of allegiance seems to be based on philosophy. Many of the bitter feuds and ornate wars-of-honor dividing Galactic culture arose out of disputes no member of the Six can now recall or comprehend. Great alliances fought over arcane differences in theology, such as the nature of the long-vanished Progenitors.

It is said that when qheuens dwelled among the stars, they were members of the Awaiters Alliance—a fealty they inherited from their Zhosh patrons, who found and adopted primitive qheuens from sea-cliff hives, dominated by fierce gray queens.

Things might have been simpler had the Zhosh only uplifted the grays, but they gave the same expansion of wit and mind to the servant castes as well. Nor was this the end, for according to lore, the Awaiter philosophy is egalitarian and pragmatic. The alliance saw useful talents in the reds and blues. Rulings were made, insisting that the bonds of obeisance to the grays be loosened.

Certain qheuens fled this meddling, seeking a place to preserve their "natural way" in peace.

That, in brief, is why they came here.

On Jijo, the three types disagree to this day over who first betrayed whom. Grays claim their colony began in harmony, discipline, and love. All went well until urs, and then humans, stirred up blue discontent. Other historians, such as River-Knife and Cuts-Coral, forcefully dissent from this view.

Whatever the cause, all agree that Jijo's qheuenish culture is now even more untraditional than the one their ancestors fled.

Such are the ironies when children ignore their parents' wishes and start thinking for themselves.

—*Collected Fables of Jijo's Seven.*
Third Edition. Department of Folklore and Language, Biblos. Year 1867 of Exile.

Asx

SUDDENLY, THEIR QUESTIONS TAKE A NEW TURN. An edge of tension—not quite fear, but a cousin to that universal passion—abruptly colors the invaders' speech.

Then, in a single night, their apprehension takes hasty physical form.

They have buried their black station!

Do you recall the surprise, my rings? At dusk there it was, serene, arrogantly uncaring of the open sky. A cubic shape, blatant in its artificiality.

When we returned at dawn, a great heap of dirt lay there instead. From the size of the mound, Lester surmised the station must have scooped a hole, dropped itself inside, and piled the detritus on top, like a borerbeetle fleeing a digbat.

Lester's guess is proven right when Rann, Kunn, and Besh emerge from below, ascending a smooth, dark tunnel to resume discussions under the canopy-of-negotiation. This time they choose to focus on *machines*. Specifically—what devices remain from Buyur days? They want to know if ancient relics still throb with vital force.

This happens on some fallow worlds, they say. Sloppy races leave countless servant drones behind when they depart, laying their worlds down for an aeon of rest. Near-perfect and self-repairing, the abandoned mechanisms can last a long time, wandering masterless across a terrain void of living voices.

They ask—have we seen any mechanical orphans?

We try to explain that the Buyur were meticulous. That their cities were dutifully scraped away, or crushed and seeded with deconstructors. Their machine servants were infected with meme-compulsions, driving those still mobile to seek nests in the deep trench we call the Midden. All this we believe, yet the sky-humans seem to doubt our word.

They ask (again!) about *visitations*. What clues have we seen of other ships coming stealthfully, for purposes vaguely hinted at but never said aloud?

As planned, we dissemble. In old human tales and books, it is a technique oft used by the weak when confronted by the strong.

Act stupid, the lore suggests. *Meanwhile, watch and listen closely.*

Ah, but how much longer can we get away with it? Already Besh questions those who come for healing. In their gratitude, some will surely forget our injunctions.

The next stage will start soon, while our preparations are barely begun.

The fourth human forayer, Ling, returns from her research trip. Did she not leave with the young heretic, Lark? Yet she comes back alone.

No, we tell her. *We have not seen him. He did not come this way. Can you tell us why he abandoned you? Why he left you in the forest, his assigned task undone?*

We promise her another guide. The qheuen naturalist, Uthen. Meanwhile, we placate.

If only our rewq had not abandoned us! When i/we ask Lester about the woman's mood—what he can read from her demeanor—he only shudders and says he cannot say.

A CONCERT WAS ARRANGED BY AN IMPROMPTU group of passengers and crew, on the fantail of the *Hauph-woa*, to welcome the Stranger back among the living.

Ulgor would play the violus, a stringed instrument based on the Earthling violin, modified to suit deft, urrish fingers. While Ulgor tuned, Blade squatted his blue-green carapace over a mirliton-drum, stroking its taut membrane with his massive, complex tongue, causing it to rumble and growl. Meanwhile, all five legs held jugs filled to varied levels with water. Tentative puffs from his speech vents blew notes across each opening.

Pzora, the traeki pharmacist, modestly renounced any claim to musical talent but agreed to take up some metal and ceramic chimes. The hoonish helmsman would sing, while the professional scriven-dancer honored the makeshift group by agreeing to accompany them in the g'Kek manner, with graceful motions of his eyestalks and those famous dancing arms, calling to mind the swaying of trees, or wind-driven rain, or birds in flight.

They had asked Sara to round out a six, but she declined. The only instrument she played was her father's piano, back in Nelo's house by the great dam, and even at that her proficiency was unremarkable. *So much for the supposed correlation between music and mathematics,* she thought ironically. Anyway, she wanted to keep an eye on the Stranger, in case events threw him into another hysterical fit. He seemed calm so far, watching through dark eyes that seemed pleasantly surprised by nearly everything.

Was this a symptom? Head injuries sometimes caused loss of memory—or even ability to *make* memories—so everything was forever new.

At least he can feel some joy, she thought. Take the way he beamed, every time she approached. It felt strange and sweet for someone to be so reliably happy to see her. Perhaps if she were prettier, it wouldn't be so befuddling. But the handsome dark outlander was a sick man, she recalled. Out of his proper mind.

And yet, she pondered further, *what is the past but a fiction, invented by a mind in order to go on functioning?* She had spent a year fleeing memory, for reasons that had seemed important then.

Now it just doesn't amount to much.

She worried about what was going on up in the Rimmers. Her brothers stayed close to her thoughts.

If you'd accepted Taine's original proposal of marriage, you might have had little ones by now, and their *future to fret about, as well.*

Refusing the august gray-headed sage had caused a stir. How many other offers would there be for the hand of a shy papermaker's daughter without much figure, a young woman with more passion for symbols on a page than dancing or the other arts of dalliance? Soon after turning Taine down, Joshu's attentions had seemed to ratify her decision, till she realized the young bookbinder might only be using her as a diversion during his journeyman year in Biblos, nothing more.

Ironic, isn't it? Lark could have his pick of young women on the Slope, yet his philosophy makes him choose celibacy. My conclusions about Jijo and the Six are the opposite to his. Yet I'm alone too.

Different highways, arriving at the same solitary dead end.

And now come gods from space, diverting us all onto a road whose markings we can't see.

They still lacked a sixth for the concert. Despite having introduced string instruments to Jijo, humans traditionally played flute in a mixed sextet. *Jop* was an adept, but the farmer declined, preferring to pore over his book of scrolls. Finally, young Jomah agreed to sit in for luck, equipped with a pair of spoons.

So much for the vaunted contribution of Earthlings to musical life on Jijo.

Hidden under Blade's heavy shell, the mirliton groaned a low, rumbling note, soon joined by a mournful sigh from one of the jugs under Blade's left-front leg. The qheuen's seeing-band winked at Ulgor, and the urs took her cue to lift the violus, laying the double bow across the strings, drawing twin wavering notes, embellishing the mirliton's basso moan. A multilevel chord was struck. It held. . . .

The moment of duet harmony seemed to stretch on and on. Sara stopped breathing, lest any other sound break the extraordinary consonance. Even Fakoon rolled forward, visibly moved.

If the rest is anything like this . . .

Pzora chose the next instant to pile in, disrupting the aching sweetness with an eager clangor of bells and cymbals. The Dolo pharmacist seemed zealously unaware of what er had shattered, rushing ahead of the beat, halting, then pushing on again. After a stunned instant, members of the hoonish crew roared with laughter. Noor on the masts chittered as Ulgor and Blade shared looks that needed no rewq to interpret— equivalents to a shrug and a wink. They played on, incorporating Pzora's enthusiasm in a catchy four-part rhythm.

Sara recalled being taught piano by her mother, from music that was actually *written down,* now a nearly forgotten art. Jijoan sextets weaved their impromptu harmonies out of separate threads, merging and diverging through one congenial coincidence after another. *Human* music used to work that way in most pre-Contact cultures, before the Euro-West hit on symphonies and other more rigorous forms. Or so Sara had read.

Overcoming shyness, Jomah started rattling his spoons as Blade puffed a calliope of breathy notes. The hoonish helmsman inflated his air sac to answer the mirliton's rumble, singing an improvisation, without words in any known language.

Then Fakoon wheeled forward, arms swaying delicately, reminding Sara of gently rising smoke.

What had been exquisite, then humorous, soon took on a quality even more highly prized.

Unity.

She glanced at the Stranger, his face overcome with emotion, eyes delighting in Fakoon's opening moves. The left hand thumped his blanket happily, beating time.

You can tell what kind of man he used to be, she mused. *Even horribly mutilated, in awful pain, he spends his waking time enthralled by good things.*

The thought seemed to catch in her throat. Taken by surprise, Sara turned away, hiding a choking wave of sadness that abruptly blurred her vision.

Tarek Town appeared soon after, perched between the merging rivers Roney and Bibur.

From afar it seemed no more than a greenish knoll, like any other hill. Grayish shapes studded the mound, as if boulders lay strewn over the slopes. Then the *Hauph-woa* rounded one last oxbow turn, and what had seemed solid from a distance now spread open—a huge, nearly hollow erection of *webbing,* festooned with greenery. The "boulders" were the protruding *tips* of massive towers, enmeshed in a maze of cables, conduits, rope bridges, netting, ramps, and sloping ladders, all draped under lush, flowing foliage.

The air filled with a humid redolence, the scent of countless flowers.

Sara liked to squint and imagine Tarek in other days, back when it was but a hamlet to the mighty Buyur, yet a place of true civilization, humming with faithful machines, vibrant with the footsteps of visitors from far star systems, thronging with sky-craft that settled gracefully on rooftop landing pads. A city lively with aspirations that she, a forest primitive, might never imagine.

But then, as the hoon crew poled the *Hauph-woa* toward a concealed dock, no amount of squinting could mask how far Tarek had fallen. Out of a multitude of windows, only a few still shone with million-year-old glazing. Others featured crude chimneys, staining once-smooth walls with the soot of cook fires. Wide ledges where floating aircraft once landed now supported miniature orchards or coops for noisy herd chicks. Instead of self-propelled machines, the streets swarmed with commerce carried on the backs of tinkers and traders, or animal-drawn carts.

High up a nearby tower, some young g'Kek sped around a rail-less ramp, heedless of the drop, their spokes blurry with speed. Urban life suited the wheeled sept. Rare elsewhere, g'Kek made up the town's largest group.

Northward, crossing Tarek's link to the mainland, lay a "recent" ruin of stone blocks—the thousand-year-old city wall, erected by the Gray Queens who long ruled here, until a great siege ended their reign, back when the Dolo paper mill was new. Scorch marks still smeared the fallen bulwark, testimony to the violent birth of the Commons-of-Six.

However many times she passed through Tarek Town, it remained a marvel. Jijo's closest thing to a cosmopolitan place, where all races mixed as equals.

Along with hoon-crewed vessels, countless smaller boats skimmed under lacy, arching bridges, rowed by human trapper-traders, bringing hides and wares to market. River-traeki, with amphibious basal segments, churned along the narrow canals, much faster than their land-bound cousins managed ashore.

Near the river confluence, a special port sheltered two hissing steam-ferries, linking forest freeholds on the north bank to southern grasslands where urrish hordes galloped. But on a sloping beach nearby, Sara saw some blue qheuens climb ashore, avoiding ferry tolls by *walking* across the river bottom, a talent useful long ago, when blue rebels toppled the Queens' tyranny—helped by an army of men, traeki, and hoon.

In all the tales about that battle, none credits the insurgents with a weapon I think crucial—that of language.

It took some time for the *Hauph-woa* to weave through a crowd of boats and tie up at a cramped wharf.

The jammed harbor helped explain the lack of upstream traffic.

Soon as the moorings were tied, *Hauph-woa*'s contingent of noor squalled and blocked the gangways, demanding their pay. Rumbling a well-pleased umble song of gratitude, the ship's cook went down the row of black-furred creatures, handing out chunks of hard candy. Each noor tucked one sourball in its mouth and the rest into a waterproof pouch, then leaped over the rail to cavort away between bumping, swaying hulls, risking death by narrow margins.

As usual, the Stranger watched with a complex mixture of surprise, delight, and sadness in his eyes. He spurned a stretcher, and went down the ramp leaning on a cane, while Pzora puffed with pride, having delivered a patient from death's door to the expert healers of Tarek Town. While Prity went to hail a rickshaw, they observed the hoonish crew strain with block and tackle, lifting crates from the hold, many of them bound from Nelo's paper works for various printers, scribes, and scholars. In their place, stevedores gently lowered ribboned packages, all bound from Tarek for the same destination.

—Pottery shards and slag from urrish forges.

—Used-up ceramic saws from qheuenish woodcarving shops.

—Worn-out printers' type and broken violin strings.

—Whatever parts of the deceased that could not be counted on to rot away, such as the bones of cremated humans and urs, hoonish vertebrae, g'Kek axles, and traeki wax crystals. The glittering dust of ground-up qheuen carapaces.

—And always lots of ancient Buyur junk—it all wound up on dross boats, sent to the great Midden, to be cleansed by water, fire, and time.

An urrish rickshaw driver helped them usher the injured man onto her low four-wheeled cart, while Pzora stood behind, holding the Stranger's shoulders with two tendril-hands. "You're sure you don't need me to come along?" Sara asked, having second thoughts.

Pzora waved her gently away. "It is a short distance to the clinic, is it not? Have you not urgent matters to attend? Have i not our own tasks to perform? All-of-you shall meet all-of-us again, tonight. And our lucky patient will your fine selves perceive on the morrow."

The Stranger's dark eyes caught hers, and he smiled, patting her hand. There was no sign of his former terror of the traeki.

I guess I was wrong about his injury. He does acquire memories.

Maybe in Tarek we can find out who he is. If family or friends can be brought, they'll help him more than I ever could. That evoked a pang, but Sara reminded herself that she was no longer a child, tending a wounded chipwing. *What matters is that he's well cared for. Now Pzora's right. I've got other matters to attend.*

The anarchic style of Tarek Town meant there was no one "official" at the dock to greet them. But merchants hurried to the quay, eager for their cargoes. Others came in search of news. There were rumors of horrible events up north and east. Of landings by frost-covered Zang ships, or whole towns leveled by titanic rays. Gossip told of a populace herded toward mass trials, conducted by insectoid judges from the Galactic Institute of Migration. One credulous human even argued with Jop, insisting the farmer was mistaken, since everyone knew Dolo Village was destroyed.

That explains why no boats came upstream, Sara thought. From Tarek, the intruder ship must have seemed to lay a streak of fire right over Sara's hometown.

Rumors were a chief stock in trade of all harbors, but surely cooler heads prevailed elsewhere?

Prity signaled that all of Nelo's crates were signed for, save the one she pulled on a wheeled dolly to be hand carried to Engril the Copier. Sara bade farewell to the other Dolo emissaries, agreeing to meet them again tonight and compare notes.

"Come, Jomah," she told Henrik's son, who was staring at the bustle and tumult of city life. "We'll take you to
your uncle first."

Voices seemed subdued in the harborside market; the
haggling was sullen, perfunctory. Most buyers and sell-
ers did not even wear rewq while dickering with members of other races—a sure sign they were only going
through the motions.

One shopkeeper, an elegant gray qheuen with intri-
cate, gold-fleck shell decorations, held up two claw-
hands and counted nine jagged toe-pads, indicating by a
slant of her cupola that it was her final offer. The trader,
a rustic-looking red, hissed in dismay, gesturing at the
fine salt crystals she had brought all the way from the
distant sea. While passing, Sara overheard the city
qheuen's reply.

*"Quality or amount, what difference does it make?
The price, why should you or I care?"*

The answer shocked Sara. An urbane gray, indifferent
over a commercial transaction? The locals must be in a
state, all right.

As if we in Dolo were any better?

Townsfolk mostly gathered in small groups, gossiping
in dialects of their own kind. Many of the hoons carried
iron-shod canes—usually a perquisite of captains—
while urrish tinkers, herders, and traders kept close to
their precious pack beasts. Each urs carried an ax or
machete sheathed at her withers, useful tools in the dry
woods and plains where they dwelled.

So why did the sight make Sara feel edgy?

Come to think of it, many *humans* were behaving
much the same, walking in close company, armed with
tools suitable for chopping, digging, hunting—or uses
Sara did not want to think about. The g'Kek populace
kept to their apartments and studios.

I'd better find out what's going on, and soon, Sara
thought.

It was a relief when the tense market zone ended at the glaring brightness of the Jumble.

Till now, they had walked in shade, but here an opening gaped under the shelter-canopy. Once towering structures lay in heaps, their neat geometries snapped, splintered and shoved together, giving the place its name. Scummy fluid shimmered between the shattered stones, where oily bubbles formed and popped, relics of a time when this place was caustic, poisonous, and ultimately restoring.

Jomah shaded his eyes. "I don't see it," he complained.

Sara resisted an impulse to pull him back out of the light. "See what?"

"The *spider*. Isn't it s'pozed to be here, in the middle?"

"This spider's dead, Jomah. It died before it could do much more than get started. That's why Tarek Town isn't just another swamp full of chewed-up boulders, like we have east of Dolo."

"I know *that*. But my father says it's still here."

"It is," she agreed. "We've been passing beneath it ever since the boat docked. See all those cables overhead? Even the ramps and ladders are woven from old mulc-spider cords, many of them still living, after a fashion."

"But where's the *spider*?"

"It was in the cables, Jomah." She motioned toward the crisscrossing web, twining among the towers. "United, they made a life form whose job was to demolish this old Buyur place. But then one day, before even the g'Kek came to Jijo, this particular spider got sick. The vines forgot to work together. When they went wild, the spider was no more."

"Oh." The boy pondered this awhile, then he turned around. "Okay, well there's another thing I *know* is around here—"

"Jomah," Sara began, not wanting to squelch the child, who seemed so much like Dwer at that age. "We have to get—"

"I heard it's here near the Jumble. I want to see the horse."

"The ho—" Sara blinked, then exhaled a sigh. "Oh! Well, why not. If you promise we'll go straight to your uncle's, right after. Yes?"

The boy nodded vigorously, slinging his duffel again. Sara picked up her own bag, heavy with notes from her research. Prity wheeled the dolly behind.

Sara pointed. "It's this way, near the entrance to Earthtown."

Ever since the Gray Queens' menacing catapults were burned, Tarek Town had been open to all races. Still, each of the Six had a favored section of town, with humans holding the fashionable south quarter, due to wealth and prestige generated by the book trade. The three of them walked toward that district under a shaded loggia that surrounded the Jumble. The arching trellises bloomed with fragrant bowlflowers, but even that strong scent was overwhelmed as they passed the sector where urs traders kept their herds. Some unmated urrish youths loitered by the entrance. One lowered her head, offering a desultory snarl at Sara.

Suddenly, all the urs lifted their long necks in the same direction, their short, furry ears quivering toward a distant rumble that came rolling from the south. Sara's reflex thought was *thunder*. Then a shiver of concern coursed her spine as she turned to scan the sky.

Can it be happening again?

Jomah took her arm and shook his head. The boy listened to the growling echo with a look of professional interest. "It's a test. I can tell. No muffling from confinement or mass loading. Some exploser is checking his charges."

She muttered—"How reassuring." But only compared to the brief, fearsome thought of more god-ships tearing across the heavens.

The young urs were eyeing them again. Sara didn't like the look in their eyes.

"All right then, Jomah. Let's go see the horse."

The Statuary Garden lay at the Jumble's southern end. Most of the "art works" were lightly scored graffiti, or crude caricatures scratched on stone slabs during the long centuries when literacy was rare on the Slope. But some rock carvings were stunning in their abstract intricacy—such as a grouping of spherical balls, like clustered grapes, or a jagged sheaf of knifelike spears, jutting at pugnacious angles—all carved by the grinding teeth of old-time gray matriarchs who had lost dynastic struggles during the long qheuenish reign and were chained in place by victorious rivals, whiling away their last days under a blazing sun.

A sharply realistic bas relief, from one of the earliest eras, lay etched on a nearby pillar. Slow subsidence into corrosive mud had eaten away most of the frieze. Still, in several spots one could make out *faces*. Huge bulging eyes stared acutely from globelike heads set on bodies that reared upward with supple forelegs raised, as if straining against the verdict of destiny. Even after such a long time, the eyes seemed somehow lit with keen intelligence. No one on Jijo had seen expressions of such subtlety or poignancy on a glaver's face for a very long time.

In recent years, Tarek's verdant canopy had been diverted over this part of the Jumble, putting most of the carvings under shade. Even so, orthodox zealots sometimes called for all the sculptures to be razed. But most citizens reasoned that Jijo already had the job in hand. The mulc-spider's ancient lake still dissolved rock, albeit slowly. These works would not outlive the Six themselves.

Or so we thought. It always seemed we had plenty of time.

"There it is!" Jomah pointed excitedly. The boy dashed toward a massive monument whose smooth flanks appeared dappled by filtered sunshine. *Humanity's Sacrifice* was its title, commemorating the one thing men and women had brought with them to Jijo that they esteemed above all else, even their precious books.

Something they renounced forever, as a price of peace.

The sculpted creature seemed poised in the act of bounding forward, its noble head raised, wind brushing its mane. One had but to squint and picture it in motion, as graceful in full gallop as it was powerful. Mentioned lovingly in countless ancient human tales, it was one of the great legendary wonders of old Earth. The memorial always moved Sara.

"It isn't like a donkey at all!" Jomah gushed. "Were horses really that big?"

Sara hadn't believed it herself, till she looked it up. "Yes, they got that big, sometimes. And don't exaggerate, Jomah. Of *course* it looks quite a bit like a donkey. They were cousins, after all."

Yeah, and a garu tree is related to a grickle bush.

In a hushed voice Jomah asked, "Can I climb up on top?"

"Don't speak of that!" Sara quickly looked around. No urrish faces were in sight, so she relented a little and shook her head. "Ask your uncle. Maybe he'll take you down here at night."

Jomah looked disappointed. "I bet *you've* been up there, haven't you?"

Sara almost smiled. She and Dwer had indeed performed the ritual when they were teens, late on a chill winter's eve, when most urs were snug among their wallow mates. No triple-eyes, then, to grow inflamed at a sight that so enraged them for the first century after Earthlings landed—that of human beings magnified by symbiosis with a great beast that could outrun any urs. Two creatures, amplified into something greater than either one alone.

They thought, after the second war, that it would put us down forever to demand all the horses, then wipe the species out.

I guess they learned different.

Sara shook off the bitter, unworthy thought. It all happened so long ago, before the Great Peace or the coming of the Egg. She glanced up past the stone figure and the flower-draped skeleton of the ancient Buyur town, toward a cloud-flecked sky. *They say when poison falls from heaven, its most deadly form will be suspicion.*

The Explosers Guild occupied a building whose formal name was Tower of Chemistry, but that most Tarekians called the Palace of Stinks. Tubes of treated boo climbed the spire's flank like parasitic vines, puffing and steaming so the place vaguely resembled Pzora after a hard day in the pharmacy. Indeed, after humans, traeki were most numerous among those passing through the front portal, or riding a counterweighted lift to upper floors, where they helped make items coveted throughout the Slope—matches for lighting cook stoves, oils to treat qheuen shells against Itchyflake, soaps for cleaning human and hoon garments, lubricants to keep elderly g'Kek rolling after Dry-Axle set in—as well as paraffin for reading lamps, ink for writing, and many other products, all certified to leave no lasting trace in Jijo's soil. Nothing to worsen punishment when the inevitable Day of Days came.

Despite smells that made Prity chuff in disgust, Sara felt a lightening of her spirit inside the tower. All races mixed in the lobby, without any of the cliquishness she'd seen elsewhere in town. The hustle of commerce, with crisp murmurs in the language of science, showed some folk weren't letting the crisis drive them to gloom or hostility. There was just too much to do.

Three floors up, Explosers Hall seemed to boil with confusion. Men and boys shouted or hurried by, while guildswomen with clipboards told hoon helpers where to push barrels of ingredients. Off in a corner, gray-headed human elders bent over long tables, consulting with traeki colleagues whose hardworking secretion rings were adorned with beakers, collecting volatile drippings. What had seemed chaotic gradually resolved as Sara saw patterned order in the ferment.

This crisis may be confusing to others, but it's what explosers have spent all their lives thinking about. In this place, the mood would be fierce dedication. It was the first justification for optimism Sara had seen.

Jomah gave Sara a swift, efficient hug, then marched over to a man with a salt-and-pepper beard, poring over schematics. Sara recognized the paper, which Nelo made in special batches once a year, for painters and explosers.

A family resemblance went beyond features of face or posture, to the man's expression when he set eyes on Jomah. A lifted eyebrow was all Kurt the Exploser betrayed as Jomah placed a long leather tube in his calloused palm.

Is that all? I could have delivered it for Henrik myself. No need to send the boy on what might be a perilous mission.

If anyone knew about events up the Rimmers, it would be those in this room. But Sara held back. The explosers seemed busy. Besides, she had her own source of information, nearby. And now it was time to go there.

Engril the Copier refilled cups of tea while Sara read a slim sheaf of pages—a chronology of events and conjectures that had arrived from the Glade of Gathering, by urrish galloper, this very morning. Sara's first emotion was a flood of relief. Till now, there had been no way of knowing which rampant rumor to believe. Now she knew the landing in the mountains had occurred without casualties. Those at Gathering were safe, including her brothers. For the time being.

In the next room, Engril's aides could be seen duplicating photostats of the report's pen-and-ink illustrations, while an offset press turned out printed versions of the text. Soon copies would reach notice boards in

Tarek Town, then surrounding hives, hamlets, and herds.

"Criminals!" Sara sighed, putting down the first page. She couldn't believe it. "Criminals from space. Of all the possibilities—"

"It always seemed the most far-fetched," Engril agreed. She was a portly, red-headed woman, normally jovial and motherly but today more somber than Sara recalled. "Perhaps it wasn't much discussed because we dared not think of the consequences."

"But if they came illegally, isn't that better than Institute police putting us all under arrest? Crooks can't report us without admitting their own crime."

Engril nodded. "Unfortunately, that logic twists around the other way. Criminals cannot afford to let *us* report *them*."

"How reasonable a fear is that? It's been several thousand years since the g'Kek came, and in all that time there's been just this one direct contact with Galactic culture. The ancients calculated a half-million-year gap before the next orbital survey, and *two* million before a major inspection."

"That's not so very long."

Sara blinked. "I don't get it."

The older woman lifted a steaming pot. "More tea? Well, it's like this. Vubben suspects these are gene raiders. If true, the crime has no—what did the ancients call it?—no *sculpture of limitations*? No time limit for punishing perpetrators. Individuals from the foray party might be long dead, but not the species or Galactic clan they represent, which can still be sanctioned, from the eldest patron race down to the youngest client. Even a million years is short by the reckoning of the Great Library, whose memory spans a thousand times that long."

"But the sages don't think we'll even be around in a million years! The ancestors' plan—the Scrolls—"

"Gene raiders can't count on that, Sara. It's too serious a felony."

Sara shook her head. "All right, let's say some distant descendants of the Six are still around by then, telling blurry legends about something that happened long ago. Who would believe their story?"

Engril lifted her shoulders. "I can't say. Records show there are many jealous, even feuding, factions among the oxygen-breathing clans of the Five Galaxies. Perhaps all it would take is a hint, just a clue, to put rivals on the scent. Given such a hint, they might sift the biosphere of Jijo for stronger proof. The entire crime could come unraveled."

Silence fell as Sara pondered. In Galactic society, the greatest treasures were biological—especially those rare natural species rising now and then out of fallow worlds. Species with a spark called Potential. Potential to be *uplifted*. To be adopted by a patron race and given a boost—through teaching and genetic manipulation—crucial to cross the gap from mere clever beasts to starfaring citizens. Crucial, unless one believed the Earthlings' legend of lonely transcendence. But who in all the Five Galaxies credited *that* nonsense?

Both wilderness and civilization had roles to play in the process by which intelligent life renewed itself. Neither could do it alone. The complex, draconian rules of migration—including forced abandonment of planets, systems, even whole galaxies—were meant to give biospheres time to recover and cultivate feral potential. New races were then apportioned for adoption, according to codes time-tested over aeons.

The raiders hoped to bypass those codes. To find something precious here on Jijo, off limits and ahead of schedule. But then, even if they made a lucky strike, what could they do with their treasure?

Take some mated pairs far away from here, to some world the thieves already control, and seed the stock quietly, nudging them along with gene infusions so they fit into a natural-seeming niche. Then wait patiently for millennia, or much longer, till the time seems right to "find" the treasure, right under their noses. Eureka!

"So you're saying," she resumed, "the raiders may not want to leave witnesses. But then why land here on the Slope? Why not beyond the Sunrise Desert, or even the small continent on the far side of Jijo, instead of barging in on us!"

Engril shook her head. "Who can say? The forayers claim to want our expertise, and they say they're willing to pay for it. But we are the ones likely to pay in the end."

Sara felt her heart thud. "They—have to kill us all."

"There may be less drastic answers. But that's the one that strikes the sages as most practical."

"Practical!"

"From the raiders' point of view, of course."

Sara absorbed this quietly. *To think, part of me looked forward to meeting Galactics, and maybe asking to peek at their portable libraries.*

Through the door to Engril's workshop, she glimpsed the copier's assistants hard at work. One girl piloted a *coelostat*, a big mirror on a long arm that followed the sun, casting a bright beam through the window onto whatever document was being duplicated. A moving slit scanned that reflected light across a turning drum of precious metal, cranked by two strong men, causing it to pick up carbon powder from a tray, pressing it on fresh pages, making photostatic duplicates of drawings, art works, designs—anything but typescript text, which was cheaper to reproduce on a printing press.

Since this technology came to Jijo, nothing so dire had ever been copied.

"This is awful news," Sara murmured.

Engril agreed. "Alas, child, it's not the worst. Not by far." The old woman motioned toward the report. "Read on."

Hands trembling, Sara turned more sheets over. Her own memory of the starship was of a blurry tablet, hurtling overhead, shattering the peaceful life of Dolo Village. Now sketches showed the alien cylinder plain as day, even more fearsome standing still than it had seemed in motion. Measurements of its scale, prepared by engineering adepts using arcane means of triangulation, were hard to believe.

Then she turned another page and saw two of the plunderers themselves.

She stared, dismayed, at the portrayal.

"My God."

Engril nodded. "Indeed. Now you see why we delayed printing a new edition of the *Dispatch*. Already some hotheads among the qheuens and urs, and even a few traeki and hoon, have begun muttering about *human collusion*. There's even talk of breaking the Great Peace.

"Of course, it may never come to that. If the interlopers find what they seek soon enough, there may not be time for war to break out among the Six. We human exiles may get to prove our loyalty in the most decisive way—by dying alongside everyone else."

Engril's bleak prospect made awful sense. But Sara looked at the older woman, shaking her head.

"You're wrong. That's *not* the worst thing."

Her voice was hoarse with worry.

Engril looked back at her, puzzled. "What could be worse than annihilation of every sapient being on the Slope?"

Sara lifted the sketch, showing a man and a woman, unmistakably human, caught unawares by a hidden artist as they looked down haughtily on Jijo's savages.

"Our lives mean nothing," she said, tasting bitter words. "We were doomed from the moment our ancestors planted their outlaw seed on this world. But these"—she shook the paper angrily—"these fools are dabbling in an ancient game no human being could possibly know how to play well.

"They'll perform their theft, then slay us to erase all witnesses, only to get caught anyway.

"And when that happens, the real victim will be *Earth*."

Asx

THEY HAVE FOUND THE VALLEY OF THE IN-
nocents.

We tried hard to conceal it, did we not, my rings?
Sending them to a far-off vale—the glavers, lorniks,
chimpanzees, and zookirs. And those children of our Six
who came to Gathering with their parents, before the
ship pierced our lives.

Alas, all efforts at concealment were unavailing. A
robot from the black station followed their warm trail
through the forest to a sanctuary that was not as secret as
we hoped.

Among our sage company, Lester was the least surprised.

"They surely expected us to try hiding what we value
most. They must have sought the deep-red heat spoor of
our refugees, before it could dissipate." His rueful smile
conveyed regret but also respect. "It's what I would have
done, if I were them."

Anglic is a strange language, in which the subjunctive
form allows one to make suppositions about impossible
might-have-beens. Thinking in that tongue, i (within
my/our second ring-of-cognition) understood Lester's
expression of grudging admiration, but then i found it
hard to translate for my/our other selves.

No, our human sage is not contemplating betrayal.

*Only through insightful empathy can he/we learn to
understand the invaders.*

Ah, but our foes learn about *us* much faster. Their
robots flutter over the once-secret glen, recording, analyzing—then swooping to nip cell or fluid samples from
frightened lorniks or chimps. Next, they want us to send
individuals of each species for study, and seek to learn
our spoken lore. Those g'Kek who know zookirs best,
the humans who work with chimps, and those qheuens
whose lorniks win medallions at festivals—these "native
experts" must come share their rustic expertise. Though

the interlopers speak softly of paying well (with trinkets and beads?), there is also implied compulsion and threat.

our rings quiver, surprised, when Lester expresses satisfaction.

"They must think they've uncovered our most valued secrets."

"Have they not?" complains Knife-Bright Insight, snapping a claw. "Are not our greatest treasures those who depend on us?"

Lester nods. "True. But we could never have hidden them for long. Not when higher life-forms are the very thing the invaders desire. It's what they *expect* us to conceal.

"But now, if they are smug, even satiated for a while, we may distract them from learning about *other* things, possible advantages that offer us—and our dependents—a slim ray of hope."

"How can that ve?" demanded Ur-Jah, grizzled and careworn, shaking her black-streaked mane. "As you said—what can we conceal? They need only pose their foul questions, and those profane rovots gallop forth, piercing any secret to its hoof and heart."

"Exactly," Lester said. "So the important thing is to keep them from asking the right questions."

Dwer

HIS FIRST WAKING THOUGHT WAS THAT HE MUST be buried alive. That he lay—alternately shivering and sweltering—in some forgotten sunless crypt. A place for the dying or the dead.

But then, he wondered muzzily, what stony place ever felt like this? So *sweaty*. Threaded by a regular, thudding rhythm that made the padded floor seem to tremble beneath him.

Still semi-incoherent—with eyelids stubbornly stuck closed—he recalled how some river hoons sang of an afterlife spent languishing within a narrow fetid space, listening endlessly to a tidal growl, the pulse-beat of the universe. That fate seemed all too plausible in Dwer's fading delirium, while he struggled to shake off the wrappers of sleep. It felt as if fiendish imps were poking away with sharp utensils, taking special pains with his fingers and toes.

As more roiling thoughts swam into focus, he realized the clammy warmth was *not* the rank breath of devils. It carried an aroma much more familiar.

So was the incessant vibration, though it seemed higher-pitched, more uneven than the throaty version he'd grown up with, resounding through each night's slumber, when he was a boy.

It's a water wheel. I'm inside a dam!

The chalky smell stung his sinuses with memory. *A qheuen dam.*

His rousing mind pictured a hive of twisty chambers, packed with spike-clawed, razor-tooth creatures, scrambling over each other's armored backs, separated by just one thin wall from a murky lake. In other words, he was in one of the safest, most heartening places he could ask.

But . . . how? The last thing I recall was lying naked in a snowstorm, halfway gone, with no help in sight.

Not that Dwer was astonished to be alive. *I've always been lucky,* he thought, though it dared fate to muse on it. Anyway, Ifni clearly wasn't finished with him quite yet, not when there were still more ways to lure him down trails of surprise and fate.

It took several tries to open his heavy, reluctant eyelids, and at first the chamber seemed a dim blur. Tardy tears washed and diffused the sole light—a flame-flicker coming from his left.

"Uh!" Dwer jerked back as a dark shape loomed. The shadow resolved into a stubby *face,* black eyes glittering, tongue lolling between keen white teeth. The rest of the creature reared into view, a lithe small form, black pelted, with agile brown paws.

"Oh . . . it's you," Dwer sighed in a voice that tasted scratchy and stale. Sudden movements wakened flooding sensations, mostly unpleasant, swarming now from countless scratches, burns, and bruises, each yammering a tale of abuse and woe. He stared back at the grinning noor beast, amending an earlier thought.

I was always lucky, till I met you.

Gingerly, Dwer pushed back to sit up a bit and saw that he lay amid a pile of furs, spread across a sandy floor strewn with bits of bone and shell. That untidy clutter contrasted with the rest of the small chamber—beams, posts, and paneling, all gleaming in the wan light from a candle that flickered on a richly carved table. Each wooden surface bore the fine marks of qheuen tooth-work, all the way down to angle brackets sculpted in lacy, deceptively strong filigrees.

Dwer held up his hands. White bandages covered the fingers, too well wrapped to be qheuen work. He felt hesitant relief on counting to ten and gauging their length to be roughly unchanged—though he knew sometimes frostbite stole the tips even when doctors saved the rest. He quashed an urge to tear the dressings with his teeth and find out right away.

Patience. Nothing you do now will change what's happened. Stabbing pins-and-needles told him that he was alive and his body was struggling to heal. It made the pain easier to handle.

Dwer kicked aside more furs to see his feet—which were still there, thank the Egg, though his toes also lay under white wrappings. *If* there were still any toes down there. Old Fallon had gone on hunting for many years, wearing special shoes, after one close call on the ice turned his feet into featureless stumps. Still, Dwer bit his lip and concentrated, sending signals, meeting resistance, nevertheless *commanding* movement. Tingling pangs answered his efforts, making him wince and hiss, but he kept at it till both legs threatened cramps. At last, he sagged back, satisfied. He could wriggle the critical toes, the smallest and largest on each foot. They might be damaged, but he would walk or run normally.

Relief was like a jolt of strong liquor that went to his head. He even laughed aloud—four short, sharp barks that made Mudfoot stare. "So, do I owe you my life? Did you dash back to the Glade, yapping for help?" he crooned.

For once, Mudfoot seemed set aback, as if the noor knew it was being mocked.

Aw, cut it out, Dwer told himself. *For all you know, it might even be true.*

Most of his other hurts were the sort he had survived many times before. Several were sewn shut with needle and thread, cross-stitched by a fine, meticulous hand. Dwer stared at the seam work, abruptly recognizing it from past experience. He laughed again, knowing his rescuer from tracks laid across his own body.

Lark. How in the world did he know?

Clearly, his brother had managed to find the shivering group amid the snowdrifts, dragging him all the way to one of the qheuen freeholds of the upper hills. *And if I made it, Rety surely did. She's young and would chew off Death's arm, if He ever came for her.*

Dwer puzzled for a while over blotchy, pale stains on his arms and hands. Then he recalled. *The mulc-spider's golden fluid—someone must have peeled it off, where it stuck.*

Those places still felt strange. Not exactly *numb* so much as *preserved*—somehow offset in time. Dwer had a bizarre inkling that bits of his flesh were *younger* now than they had been before. Perhaps those patches would even outlive his body for a while, after the rest of him died.

But not yet, One-of-a-Kind, he mused.

It's the mulc-spider who's gone. Never got to finish her collection.

He recalled flames, explosions. *I better make sure Rety and the glaver are all right.*

"I don't guess you'd run and fetch my brother for me, would you?" he asked the noor, who just stared back at him.

With a sigh, Dwer draped a fur over his shoulders, then gingerly pushed up to his knees, overruling waves of agony. Lark would resent him popping any of those fine stitches, so he took it easy, standing with one hand pressed against the nearest wall. When the dizziness passed, he shuffled on his heels to the ornate table, retrieving the candle in its clay holder. The doorway came next, a low, broad opening covered by a curtain of hanging wooden slats. He had to stoop, pushing through the qheuen-shaped portal.

A pitch-black tunnel slanted left and right. He chose the leftward shaft, since it angled upward a bit. Of course, blue qheuens built their submerged homes to a logic all their own. Dwer used to get lost even in familiar Dolo Dam, playing hide-and-seek with Blade's creche-mates.

It was painful and awkward keeping most of his weight gingerly on the heels. Soon he regretted the stubborn impulse that sent him wandering like this, away from his convalescent bed. But a few duras later, his stubbornness was rewarded by sounds of anxious conversation, echoing from somewhere ahead. Two speakers were clearly human—male and female—while a third was qheuen. None were Lark or Rety, though mumbled snatches rang familiar. And *tense*. Dwer's hunter-sensitivity to strong feelings tingled like his frostbitten fingers and toes.

". . . our peoples are natural allies. Always have been. Recall how our ancestors helped yours throw off the tyranny of the grays?"

"As my folk succored *yours* when urrish packs stalked humans everywhere outside Biblos Fortress? Back when our burrows sheltered your harried farmers and their families, till your numbers grew large enough to let you fight back?"

The second voice, aspirated from two or more leg-vents, came from a qheuen matron, Dwer could tell. Probably lord of this snug mountain dam. He didn't like the snatches of conversation he had heard so far. He blew out the candle, shuffling toward the soft glow of a doorway up ahead.

"Is that what you are asking of me now?" the matri-arch went on, speaking with a different set of vents. The timbre of her Anglic accent changed. "If refuge is your need against this frightful storm, then I and my sisters offer it. Five fives of human settlers, our neighbors and friends, may bring their babes and chimps and smaller beasts. I am sure other lake-mothers in these hills will do the same. We'll protect them here until your criminal cousins depart, or till they blast this house to splinters with their almighty power, setting the lake waters boiling to steam."

The words were so unexpected, so free of any context in Dwer's foggy brain, that he could not compass them.

The male human grunted. "And if we ask for more?"

"For our *sons*, you mean? For their rash courage and spiky claws? For their armored shells, so tough and yet so like soft cheese when sliced by Buyur steel?" The qheuen mother's hiss was like that of a bubbling kettle. Dwer counted five overlapping notes, all vents working at once.

"That *is* more," she commented after a pause. "That is very much more indeed. And knives of Buyur steel are like whips of soft boo, compared to the new things we all fear."

Dwer stepped around the corner, where several lanterns bathed the faces of those he had been listening to. He shielded his eyes as two humans stood—a dark stern-looking man in his mid-forties and a stocky woman ten years younger, with light-colored hair severely tied back from a broad forehead. The qheuen matron rocked briefly, lifting two legs to expose flashes of claw.

"What new things do you fear, revered mother?" Dwer asked hoarsely. Turning to the humans, he went on. "Where are Lark and Rety?" He blinked. "And there . . . was a glaver, too."

"All are well. All have departed for the Glade, bearing vital information," the qheuen whistle-spoke. "Meanwhile, until you recover, you honor this lake as our guest. I am known as Tooth Slice Shavings." She lowered her carapace to scrape the floor.

"Dwer Koolhan," he answered, trying awkwardly to bow with arms crossed over his chest.

"Are you all right, Dwer?" the man asked, reaching toward him. "You shouldn't be up and about."

"I'd say that's up to Captain Koolhan himself," the woman commented. "There's much to discuss, if he's ready."

Dwer peered at them.

Danel Ozawa and . . . Lena Strong.

He knew her. They had been scheduled to meet at Gathering, in fact. Something having to do with that stupid *tourism* idea.

Dwer shook his head. She had used a word, strange and dire-sounding.

Captain.

"The militia's been called up," he reasoned, angry with his mind for moving so slowly.

Danel Ozawa nodded. As chief forester for the Central Range, he was nominally Dwer's boss, though Dwer hardly saw him except at Gatherings. Ozawa was a man of imposing intellect, a deputy sage, sanctioned to make rulings on matters of law and tradition. As for Lena Strong, the blond woman was aptly named. She had been a crofter's wife until a tree fell—accidentally, she claimed—on her shiftless husband, whereupon she left her home village to become one of the top lumberjack-sawyers on the river.

"Highest-level alert," Ozawa confirmed. "All companies activated."

"What . . . *all*? Just to collect a little band of *sooners*?"

Lena shook her head. "The girl's family beyond the Rimmers? This goes far beyond that."

"Then—"

Memory assailed Dwer. The blurry image of a hovering monster, firing bolts of flame. He croaked, "The flying machine."

"That's right." Danel nodded. "The one you encountered—"

"Lemme guess. Some hotheads dug up a *cache*."

Dreamers and ne'er-do-wells were always chasing rumors of a fabled hoard. Not rubble but a sealed trove buried on *purpose* by departing Buyur. Dwer often had to round up searchers who strayed too far. What if some angry young urs actually found an ancient god-weapon? Might they test it first on two isolated humans, trapped in a mulc-spider maze, before going on to settle larger grudges?

Lena Strong laughed out loud.

"Oh, he's a wonder, Danel. What a theory. If only it were true!"

Dwer lifted a hand to his head. The vibration of the water wheel seemed labored, uneven. "Well? What *is* true?" he demanded testily, then stared at the expression on Ozawa's face. The older man answered with a brief eye-flick heavenward.

"No," Dwer whispered.

He felt strangely remote, detached.

"Well then iz all over, an' I'm out of a job—no?"

The two humans grabbed his arms as he let go of the thing that had kept him going until now, the force that had dragged him upward out of unconsciousness in the first place: duty.

Galactics. Here on the Slope, he thought as they bore his weight back down the hall. *So it's come at last. Judgment Day.*

There was nothing more to do. No way he could make any difference at all.

Apparently, the sages didn't agree. They thought fate might yet be diverted, or at least modified somehow.

Lester Cambel and his aides are making plans, Dwer realized the next morning as he met the two humans again, this time by the shore of the forest-shrouded mountain lake. Even the dam wore trees, softening its graceful outline, helping root the structure firmly to the landscape. Stretched out on an elegant wooden bench, Dwer sipped a cool drink from a goblet of urrish glass as he faced the two envoys who had been sent all the way to see him.

Clearly the leaders of Earthling-Sept were playing a complex, multilayer game—balancing species self-interest against the good of the Commons as a whole. Bluff, open-faced Lena Strong seemed untroubled by this ambivalence, but not Danel Ozawa, who explained to Dwer the varied reactions of other races to the invaders being human.

I wish Lark had stayed. He could have made sense of all this. Dwer's mind still felt woozy, even after a night's restoring sleep.

"I still don't get it. What are *human* adventurers doing out here in Galaxy Two? I thought Earthlings were crude, ignorant trash, even in their own little part of Galaxy Four!"

"Why are *we* here, Dwer?" Ozawa replied. "Our ancestors came to Jijo just decades after acquiring star drive."

Dwer shrugged. "They were selfish bastards. Willing to endanger the whole race just to find a place to breed."

Lena sniffed, but Dwer kept his chin raised. "Nothing else makes sense."

Our ancestors were self-centered scoundrels—Lark had put it one day.

"You don't believe the stories of persecution and flight?" Lena asked. "The need to hide or die?"

Dwer shrugged.

"What of the g'Keks?" Ozawa asked. "Their ancestors claimed persecution. Now we learn their race *was* murdered by the Inheritors' Alliance. Does it take genocide to make the excuse valid?"

Dwer looked away. None of the g'Keks *he* knew had died. Should he mourn millions who were slaughtered long ago and far away?

"Why ask me?" he murmured irritably. "Can anything I do make a difference?"

"That depends." Danel leaned forward. "Your brother is brilliant but a heretic. Do you share his beliefs? Do *you* think this world would be better off without us? *Should* we die out, Dwer?"

He saw they were testing him. As a top hunter, he'd be valuable to the militia—if he could be trusted. Dwer sensed their eyes, watching, weighing.

Without doubt, Lark was a deeper, wiser man than anyone Dwer knew. His arguments made sense when he spoke passionately of higher values than mere animal reproduction—certainly more sense than *Sara's* weird brand of math-based, what-if optimism. Dwer knew firsthand about species going extinct—the loss of something beautiful that would never be recovered.

Maybe Jijo *would* be better off resting undisturbed, according to plan.

Still, Dwer knew his own heart. He would marry someday, if he found the right partner, and he would sire as many kids as his wife and the sages allowed, drinking like a heady wine the love they gave, in return for his devotion.

"I'll fight, if that's what you're askin'," he said in a low voice, perhaps ashamed to admit it. "If that's what it takes to survive."

Lena grunted with a curt, satisfied nod. Danel let out a soft sigh.

"Fighting may not be necessary. Your militia duties will be taken up by others."

Dwer sat up. "Because of this?" He motioned toward the bandages on his feet and left hand. Those on the right were already off, revealing that the middle finger was no longer the longest, a disconcerting but noncrippling amputation, healing under a crust of traeki paste.

"I'll be up and around soon, good as ever."

"Indeed, I am counting on it." Ozawa nodded. "We need you for something rather arduous. And before I explain, you must swear never to inform another soul, *especially* your brother."

Dwer stared at the man. If it were anyone else, he might have laughed scornfully. But he trusted Ozawa. And much as Dwer loved and admired his brother, Lark was without any doubt a heretic.

"It's for the good?" he asked.

"I believe so," the older man said, in apparent sincerity.

Dwer sighed unhappily. "All right then. Let's hear what you have in mind."

A_{sx}

THE ALIENS DEMANDED TO SEE CHIMPANZEES, then marveled over those we brought before them, as if they had never seen the like before.

"Your chimps do not speak! Why is that?"

Lester proclaims mystification. Chimpanzees are capable of sign language, of course. But have other traits been added since the *Tabernacle* fled to Jijo?

The invaders seem unimpressed with Lester's demurral, and so are some of our fellow Sixers. For the first time, i/we sense something hidden, deceitful, in the manner of my/our human colleague. He knows more than he tells. But our skittish rewq balk at revealing more.

Nor is this our sole such worry. Qheuens refuse to speak further regarding lorniks. Our g'Kek cousins reel from the news that they are the last of their kind. And all of us are appalled to witness alien robots returning to base laden with gassed, sleeping *glavers,* kidnapped from faraway herds for analysis under those once-gay pavilions we lent our guests.

"Is *this* the return of innocence, promised in the Scrolls?" Ur-Jah asks, doubt dripping like fumes from her lowered snout. "How could a blessing arise out of base crime?"

If only we could *ask* the glavers. Is this what they wanted, when they chose the Path of Redemption?

Lark

"**W**ELL, LOOK WHO IT IS. I'M SURPRISED YOU HAVE the nerve to show your face around here."

The forayer woman's grin seemed at once both sly and teasing. She peeled off elastic gloves, turning from a glaver on a lab bench with wires in its scalp. There were several of the big trestle tables, where human, g'Kek, and urrish workers bent under cool, bright lamps, performing rote tasks they had been taught, helping their employers test animals sampled from sundry Jijoan ecosystems.

Lark had dropped his backpack by the entrance. Now he picked it up again. "I'll go if you want."

"No, no. Please stay." Ling waved him into the laboratory shelter, which had been moved to a shielded forest site the very night Lark last saw the beautiful intruder, the same evening the black station buried itself under a fountain of piled dirt and broken vegetation. The basis for both actions was still obscure, but Lark's superiors now thought it must have to do with the violent destruction of one of the interlopers' robots. An event his brother must have witnessed at close hand.

Then there was the testimony of Rety, the girl from over the mountains, supported by her treasure, a strange metal machine, once shaped like a Jijoan bird. Was it a Buyur remnant, as some supposed? If so, why should such a small item perturb the mighty forayers? Unless it was like the tip of a red qheuen's shell, innocuous at first sight, poking over a sand dune, part of much more than it seemed? The "bird" now lay in a cave, headless and mute, but Rety swore it used to move.

Lark had been ordered back down to the Glade before his brother could confirm the story. He knew he shouldn't worry. Danel Ozawa was qualified to tend Dwer's wounds. Still, he deeply resented the recall order.

"Will you be needing me for another expedition?" he asked Ling.

"After you abandoned me the last time? We found human tracks when we finally got to where our robot went down. Is that where you rushed off to? Funny how you knew which way to go."

He shouldered his pack. "Well, if you don't need me, then—"

She swept a hand before her face. "Oh, never mind. Let's move on. There's plenty of work, if you want it."

Lark glanced dubiously at the lab tables. Of Jijo's Six, all three of the races with good hand-eye coordination were employed. Outside, hoons and qheuens also labored at the behest of aliens whose merest trinkets meant unimaginable wealth to primitive savages. Only traeki were unseen among the speckled tents, since the ringed ones seemed to make the raiders nervous.

Sepoy labor. That was the contemptuous expression Lena Strong had used when she brought Lark new orders at Tooth-Slice Shavings' Dam. An old Earth term, referring to aborigines toiling for mighty visitors, paid in beads.

"Oh, don't look so sour." Ling laughed. "It *would* serve you right if I put you to work staining nerve tissue, or shoveling the longsnout pens. . . . No, stop." She grabbed Lark's arm. All signs of mockery vanished. "I'm sorry. There really *are* things I want to discuss with you."

"Uthen is here." He pointed to the far end of the tent, where his fellow biologist, a large male qheuen with a slate gray carapace, held conference with Rann, one of the two male forayers, a tall massive man in a tight-fitting uniform.

"Uthen knows incredible detail about how different species relate to each other." Ling agreed with a nod. "That's not easy on a planet that has had infusions of outsider species every twenty million years or so, for aeons. Your lore is impressive, given your limitations."

Had she any idea how far Jijoan "lore" really went? So

far, the sages had not released his detailed charts, and
Uthen must be dragging all five feet, cooperating just
enough to stay indispensable. Yet the aliens seemed easily impressed by sketchy glimmers of local acumen,
which only showed how insultingly low their expecta-
tions were.

"Thanks," Lark muttered. "Thanks a lot."

Ling sighed, briefly averting her dark eyes. "Crampers,
can't I say *anything* right, today? I don't mean to offend.
It's just . . . look, how about we try starting from
scratch, all right?" She held out a hand.

Lark looked at it. What was he expected to do now?

She reached out with her left hand to take his right
wrist. Then *her* right hand clasped *his*.

"It's called a handshake. We use it to signify respect,
amicable greeting, or agreement."

Lark blinked. Her grip was warm, firm, slightly moist.

"Oh, yes . . . I've rea—heard of it."

He tried to respond when she squeezed, but it felt so
strange, and vaguely *erotic,* that Lark let go sooner than
she seemed to expect. His face felt warm.

"Is it a common gesture?"

"Very common, I hear. On Earth."

You hear? Lark leaped on the passing phrase and
knew it had begun again—their game of hints and reve-
lations, mutual scrutiny of clues and things left unsaid.

"I can see why we gave it up, on Jijo," he commented.
"The urs would hate it; their hands are more personal
than their genitals. Hoons and qheuens would crush *our*
hands and we'd squash the tendrils of any g'Kek who
tried it." His fingers still felt tingly. He resisted an urge to
look them over. Definitely time to change the subject.

"So," Lark said, trying for a businesslike tone of equality, "you've never been to Earth?"

One eyebrow raised. Then she laughed. "Oh, I knew
we couldn't hire *you* for just a handful of biodegradable
toys. Don't worry, Lark; you'll be paid in answers—*some*
answers—at the end of each day. After you've earned
them."

Lark sighed, although in fact the arrangement did not sound unsatisfactory.

"Very well, then. Why don't you tell me what it is you want to know."

Asx

EACH DAY WE STRIVE TO MEDIATE STRESS AMONG our factions, from those urging cooperation with our uninvited guests, to others seeking means to destroy them. Even my/our own sub-selves war over these options.

Making peace with felons, or fighting the unfightable. Damnation or extinction.

And still our guests question us about *other visitors!* Have we seen other outsiders lately, dropping from the sky? Are there Buyur sites we have not told them about? Sites where ancient mechanisms lurk, alert, still prone to vigorous action?

Why this persistence? Surely they can tell we are not lying—that we know nothing more than we have told.

Or is that true, my rings? Have all Six shared equally with the Commons, or are some withholding vital information, needed by all?

That i should think such a thing is but another measure of how far we are fallen, we unworthy, despicable sooners. We, who surely have farther yet to fall.

Rety

UNDER A SMALLER, SHABBIER TENT, IN A DENSE grove some secret distance from the research station, Rety threw herself onto a reed mat, pounding it with both fists.

"Stinkers. Rotten guts an' rancy meat. Rotten, rotten, *rotten!*"

She had good reason to thrash in outrage and self-pity. That liar, Dwer, had told her the sages were good and wise. But they turned out to be horrid!

Oh, not at the beginning. At *first,* her hopes had shot up like the geysers back home in the steaming Gray Hills. Lester Cambel and the others seemed *so* kind, easing her dread over being punished for her grandparents' crime of sneaking east, over the forbidden mountains. Even before questioning her, they had doctors tend her scrapes and burns. It never occurred to Rety to fear the unfamiliar g'Kek and traeki medics who dissolved away drops of clinging mulc-fluid, then used foam to drive off the parasites that had infested her scalp for as long as she could remember. She even found it in her to forgive them when they dashed her hopes of a cure for the scars on her face. Apparently, there was a limit even to what Slopies could accomplish.

From the moment she and Lark strode into the Glade of Gathering, everyone seemed awfully excited and distracted. At first Rety thought it was because of her, but it soon grew clear that the real cause was visitors from the sky!

No matter. It still felt like coming home. Like being welcomed into the embrace of a family far bigger and sweeter than the dirty little band she had known for fourteen awful years.

At least it felt that way for a while.

Till the betrayal.

Till the sages called her once again to their pavilion and told her their decision.

"It's all Dwer's fault," she muttered later, nursing hot resentment. "Him an' his rotten brother. If only I could've snuck in over the mountains without being seen. No one would've noticed me in all this ruckus." Rety had no clear notion what she would have done after that. The oldsters back home had been murky in their handed-down tales about the Slope. Perhaps she could make herself useful to some remote village as a trapper. Not for food—Slopies had plenty of that—but for soft furs that'd keep townfolk from asking too closely where she came from.

Back in the Gray Hills, such dreams used to help her pass each grinding day. Still, she might never have found the guts to flee her muddy clan but for the beautiful bright bird.

And now the sages had taken it away from her!

"We are grateful for your part in bringing this enigmatic wonder to us," Lester Cambel said less than an hour ago, with the winged thing spread on a table before him. "Meanwhile though, something terribly urgent has come up. I hope you'll understand, Rety, why it's become so necessary for you to go back."

Back? At first, she could not bring herself to understand. She puzzled while he gabbled on and on.

Back?

Back to Jass and Bom and their strutting ways? To the endless bullying of those *big, strong hunters*? Always boasting around the campfire about petty, vicious triumphs that grew more exaggerated with each telling? To those wicked oafs who used fire-tipped sticks to punish anyone who dared to talk back to them?

Back to where mothers watched half their babies waste away and die? To where that hardly mattered, because new babies kept on coming, coming and coming, till you dried up and died of old age before you were forty? Back to all that hunger and dirt?

The human sage had muttered words and phrases that were supposed to sound soothing and noble and logical. But Rety had stopped listening.

They meant to send her back to the tribe!

Oh, it might be fine to see Jass's face when she strode into camp, clothed and equipped with all the wonders the Six could offer. But then where would she be? Condemned once more to that awful life.

I won't go back. I won't!

With that resolution, Rety rolled over, wiped her eyes, and considered what to do.

She could try running away, taking shelter elsewhere. Rumors told that all was not in perfect harmony among the Six. So far, she had obeyed Cambel's request not to blab the story of her origins. But Rety wondered—might some urrish or qheuen faction *pay* for the information? Or invite her to live among them?

It's said the urs sometimes let a chosen human ride upon their backs, when the human's light enough, and worthy.

Rety tried to picture life among the galloping clans, roaming bold and free across the open plains with wind blowing through her hair.

Or what about going to sea with hoons? There were islands nobody had ever set foot on, and flying fish, and floating mountains made of ice. What an adventure *that* would be! Then there were the traeki of the swamps . . .

A new thought abruptly occurred to her. *Another* option that suddenly appeared to lie open. One so amazing to contemplate that she just lay there silently for several duras, hands unclenching at last from their tightly clutched fists. Finally, she sat up, pondering with growing excitement a possibility beyond any other ambition she had ever conceived.

The more she thought about it, the better it began to seem.

XI. THE BOOK OF THE SEA

Animals think nothing of race, clan,
or philosophy.
Nor of beauty, ethics, or investment
in things that will long outlast their
lives.
All that matters to beasts is the
moment.
All that counts is self.

Mates, offspring, siblings, and hive-
consorts,
All these offer continuity of self.
To even a loving beast, altruism has
deep roots, founded in self-interest.

Sapient beings are not beasts.
Loyalty binds even the innately
egotistic to things nobler, more
abstract, than mere continuity, or self.
To race, clan, or philosophy.
To beauty, ethics, or investment
in fruits you and I will never harvest.

If you seek the downward trail, the
long road to redemption—

If you want a second chance, shriven
of your grief and worry—
Seek that path by returning to the
soil,
In forgetfulness of race, clan, or
philosophy.
Yet beware! Lest the road take you
too far.
Keep faith in something greater than
you are.
Beware resumed obsession with the
self.

To those who have tasted vacuum
and stardust,
that way lies damnation.

—The Scroll of Redemption

Alvin's Tale

THE OTHERS ARE ASLEEP NOW. IT'S LATE, BUT I want to get all this down, 'cause things are about to get busy and I don't know when I'll have another chance.

Tomorrow we head back down the mountain, loaded with all kinds of gear lent to us by Uriel the Smith—so much good stuff that we're feeling pretty dumb right now about our former plans.

To think, we were willing to trust our lives to some of the junk *we* designed!

Uriel already sent messages to our parents, calligraphed on heavy cloth paper and sealed with her signet as a sage of the Commons. So there's not much Huck's folks or mine can do to stop us.

Not that I looked forward to facing them, anyway. What would I say? *"Hey, Pop. It'll be just like* Twenty Thousand Leagues Under the Sea*! Remember how often you read it to me, when I was little?"*

I recall now how that tale ended for Captain Nemo's submarine crew, and I can see why Yowg-wayuo regrets what a humicker I've become. If my father confronts me over this, I'll discuss it in a language other than Anglic, to show that I really have thought it out several ways. This trip is more than a passing kid-obsession but something meaningful for our village and our race. Me and the others are going to make history. It's important for a hoon to be involved, from notion to motion to recollection.

·   ·   ·

Once she decided, Uriel really got things rolling. Pincer-Tip headed out the very same evening after Ziz was vlenned, taking the newly budded traeki to his home hive for water-adapting in the tidepools south of Wuphon. Pincer will also use the smith's authority to hire some red-shelled cousins to haul the bathy's wooden hull to a meeting point down near the Rift. The rest of us will come overland with supply wagons.

Test dives start in just five days!

The choice of a site was vital. There's just one place where the Midden's deep watery trench plunges like a scythe blade toward the coast. Where it sends a deep rupture of jagged canyons passing right next to Terminus Rock. By deploying a boom from an overhanging ledge, we won't even need to hire a ship.

It's a relief to have a decision made at last. Even Huck admits the die is cast, accepting destiny with a shrugged rubbing of two eyestalks.

"At least we'll be right there at the border, where I want to be anyway. When we finish, Uriel will owe us. She'll *have* to write us a warrant to go over the line and visit some Buyur ruins."

There's an Anglic word—*tenacity*—that comes out as *stubbornness* when I translate into GalSix. Which is one more reason why human speech best describes my pal Huck.

All of us, even Ur-ronn, are more than a little surprised by how Uriel is throwing resources at our "little adventure" all of a sudden. We talked about the smith's outbreak of helpfulness during our last evening on Mount Guenn, after a long day spent packing crates and going over inventory lists, waiting for the factory complex to settle down for the night.

"It nust have to do with the *starshifs*," Ur-ronn said, lifting her muzzle from the straw of her sleeping pallet.

Huck turned two stalks toward Ur-ronn—leaving just one buried in her well-thumbed copy of *Lord Valentine's Castle*. She groaned. "Not that again! What in the world could *our* dumbass little diving trip have to do with Galactic cruisers coming to Jijo? Don't you think Uriel would have more important things on her mind?"

"Vut Gyfz said, a week ago—"

"Why not just admit you overheard Gybz wrong? We asked er again today, and that traeki doesn't recall seeing any spaceships."

"Not *that* tracki," I corrected. "We never had a chance to ask *Gybz* anything, before the vlenning. It's *Tyug* who said er doesn't remember."

"Tyug, Gybz. The difference can't be that great. Not even a vlenned traeki would forget something like that!"

I wasn't so sure about that. Traeki memory wax can be tricky stuff, I hear.

Then again, I'm hardly ever as sure of *anything* as Huck is of *everything*.

Of course, there was one other person we could ask, but in the course of stowing gear and going over plans, I guess the fiery old smith dazzled us out of bringing the subject up. *Intimidated* may be a better word, though I'm not sure, since I'm writing this by candlelight without my handy dictionary. All during the last few days, Uriel galloped from her normal duties, to talks with her human guest, to tending her precious hall of disks, to flooding us with more details we never thought of during all our long months planning an undersea adventure—a voyage none of us ever *really* expected to come true. In all the rushing about, there never seemed time to raise other questions. Or else Uriel made it plain that some things weren't any of our business.

At one point I did try to ask about all the changes she had made in our plan.

"We always figured on starting by exploring the shallows near home. Then redesign and refit before trying deeper water from a boat. Maybe going down ten or twenty cords. Now you're talking about doing *thirty,* right from the start!"

"Thirty cords is not so very nuch," Uriel dismissed with a snort. "Oh, I agree that your old air circulators wouldn't have veen uf to it. That's why I reflaced the systen with a suferior one we had on hand. Also, your gaskets would have leaked. As for the hull itself, your design will do."

I couldn't help wondering—where did all the equipment come from? We hadn't figured on needing a gas pressure regulator, for instance. Good thing Uriel pointed out the mistake and happened to have a beautiful handmade one in stock. But *why* did she already have one? Why would even the Smith of Guenn Volcano need such a thing?

Huck admitted, it wasn't hurting our chances to have Uriel's competence behind us. Yet I worried. An air of mystery shrouded the enterprise.

"All will ve nade clear when you get to the Rock, and everything is ready to go. I'll check the gear out nyself, then I'll exflain what *you* can do for *ne*."

Barring day trips to Wuphon, Uriel hardly ever left her forge. Now she wanted to take two *weeks* off, adventuring with us? Never in my life has a single piece of news struck me the way that one did—at once both reassuring and terrifying. Perhaps my nick-namesake felt the same way when, exploring the deep catacombs under Diaspar, he found something unimaginable, a mystery tunnel leading all the way to faraway Lys.

So there we were, Huck, Ur-ronn, and me, all packed up and ready to set off in the morn, on an exploit that would either make us famous or kill us. Before that, though, there was one bit of business we *had* to take care of. We waited till night settled fully over Mount Guenn, when sunshine no longer filled the hundred clever sky-lights, leaving nothing to compete with the lava pools and glowing forges. The ore buckets and casting furnaces went silent and laborers downed tools. Soon after evening meal, seven gongs clanged, summoning urrish workers to perform their ritual grooming before settling down to sleep.

Ur-ronn didn't like moving about at that hour—what urs does?—but she knew there was no other choice. So we set forth single file from the warehouse chamber where Urdonnol had us barracked, picking our way without lanterns. Huck led, with two eyestalks stretched ahead as she spun quickly along a swooping stone ramp. The eyes facing backward seemed to glare at us each time she passed under a sky-duct, catching glimmers of moonlight.

"Come on, you guys! You're so jeekee slow!"

Ur-ronn muttered, "Who had to carry *her* across rock-fields for three days, when we went exfloring the Yootir Caves? I still have sfoke scars in ny flanks."

An exaggeration. I know how tough urrish hide is. Still. Huck does have a way of recalling only whatever seems convenient at the time.

She had to stop and wait, huffing impatiently, at intersections to let Ur-ronn show the way. Soon that meant exiting the warren of underground passages and following a trail of pounded pumice across a rocky plain that looked even more eerily alien, more starkly un-Jijoan, by night than it did by day. In fact, we were crossing terrain much like pictures I've seen of Earth's moon.

Speaking of moons, great Loocen sat low in the west, the largest of Jijo's satellites, a familiar reddish crescent, though right now the main part facing us was dark, so no sunlight sparkled off the cold, dead cities the Buyur left there intact, as if to taunt us.

Stars glittered overhead like . . . well, before writing this down, I wracked my brain for a comparison out of some book I've read, but Earthling authors never had anything in their sky like the Dandelion Cluster, a giant puff-ball of sparkling pinpoints taking up almost a quarter of the sky, skimming the southern horizon. I know 'cause if they did, they'd have competed to describe it over and over, in a million different ways. Visitors from the crowded north part of the Slope always act amazed to see it in its glory, so I guess the Dandelion's one good thing about living here at the southmost boonies.

It's also one chief reason why Uriel's predecessor built a telescope on that spot, and a dome to protect it against rain and ash from old Guenn's frequent mini-eruptions.

Ur-ronn says there's just one part of the mountain where the observatory can take advantage of the sea breeze and not have heat currents ruin the seeing. There are probably much better places for astronomy on the Slope. But this spot has one advantage—it's where Uriel lives. Who else has the time, wealth, and knowledge to maintain such a hobby? No one, except perhaps the savants of Great Biblos.

The heavy cinderblock structure seemed to rise against the dazzling starry cluster, reminding me of a glaver's muzzle, taking a bite out of a big gutchel pear. The sight made my back scales frickle. Of course at this altitude, with no clouds in the sky, the air had a chilly bite.

Whistling dismay, Ur-ronn halted in a sudden plume of dust, causing Huck to ram into me, eyestalks pronging outward, squinting in all directions at once. Little Huphu reacted by digging her claws into my shoulder, ready to leap and abandon us at the first sign of peril.

"What is it!" I whispered urgently.

"The roof is open," Ur-ronn explained, slipping into GalTwo as her pointed snout sniffed greedily. *"The mercury float bearing, I do scent; therefore the telescope (probably) is in use. We must now undertake (swiftly) to return to our beds, not raising suspicion."*

"The hell you say," Huck cursed. "I'm for sneakin' in."

They looked to me for the deciding vote. I shrugged, human-style. "We're here. Ought to at least take a look."

Ur-ronn corkscrewed her neck. She snorted a sigh. *"Stay behind me, in that case. And in vain hope of Ifni's luck, do remain quiet!"*

So we neared the dome and made out that the roof line was split open, exposing blocky shapes to the shimmering sky. The path ended at a ground-level door—ajar—revealing dim shadows within. Huphu trembled on my shoulder, either from eagerness or from anxiety. I already regretted taking her along.

Ur-ronn was an outline, pressed against the outer wall, snaking her head through the door.

"Of all utterjeekee things, what could top *her* scouting ahead at night?" Huck groused. "Urs can't see in the dark any better'n a glaver can at noon. Oughta let me do it."

Yeah, I thought. *As if g'Keks are built for stealth.* But I kept silent, except for a low umble to prevent Huphu jumping off.

Switching her braided tail nervously, Ur-ronn twisted her neck inside—and her long body followed, twisting nimbly through the doorway. Huck followed close behind, all eyestalks erect and quivering. Taking up the rear, I kept swiveling to check for anyone creeping *behind,* though of course there was no reason to imagine someone would want to.

The main floor of the observatory looked deserted. The big scope glittered faintly under starlight. On a nearby table, one hooded lantern spilled a red-filtered glow onto a clipboarded sky chart and a pad covered with what might be mathematical markings—lots of numbers plus some symbols that weren't part of any alphabet . . . though now that I think about it, maybe Mister Heinz *did* show some of them to our class, hoping to hook an interest.

"Listen and note," Ur-ronn said. *"The motor for tracking objects in compensation against Jijo's rotation; that device is still turned on."*

Sure enough, a low, hoonlike rumble transmitted from the telescope's case, and I smelled faint exhaust from a tiny fuel cell motor. Another extravagance almost unknown elsewhere on the Slope but allowed here because Mount Guenn is a sacred place, certain to cleanse itself of all toys, conceits, and unreverent vanities, if not tomorrow then sometime in the next hundred years.

"That means it may still be pointed wherever they were looking before they left!" Huck responded eagerly.

Who says "they" have left?—I was about to add. Turning around again, I noticed a closed door outlined by a pale rim of light. But Huck rushed on.

"Alvin, give me a boost so I can look!"

"Hr-r-rm? But—"

"Alvin!" A wheel stroked one of my footpads, as a warning to do what I was told.

"What? A boost?" I saw no ramp or other way for Huck to reach the scope's eyepiece, only a chair resting next to the table. Still, the best course would be to let her have her way, as quickly and silently as possible, rather than forcing an argument.

"Hrrrm . . . well, all right. But keep it quiet, will you?"

I stepped behind Huck, squatted down, and slung both arms under her axle frame. I grunted, lifting her to bring one stalk level with the eyepiece.

"Hold still!" she hissed.

"I am . . . hrm-rm . . . *trying* . . ."

I let my arm bones slip slightly, so the elbow joints clicked into a locked position—a trick I'm told humans and urs are jealous of, since even the strongest human who tried this would have to do it using muscle power alone. Even so, Huck had put on weight, and holding her in place meant standing in a bent-over half-squat. Whenever I grunted, she'd twist a free stalk round to glare, just a handsbreadth from my face, as if I was annoying her on purpose.

"Hold it, you unbuff hoon! . . . Okay, I can see now . . . a whole lot of stars . . . more stars. . . . Hey, there's *nothing* but stars in here!"

"Huck," I murmured, "did I ask you to keep it quiet?"

Ur-ronn whistled a sigh. "Of *course* there's only stars, you hoof-stinky g'Kek! Did you think you could count the fortholes on an orviting starshif with this little telescofe? At that height, it'll twinkle like any other foint source."

I was impressed. We all know Ur-ronn is the best mechanic in our bunch, but who figured she knew astronomy, as well?

"Here, give ne a chance to look. It's fossible I can tell which star *isn't* a star, if its fosition changes in relation to others."

Huck's wheels spun angrily in air, but she could no more deny the fairness of Ur-ronn's request than keep me from lowering her to the ground. I straightened with relief, and some crackling of cartilage, as she rolled away, grumbling. Ur-ronn had to put both forehooves on the chair in order to rise up and peer through the eyepiece.

For a few moments, our urrish pal was silent; then she trilled frustration. "They really *are* all just stars, far as I can tell. Anyway, I forgot—a starshif in orvit would drift out of view in just a few duras, even with the tracking engine turned on."

"Well, I guess that's it," I said, only half disappointed. "We'd better head on back now—"

That's when I saw that Huck was gone. Whirling, I finally spied her, heading straight for the doorway I had seen earlier!

"Remember what we discussed?" she called rearward at us, speeding toward the back-lit rectangle. "The *real* evidence will be on those photographic *plates* you say Gybz spoke of. That's what we came up here to look at in the first place. Come on!"

I admit staring like a stranded fish, my throat sac blatting uselessly while Huphu gouged my scalp, gathering purchase for a spring. Ur-ronn took off in a mad scramble after Huck, trying desperately to tackle her by the spokes before she reached the door—

—which *swung open,* I swear, at that very instant, casting a painful brightness that outlined a *human* silhouette. A short, narrow-shouldered male whose fringe of head hair seemed aflame in the glare of several lanterns behind him. Blinking, raising a hand to shade my eyes, I could dimly make out several easels in the room beyond, bearing charts, measuring rules, and slick glass plates. *More* square plates lay racked on shelf after shelf, crowding the walls of the little room.

Huck squealed to a stop so suddenly her axles glowed. Ur-ronn nearly rammed her, halting in frantic haste. We all froze, caught in the act.

The human's identity wasn't hard to guess, since only one of his race lived on the mountain at the time. He was *only* known far and wide as the most brilliant of his kind, a sage whose mind reached far, even for an Earthling, to grasp many of the arcane secrets that our ancestors once knew. One whose intellect even the mighty self-assured *Uriel* bowed before.

The Smith of Mount Guenn was *not* going to be pleased with us for intruding on her guest.

Sage Purofsky stared for a long moment, blinking into the darkness beyond the doorway, then he raised a hand straight toward us, pointing.

"You!" he snapped in a strangely distracted tone of voice. "You surprised me."

Huck was the first of us to recover.

"Um, sorry . . . uh, master. We were just, er . . ."

Cutting her off, but without any trace of rancor, the human went on.

"It's just as well, then. I was about to ring for somebody. Would you kindly take these notes to Uriel for me?"

He held out a folded sheaf of papers, which Huck accepted in the grasp of one quivering tentacle-arm. Her half-retracted eyestalks blinked in surprise.

"That's a good lad," the savant went on absentmindedly, and turned to go back into the little room. Then Sage Purofsky stopped and swiveled to face us once more.

"Oh, please also tell Uriel that I'm now sure of it. Both ships are gone. I don't know what happened to the bigger one, the first one, since it appeared only by lucky accident on one early set of plates, before anyone knew to look for it. That orbit can't be solved except to say I think it may have landed. But even a rough calculation based on the last series shows the *second* ship deorbiting, heading into an entry spiral down to Jijo. Assuming no later deviations or corrections, its course would have made landfall some days ago, north of here, smack dab in the Rimmers."

His smile was rueful, ironic.

"In other words, the warning we sent up to the Glade may be somewhat superfluous." Purofsky rubbed his eyes tiredly and sighed. "By now our colleagues at Gathering probably know a lot more about what's going on than we do."

I swear, he sounded more disappointed than worried

over the arrival of something the exiles of Jijo had feared for two thousand years.

We all, even Huphu, stared for a long time—even after the man thanked us again, turned around, and closed the door behind him, leaving us alone with our only company millions of stars, like pollen grains scattered on a shimmering ocean, stretching over our heads. A sea of darkness that suddenly felt frighteningly near.

XII. THE BOOK OF THE SLOPE

Legends

There is a word we are asked not to say too often. And to whisper, when we do.

The *traeki* ask this of us, out of courtesy, respect, and superstition.

The word is a name—with just two syllables—one they fear ever to hear again.

A name they once called themselves.

A name presumably still used by their cousins, out on the star-lanes of the Five Galaxies.

Cousins who are mighty, terrifying, resolute, pitiless, and single-minded.

How different that description seems to make our *own* sept of ringed ones, from those who still roam the cosmos, like gods. Those *Jophur*.

Of all the races who came to Jijo in sneakships, some, like qheuens and humans, were obscure and almost unknown in the Five Galaxies. Others, like g'Keks and glavers, had reputations of modest extant, among those needing their specialized skills. Hoon and urs had made a moderate impression, so much that Earthlings knew of them before landing, and worried.

But it is said that every oxygen-breathing, starfaring clan is familiar with the shape of stacked rings, piled high, ominous and powerful.

When the traeki sneakship came, the g'Kek took one look at the newcomers and went into hiding for several generations, cowering in fright until, at last, they realized—these were *different* rings.

When qheuen settlers saw them already here, they very nearly left again, without unloading or even landing their sneakship.

How came our beloved friends to have such a reputation to live down? How came they to be so different from those who still fly in space, using that awful name?

—Reflections on the Six,
　Ovoom Press,
　Year-of-Exile 1915

A~sx~

ITHER THE INVADERS ARE TRYING TO CONFUSE
us, or else there is something strange about them.

At first, their powers and knowledge appeared as
one might expect—so far above us that we seem as
brutish beasts. Dared we contrast our own meager wisdom, our simple ways, against their magnificent, unstoppable machines, their healing arts, and especially the
erudition of their piercing questions about Jijoan life?
Erudition showing the vast sweep and depth of records
at their command, surely copied from the final survey of
this world, a million years ago. Yet . . .

They seem to know nothing about lorniks or zookirs.

They cannot hide their excitement, upon measuring
specimen glavers, as if they have made a great discovery.

They make puzzling, nonsensical remarks concerning
chimpanzees.

And now they want to know everything about mulc-
spiders, asking naïve questions that even this inexpert
stack of manicolored rings could answer. Even if all of
our/my toruses of sapiency were vlenned away, leaving
nothing but instinct, memory, and momentum.

The sigil of the Great Library was missing from the
bow of the great vessel that left their station here. We
thought its absence a mere emblem of criminality. A
negative symbol, denoting a kind of skulking shame.

Can it mean more than that? Much more?

Sara

FROM ENGRIL'S SHOP ON PIMMIN CANAL, IT WAS but a short walk to the clinic where Pzora had taken the Stranger yesterday. Engril agreed to meet Sara there with Bloor the Portraitist. Time was short. Perhaps Sara's idea was foolish or impractical, but there would be no better moment to broach it, and no better person to present it to than Ariana Foo.

A decision had to be made. So far, the omens weren't good.

The emissaries from Dolo Village had gathered last night, in a tavern near the Urrish Quarter, to discuss what each of them had learned since the *Hauph-woa* docked. Sara showed a copy of the sages' report, fresh from Engril's copy shop, expecting it to shock the others. But by that evening even Pzora knew most of the story.

"I see three possibilities," the stern-browed farmer Jop had said, nursing a mug of sour buttermilk. "First—the story's an Egg-cursed lie. The ship really *is* from the great Institutes, we're about to be judged as the Scrolls say, but the sages are spreading a pebble-in-my-hoof fable about bandits to justify musterin' the militia, preparin' for a fight."

"That's absurd!" Sara had complained.

"Oh yeah? Then why've all the units been called up? Humans drilling in every village. Urrish cavalry wheelin' in all directions, and the hoons oilin' their old catapults, as if they could shoot down a starship by hurlin' rocks." He shook his head. "What if the sages've got some fantasy about resisting? It wouldn't be the first time leaders were driven mad by an approaching end to their days of petty power."

"But what of these sketches?" asked the scrivendancer, Fakoon. The g'Kek touched one of Engril's reproductions, portraying a pair of humans dressed in one-piece suits, staring brazenly at sights both new to them and yet somehow pathetic in their eyes.

Jop shrugged. "Ridiculous on the face of it. What would *humans* be doin' out here? When our ancestors left Earth on an aged thirdhand tub, not a single human scientist understood its workings. The folks back home couldn't have caught up with galactic standard tech for another ten thousand years."

Sara watched Blade and the hoon captain react with surprise. It was no secret, what Jop had said about human technology at the time of exile, but they must find it hard to picture. On Jijo, *Earthlings* were the engineers, the ones most often with answers.

"And who would want to ferfetrate such a hoax?" Ulgor asked, lowering her conical head. Sara read tension in the urs's body stance. *Uh-oh,* she thought.

Jop smiled. "Why, maybe some bunch that sees opportunity, amid the chaos, to besmirch our honor and have one last chance at revenge before Judgment Day."

Human and urs faced each other, each grinning a bright display of teeth—which could be taken equivocally as either friendly or threatening. For once, Sara blessed the sickness that had caused nearly everyone's rewq to curl up and hibernate. There would have been no ambiguity with symbionts to translate the meaning in Jop's and Ulgor's hearts.

At that moment, a squirt of pinkish steam jetted between the two—a swirling fume of cloying sweetness. Jop and Ulgor retreated from the cloud in opposite directions, covering their noses.

"Oops. i express repentance on our/my behalf. This pile's digestive torus still retains, processes, deletes the richness of esteemed hoonish shipboard fare."

Unperturbed, the captain of the *Hauph-woa* said— "How fortunate for you, Pzora. As to the subject at hand, we must still decide what advice to send back to Dolo Village and the settlements of the Upper Roney. So let me ask Jop. . . . *Hrrrm*—what if we consider a simpler theory—there is *no* hoax by the honored sages, *hrr*?"

Jop still waved the air in front of his face, coughing. "That brings us to possibility number two—that we are being tested. The Day has come at last, but the noble

Galactics are undecided what to do with us. Maybe the great Institutes hired human actors to play this role, offering us a chance to tip the scales one way through right action, or the other by choosing incorrectly. As for what advice we send upriver, I say we counsel that demolition should proceed according to the ancient plan!"

Blade, the young qheuen delegate, reared back on three legs, lifting his blue carapace, stammering and hissing so that his initial attempts at Anglic came out garbled. He switched to Galactic Two.

"Madness you betray! This (lunatic) thing, how can you say? Our mighty dam (glorious to see and smell) must fall? For what reason, if our (illicit) existence on Jijo be already known?"

Jop explained, "True, we can't hide our crime of colonization. But we *can* start the process of removing our works from this scarred world. By showing our good intentions, we'll prove we merit leniency.

"What we must *not* do—and I fear our sages may be fooled—is offer any cooperation to these humans who pretend to be gene raiders. No bribes or service, since that, too, must be part of the test."

Ulgor snorted doubt. "And fossivility three? What if they turn out to ve felons, after all?"

Jop had shrugged. "Then the same answer holds. Passive resistance. Fade into the countryside. Tear down our cities—"

"Burn the libraries," Sara cut in, and Jop glanced her way, then nodded, curtly.

"Above all else. They are the roots of conceit. Our outrageous pretense at remaining civilized." He waved around him at the old Buyur chamber that had been converted to a tavern, the soot-stained walls adorned with spears, shields, and other souvenirs of the bloody siege of Tarek Town. "Civilized!" Jop laughed again. "We're like parrot-ticks, reciting verses we do not understand, pathetically miming the ways of the mighty. If pirates have indeed come, such vanities can only lessen our skill at burrowing down. Our only chance of survival will be to blend in with Jijo's animals. To *become* the innocents that glavers are, in their blessed salvation. A salvation we might have achieved by now, had humans not foiled nature with our so-called Great Printing.

"So you see it does not matter," he concluded with a shrug of finality. "Whether the visitors from space are noble chancellors from the Institute of Migration or the foulest criminals to prowl space. Either way, they are our judgment, come at last. Our sole option remains the same."

Shaking her head in bemusement, Sara had commented, "You're starting to sound like Lark."

But Jop saw nothing ironic in that. His radicalization had intensified each day since the deafening, terrifying specter shook the tree farms, leaving trails of noise and heat that seared the sky.

"This is a bad thing," Blade had said to Sara, later that evening, after Jop left to meet friends and fellow believers. "He seems sure of his reasoning and virtue—like a gray queen, unshakably convinced of her righteousness."

"Self-righteousness is a plague that afflicts all races, except the traeki," answered Fakoon, bowing two stalks toward Pzora. "Your folk are lucky to be spared the curse of egotism."

The Dolo Village pharmacist had vented a soft sigh. "i/we urge you to make no simple assumptions, dear comrades. It is said that we, too, once possessed that talent, whose partner is the gift/curse of ambition. To excise it from our natures meant leaving behind some of our greatest treasures, our finest rings. It must not have been an easy thing to do.

"One of the things we/i fear most about restored contact with Galactics is something you other species and beings may not understand—we fear temptation by an enticing offer.

"We fear an offer to be made whole."

• • •

The clinic was a place of wheels—of g'Kek surgeons and patients on push-chairs. Many of the traeki pharmacists used skooter-wagons, pushing along faster than most could walk alone. No wonder the smooth planarity of city life appealed to two of the Six.

The Stranger's room was on the fifth floor, looking out across the confluence of the rivers Roney and Bibur. Both steam ferries could be seen moored under screening arbors, now operating only at night, since vigilante groups had threatened to burn them if they budged by day. And this morning confirming word came down from the Glade. The High Sages, too, wanted no unnecessary signs of technology revealed by the Six. *Destroy nothing. Conceal everything.*

It only added to a growing sense of confusion among common folk. Was this Judgment Day or not? Sounds of raucous argument were heard in all parts of town. *We need some goal to unite us,* Sara thought, *or we'll start coming apart, skin and pelt, shell and spokes.*

A traeki attendant motioned Sara through to the private chamber that had been given the Stranger. The dark man looked up when she entered, and smiled with clear delight to see her. He laid aside a pencil and pad of pale paper, on which Sara glimpsed the scene outside the window—one of the steam ferries, outlined with subtle countershading. Pinned to the wall was another sketch depicting the shipboard concert on the fantail of the *Hauph-woa,* capturing a gentle interlude amid the storm of crisis.

"Thank you for coming," said an elderly, sallow-faced woman seated by the Stranger's bedside, looking surprisingly like a g'Kek, in coloration, her startling blue eyes, and also the way a wheelchair framed her blanket-shrouded form. "We have been making progress, but there are some things I wanted to try only after you arrived."

Sara still wondered why Ariana Foo, of all people, had taken an interest in the wounded man. With Lester Cambel and most other sages away, she was the highest ranking human savant left this side of Biblos. One might expect her to have more urgent things on her mind right now, than focusing her keen intellect on the problem of the Stranger's origins.

The g'Kek doctor rolled forward, his voice mellow, with a cultured accent.

"First, Sara, please tell us—have you recalled anything further about our patient's aspect, the day you pulled him from the swamp all burned and torn?"

She shook her head silently.

"His clothing, none was recovered?"

"There were a few scraps, mostly charred. We threw them out while treating his burns."

"Did those scraps go to dross barrels?" he asked eagerly. "Those very barrels aboard the *Hauph-woa* right now?"

"There were no ornaments or buttons, if that's what you're looking for. The scraps went to recycling, which in the case of old cloth means going straight to my father's pulping machine. Would they have helped?"

"Perhaps," answered the old woman, clearly disappointed. "We try to consider all possibilities."

The Stranger's hands lay folded on his lap, and his eyes darted back and forth, focusing on faces as if he were fascinated not by words but the sounds themselves.

"Can"—she swallowed—"can you do anything for him?"

"That depends," the doctor replied. "All burns and contusions are healing well. But our finest unguents are useless against structural damage. Our enigmatic guest has lost part of his left temporal lobe, as though it had been torn out by some horrid predator. I am sure you know this area is where you humans process speech."

"Is there any chance—"

"Of recovering what he has lost?" A g'Kek shrug, twining two eyestalks, had never became fashionable among the other races. "If he were very young or female, there might be some transfer of speech facility to the *right* lobe. A few stroke victims do this. But the feat is rare for adult males, whose brain structures are more rigid, alas."

The light in the dark Stranger's eyes was deceptive. He smiled amiably, as if they were discussing the weather. His reliable cheerfulness tore at Sara's heart.

"Nothing can be done?"

"Out in the Galaxy, perhaps."

It was an old expression, almost habitual, whenever one hit the limits of the crude arts available on the Slope.

"But we can do no more. Not in *this* place."

There was something in the doctor's tone. All four eyes stared inward—as if a human being were studying his fingernails, waiting for someone else to say the unspoken. Sara looked to Ariana Foo, whose face was composed.

Too composed. Sara leaped on the doctor's hanging implication.

"You can't be serious."

The sage briefly closed her eyes. When they reopened, there was a daring glitter.

"Word comes down that our invaders are plying mass opinion, winning converts with drugs, potions, and miracle cures. Already, unsanctioned caravans of the sick and lame have set out from Tarek and other sites, hobbling up the hard trails in desperate search of remedies. I admit, the thought even crossed *my* mind." She lifted her stick-thin arms from her fragile body. "Many may die on the trek, but what matters such risk against the lure of hope?"

Sara paused. "Do you think the outsiders can help him?"

Ariana shrugged in the hoonish manner, with a puff of air in her cheeks. "Who can say? Frankly, I doubt even Galactics could repair such damage. But they may have palliatives to improve his lot. Anyway, all bets are off if my suspicion is true."

"What suspicion?"

"That our Stranger is no poor savage at all."

Sara stared, then blinked. *"Ifni,"* she breathed.

"Indeed." Ariana Foo nodded. "Shall we see if our guest truly was delivered to us by our goddess of luck and change?"

Sara could barely manage a nod. While the old woman rummaged in her valise, Sara pondered. *This must be why everyone was in awe of her, when she was chief human sage before Cambel. They say genius is a knack for seeing the obvious. Now I know it's true.*

How could I have been so blind!

Ariana took up several of the sheets recently copied on Engril's machine. "I thought of asking a Sensitive to sit in, but if I am right, we'll want this kept quiet. So we'll make do by watching how he reacts. Note that he is probably the only person in Tarek Town who has not seen these yet. Everybody pay close attention, please."

She rolled closer to the patient, who watched attentively as Ariana laid a single sheet on the coverlet.

His smile gradually thinned as he picked up the drawing, touching the fine expert lines. Mountains framed a bowllike vale littered with shattered trees—nest lining for a thick javelin, adorned with jutting spines, whose contours Sara had first seen hurtling above her shaken home. Fingertips traced the sloping curves, trembling. The smile was gone, replaced by a look of agonized perplexity. Sara sensed that he was trying to *remember* something. Clearly there was familiarity here, and more, much more.

The Stranger looked up at Ariana Foo, eyes filled with pain and questions he could not pose.

"What can this prove?" Sara asked, writhing inside.

"He finds the image of the ship troubling," Ariana answered.

"As it would any thoughtful member of the Six," Sara pointed out.

The older woman nodded. "I had expected a happier response."

"You think he's one of *them,* don't you?" Sara asked. "You think he *crashed* into the swamp east of Dolo, aboard some kind of flying machine. He's a Galactic. A criminal."

"It seemed the simplest hypothesis, given the coincidence in timing—a total stranger, burned amid a humid swamp, appearing with injuries unlike anything our doctors have seen. Let's try another one."

The next sketch showed the same little valley, but with the starship replaced by what the sages called a "research station," assigned the task of analyzing Jijoan life. The Stranger peered at the black cube, intrigued and perhaps a little frightened.

Finally, Ariana presented a drawing showing two figures with strong, confident faces. A pair who had come a hundred thousand light-years to plunder.

This time a sharp gasp escaped him. The Stranger stared at the human forms, touching the symbol-patches on their one-piece exploration suits. It did not require fey sensitivity to read despair in his eyes. With an incoherent cry, he crumpled the sketch and flung it across the room, then covered his eyes with an arm.

"Interesting. *Very* interesting," Ariana murmured.

"I fail to understand," the doctor sighed. "Does this mean he is from off-Jijo or not?"

"It is too soon to tell, I fear." She shook her head. "But let's say it turns out he *is* from the Five Galaxies? If the forayers are seeking a mislaid confederate, and we have him in hand to offer in trade, it might work to our advantage."

"Now just a darn—" Sara began, but the older human only continued, thinking aloud.

"Alas, his reaction isn't one I'd call *eager* to be reunited with lost comrades. Do you think he might be an escaped foe? That somehow he survived imprisonment, even attempted murder, just a day or so before the foray ship came down to land? If so, how ironic his particular injury, which prevents him from telling so much! I wonder if *they* did it to him . . . the way barbaric kings of old Earth used to rip out an enemy's tongue. How horrible, if true!"

The range of possibilities rattled off by the sage left Sara momentarily stunned. There was a long stretch of silence, until the doctor spoke once more.

"Your speculations intrigue and terrify me, old friend.

Yet now I must ask that you not agitate my patient further."

But Ariana Foo only shook her head in somber pondering. "I had thought to send him up to the Glade right away. Let Vubben and the others decide for themselves what to do next."

"*Indeed?* I could never allow you to move one so seriously—"

"Of course an opportunity to offer him Galactic-level treatment of his injuries would make a fine synergy, combining pragmatism with kindness."

The g'Kek medic's oral flap opened and shut soundlessly, as he worked to find a way past Ariana's logic. Finally, his stalks contracted unhappily.

The retired sage sighed. "Alas, the point seems moot. From what we've seen, I doubt very much that our guest here will be willing to go."

Sara was about to tell the old woman where *she* could go, with her intent to meddle in a man's life. But just then the subject of their deliberations lowered his arm. He looked at Ariana and Sara. Then he picked up one of the sketches.

"G-guh . . . ?" He swallowed, and his brow furrowed with intense concentration.

All eyes stared back at him. The man lifted one of the drawings, showing the starship nestled in a bower of shattered trees. He stabbed the scene with his index finger.

"G-g-g-oh!"

Then he looked into Sara's eyes, pleadingly. His voice dropped to a whisper.

"*Go.*"

After that, discussion of Sara's plan seemed almost anticlimactic. *I won't be going back to Dolo on the next boat, after all. I'm on my way to see the aliens.*

Poor Father. All he ever wanted was to raise a gaggle of safe little papermakers. Now every heir goes rushing into danger's pincers, just as fast as our legs can carry us!

Engril and Bloor, the portraitist, arrived, bearing portable tools of their trades.

Bloor was a short, fair-skinned man with ringlets of yellow hair showering over his shoulders. His hands were stained blotchy from years creating the delicate emulsions required by his art. He held up a plate of metal, as wide as his palm, which shimmered with finely etched lines and depressions. From certain angles, those acid-cut shapes coalesced to form sharp profiles of shadow and light.

"It's called the *Daguerre* process," he explained. "Actually, it is quite a simple technique for creating permanent images. One of the first methods of photography ever invented by wolfling humans, back on Old Earth. Or so say our reference books. We don't employ the procedure for portraits nowadays, as paper is faster and safer."

"And paper decays," Ariana Foo added, turning the plate over in her hands. Depicted on the etched metal was an urrish warrior of high rank, with both husbands perched on her back in a formal pose. The female's sinuous neck was painted with garish, zigzag stripes, and she held a large crossbow, as if cradling a beloved scent-daughter.

"Indeed." The portraitist conceded. "The fine papers produced by Sara's father are guaranteed to corrupt in less than a century, leaving no traces to betray our descendants. This sample daguerreotype is one of only a few not sent to the dross middens since our strengthened Commons started promoting wider respect for the Law. I have special permission to hold on to this excellent example. See the fine detail? It dates from before the third urrish-human war. The subject is a chieftain of the Sool tribes, I believe. Note the tattoo scars. Marvelous. As crisp and clear as the day it was taken."

Sara leaned forward as Ariana passed the slim plate over. "Has anyone used this process on Jijo since then?"

Bloor nodded. "All members of my guild create one

daguerreotype, as part of our master work. Nearly all are then sent to the Midden, or given to smiths for remelting, but the capability remains." He lifted a satchel, causing a faint clinking of bottles. "There's enough acid and fixative here to treat and develop several dozen plates—but I have only about twenty of the plates themselves. If we want more, they must be ordered from Ovoom Town, or one of the volcano smithies."

Sara felt a tap on her shoulder and turned to see the Stranger holding out his hand. She gave him the small photograph, and he traced the finely etched grooves with his fingertips.

Now that her mind had shifted to encompass Ariana's theory, everything the wounded man did seemed to refract differently. Was he smiling now over the crudeness of this photographic technology, or expressing enchantment at its cleverness? Or was the sparkling delight in his eyes a reaction to the depicted image of a savage warrior, whose bow and lance had been such a scourge during that age of heroic struggle, ten generations ago?

Ariana Foo rubbed her chin. "Twenty plates. Let's say you get good pictures with just half—"

"A generous estimate, my sage, since the technique requires long exposure times."

Ariana grunted. "A half-dozen successes, then. And several must be handed over to the forayers, in order for a threat to be believable."

"Copies can be made," Engril put in.

"We won't need copies," Sara said. "They'll *have* to assume we have plenty of others. The crucial point is, can these pictures last a million years?"

The portraitist blew at a strand of yellow hair. From his throat, there emerged a soft strangling sound, like a qheuen sigh. "Given the right storage conditions, this metal oxidizes a nice protective layer. . . ." He laughed nervously, looking from Sara to Ariana. "You aren't *serious,* are you? A bluff is one thing. We're desperate enough to clutch at straws, but do you *really* imagine you can store evidence somewhere until the next Galactic survey?"

The g'Kek doctor twisted two eyestalks to stare in opposite directions. "It appears we have entered into entirely new realms of heresy."

A_{SX}

IT MAY HAVE BEEN A MISTAKE TO HAVE STRIVEN SO hard to suppress psi powers among the Six.

For most of the long millennia of our exile, it seemed the wisest move. Was not our greatest goal to remain hidden? We had only to build modestly, in harmony with nature, and let the inverse square law do the rest.

But psi channels are fey, nonlinear. Or so say books printed by the humans, who admit that their kind knew little about the subject when their ancestors fled this way.

When the Holy Egg first gave us rewq, some among the Six feared the symbionts worked by psi, which might make our fugitive enclave more detectable. Despite satisfying proof it is not so, that old slander has now returned, once more stirring friction among us.

Some even contend that the Holy Egg *itself* may have attracted our ruin! After all, why do pirates come *now,* a mere century after the blessed day the Egg emerged? Others point out that we might by now know much more about our invaders, if only we had bred adepts of our own, instead of the few sensitives and truth-scryers we have today.

Regret is a silly, useless thing. i might as well pine for the rings our ancestors were said to have abandoned, simply because those toroids were tainted with sin.

Oh, how many things the legends say those rings once let us do! To run before the wind, as fleet as any urs. To swim like qheuens and walk beneath the sea. To touch and handle the world at all levels of its grainy texture. Above all, to face this dire, dread-filled universe with a self-centered confidence that was utterly, biologically se-

rene. No uncertainty to plague our complex community
of selves. Only the towering egotism of a central, confident "I."

Dwer

THE BLUE QHEUENS OF THE MOUNTAINS HAD DIF-
ferent traditions than their cousins who lived behind
mighty Dolo Dam. Molting rituals back home always
seemed informal. Human youngsters from the nearby
village ran free with their chitinous friends, while grown-
ups shared nectar-beer and celebrated the coming-of-
age of a new generation.

In this alpine sanctuary, the chants and hissing rituals
felt more solemn. Guests included the local g'Kek doctor, some traeki gleaners, and a dozen human neighbors,
who took turns at a warped window pane, to view
events in the larva creche next door. The hoons who
fished the lake behind the dam had sent the usual regrets. Most hoon felt incurably squeamish toward the
qheuen way of reproduction.

Dwer was here out of gratitude. If not for this kindly
hive, he might be flexing stumps instead of a nearly full
set of fingers and toes, still tender but recovering. The
occasion also came as a break from tense preparations
with Danel Ozawa. When beckoned to the window by
Carving Tongue, the local matriarch, Dwer and Danel
bowed to the matriarch, and to the human tutor, Mister
Shed.

"Congratulations to you both," Ozawa said. "May you
have a fine clutch of graduates."

"Thank you, honored sage." Carving Tongue's
breathy sigh seemed edgy. As head female, she laid
more than half the eggs. Many of the throbbing shapes
next door would be her offspring, preparing to emerge
at last. After waiting twenty years or more, some strain
was expected.

Mister Shed had no genetic investment in the young

qheuens transforming next door, but anxiety wrote across the instructor's gaunt face.

"Yes, a fine clutch. Several will make excellent senior students, when their shells harden and they take names."

Carving Tongue added—"Two are already precocious chewers of wood—though I believe our tutor refers to other talents."

Mister Shed nodded. "There is a school downslope, where local tribes send their brightest kids. Elmira should qualify, if she makes it through—"

The matriarch erupted a warning hiss. *"Tutor! Keep your private nicknames to yourself. Do not jinx the larvae on this sacred day!"*

Mister Shed swallowed nervously. *"Sorry, matron."* He rocked side to side, in the manner of a qheuen boy, caught stealing a crayfish from the hatchery ponds.

Fortunately, a traeki caterer arrived then with a cauldron of vel nectar. Humans and qheuens crowded the table. But Dwer saw that Ozawa felt as he did. Neither of them had time for a euphoric high. Not while preparing for a deadly serious mission.

Too bad, though, Dwer thought, noting how the traeki spiked each goblet with a race-specific spray from its chem-synth ring. Soon the mood in the chamber lightened as intoxicants flowed. Carving Tongue joined the throng at the cauldron, leaving the three humans alone by the window.

"That's it, my beauties. Do it gently," murmured the scholar contracted to teach qheuen children reading and math—a long patient task, given the decades larvae spent in one muddy suite, devouring wrigglers and slowly absorbing the mental habits of sapient beings. To Dwer's surprise, Mister Shed slipped a functioning rewq over his face. Lately, most of the symbionts had gone dormant, or even died.

Dwer peered through the window, a rippled convex lens with a broken stem in the middle. A greasy pool filled the center of the next room, which dim shapes traversed, casting left and right as if in nervous search.

Those may have been Mister Shed's beloved pupils a few days ago, and some would be again, after molting into adolescent qheuens. But this play hearkened back millions of years, to a time long before the patrons of the qheuen race meddled and reshaped them into starfarers. It had a bloody logic all its own.

"That's right, children, do it softly—"

Shed's hopeful sigh cut off with a yelp as the pond erupted in froth. Wormlike forms flipped out of the water in a thrashing tangle. Dwer glimpsed one shape that was already nearly five-sided, with three legs flailing under a glistening carapace of aquamarine. The new shell bore livid marks of recent raking. Trailing were tatters of white tissue, the larval body mass that must be sloughed.

Legend said that qheuens who still roamed the stars had ways to ease this transition—machines and artificial environments—but on Jijo, molting was much the same as when qheuens were clever animals, hunting the shallows of the world that gave them birth.

Dwer recalled running home in tears, the first time he saw a molting, seeking comfort and understanding from his older brother. Even then, Lark had been serious, learned, and a bit pedantic.

"Sapient races have many reproductive styles. Some focus all their effort on a few offspring, which are cherished from the start. Any good parent will die to save her child. Hoons and g'Keks are like humans in this so-called High-K approach.

"Urs breed much like fish in the sea—that's Low-K—casting hordes of offspring to live wild in the bush, until the survivors sniff their way back to blood relatives. Early human settlers thought the urrish way heartless, while many urs saw our custom as paranoid and maudlin.

"Qheuens fall in between. They care about their young but also know that many in each clutch must die, so that others can live. It's a sadness that lends poignancy to qheuen poetry. Truly, I think the wisest of them have a better grasp of life and death than any human ever could."

Sometimes Lark got carried away. Still, Dwer saw truth in what his brother said. Soon a new generation would shamble out of the humid nursery, to a world that would dry their shells and make them citizens. Or else no survivors would emerge at all. Either way, the bitter-sweetness was so intense, anyone wearing rewq, like Mister Shed, must be crazy or a masochist.

He felt a touch on his arm. Danel motioned—time to make a polite exit, before the rituals resumed. They had work, provisions and weapons to prepare, as well as the *Legacy* they were to take over the mountains.

This morning, Lena Strong had returned from the Glade with another young woman Dwer recognized with a wince—Jenin, one of the big, strapping Worley sisters—along with five donkey-loads of books, seeds, and ominous sealed tubes. He had been expecting Rety as well, but Lena reported that the sages wanted to talk to the sooner girl for a while longer.

No matter. With or without her as a guide, Dwer was ultimately responsible for getting the small expedition to its goal.

And once there? Would there be violence? Death? Or a brave beginning?

Sighing, Dwer turned to follow Ozawa.

Now we'll never know if Sara would've turned out to be right, or Lark. Whether the Six were bound on the Low Road, or the High.

From here on, it's all about survival.

Behind him, Mister Shed pressed both hands against the warped pane, his voice hoarse with anguish over small lives that were not his to adore or rightfully to mourn.

The Stranger

He wonders how he knows the thing he knows.

It used to be so easy, back when wisdom came in compact packages called words. Each one carried a range of meanings, subtly shaded and complex. Strung together, they conveyed a multitude of concepts, plans, emotions . . .

And lies.

He blinks as that one word comes slickly into mind, the way so many used to do. He rolls it around his tongue, recognizing both sound and meaning at the same time, and this brings on a wash of joy mixed with awe. Awe to imagine that he once did the same thing countless times during the span of any breath, knowing and using innumerable words.

He relishes this one, repeating it over and over.

Lies . . . lies . . . lies . . .

And the miracle redoubles as another, related word slips in—

Liars . . . liars . . .

On his lap he sees the crumpled sketch, now smoothed almost flat again, a detailed rendition of human figures with expressive faces, staring disdainfully past a multirace crowd of primitive beings. The newcomers wear uniforms with bright emblems he finds somehow familiar.

He used to know a name for people like this. A name—and reasons to avoid them.

So why had he been so eager to go see them, just a little while ago? Why so insistent? At the time it seemed as if *something welled up from deep inside him. An urgency. A need to travel, whatever the cost, to the far-off mountain glen shown in the drawing. To go confront those depicted on a rumpled sheet of off-white paper. The journey had seemed terribly important, though right now he cannot quite remember why.*

A cloudy haze covers most of his memory. Things that had waxed vivid during his delirium now can barely be glimpsed as fleeting images—

—like a star *that appears dwarfed by a surrounding* structure, *a made-thing consisting of countless angles and divided ledges, enclosing a reddish sun's brittle heat within a maze of plane surfaces.*

—or a world of water, where metal isles jut like mushrooms and the sea is a slow poison to touch.

—or one particular shallow place in space, far from the deep oases where life normally gathers. Nothing lives in that shoal, far beyond the shining spiral arm. Yet amid the strange flatness there clusters a vast formation of globelike forms, strangely bright, floating timelessly, resembling a fleet of moons. . . .

His mind flees from that last impression, reburying it with all the other half-real memories. Losing it along with his past, and almost certainly his future.

XIII. THE BOOK OF THE SEA

*Sapient beings are frequently tempted
to believe in purpose.
That they exist in the universe
for a reason.*

*To serve something greater—
—a race or clan,
—patrons or gods,
—or an esthetic aim.*

*Or else to seek individual goals—
—wealth and power,
—reproduction,
—or enhancement of a personal soul.*

*Deep Philosophers call this search for
purpose nothing more than vanity, a
frantic need to justify an inherited
drive to exist.*

*But why would our ancestors
have brought us here, so far from
race, clan, patrons, gods, or wealth or
power,
if not to serve a purpose higher than
all those things?*

—The Scroll of Contemplation

Alvin's Tale

ALWAYS THOUGHT MYSELF A CITY BOY. AFTER ALL,
Wuphon is the biggest port in the south, with almost a
thousand souls, if you include nearby farmers and
gleaners. I grew up around docks, warehouses, and
cargo hoists.

Still, the Deploying Derrick is really something. A
long, graceful shape made of hundreds of tubes of
reamed and cured boo, it was pieced together in a matter of days, crisscrossed and joined by a team of qheuen
carpenters, who listened politely each time Urdonnol
berated them for straying from the design illustrated on
page five hundred and twelve of her precious text, *Pre-
Contact Terran Machinery, Part VIII: Heavy Lifting
Without Gravitics*. Then, with a respectful spin of their
cupolas, the qheuens went back to lacing and gluing the
crane in their own way, applying lessons learned in real
life.

Urdonnol should be more flexible, I thought, watching
Uriel's humorless assistant grow ever more frustrated.
*True, the books hold great wisdom. But these guys aren't
exactly working with titanium here. We're castaways
who must adapt to the times.*

I was glad to see that our pal, *Ur-ronn,* seemed satisfied with the work so far, after peering and sniffing at
every brace, strut, and pulley. Still, I'd rather *Uriel* were
here, supervising as she had for the first two days, when
our group set up camp under the stark shadow of Terminus Rock. The master smith was a persnickety, demand-

ing taskmistress, often insisting a job be done over, and over again, till it was damn well perfect.

I guess we four *might* resent the bossy way she took over what used to be our own private project. But we didn't. Or not much. Her attention to detail was nerve-wracking, but each time Uriel finally admitted something was done right, my confidence rose a notch that we might actually come back alive. It came as a blow when she went away.

An urrish courier had raced into camp—breathless, exhausted, even *thirsty,* for Ifni's sake—holding an envelope for Uriel to snatch and tear open. On reading the message, she drew aside Tyug, the traeki, and whispered urgently. Then she galloped off, hurrying back toward her precious forge.

Since then, things didn't exactly fall apart. The plan moves ahead step by step. But I can't say our mood's quite the same. Especially after our first test dive near-to drowned the passenger.

By then the crane was a beautiful thing, a vaulting arm so graceful, you'd never guess sixteen steel bolts thick as my wrist anchored it to the ledge, hanging far over the deep blue waters of the Rift. A big drum carried more than thirty cables of Uriel's best hawser, all of it ending at our gray-brown vessel, which we named *Wuphon's Dream,* in hope of placating our parents—and those in the local community who think we're doing blasphemy.

Another derrick stands alongside the first, linked to an even bigger drum. This one doesn't have to carry the bathy's weight, but its job is just as vital—keeping a tangle-free length of double *hose* attached to our little craft, so that clean air goes in and bad air goes out. I never got a chance to ask what the hoses are made of, but it's much stronger than the stitched skink bladders we four had planned using, back when we started thinking about this adventure.

Uriel had made other changes—a big pressure regulator, high strain gaskets, and a pair of *eik lights* to cast bright beams down where sunshine never reaches.

Again, I wondered—where did all this stuff come from?

It surprised us that Uriel never messed much with the bathy itself—carved from a single hollowed-out garu trunk, with Ur-ronn's beautiful window sealed at one end. In front, we installed two hinged grabber arms that Ur-ronn copied out of a book. Our little craft also bore *wheels,* four in all, mounted so *Wuphon's Dream* might roll along the muddy sea bottom.

Even after being fitted with superwide treads, the wheels looked familiar. Especially to Huck. She had kept them as private mementos out of the wreckage of her home, back when her real g'Kek parents were killed in that awful avalanche. With typical grim humor, Huck named them Auntie Rooben, Uncle Jovoon Left, and Uncle Jovoon Right. The fourth one was simply Dad—till I made her stop the grisly joke and call them One through Four instead.

Using wheels would normally be impossible without Galactic technology. A turning axle would tear any gasket apart. But Huck's macabre stash of spare parts offered a solution. Those wondrous g'Kek magnetic hubs and motivator spindles can be placed on either side of the hull, without actually piercing the wood. Huck will steer the forward pair of wheels, while I'll use a rotary crank to power the driver pair in back.

Which covers all our jobs during a dive, except "Captain" Pincer-Tip, whose world of bright blue water we'll pass through on our way to depths no qheuen has seen since their sneakship sank, a thousand years ago. His place is right in the bubble nose, controlling the eik-lamps and shouting instructions how the rest of us are to steer and push or grab samples.

Why does *he* get to be in charge? Pincer surely never impressed anyone as the brightest member of our gang.

First, all this was his idea from the start. He hand—or rather mouth—carved most of the *Dream* all by himself, during scarce free time between school and day-work in the crustacean pens.

More important, if that beautiful window ever starts to

fail—or any of the other gaskets—he's the one least likely to panic when salt water starts spraying about the cabin. If that ever happens, it'll be up to Pincer to get the rest of us out somehow. We've all read enough sea and space tales to know *that's* a pretty good definition of a captain—the one you all better listen to when seconds count the difference 'tween life and death.

He'd have to wait awhile, though, before taking command. Our first test dive would have just one passenger, a volunteer who was literally "born" for the job.

That morning, Tyug, the traeki, laid a trail of scentomones to draw the little partial stack, Ziz, from its pen to where *Wuphon's Dream* waited, gleaming in the sunshine. Our good ship's hull of polished garuwood was so bright and lovely—too bad the open blue sky is normally taken as a bad omen.

So it seemed to the onlookers watching our crew from a nearby bluff. There were hoon from Wuphon Port, plus some local reds, and urs with caravan dust on their flanks, as well as three humans who must have come a hard three-day trek from The Vale—all of them with nothing better to do than trade hearsay about the starship, or ships, said to have landed up north. One rumor said everyone at the Glade was already dead, executed on the spot by vengeful Galactic judges. Another claimed the Holy Egg had wakened fully at last, and the lights some saw in the sky were the *souls* of those lucky enough to be at Gathering when the righteous of the Six were transformed and sent back as spirits to their ancient homes among the stars.

Shave my legs if some of the stories weren't beautiful enough to make me wish I'd made 'em up.

Not all the onlookers were protestors. Some came out of curiosity. Huck and I had some fun with Howerr-phuo, who is second nephew by adoption to the Mayor's junior half-mother, but who dropped out of school anyway, on account of he claimed not to like the way Mister Heinz smells. But everyone knows Howerr-phuo is lazy, and anyway, *he* shouldn't talk about the hygienic habits of *others*.

At one point Howerr slinked up to ask about the *Dream* and its mission. Nice polite questions, mind you. But he seemed to barely hear our answers.

Then he sort of eased over to asking questions about *traekis,* gesturing over at Tyug, who was feeding Ziz in ers pen.

True, we have a pharmacist in Wuphon Town, but still there's some mystery about the ringed ones. Sure enough, Huck and I soon got the gist of what Howerr-phuo was going on about. He and some of his backwash friends had a wager going, about *traeki sex life,* and he'd been elected to run the matter past *us,* as local experts!

Sharing a wink, Huck and I quickly emptied his head of all the nonsense it had been stuffed with—then proceeded to fill it back up with our own imaginative version. Howerr soon looked like a sailor who just had a loose tackle-pulley carom off his skull. Glancing furtively at his feet, he hurried off—no doubt to check for "ring spores," lest he start growing little traekis in places where he'd been neglectful about washing.

I don't feel much guilt over it. Anyone standing downwind from Howerr-phuo, from now on, oughta thank us.

I was going to ask Huck if we were ever that dumb—then I recalled. Didn't *she* once convince me that a g'Kek can manage to be her own mother *and* father? I swear, she had made it sound plausible at the time, though for the life of me, I still can't figure out how.

For the first couple of days, the spectators mostly lurked beyond a line in the sand, drawn by Uriel with her sage's baton. No one said much while the master smith was around. But after she left, some took to yelling slogans, mostly objecting that the Midden is sacred, not a place for conceited gloss-addicts to go sight-seeing. Once the Vale humans arrived, the protests got better organized, with banners and slogans chanted in unison.

I found it pretty exciting, like a scene from *Summer of Love* or *Things to Come,* all full of righteous dissent for a cause. To a humicker like me, nothing could be more buff than forging ahead with an adventure *against* popular opinion. Seems nearly all the romantic tales I've read were about intrepid heroes persisting despite the doubts of stick-in-the-mud parents, neighbors, or authority figures. It reminded me of the book my nickname comes from—where the people of Diaspar try to keep Alvin from making contact with their long-lost cousins in faraway Lys. Or when the Lysians don't want him going back home with news of their rediscovered world.

Yeah, I know that's fiction, but the connection stoked my resolve. Huck and Ur-ronn and Pincer-Tip said they all felt the same.

As for the mob, well, I know that folks who're scared can get unreasonable. I even tried once or twice to see it from their point of view. Really, I did.

Boy, what a bloat-torus of jeekee, Ifni-slucking skirls. Hope they all sit on bad mulch and get spin vapors.

XIV. THE BOOK OF THE SLOPE

Legends

It is said that humans on Earth spent untold generations living in brute fear, believing a myriad things that no *sensible* person would ever imagine. Certainly not anyone who had been handed truth on a silver platter—the way it was given to nearly every sapient race in the Five Galaxies.

Earthlings had to figure it all out for themselves. Slowly, agonizingly, humans learned how the universe worked, abandoning most of the fanciful beliefs they carried through their long, dark loneliness. This included belief in—

—the divine right of egotistical kings,

—the mental incapacity of women,

—the idea that a wise *state* knows all,

—the idea that the *individual* is always right,

—the sick-sweet addiction that transforms a doctrine from a mere model of the world into something sacred, worth killing for.

These and many other wild concepts eventually joined pixies and ufos in the trunk where humans finally put away such childish things.

A very large trunk.

Even so, the newly contacted Galactics saw Earthlings as superstitious primitives, as *wolflings*, prone to weird enthusiasms and peculiar, unprovable convictions.

How ironic, then, is the role reversal that we see on *Jijo*, where Earthlings found the other five far regressed down a road humans had traveled before, wallowing in a myriad of fables, fantasies, grudges, and vividly absurd notions. To this maelstrom of superstition, settlers fresh off the *Tabernacle* contributed more than paper books. They also brought tools of logic and verification—the very things Earthlings had to fight hardest to learn, back home.

Moreover, with their own history in mind, Earthlings became voracious *collectors* of folklore, fanning out among the other five to copy down every tale, every belief, even those they demonstrated to be false.

Out of their wolfling past came this strange mixture—reasoning skepticism, plus a deep *appreciation* of the peculiar, the bizarre, the extravagantly vivid.

Amid the darkness, humans know

that it is all too easy to lose your way,
if you forget how to tell what is true.

But it is just as urgent never to let
go of the capacity to dream. To weave
the illusions that help us all make it
through this dark, dark night.

—from *The Art of Exile,*
by Auph-hu-Phwuhbhu

Asx

THE TINY ROBOT WAS A WONDER TO BEHOLD. NO larger than a g'Kek's eyeball, it lay pinned down to the ground by a horde of attacking *privacy wasps*, covered by their crowded fluttering wings.

Lester was the first sage to comment, after the initial surprise.

"Well, now we know why they're called *privacy wasps*. Did you see the way they swarmed over that thing? Otherwise, we'd never have known it was there."

"A device for spying," surmised Knife-Bright Insight, tipping her carapace to get a closer look at the machine. "Minuscule and mobile, sent to listen in on our council. We would have been helpless, all our plans revealed, if not for the wasps."

Phwhoon-dau concurred with a deep umble.

"Hr-rm. . . . We are used to seeing the insects as minor irritants, their presence required by tradition for certain ceremonies. But the Buyur must have designed the wasps for just such a purpose. To patrol their cities and homes, thwarting would-be eavesdroppers."

"Using a (specifically) designed life-form to deal with the (annoying) threat—indeed, that would have been the Buyur way," added Ur-Jah.

Lester leaned close to peer at the wasps, whose wings rippled in front of the robot's tiny eyes, beating a maze of colors that reminded me/us of rewq.

"I wonder what the wasps are showing it," murmured our human sage.

Then Vubben spoke for the first time since the wasps attacked the intruder.

"Probably exactly what it *wants* to see," he suggested confidently.

Do you recall, my rings, how we all nodded, sighed, or umbled respectful agreement? Vubben spoke the words so well, in such tones of wise credibility. Only later did it occur to we/us to ask ourselves—

What?

What in the world could he possibly mean by that?

Lark

DURING TWO THOUSAND YEARS OF ILLICIT SET-tlement, Lark was hardly the first member of the Six to fly. He wasn't even the first human.

Soon after the sneakship *Tabernacle* sank forever into the Midden's sucking embrace, men and women used to soar like kites, riding steady offshore winds from the blue ocean all the way to the white peaks of the Rimmer Range. Back in those days, lacy airfoils used to catch sky-currents, lofting brave pilots to survey their new world from above.

The last silky glider now lay under glass in a Biblos museum, a wonder to behold, made of the mystical materials *monomolecular carbon* and *woven stress polymer,* which the brightest wizards of the Chemists' Guild could not reproduce today, even if the sages allowed it. Time and mishaps eventually smashed all the others, leaving later human generations to walk the heavy ground like everybody else, and erasing one more cause of jealousy among the Six—though lately, since the Great Peace, groups of ambitious youths had resumed a crude version of the pastime, occasionally risking their lives on spindly frames of hollow boo, covered with hand-woven sheets of wic-cotton. Or else urrish middlings rode bulging *balloons,* wafting upward on puffs of torrid air. Sometimes success caused a local sensation, but none of the efforts had much lasting effect. Available materials were too heavy, weak, or porous. The wind was much too strong.

Some, with ardent piety, claimed this was a good thing. The sky was not where redemption would be found. Nor in clinging to vanities of the past. Lark normally agreed with the orthodox view, but in this case, he mused—

Such a modest dream. To waft a few leagues through the lower air. Is that so much to ask, when once we had the stars?

He was never one to waste time on idle fancies, though. Certainly Lark never expected *personally* to spy down on Jijo's mountains from a great height.

But look at me now!

Ling had clearly enjoyed watching his expression, when she told him of today's plan.

"We'll be gone most of the day, to pick up some specimens our robots have snared. Later, as the drones roam farther afield, we'll go for trips of several days at a time."

Lark had stared at the alien flying machine, a slender arrow with stubby wings that unfolded after it exited a narrow tunnel from the buried research station. The hatch gaped like a pair of hungry jaws.

How like Ling to spring this on him without warning!

While Besh loaded supplies, the big blond man, Kunn, shouted, "Come on, Ling! We're running late. Coax your pet aboard or get another."

Lark set his jaw, determined to show no emotion as he followed her up a ramp. He expected a cave-like interior, but it turned out to be more brightly lit than any enclosed space he'd ever seen. There was no need to let his eyes adapt.

Not wanting to gawk like a yokel, he aimed for a padded seat next to a window and dropped his pack nearby. Lark sat down gingerly, finding the voluptuous softness neither comfortable *nor* comforting. It felt as if he had settled onto the lap of something fleshy and perhaps queerly amorous. Moments later, Ling added to his unease by strapping a belt across his waist. The hissing closure of the metal hatch made his ears feel funny, increasing his disorientation. The moment the engines came on, Lark felt a strange tickling at the base of his neck, as if a small animal were breathing on the hairs back there. He could not help lifting a hand to brush away at the imaginary creature.

Takeoff was surprisingly gentle, a wafting motion, rising and turning, then the sky-boat swept away so quickly that he had no chance to survey the Glade and its surroundings, or to seek the hidden valley of the Egg. By the time he turned around to press close against the window, the continent was already sweeping underneath as they hurtled southward, many times faster than a catapulted stone. Only minutes later, they dropped away from the alpine hills, streaking over a wide-open plain of steppe grass, which bowed and rippled like the ever-changing surface of a phosphorescent sea. At one point, Lark spotted a drove of galloping stem-chompers, a genus of native Jijoan ungulates, which trumpeted distress and reared away from the airboat's passing shadow. A band of urrish herders stretched their sinuous necks in expressions of curiosity mixed with dread. Near the adults, a group of early middlings gamboled and snapped in mock battle, ignoring their elders' sudden, dark focus on the heavens.

"Your enemies certainly are graceful creatures," Ling commented.

Lark turned and stared at her. *What's she going on about now?*

Ling must have misinterpreted his look, hurrying as if to placate. "Of course I mean that in a strictly limited sense, the way a horse or other animal can be graceful."

Lark pondered before answering. "Hrm. It's too bad your visit disrupted Gathering. We'd normally be having the Games about now. That's when you'd see real grace in action."

"Games? Oh, yes. Your version of the fabled Olympics. Lots of running and jumping around, I suppose?"

He nodded guardedly. "There are speed and agility

events. Others let our best and bravest test their endurance, courage, adaptability."

"All traits highly prized by those who brought humanity into being," Ling said. Her smile was indulgent, faintly condescending. "I don't imagine any of the six species go up against each other *directly* in any events, do they? I mean, it's hard to picture a g'Kek outrunning an urs, or a qheuen doing a pole vault!" She laughed.

Lark shrugged. Despite Ling's hint regarding a subject of great moment—the question of human origins—he found himself losing interest in the conversation.

"Yes, I suppose it could be. Hard. To picture."

He turned to look back out the window, watching the great plain sweep by—wave after wave of bending grass, punctuated by stands of dark boo or oases of gently swaying trees. A distance requiring several days to cross by caravan was dismissed in a few brief duras of blithe flight. Then the smoldering mountains of the southern range swarmed into view.

Besh, the forayer pilot, banked the craft to get a closer look at Blaze Mountain, circling at an angle so that Lark's window stared vertiginously on a vast lava apron where past eruption layers spilled across a country that was both ravaged and starkly renewed. For an instant, he glimpsed the smelters that lay clustered halfway up the mighty eminence. Fashioned to resemble native magma tubes and floes, the forge vented steam and smoke no different from that exhaled by nearby wild apertures. Of course, the camouflage was never meant to endure scrutiny as close as this.

Lark saw Besh share a knowing glance with Kunn, who tapped one of his magical viewing screens. Out of several score glowing red lights, outlining the mountain's shape, *one* was marked by sharp symbols and glowing arrows. Dotted lines traced underground passages and workrooms where famed urrish smiths labored to make tools out of those special alloys sanctioned by the sages, second in quality only to those produced farther south, near the peak of towering Mount Guenn.

Incredible, Lark thought, trying to memorize the level of detail shown on Kunn's screen, for his report to Lester Cambel. Clearly that monitor had little to do with the ostensible purpose of this mission—scouting for advanced "candidate" life-forms. From a few brief exchanges, Lark reckoned Kunn was no biologist. Something in the man's stance, his way of moving, reminded one of Dwer stalking through a forest, only *more* deadly. Even after generations of relative tranquillity, a few men and women on the Slope still carried themselves like that, experts whose chief job was to circulate each summer from village to village, training local human militias.

Just in case.

Each of the other five races had similar specialists. A prudent policy, since even now there were regular minor crises—a criminal act here, a wayward tribe of sooners there, and spates of hot-tempered friction between settlements. Enough to make "peacetime warrior" no contradiction in terms.

The same *might* also be true of Kunn. Looking lethally competent didn't mean he was coiled, preparing to wreak murder.

What's your purpose, Kunn? Lark wondered, watching symbols flash across the screen, crisscrossing reflections of the outlander's face. *What, exactly, are you looking for?*

Blaze Mountain fell behind them as the little vessel now seemed to leap ahead at a new angle, spearing across a brilliant whiteness known as the Plain of Sharp Sand. For a long time, low dunes swept past, undulating in windswept perfection. Lark saw no caravans laboring across the sparkling desert, carrying mail or trade goods to isolated settlements of The Vale. But then, no one sane ranged those searing wastes by day. There were hidden shelters down there, where travelers awaited nightfall, which even Kunn's rays shouldn't be able to pick out, amid the glaring immensity.

That pale dazzle was nothing compared to the *next* sudden transition, crossing over from the sand ocean to the Spectral Flow, a blurry expanse of shifting colors that made Lark's eyes sting. Ling and Besh tried to peer at it past their sheltering hands, before finally giving up, while Kunn muttered sourly at the static on his display. Lark struggled against a natural reflex to squint, endeavoring instead to *loosen* his habitual way of focusing. Dwer had once explained that it was the only way to let oneself see in this realm where exotic crystals cast an ever-changing wildness of luminance.

That had been shortly after Dwer won master hunter status, when he hurried home to join Lark and Sara at their mother's bedside, during the illness that finally took her away, turning Nelo almost overnight into an old man. Melina accepted no food during that final week, and very little drink. Of her two eldest, whose minds she had doted on, day in, day out, ever since arriving in Dolo to be a papermaker's wife, she now seemed to need nothing. But from her youngest child, she devoured tales of his wanderings, the sights, sounds, and sensations of far corners of the Slope where few ever trod. Lark recalled feeling a jealous pang when he saw the contentment Dwer's stories gave in her last hours, then chiding himself for having such unworthy thoughts.

That memory swept over him starkly, apparently triggered by the stabbing colors.

Some credulous folk among the Six said these layers of poison stone had magical properties, poured into them by aeons of overlapping volcanic effusions. "Mother Jijo's blood," they called it. At that moment, Lark could almost credit the superstition, so struck was he by uncanny waves of *familiarity*. As if he had been here before, sometime long ago.

With that thought, his eyes seemed to adjust—to *open up,* letting the muddle of swirling hues blossom into mirage canyons, figment valleys, ghost cities, and even whole phantom civilizations, vaster than the greatest Buyur sites. . . .

Then, just as he was starting to enter fully into the experience, the blur of illusion suddenly ended, cut off as the Spectral Flow plunged into the sea. Besh banked the craft again, and soon the sweeping domain of color vanished like a dream, replaced on the left by a more normal desert of windswept igneous rock.

The line of crashing surf became like a fabled highway, pointing toward lands unknown. Lark fumbled to unfasten his seat belt, moving across the aisle to stare over the great ocean. *So vast,* he thought. Yet this was nothing compared to the immensities Ling and her comrades spanned with hardly a thought. His eyes peered in hopes of spotting a camouflaged dross-hauler, its graygreen sails slicing the wind, bearing sacred caskets to their final rest. From this height, he might even glimpse the Midden itself, dark blue waters-of-forgetfulness covering a plunge so deep that its trench could take all the arrogant excesses of a dozen mighty civilizations and still bless them with a kind of absolution—oblivion.

They had already dashed beyond the farthest of Lark's lifetime travels, seeking data for his ever-hungry charts. Even looking with a practiced eye, he found few scattered traces of sapient habitation—a hoonish fishing hamlet, a red qheuen rookery—tucked under rocky clefts or bayou-root canopies. Of course, at this speed something important might sweep by in the time it took to switch windows, which he did frequently as Besh rolled the craft, playing instruments across both shore and sea.

Even those few signs of settlement ceased when they reached the Rift, crossing a few hundred arrowflights west of the distant, hatchet-shape of Terminus Rock.

A series of towering cliffs and deep subsea canyons split the land here. Jagged promontories alternated with seemingly bottomless fingers of dark sea, as if some great claw had gouged parallel grooves almost due east, to form a daunting natural barrier. Dwelling beyond this border labeled you an outlaw, cursed by the sages and by the Holy Egg. But the alien flier made quick work of the realm of serrated clefts and chasms, dismissing them like minor ruts across a well-traveled road.

League after league of sandy scrublands soon passed by, punctuated at long intervals by stark fragments of ancient cities, eroded by wind, salt, and rain. Explosions and pulverizing rays must have shattered the mighty towers, just after the last Buyur tenant turned off the lights. In time, the ceaseless churning of the Midden and its daughter volcanoes would grind even these sky-stabbing stumps to nothing.

Soon the sky-boat left the continent altogether, streaking over chains of mist-shrouded isles.

Even Dwer never dreamed of going this far.

Lark decided not to mention this trip to the lad without discussing it first with Sara, who understood tact and hurt feelings better than either brother.

Then reality hit home. *Sara's back in Dolo. Dwer may be sent off east, hunting glavers and sooners. And when the aliens finish their survey, we all may meet our end, far from those we love.*

Lark sank into his seat with a sigh. For a while there, he had actually been enjoying himself. *Damn* memory, for reminding him the way things were!

For the rest of the trip he kept low-key and business-like, even when they finally landed near forests eerily different from those he knew, or while helping Ling haul aboard cages filled with strange, marvelous creatures. Professionalism was one pleasure Lark still allowed himself—a relish for studying nature's ways. But there remained little zest or wonder in the thought of flying.

It was after nightfall when Lark finally shuffled back to his own shabby tent near the Glade—only to find Harullen waiting there with news.

The low massive figure took up fully half the shelter. At first, standing in the entry with only dim moonlight behind him, Lark thought it was *Uthen,* his friend and fellow naturalist. But this qheuen's ash-colored carapace wasn't scarred from a lifetime digging into Jijo's past. *Harullen* was a bookworm, a mystic who spoke with aristocratic tones reminiscent of Gray Queens of old.

"The zealots sent a message," the heretic leader announced portentously, without even asking Lark about his day.

"Oh? Finally? And what do they say?" Lark dropped his daypack by the entrance and sagged onto his cot.

"As you predicted, they desire a meeting. It is arranged for tonight at midnight."

Echo-whispers of the final word escaped speaking vents in back, as the qheuen shifted his weight. Lark suppressed a groan. He still had a report to prepare for the sages, summarizing everything he'd learned today. Moreover, Ling wanted him bright and early the next morning, to help evaluate the new specimens.

And now this?

Well, what can you expect when you play games of multiple loyalty? Old-time novels warn how hard things can get when you serve more than one master.

Events were accelerating. Now the rumored, secretive rebel organization had finally offered to talk. What choice had he but to go?

"All right," he told Harullen. "Come get me when it's time. Meanwhile, I have work to do."

The gray qheuen departed silently, except for a faint clicking of claws on the rocky trail. Lark struck a match that sputtered rank fumes before settling enough to light his tiny oil lamp. He unfolded the portable writing table Sara had given him when he graduated from the Roney School, what seemed a geologic age ago. Pulling out a sheet of his father's best writing paper, he then shaved black powder from a half-used ink stick into a clay mortar, mixed the dust with fluid from a small bottle, and ground the mixture with a pestle till all the lumps were gone. Lark used his pocket knife to sharpen his tree-staller quill pen. At last he dipped the tip into the ink, paused for a moment, and began to write his report.

It was true, Lark realized later, during a tense conclave by the wan opal glow of Torgen, the second moon. Tentatively, suspiciously, the zealots were indeed offering alliance with Harullen's loose-knit society of heretics.

Why? The two groups have different aims. We seek to reduce, then end, our illegal presence on this fragile world. The zealots only want the old status quo back, our hidden secrecy restored, as it was before the raider ship came—and perhaps a few old scores settled along the way.

Still, envoys of the two groups gathered in the dead of night, near a steaming fumarole, by the winding path leading to the silent nest of the Egg. Most of those in the conspiracy wore heavy cloaks to hide their identities. Harullen, who was among the few still to possess a functioning rewq, was asked to remove the squirming symbiont from his sensory cupola, lest the delicate creature burn itself out in the atmosphere of strained intrigue. Creatures of the Great Peace, rewq were not suited for times of war.

Or is it because the zealots don't want us to see too much, Lark pondered. Not for nothing were rewq called the "mask that reveals." Their near-universal hibernation was as troubling as the heavy silence of the Egg itself.

Before starting, the zealots first cracked open several jars, releasing swarms of privacy wasps around the periphery—an ancient ritual whose origins had been lost but that now made earnest sense, after discoveries of the last few days. Then the urrish spokesman for the cabal stepped forward, speaking in Galactic Two.

"Your association sees opportunity in the (greatly lamented) coming of these felons," she accused. The whistles and clicks were muffled by a cowl, obscuring all but the tip of her muzzle. Still, Lark could tell she wasn't many seasons past a middling, with at most one husband pouched under an arm. Her diction implied education, possibly at one of the plains academies where young urs, fresh from the herd, gathered within sight of some steaming volcano, to apprentice in their finest arts. *An intellectual, then. All full of book learning and the importance of her own ideas.*

Yeah, a part of him answered honestly. *In other words, not too different from yourself.*

Harullen answered the rebel's challenge, making a political point by speaking Anglic.

"What do you mean by that strange proposition?"

"We mean that you perceive, in these (disliked/unwelcome) aliens, a chance to see your ultimate goals fulfilled!"

The urs stamped a foreleg. Her insinuation sent angry murmurs through the heretic delegation. Yet Lark had seen it coming.

Harullen's gray carapace rocked an undulating circle. A traeki gesture, which the ringed ones called Objection to Unjust Impeachment.

"You imply that we condone our own murder. And that of every sapient on Jijo."

The urrish conspirator imitated the same motion, but in reverse—Reiteration of Indictment.

"I do so (emphatically) imply. I do so (in brutal frankness) mean. All know this is what you heretics (misguidedly) desire."

Lark stepped forward. If the zealots' murmur included any anti-human slurs, he ignored them.

"That is not (negation reiterated) what we desire!" Lark complained, garbling the qualifier trill-phrase in his haste to speak up.

"There are two reasons for this," he continued, still struggling in GalTwo.

"First among our grounds (for rebuttal) is this—the aliens (greedy to extreme fault) must not only eliminate all sapient witnesses (to crime/to theft) who might testify in a Galactic court. They must also wipe out the native stock of any (unlucky) species they steal from Jijo! Otherwise, how embarrassing would it be someday, when the (foolish) thieves announce their adoption of a new client race, only to be confronted with proof that it was stolen from this world? For this reason they must exterminate the original population, when they depart.

"This we (in righteousness) cannot allow! Genocide of innocent life is the very crime our group was (in selfless righteousness) formed to fight!"

Harullen and the other heretics shouted approval.

Lark found his throat too dry to continue in Galactic Two. He had made the gesture. Now he switched to Anglic.

"But there is another reason to resist being slaughtered by the aliens.

"There is no honor in simply being killed. Our group's goal is to seek agreement, consensus, so that the Six shall do the right thing slowly, painlessly, *voluntarily,* by means of birth control, as an act of nobility and devotion - to this world we love."

"The effect, in the end, would ve identical," the urrish speaker pointed out, slipping into the same language Lark used.

"Not when the truth is finally revealed! And it *will* be, someday, when this world has new legal tenants, who take up the common hobby of archaeology."

That statement triggered confused silence. Even Harullen rotated his cupola to stare at Lark.

"Exflain, flease." The urrish rebel bent her forelegs, urging him to continue. "What difference will archaeology signify, once we and all our descendants are long gone, our hoof bones littering the wallows of the sea?"

Lark drew himself up, fighting fatigue.

"Eventually, despite all efforts to live by the Scrolls and leave no permanent marks, this story *will* someday be told. A million years from now, or ten, it will become known that a society of sooners once dwelled here, descendants of selfish fools who invaded Jijo for reasons long forgotten. Beings who nonetheless *transcended* their ancestors' foolishness, teaching themselves where true greatness lies.

"*That* is the difference between seeking dignified self-extinction and being foully murdered. For honor's sake, and by all the blessings of the Egg, the choice must be *ours,* every individual's, not imposed on us by a pack of criminals!"

Harullen and his other friends were clearly moved. They shouted, hissed, and umbled fervent support. Lark even heard some approving murmurs among the cowled zealots. Without benefit of rewq, he could tell he was managing to sound convincing—although deep inside, he scarcely believed his own words.

Ling's bunch don't seem to fear archaeological hobbyists of some future aeon.

In fact, Lark didn't give a damn either, whether some obscure historical footnote said nice things about the Six, far in the distant future.

Good laws don't need rewards or recognition to make them right. They're true and just on their own account and should be honored even if you know that no one else is watching. Even if no one ever knows.

Despite all the well-recited flaws of Galactic civilization, Lark knew the rules protecting fallow worlds were *right*. Though he'd been born flouting them, it was still his duty to help see to it they were obeyed.

Contrary to his own words, he had no objection, in principle, to Ling's bunch eliminating local witnesses, if the means were gentle. *Take a gene-tailored plague, one leaving everyone healthy but sterile. That might handle their witness predicament and solve Jijo's problem as well.*

Ah, but Lark also had a duty to oppose the raiders' gene-stealing scheme. That, too, was a violation of Jijo, not unlike rape. With the sages apparently waffling, only the zealot conspiracy seemed willing to fight the alien threat.

Hence Lark's impassioned lie, meant to build trust between two very different radical bands. He wanted a coalition with the zealots, for one simple reason. If there were plans afoot, Lark wanted a say in them.

Cooperate for now, he told himself as he spoke on, using his best oratorical skills to soothe their suspicions, arguing persuasively for alliance.

Cooperate, but keep your eyes open.

Who knows? There may come a way to accomplish both goals with a single stroke.

A_{SX}

THE UNIVERSE DEMANDS OF US A SENSE OF IRONY. For example, all the effort and good will that forged the Great Peace was worthwhile. We folk of the Commons became better, wiser because of it. We also supposed it would work in our favor, if/when Galactic inspectors came to judge us. Warring nations do more harm to a world than those who calmly discuss how best to tend a shared garden. It would surely weigh well that we were courteous and gentle criminals, not rapacious ones.

Or so we reasoned. Did we not, my rings?

Alas, no judges dropped from the sky, but thieves and liars. Suddenly, we must play deadly games of intrigue, and those skills are not what they were in days before Commons and Egg.

How much more capable we might have been, if not for peace!

We rediscovered this truth with sharp pangs today, when a panting galloper showed up with dispatches from the forge-study of Uriel the Smith. Words of warning. Dire admonitions, telling of sky-portents, urging that we brace ourselves for visitation by a starship!

Oh, tardy premonition! A caution that arrived too late by far.

Once, stone citadels nestled on bitter-cold peaks, from north of Biblos all the way down to the tropic settlements of the Vale, flashing messages via cleverly fashioned mirrors, outracing the swiftest urrish couriers or even racing birds. With their semaphore, humans and their allies mobilized speedily for battle, making up skillfully for their lack of numbers. In time, urs and hoon developed systems of their own, each clever in its way. Even we traeki formed a network of scent-spore trackers, to warn of possible danger.

None of these feats survived peace. The semaphore was abandoned, the system of signal rockets allowed to lapse. Until lately, commerce alone simply did not justify such costly media—though ironically just last year investors had begun speaking of reoccupying those frigid stone aeries, resuming the network of flashed messages.

Had they moved faster, would we have received Uriel's warning in time?

Would receiving it have made any difference in our fate?

Ah, my rings. How vain it is to dwell on might-have-beens. Other than solipsism, it may be the most mad thing that unitary beings waste their time doing.

Rety

DO YOU HAVE SOMETHING FOR ME?"

Rann, the tall, stern-looking leader of the sky-humans, held out his hand toward her. In the late twilight, with wind rustling a nearby thicket of pale boo, it seemed to Rety that each of his calloused fingers was like her entire wrist. Moonlight brought out shadows on Rann's craggy features and wedgelike torso. She tried not to show it, but Rety felt all too insignificant in his presence.

Are all men like this, out there among the stars?

The thought made her feel funny, like earlier, when Besh told her it was possible to smooth away her scars.

First had come bad news.

"We cannot do anything about it here in our little clinic," the forayer woman had told her, during Rety's brief turn at the aliens' sick call, near their buried station.

She had been standing in line for half the morning, a horrid wait, spent shuffling between a g'Kek with a wheezy, lopsided wheel and an aged urs whose nostril dripped a ghastly gray fluid. Rety tried hard not to step in it each time the queue moved forward. When her chance finally came to be examined under bright lights and probing rays, her hopes soared, then crashed.

"This kind of dermal damage would be easy to repair back home," Besh had said, while ushering Rety toward the tent flap. "Bio-sculpting is a high art. Experts can mold a pleasant form out of even primitive material."

Rety wasn't offended. *Primitive material. It's what I am, all right.* Anyway, at the time she was dazed from imagining—what if Galactic wizardry could give her a face and body like Besh, or Ling?

She set her feet, refusing to budge till Besh let her speak.

"They—they say you may take some humans with you, when you go."

Besh had looked down at her with eyes the color of golden-brown gemstones.

"Who says such things?"

"I . . . hear stuff. Rumors, I guess."

"You should not believe all rumors."

Had there been extra emphasis on the word *all*? Rety leaped on any excuse for hope.

"I also hear you pay good when folks bring things you want—or news you need."

"That much is true." Now the eyes seemed to glitter a little. From amusement? Or greed?

"And if the news is really, *really* valuable? What'd be the reward then?"

The star-woman smiled, a grin full of friendship and promise. "Depending on how helpful or precious the information—the sky's the limit."

Rety had felt a thrill. She started to reach into her belt pouch. But Besh stopped her. "Not now," the woman said in a low voice. "It is not discreet."

Looking left and right, Rety realized there were other patients around, and employees of the forayers—members of the Six serving as assistants in the aliens' many enterprises. Any one could be a spy for the sages.

"Tonight," Besh had told her in a low voice. "Rann goes walking each evening, down by the stream. Wait next to the stand of *yellow* boo. The one just coming into bloom. Come alone, and speak to no one you see along the way."

Great! Rety had thought jubilantly on leaving the tent. *They're interested! It's exactly what I was hoping for. And just in the nick o' time.*

All might have been lost if it had taken much longer to make contact. The chief human sage had decreed she must leave tomorrow, accompanying a small donkey caravan aimed up into the mountains, along with two silent men and three big women she had never met before. Nothing was said, but she knew the goal was to catch up with Dwer, and from there head back to the wilderness she came from.

No chance of that! she had thought, relishing tonight's rendezvous. *Dwer's welcome to go play hunter in the forest. While he's scratchin' for eats in the Gray Hills, I'll be living high an' mighty, up on the Dolphin's Tail.*

That was the constellation where, rumor had it, the forayers came from, although the crablike sage, Knife-Bright Insight, once tried explaining to Rety about galaxies and "transfer points" and how the route back to civilization was twisty as a mulc-spider's vine. None of it made sense, and she figured the old qheuen was probably lying. Rety far preferred the idea of going to a star she could clearly see—which meant she would someday look *back* at Jijo from the beautiful Galactic city where she'd gone to live, and stick her tongue out every night at Jass and Bom and their whole stinking tribe. And Dwer and the sages, for that matter, along with everyone else on this rancy planet who was ever mean to her.

All day after meeting Besh she had avoided the sages and their servants, seeking the clearings several arrow-flights to the west, where some pilgrims were trying to restore a few of the festivities of Gathering. Pavilions that had been taken down in panic were now restored, and many folk had come out of hiding. There was still plenty of tension. But some people seemed determined to get on with life, even if just for a little while.

She visited one tent where craft workers showed wares brought from all over the Slope. Their goods would have impressed Rety even yesterday. But now she smiled scornfully, having seen the bright machines the sky-humans used. At one panel discussion, she watched hoon, g'Kek, and human experts discuss improved techniques for weaving rope. The atmosphere was hushed, and few in the audience asked questions.

Nearby, a traeki ring-breeder displayed some flabby donut shapes with slender arms, eye buds, or stubby feet. A trio of mature traeki stood near the pen, perhaps pondering additions to a newborn stack they were building back home. Or maybe they were just browsing.

Farther along, in a sun-dappled glade, chimp acrobats performed for a crowd of children, and an all-race sextet played by a simmering hot spring. It all might have seemed quite gay if Rety didn't sense a pall, spoiling the mood. And if she had not already hardened her heart to all things Jijoan.

These Slopies think they're so much better than a pack of dirty sooners. Well, maybe it's so. But then, everybody on Jijo is a sooner, ain't they?

I'm going far away, so it won't matter to me anymore.

In a rougher clearing, she passed much of the afternoon watching human kids and urrish middlings vie in a game of Drake's Dare.

The playing field was a strip of sand with a stream along one side. The other border was a long pit filled with coals, smoldering under a coating of gray ash. Wisps of hot smoke wafted into Rety's face, tugging painful memories of Jass and Bom. Her scars tightened till she moved a ways uphill, sitting under the shade of a dwarf garu.

Two contestants arrived—a human boy starting at the north end of the field and a burly urrish middling at the south—sauntering and hurling insults as they neared the center, where two umpires waited.

"Hey, hinney! Get ready to take a bath!" the boy taunted, trying to swagger but hindered by his left arm, which was trussed back with cloth bindings. He wore a leather covering from crotch to chin, but his legs and feet were bare.

The young urs had her own protections and handicaps. Tough, transparent junnoor membranes stretched
tight over her delicate pouches and scent glands. As the
middling drew close, she tried to rear up threateningly—
and almost fell over, to the amusement of onlookers.
Rety saw the reason—her hind pair of legs were hobbled
together.

"Silly skirl!" the urs shouted at her adversary, regaining her balance to hop forward once more. "Vavy skirl
gonna get vurned!"

Along both boundaries—beyond the coal bed and
across the stream—crowds of other youths gathered to
watch. Many wore leather or membrane protectors,
hanging jauntily open, while waiting for their own turn
in the arena. Some boys and girls smeared salve over
livid reddish streaks along their calves and thighs and
even their faces, making Rety wince. True, none of the
burns looked anywhere near as deep or wounding as
her own. No blisters or horrid, charred patches. Still,
how could they risk getting scorched *on purpose*?

The thought both nauseated and queerly fascinated
Rety.

Was this so very different from her own story, after all?
She had known that standing up to Jass would have
consequences, yet she did it anyway.

Sometimes you just gotta fight, that's all. Her hand
lifted briefly to touch her face. She regretted nothing.
Nothing.

Some urrish spectators also bore marks of recent combat, especially on their legs, where swaths of fur had
gone mangy or sloughed off. Strangely, there wasn't any
clear separation along race lines—no human cheering
section versus an urrish one. Instead, there was a lot of
mixing, preliminary sparring, and friendly comparing of
techniques and throws. Rety saw one human boy joke
with a middling urs, laughing with his arm on her sleek
mane.

A sizable group of zookirs and chimps screeched at
each other in excitement, making wagers of piu nodules
and pounding the ground with their hands.

Some distance beyond the coals, Rety saw another makeshift arena being used by juvenile traekis with newly wedded rings, engaged in a different kind of sport with g'Kek youngsters so light and agile, they spun wheelies and even lifted to stride briefly on their rear pusher legs. That tournament seemed to involve a sort of rolling, whirling dance. Rety couldn't make out the point, but clearly the pastime was less violent than Drake's Dare.

A pair of qheuen umpires—one gray and one blue—awaited the two contestants in the middle of the sandy strip. They carefully inspected the human's sleeve for weapons, then checked the middling's teeth for caps on her scythelike incisors. The blue qheuen then backed away into the stream while the gray extended armored legs and, to Rety's blinking surprise, stepped daintily onto the bed of steaming coals! From then on it kept shifting its weight, lifting two clawed feet at a time high above the fuming surface, then switching to another pair, and so on.

After ritually—and warily—bowing to each other, the boy and middling began circling, looking for weakness.

Abruptly, they sprang at each other, grappling, each trying to push, twist, or throw the other in the direction he or she least wanted to go. Now Rety saw the reason for the handicaps. With both hind legs tied, the urs could not stomp her opponent or simply power her way to victory. Likewise, the boy's strong, agile arms might throttle the middling, unless one was bound to his side.

"drak's dare! drak's dare! yippee yooee!"

The tiny, squeaky voice startled Rety, coming from much closer than the crowd of shouting onlookers. She swiveled, seeking the source, but saw no one nearby till a tug on her tunic made her look down.

"pouch-safe? yee talk! you me pouch-safe and yee talk you!"

Rety stared. It was a tiny urs! No bigger than her foot, it danced delicately on four miniature hooves while still plucking at her garment. The little creature tossed its mane, rotating a sinuous neck to peer around behind it, nervously. *"yee need pouch! need pouch!"*

Rety turned to follow its anxious stare and glimpsed what had it terrified. A sleek black shape crouched in the undergrowth, panting slightly, a lolling tongue hanging between rows of sharp white teeth. At first, Rety felt a shock of recognition, thinking it was Mudfoot, grouchy old Dwer's funny companion in the mountains. Then she saw this one had no brown paw patches. A different noor, then.

The predator raised its head and leered at the tiny urs, taking a step, then another.

On impulse, Rety scooped up the quivering prey and slipped it in her leather hip-pouch.

The noor gave her a look of puzzled disappointment, then turned to vanish in the shrubs.

Cheers, boos, and excited snorts made her look up in time to see the human contestant tumble through a cloud of billowing ash. To Rety's amazement, the boy was not instantly set ablaze but rolled erect, dancing from bare foot to bare foot on the coals, swiftly but calmly brushing embers from crevices in his leather garment. He waved off the gray qheuen, who had hurried protectively to his side. The youth ran a hand along his collar one more time, then sauntered across more glowing cinders back to the sandy arena.

Rety was impressed. Slopies seemed tougher than she'd thought.

"hot-hot, but not much heat!" the little voice squeaked from her pouch, as if pleased by her surprise. All memory of flight from the hungry noor seemed forgotten. *"boy make boo-boo. slip and fall. but not again. not this boy! he tops! watch silly hinney get wet!"*

Rety wrestled with her own amazement, unable to decide which thing dumbfounded her more, the contest below or the entity in her pocket, providing running commentary.

Combat won her attention as the young human launched at his opponent once more. Whatever his mistake the first time, the boy seemed bent on making up for it as he bobbed and weaved, then leaped to catch a handful of the middling's mane. She snorted and snapped, pushing vainly with both slim handling-arms to break his grip. She tried lifting a foreleg to tug with its stubby grasping paw, but that just left her teetering dangerously.

"drak's dare!" the tiny urs shouted gleefully. *"drak say to Ur-choon. you-me tussle. tussle 'stead of kill!"*

Rety caught her breath.

Oh, I remember now.

She had heard the legend when she was little, told round the campfire by one of the old grandpas. A tale that died with the old man, since Jass and the young hunters preferred exaggerated retellings of their own exploits over stories of life beyond the mountains.

To Rety's best recollection, there once had been a man named Drak—or Drake—a hero mightier and bolder than any human before or since. Once, when Earthlings were still new on Jijo, a giant urrish chieftain fought Drak in a wrestling match. For three days and nights they grappled, pounding and tearing at each other, making the ground shake, drying up rivers, ripping all the countryside between a fiery mountain and the sea, till both volcano and ocean vanished in curling steam. When the clouds finally cleared, a bright region glowed from horizon to horizon with all the colors one could paint by mixing urrish and human blood.

Then, out of the smoke and mist, two heroes strode forth—he missing an arm and she a leg—leaning on each other, inseparable from that day forth.

While there would be more wars between the tribes, from that day forth all were fought with honor, in memory of Drak and Ur-choon.

"watch!" the little urs called.

The boy faked a leftward lean, then planted his right foot and heaved. Snorting dismay, the urs could not keep her greater weight from pivoting over his hip, sailing head-over-withers to crash into the nearby stream. There came a shrill sigh as she floundered, slipping in the mud. Finally, the blue qheuen surfaced behind her, using one clenched foot to give a helpful shove. With a grateful cry, the middling dove into the sand, raising plumes of dust.

"hee! go roll in hot ash, silly hinney! sand too slow! hair gonna rot!"

Rety gazed down at the tiny urs. It was no baby, as first she thought. Somewhere she recalled hearing that urrish newborns stayed in their mothers' pouches for a few months, then were spilled by the dozen into tall grass to fend for themselves. Anyway, infant urs couldn't talk.

It must be a male! Rety saw that its throat and muzzle looked unlike a female's, lacking the flashy neck colors or pendulous cloven lip, which explained why it could speak Anglic sounds a female could not.

Back in the arena, the boy crouched for a third round, but the urrish youth lowered her head, conceding. The human raised a red-streaked arm in victory, then helped guide the limping loser off the playing field. Meanwhile, two new contestants flexed and stretched, while helpers trussed their handicapped limbs.

Wistfully, Rety watched the human kids, joking with friends from the other septs. She wondered how the boy had managed to get just slightly singed by the coals—but could not bring herself to approach with questions. They might only laugh at her unkempt hair, her uncouth speech, and her scars.

So forget 'em, anyway, she thought bitterly. All the dry heat and smoke was making her face itch. In any case, she had important business. An item to retrieve from her tent before dark. Something to use as down payment on a ticket *away* from here, to a place none of these big handsome kids would ever see, despite all their pride and skill and strutting around. A place where no one from her past would bother her. That was lots more important than watching savages play violent games with fire and water.

"Look, I gotta go," she told the little urrish male, rising to her feet and looking around. "I think the nasty ol' noor's gone away, so you can be off now too."

The tiny creature peered at her, his tail and muzzle drooping. Rety cleared her throat.

"Um, can I drop you off somewhere? Isn't your—uh—*wife* prob'ly worried about you?"

The dark eyes glittered sadly. *"Uf-roho need yee no more. pouch home now full of slimy newbrats. push yee out. right-pouch still husband-full. yee must find new pouch. or grass burrow to live/die in. but no sweet grass in mountain! just rocks!"*

That last was sung mournfully. It sounded like an awful thing to do to a helpless little guy, and Rety felt mad just thinking about it.

"this nice pouch, this one." He crooned a strange reverberating melody, surprisingly low for a creature so small. Rety's skin tingled where he lay closest.

"yee serve new wife good. do good things she want."

Rety stared at him, dazed to think of what he offered. Then she burst out laughing, leaning on a tree, guffawing till her sides hurt. Through clouded eyes, she saw that *yee* seemed to laugh too, in his own fashion. At last she wiped her face and grinned. "Well, you done one thing for me, already. Ain't chortled so good in I dunno how long.

"An' you know what else? Come to think of it, there *is* somethin' you might be able to do. Somethin' that'd make me even happier."

"yee do anything! new wife feed yee. yee make wife happy!"

Rety shook her head, amazed once more at the twists and turns life seemed to push on the unwary. If her new idea worked out, this could turn out to be an awfully lucky break.

"Do you have something for me?"

Rann held out his enormous hand. In the dim twilight, with the yellow boo rustling nearby, Rety stared at the man's calloused fingers, each like her wrist. His craggy features and massive torso—so much greater than the biggest boy-wrestler playing Drake's Dare that day—made her feel callow, insignificant.

Rety wondered—*Are all men like this, out there among the stars?*

Could I ever trust anyone with hands like those, to have a husband's power over me?

She had always thought she'd rather die than marry.

Yet now she *had* a husband, purring next to her belly. Rety felt yee's warm tongue on her hand as she stroked his silky neck.

Rann seemed to note her ironic smile. Did it make her seem more confident?

She reached past yee to pluck a slender object, fluffy at one end, pointy-hard at the other, and laid the feather on Rann's open palm. Puzzled, he drew forth an instrument to shine at it from several sides, while her mind still cycled round-and-round the events leading to this moment, when her hopes hung in the balance.

On her way here, Rety had passed other members of the Six, each waiting alone by some landmark along Rann's regular evening stroll. As instructed, no one spoke or made eye contact, though Rety spied observers—a g'Kek, two hoons, and a human—taking notes from a distance.

Rety didn't give a damn what they told Lester Cambel about her "treason." After tonight, the sages wouldn't make plans for her anymore.

On arriving at the yellow boo, she had waited nervously, petting yee and biting her fingernails. A few duras before Rann appeared, a soft whine announced one of the mighty robots—eight-sided, intimidating—and a wave of horrid memory recalled another floating monster, firing savagely into the mulc-spider's lair . . . and Dwer's strong arms yanking her out of the path of a searing beam, holding her fiercely against falling, sheltering her with his body.

Rety bit her lip, quashing any thought, any memory, that might shake her resolve. Now was no time to go sappy and soft. That was what the sages wanted.

As she had done countless times back home—making

herself stand up to Jass despite horrid punishments—she had stopped cowering from the dark robot, standing straight, forcing her chin out.

You can't harm me, she projected defiantly. *You wouldn't dare!*

But an unwelcome thought fizzed up from below.

One of these killed the bird.

The bird fought it and died.

A surge of guilt nearly made her spin around and flee. But then the robot had swerved aside, vanishing into the night, and Rann took its place, holding out his massive hand.

"Do you have something for me?" he had asked, smiling till Rety handed over the feather.

Now she watched him grow excited as he played instruments over the souvenir, once her prize possession. Pressing lips together, she bore down to reinforce her resolve.

Hell yes, I have somethin' for you, Mister Star-Man. Somethin' I bet you want pretty bad.

The point is—you better have somethin' for me, too!

XV. THE BOOK OF THE SEA

The Path takes time,
so time you must dearly buy.

When the lawful seek you—hide.
When they find you—be discreet.
When you are judged—do not
quail.

What you have tried to do is
rightly banned.
But there is a beauty in it, if done
well.

On this, most agree.

—The Scroll of Redemption

Alvin's Tale

I'VE GOT MY ANGLIC DICTIONARY AND USAGE Guide with me right now, so I'm going to try an experiment. To capture some of the drama of what happened next, I'm going to try my narrative skill in *present tense*. I know it's not used in many of the Old Earth stories I've read, but when it's done right, I think it lends a buff sense of *immediacy* to a story. Here goes.

I left off with little Ziz—the traeki partial we all witnessed being vlenned a week ago, on the day Gybz turned erself into Tyug and forgot all about starships—slithering its way from pen to derrick, where we were about to test the bathy for the first time. Ziz had spent the last week voring a rich feed-mix and had grown a lot. Still, it made a pretty short stack. Nobody expects miracles of strength or brilliance from a half-pint traeki that barely reaches my bottom set of knees.

Ziz follows Tyug's scentomone trail almost to the edge of the cliff, where you can stare straight down into the Great Midden as it takes a sharp hook, stabbing the continent with a wound so deep and wide, our ancestors chose it as a natural boundary for settler life on Jijo.

The towering bulk of Terminus Rock casts a long morning shadow, but *Wuphon's Dream,* our pride and joy, dangles just beyond, shimmering in a blaze of sunlight. Instead of slithering up the ramp to the sealed cabin hatch, Ziz glides into a little cage mounted under the bulb window, in front of eighteen heavy ballast stones. As it passes Tyug, Ziz and the full-size traeki exchange puffs of vapor in a language no other member of the Six is equipped to even try to understand.

The cage closes. Urdonnol whistles a call, and gangs of hoon and qheuens set to work, first swinging the bathy gently away, then lowering it toward the sea, unreeling both the taut hawser and the double hose. The drums turn to a slow steady beat, singing over and over—

rumble-dum-dumble-um-rumble-dum-dumble-um . . .

It draws us. Hoon all over the mesa—even protestors—get caught up in the pulselike cadence of joyful labor. A rhythm of teamwork, sweat, and a job under way.

Being the only noor present, Huphu seems to think it her duty to scamper like a wild thing, taking perches high on the derricks like they're ship masts, arching her back and stretching as if the umble is being sung just for her, a physical hand petting her back, stroking the bristles on her head. Her eyes sparkle, watching our bathy dip lower and lower with Ziz visible as a single tentacle dangling from the wire cage.

It occurs to me that maybe Huphu thinks the little traeki is being used as *bait* at the end of a really big fishing line! Maybe Huphu's curious what we're trying to catch.

That, in turn, brings to mind Pincer's wild tales of "monsters" in the deep. Neither he nor Huck has mentioned a word about it since we arrived, each for his or her own reasons, I guess. Or am I the only one who hasn't forgotten, amid all the recent excitement?

Wuphon's Dream descends below the cliff face, and we rush near the edge to keep her in sight. Qheuens don't like heights and react by hunkering down, scraping their abdomens, clutching the ground. That's where I go too, lying prone and screwing up my courage to slide forward. Huck, on the other hand, just rolls up to the stony rim, teeters with her pusher legs jutting back for balance, then sticks two of her eyestalks over as far as they'll go.

What a girl. So much for g'Keks being cautious, High-K beings. Watching her, I realize I can't do any less, so I creep my head over the rim and force my eyelids apart.

Looking west, the ocean is a vast carpet stretching to a far horizon. Pale colors dominate where the sea covers only a few cables' depth of continental shelf. But a band of dark blue-gray tells of a *canyon*, stabbing our way from the giant planetary scar called the Midden. That deep-deep gorge passes almost directly under our aerie, then drives on farther east, splitting the land like a crack in the clinker boards of a doomed ship. The far shore is just a hundred or so arrowflights away, but rows of razor-sharp crags and near-bottomless ravines parallel the Rift, making it a daunting barrier for anyone wishing to defy the Law.

I'm no scientist; regrettably, I don't have the mind for it. But even I can tell the jagged spires must be new, or else wind and surf and rain would've worn them down by now. Like Mount Guenn, this is a place where Jijo is actively renewing itself. (We felt two small quakes since setting up camp here.) No wonder some think Terminus Rock a sacred spot.

The surf is a crashing, spuming show elsewhere, but here the sea settles down mysteriously—glassy smooth. A slight out-tow draws gently *away* from the cliff. Ideal conditions for our experiment—*if* they're reliable. No one ever thought to make soundings in the Rift before, since no dross ships ever come this way.

Wuphon's Dream drops lower, like a spiderfly trailing twin filaments behind her. It gets hard to tell exactly how far she is from the surface. Huck's eyestalks are spread as far apart as possible, trying to maximize depth perception. She murmurs.

"Okay, here we go, into the drink . . . *now!*"

I hold my breath, but nothing happens. The big drums keep feeding out cable and hose. The bathy gets smaller.

"Now!" Huck repeats.

Another dura passes, and *Wuphon's Dream* is still dry.

"Sure is a long way down-own-own," Pincer stutters.

"You can say that again," adds Ur-ronn, stamping nervously.

"But please don't," Huck snaps, showing pique. Then in GalSix—*"Reality merges with expectation when—"*

It serves her right—a splash cuts off whatever deep insight she was about to share. The big drums' song slows and deepens as I stare across the vast, wet stillness where the *Dream* vanished.

roomble-doom-doomble-oom-roomble-doom-doomble . . .

It sounds like the world's biggest hoon. One who never has to take a break or a breath. Based on that umble, the big derrick would've won the title of Honorary Captain of the South if it came to a vote then and there.

Huphu is all the way out at the end of the deployer crane, back arched with pleasure. Meanwhile, someone counts off.

"One cable, *forty* . . .

"One cable, *sixty* . . .

"One cable, *eighty* . . .

"Two cables!

"Two cables, *twenty* . . ."

The chant reminds me of Mark Twain's tales of river pilots on the romantic Mississippi, especially one scene with a big black man-human up at the bow of the *Delta Princess,* swinging a weight on a line, calling out shoals in a treacherous fog, saving the lives of everyone aboard.

I'm an ocean hoon. My people sail *ships,* not sissy boats. Still, those were among my father's favorite tales. And Huck's too, back when she was a little orphan, toddling around on her pusher legs, four eyes staring in lost wonder as Dad recited tales set on a wolfling world that never knew the stifling wisdom of Galactic ways. A world where ignorance wasn't exactly noble, but had one virtue—it gave you a chance to see and learn and do things no one else had ever seen or learned or done before.

Humans got to do that back on Earth.

And now we're doing it here!

Before I even know I'm doing it, I sit up on my double-fold haunches, rock my head back, and belt out an umble of joy. A mighty, rolling hoot. It resounds across the mesa, strokes the grumbling equipment, and floats over the serrated stones of the Great Rift.

For all I know, it's floating out there still.

Sunshine spills across calm waters at least twenty cables deep. We imagine *Wuphon's Dream,* drifting ever downward, first through a cloud of bubbles, then a swollen wake of silence as the light from above grows dimmer and finally fails completely.

"Six cables, *sixty* . . .

"Six cables, *eighty* . . .

"Seven cables!"

When we go down, this is where we'll turn on the eik lights and use the acid battery to send sparks up the hawser, telling those above that all is well. But *Ziz* has no lights, or any way to signal. The little stack is all alone down there—though I guess no traeki ever feels entirely lonely. Not when its rings can argue endlessly among themselves.

"Eight cables!"

Someone brings a jar of wine for me and some warm simla blood for Ur-ronn. Huck sips pungent galook-ade from a long curvy straw, while Pincer sprays his back with salt water.

"Nine cables!"

This experiment's only supposed to go to ten, so they begin gently increasing pressure on the brake. Soon they'll reverse the drums to bring *Wuphon's Dream* back to the world of air and light.

Then it happens—a sudden twang, like a plucked violus string, loud as thunder.

The deployer chief cries— *"Release the brake!"*

An operator leaps for a lever . . . too late as bucking convulsions hit the derrick, like backlash on a fishing pole when a big one gets away. Only this recoil is massive, unstoppable.

We all gasp or vurt at the sight of *Huphu,* a small black figure clinging to the farthest spar as the crane whips back and forth.

One paw, then another, loses its grip. She screams.

The tiny noor goes spinning across space, barely missing the hawser's cyclone whirl amid a frothing patch of sea. Staring in helpless dismay, we see our mascot plunge into the abyss that already swallowed Ziz, *Wuphon's Dream,* and all the hopes and hard work of two long years.

XVI. THE BOOK OF THE SLOPE

Legends

The urs tell of a crisis of breeding.

Out among the stars, they were said to live longer than they do on Jijo, with spans much enhanced by artificial means. Moreover, an urs never stops wanting a full pouch, tenanted either with a husband or with brooding young. There were technical ways to duplicate the feeling, but to many, these methods just weren't the same.

Galactic society is harsh on overbreeders, who threaten the billion-year-old balance. There is constant dread of another "wildfire"—a conflagration of overpopulation, like one that burned almost half the worlds in Galaxy Three, a hundred or so million years ago.

Especially, those species who reproduce slowly, like hoon, seem to have a deep-set fear of "low-K" spawners, like urs.

Legend tells of a conflict over this matter. Reading between the lines of ornate urrish oral history, it seems the bards must be telling of a *lawsuit*—one judged at the higher levels of Galactic society.

The urs lost the suit, and a bitter war-of-enforcement that followed.

Some of the losers did not wish to settle, even then. They turned one ship toward forbidden spaces, there to search for a wild prairie they could call home.

A place to hear the clitter-clatter of myriad little urrish feet.

A_{sx}

A STRANGE MESSAGE HAS COME ALL THE WAY from Tarek Town, sent by Ariana Foo, emeritus High Sage of human sept.

The exhausted urrish runner collapsed to her knees after dashing uphill from the Warril Plain, so spent that she actually craved water, raw and undiluted.

Center now, my rings. Spin your ever-wavering attention round the tale of Ariana Foo, as it was read aloud by Lester Cambel, her successor. Did not the news send vaporous wonder roiling through my/our core—that a mysterious injured outlander showed up one day near the Upper Roney? A stranger who might possibly be some *lost comrade* of the star-god visitors who now vex our shared exile! Or else, she speculates, might he be one who *escaped* these far-raiding adventurers? Could his wounds show evidence of shared enmity?

Ariana recommends we of the Council cautiously investigate the matter at our end, perhaps using truth-scryers, while she performs further experiments at Biblos.

The forayers *do* seem to have other interests, beyond seeking pre-sentient species to ravish from Jijo's fallow peace. They feign nonchalance, yet relentlessly query our folk, offering rewards and blandishments for reports of "anything strange."

How ironic those words, coming from *them*.

Then there is the bird.

Surely you recall the metal bird, my rings? Normally, we would have taken it for yet another Buyur relic, salvaged from the entrails of a dead-dying mulc-spider. Yet the sooner girl swears she saw it move! Saw it travel great distances, then fight and kill a Rothen machine!

Was that not the very evening the forayers buried their station, as though *they* were now fearful of the dread sky?

Our finest techies examine the bird-machine, but with scant tools available they learn little, save that energies still throb within its metal breast. Perhaps the contingent Lester has sent east—to ingather the human sooner band according to our law—will find out more.

So many questions. But even with answers, would our dire situation change in the least?

Were there time, i would set my/our varied rings the task of taking up different sides and arguing these mysteries, each question pouring distinct scents to coat our moist core, dripping syllogisms like wax, until only truth shines through a lacquered veneer. But there is no time for the traeki approach to problem solving. So we sages debate in the dry air, without even rewq to mediate the inadequacies of language. Each day is spent buying futile delays in our destiny.

As for Ariana's other suggestion, we *have* employed truth-scryers during discussions with the sky-humans. According to books of lore, this passive form of psi should be less noticeable than other techniques.

"Are you seeking anybody in particular? This we asked, just yesterday. *Is there a person, being, or group we should look for in your name?"*

Their leader—the one answering to the name-label Rann—seemed to grow tense, then recovered swiftly, confidently, smiling in the manner of his kind.

"It is always our desire to seek strangeness. Have you observed strange things?"

In that moment of revealed strain, one of our scryers claimed to catch something—a brief flash of *color*. A dark shade of gray, like the hue of a Great Qheuen's carapace. Only this surface seemed more supple, with a lissome litheness that undulated nimbly, free of adornment by hair, scale, feather, or torg.

The glimpse ended quickly. Still the scryer felt an association—with *water*.

What else did she describe, my rings, during that scant fey moment?

Ah, yes. A swirl of bubbles.

Scattered in formations, numerous as stars.

Bubbles growing into globes the size of Jijo's moons. Glistening. Ancient. Ageless.

Bubbles filled with distilled wonder . . . sealed in by time.

Then nothing more.

Well and alas, what more could be asked? What are we but amateurs at this kind of game? Phwhoon-dau and Knife-Bright Insight point out that even this slim "clue" might have been laid, adroitly, in the scryer's thoughts, in order to distract us with a paradox.

Yet at times like these, when our rewq and the Holy Egg seem to have abandoned us, it is such slender stems that offer wan hope to the drowning.

In her message, Ariana promised to send another kind of help. An expert whose skill may win us leverage with our foes, perhaps enough to make the invaders willing to bargain.

Oh, Ariana, how we/i have missed your wily optimism! If fire fell from heaven, you would see a chance to bake pots. If the entire Slope shuddered, then sank into the Midden's awful depths, you would find in that event cause to cry out—*opportunity!*

Sara

DESPITE URGENT ORDERS TO HIDE BY DAY, THE steamship *gopher* broke her old record, bolting upstream from Tarek Town, against the Bibur's springtime flood, boilers groaning as pistons beat their casings, an exuberance of power unsurpassed by anything else on Jijo, save her sister ship, the *mole*. Mighty emblems of human technology, they were unapproachable even by clever urrish smiths, laboring on high volcanoes.

Sara recalled her own first ride, at age fifteen, newly recruited to attend advanced studies in Biblos and fiercely proud of her new skills—especially the knack of seeing each clank and chug of the growling steam engine in terms of temperatures, pressures, and pounds of force. Equations seemed to tame the hissing brute, turning its dismaying roar into a kind of music.

Now all that was spoiled. The riveted tanks and pulsing rocker-arms were exposed as primitive gadgets, little more advanced than a stone ax.

Even if the star-gods leave without doing any of the awful things Ariana Foo predicts, they have already harmed us by robbing us of our illusions.

One person didn't seem to mind. The Stranger lingered near the puffing, straining machinery, peering under the rockers, insisting with gestures that the engine chief open the gear box and let him look inside. At first, the human crew members had been wary of his antics; but soon, despite his mute incapacity with words, they sensed a kindred spirit.

You can explain a lot with hand motions, Sara noted. Another case of language adapting to needs of the moment—much as each wave of Jijoan colonists helped reshape the formal Galactic tongues they had known, culminating when humans introduced half a million texts printed mostly in Anglic, a language seemingly built *out of* chaos, filled with slang, jargon, puns, and ambiguity.

It was a warped mirror image of what had happened back on Earth, where billion-year-old grammars were pushing human culture *toward* order. In both cases the driving force was a near monopoly on knowledge.

That was the *obvious* irony. But Sara knew another— her unusual theory about language and the Six—so heretical, it made *Lark's* views seem downright orthodox.

Maybe it is *past time I came back to Biblos, to report on my work . . . and to confront everything I'm afraid of.*

The Stranger seemed happy, engrossed with his fellow engineers and closely observed by Ariana Foo from her wheelchair. So Sara left the noisy engine area, moving toward the ship's bow, where a thick mist was cleaved by the *gopher's* headlong rush. Tattered breaks in the fog showed dawn brightening the Rimmer peaks, south and east, where the fate of the Six would be decided.

Won't Lark and Dwer be surprised to see me!

Oh, they'll probably yell that I should have stayed safe at home. I'll answer that I have a job to do, just as important as theirs, and they shouldn't be such gendermenders. And we'll all try hard not to show how happy we are to see each other.

But first, Sage Foo wanted this side trip to check her notion about the Stranger, despite Sara's instinct to protect the wounded man from further meddling.

Those instincts have caused me enough trouble. Is it not time to temper them with reason?

One ancient text called it "nurturing mania," and it might have seemed cute when she was a child, nursing hurt creatures of the forest. Perhaps it would have posed no problem, if she followed the normal life path of Jijoan women, with children and a fatigued farmer-husband tugging at her, demanding attention. What need, then, to *sublimate* maternal instincts? What time for other interests, without all the labor-saving tools tantalizingly described in Terran lore? Plain as she was, Sara felt certain she would have been successful at such a modest life and made some simple, honest man happy.

If a simple life was what I wanted.

Sara tried to shrug the wave of introspection. The cause of her funk was obvious.

Biblos. Center of human hopes and fears, focus of power, pride, and shame, the place where she once found love—or its illusion—and lost it. Where the prospect of a "second chance" drove her off in panicked flight. Nowhere else had she felt such swings of elation and claustrophobia, hope and fear.

Will it still be standing when we round the final bend?

If the roof-of-stone had already fallen—

Her mind shied away from the unendurable. Instead, she drew from her shoulder bag the draft manuscript of her second paper on Jijoan language. It was past time to consider what to say to Sage Bonner and the others, if they confronted her.

What have I been doing? Demonstrating on paper that chaos *can be a form of progress. That noise can be informing.*

I might as well tell them I can prove that black is white, and up is down!

> Evidence suggests that long ago, when terran tribes were nomadic or pre-agricultural, most language groups were more rigidly structured than later on. For example, Earth scholars tried rebuilding proto-Indo-European, working backward from Latin, Sanskrit, Greek, and German, deriving a mother tongue strictly organized with many cases and declensions. A rule-based structure that would do any Galactic grammar proud.

In the margin, Sara noted a recent find from her readings, that one native North American tongue, Cherokee, contained up to seventy pronouns—ways to say "I" and "you" and "we"—depending on context and personal relationship—a trait shared with GalSix.

> To some, this implies humans must have once had patrons, who uplifted Earthling man-apes. Teachers who altered our bodies and brains and also taught a stern logic, through languages tailored to our needs.
>
> Then we lost our guides. Through our own fault? Abandonment? No one knows.
>
> After that, the theory goes, all Earthly languages devolved, spiraling back toward the apelike grunts protohumans used before uplift. At the time our ancestors left Earth for Jijo,

Galactic advisers were counseling that Anglic and other "wolfling" tongues be dropped in favor of codes designed for thinking beings.

Their argument can be illustrated by playing the game of Telephone.

Take a dozen players, seated in a circle. Whisper a complex sentence to one, who then whispers the same message to the next, and so on. Question: how soon is the original meaning lost amid confusion and slips of the tongue? Answer: in Anglic, noise can set in from the very start. After just a few relays, a sentence can become hilariously twisted.

The experiment yields different results in Rossic and Nihanic, human grammars that still require verb, noun, and adjective endings specific to gender, ownership, and other factors. If a mistake creeps into a Rossic Telephone message, the altered word often stands out, glaringly. Acute listeners can often correct it automatically.

In pure Galactic languages, one might play Telephone all day without a single error. No wonder the game was unknown in the Five Galaxies, until humans arrived.

Sara had quickly recognized a version of *Shannon coding,* named after an Earthling pioneer of information theory who showed how specially coded messages can be restored, even from a jumble of static. It proved crucial to digital speech and data transmission, in pre-Contact human society.

Indo-European was logical, error-resistant, like Galactic tongues that suit computers far better than chaotic Anglic.

To many, this implied Earthlings *must* have had patrons in the misty past. But watching the Stranger commune happily with other engineers, in a makeshift language of grunts and hand gestures, reminded Sara

It wasn't Indo-European speakers who invented *com-*

puters. Nor users of any prim Galactic language. The star-gods received their mighty powers by inheritance.

In all the recent history of the Five Galaxies, just one folk independently invented computers—and nearly everything else needed for starfaring life—from scratch.

Those people spoke Rossic, Nihanic, French, and especially the forerunner of Anglic, wild, undisciplined English.

Did they do it despite their chaotic language?

Or because of it?

The masters of her guild thought she chased phantoms—that she was using this diversion to evade other obligations.

But Sara had a hunch. Past and present held clues to the destiny awaiting the Six.

That is, if destiny had not already been decided.

Dawn spilled quickly downslope from the Rimmers. It was in clear violation of emergency orders for the *gopher* to continue, but nobody dared say it to the captain, who had a crazed look in his eye.

Probably comes from spending so much time around humans, Sara thought. The steamers had as many men and women on the crew—to tend the machines—as hoon sailors. Grawph-phu, the pilot and master, knew the river with sure instincts that arose out of his heritage. He also had picked up more than a few Earthling mannerisms, like wearing a knit cap over his furry pate and puffing a pipe that fumed like the steamer's chimney. Peering through the dawn haze, the captain's craggy features might have come from the flyleaf of some seafaring adventure tale, chosen off the shelves in the Biblos Library—like some piratical old-timer, exuding an air of confidence and close acquaintance with danger.

Grawph-phu turned his head, noticed Sara looking at him, and closed one eye in a sly wink.

Oh, spare me, she sighed, half expecting the hoon to spit over the side and say—*"Arr, matie. 'Tis a fine day for sailin'. Full speed ahead!"*

Instead, the *gopher*'s master pulled the pipe from his mouth and pointed.

"Biblos," he commented, a low, hoonish growl accented by a salty twang. "Just beyond the curve after next. Hr-rm. . . . A day sooner 'n you expected to arrive."

Sara looked ahead once more. *I should be glad,* she thought. *Time is short.*

At first she could make out little but Eternal Swamp on the left bank, stretching impassably all the way to the Roney, an immensity of quicksand that forced the long detour past Tarek Town. On the right began the vast Warril Plain, where several passengers had debarked earlier to arrange overland passage. Taking a fast caravan were Bloor, the portraitist, and a petite exploser carrying dispatches for her guild. Both were slight enough to ride donkeys all the way and with luck might reach the Glade in three days. Prity and Pzora also went ashore at Kandu Landing to hire carts in case the Stranger must be taken before the High Sages—to be decided during this trip to Biblos.

As the fog cleared, there now reared to the right a wall of stone, rising from the water line, getting taller with each passing dura. The cliff shimmered, almost glassy smooth, as though impervious to erosion or time. Arguments raged as to whether it was natural or a Buyur relic.

Against these mirror-like cliffs, Ulgor had said the citizens of Dolo Village might see flames from burning books. Two centuries ago, settlers *had* witnessed such a sight, horrible even from afar. A disaster never equaled since, not by the massacre at Tolon, or when Uk-rann ambushed Drake the Elder at Bloody Ford.

But we saw no flames.

Still, tension reigned until the steamer turned a final bend. . . .

Sara let out a tense sigh. *The Archive . . . it stands.*

She stared for some time, awash in emotion, then hurried aft to fetch the Stranger and Ariana Foo. Both of them would want to see this.

· · · ·

It was a *castle,* adamant, impervious, carved with tools that no longer existed. Godlike tools, sent to the deep soon after they cut this stronghold. A citadel of knowledge.

The original granite outcrop still jutted like a finger into the curving river, with its back braced against the shiny-smooth cliff. From above, it probably looked much as it always had, with woody thickets disguising atrium openings that let filtered daylight into courtyards and reading groves below. But from the dock where the *gopher* tied up, one saw imposing defensive battlements, then row after row of massive, sculpted pillars that held up the natural plateau, suspending its undermined weight as a roof against the sky.

Inside this abnormal cave, wooden buildings protected their precious contents against rain, wind, and snow—all except the inferno that once rocked the southern end, leaving rubble and ruin. In a single night, fully a third of the wisdom left by the Great Printing had gone up in smoke and despair.

The sections that would have been most useful today. Those devoted to Galactic society, its many races and clans. What remained gave only sketchy outlines of the complex bio-social-political relationships that fluxed through the Five Galaxies.

Despite the crisis, dawn summoned a stream of pilgrims from hostelries in the nearby tree-shrouded village, scholars who joined the *gopher* passengers climbing a zigzag ramp toward the main gate. Traeki and g'Kek students caught their breath at resting spots. Red qheuens from the distant sea paused now and then to spray saltwater over their cupolas. Ulgor and Blade gave them wide berth.

A donkey-caravan edged by the line of visitors, heading downhill. Wax-sealed crates told of precious contents. *They're still evacuating,* Sara realized. *Taking advantage of the sages' delaying tactics.*

Would she find empty shelves inside, as far as the eye could see?

*Impossible! Even if they could somehow move so many
volumes, where would they store them all?*

The Stranger insisted on pushing Ariana's wheelchair,
perhaps out of respect, or to show how far his physical
recovery had come. In fact, his dusky skin now had a
healthy luster, and his deep laughter was hearty. He
stared in wonder at the mighty stone walls, then the
drawbridge, portcullis, and militia guards. Instead of the
token detail Sara recalled, now a full platoon patrolled
the parapets, equipped with spears, bows, and arbalests.

Ariana looked pleased by the Stranger's reaction. The
old woman glanced at Sara with an expression of satisfaction.

*He's never been here before. Even the damage he's
suffered could not have erased a memory as vivid as
Biblos. Either he is a rube from the farthest, most rustic
human settlements, or else . . .*

They passed the final battlements, and the Stranger
gazed in amazement at the buildings of the Archive itself. Wooden structures, modeled after stone monu-
ments of Earth's revered past—the Parthenon, Edo
Castle, and even a miniature Taj Mahal, whose minarets
merged into four heavy pillars holding up part of the
roof-of-stone. Clearly, the founders had a taste for the
dramatically ironic, for all the ancient originals had been
built to *last,* dedicated in their day to vain resistance
against time, while *these* buildings had a different goal—
to serve a function and then vanish, as if they had never
been.

Even that was too much for some people.

"Arrogance!" muttered Jop, the tree farmer, who had
chosen to come along when he learned of this expedition. "It all has to go, if we're ever to be blessed."

"In time, it must," Ariana Foo nodded, leaving vague
whether she meant next week, or in a thousand years.

Sara saw fresh clay smeared over holes at the base of
several great pillars. *Just like back home,* she realized.
The explosers are making sure all is ready.

She could not help turning to glance behind Jop. Taking up the rear were the last two *gopher* passengers,

young Jomah, Henrik's son, and his uncle, Kurt. The elder exploser bent to point out structural features to the boy, using hand motions that made Sara think of tumbling chunks of ancient granite. She wondered if the Stranger, staring about in apparent delight, had any idea how little it would take to turn all this into rubble, indistinguishable from a hundred other places demolished by the Buyur when they departed, leaving the planet to revert to nature.

Sara felt a return of the old tightness in her shoulder blades. It hadn't been easy, at first, being a student in this place. Even when she had taken her books to the forest up top, to read under the shade of a homey garu tree, she could never shake off a sense that the whole plateau might shudder and collapse beneath her. For a while, the nervous fantasies had threatened her studies—until Joshu came along.

Sara winced. She had known it would all come back if she returned to this place. Memories.

"Nothing lasts forever," Jop added as they neared the Athenian portico of Central Hall, unaware how stingingly the words struck Sara's private thoughts.

Ariana agreed. "Ifni insists on it. Nothing can resist the goddess of change."

If the elder sage meant the remark to be sardonic, Sara missed her point. She was too deep in reminiscence to care, even as they neared the giant double doors— carved from the finest wood as a gift from the qheuen race, then bound with urrish bronze, lacquered by traeki secretions and painted by g'Kek artists. The work towered ten meters high, depicting in ornate symbolism the thing most treasured by all, the latest, best, and most hard-won accomplishment of Jijo's Commons in Exile.

The Great Peace.

This time, Sara hardly noticed when the Stranger gasped in appreciation. She couldn't share his pleasure. Not when all she felt within this place was sadness.

Asx

THE PORTRAITIST DID NOT EVEN ASK TO REST AFter the long, hard trek from Kandu Landing. He set to work at once, preparing his materials—caustic chemicals and hard metals whose imperviousness to time make them suspect under Commons law—yet ideal for blackmail.

Others of his guild were already here, having come to Gathering in order to sell paper photographs of visitors, guildmasters, winners at the games—anyone vain enough to want a graven image keepsake to last out a lifetime, maybe two. A few of these skilled likeness-peddlers had offered to secretly record the invaders, but to what purpose? Paper portraits are designed to fade and rot, not last aeons. Better not to risk the aliens catching them in the act, and so discovering some of our hidden arts.

But Ariana, Bloor, and young Sara Koolhan appear to have come up with something different, have they not, my rings? Despite exhaustion from the road, Bloor appeared at once before us to show off the *daguerreotype*. An implausibly precise image stored on etched metal, centuries in age. Ur-Jah trembled as she fondled the accurate depiction of a great tattooed chieftain of old.

"If we attempt this, secrecy is essential. Our foes must not know how few pictures were taken," Phwhoon-dau pointed out, while privacy wasps swarmed our hidden tent-of-conclave, fluttering drops of bitter color from their glowing wings.

"The sky-gods must imagine that we have scribed *hundreds* of plates already safely hidden far from here, in so many deep places they could never find them all."

"True," Vubben added, his eyestalks weaving a dance of caution. "But there is more. For this to work, the portraits cannot simply show the human invaders' faces. Of what use will that be as evidence, a million years hence? They must include the aliens' machines, and clear Jijoan landmarks, and also the local animals they inspect as candidates for ravishment."

"And their costumes, their garish garb," Lester Cambel inserted urgently. "Any identifiers to show they are *renegade* humans. Not representatives of our sept on Jijo, or of Earth."

We all assented to this last request, though it seems futile to satisfy. How could a few etched plates express such fine distinctions to prosecutors so long after we are gone?

We asked Bloor to consult with our agents, bearing all these criteria in mind. If anything comes of this, it will indeed be a miracle.

We *believe* in miracles, do we not, my rings? Today, the rewq in our/my pouch came out of dormant state. So did that of Vubben, our Speaker of Ignition. Others report stirrings.

Is it possible to call this cause for hope? Or have they only begun awakening, as rewq sometimes do in the last stages of illness, shortly before they roll up and die?

Dwer

THE TRAIL OVER THE RIMMERS WAS STEEP AND broken.

That never mattered during Dwer's prior trips into the eastern wilderness—survey sweeps sanctioned by the sages—carrying just his bow, a map, and a few necessities. The first time, right after old Fallon's retirement, he got so elated that he *ran* down to the misty plains letting gravity yank him headlong, yelling as he leaped from one teetering foothold to the next.

There was none of that now. No exhilaration. No contest of youth and skill against Jijo's ardent hug. This was a sober affair, coaxing a dozen heavily laden donkeys over patches of unsteady footing, using patient firmness to overcome the animals' frequent bouts of stubbornness. He wondered how Urrish traders made it look so easy, guiding their pack trains with shrill, clipped whistles.

And they say these things come from Earth? he wondered, dragging yet another donkey out of trouble. Dwer wasn't warm to the idea of being a close genetic cousin to such creatures.

Then there were the *human* charges he must also shepherd into the wilderness.

In fairness, it could have been worse. Danel Ozawa was an experienced forester, and the two women were strong, with their own unique skills. Still, nothing back on the tame Slope compared to this kind of trekking. Dwer found himself frequently moving up and down the train, helping his companions out of jams.

He wasn't sure which unnerved him more, the stolid indifference of Lena Strong or the gawky friendliness of Jenin Worley, frequently catching his eye with a shy smile. They had been obvious choices, since Jenin and Lena were already at Gathering to lobby for their "tourism" idea—hoping to enlist Dwer's help, and approval from the sages, to start taking groups of "sight-seers" over the Rimmers.

In other words, bright people with too much time on their hands, overly influenced by notions they found in old Earth books.

I was going to fight it. Even same-sex groups risked violating the anti-sooner covenant.

But now—I'm part of a scheme to break the law I'm sworn to uphold.

He couldn't help glancing repeatedly at the two women, the same way they were surely appraising him.

They sure looked . . . healthy.

You're a true wild man now. Learn to prize the honest virtues of wild females.

There would be women in the Gray Hills, too, but Rety said most of them began childbirth at fourteen. Few kept more than half their teeth past age thirty.

There was supposed to be a second group of volunteer exiles from the Slope, following behind this one. For their sake, Dwer smeared dabs of porl paste on prominent landmarks every half a midura or so, blazing a trail any moderately competent Jijoan could follow, but that should be untraceable by Galactic raiders or their all-seeing machinery.

Dwer would rather be home at the bitter end, preparing to fight hopelessly against the aliens, alongside other militia soldiers of the Six. But no one was better qualified to lead this expedition to the Gray Hills, and he had given Danel his word.

So now I'm a tour-guide, after all, he thought.

If only he felt sure it was right.

What are we doing? Fleeing to another place we don't belong, just like our sinner ancestors? It made Dwer's head ache to think about such things. *Just please don't let Lark find out what I'm doing. It'd break his heart.*

The trek grew a little easier when they spilled off the mountain onto a high steppe. But unlike his other expeditions, this time Dwer turned *south,* toward a rolling domain of bitter yellow grass. Soon they were stomping through a prairie of calf-high shoots, whose florets had sharp tips, forcing the humans—and even the donkeys—to wear leather leggings for protection.

No one complained, or even murmured discomfort. Danel and the others took his guidance without question, wiping sweat from their hat brims and collars as they slogged alongside the stolid donkeys. Fortunately, scattered oases of real forest helped Dwer pilot the company from one water source to the next, leaving markers for the next group.

Rety must've been dogged to cross all this, chasing after her damn bird.

Dwer had suggested waiting for the girl. "She's your real guide," he had told Danel.

"Not true," Ozawa demurred. "Would you trust her advice? She might steer us wrong in some misguided gesture to protect her loved ones."

Or to avoid ever seeing them again. Still, Dwer wished

Rety had made it back in time to depart with this group. He kind of missed her, sullen sarcasm and all.

He called a halt at a large oasis, more than an hour before sunset. "The mountains will cut off daylight early," he told the others. Westward, the peaks were already surrounded by a nimbus of yellow-orange. "You three should clear the water hole, tend the animals, and set up camp."

"And where are *you* going?" Lena Strong asked sharply, mopping her brow.

Dwer strapped on his hip quiver. "To see about shooting some supper."

She gestured at the sterile-looking steppe. "What, here?"

"It's worth a try, Lena," Danel said, slashing at some yellow grass with a stick. "With the donkeys unable to eat this stuff, our grain must last till we hit hill country, where they can forage. A little meat for the four of us could help a lot."

Dwer didn't bother adding anything to that. He set out down one of the narrow critter byways threading the spiky grass. It was some distance before he managed to put the donkey stench behind him, as well as the penetrating murmur of his companions' voices.

It's a bad idea to be noisy when the universe is full of things tougher than you are. But that never stopped humans, did it?

He sniffed the air and watched the sway of thigh-high grass. In this kind of prairie, it was even more imperative to hunt upwind not only because of scent, but so the breeze might help hinder the racket of your own trampling feet from reaching the quarry—in this case a covey of bush quaile he sensed pecking and scratching, a dozen or so meters ahead.

Dwer nocked an arrow and stepped as stealthfully as he could, breathing shallowly, until he picked out soft chittering sounds amid the brushing stems . . . a tiny ruckus of claws scratching sandy loam . . . sharp beaks pecking for seeds . . . a gentle, motherly cluck . . . answering peeps as hatchlings sought a feathery breast . . . the faint puffs of junior adults, relaying news from the periphery that all is well. All is well.

One of the sentries abruptly changed its muted report. A breath of tentative alarm. Dwer stooped to make his profile lower and kept stock still. Fortunately, the twilight shadows were deepest to his back. If only he could manage to keep from spooking them for a few more . . .

A sudden crashing commotion sent four-winged shapes erupting into the air. *Another predator,* Dwer realized, raising his bow. While most of the quaile scattered swiftly across the grasstops and vanished, a few spiraled back to swoop over the intruder, distracting it from the brood-mother and her chicks. Dwer loosed arrows in rapid succession, downing one—then another of the guardians.

The ruckus ended as swiftly as it began. Except for a trampled area, the patch of steppe looked as if nothing had happened.

Dwer shouldered his bow and pulled out his machete. In principle, nothing that could hide under grass should be much of a threat to him, except perhaps a root scorpion. But there were legends of strange, nasty beasts in this realm southeast of the gentle Slope. Even a famished ligger could make a damned nuisance of itself.

He found the first bird where it fell.

This should make Lena happy for a while, he thought, realizing that might be a lifelong task, from now on.

The grass swayed again, near where he'd shot the second bird. He rushed forward, machete upraised. "Oh, no you don't, thief!"

Dwer braked as a slinky, black-pelted creature emerged with the other quaile clutched between its jaws. The bloody arrow trailed in the dust.

"You." Dwer sighed, lowering the knife. "I should've known."

Mudfoot's dark eyes glittered so eloquently, Dwer imagined words.

That's right, boss. Glad to see me? Don't bother thank-

ing me for flushing the birds. I'll just keep this juicy one as payment.

He shrugged in resignation. "Oh, all right. But I want the arrow back, you hear?"

The noor grinned, as usual betraying no sign how much or how little it understood.

Night fell as they ambled toward the oasis. Flames flickered under a sheltering tree. The shifting breeze brought scents of donkey, human, and simmering porridge.

Better keep the fire small enough to seem a natural smolder, he reminded himself.

Then another thought occurred to Dwer.

Rety said noor never came over the mountains. So what's this one doing here?

Rety hadn't lied about there being herds of *glaver*, southeast of the Rimmers. After two days of swift trekking, loping at a half-jog beside the trotting donkeys, Dwer and the others found clear signs—the sculpted mounds where glavers habitually buried their feces.

"Damn . . . you're right . . ." Danel agreed, panting with hands on knees. The two women, on the other hand, seemed barely winded.

"It looks . . . as if things . . . just got more complicated."

You could say that, Dwer thought. Years of careful enforcement by hunters like himself had all been in vain. *We always figured the yellow grass could be crossed only by well-equipped travelers, never glavers. That's why we aimed most of our surveys farther north.*

The next day, Dwer called a halt amid another jog, when he spied a throng of glavers in the distance, scrounging at one end of a scrub wadi. All four humans took turns observing through Danel Ozawa's urrish-made binoculars. The pale, bulge-eyed creatures appeared to be browsing on a steppe-gallaiter, a burly, long-legged beast native to this region, whose corpse lay sprawled across a patch of trampled grass. The sight stunned them all, except Jenin Worley.

"Didn't you say that's how to survive on the plains? By eating animals who *can* eat this stuff?" She flicked a stem of the sharp yellow grass. "So the glavers have adapted to a new way of life. Isn't that what we're gonna have to do?"

Unlike Danel Ozawa, who seemed sadly resigned to their mission, Jenin appeared almost *avid* for this adventure, especially knowing it might be their destiny to preserve the human race on Jijo. When he saw that zealous eagerness in her eyes, Dwer felt he had more in common with the sturdy, square-jawed Lena Strong. At least Lena looked on all this much the way he did—as one more duty to perform in a world that didn't care about anyone's wishes.

"It's . . . rather surprising," Danel replied, lowering the glasses and looking upset. "I thought it wasn't possible for glavers to eat red meat."

"Adaptability," Lena commented gruffly. "One of the hallmarks of presentience. Maybe this means they're on their way back up, after the long slide down."

Danel seemed to consider this seriously. "So soon? If so, I wonder. Could it mean—"

Dwer interrupted before the sage had a chance to go philosophical on them. "Let me have those," he said, taking the glass-and-boo magnifiers. "I'll be right back."

He started forward at a crouch. Naturally, Mudfoot chose to tag along, scampering ahead, then circling repeatedly to stage mock-ambushes. Dwer's jaw clenched, but he refused to give the beast the satisfaction of reacting. *Ignore it. Maybe it'll go away.*

That hadn't worked so far. Jenin seemed thrilled to have Mudfoot as a mascot, while Danel found its tenacity intriguing. Lena had voted with the others, overruling Dwer's wish to send it packing. *"It weighs next to nothing,"* she said. *"Let it ride a donkey, so long as it fetches its own food and stays out of the way."*

That it did, scrupulously avoiding Lena, posing for

Danel's pensive scrutiny, and purring contentedly when Jenin petted it by the campfire each evening.

In my case, it acts as if being irritated were my heart's desire.

While creeping toward the wadi, Dwer kept mental notes on the lay of the land, the crackling consistency of the grass stems, the fickleness of the breeze. He did this out of professional habit, and also in case it ever became necessary to do this someday for real, pursuing the glaver herd with arrows nocked and ready. Ironically that would happen only in the event of *good* news. If word came from the Slope that all was well—that the gene-raiders had departed without wreaking the expected genocide—then this expedition would revert to a traditional Mission of Ingathering—a militia enterprise to rid this region of all glavers *and* humans, preferably by capture, but in the end by any means necessary.

On the other hand, assuming the worst did happen out west and all the Six Races were wiped out, their small group would *join* Rety's family of renegades as exiles in the wilderness. Under Danel's guidance, they would tame Rety's cousins and create simple, wise traditions for living in harmony with their new home.

One of those traditions would be to forbid the sooners from ever again hunting glavers for food.

That was the bloody incongruity Dwer found so hard to take, leaving little option or choice. *Good* news would make him a mass-killer. Contrariwise, horrible news would make him a gentle neighbor to glavers and men.

Duty and death on one side. Death and duty on the other. Dwer wondered, *Is survival really worth all this?*

From a small rise, he lifted the binoculars. Two families of glavers seemed to be feeding on the gallaiter, while others kept watch. Normally, such a juicy corpse would be cleaned down to a white skeleton, first by liggers or other large carnivores, then hickuls with heavy jaws for grinding bones, and finally by flyers known simply as vultures, though they looked like nothing in pictures from Old Earth.

Even now, a pack of hickuls swarmed the far periphery of the clearing. A glaver rose up on her haunches and hurled a stone. The scavengers scattered, whining miserably.

Ah. I see how they do it.

The glavers had found a unique way to live on the steppe. Unable to digest grass or boo, or to eat red meat, they apparently used cadavers to attract hordes of *insects* from the surrounding area, which they consumed at leisure while others in the herd warded off all competition.

They seemed to be enjoying themselves, holding squirmy things before their globelike eyes, mewling in approval, then catching them between smacking jaws. Dwer had never seen glavers act with such—*enthusiasm*. Not back where they were treated as sacred fools, encouraged to root at will through the garbage middens of the Six.

Mudfoot met Dwer's eyes with a revolted expression.

Ifni, what pigs! All right if we charge in there now? Bust 'em up good, boss. Then herd 'em all back to civilization, like it or not?

Dwer vowed to curb his imagination. Probably the noor simply didn't like the smell.

Still he chided Mudfoot in a low voice.

"Who are *you* to find *others* disgusting, Mister lick-myself-all-over? Come on. Let's tell the others, glavers haven't gone carnivorous, after all. We have more running ahead, if we're to make it out of this sting-grass by nightfall."

Asx

MORE WORD ARRIVES FROM THE FAR SOUTH, SENT by the smith of Mount Guenn Forge.

The message was sparse and distorted, having come partly by courier, and partly conveyed between mountain peaks by inexperienced mirror-flashers, in the partly-restored semaphore system.

Apparently, the alien forayers have begun visiting all the fishing hamlets and red qheuen rookeries, making pointed inquiries. They even landed in the water, far out at sea, to badger the crew of a dross-hauler, on its way home from holy labors at the Midden. Clearly the interlopers feel free to swoop down and interrogate our citizens wherever they dwell, with questions about "strange sights, strange creatures, or lights in the sea."

Should we make up a story, my rings? Should we fabulate some tale of ocean monsters to intrigue our unwanted guests and possibly stave off fate for a while?

Assuming we dare, what would they do to us when they learn the truth?

Lark

ALL THAT MORNING, LARK WORKED NEXT TO LING in a state of nervous tension, made worse by the fact that he did not dare let it show. Soon, with luck, he would have his best chance to line things up just right. It would be a delicate task though, doing spywork at the behest of the sages while also probing for information *he* needed, for reasons of his own.

Timing would be everything.

The Evaluation Tent bustled with activity. The whole rear half of the pavilion was stacked with cages made by qheuenish crafters out of local boo, filled with specimens brought from all over this side of Jijo. A staff of humans, urs, and hoon labored full-time to keep the animals fed, watered, and healthy, while several local g'Kek had shown remarkable talent at running various creatures through mazes or performing other tests, supervised by robots whose instructions were always in prim, flawless Galactic Two. It had been made clear to Lark that it was a mark of high distinction to be asked to work *directly* with one of the star-humans.

His second airborne expedition had been even more exhausting than the first, a three-day voyage beginning with a zigzag spiral far out to sea, cruising just above the waves over the dark blue expanse of the Midden, then hopping from one island to the next along an extended offshore archipelago, sampling a multitude of wildly varied life-forms Lark had never seen before. To his surprise, it turned out to be a much more enjoyable trip than the first.

For one thing, Ling grew somewhat less condescending as they worked together, appreciating each other's skills. Moreover, Lark found it stirring to see what evolution had wrought during just a million fallow years, turning each islet into a miniature biological reactor, breeding delightful variations. There were flightless avians who had given up the air, and gliding reptiloids that seemed on the verge of earning wings. Mammiforms whose hair grew in horny protective spikes, and zills whose coatings of fluffy torg shimmered with colors never seen on their bland mainland cousins. Only later did he conclude that some of the diversity might have been enhanced from the start, by Jijo's last legal tenants. Perhaps the Buyur seeded each isle with different genetic stock as part of a *very* long scale experiment.

Ling and Besh often had to drag him away when it came time to leave a sampling site, while Kunn muttered irascibly by his console, apparently happy only when they were aloft. On landing, Lark was always first to rush out the hatch. For a while, all the dour brooding of his dreams lay submerged under a passion for discovery.

Still, as they cruised home on the last leg—another unexplained back-and-forth gyration over open sea—he had found himself wondering. *This trip was marvelous, but* why *did we go? What did they hope to accomplish?* Even before humans left Earth, biologists knew—higher life-forms need *room* to evolve, preferably large continents. Despite the wild variety encountered on the archipelago, there wasn't a single creature the star-folk could hope to call a candidate for uplift.

Sure enough, when he rejoined Ling the next day, the outlander woman announced they would return to analyzing rock-stallers, right after lunch. Besh had already resumed her intensive investigation of glavers, clearly glad to be back to work on her best prospect.

Glavers. The irony struck Lark. Yet he held back his questions, biding his time.

Finally, Ling put down the chart they had been working on—duplicating much that already covered the walls of his Dolo Village study—and led him to the table where machines offered refreshments in the sky-human fashion. The light was very good there, so Lark gave a furtive nod to a small man cleaning some animal pens. The fair-haired fellow moved toward a stack of wooden crates, used for hauling foodstuffs for the raucous zoo of captive creatures.

Lark positioned himself at the south end of the table so he would not block the man's view of Ling, as well as Besh and everything beyond. Especially Ling. For this to work, he must try to keep her still for as long as possible.

"Besh seems to think you've found yourselves a first-class candidate species."

"Mm?" The dark-eyed woman looked up from a complex machine lavishly dedicated to producing a single beverage—a bitter drink Lark had tried just once, appropriately named *coughee.*

"Found what?" Ling stirred a steaming mug and leaned back against the edge of the table.

Lark gestured at the subject Besh studied, complacently chewing a ball of sap while a contraption perched on its head, sifting neurons. There had been a spurt of excitement when Besh swore she heard the glaver "mimic" two spoken words. Now Besh seemed intent, peering through her microscope, guiding a brain probe with tiny motions of her hands, sitting rock still.

"I take it glavers have what you seek?" Lark continued.

Ling smiled. "We'll know better when our ship returns and more advanced tests are made."

Out the corner of his eye, Lark saw the small man remove the cover from a hole in one side of a box. There was a soft sparkle of glass.

"And when *will* the ship be back?" he asked, keeping Ling's attention.

Her smile widened. "I wish you folks would stop asking that. It's enough to make one think you had a reason for caring. Why should it matter to you when the ship comes?"

Lark blew his cheeks, hoon fashion, then recalled that the gesture would mean nothing to her. "A little warning would be nice, that's all. It takes *time* to bake a really big cake."

She chuckled, more heartily than his joke deserved. Lark was learning not to take umbrage each time he suspected he was being patronized. Anyway, Ling wouldn't be laughing when shipboard archives revealed that glavers—their prime candidate for uplift—were *already* Galactic citizens, presumably still flitting around their own backwater of space, in secondhand ships.

Or would even the star-cruiser's onboard records reveal it? According to the oldest scrolls, glavers came from an obscure race among the myriad sapient clans of the Five Galaxies. Maybe, like the g'Kek, they had already gone extinct and no one remembered them, save in the chilly recesses of the largest-sector branch Libraries.

This might even be the moment foretold long ago by the final glaver sage, before humans came to Jijo. A time when restored innocence would shrive their race, peel away their sins, and offer them a precious second chance. A new beginning.

If so, they deserve better than to be adopted by a pack of thieves.

"Suppose they prove perfect in every way. Will you take them with you when you go?"

"Probably. A breeding group of a hundred or so."

Peripherally, he glimpsed the small man replacing the cover of the camera lens. With a satisfied smile, Bloor the Portraitist casually lifted the box, carrying it outside through the back tent flap. Lark felt a knot of tension release. Ling's face might be a bit blurry in the photo, but her clothes and body stood a good chance of coming through, despite the long exposure time. By good fortune, Besh, the glaver, a robot, and a sleeping rock-staller had remained still the entire time. The mountain range, seen through the open entrance, would pin down location and season of the year.

"And what of the rest?" he asked, relieved to have just one matter on his mind now.

"What do you mean?"

"I mean what will happen to all the glavers you leave behind?"

Her dark eyes narrowed. "Why should anything happen to them?"

"Why indeed?" Lark shifted uncomfortably. The sages wanted to maintain the atmosphere of tense ambiguity for a while longer rather than confront the aliens directly over their plans. But he had already done the sages' bidding by helping Bloor. Meanwhile, Harullen and the other heretics were pressuring Lark for answers. They must decide soon whether to throw their lot in with the zealots' mysterious scheme.

"Then . . . there is the matter of the rest of us."

"The rest of you?" Ling arched an eyebrow.

"We Six. When you find what you seek, and depart— what happens to us?"

She groaned. "I can't count the number of times I've been asked about this!"

Lark stared. "Who—?"

"Who *hasn't*?" She blew an exasperated sigh. "At least a third of the patients we treat on clinic day sidle up afterward to pump us about how we'll *do it*. What means do we plan to use when we finally get around to killing every sentient being on the planet! Will we be gentle? Or will it come as firebolts from heaven, on the day we depart? It gets so repetitious, sometimes I want to—agh!" She clenched her fist, frustration apparent on her normally composed features.

Lark blinked. He had planned edging up to the very same questions.

"Folks are frightened," he began. "The logic of the situation—"

"Yes, yes. I know," Ling interrupted impatiently. "If

we came to steal presapient life-forms from Jijo, we can't afford to leave any witnesses. And especially, we can't leave any native stock of the species we stole! Honestly, where do you people get such ideas?"

From books, Lark almost answered. *From the warnings of our ancestors.*

But, indeed, how well could those accounts be trusted? The most detailed had been lost to fire soon after humans arrived. Anyway, weren't humans naïve newcomers on the Galactic scene back in those days, worried to the point of paranoia? And wasn't it the *most* paranoic who had boarded the *Tabernacle,* smuggling themselves to a far, forbidden world to hide?

Might the danger be exaggerated?

"Seriously, Lark, why should we fear anything a bunch of sooners might say about us? The odds of another Institute inspection team arriving at Jijo in under a hundred thousand years are very small. By the time one does, if any of you are still around, our visit will surely have dissolved into vague legends. We have no need to commit genocide—as if we could *ever* bring ourselves to do such a horrid thing, however strong the reason!"

For the first time, Lark saw beyond Ling's normal mask of wry sardonicism. Either she deeply believed what she was saying, or she was a very skilled actress.

"Well then, how *do* you plan to adopt any presentient species you find here? Surely you can't admit you picked them up on a restricted world."

"At last, an intelligent question." She seemed relieved. "I confess, it won't be easy. They must be planted in another ecosystem for starters, along with any symbionts they need, and other evidence to imply they've been there for some time. Then we must wait quite a while—"

"A million years?"

Ling's smile returned, thinly. "Not quite so long. We have a couple of advantages going for us, you see. One is the fact that on most worlds the bio-record is a jumble of phylogenic anomalies. Despite rules to minimize harmful cross-flow, each time a new starfaring clan wins tenant rights to a world, they inevitably bring in their

favorite plants and animals, along with a host of parasites and other hangers-on. Take glavers, for instance."
She nodded over at the subject. "I'm sure we'll find
records of places where similar genes flowed in the
past."

Now it was Lark's turn to smile, briefly. *You don't
know the half of it.*

"So you see," Ling went on. "It won't matter much if a
residual population stays on Jijo, as long as we have time
to modify the borrowed stock, artificially enhancing the
apparent rate of genetic divergence. And that will happen anyway when we begin the process of uplift."

So, Lark realized, *even if the forayers eventually find
glavers unsuitable, they might still make off with some
other promising species and turn a nice profit from their
crime.*

Moreover, they appeared completely comfortable seeing it as no crime at all.

"And your other advantage?" he asked.

"Ah, now that's the real secret." A shine seemed to
enter the woman's dark eyes. "You see, what it really
comes down to is a matter of *skill.*"

"Skill?"

"On the part of our blessed patrons." Now her words
struck a reverent tone. "The Rothen are past masters at
this art, you see. Witness their greatest success so far—
the human race."

There it was again, mention of the mysterious clan
that had the utter devotion of Ling, Rann, and the others.
The star-humans had started out reticent. Ling had even
made it clear that Rothen was not their real name. But
with time she and the others grew more talkative, as if
their pride could not be contained.

Or else, because they had no fear the tale would
spread.

"Imagine. They managed to uplift humanity in complete secrecy, subtly altering the records of the Migration
Institute so that our homeworld, Earth, remained untouched, on fallow status, for an incredible half a *billion*
years! They even kept their gentle guidance unknown to

our own ancestors, leaving them with the fantastic but useful illusion that they were uplifting themselves!"

"Amazing," Lark commented. He had never seen Ling so animated. He wanted to ask, *"How could such feats be feasible?"* But that might imply he doubted her, and Lark wanted this openness to continue. "Of course, self-uplift is impossible," he prompted.

"Completely. It's been known since the fabled days of the Progenitors. Evolution can bring a species all the way up to *pre*-sapience, but the final leap needs help from another race that's already made it. This principle underlies the life-cycle of all oxygen-breathing races in the Five Galaxies."

"So why did our ancestors believe they raised themselves up?"

"Oh, the most insightful always suspected we had help from beyond. It explains the depth of feeling underlying most religions. But the true source of our gift of sapiency remained mysterious for most of the time that hidden hands guided our path. Only the Danikites—early precursors of our group—knew the secret all along."

"Even the Tergens Council—"

"The *Terragens* Council." Her voice soured. "The idiots guiding Earth and her colonies during these dangerous times? Their obstinacy hardly matters. Even this *Streaker* business, sending half the fanatics in the universe into a frenzy, howling for Earthling blood, even this will come out all right, despite the Terragens fools. The Rothen will see to things. Don't worry."

Lark *hadn't* been worried. Not on the scale she referred to. Not till that moment. Now he found her words anything but reassuring.

From other conversations with the Danik sky-humans, the sages had already pieced together hints that some great crisis was setting the Five Galaxies in an uproar. It might even explain why the gene raiders were here right now, taking advantage of the turmoil to do a little burglary.

What could a feeble clan of Earthlings have done to cause such commotion? Lark wondered.

With some effort, he pushed the thought aside as much too vast to be grappled with right now.

"When did the Rothen reveal the truth to you . . . Danikites?"

"Longer back than you might think, Lark. Even before your ancestors headed off in their creaky junkyard starship, taking their foolish wild gamble in coming to this world. Soon after humanity entered interstellar space, a few men and women were chosen by the Rothen to receive the word. Those who had already been keeping faith, holding steadfast vigil. Some stayed on Earth to help guide the race in secret, while others went off to dwell in joy among the Rothen, aiding them in their work."

"And what work is that?"

She had a look Lark sometimes saw on the faces of those returning from pilgrimages to the Egg, on those blessed occasions when the sacred stone sang its serene harmonies. An expression of having experienced splendor.

"Why, rescuing the lost, of course. And nurturing what might-yet-be."

Lark worried she might drift into complete mysticism. "Will we get to meet some Rothen?"

Her eyes had defocused while pondering vistas of time and space. Now they turned and glittered sharply.

"Some of you may, if you are lucky.

"In fact, a few of you may get luckier than you ever dreamed."

Her implication set his head awhirl. Could she mean what he thought she meant?

That evening, by candlelight, he went over his calculations one more time.

From our best measurements, the starship had a volume of about half a million cubic meters. If you stacked

every human on Jijo like frozen cordwood, we just might
fit—providing you left no room for anything else.

The first time he had worked out the numbers, his
intent was simply to dispel rumors among some younger
urs and qheuens that the human settlers would soon
abandon Jijo. It was physically impossible, he showed,
for the youngest sept to forsake the Commons for a
ticket back to the stars. At least with this ship alone.

But she said "some of you."

Even after loading aboard hundreds of wuankworms,
longsnouts, or glavers, there'd still be room for a few lost
cousins. Those who had proved useful.

Lark knew a bribe when he heard one.

Much as he condemned the ancestors' choice to come
here, Lark loved this world. He would feel a pang if he
ever left, and for all his days thereafter.

Yet if things were different, I'd go in a shot. Who
wouldn't?

The zealots are right. No human can be completely
trusted these days. Not when any of us might be sub-
orned. Bought with an offer to be made into a god.

In fact, he had no idea what the zealots planned. Only
that they felt free to act without advice or approval from
the dithering sages. There were humans in the cabal, of
course. What could be accomplished without Earthling
skill and lore? But men and women were excluded from
the inner circle.

So what have I learned?

He looked down at a blank sheet. Surely the sages and
zealots had other feelers out. Even Harullen must be
hedging his bets. Still, Lark knew his words carried
weight.

If Ling is telling the truth, and the zealots believe it,
they might call off whatever action they planned. What
do they care if a few glavers or rock-stallers are taken
off-planet, so long as the intruders leave us in peace, as
we were before?

But what if Ling was lying? Might the zealots lose their
best chance to strike, for nothing?

On the other hand, suppose no one believed Ling, but

she really *was* telling the truth? The zealots might attack, and fail, only to goad the very response they feared!

At the opposite extreme of radicalism from the fiery zealots, some of the most radical *heretics* actually *favored* their own destruction, along with the rest of the Six. Some hoon and urs members of Harullen's society yearned for a time of transcendent ending—the urrish apostates because of their hot blood, and the hoon preciscly *because* their passions stirred slowly, but once whipped, they stopped for nothing.

If our extremists think Ling's folk haven't the guts to do the job, they may plot to provoke genocide! This despite his speech, urging that the Six cede their place on Jijo by consensus and birth control.

Then there was this scheme to try *blackmailing* the forayers. Lark had helped Bloor set up candid shots, but were the sages aware of how the scheme might backfire?

Did they think they had nothing to lose?

Lark rubbed his stubbled chin, feeling wearier than his years. *What a tangled web we weave,* he pondered. Then he licked the tip of his pen, dipped it in the ink, and began to write.

The Stranger

This place makes him want to laugh. It makes him want to cry.

So many books—*he even remembers that word for them—lay stacked high all around him, in row after mighty row, vanishing around corners or up twisty, spiral ramps. Books bound in the leather of unknown animals, filling the air with strange scents, especially when he cracks some volume taken off a shelf at random and inhales the fumes of paper and ink.*

It jolts something within him, dredging up memories more effectively than anything since he regained consciousness.

Suddenly, he recalls a cabinet of books like these, in his room when he was very young . . . and that brings back the pinch and crinkling flex of paper pages, covered with bright pictures. Grown-ups did not use books very much, he remembers. Adults needed the constant flash and jangle of their machines. Machines that talked at you faster than a child was trained to hear, or cast flickering beams directly at the eyeball, filling it with facts that faded the moment you blinked. That was one reason he used to like the solid promise of paper—where a favorite story would not go away like smoke, or vanish when the info-screens went dark.

Another image leaps out from childhood—holding his mother's hand while strolling in a public place filled with busy, important people. Several walls were rimmed with bound volumes, much like the books surrounding him right now. Big books without pictures, filled with black, unmoving dots. Filled with words and nothing else. Hardly anyone used them anymore, his mother had explained. But they were important nonetheless, as decorations lining many of the places most sacred or important to human beings.

They were reminders of something . . . of something he cannot quite recall right now. But it must have been important. That much he knows.

Patiently, he waits for the two women—Sara and Arianafoo—to finish their meetings and return for him. Passing the time, he sketches on a pad of rich, almost luminous paper, first refining some of his drawings of the machinery aboard the steamship, then trying to capture the eerie perspectives of the stone cavern where all these odd wooden buildings lay sheltered from the sky— under a cave whose roof is propped up by incredible, massive stone pillars.

A few names are coming easier now, so he knows that it is Prity *who brings him a cup of water, then checks his dressing to make sure it's still tight. Her hands seem to flutter and dance before her, then* his *do likewise. He watches, fascinated, as his own fingers make movements independent of his will or command. It might be frightening to behold . . . except that Prity suddenly grins broadly and slaps her knee, chuffing hoarse, appreciative chimpanzee laughter.*

He feels a wash of pleasure to know his joke had pleased her. Though it puzzles and slightly miffs him that his hands never saw fit to share the humor with him.

Well, well. The hands seem to know what they are doing, and he draws some satisfaction from their work. Now they pick up the pencil once again, and he lets time slip away, concentrating on the moving pencil, and on the stretch and tilt of line and shadow. When Sara *returns for him, he will be ready for whatever comes next.*

Perhaps it might even be possible to find a way to save her and her people.

Maybe that *was what his hands had said to Prity, just a little while ago.*

If so, no wonder the little chimp broke out in wry, doubtful laughter.

XVII. THE BOOK OF THE SEA

Should you succeed in following
the Path of Redemption—
to be re-adopted, uplifted anew,
given a second chance—
that will not mean an end
to all your strivings.

First you must prove yourselves
as noble clients, obedient and true
to the new patrons who redeemed
you.

Later you will rise in status,
and uplift clients of your own,
generously passing on the
blessings that you earned.

But then, in time, there oft
begins to glimmer a light
on the horizon of a species' life,
hinting at other realms,
beckoning the tired, the worthy.

This is said to be a sign post.
Some will call it The Lure,
or else The Enticement.

Aeon after aeon, old ones depart,
seeking paths that younger
races can't perceive.

They vanish from our midst,
those who find these paths.

Some call it transcendence.
Others call it death.

—The Scroll of Destiny

Alvin's Tale

ONE THING ALWAYS STRUCK ME ABOUT THE WAY tales are told in Anglic—or any of the other Earthling tongues I've learned—and that's the problem of keeping up *suspense.*

Oh, some human authors of Twencen and Twenty-One had it down cold. There've been times that I stayed up three nights straight, taken with some yarn by Conrad or Cunin. What's puzzled me, ever since I got the notion of becoming a writer myself, is *how* those old-timers managed it.

Take this account I've been scribbling lately, whenever I get a chance to lie down on this hard deck with my notebook, already gone all ragged at the corners from the places I've taken it, scrawling clumsy hoon-sized letters with a chewed-up pencil clutched in my fist. From the very start I've been telling my story in "first person"—like in a diary, only with all sorts of fancy-gloss tricks thrown in that I've picked up from my reading over the years.

Why first person? Well, according to *Good Fiction* by Anderson, that "voice" makes it a whole lot easier to present the reader with a single, solid-feeling point-of-view, even though it means my book will have to be translated if a traeki's ever to understand it.

But the trouble with a first person chronicle is this— whether it's real-life history or a piece of make-believe, *you know the hero survived!*

So during all of the events I'm about to relate, you who are reading this memoir (hopefully after I've had a chance to rewrite it, have a human expert fix my grammar, and pay to have it set in type) you already know that I, Alvin Hph-wayuo, son of Mu-phauwq and Yowgwayuo of Wuphon Port, and intrepid explorer extraordinaire, simply *have* to escape alive the jam I'm about to describe, with at least one brain, one eye, and a hand to write it all down.

I've lain awake some nights, trying to see a way around this problem using some other language. There's the GalSeven tentative case, for instance, but that doesn't work in past-explicit tense. And the quantum-uncertain declension, in Buyur-dialect GalThree, is just too *weird*. Anyway, who would I be writing for? Huck's the only other GalThree reader I know, and getting praise from *her* is kind of like kissing your sister.

Anyway, the waters of the Rift were all a-froth at the point where I last left our tale. The hatchet shadow of Terminus Rock cut across a patch of ocean where both hawser and hose still whirled, chopping the normally placid surface, spinning with tension energy released just moments before, by a disaster.

It was all too easy to picture what had happened to *Wuphon's Dream,* our little vessel for exploring the great unknown below. In reluctant imagining I saw the hollow wooden tube—its wheels spinning uselessly, the bulbous glass nose broken—tumbling into black emptiness trailing its broken leash, carrying Ziz, the little traeki partial stack, to perdition along with it.

As if that weren't enough, we all had fresh in memory the sight of little *Huphu,* our noor-beast mascot, thrown by the recoiling crane, screeching and gyrating till her tiny black figure vanished into the blue waters of the Rift. As Huck's Earthling nicknamesake might've said— "It warn't a happy sight. Nor a lucky wun."

For a long time, everybody just stared. I mean, what could we do? Even the protestors from Wuphon Port and The Vale were silent. If any felt smug over our comeuppance as heretics, they felt wiser to withhold jubilation.

We all backed away from the ledge. What point in peering at a velvety-smooth grave?

"Retract the hawser and hose," Urdonnol commanded. Soon the drums began rotating the other way, rewinding what had unreeled so hopefully just duras before. The same hoonish voice called out depths, only this time the numbers grew steadily smaller, and there was no great, booming enthusiasm in the throaty baritone. Finally, at two and a half cables, the hawser's frayed end popped out of the sea, dripping water like white lymph fluid from a traeki's wounded, dangling tentacle. Those cranking the drum sped up, eager to see what had happened.

"Acid vurn!" Ur-ronn declared in shock, when the severed end was swung onto the bluff. She lisped in anger. "Savotage!"

Urdonnol seemed reluctant to leap to conclusions, but the older urs technician kept swinging her narrow head back and forth, low and snakelike, from the burned cable to the crowd of protestors standing on the bluff, gaping at our tragedy. The urrish apprentice's dark suspicion was clear.

"Get away from here!" Huck shouted angrily, rolling toward the dissenters, spinning up gravel with her rims. She swerved, just missing the toes of several humans and hoon, who backed off nervously. Even a couple of reds withdrew their clawed, armored legs, scuttling away a pace or two, before recalling that a flail-eyed g'Kek isn't much physical threat to a qheuen. Then they moved forward again, hissing and clicking.

Pincer and I rushed to Huck's side. It might've gotten ugly, but then a bunch of big grays and burly urrish smiths from Mount Guenn Forge hurried up behind us, some carrying cudgels, ready to back up Huck's demand with angry force. The rabble took note and quit our worksite, moving toward their makeshift camp.

"Bastards!" Huck cursed after them. "Horrid, jeekee murderers!"

Not by law, I thought, still numb from shock. Neither Huphu nor little Ziz had strictly been citizens of the

Commons. Nor even honorary ones, like glavers, or members of any threatened species. So it wasn't murder, exactly.

But close enough, by my reckoning. My hands clenched, and I sensed something *give* as my back flexed with fight-hormones. Anger is slow to ignite in a hoon and hard to snuff once lit. It's kind of disturbing to look back on how I felt then, even though the sages say what you feel isn't evil, only what you do about it.

No one said a word. We must've moped for a while. Urdonnol and Ur-ronn argued over what kind of a message to send to Uriel.

Then a stuttering whistle pierced our pit of mourning, coming from behind us, toward the sea. We turned to see Pincer-Tip, teetering bravely at the edge, blowing dust as he piped shrilly from three leg-vents while motioning with two claws for us to come back.

"Look-ook-ook!" came his aspirated stammer. "Huck, Alvin—hurry!"

Huck claimed later she realized right off what Pincer must've seen. I guess in retrospect it *is* kind of obvious, but at the time I had no idea what could have him so excited. On reaching the edge, I could only peer down in amazement at what had popped out of the belly of the Rift.

It was our bathy! Our beautiful *Wuphon's Dream* floated upright, almost peaceful in the bright sunshine. And on its curved top sat a small black figure, wet and bedraggled from nose to tail. It didn't take a g'Kek's vision to tell that our little noor was as amazed to be alive as we were to see her. Faint whispers of her yelping complaint floated up to us.

"But how—" Urdonnol began.

"Of course!" Ur-ronn interrupted. "The vallast cane loose!"

I blinked a couple of times.

"Oh, the *ballast*! Hr-rm. Yes, the *Dream*'d be buoyant without it. But there was no crew to pull the release, unless—"

"Unless *Ziz* did it!" Huck finished for me.

"Insufficient explanation," Urdonnol interjected in GalTwo. *"With eight cables of (heavy, down-seeking) metal hawser weighing the diving device, the (minuscule) air pocket within our vessel ought to have been (decisively) overwhelmed."*

"Hrm-rm, I think I see what made the difference," I suggested, shading my eyes with both hands. "Huck, what is that . . . *thing* surrounding the bathy?"

Again, our wheeled friend teetered at the edge, spreading two eyestalks far apart and sticking out a third for good measure. "It looks like a *balloon* of some sort, Alvin. A tube, wrapped around the *Dream* like a life preserver. A circular—*Ziz*!"

That matched my own guess. A traeki torus, inflated beyond anything we might have thought possible.

Everybody turned to stare at Tyug, the Mount Guenn Master of Mixes. The full-sized traeki shuddered, letting out a colored cloud that smelled like released tension.

"A precaution. One that i/we contemplated in consultation with our lord, Uriel. A safeguard of unknown, untried efficacy.

"Glad we/i are to have vlenned a success. These rings, and those below, anticipate relishing recent events. Soon. In retrospect."

"In other words-ords," Pincer interpreted, "stop staring like a bunch of day-blind glavers. Let's go fetch 'em *back-ack-ack*!"

XVIII. THE BOOK OF THE SLOPE

Legends

It is said that earlier generations interpreted the Scrolls in ways quite different than we do now, in our modern Commons.

Without doubt, each wave of immigrants brought to the Slope a new crisis of faith, from which beliefs emerged restructured, changed.

At the start, every fresh arrival briefly held advantages, bearing godlike tools from the Five Galaxies. Newcomers kept these powers for intervals ranging from a few months to more than eight years. This helped each sept establish a secure base for their descendants, as humans did at Biblos, the hoon on Hawph Island, and the g'Kek at Dooden Mesa.

Yet each also knew its handicaps—a small founding population and ignorance about how to live a primitive existence on an unknown world. Even the haughty gray queens conceded they must accept certain principles, or risk vendetta from all the others combined. The Covenant of Exile set rules of population control, concealment, and Jijo-preservation, as well as proper ways to handle dross. These fundamentals continue to this day.

It is all too easy to forget that other matters were settled only after mordant struggle.

For instance, bitter resistance to the reintroduction of metallurgy, by urrish smiths, was only partly based on qheuens protecting their tool-monopoly. There was also a sincere belief, on the part of many hoon and traeki, that the innovation was sacrilege. To this day, some on the Slope will not touch reforged Buyur steel or let it in their villages or homes, no matter how many times the sages rule it safe for "temporary" use.

Another remnant belief can be seen among those puritans who despise *books*. While paper itself can hardly be faulted—it decays well and can be used to reprint copies of the Scrolls—there is still a dissident minority who call the Biblos trove a vanity at best, and an impediment to those whose goal should lie in blessed ignorance. In the early days of human life on Jijo, such sentiments were exploited by urrish and qheuen foes—until the great smiths discovered profit in the forging of type, and book-addiction spread unstoppably throughout the Commons.

Strangely, it is the most recent crisis-of-faith that shows the least leftover effects today. If not for written accounts, it would be difficult to believe that, only a century ago, there were many on the Slope who loathed and feared the newly arrived Holy Egg. Yet at the time there were serious calls for the Explosers Guild to destroy it! To demolish the stone-that-sings, lest it give away our hiding place or, worse, distract the Six away from following the same path already blazed by glavers.

"If it is not in the Scrolls, it cannot be sacred."

That has always been the declaration of orthodoxy, since time immemorial. And to this day it must be confessed—there is no mention in the Scrolls of anything even remotely like the Egg.

Rety

DARK, CLAMMY, STIFLING.

Rety didn't like the cave.

It must be the stale, dusty air that made her heart pound so. Or else the painful scrapes on her legs, after sliding down a twisty chute to this underground grotto, from a narrow entrance in a boo-shrouded cleft.

Or maybe what made her jumpy was the way *shapes* kept crowding in from all sides. Each time Rety whirled with her borrowed lantern, the creepy shadows turned out to be knobs of cold, dead rock. But a little voice seemed to say—*Always . . . so far! But a real monster may wait around the next bend.*

She set her jaw and refused to listen. Anyone who called *her* scared would be a liar!

Does a scared person slink into dark places at night? Or do things they was told not to do, by all the big fat chiefs of the Six?

A weight wriggled in her belt pouch. Rety reached past the fur-lined flap to stroke the squirming creature. "Don't spook, yee. It's just a big hole in the groun'."

A narrow head and a sinuous neck snaked toward her, three eyes glittering in the soft flamelight. A squeaky voice protested.

"yee *not* spooked! dark good! on plains, li'l man-urs love hidey-holes, till find warm wife!"

"Okay, okay. I didn't mean—"

"yee *help* nervous wife!"

"Who're *you* calling nervous, you little—"

Rety cut short. Maybe she should let yee feel needed, if it helped him keep his own fear under control.

"ow! not so tight!" The male yelped, echoes fleeing down black corridors. Rety quickly let go and stroked yee's ruffled mane. "Sorry. Look, I bet we're gettin' close, so let's not talk so much, okay?"

"okay. yee shut up. wife do too!"

Rety's lips pressed. Then anger flipped into a sudden urge to laugh. Whoever said male urs weren't smart must've never met her "husband." yee had even changed his *accent,* in recent days, mimicking Rety's habits of speech.

She raised the lantern and resumed picking her way through the twisty cavern, surrounded by a sparkle of strange mineral formations, reflecting lamplight off countless glittering facets. It might have been pretty to look at, if she weren't obsessed with one thing alone. An item to reclaim. Something she once, briefly, had owned.

My ticket off this mudball.

Rety's footprints appeared to be the first ever laid in the dust—which wasn't surprising, since just qheuens, and a few humans and urs, had a knack for travel underground, and she was smaller than most. With luck, this tunnel led toward the much larger cave she had seen Lester Cambel enter several times. Following the chief human sage had been her preoccupation while avoiding the group of frustrated men and women who wanted her to help guide them over the mountains. Once she knew for sure where Cambel spent his evenings, she had sent yee scouring the underbrush till he found this offshoot opening, bypassing the guarded main entrance.

The little guy was already proving pretty darn useful. To Rety's surprise, married life wasn't so bad, once you got used to it.

There was more tight wriggling and writhing. At times, she had to squirm sideways or slide down narrow chutes, making yee complain when he got squeezed. Beyond the lantern's dim yellow puddle, she heard soft tinkling sounds as water dripped into black pools, slowly sculpting weird underground shapes out of Jijo's raw mineral juices. With each step Rety fought a tightness in her chest, trying to ignore her tense imagination, which pictured her in the twisty guts of some huge slumbering beast. The rocky womb kept threatening to close in from all sides, shutting the exits, then grinding her to dust.

Soon the way narrowed to a corkscrew horizontal tube that was tight even for her. She had to send yee ahead before attempting the contorted passage, pushing the lantern along in front of her.

yee's tiny hooves clattered on gritty limestone. Soon she heard a welcome hoarse whisper.

"is good! hole opens up, little ways more. come wife, faster!"

His chiding almost made her snort angrily—not a wise idea with her cheek, nose, and mouth scraping rank dust. Contorting her body to turn the next corner, she suddenly felt *certain* the walls were moving!

She recalled what Dwer's brother had said about this region, when he led her down that last stretch to the Glade, past steaming sulfur vents. Lark had called this a land of earthquakes, and seemed to think it a *good* thing!

Twisting uneasily, her hip jammed in a stone cleft.

I'm caught!

Thought of entrapment sent a whimpering moan surging past flecked lips as she thrashed, banging her knee agonizingly. The world really was closing in!

Her forehead struck stone, and pain-dazzles swarmed her dimming vision. The candle lantern rattled from her clutching fingertips, almost toppling over.

"easy, wife! stop! stay!"

The words bounced off the warped mirror of her panic. Stubbornly, Rety kept striving against cold stone, groaning and pushing futilely . . . until . . .

Something *clicked* inside her. All at once, she went limp, suddenly resigned to let the mountain do whatever it wanted with her.

Moments after she stopped fighting, the walls miraculously seemed to stop moving. Or had it been her, all along?

"better now? good-good. now move left leg . . . left! good. stop now. okay roll other way. go-o-o-ood wife!"

His tiny voice was a lifeline she clutched for the few duras—for the *eternity*—that it took to win free. At last, the clutch of the stony passage eased, and she slithered down a sandy bank in a flowing, almost liquid liberation that felt just like being born.

When next she looked up, yee had the lantern cradled in both arms, bowing with forelegs bent.

"good brave wife! no wife *ever* like yee's amazing wife!"

This time Rety could not hold it in. She covered her mouth with both hands, yet her escaping laughter bounced off the fluted walls. Combed by stalactites, it came back as a hundred soft echoes of her joy to be alive.

The sage was pondering *her* bird.

He peered at it, wrote on a notepad, then poked it with some shiny tool.

Rety seethed. The gold-green machine was hers. Hers! She had pursued it from the southern marshes to the Rimmers, rescued it from a greedy mulc-spider, *won* it with her sweat, suffering, and dreams. *She* would choose who, if anybody, got to study it.

Anyway, what was a savage shaman going to achieve with his crude glass lenses and such? The tools lying near the bird might have impressed the old Rety, who thought Dwer's hunting bow was so great. But all that changed after meeting Besh, Rann, and the other star-humans. Now she knew—despite all his airs, Lester Cambel was just like Jass or Bom, or any of the other idiots back in the Gray Hills. Stupid braggarts. Bullies. Always taking things that didn't belong to them.

Under the bright flare of a mirrored oil lamp, Cambel flipped through a book. Its pages crackled, as if they had not been turned in a very long time. Rety couldn't make out much from her vantage point, perched on a cleft high up one craggy cavern wall. Not that she could read, anyway. Most of each page seemed to be taken up with drawings with lots of little crisscrossing lines. Nothing much resembled a bird.

Come on, yee, she thought, restlessly. *I'm countin' on you!*

She was taking a big risk. The little male had assured her he could handle it, but what if he got lost while sneaking around to the other side? Or forgot his lines? Rety would be furious if the little guy wound up getting hurt!

Cambel's assistant stood up and left the chamber, perhaps on some brief errand, or else to retire for the night. Either way, this was a perfect time! *Come on, yee!*

After so long writhing through dark passages, always fearful the little candle would go out, Rety found the cool brilliance of the sage's lamp harsh to the eyes. With reluctance she had blown out her own light while creeping the last few meters, lest its glow draw attention. Now she regretted it. *What if I have to retreat the way I came?* She couldn't willingly face that path again. But as a last resort, if someone were chasing her . . . ?

Too bad she had no way to restart the candle. *Maybe I should've learned to use one of those "match" things the Slopies boast about.* She had been too awed by the sudden burst of flame to pay close attention when Dwer, and later Ur-Jah, tried showing how they worked. It was all the fault of Jass and Bom, of course, who didn't like womenfolk controlling fire on their own.

But fire's just fine for scaring or burning women, ain't it? she pondered angrily, touching her face. *Maybe I'll come back someday, Jass. Maybe I'll bring another kind of fire.*

Rety reentered her favorite fantasy, flying off to live with the sky-humans on their home star. Oh, at first she'd start out as a sort of pet or mascot. But just give her time! She'd learn whatever it took in order to rise up, until she became so important . . .

So important that some great Rothen prince would put

a ship—a *fleet* of ships!—at her command, to go with her
back to Jijo.

It was fun picturing the look on Jass's smug handsome
face, when the sky over the Gray Hills went dark at
noon, and then *her* words booming from above—

"you wise mister human sir?"

The tiny voice shook her back to the present. She
sought down below—and spied yee trotting nervously
near the leg of Lester Cambel's chair.

"Hm? What was that?" Cambel asked. yee jumped as
the chair scraped back, pushed by the sage, who peered
about in confusion.

"message for wise human! message from wise
grandma urs, Ur-Jah!"

Now Cambel looked down, first amazed, then quizzi-
cally intrigued.

"Yes, small one? And how did you get down here past
the guard?"

"guard he look out for danger. look right past yee. is
yee danger?"

The tiny urs laughed, mimicking Rety's own nervous
giggle. She hoped Cambel didn't recognize the similarity.

The sage nodded, gravely. "No, I suppose not. Unless
someone gets you angry, my friend, which I'll strive not
to do. So now, what's this about a message at this time of
night?"

yee did a little dance with his hooves and lifted both
arms dramatically. "urgent time for talk-talk. look at
dead birdie later! go Ur-Jah now. now!"

Rety feared his vehemence would rouse suspicion.
But the balding human put down his tools at once and
stood up. "Well then, let's go."

Rety's hopes soared, then sank as Cambel lifted the
bird with both hands.

No! Put it down!

As if prodded by her tense mental urging, the sage
paused, shook his head, and put the machine back,
picking up his notebook instead.

"Lay on, Macduff," he said to yee, motioning with a sweep of one arm.

"great sage says what?" the small urs tilted his head.

"I said . . . oh, never mind. An obscure allusion. Guess I'm just tired. Shall I carry you, sir?"

"no! yee lead wise human. walk this way! *this* way!" and he scampered off eagerly, pausing impatiently and backtracking several times as the sage followed plod-dingly behind.

When they both had vanished up the tunnel leading toward the main entrance, Rety wasted no time slither-ing down the crumbly, slanting limestone wall till she tumbled bottom-first onto the floor of the laboratory cave. She scrambled up and hurried to the table where her bird lay, headless as it had been ever since the fight with the alien robot.

Its breast lay spread open like a carcass at a feast, exposing innards like none Rety had ever seen, glittering like jewels. *What did the stinker do, gut it like a herd chick?* She fought to check her rage. *Rann might not pay if the fools have ruined it by mucking inside!*

She looked closer. The opening was too clean to have been hacked with a knife. In fact, when she hesitantly touched the bird's ribcage, it seemed to roll smoothly around the line where it was still connected—like the *hinged* door she had seen on a big cabinet, and mar-veled at, while visiting the forayers' medical tent.

I see. You just close it like . . . this.

She lifted the smaller section through an arc, till it swung shut with a decisive click.

Now Rety regretted her haste. There was no more chance to look closer at the little flashings inside. *Oh, well. None of my biznis, anyway,* she thought, and plucked up her prize. *At least I don't pretend I'm any-thin' but a sooner an' a savage.*

Though not forever. Once I get off Jijo, I'll learn. I'll learn all right!

The bird was heavier than she recalled. Briefly, her heart felt full. She had her treasure back! She crammed the heavy bird-thing into her pouch, bypassing the books strewn across the table as she hurried off, following the same path yee and Lester Cambel had taken, an easy stand-up trail leading toward the outside world.

The way was lit by little lamps, hanging from a thin boo pipe stapled to the hall. Tiny flames flickered an eerie blue color, leaving wide pools of shadow in between. Dim light also spilled from several side chambers, now mostly empty of workers as it was nighttime outside. One cell, however, seemed to blaze with bulky lanterns. Before tiptoeing past, Rety warily eyed two human occupants—who were luckily turned away, murmuring with low voices. Drawings of the star-gods, their aircraft, and other tools lay tacked on a dozen or so easels. The cube-shaped station—which Rety had never seen unburied—lay revealed in fine detail, more grand than some shattered Buyur site. Yet it seemed minute next to the monstrous tube depicted on the *next* sketch, floating above the forest.

My starship, she mused, though cowed by the thought of boarding the huge vessel when it returned for the forayers. She must remember to hold her chin up that day and show no fear.

The artists had caught Rann's distant amused gaze, and Kunn's sharp hunter's glare as he adjusted the claw arm of a hovering robot. The pale intensity of Besh balanced Ling's dusky half-cynical expression. Rety knew they were only drawings, like the ones some old grandpas used to scratch on a cliff overlooking the wintering cave, back in the Gray Hills. Still, the lifelike accuracy seemed spooky and magical. *The Slopies are studying the star-men. What could it mean?*

Rety almost tripped in her haste to get away. *Whatever they're planning, it won't come to much.* She set her mind back to getting out of this place and making the rendezvous in time.

The mustiness began to lift and the harsh echoes softened. Soon she heard voices ahead . . . . Lester Cambel trading words with a second human. Rety tiptoed to the next bend and peered around. The human sage could be seen talking to the cave guard, who looked down at yee with a chagrined expression.

"Privacy wasps may stop the tiniest robots," Cambel said. "But what about something the size of this little fellow?"

"Honestly, sir. I can't imagine how he got past—"

Cambel waved off the apology. "There was no harm done this time, son. It's mostly their contempt that protects us—their confidence we have nothing worth spying on. Just be more careful from now on, eh?"

He patted the young man's arm and turned to follow as yee hurried outside. The path seemed brightly lit by moonshine, piercing through gently waving forest branches. Still clearly perplexed, the guard set his jaw and gripped his weapon—a kind of pole with a sharp-looking knife-thing at one end—standing with legs slightly apart, in the center of the entrance. When the scrape of Cambel's footsteps faded, Rety counted twenty duras, then made her own move. Faking calm, she sauntered toward the young guard, who swiveled when she was close.

Rety gave a smile and an easygoing wave. "Well, guess I'm all done for the night." She yawned, sidling past his bulk, sensing his startled indecision. "Boy I'll tell ya, that science sure is hard work! Well, g'night."

Now she was outside, gratefully inhaling fresh mountain air and trying not to break into a run. *Especially* when he shouted—"Hey, stop right there!"

Swiveling around but continuing to walk backward down the path, Rety delayed him a few more seconds by grinning broadly. "Yeah? You need somethin'?"

"What . . . who *are* you—?"

"Got something here I figure the sage'd want to be seein'," she replied with deceptive truthfulness, patting her belt pouch and still backing away.

The guard started toward her.

With a joyful shout, Rety spun about and took off into

the forest, knowing pursuit was hopeless at this point.
He had lost his chance, the stinker!

Still, she was kind of glad that he tried.

yee met her where they had agreed, by the log bridge,
halfway to the place where she was to join Rann. On
spying her, the little urs yelped and seemed to fly into
her arms.

He was less pleased on trying to burrow into his accustomed place, only to find a cold hard object taking up
the pouch. Rety tucked him into the folds of her jacket,
and after a moment he seemed to find that acceptable.

"yee tell wife. yee see—"

"We did it!" Rety chortled gleefully, unable to contain
the rush of an adventure so well closed. The chase had
been a perfect way to finish, leaping and laughing as she
ran through the forest, leaving the big oaf to flounder in
the dark while she circled around, then slinked right past
the noisy guard on her way back to the Glade.

"You were great, too," she told yee, sharing credit.
"Would've been harder to do it without you." She
hugged his little body till he complained with a series of
short grunts. "Did you have any trouble getting away
from Cambel?" she asked.

"wiseman human no problem. yee get 'way good. but
then—"

"Great, then it's over. We better go now, though. If
Rann has to wait, he may not be in as good a mood
as—"

"—but then yee *see* something on way to meet wife!
whole *herd* of urs . . . qheuens . . . hoons . . .
men . . . all going sneak-sneak in dark. carry big
boxes!"

Rety hurried down a side trail leading toward the rendezvous point. "Hm-hm? Do tell? Prob'ly one of those
silly pilgrim things, headin' up to pray to that big rock
they think is a god." She had only contempt for the
superstitions of planet-grubbing sooners. To her, all the
talk she'd heard about the Slopies' fabulous "Egg" was

just more scare-you-in-the-dark stuff, like those tales of ghosts and huge beasts and spirit glavers that were common campfire fare back in the Gray Hills, especially since Jass and Bom took over. Whenever times were hard, the hunters would argue into the night, seeking some reason why the prey animals might be angry, and ways to appease them.

"herd of sneakers *not* go holy rock!" yee protested. "head wrong way! no white robes. no sing-songs! just sneak-sneak, I say! sneak with boxes to 'nother cave!"

Rety's interest was almost piqued. yee sure seemed to think it important. . . .

But just then the trail turned to overlook the little valley where the sky-humans dwelled. Moonlight spilled across pavilions that seemed strangely less well camouflaged now, in the vivid dimness.

A soft hum warbled from the west, and a *glint* drew her eye as a glistening teardrop shape floated into view, folding away two delicate wings as it descended. Rety felt a tingle, recognizing the small flying boat of the forayers, returning from another mysterious expedition. She watched, transfixed, as the lovely thing settled gracefully to the valley floor. A hole opened, swallowing it into the ground.

Excitement filled Rety's lungs, and her heart felt light.

"Hush, husband," she told yee when he complained of being ignored. "We got some tradin' and dickerin' to do.

"Now's when we'll see if they pay what they promised."

A<small>sx</small>

MY RINGS, YOU NEED NOT MY WEAKLY FOCUSED musings to inform you. Surely all of you must feel it, deep within each oily torus core?

The Egg. Slowly, as if rising from a deep torpor, it wakens!

Perhaps now the Commons will be filled once more with comity, with union of spirit, with the meshed resolve that once bound jointly our collective wills.

Oh, let it be so!

We are so fractured, so far from ready. So far from worthy.

Oh, let it be so.

Sara

THE STACKS WERE INFESTED WITH POLISHER BEES, and the music rooms thronged with hungry, biting parrot fleas, but the chimps on the maintenance staff were too busy to fumigate for minor pests.

While taking some air in the west atrium, Sara watched several of the hairy workers help a human librarian pack precious volumes into fleece-lined crates, then seal them with drippings from a big red candle. Gobbets of wax clung to the chimps' matted fur, and they complained to each other with furtive hand signs.

This is not correct, Sara interpreted one worker's flurry of gestures and husky grunts. *In this intemperate haste, we are making regrettable errors.*

The other replied, *How true, my associate! This volume of Auden should not go in among Greek classics! We shall never get these books properly restacked when this crisis finally blows over, as surely it must.*

Well, perhaps she was generous in her mental translation. Still, the chimps who labored in these hallowed halls were a special breed. Almost as special as Prity.

Overhead towered the atrium of the Hall of Literature, spanned by bridges and ramps that linked reading rooms and galleries, all lined with shelves groaning under the weight of books, absorbing sound while emitting a redolence of ink, paper, wisdom, and dusty time. Weeks of frantic evacuation, hauling donkey-loads to faraway caves, had not made a dent in the hoard—still crammed with texts of every color and size.

Sage Plovov called this hall—dedicated to *legend, magic,* and *make-believe*—the House of Lies. Yet Sara always felt this place less burdened by the supremacy of the past than in those nearby structures dedicated to science. After all, what could Jijo's savages ever add to the mountain of facts brought here by their godlike ancestors? A mountain said to be like a sand grain next to the Great Galactic Library. But the tales in *this* hall feared no refutal by ancient authority. Good or bad, great or forgettable, no work of literature was ever provably "false."

Plovov said—*"It's easy to be original when you don't have to care whether you're telling the truth. Magic and art arise from an egomaniac's insistence that the artist is right, and the universe wrong."*

Of course, Sara agreed. On the other hand, she *also* thought Plovov was jealous.

When humans came to Jijo, the effect on the other five races must have been like when Earth met Galactic culture. After centuries with just a handful of engraved scrolls, the urs, g'Kek, and others reacted to the flood of paper books with both suspicion and voracious appetite. Between brief, violent struggles, nonhumans devoured Terran fables, dramas, and novels. When they wrote stories of their own, they imitated Earthly forms—like ersatz Elizabethan romances featuring gray-shelled queens, or Native North American legends recast for urrish tribes.

But lately, a flowering of new styles had also started emerging, from heroic adventures to epic poems set in strange meters and rhymes, unraveling the last shreds of order from dialects of GalSeven, and even GalTwo. Printers and binders had as many orders for new titles as reprints. Scholars debated what it all might mean—an outbreak of heresy? Or a freeing of the spirit?

Few dared use the term *renaissance.*

All of which may end in a matter of days or weeks, Sara pondered glumly. News from the Glade—brought by a kayak pilot braving the Bibur rapids—showed no change in the sages' grim appraisal of the alien gene-raiders, or their intent.

Well, Bloor should be there by now. Sara's plan might not dissuade the sky-humans from genocide, but a folk as helpless as the Six must be willing to try anything.

Including Ariana's crazy notion. Even if it's cruel.

The voice of the elderly sage carried from the chamber behind Sara.

"There now, dear. You've struggled long enough with that one. Let's see what you can make of this nice book. Have you ever seen symbols and words like these before?"

Sighing, Sara turned around to reenter the Children's Wing.

The Stranger sat near Ariana Foo's wheelchair, surrounded by volumes bearing bright colors and simple text, printed in large friendly type. Though his face was haggard, the tall dark man resignedly accepted yet another book and ran his hand over the dots, slashes, and bars of a GalTwo teaching rhyme—a primer meant for young urrish middlings. Sara was unsurprised when his lips pursed and his tongue clicked as he worked across the page, laboriously. His eyes recognized the symbols, but clearly, no sense was being made of the sentence-phrase itself.

It had been the same with books in GalSix, Anglic, and GalSeven, tearing Sara's heart to see his frustration turn into torment. Perhaps only now was the injured man coming to know fully what had been ripped away from him. What he had forever lost.

Ariana Foo, on the other hand, seemed eminently satisfied. She beamed at Sara. "This is no rube from the outer hamlets," the old woman ruled. "He was an educated person, familiar with every language currently in use among the Six. If we have time, we *must* take him to the Linguistics Wing and try some of the forgotten dialects! Galactic Twelve would clinch it. Only three scholars on Jijo know any of it today."

"What's the point?" Sara asked. "You've made your case. Why not let him be?"

"In a minute, dear. One or two more, then we'll be off. I've saved the best for last."

Two library staff members watched nervously as Ariana reached over to a stack of books by her side. Some were priceless, with rings set in their spines where chains normally kept them locked to their shelves. The archivists clearly did not like seeing them pawed by a speechless barbarian.

Unwilling to watch, Sara turned away.

The rest of the Children's Wing was placid—and contained few children. Scholars, teachers, and traveling librarians from all six races came here to study, copy, or select books to borrow, carrying their precious cargo by cart, boat, or pack donkey to settlements throughout the Slope. Sara observed a red qheuen carefully gather some of the heavy, brass-bound albums required by her kind, assisted by two lorniks trained as assistants and page-turners. One lornik swatted at a polisher bee that was working its way across the cover of a book, rubbing its abdomen amorously across the jacket, buffing it to a fine sheen and erasing part of the title. No one knew what function the insectoids once served for the departed Buyur, but they were a damned nuisance nowadays.

Sara saw others from every race, educators who refused to let a mere crisis interfere with the serious task of instructing the next generation. Beyond the qheuen, an elderly traeki selected volumes treated to resist the fluids emitted by new stacks of rings, too clumsy to control their secretions.

A low moan brought Sara back around to see the Stranger holding before him a long, slim book so old, the colors had gone all dingy and gray. The man's dark features clouded with clashing emotions. Sara had no time to read the title, only to glimpse a skinny black feline figure on the cover, wearing a red-and-white-striped stovepipe hat. Then, to the librarians' gasping dismay, he clutched the volume tightly to his chest, rocking back and forth with eyes closed.

"Something from his childhood, I'll warrant," Ariana Foo diagnosed, scribbling on her pad. "According to the indexes, this fable was widely popular among children in northwestern Earth civilization almost continuously for over three centuries, so we can tentatively localize his cultural origins. . . ."

"How nice. Then you're finished?" Sara demanded, caustically.

"Hm? Oh, yes, I suppose so. For now. Get him settled down will you, pet? Then bring him along. I'll be waiting in the main Listening Parlor." With that, Ariana nodded briskly to the chim assigned to push her chair, leaving Sara behind to deal with the upset Stranger.

He was muttering to himself, as he did from time to time, repeating the same short phrase, over and over. Something that wormed its way out, despite the damage to his brain. In this case, it was clearly nonsense, sparked by intense emotion.

". . . *a wocket in my pocket . . .*" he said again and again, chortling poignantly, ". . . *a wocket in my pocket . . .*"

Gently, firmly, Sara managed to pry the ancient tome out of his trembling hands, returning the treasure to the disapproving librarians. With patience she encouraged the wounded man to stand, though his dark eyes were fogged with a kind of misery Sara found she could fathom. She, too, had lost someone precious to her.

Only the one *he* was mourning was himself.

Two g'Kek savants met them by the entrance to the Listening Parlor, physician researchers who had examined the Stranger soon after he arrived in Biblos. One now took him by the hand.

"Sage Foo wishes you to attend her in the observing room, next door," the other one said. One eyestalk gestured toward an opening farther down the hall. When the Stranger looked at Sara questioningly, she gave him an encouraging nod. His trusting smile only made her feel worse.

The observing room was dimly illuminated by light streaming in through two circular windows—exquisite slabs of spun glass, flawless except for the characteristic central stem—which looked into another chamber where the two g'Kek doctors could be seen seating the Stranger before a large box with a crank on one side and a trumpetlike horn rising from the other.

"Come in, pet. And please close the door."

It took several duras for Sara's eyes to adapt and see who sat with Ariana. By then it was too late to flee.

The whole party from Tarek Town was present, along with two humans dressed in scholars' robes. Ulgor and Blade had reason to be here, of course. Blade had helped rescue the Stranger from the swamp, and Ulgor was an honorary delegate from Dolo Village. Even Jop had an official interest. But why were Jomah and Kurt the Exploser in the room? Whatever cryptic guild business brought them from Tarek, the old man and boy now watched the proceedings with the silent intensity that was a trademark of their family and craft.

The human scholars turned toward her.

Bonner and Taine—the very persons she had hoped to avoid during this visit.

Both men rose to their feet.

Sara hesitated, then bowed at the waist. "Masters."

"Dear Sara." Bonner sighed, leaning on his cane more than she recalled when she had last seen the balding topologist. "How we've missed you in these dusty halls."

"As I've missed you, master," she replied, surprised how true it was. Perhaps in the numbness after Joshu's passing, she had closed off too many good memories as well as bad. The warmth of the old savant's hand on her arm recalled their many walks, discussing the arcane, endlessly fascinating habits of *shapes,* the sort that could be described with symbols but never seen by human eyes.

"Please don't call me master anymore," he asked. "You are an adept now, or should be soon enough. Come, have a seat between us, like old times."

A bit *too* much like old times, Sara realized, meeting the eyes of the other mathematician-sage. The tall, silver-haired algebraist seemed unchanged, still distant, enigmatic. Taine nodded and spoke her name, then sat again facing the windows. Typically, he had chosen the position farthest from the nonhumans in the room.

Sage Taine's discomfort around the other septs was not rare. A minority felt that way in every race, a reaction deep-rooted in ancient drives. What mattered was how you dealt with it, and Taine was unfailingly polite to the urs or g'Kek teachers who came to consult him about the binomial theorem. Given the handicap, it was just as well the tall savant could live a scholar's cloistered life . . . like the one Sara herself had expected—

—until a visiting bookbinder became an unlikely suitor, filling Sara's heart with unexpected possibilities.

—until she boldly announced to her confused colleagues a new focus for her studies, *language,* of all things.

—until Joshu sickened when pepper pox swept through the Valley of the Bibur, a plague that took its victims with agonizing suddenness, and she had to watch another woman perform the rites of mourning, knowing that everyone was watching, to see how she'd react.

—until, after the funeral, Sage Taine approached her with stiff formality and renewed his earlier proposal of marriage.

—until, in a rush, she fled this place of dust and memories, running home to her treehouse overlooking the great dam where she was born.

Now it all circled around again. Taine had seemed so austerely beautiful when she first came to Biblos in her teens, a towering figure, impressive beyond compare. But things had changed inside her since. *Everything* had changed.

Abruptly, Taine's aristocratic bearing broke as he cursed and slapped his neck, then peered at his hand, frowning in disappointment. Sara glanced at Bonner, who whispered, "Parrot ticks. Such annoyances. If one gets in your ear, Ifni help you. I heard everything double for a week, till Vorjin fished the damn thing out."

Ariana Foo made an emphatic throat-clearing sound,

drawing their attention forward. "I've already explained to the others, Sara, my belief that your Stranger is a man from the stars. Further research illuminates the nature of his injuries."

Her chimp assistant passed out sheets of paper, streaked from hasty, hand-cranked photocopying, showing the stylized profile of a man's head, with arrows and captions pointing to parts. Most of the words were gibberish to Sara, though Lark might have found them familiar.

"I recalled reading about this once and was lucky enough to find the reference quickly. It seems that when our ancestors departed Earth, experiments had been taking place with the objective of creating direct connections between computers and living human brains."

Sara heard an awed hiss from somewhere in back. To many of the Six, the word *computer* carried superstitious power. The crews of every sneakship to reach Jijo had melted all their digital calculating engines, down to the very smallest, before sinking their star-cruisers in the depths of the Midden. No other possession had such potential for betraying illegal sapience on a forbidden world.

Sara had read a few gaudy stories from Earth days, in which the author used mind-to-computer links in the narrative. She had always dismissed them as a metaphor, like legends of humans flying with feathers glued to their arms. But Ariana said the notion was once taken seriously.

"This illustration shows some of the brain areas being proposed for neural-electronic junctions at the time our ancestors departed," Ariana continued. "Research surely proceeded during the three hundred years since. In fact, it's my belief that our Stranger possessed the product—an aperture which let him commune with computers and other devices, inset just above the left ear."

Now it was Sara's turn to gasp. "Then his—"

Ariana held up a hand. "It is a safe guess that his burns and lesser injuries resulted when his ship or flying craft crash-landed in the Eternal Swamp, not far from where

Sara and her friends found him. Alas, his miraculous escape from fiery death was spoiled by one bit of bad luck, when the artificial connector attached to his head was violently ripped away, taking with it portions of his left temporal lobe.

"I needn't add, this is the portion of the human brain most closely identified with speech."

Sara could only blink. Through the glass, she saw the man Ariana referred to, eyes bright and interested, watching the g'Kek doctors prepare their apparatus.

"I'd have thought such damage would kill him," Bonner said, summarizing her own surprise.

"Indeed, he seems to have made a remarkable recovery. Were he not adult and male, with a rigid synaptic structure, perhaps he might have roused speech from the semidormant *right* temporal lobe, as some children and women do, after suffering damage to the left side. As things stand, there remains one possib—" She paused, noticing a waving of eyestalks in the next room.

"Well, I see our good doctors are ready, so let's proceed."

Ariana opened a listening vent under the nearest pane of glass. At almost the same moment, Sara felt a sudden sharp pain on her thigh, and Taine slapped his neck again. "Damn pests!" he muttered, and glanced sideways at Sara. "Things have been going to hell in more ways than one around here."

Good old, cheerful Taine, she thought, quashing an urge to brush at her own neck. Parrot ticks were generally harmless—another mysterious vestige of Buyur times. Who would ever want the "symbiosis" of a creature who attached itself to one of your veins and repaid you by reiterating every sound you heard? The Buyur must have been strange beings indeed.

In the next room, one of the g'Kek doctors opened a large album whose thick sleeves held several dozen slim black disks. The physician delicately removed one and laid it on a round platform which began to spin.

"An elenentary sfring action device," Ulgor explained. "Easily constructed fron scraf netal and slices of voo."

"A primitive but effective analog storage and retrieval system," Taine elucidated.

"Safely nondigital," Bonner added.

"Yesss," the blue qheuen, Blade, hissed in agreement. "And I hear it plays *music*. Sort of."

The g'Kek doctor gently lowered a wooden armature until a slender stylus touched the rim of the spinning disk. Almost at once, low strains of melody began crooning from the machine's hornlike speaker. A strange *tinny* melody—accompanied by faint crackling pops—which seemed to tickle the roots of Sara's hair.

"These disks are originals," Ariana Foo said, "pressed by the *Tabernacle* colonists at the same time as the Great Printing. Nowadays, only a few experts play them. Earthly musical forms aren't popular in the modern Commons, but I'm betting our Stranger won't agree."

Sara had heard of the disk-playing device. It seemed bizarre to listen to music with no living performer involved. Almost as bizarre as the music itself, which sounded unlike anything she had heard. Sara quickly recognized some instruments—violins, drums, and horns—which was natural, since string and wind instruments had been introduced to Jijo by Earthlings. But the arrangement of notes was strange, and Sara soon realized—what seemed most eerie was its *orderliness*.

A modern Jijoan sextet involved the blending of six solo performers, each spontaneously merging with the others. Half the excitement came from waiting for unpredictable, felicitous blendings of harmony, emerging and then vanishing once more, much like life itself. No two performances were ever the same.

But this is purely human music. Complex chords coiled and gyred in sequences that reiterated with utter disciplined precision. *As in science, the point is to make something repeatable, verifiable.*

She glanced at the others. Ulgor seemed fascinated, twitching her left hand-cluster—the one used for fingering notes on a violus. Blade rocked his heavy carapace in bewilderment, while young Jomah, sitting next to his stolid uncle, seemed twitchy with confused ennui.

Although she'd never heard its like, something felt ineffably familiar about the orderly sweep and flow of harmony. The notes were like . . . *integers,* the phrases like geometric figures.

What better evidence that music can be like mathematics?

The Stranger was reacting, as well. He sat forward, flushed, with clear recognition in his squinting eyes. Sara felt a wave of concern. Too much more emotional turbulence might push the poor exhausted man past his limit.

"Ariana, is all of this going somewhere?" she asked.

"In a minute, Sara." The sage held up her hand once more. "That was just the overture. Here comes the part we're interested in."

How does she know? Sara wondered. Apparently, the breadth of Ariana's eclectic knowledge stretched even to obscure ancient arts.

Sure enough, in moments the instrumental arrangement crescendoed and paused. Then a new element joined in—the unmistakable twang of human voices. After missing the first few stanzas, Sara bent forward, concentrating to make out queerly accented words.

> *For today our pirate 'prentice*
> *rises from indenture freed,*
> *Strong his arm and keen his scent is,*
> *he's a pirate now indeed.*

The effect on the Stranger was profound. He stood up, trembling. The emotion spilling across his face was not simply recognition, but joyful *surprise.*

Then—to his own clear amazement as much as Sara's—he opened his mouth and sang along!

> *Pour, oh pour, the pirate sherry,*
> *fill, oh fill, the pirate glass.*
> *And to make us more than merry,*
> *let the pirate bumper pass!*

Sara stood up, too, staring in astonishment. From Ariana Foo came a shout of satisfaction.

"Aha! A hit with the very first try! Even with the cultural cue, I expected to work through many before finding one he knew."

"But his injury!" objected Taine. "I thought you said—"

"Quite right," Bonner cut in. "If he can't speak, how can he sing?"

"Oh, that." Ariana dismissed the miracle with a wave. "Different functions. Different parts of the brain. There are precedents in the medical references. I'm told it's even been observed here on Jijo, once or twice.

"No, what startles *me* is the cultural persistence this experiment demonstrates. It's been three hundred years. I'd have thought by now Galactic influences would overwhelm all native Earthly—" The old woman paused, as if realizing she was running off on a tangent. "Well, never mind that. Right now what matters is that our off-planet visitor seems to have found a way to communicate, after all."

Even in the dimness, Ariana's smile was broad and anything but humble.

Sara laid her hand on the glass, feeling its cool slickness vibrate to the music in the next room, which had passed on to a new song. The cadence slowed and melody changed, though apparently not the topic.

She closed her eyes and listened as the Stranger plunged ahead with throaty joy, outracing the recording in his eagerness to be heard at last.

> *Away to the cheating world go you,*
> *where pirates all are well-to-do.*
> *But I'll be true to the song I sing . . .*
> *and live and die a Pi-i-rate King!*

XIX. THE BOOK OF THE SEA

Scrolls

Of galaxies, it is said,
there were once seventeen,
linked and bound together,
by tubes of focused time.
One by one, those frail tubes
snapped,
sundered as the universe
stretched its ageing seams.
Of galaxies, the Progenitors
knew eleven.

Six more have parted ways,
in the ages since, stranding
distant cousins to unknown fates.
Of galaxies, our immediate ancestors
knew five.

What if it should happen
once again, while we seek redemption
in this fallow spiral?
Will anyone come down to claim us,
once our innocence is restored?
In our own sky, of Galaxies we see
but one.

—The Scroll of Possibilities

Alvin's Tale

I DON'T WISH TO DWELL TOO MUCH ON MY OWN role in what came next. Let's just say that as a young male hoon, I seemed best suited to dangle at the end of the redeployed hawser, sitting in a makeshift sling while the crew lowered me toward the dark blue waters of the Rift.

After dropping below the edge, all I could see of the others were a few hoon and urrish faces, plus a pair of g'Kek eyestalks, peering down at me. Then even those blended into the rocks and I was alone, dangling like bait on a hooked line. I tried not to look at the long drop below, but soon a gusting wind set the hawser swaying, reminding me of the slender support overhead.

During the lonely descent I had time to ask myself— *"What the heck am I doing here?"*

It became a kind of *mantra*. (If I recall that word right, since it's not in the dictionary I have with me in this cold, hard place.) Repeated often enough, the phrase soon lost some of its horrid fascination, instead taking on a queerly pleasant cadence. By the halfway point, I was umbling—

"What the heck. I am *doing*. Here!"

In other words, a deed is being done, and I'm the one doing it, so why not do it right? An Anglic way of phrasing a very hoonish thought.

Anyway, I guess I did a good job of convincing myself, 'cause I didn't panic when they overshot at the end. My furry legs got well dunked before the brakes firmed and the tether stopped jouncing. It took a moment to gather breath and start umbling at Huphu, calling her to swim over from *Wuphon's Dream,* almost an arrowflight away. Haste was vital, since the bathy was slowly drifting out from the placid water under Terminus Rock. Soon she'd hit the Rift Current, and we might never see her again.

This time Huphu didn't make me wait. She dove in and swam toward me like a little black dartfish, clearly not badly harmed by her plummet off the bluff.

What's that sick joke they tell about noors? If you ever *have* to kill one, it will take a quart of traeki poison, a qheuen's claw, a human's arrow, and a rack of urrish insults. That assumes a hoon first distracts the beast with a first-class umble, and even so, it's best to have a g'Kek roll back and forth over the corpse a few times, just to be sure.

All right, it's juvenile humor, but also *respectful* in a way. I couldn't help spine-laughing over it while waiting for our indestructible Huphu. Finally, she clambered up my leg and into my arms, wallowing in my happy umble. I sensed she was still frightened, since for once she made no effort to pretend nonchalance or to hide her happiness to see me.

Still, time was short. Soon as I could, I slipped a harness of tough cord over Huphu's shoulders and urged her back down to the sea.

Urdonnol's plan seemed a good one . . . that is, *if* Huphu understood my instructions . . . *if* the *Dream* hadn't already drifted beyond reach . . . *if* Huphu managed to hook the cable's end onto the bathy's grommet fixture . . . *if* the subtraeki, Ziz, could hold on awhile longer in its hugely distended form, bearing up the weight of all that dangling metal . . . *if* the re-spliced hawser would bear the burden when the crew above hauled away . . .

There were so many ifs. Is this why Earthlings chose to call their goddess of luck and chance Ifni? Her capricious whims sure do swing back and forth. As on that day, when she first cursed our enterprise with calamity, then tossed her dice again the other way. Throughout the following tense midura, we all worried and wondered what her next clattering roll would bring—till at last Huphu and I stood atop the cliff together, dripping beside the beautiful flank of *Wuphon's Dream,* staring in amazement as Tyug carefully deflated and tended Ziz. Meanwhile, Pincer and Huck rolled round and round the bathy, inspecting nervously for damage, and Ur-ronn supervised the crew hauling in the rest of the dangling cable.

Finally, the two severed ends lay side by side on the stony mesa, burned, frayed, and torn.

"This will *not* haffen again!" I overheard our urrish friend mutter. It was in that tone of voice an urs uscs when she makes a prediction, a vow, and means she'll rip the neck off anyone who tries to make a liar out of her.

The next day Uriel returned, galloping into camp accompanied by armed assistants and a retinue of pack donkeys. With her came messages that had arrived by semaphore-and-runner relay from the far north, which she read aloud that evening, with the Dandelion Cluster as a shimmering backdrop above the glistening Rift. Wearing the robes of a lesser sage, the smith summarized what had occurred at Gathering—the coming not just of starships but star-*criminals.* Beings capable of bringing an end to the Great Peace, the Commons, and perhaps every member of the Six.

I couldn't see Huck's reaction when Uriel told in passing that the g'Kek race was now extinct among the stars, their last survivors reduced to savages, wheeling primitive tracks in the dust of Jijo. My tunnel of attention was still centered on other startling news.

The forayers were humans!

Everyone knows Earthlings weren't much more than animals in the eyes of the Galactic god-clans, only three hundred years ago. So what were mere *humans* doing, trying to pull a complicated theft across such distances?

Then I realized, since Uriel was addressing us in formal GalTwo, I'd been thinking in that tongue, seeing events the way a Galactic would. Things looked quite different when I rephrased the question in Anglic.

Three hundred years? That's an eternity! In that time humans moved from sailboats to their first starships. By now, who knows? Maybe they own half the universe!

All right, I've probably read way too much stuff by Doc Smith and "Star-Smasher" Feng. But while most folks on the bluff that night expressed shock that wise, cultured human beings could ever do such things, I knew an inner truth about them. One that weaves through Earthling literature like a never-absent umble tone.

As long as their race survives, some among them will be wolves.

It amazed us all when Uriel said the project would continue.

Amid talk of militia call-ups, emergency camouflage repairs, and possibly having to fight for our lives against overwhelming power, I expected the smith to order us all back to Wuphon and Mount Guenn at once, putting our backs to labor for the common good. So we stared when instead she acted as if *this* were important, this silly diving expedition of ours.

I even said so to her face.

"Why are you doing this?" I asked the next day as Uriel oversaw resplicing the hawser and air hose. "Don't you have urgent things to worry about?"

Her neck stretched upward, lifting the center, pupil-less eye almost even with my own.

"And what would you have us do instead? Turn out *weafons*? Convert our forge into a factory of death?" Her single nostril flared, revealing the twisty membranes that lock in moisture, making urrish breath as dry as wind off the Plain of Sharp Sand.

"We urs know death well, young Hph-wayuo. It scales our legs and dries our husvand fouches all too soon. Or else we hurry it along with fights and feuds, as if glory could ever requite our haste to die. A great nany urs look fondly on those days when Earthlings were our finest foes, when heroes roared across the frairie, wheeling and charging recklessly.

"I, too, feel that call. And like others, I resist. This is an age for another kind of hero, young fellow. A warrior who *thinks*."

Then she turned back to her labors, directing workers with severe attention to detail. Her response left me confused, unsatisfied . . . but also, in some way I could not quite fathom, just a bit more proud than I had been before.

It took two days to complete the overhaul and triple-check all systems. By that time, the mass of onlookers had changed. Many of the originals had hurried home on hearing Uriel's news. Some had militia duties, or were eager to perform destructive sacraments prescribed by the oldest scrolls. Others rushed back to save their property *against* premature drossing by the devout, or simply to be with loved ones during the expected last of days.

Those departing were replaced by others even angrier than the first, or frightened by things they had seen. Only yesterday, observers from Wuphon Port all the way to Finaltown Bay beheld a narrow, winged specter—a pale *aircraft*—that paused over the useless camouflage lattices, as if to say *I see you,* before resuming a twisty course along the coast, then out to sea.

No one had to say it. Whatever Uriel wanted to accomplish here, we didn't have a lot of time.

XX. THE BOOK OF THE SLOPE

Legends

The first sooner races arrived at Jijo knowledgeable, but they lacked a safe way to store that knowledge. The names of many archival tools come down to us, from *data plaques* to *memo-slivers* and *info-dust*, but all of these had to be consigned to the deep.

Earthlings possessed a secure, undetectable way to store information. The secret of paper—pulping and screening vegetable fibers with clays and animal products—was a uniquely wolfling invention. But the *Tabernacle* crew left Earth so soon after Contact, the data published in the Great Printing was sparse in galactology, especially concerning other "sooner infections" elsewhere in the Five Galaxies.

This makes it hard to put our Jijoan Commons in perspective. How different are we from other cases of illegal settlement on fallow worlds? Have we done a better job at minimizing the harm we do? What are our chances of avoiding detection? What kinds of justice were meted out to other squatters who were caught? How far down the Path of Redemption must a race travel before they cease being criminals and become blessed?

The Scrolls offer some guidance on these matters. But since most date from the first two or three landings, they shed little light on one of the greatest mysteries.

Why did so many come to this small patch of ground, in such a short span of time?

Against the half a million years since the Buyur left, two thousand years is not very much. Moreover, there are many fallow worlds—so why Jijo? There are many sites on Jijo—so why the Slope?

Each question has answers. The great carbon-spewing star, Izmunuti, began shielding local space only a few millennia ago. We are told this phenomenon somehow disabled robot sentinels patrolling routes to this system, easing the way for sneakships. There are also vague references to omens that a "time of troubles" would soon spread upheavals across the Five Galaxies. As for the Slope, its combination of robust biosphere and high volcanic activity assures that our works will be destroyed, leaving few traces we were ever here.

To some, these answers suffice. Others wonder, still.

Are we unique?

In some Galactic languages, the question does not even parse as sane. One can find a precedent for anything in the archives of a billion years. Originality is an illusion. Everything that *is* also *was*.

Perhaps it is symptomatic of our low state—our uncivilized level of consciousness, compared with the godlike heights of our ancestors—but one still is tempted to wonder.

Might something unusual be going on here?

—Spensir Jones, *A Landing Day Homily*

Asx

WE SAGES PREACH THAT IT IS FOOLISH TO ASSUME. Yet, during this, our greatest crisis, the invaders often turn out to know much that we thought safely hidden.

Should this surprise us, my rings? Are they not stargods from the Five Galaxies?

Worse, have *we* been united? Have not many of the Six rashly exercised their right of dissent, currying favors from the sky-humans against our advice? Some of these have simply vanished—including the sooner girl who so vexed Lester with her ingratitude, daring to steal back the treasure she had brought, which intrigued our human sage for days on end. Does she even now dwell within the buried station, pampered as a g'Kek might groom a favorite zookir? Or else, did the sky-felons simply delete her, as a traeki voids its core of spent mulch, or as Earthling tyrants used to eliminate quislings who had finished serving their purpose?

For every secret the raiders uncover, there are as many ways they seem shockingly ignorant, for sky-gods.

It is a puzzlement—and small solace as we contemplate the proud, intimidating visitor who this morn came before the Council of Sages.

My rings, has memory of this event yet coated your waxy cores? Do you recollect the star-human, Rann, making his request? Asking that several from his group be invited along, when next we commune with the Holy Egg?

The request was courteous, yet it had aspects of a command.

We should not be surprised. How could the aliens *not* notice what is happening?

At first discernible only to the most sensitive, the tremors strengthen till now they pervade this corner of our world.

—curling the mists that rise from geysers and steam pools,

—guiding patterned flocks of passing birdlings,

—waking dormant rewq, both in caves and in our pouches,

—even permeating the myriad blue colors of the sky.

"We have heard much about your sacred stone," Rann said. "Its activity triggers fascination in our sensoria. We would see this wonder for ourselves."

"Very well," Vubben answered for the Six, wrapping three eyestalks in a gesture of assent. Indeed how could we refuse?

"Pray tell—how many will be in your party?"

Rann bowed again, imposing for a human, as tall as any traeki, broad in the shoulders as a young hoon. "There will be three. Myself and Ling, you have met. As for the third, his revered name is *Ro-kenn,* and it is incumbent to realize how you are about to be honored. Our master must be shown all expressions of courtesy and respect."

With varied eyes, visors, and sight patches, we sages winked and winced amazement. All save Lester Cambel, who muttered softly next to our traeki stack,

"So the bloody Danikites had one underground with them, all along."

Humans are surprising creatures, but Lester's breach in tact so stunned our rings that "i" was unanimously amazed. Did he not fear being overheard?

Apparently not. Through our rewq, i read Lester's ill-regard for the man across from us, and for this news.

As for the rest of the Council, it did not take rewq to note their *curiosity*.

At long last, we were about to meet the Rothen.

Lark

Dear Sara,

The caravan bearing your letter took some time to get here, because of troubles on the plains. But how wonderful to see your familiar scrawl, and to hear you're well! And Father, when you saw him last. These days, there are few enough reasons to smile.

I'm dashing this off in hopes of catching the next brave kayak-courier to head down the Bibur. If it reaches Biblos before you leave, I hope I can persuade you not to come up here! Things are awful tense. Recall those stories we told each other about the dam, back home? Well, I wouldn't sleep in that attic room right now, if you smell my smoke. Please stay somewhere safe till we know what's happening.

As you asked, I've inquired carefully about your mysterious stranger. Clearly the aliens are seeking someone or something, beyond their goal of illicitly adopting a candidate species for uplift. I can't prove your wounded enigma-man isn't the object of their search, but I'd bet he's at most a small part of the picture.

I could be wrong. Sometimes I feel we're like kitchen-ants peering upward, trying to comprehend a human quarrel from the stir of shadows overhead.

Oh, I can picture your look right now! Don't worry, I'm not giving up! In fact, I have a different answer to the question you're always asking me. . . . Yes, I have met a girl. And no, I don't think you'd approve of her. I'm not sure this boy does, either.

·   ·   ·

Smiling ironically, Lark finished the first page of the letter and put down his pen. He blew on the paper, then picked up his portable blotter, rolling the felt across the still damp lines of ink. He took a fresh sheet out of the leather portfolio, dipped the pen in the ink cup and resumed.

Along with this note you'll get a hand-cranked copy of the latest report the sages are sending throughout the Commons, plus a confidential addendum for Ariana Foo. We've learned some new things, though so far nothing likely to assure our survival when the Rothen ship returns. Bloor is here, and I've been helping him put your idea into effect, though I see potential drawbacks to threatening the aliens, the way you recommend.

Lark hesitated. Even such veiled hints might be too much to risk. In normal times it would be unthinkable for anyone to tamper with someone else's mail. But such things used to be done by frantic factions during ancient Earthly crises, according to historical accounts. Anyway, what good would it do Sara to worry? Feeling like a wastrel, he crumpled the second sheet and started fresh.

Please tell Sage Foo that young Shirl, Kurt's daughter, arrived safely along with B—r, whose work proceeds as well as might be expected.

Meanwhile, I've followed up on your other queries. It's delicate questioning these space people, who always make me pay with information useful to their criminal goals. I must also try not to arouse suspicion over why I want to know certain things. Still, I managed to bargain for a few answers.

One was easy. The star humans do not routinely use Anglic, or Rossic, or any other "barbaric wolfling tongue." That's how Ling put it the other day, as if those languages were much too vulgar and unrigorous for a properly scientific person to use. Oh, she and the others speak Anglic well enough to converse. But among themselves, they prefer GalSeven.

He paused to dip his pen in the cup of fresh ink.

It fits our notion that these humans do not come from the main branch of the race! They aren't representatives of Earth, in other words, but come instead from an offshoot that's bound in loyalty to the Rothen, a race claiming to be the long-lost patrons of humankind.

Recall how Mother used to have us debate the Origins Question? One of us arguing the Danikenite side and the other supporting the Darwinists? At the time it seemed interesting but pretty pointless, since all our facts were out of texts three hundred years old. Who would think we'd live to see an answer proclaimed on Jijo, before our eyes?

As to the validity of the Rothen claim, I can't add anything to the report except that Ling and the others seem passionately to believe.

Lark took a sip from an earthenware cup of springwater. He dipped the pen again.

Now for the big news everyone's excited about. It seems we're about to get our first glimpse of one of these mysterious beings! Within hours, one or more Rothen are scheduled to emerge from their buried station and join a pilgrimage to the reawakening Egg! All this time, we never guessed their starship had left any of them behind with Rann and the others.

The Commons is tense as a violus that's been strung too tight. You could cut the anxiety here with an overused metaphor.

I'd better wrap this up if I'm to slip it in the mail packet.

Let's see. You also asked about "neural taps." Do the aliens use such things to communicate directly with computers and other devices?

I was going to answer yes. Ling and the rest do carry tiny devices that bring them voice and data information, arriving as if by magic from afar.

Then I reread your account of the Stranger's injury and reconsidered. The forayers command their machines by voice and gesture. I never saw anything like a brain-direct computer link, or the sort of "instant man-machine rapport" Ariana spoke of.

Now that I think about it

Lark dipped the pen again, poised to continue, then stopped.

Footsteps clattered on the gravel path beyond his tent. He recognized the heavy, scrape-ratchet of a gray qheuen. Nor was it the casual, unpretentious rhythm of Uthen. This was a stately twist-and-swivel cadence, using a complex ripple of alternating feet—a difficult aristocratic step, taught by chitinous matriarchs who sometimes styled themselves royal queens.

Lark laid down his pen and closed the portfolio. A low, wide silhouette loomed against the tent flap. Harullen's voice was accompanied by fluting sighs from three speech vents, each singing a different note in a high qheuenish dialect of Galactic Six.

"Friend Lark, are you within? Please greet me. I come bearing precious gifts."

Lark lifted the flap, shading his eyes as he emerged from dimness to face the lowering sun, poking sharp rays between rows of forest giants. "I greet you, Harullen, faith-comrade," he replied in the same language.

Harullen wore pilgrim's robes draped across his pentagonal carapace, leaving the central cupola uncovered. The g'Kek-woven finery shimmered under glancing sunshine. It took a moment for Lark's adapting eyes to spot what else was different—something wound around the qheuen's ash-colored cupola.

"Aha," he commented, slipping into a more relaxed sevenish dialect. "So it's true. The mask renews its offer."

"To take nourishment of our bodies in exchange for revelation of the soul. Indeed. The mask returns among us. Caves which had seemed barren now swarm with labile young rewq, even as the Egg resumes its patterning song. Are these not good omens? Shall we rejoice?"

With a snap of one claw, Harullen signaled to a lornik, which had been crouching out of view behind its master. The small servant creature hurried around the qheuen's great flank, scuttling and twisting in a four-legged imitation of Harullen's own stately walk. With small, three-fingered hands it bore a box of polished wood, showing fluted traces of personal tooth-carving.

"From among this crop of cave fledglings, there were many shaped for noble human brows," Harullen continued. "Please accept these to choose from, as offerings of deep esteem."

Lark took the box from the lornik, knowing better than to thank or make eye contact with the shy creature. Unlike chimps and zookirs, lorniks seemed able to bond only with the race that brought their ancestors to Jijo, nearly a thousand years ago.

He lifted the delicately grooved lid of the gift box, which by qheuenish tradition had been gnawed by the giver and could never be used again for any other purpose. Inside, resting on a bed of garu sawdust, several clusters of brown-speckled tendrils quivered, coupled by colored bands of translucent film.

There's been so little time. I've had so many duties. This really is a fine favor. . . .

Still, all told, Lark would rather have gone to the caves and picked his next rewq for himself, as he had done on three other occasions since passing puberty. It seemed strange to choose one out of a box. What was he to do with the others?

Several tentacles raised tentatively, reaching toward the light, then twisting, searching. Only one pair showed no indecision, wafting gently in Lark's direction, spreading a gossamer web between them.

Well, it's a humaniform rewq, all right, he thought. *It looks new, robust.*

To feel diffident was only natural. A person usually held on to a personal rewq for many years. It had been painful to watch helplessly as the last one wasted in its moss-lined pouch, during the many weeks the Egg was silent. Nor could he share someone else's symbiont. Among humans, one was more likely to pass around a toothbrush than a rewq.

"My gratitude is manifest in acceptance of this unexcelled gift," he said. Though reluctant, Lark lifted the squirming mass to his brow.

His former rewq had been like a pair of old shoes—or a favorite pair of urrish-made sunglasses—comfortable and easy to use. This one twitched and wriggled in agitated eagerness, palpating his temples in avid search of rich surface veins where it might feed. The gauzy membrane spread taut over Lark's eyes, rippling with the rewq's own excitement, conveying nothing more useful than a wave of vertigo. It would take time to reach an understanding with the new creature. Ideally you let your old one teach the new, during an overlapping time before the elderly rewq died.

Ifni's miracles often have ironic timing. We had to face the aliens for so long without the help rewq might have offered. Now, at a critical moment, they return so suddenly that they may only prove a distracting hindrance.

Still, for courtesy's sake, he pretended pleasure, bowing and thanking Harullen for the fine gift. With luck, Harullen's own rewq would be noisy too, and not convey any of Lark's own mixed feelings.

The heretic leader's satisfaction was evident in a mincing, clattering dance of feet and dangling claws. The film over Lark's eyes added a blur of sparks that *might* be translated qheuenish emotions—or else just static from the excited, untrained rewq.

Then Harullen abruptly changed the subject, slipping into Anglic.

"You know that the time of pilgrimage is almost at hand?"

"I was just writing a letter. I'll don my robe and join our group at the Wheel Stone in a midura."

Partly because Ling requested Lark's presence, the Sages had granted the heretical faction two sixes among the twelve twelves selected to make the first climb, setting forth to greet the rousing Egg. Since hearing the news, Lark had felt a familiar heat coming from the knob of stone that hung by a thong around his neck. His reminder and penance. No pilgrimage was ever easy wearing that amulet.

"Very well, then," Harullen replied. "At the Wheel Stone we shall consider the zealots' latest entreaty before proceeding to join . . ."

The heretic's voice trailed off, muffling as he crouched down, drawing all five legs into his carapace, bringing his sensitive tongue into contact with the ground. This time, Lark's rewq conveyed a vivid image of emotions— a halo depicting distaste mixed liberally with disapproval.

Harullen resumed. "There is another on the trail. One whose stone-hard lineage is belied by disorderly foot-haste."

One whose *what* is *what*? Lark puzzled. Sometimes the way other races used Anglic left him confused. Maybe it wasn't such a good thing the chaotic human language had become so popular on Jijo.

Soon he also felt ground-tremors, tickling the soles of his feet. A five-beat vibration even more familiar than Harullen's earlier footsteps. *Similar* to that rhythmic beat, yet simpler, less aristocratic, a pace too hurried and eager to waste time on etiquette or show.

Another armored form burst into view, trailing twigs and leaves.

Like Harullen, Uthen the Taxonomist was dressed for pilgrimage—in a carelessly draped, once-white rag that flapped behind him like somebody's old bedsheet. His carapace was a slightly deeper shade of slate than his disdainful cousin's. Like Harullen, Uthen wore a new rewq, which might explain his stumbling progress, twice veering off the path as if distracted by swarms of buzzing insects. Lark peeled his own reluctant symbiont back from his eyes. He needed no help reading his colleague's excitement.

"Lark-ark, Harullen-en," Uthen stammered out several vents, in unmatched timbres. Harullen scornfully turned his cupola while the newcomer caught his breath.

"Come quickly, both of you. They've come out!"

"*Who's* come—?" Lark began, before realizing that Uthen could mean but one thing.

He nodded. "Just give me a dura."

Lark ducked back under the tent flap, fumbled for his own pilgrimage robe, then paused by the writing desk. He snatched the unfinished letter from under the folio and slid it into a sleeve, along with a sharpened pencil. Ink was more elegant and wouldn't smudge. Still, Sara wouldn't give a damn, so long as the letter got there and contained the latest news.

"Come on!" Uthen urged, impatiently, when Lark reemerged. "Hop aboard and let's hoof it!" The gray qheuen scientist dipped one end of his shell to the ground. This time, Harullen groaned annoyance. Sure, kids did it all the time, but it wasn't dignified for an adult gray—especially one with ancestry like Uthen's—to go around carrying a human on his back. Still, they would move faster now, toward the Meadow of Concealed Aliens, hurrying to see the wonder that had emerged.

If anything, Ling understated when she called them beautiful.

Lark had never envisioned anything quite like them. Not when leafing through ancient picture books, or reading pre-Contact works of space fiction. Not even in his dreams.

In the vernacular of Jijo's exiled tribes, it was common to call all Galactics "star-gods." Yet here, strolling a forest clearing, were beings that seemed all but literally worthy of the name, so exquisite were they to behold. Lark could stand it only for moments at a stretch, then had to look away lest his eyes fill with tears and his chest begin to ache.

Ling and the other forayer humans formed a guard of honor around their noble patrons, while vigilant robots hovered. Occasionally, one of the tall stoop-shouldered Rothen crooked a finger, beckoning Rann or Besh to lean upward and explain something, like children called on to recite, gesturing at a nearby tree, one of the tent-pavilions, a herd of spline beasts, or a shy infant g'Kek.

Crowds gathered. Proctors of Gathering, armed with red-dyed sticks, kept people from pressing too close, but there seemed small likelihood of a shameful outburst. Hardly anyone even whispered, so thick was the atmosphere of awe.

The effect seemed greatest on the humans present, most of whom stared with hushed wonderment and bewildered *familiarity*. Rothen were humanoid to an uncanny degree, with high noble foreheads, wide sympathetic eyes, eloquent noses, and droopy, soft-fringed eyebrows that seemed to purse with sincere, attentive interest in anyone or everything they encountered. Nor were these parallels coincidental, Lark supposed. Physical and emotional affinities would have been cultivated during the long process of uplift, tens of thousands of years ago, when Rothen experts tinkered and modified a tribe of graceless but promising apes back on Pliocene Earth, altering them gradually into beings almost ready for the stars.

That assumed these creatures really *were* humanity's long-hidden patrons, as Ling claimed. Lark tried to retain an attitude of cautious neutrality but found it hard in the face of such evidence. How could this race be any other than humankind's lost patrons?

When the two august visitors were introduced to the assembled High Sages, Lark drew comfort from the serene expressions of Vubben, Phwhoon-dau, and the others, none of whom wore rewq for the occasion. Even

Lester Cambel remained composed—at least on the outside—when presented to *Ro-kenn* and *Ro-pol,* whose
names Rann proclaimed for all to hear.

By human standards, Ro-kenn appeared to be male.
And though Lark tried not to be overly influenced by
analogies, the more delicate-featured Ro-pol struck him
as possibly female. The crowd murmured when the two
smiled—revealing small white teeth—conveying apparent pleasure at the meeting. Ro-pol's grin creased in
ways that might even be called dimples. The word *merry*
tempted Lark, as a way to describe the slighter Rothen's
cheerful mien. It wouldn't be hard to like a face like that,
so warm, open, and filled with understanding.

It makes sense, Lark thought. *If the Rothen really are
our patrons, wouldn't they have ingrained us with similar esteem patterns?*

Nor were Earthlings alone affected. After all, the Six
Races had a lot of experience with each other. You didn't
have to be a qheuen to sense the charisma of a stately
queen, so why shouldn't an urs, or hoon, or g'Kek sense
this potent humanoid magnetism? Even without rewq,
most of the nonhumans present seemed caught up in the
prevailing mood—*hope.*

Lark recalled Ling's assurance that the forayer mission
would succeed without incident, and Jijo's Commons
needn't be changed in any but positive ways. *"It will all
work out,"* she had said.

Ling had also told him the Rothen were special beings,
even among high Galactic clans. Operating in deliberate
obscurity, they had quietly arranged for Old Earth to lie
fallow, off the colonization lists, for half a billion years,
an accomplishment with implications Lark found hard to
imagine. Needing no fleets or weapons, the Rothen were
influential, mystical, mysterious—in many ways godlike
even compared with those beings whose vast armadas
thundered across the Five Galaxies. No wonder Ling and
her peers thought themselves above so-called "laws" of
migration and uplift, as they sifted Jijo's biosphere for
some worthy species to adopt. No wonder she seemed
fearless over the possibility of being caught.

The newly cave-fledged rewq also appeared dazzled, ever since the tall pair emerged from the buried research station. The one on Lark's brow trembled, casting splashy aurae around the two Rothen till he finally had to peel it back.

Lark tried to wrest control over his thoughts, reclaiming a thread of skepticism.

It may be that all advanced races learn to do what the Rothen are doing now—impressing those beneath them on the ladder of status. Perhaps we're all extra-susceptible on account of being primitives, having no other experience with Galactics.

But skepticism was slippery as the Rothen emissaries conversed with the sages in voices that seemed warm, compassionate. A robot amplified the discourse for all to hear.

"We two now express grateful and respectful honors for your hospitality," Ro-kenn said in a very prim, grammatically perfect GalSixish.

"Furthermore, we now express regret for any anxiety our presence may have generated among your noble Commons," Ro-pol added. *"Only of late have we come to realize the depth of your unease. Overcoming our natural reticence—our shyness, if you will—we now emerge to soothe your quite unwarranted fears."*

Again, whispers of tentative hope from the crowd—not an easy emotion for Jijoan exiles.

Ro-kenn spoke again.

"Now we express joy and appreciation to have been invited to attend your sacred rites. One of us shall accompany you on this eve, to witness the wonderment inherent in, and remarkably expressed by, your renowned and Holy Egg."

"Meanwhile," Ro-pol continued, *"the other of us shall withdraw to contemplate how best to reward your Commons for your pains, your worries, and your hard sequestered lives."*

Ro-pol appeared to muse on the problem for a moment, choosing her words.

"Some gift, we foresee. Some benefaction to help you

through the ages ahead, as each of your cojoined races
seeks salvation down the long, courageous path known
as Return-to-Innocence."

A murmur coursed the ranks of onlookers—pleasure
at this surprising news.

Now each of the sages took turns making a welcom-
ing speech, starting with Vubben, whose aged wheels
squeaked as he rolled forward to recite from one of the
oldest scrolls. Something apropos about the ineffable
nature of mercy, which drifts upward from the ground
when least expected, a grace that cannot be earned or
even merited, only lovingly accepted when it comes.

Lark let the neophyte rewq slip back over his eyes.
The Rothen pair remained immersed in a nimbus of confused colors, so while Vubben droned on, he turned and
scanned the assembled onlookers.

Of course rewq offered no magic window to the soul.
Mostly, they helped make up for the fact that each race
came equipped with brain tissue specifically adapted for
reading emotional cues from its own kind. Rewq were
most effective when facing *another* rewq-equipped being, especially if the two symbionts first exchanged empathy hormones.

Is that why the sages aren't wearing theirs now? In
order to protect secret thoughts?

From the throng he picked up ripples of fragile optimism and mystical wonder, cresting here and there with
spumelike waves of near-religious fervor. There were
other colors, however. From several dozen qheuens,
hoon, urs, and men—proctors and militia guards—there
flowed cooler shades of duty. Refusal to be distracted by
anything short of a major earthquake.

Another glittering twinkle Lark quickly recognized as
a *different* kind of duty, more complex, focused, and
vain. It accompanied a brief reflection off a glass lens.
Bloor and his comrades at work, Lark guessed. *Busy*
recording the moment.

Lark's symbiont was working better now. In fact, despite its lack of training, it might never again be quite
this sensitive. At this moment almost every rewq in the

valley was the same age, fresh from caves where they had lately mingled in great piles, sharing unity enzymes. Each would be acutely aware of the others, at longer than normal range.

I should warn Bloor. His people shouldn't wear rewq. If it lets me spot them, it might help robots, too.

Another swirl caught his eye, flashing bitterly from the far end of the Glade, standing out from the prevailing mood like a fire burning on an ice-field. There was no mistaking a flare of acrid *hate*.

Finally he made out a shaggy snakelike neck, rising from the profile of a small centaur. Rewq-mediated colors, like a globe of distilled loathing, obscured the head itself.

The wearer of that distant, powerful symbiont suddenly seemed to notice Lark's focused regard. Shifting her attention from aliens and sages, she turned to face Lark directly. Across a crowd of shifting, sighing citizens, they watched each other's colors. Then, in unison each pulled back their rewq.

In clear light, Lark met her unblinking stare—the urrish leader of the zealot cause. A rebel whose malice toward invaders was stronger than Lark had realized. With those three fierce eyes turned his way, Lark needed no symbiont to translate the zealot's feelings toward *him*.

Under the late afternoon sun, her neck twisted and she snarled an urrish smile of pure, disdainful contempt.

The pilgrimage commenced at dusk, with long forest shadows pointing toward a hidden mountain pass. Twelve twelves of chosen citizens represented all the Commons, along with two star-humans, four robots, and one tall ancient being whose shambling gait hinted great strength under glossy white robes.

Judging by his so-humanlike smile, Ro-kenn seemed to find delight in countless things, especially the rhythmic chanting—a blending of vocal contributions from all races—as the assembly set out past steaming vents and sheer clefts, weaving its slow way toward the hidden oval Valley of the Egg. The Rothen's long-fingered hands stroked slim-boled welpal trees, whose swaying resonated with emanations from that secret vale. Most humans would hear nothing till they got much closer.

In Lark's heart, dark feelings churned. Nor was he alone. Many, especially those farthest from Ro-kenn's cheerful charisma, still felt uneasy about guiding strangers to this sacred place.

The procession marched, rolled, and slithered, wending higher into the hills. Soon the heavens glittered with formations of sparkling lights—brittle bright clusters and nebulae—divided by the dark stripe of the Galactic disk. If anything, the sight reinforced the starkly uneven order of life, for tonight's guests would shortly cross those starscapes, whether they departed in peace or betrayal. To them, Jijo would become another quaint, savage, perhaps mildly interesting spot they had visited once in long, deified lives.

The last time Lark came up this way—so earnest about his self-appointed mission to save Jijo from invaders like himself—no one had any thought of starships cruising Jijo's sky.

Yet they were already up there, preparing to land.

What is more frightening? The danger you already dread, or the trick the universe hasn't pulled on you yet? The one to make all prior concerns seem moot.

Lark hoped none of this gloom carried into his letter to Sara, which he had finished in a hurried pencil scrawl by the headwaters of the Bibur after the Rothen emerged. The kayak pilot added Lark's note to a heavy bundle from Bloor, then set off in a flash of oars, speeding down the first set of spuming rapids in a pell-mell rush toward Biblos, two days' hard rowing away.

On his way back to rendezvous with the other heretics, he had stopped to watch the alien aircraft glide out of its dark tunnel like a wraith, rising on whispering engines. Lark glimpsed a small human silhouette, hands and face pressed against an oval window, drinking in the view. The figure looked familiar . . . but before he could raise his pocket ocular, the machine sped away, eastward, toward a cleft where the largest moon was rising above the Rimmer Range.

Now, as the evening procession entered a final twisty canyon leading to the Egg, Lark tried putting temporal concerns aside, preparing for communion. *It may be my last chance*, he thought, hoping this time he might fully take part in the wholeness others reported, when the Egg shared its full bounty of love.

Drawing his right arm inside his sleeve, he grasped the rocky flake, despite its growing heat. A passage from the Scroll of Exile came to mind—an Anglic version, modified for Earthlings by one of the first human sages.

We drift, rudderless, down the stream of time,
betrayed by the ancestors who left us here,
blind to much that was hard-learnt by other ages,
fearful of light and the law,
but above all, anxious in our hearts
that there might be no God,
no Father,
no heavenly succor,
or else that we are already lost to Him,
to fate,
to destiny.

Where shall we turn, in banished agony,
with our tabernacle lost,
and faith weighed down by perfidy?
What solace comes to creatures lost in time?

One source of renewal,
never fails.
With rhythms long,
its means are fire and rain,
ice and time.
Its names are myriad.
To poor exiles it is home.
Jijo.

The passage ended on a strange note of combined reverence and defiance.

> *If God still wants us, let him find us here.*
> *Till then, we grow part of this,*
>   *our adopted world.*
> *Not to hinder, but to serve Her cyclic life.*
>
> *To sprout humble goodness out of the foul seed of crime.*

Not long after that scroll gained acceptance in the human sept, one winter's day, ground tremors shook the Slope. Trees toppled, dams burst, and a terrible wind blew. Panic swept from mountains to sea amid reports that Judgment Day had come.

Instead, bursting through a cloud of sparkling dust, the *Egg* appeared. A gift out of Jijo's heart.

A gift which must be shared tonight—with aliens.

What if they achieved what he had always failed? Or worse, what if they reacted with *derisive laughter,* declaring that the Egg was a simple thing that only yokels would take seriously—like fabled Earth-natives worshipping a music box they found on the shore?

Lark struggled to push out petty thoughts, to tune himself with the basso rumble of the hoon, the qheuens' calliope piping, the twanging spokes of the g'Keks, and all of the other contributions to a rising song of union. He let it take over the measured pace of his breathing, while warmth from the stone fragment seemed to swell up his hand and arm, then across his chest, spreading relaxed detachment.

Close, he thought. A tracery of soft patterns began taking shape in his mind. A weblike meshing of vague spirals, made up partly of images, partly of sound.

It's almost as if something is trying to—

"Is this not *exciting?*" a voice broke in from Lark's right, splitting his concentration into broken shards. "I believe I can feel something now! It's quite unlike any psi phenomenon I have experienced. The motif is highly unusual."

Ignore her, Lark thought, clinging to the patterns. *Maybe she'll go away.*

But Ling kept talking, sending words clattering up avenues that could not help hearing them. The harder he tried holding on, the quicker detachment slipped away. Lark's hand now clenched a clammy ball of rock and twine, warm with his body heat alone. He let go in disgust.

"We picked up some tremors on instruments several days ago. The cycles have been rising in strength and complexity for some time."

Ling seemed blithely unaware of having done anything wrong. That, in turn, made Lark's simmering resentment seem both petty *and* futile. Anyway, her beauty by moonlight was even more unnerving than usual, cutting through his anger to a vulnerable loneliness within.

Lark sighed. "Aren't you supposed to be guarding your boss?"

"Robots do the real guarding—as if we have anything to fear. Ro-kenn gave Rann and me permission to look around while he talks to your sages, preparing them for what's about to happen."

Lark stopped so suddenly, the next pilgrim in line had to stumble to avoid him. He took Ling's elbow. "What are you talking about? *What's* about to happen?"

Ling's smile carried a touch of the old sardonicism.

"You mean you haven't guessed by now? Oh, Lark. Think about the *coincidences.*

"For two thousand years sooners of various races lived on this world, squabbling and slowly devolving. Then humans came and everything changed. Though you started few and helpless, soon your culture became the most influential on the planet.

"Then, just a few generations after your arrival, a miracle suddenly erupts out of the ground, this spirit guide you all revere."

"You mean the Egg," he said, brow furrowing.

"Exactly. Did you really think the timing *accidental*? Or that your patrons had forgotten you?"

"Our patrons." Lark frowned. "You mean . . . you're implying the Rothen knew all along—"

"About the voyage of the *Tabernacle*? Yes! Ro-kenn explained it to us this morning, and now everything makes sense! Even our own arrival on Jijo is no accident, dear Lark. Oh, our mission *is* partly to seek deserving presapients, to join our clan. But more than that, we came for *you*. Because the experiment is finished!"

"Experiment?" He felt an involuntary disorientation.

"An arduous trial for your small branch of humanity, castaway and forgotten—or so you thought—on a savage world. It sounds harsh, but the road of uplift is hard when a race is destined for the heights our patrons plan for us."

Lark's mind whirled. "You mean our ancestors were *meant* to sneak down to Jijo? As part of an ordeal that's supposed to . . . transform us somehow? The Egg was—is—part of some Rothen scheme—"

"Design," Ling corrected, a kind of elation invading her voice. "A *grand* design, Lark. A *test,* which your folk passed brilliantly, I'm told, growing stronger, smarter, and more noble even as this awful place tried to grind you down.

"And now the time has come to graft this successful offshoot back onto the main trunk, helping all of humanity to grow, thrive, and better face the challenges of a dangerous universe."

Her grin was joyful, exuberant.

"Oh, Lark, when I spoke to you last, I thought we might be taking a few human castaways with us, when we go.

"But *now* the news is pure and grand, Lark.

"*Ships* are coming. So many ships!

"It is time to bring you *all* back home."

Asx

ASTONISHMENT!
This news bellows through our waxy cavities, driving out the Egg's pattern/resonance with acrid vapors of surprise.

we/i/we/i/we . . . cannot coalesce as Asx. Nor contemplate these tidings with any sense of unity.

The worst rumors of recent months—spread by irredentist urrish chiefs and bitter gray queens—claimed that humans might abandon Jijo, departing with their sky-cousins, leaving the other five to fester and be damned.

Yet even *that* dark fantasy left one solace to the rest of us.

One comfort.

The Egg.

Now, we are told—
(disbelieve it!)
(but how?)
—that the holy ovoid was *never* ours! Only *humans'*, all along! Its dual purpose—to guide Earthlings toward greatness while at the same time soothing, *domesticating* we other Five!

Taming the other septs, in order to keep humans safe during their brief stay on Jijo.

Now this is topped by insulting "kindness," as Rokenn says the Egg will be left as a parting gift.

Left as a token,
a trifle,
a gratuity for our pains.

Left to shame us all!

Pause, my rings. Pause. Ensure fairness. Stroke vapors across the wax drippings. Remember.

Did not Lester Cambel seem as dismayed as the rest of us?

Did not all the sages resolve to conceal this news? Lest rumors do great harm?

It is useless. Even now, eavesdropping citizens rush off, dispersing exaggerated versions of what they overheard, casting a poison up and down the chain of pilgrims, shattering the rhythms that had been uniting us.

Yet from the majestic Rothen, we sense cheerful unawareness that anything is wrong!

Is this what it means to be a god? To know not what harm you do?

Ripples of infection spread along the twisty trail. The worship-chant breaks apart, dissolving into many twelves of muttering individuals.

Now, from my/our highest peak, we perceive *another* disturbance, propagating from the *front* of the procession! The two disruptions meet like waves on a storm-tossed lake, rolling through each other in a great spume of noise.

"The way is blocked," a galloping messenger cries, hastening back with word. *"A rope barrier bars the path, with a banner upon it!"*

NO INFIDEL DESECRATION
KEEP SKY FILTH AWAY
JIJO WILL NOT BE MOCKED!

This can only be the work of zealots.

Frustration spins round our core. The fanatics chose a fine time to make their gesture!

We sages must go see. Even Vubben makes haste, and my basal segments labor to keep up. Ro-kenn strides with graceful ease, seeming unperturbed.

And yet, my rings, is this *variance* we observe, in Ro-kenn's aura? Through our rewq, we sense discrepancy between parts of his face, as if the Rothen's outward calm masks a canker of seething *wrath*.

Can rewq read so much from an alien form we just met, this very day? Is it because i have one of the few *older* rewq, surviving from earlier days? Or do we notice this because traeki are tuned to perceive disunity of self?

. . .

Ahead—the defiant banner.

Above—perched on cliffs, shouting youths brandish foolish (but brave!) weapons.

Below—Phwhoon-dau, with his booming voice, calls to them, asking them to state their demands.

Their reply? Echoing down canyons and steam-fumaroles—a command that the aliens depart! Never to return. Or else suffer vengeance by the greatest force on Jijo.

!?!?

The zealots threaten the Rothen with the *Egg*?

But did not Ro-kenn just claim the great ovoid as *his* to command?

Across the Rothen's visage flows what i interpret as *cool amusement*. He calls the zealots' bluff.

"Shall we see who has the power to back up their claims?" the star-god asks. *"This night the Egg, and all Jijo, will sing our truth."*

Lester and Vubben plead for restraint, but Ro-kenn ignores them. Still smiling, he commands robots to each side of the gorge, to seize the anchor bolts holding the barrier in place. Overhead, the rebel leader stretches her long neck, keening a curse in plains dialect, invoking the sacred power of Jijo to renew. To cleanse impudent dross with fire.

The young zealot is a fine showman, stamping her hooves, foretelling awful punishments. Our more credulous rings find it possible, for a moment, to believe—

—to believe—

—to believe—

What is happening?
What—is—happening?
What impressions pour
　　in
　　now,
　　faster than
　　wax can melt?
Then penetrate

awareness,
ring after
ring
in a manner that
makes
all events
equal in both
timing and
import?
What is happening?

*—twin lightning bolts outline many twelves of pilgrims,
their shadows fleeing from white flame . . .*
 *—crackling metal complains . . . shattered . . .
unable to fly . . . a pair of tumbling cinders . . .*
 *—after-image of demolition . . . two junk piles smol-
der . . . more dross to collect and send to sea . . .*

With other eye-patches, we/i glimpse horrified surprise on the face of Rann, the sky-human.

*—surrounding Ro-kenn, a schism of variance . . .
like a traeki sundered between one ring that is jolly and
a neighbor filled with wrath . . .*

And now, though surfeited with impressions, suddenly there is more!

 *—with eye-patches on the opposite side, we are first to
glimpse a fiery spike . . .*
 *—a searing brightness climbs the western sky . . .
rising from the Glade of Gathering . . .*
 —the ground beneath us trembles . . .
 *—actual sound takes a while longer to arrive, battling
upward through thin air to bring us a low groan, like
thunder!*

. . .

At last, the pace of events slows enough for our spinning vapors to keep up. Happenings occur in order. Not disjointed, parallel.

Review, my rings!

Did we perceive two robots *destroyed,* even as they tore down the zealots' barrier?

Then were we dazzled by some vast explosion *behind* us? Toward the Glade of Gathering?

What had been a pilgrimage of union dissolves into a mob. Small groups hurry downhill toward a dusty, moon-lit pall, left by that brief flame. Humans hang close together, for protection, clinging to their remaining hoonish and qheuenish friends, while other qheuens and many urs clatter by, aloof, scornful, even threatening in their manner.

Ro-kenn no longer walks but rides a cushioned plate between his two remaining robots, speaking urgently into a handheld device, growing more agitated by the moment. His human servants seem in shock.

The female, Ling, holds the arm of Lark, our young human biologist. Uthen offers a ride, and they climb aboard his broad gray back. All three vanish down the trail after Ro-kenn.

Bravely, Knife-Bright Insight proposes similarly to carry *this* pile of rings, this Asx!

Can i/we refuse? Already, Phwhoon-dau totes Vubben in his strong, scaly arms. The hoon sage lugs the g'Kek so both might hurry downhill and see what has happened.

By majority ballot, our rings choose to accept the offer. But after several duras of jouncing qheuenish haste, there are calls for a recount! Somehow, we clamp down, managing to hang on to her horny shell, wishing we had walked.

Time passes through a gelatin of suspense, teasing us with idle speculation. Darkness swallows wisdom. Glittering stars seem to taunt.

Finally, at an overlooking bluff, we jostle with others for a view.

• • •

Can you sense it, my rings?

Unified now, in shock, i see a steaming *crater,* filled with twisted metal. The sanctuary where Ro-kenn and the sky-humans dwelled among us for weeks. Their buried outpost—now a fiery ruin.

Acting with hot-blooded decisiveness, Ur-Jah and Lester call for volunteers to leap into that smoky pit, reckless of their own lives, heroically attempting rescue. But how could anyone survive within the wrecked station? Can anyone be found alive?

We all share the same thought. All members of the Six. All of my rings.

Who can doubt the power of the Egg? Or the fury of a planet scorned?

The Stranger

Doors seem to open with every song he rediscovers, as if old melodies are keys to unlock whole swaths of time. The earlier the memory, the more firmly it seems attached to a musical phrase or snippet of lyrics. Nursery rhymes, especially, take him swiftly down lanes of reclaimed childhood.

He can picture his mother now, singing to him in the safety of a warm room, lying sweetly with ballads about a world filled with justice and love—sweet lies that helped fix his temperament, even when he later learned the truth about a bitter, deadly universe.

A string of whimsical ditties brings back to mind the bearded twins, two brothers who for many years shared the Father Role in his family-web, a pair of incurable jokers who routinely set all six of the young web-sibs giggling uncontrollably at their quips and good-natured antics. Reciting some of the simplest verses over and over, he finds he can almost comprehend the crude punchlines—a real breakthrough. He knows the humor is puerile, infantile, yet he laughs and laughs at the old gag-songs until tears stream down his cheeks.

Arianafoo *plays more records for him, and several release floods of excitement as he relives the operettas and musical plays he used to love in late adolescence. A* human *art form, to help ease the strain as he struggled, along with millions of other earnest young men and women, to grasp some of the lofty science of a civilization older than most of the brightest stars.*

He felt poignant pain in recovering much of what he

once had been. Most words and facts remain alien, un-obtainable—even his mother's name, or his own, for that matter—but at least he begins to feel like a living being, a person with a past. A man whose actions once had meaning to others. Someone who had been loved.

Nor is music the only key! Paper offers several more. When the mood strikes, he snatches up a pencil and sketches with mad abandon, using up page after page, compelled to draw even though he knows each sheet must cost these impoverished folk dearly.

When he spies Prity doodling away, graphing a simple linear equation, he delightedly finds that he under-stands! Math was never his favored language, but now he discovers a new love for it. Apparently, numbers hadn't quite deserted him the way speech had.

There is one more communion that he realizes while being treated by Pzora, the squishy pile of donut-rings that used to frighten him so. It is a strange rapport, as foreign to words as day is to night. Robbed of speech, he seems better attuned to notice Pzora's nuances of smell and touch. Tickling shimmers course his body, triggered by the healer's ever-changing vapors. Again, his hands seem to flutter of their own accord, answering Pzora's scent-queries on a level he can only dimly perceive.

One does not need words to notice irony. Beings shaped much like this one had been his deadly foes—this he knew without recalling how. They were enemies to all his kind. How strange then that he should owe so much to a gentle pile of farting rings.

All these tricks and surprises offer slim rays of hope through his desolation, but it is music that seems the best route back to whoever he once was. When Arianafoo offers him a choice of instruments, laid out in a glass case, he selects one that seems simple enough to experiment with, to use fishing for more melodies, more keys to unlock doors.

His first awkward efforts to play the chosen instrument send clashing noises down the twisty aisles of this strange temple of books, hidden beneath a cave of stone. He strives diligently and manages to unloose more recollections of childhood, but soon discovers that more recent memories are harder to shake free. Perhaps in later life he had less time to learn new songs, so there were fewer to associate with recent events.

Events leading to a fiery crash into that horrid swamp. The memories are there, he knows. They still swarm through his dreams, as they once thronged his delirium. Impressions of vast, vacuum vistas. Of vital missions left undone. Of comrades he feels shamed to have forgotten.

Bent over the instrument with its forty-six strings, he hammers away, one and two notes at a time, seeking some cue, some tune or phrase that might break the jam-up in his mind. The more it eludes him, the more certain he grows that it is there.

He begins to suspect it is no human song he seeks, but something quite different. Something both familiar and forever strange.

That night, he dreams several times about water. It seems natural enough, since Sara had made it clear they would be departing on the steamboat tomorrow, leaving behind the great hall of paper books, heading for the mountain where the starship landed.

Another ship voyage might explain the vague, watery images.

Later, he knew better.

XXI. THE BOOK OF THE SEA

In traveling the downward path,
that of redemption,
be not unaware of what you seek.

To divorce your racial destiny
from your former clan,
from your associations,
from the patrons who first gave
your species speech,
and reason,
and starflight.

You are saying that they failed
the first time.
That someone else should have
a new chance to adopt your kind
and try again.

There is nobility in this gamble.
Nobility and courage.

But do not expect gratitude from
those you have spurned.

—The Scroll of Exile

Alvin's Tale

THE DAY CAME. AFTER ALL OUR FANTASIES, PREPArations, and endless details, there we were at last, the four of us, standing by the open hatch of *Wuphon's Dream*.

"Shoulda built a raft instead," Huck muttered nervously, while static from her nearest wheel hub made my leg hair stand out. "There's lots of rivers we could've explored all summer, all by ourselves. Done some nice quiet fishing, too."

I was hyperventilating my throat sacs, as if packing their livid tissues with pure oxygen would help much where we were going! Fortunately, Tyug had provided each of us with mild relaxant drugs, which might explain Ur-ronn's easy composure.

"*I* couldn't've gone on a raft," Ur-ronn replied, in flat deadpan tones. "I'd've gotten wet."

We all turned to stare at her, then each of us, in our own way, burst out laughing. Pincer whistled, Huck guffawed, and I umbled till it hurt. Oh, Ur-ronn—what a character!

"You're right," added Pincer-Tip. "The hot-air balloon would have been a *much* better plan. Let's talk Uriel into doing a retrofit-fit."

"Hush up, you two!" Huck chided, a little unfairly, since she had started it. We all turned as Uriel approached, Tyug following two paces behind. The traeki's little partial, Ziz, now recovered from its distending ordeal, lay back in its assigned cage, under the *Dream*'s bubble window.

"You have your charts?" Uriel inspected Pincer's pouch to make sure. Made of laminated plastic by a human-invented process, the sheets were tough, durable, and therefore somewhat less than legal. But we were heading for the Midden anyway, so wasn't it all right? We had studied the course chosen by Uriel, to follow as soon as the *Dream*'s wheels touched the muddy bottom.

"Compass?"

Both Pincer and Ur-ronn were equipped. Huck's magnetically driven axles shouldn't interfere much, if she didn't get too excited.

"We've gone over contingency tactics and rehearsed as nuch as fossifle, given our haste. I hope." Uriel shook her head in the manner of a human expressing regret. "There's just one thing left to cover, an ovject you are to seek out, while down there. A thing I need you to find."

Huck craned an eyestalk around to semaphore me.

See? I told you so! she flashed in visual GalTwo. Huck had maintained for days that there must be some item Uriel desperately wanted. An ulterior motive for all this support. Something we alone, with our amateur bathy, were qualified to find. I ignored her smug boast. The problem with Huck is that she's right just often enough to let her think it's a law of nature.

"This is what you are looking for," Uriel said, lifting up a sketch pad so that no one but we four could see, showing a *spiky* shape with six points, like a piece in a child's game of jacks. Tendrils, or long cables, stretched outward from two of the arms, trailing in opposite directions off the page. I wondered if it might be some kind of living thing.

"It is an artifact we need rather urgently," Uriel went on. "Even nore infortant than the artifact, however, is the strand of wire running away fron it. It is this strand that you seek, that you shall seize and fasten with the retrieval cord, so that we can haul it vack."

Sheesh, I thought. The four of us were modernist gloss-junkies who would gladly raid the Midden for treasure, even in defiance of the Scrolls. But now to have a *sage* order us to do that very thing? No wonder she preferred not letting nearby citizens in on this heresy!

"Will do!" Pincer exclaimed, briefly teetering on two legs in order to salute with three. As for the rest of us, we already stood on the ramp. What were we going to do? Use this as an excuse to back out?

All right, I considered it. So strap me to the Egg and sing till I confess.

I was the last one aboard—unless you count Huphu, who scampered through my legs as I was about to dog the hatch. I tightened the wheel and the skink-bladder seals spread thin, oozing like immunity caulk between a traeki's member rings. The closing shut us off from nearly all sound—except the hissing, gurgling, rumbling, and sighing of four frightened kids just coming to realize what a fix all their humicking daydreams had gotten them into.

It took half a midura to make certain the air system and dehumidifiers worked. Pincer and Ur-ronn went over a checklist up front and Huck tested her steering bars, while I squatted in the very back with nothing to do but stroke the crank that I would use, whenever the *Dream* needed the services of an "engine." To pass the time, I umbled Huphu, whose claws were a welcome distraction, scratching a nervous itch that tickled the outer surface of my heart spine.

If we die, please let Uriel at least drag our bodies home, I thought, and maybe it was a prayer, like humans often do in tight spots, according to books I've read. *Let my folks have a life-bone for vuphyning, to help them in their grief and disappointment over how I misspent the investment of their love.*

XXII. THE BOOK OF THE SLOPE

Legends

Anyone who travels by riverboat, and listens to the compelling basso of a hoonish helmsman, knows something of the process that once made them starfaring beings.

For one thing, the sound is clearly where their race-name comes from. According to legend, the Guthatsa patrons who originally adopted and uplifted presapient hoon were entranced by the musical trait. While splicing in speech, reason, and other niceties, the Guthatsa also worked to enhance the penetrating, vibrant output of the hoonish throat sac, so that it might enrich their clients' adulthood, when they took up mature responsibilities in Galactic society.

It would, the Guthatsa predicted, help make the hoon better patrons when their turn came to pass on the gift of wisdom, continuing the billion-year-old cycle of intellect in the Five Galaxies.

Today we know our hoonish neighbors as patient, decent folk, slow to anger, though doughty in a fix. It is hard to reconcile this image with the reaction of urrish and later human settlers, on first learning that the Tall Ones dwelled on Jijo—a response of animosity and fear.

Whatever the initial reasons for that loathing, it soon ebbed, then vanished within a single generation. Whatever quarrels divided our star-god ancestors, we on Jijo do not share them. These days, it is hard to find anyone among the Six who can claim not to like the hoon.

Yet there remains a mystery—why do they dwell on Jijo at all? Unlike other races of the Six, they tell no tale of persecution, or even of a quest for breeding space. When asked why their sneakship defied great odds to seek this hidden refuge, they shrug and cannot answer.

A sole clue lies in the Scroll of Redemption, where we read of an inquiry by the last glaver sage, who asked a first-generation hoonish settler why his folk came, and got this deeply-umbled answer—

"To this (cached) haven, we came, (in hope) seeking.
"On a (heartfelt) quest to recover the (lamented) spines of (lost) youth.

"Here we were sent, on the advice of (wise, secret) oracles.
"Nor was the (danger-ridden) trip in vain.
"For behold what, in (delighted) surprise, we already have won!"

At that point, the hoon colonist was said to point at a crude raft, fashioned from boo logs and sealed with tree sap—earliest precursor of all the vessels to follow, plying Jijo's rivers and seas.

From our perspective, a thousand years later, it is hard to interpret the meaning of it all. Can any of us today imagine our shaggy friends without boats? If we try to picture them cruising space in starships, do we not envision those, too, running before storm and tide, sluicing their way between planets by keel, rudder, and sail?

By that logic, does it not follow that urs once "galloped" across Galactic prairies, with stellar winds blowing their waving tails? Or that any starcraft fashioned by humans ought to resemble a tree?

—from *A Re-Appraisal of Jijoan Folklore*, by Ur-Kintoon and Herman Chang-Jones Tarek City Printers, Year-of-Exile 1901.

Dwer

IT WAS A MIDURA PAST NIGHTFALL WHEN THE EM-
ber crossed the sky, a flicker that grew briefly as it
streaked by, crossing the heavens to descend southeast. Dwer knew it was no meteor, because the spark
traveled below the clouds.

Only after it was gone, dropping beyond the next rank
of forested knolls, did he hear a low, muttering purr,
barely above the rustling of the tree branches.

Dwer might never have noticed if his dinner had
agreed with him. But his bowels had been shaky ever
since the four humans began supplementing their meager supplies with foraged foods. So he sat at the makeshift latrine, in a cleft between two hills, waiting for his
innards to decide whether to accept or reject his hard-
won evening meal.

The others were no better off. Danel and Jenin never
complained, but Lena blamed Dwer while her intestines
growled.

"Some mighty hunter. You've been over the pass dozens of times and can't tell what's poison from what's
not?"

"Please, Lena," Jenin had asked. "You know Dwer
never crossed the Venom Plain. All he can do is look for
stuff that's like what he knows."

Danel tried his hand at peacemaking. "Normally, we'd
eat the donkeys as their packs lightened. But they're
weak after recent stream-crossings, and we can't spare
any from carrying our extra gear."

He referred to the weight of books, tools, and special

packages that were meant to make human life beyond
the Rimmers somewhat more than purely savage. *If it
was finally decided to stay here forever.* Dwer still
hoped it wouldn't come to that.

"One thing we do know," Danel went on. "Humans
can survive here in the Gray Hills, and without all the
vat processes we're used to back home. Right now we're
adjusting to some local microbes, I'm sure. If the sooner
band got used to them, so can we."

Yes, Dwer had thought, *but survival doesn't mean
comfort. If Rety's any indication, these sooners are a
grumpy lot. Maybe we're getting a taste of how they got
that way.*

Things might improve once Danel set up vats of his
own, growing some of the yeasty cultures that made
many Jijoan foods palatable to humans, but there would
be no substitutes for the traeki-refined enzymes that
turned bitter ping fruit and bly-yoghurt into succulent
treats. Above all, Dwer and the other newcomers would
count on the sooners to explain which local foods to
avoid.

Assuming they cooperate. Rety's relatives might not
appreciate having the new order-of-life explained to
them. *I wouldn't either, in their position.* While Danel
was skilled at negotiation and persuasion, Dwer's role
would be to back up the sage's words, giving them force
of law.

From Rety's testimony, her tribe likely totaled no more
than forty adults. The social structure sounded like a
typical macho-stratified hunting band—a standard human devolution pattern that old Fallon long ago taught
Dwer to recognize—with a fluid male-ranking order en-
forced by bluster, personal intimidation, and violence.

The preferred approach to ingathering such a group,
worked out by Dwer's predecessors, was to make contact swiftly and dazzle the sooners with gifts before
shock could turn into hostility, buying time to map the
web of alliances and enmities within the band. After that,
the procedure was to choose some promising middle-
ranked males and help those candidates perform a *coup,*

ousting the formerly dominant group of bully boys, whose interest lay in keeping things as they were. The new leaders were then easy to persuade to "come home."

It was a time-tested technique, used successfully by others faced with the task of retrieving wayward human clans. Ideally, it shouldn't prove necessary to kill anybody.

Ideally.

In truth, Dwer hated this part of his job.

You knew it might come to this. Now you pay for all the freedom you've had.

If gentle suasion didn't work, the next step was to call in militia and hunt down every stray. The same hard price had been agreed to by every sept in the Commons, as an alternative to war and damnation.

But this time things are different.

This time we don't have any law on our side—except the law of survival.

Instead of bringing illegal settlers back to the Slope, Ozawa planned to *take over* Rety's band. Guiding them toward a different way of life, but one still hidden from sight.

Only if the worst happens. If we're the last humans alive on Jijo.

Dwer's mind reeled away from that awful notion, as his innards wrestled with the remnants of his meal. *If this keeps on, I'll be too weak to win a wrestling match, or however else Jass and Bom settle their tribal ranking. It may come down to Lena and her tools, after all.*

Throughout the journey, the stocky blond woman carefully tended one donkey carrying the gadgets of her personal "hobby"—a human technology passed down since the first ancestors landed on Jijo, one so brutal that it had been seldom used, even during the urrish wars. "My equalizers," Lena called the wax-sealed wooden crates, meaning their contents made her able to enforce Danel's verdicts, as thoroughly as Dwer's muscle and physical skill.

It won't come to that! he vowed, commanding his

body to shape up. Dwer touched several fingertips whose frostbite damage might have been much worse. *I've always been luckier than I deserved.*

According to Sara, who had read extensively about Earth's past, the same thing could be said about the whole bloody human race.

That was when the glowing ember crossed the sky, streaking overhead while Dwer sat at the makeshift latrine. He would never have noticed the sight had he been facing another way or engaged in an activity more demanding of his attention. As it was, he stared glumly after the falling spark while the rumbling thunder of its passage chased up and down nearby canyons, muttering echoes in the night.

They faced more stream crossings the next day.

It was hard country, which must have influenced the sooners' ancestors to come this way in the first place. Guarded first by the Venom Plain, then ravines and whitewater torrents, the Gray Hills were so forbidding that surveyors checked the region just once per generation. It was easy to imagine how Fallon and the others might overlook one small tribe in the tortured badlands Dwer led the party through—a realm of sulfurous geysers and trees that grew more twisted the deeper they went. Low clouds seemed to glower and sulk, giving way to brief glimpses of sunshine. Green moss beards drooped from rocky crevices, trickling oily water into scummy pools. Animal life kept its skittish distance, leaving only faint spoor traces for Dwer to sniff and puzzle over.

They lost several donkeys crossing the next rushing stream. Even with a rope stretched from bank to bank, and both Lena and Dwer standing waist-deep in the frigid water to help them along, three tired animals lost their footing on slippery stones. One got tangled in the rope, screaming and thrashing, then perished before they could free it. Two others were carried off. It took hours, sloshing through shallows, to retrieve their packs.

Dwer's fingers and toes seemed to burn the whole time with a queer icy-hot numbness.

Finally, drying off by a fire on the other side, they measured the damage.

"Four books, a hammer, and thirteen packets of powder missing," Danel said, shaking his head over the loss. "And some others damaged when their waterproofs tore."

"Not to mention the last fodder for the beasts," Jenin added. "From now on they forage, like it or not."

"Well, we're almost there, ain't we?" Lena Strong cut in, cheerful for once as she knelt butchering the donkey that had strangled. "On the bright side, we eat better for a while."

They rested that night, feeling better—if a bit guilty—with the change in diet. The next morning they marched just one arrowflight east to face a mighty ravine, with sheer walls and a raging torrent in its heart.

Dwer headed upstream while Lena struck off to the south, leaving Jenin and Danel to wait with the exhausted donkeys. Two days out and two back, that was the agreed limit. If neither scout found a way by then, they might have to make a raft and try the rapids. Not a prospect Dwer relished.

Didn't I tell Danel we should wait for Rety? I may be a tracker, but she came out through this desolation all by herself.

More than ever he was impressed by the girl's unswayable tenacity.

If there is a second party, and she's with them, Rety's probably chortling over me falling into this trap. If she knows some secret shortcut, they may reach the tribe before us. Now won't that screw up Danel's plans!

Even moving parallel with the river was awkward and dangerous, a struggle up steep bluffs, then back down the slippery bank of one icy tributary after another. To Dwer's surprise, Mudfoot came along, forsaking Danel's campfire and Jenin's pampering attention. The trek was

too hard for any of the noor's standard antics, ambushing Dwer or trying to trip him. After a while, they
even began helping each other. He carried the noor
across treacherous, foamy creeks. At other times,
Mudfoot sped ahead to report with squeals and quivers
which of two paths seemed better.

Still, the river and its canyon tormented them, appearing almost to open up, then abruptly closing again, narrower and steeper than before. By noon of the second
day, Dwer was muttering sourly over the obstinate nasti-
ness of the terrain. *Fallon warned me about the Gray
Hills. But I always figured I'd get to go through the old
man's notes and maps. Pick a path based on the trips of
earlier hunters.*

Yet none of them had ever found any trace of Rety's
band, so maybe they relied *too* much on each other's
advice, repeatedly taking the same route in and out of
these badlands. A route the sooners knew to avoid.
Maybe all this horrid inaccessibility meant Danel's group
was getting near the tribe's home base.

*That's it, boy. Keep thinkin' that way, if it makes you
feel better.*

Wouldn't it be great to struggle all this way, and back,
only to learn that *Lena* had already found a good crossing, just a little ways downstream? That thought tortured
Dwer as he shared food with Mudfoot. Going on seemed
futile, and he'd have to call the trip a loss in a few hours
anyway. Dwer's fingers and toes ached, along with overstrained tendons across his back and legs. But it was the
pounding roar of rushing water that really wore away at
him, as if a clock teet had been hammering inside his
head for days.

"Do *you* think we oughta head back?" he asked the
noor.

Mudfoot cocked its sleek head, giving Dwer that deceptively intelligent expression, reminding him of legends that said the beasts could grant wishes—if you
wanted something so bad, you didn't care about the
cost. Workmen used the expression "Let's consult a

noor" to mean a problem couldn't be solved, and it was time to soften frustration with a set of stiff drinks.

"Well," Dwer sighed, hoisting his pack and bow, "I don't guess it'd hurt to go on a ways. I'd feel silly if it turned out we missed a good ford just over the next rise."

Thirty duras later, Dwer crawled up a thorny bank, cursing the brambles and the slippery wetness that soaked his skin, wishing he was on his way back to a hot meal and a dry blanket. Finally, he reached a place to stand, sucking an oozing scratch across the back of his hand.

He turned—and stared through a mist at what lay ahead.

A crashing waterfall, whose roar had been masked by the turbulent river, stretched low and wide from far to the left all the way to the distant right. A wide curtain of spray and foam.

Yet that was not what made Dwer gape.

Just *before* the roaring plummet, traversing the river from bank to bank, lay a broad expanse of rocky shallows that appeared nowhere more than ankle deep.

"I guess this settles the question of whether or not to *pro-ceed*." He sighed.

Shortly, he and Mudfoot stood at last on the other shore, having sloshed easily across to prove the ford was safe. From there an obvious game trail zigzagged through the forest, departing the canyon eastward.

On my way back downstream I'll scout an easier path for Danel and the others to get up here. Success took much of the sting out of his aches and pains. *There's a chance Lena beat me to a way across. Still, I found this place, and maybe I'm the first! If all this stupid alien stuff blows over and we get to go home, I'll check Fallon's maps to see if anyone's named this spot since the Buyur went away.*

The broad falls reminded him of the spillway back at Dolo Village, a thought that was sweet, but also a bitter reminder of why he was here, so far from Sara and everyone else he loved.

I'm here to survive. It's my job to cower and have babies with women I barely know, while those on the Slope suffer and die.

The pleasure of discovery evaporated. *Shame* he displaced with a wooden determination to do the job he had been commanded to do. Dwer started to head back across the shallows . . . then paused in his tracks, acutely aware of a tickling sensation in the middle of his back.

Something was wrong.

Frowning, he slipped off the bow and drew the string-tightening lever. With an arrow nocked, he flared his nostrils to suck humid air. It was hard to make out anything in the musty dankness. But judging from Mudfoot's arched spines, the noor felt it too.

Someone's here, he thought, moving swiftly inland to get under the first rank of trees. *Or was here, recently.*

Away from the shore, the place stank with a terrible muddle of scents, which was natural next to the only river crossing for many leagues. Animals would come to drink, then leave territorial markings. But Dwer sensed something else, inserting a wary hint of threat.

Painfully aware that open water lay at his back, he moved deeper into the forest.

I smell . . . burnt wood—someone had a fire, not too long ago.

He scanned. Sniffing and peering.

It was over . . . there.

Amid the shadows, half a stone's throw away, he made out the remnants, set in a modest clearing. A large pit of black ashes.

Some of Rety's band? He worried. Might Jass and Bom be watching right now, picking their best shot at an intruder from the dreaded west?

Clues lay in the brushing rustle of wind in the branches, the furtive movements of insects and birds. But this terrain and wildlife were strange to him, and the racket from the waterfall would drown out a militia company on maneuvers.

Mudfoot made a low chuffing growl and sniffed close

to the ground while Dwer scanned the complex dimness beyond the next rank of trees. "What is it?" he asked, kneeling where Mudfoot scratched a layer of freshly fallen leaves.

A familiar odor struck him fully.

"Donkey shit?"

He risked a quick glance—and didn't need a second look.

Donkeys? But Rety said the sooners didn't have any!

With dark-adapting eyes he now picked out traces of pack beasts all over the clearing. Hoofprints and droppings from at least a dozen animals. A stake where a remuda line was tethered. Flattened spots where cargo carriers must have lain.

He lowered the bow. So a second expedition *had* set out, passing the first by a better route, no doubt led by Rety herself.

Well, at least we won't be quite so outnumbered by the sooners, even if contact doesn't happen in the order Danel planned.

An element of relief was more personal, if ungallant. *My choice in a future mate might go beyond Jenin, Lena, or some surly cousin of Rety's.*

Something still nagged at Dwer, however, making him reluctant to put down the bow. He was counting wallows—the depressions made by donkeys as they lay—and realized there were just too many. Or rather, there were two different *kinds* of wallow. Nearer the fire they were smaller, closer. . . .

No. It can't be.

Anywhere else, scent would have hit him long before this. Now a sharp, familiar pungency smacked Dwer in his sinuses. He bent to pluck a clump of stringy fur, still coated from when the owner rolled in ash after an unpleasantly wet river crossing.

Glossy strands from an urrish mane.

It had been generations since the last war. Regardless, instinctive fear surged in Dwer's chest—a heart-pounding wave of angst.

An urrish caravan in these parts could not be up to anything good.

Here in the wilderness, far from the restraint of sages and the Commons, with the Six possibly already extinct back home, all the old rules were clearly moot. As in days before the Great Peace, Dwer knew how dangerous these beings would be to have as enemies.

Silent as a ghost, he crept away, then crossed the river in a zigzag dash, leaping behind a boulder, then swiveling to cover the opposite bank while Mudfoot came splashing behind, clearly as eager to get out of there as he was.

Dwer kept wary watch for a whole midura, till long after his pounding pulse finally settled.

At last, when it seemed safe, he slung his bow and set off downstream, running when and where he could, hurrying southward with news.

A<small>SX</small>

CAN YOU SEE THE SMOKE, OH MY RINGS? SPIRALing from a fresh cavity in Jijo's ruptured soil? Two moons cast wan beams through that sooty pall, piercing a crater wherein twisty metal shapes flicker and burn.

Distracting thoughts rise from our second torus-of-cognition.

What is that you say, my ring? That this is a *very* large amount of dross? Dross that will not degrade back to nature on its own?

Indeed it is. Shall we hope that the aliens themselves will clean up the mess? It would take a hundred donkey-caravans to haul so much hard waste down to the sea.

Another ring suggests a stream be diverted, to form a lake. A transplanted mulc-spider might dissolve the sinful wreckage over the course of centuries.

By mass vote, we send these thoughts to waxy storage

for later reflection. For now, let us watch events flow in real time.

A roiling mob of onlookers teems the slopes overlooking this savaged vale, held in check by stunned, overworked proctors. Higher on tree-shrouded hills, we glimpse murky ranks of disciplined silhouettes, wheeling and maneuvering—militia units taking up positions. From here we cannot tell the companies' intent. Are they preparing, counter to all hope, to defend the Commons against overpowering vengeance? Or else have intersept grudges finally torn the Great Peace, so that we hasten doomsday tearing each other apart with our own bloody hands?

Perhaps even the commanders of those dark battalions don't yet know for sure.

Meanwhile, closer to the heat, Ur-Jah and Lester Cambel supervise teams of brave urs, men, hoon, and gray qheuens, who descend into the pit armed with ropes and tools of Buyur steel.

Ro-kenn protests at first, does he not, my rings? In hasty GalSeven, the Rothen emissary decries those he calls "wanton looters." One of the remnant robots rises, unfolding spiky organs of punishment.

Vubben urges that Ro-kenn look again. Can he not recognize sincere efforts at *rescue*? For two tense duras we poise on a precipice. Then, with a grudging mutter, the Rothen recalls his death machine—for now.

From Ro-kenn's charismatic, human-handsome face, our steady old rewq translates undertones of grief and rage. True, this race is new to us, and rewq can be fooled. Yet what else should we expect from one whose home/campsite lies in ruins? Whose comrades languish, dead or dying, in the twisted tangle of their buried station?

The male sky-human, Rann, wears torment openly as he rides the other robot, shouting at those working through the rubble, directing their efforts. A tense but encouraging sign of cooperation.

Ling, the other sky-human, appears in shock, leaning against young Lark as he pokes his foot through debris at the crater's rim. He bends to lift a smoldering plank, sniffing suspiciously. We perceive his head rock back, exclaiming surprise.

Ling draws away, demanding an explanation. Through our rewq, we perceive Lark's reluctance as he shows her the smoky plank, a strip of burned wood from a Jijoan box or crate.

Ling drops her hand from his arm. She spins about, hurrying toward Rann's hovering robot steed.

Much closer to this stack of rings, Ro-kenn has become embroiled in argument. A delegation accosts the Rothen emissary, demanding answers.

Why did he earlier claim the right and power to *command* the Holy Egg, since it is now clear that the sacred stone violently rejects him and his kind?

Furthermore, why did he seek to sow dissension among the Six with his baseless calumny about the human sept? His groundless lie, claiming that our Earthling brethren are *not* descendants of sinners, just like the other Five.

"You Rothen may or may not be the high patrons of humanity," the spokesman contends. "But that takes nothing from our ancestors who came here on the *Tabernacle*. Not from their crime, or their hope, when they set us on the Path of Redemption."

There is anger in the voice of the human intercessor. But we/i also descry thick brushstrokes of *theater*. An effort to smother the fire of disharmony that Ro-kenn ignited with his tale. Indeed, urrish voices rise in approval of his anger.

Now our second cognition-torus vents yet another thought-hypothesis.

What is it, my ring? You suggest disharmony was Ro-kenn's *intent,* all along? A deliberate scheme to create strife among the Six?

Our fourth ring rebuts—what purpose might such a bizarre plot serve? To have Five gang up on One? To cause vendetta against the very sept these Rothen claim as beloved clients?

Store and wick this weird postulate, oh my rings. Argue it later. For now the Rothen prepares to respond. Drawing himself up, he surveys the crowd with an expression that seems awesome both to humans and to those who know them—to rewq-wearers and those without.

There is kindness in his expressive gaze. Overstrained patience and love.

"Dear, misguided children. This explosive manifestation was not rejection by Jijo, or the Egg. Rather, some malfunction of the mighty forces contained in our station must have released—"

Abruptly, he stops as Rann and Ling approach, each riding a robot. Each wearing looks of dark anger. They murmur into devices, and the Rothen stares back, listening. Again, my rewq reveals dissonance across his features, coalescing at last in raging fury.

Ro-kenn speaks.

"So, now the (dire) truth is known. Learned. Verified!

"No accident, this (slaying) explosion.

"No (unlikely) malfunction—nor any rejection by your (overly-vaunted) Egg.

"Now it is known. Verified. That this was (foul, unprovoked) murder!

"Murder by deceit, by subterfuge.

"By use of subterranean explosives. By sneak attack.

"By you!"

He points, stabbing with a long, graceful finger. The crowd reels back from Ro-kenn's fierce wrath, and this news.

At once it is clear what the zealots have done. Secretly, taking advantage of natural caverns lacing these hills, they must have laboriously burrowed deep beneath the station to lay chests of eruptive powder—crude but plentiful—which then awaited a signal, the right symbolic moment, to burst forth flame and destruction.

"With scanners tuned for chemical sleuthing, we now perceive the depth of your shared perfidy. How undeserved were the rewards we planned conferring on murderous half-beasts!"

He might say more to the cowering throng, adding terrible threats. But at that moment, a *new* disturbance draws our focus toward the smoldering pit. The crowd parts for a phalanx of soot-stained rescuers, coughing and gasping as they bear pitiable burdens.

Rann cries out, bounding from his mount to inspect a crumpled form, borne upon a litter. It is Besh, the other female sky-human. From her mangled figure, our rewq reads no life flicker.

Again, the crowd divides. This time it is *Ro-kenn* who exclaims a distinctly unhuman wail. The litter brought before him bears the other of his race, Ro-pol, whom we guessed to be female. (His mate?)

This time, a slim thread of *breath* swirls in the near infrared, from the victim's soot-stained but still splendid face. Ro-kenn bends close, as if seeking some private communion.

The poignant scene lasts but a few moments. Then the reed of living tension is no more. A second corpse lies in the hollow, under bitter-bright stars.

The living Rothen stands to his full height, a terrible sight, emoting vast anger.

"Now comes the reward (foul) treachery deserves!" Ro-kenn cries, reaching skyward, his voice reverberating with such wrath that every rewq in the valley trembles. Some humans drop to their knees. Do not even gray queens whistle awe and dismay?

"For so long you have feared (righteous) judgment from above. Now behold its incarnate form!"

Along with the others, we/i look up, our gaze following Ro-kenn's extended arm.

There, crossing the sky, we perceive a single glaring spark. A pitiless glimmer that ponderously *moves,* passing from the Spider's Web into the constellation humans call The Sword.

The great ship is still a distant point, but it does not wink, nor does it twinkle. Rather, it seems to *throb* with an intensity that hurts those who watch for long.

One can hardly fault the zealots' timing, suggests our

ever-thoughtful second-torus-of-cognition. *If their objective was to bring an end to pretense, they could have chosen no better way.*

_____

Sara

_____

SAGE TAINE WANTED TO SPEAK WITH HER BEFORE she left for Kandu Landing. So did Ariana Foo. Both wished she would delay her departure, but Sara was eager to be off.

Yet with just a midura to go before the *gopher* set sail, she decided on impulse to visit her old office, high in the cathedral-tower housing the Library of Material Science.

West from the Grand Staircase, her ascent first took her by the vast, rambling stacks of physics and chemistry, where the recent evacuation had taken a visible toll. The maze of shelves showed frequent gaps. Scraps of paper lay in place of absent volumes, to help staff put things back if the present crisis passed. In places, the wood surface looked almost new, implying this was the first time a book had budged since the Great Printing.

Glancing down one crooked aisle, Sara glimpsed young Jomah, teetering under a load of heavy volumes, lumbering gamely behind his uncle to begin the ornate rituals-of-borrowing. None too soon if they hoped to make the *gopher* in time. The explosers and quite a few others were bound the same way as Sara, first by boat, then donkey-caravan to the Glade of Gathering.

The winding labyrinth triggered complex emotions. She used to get lost back in the early days, but never cared, so happy had she been to dwell in this splendid place. This temple of wisdom.

Her long year away had hardly changed her little office, with its narrow window overlooking the green-flanked Bibur. Everything seemed much as she had left it, except for the dust. *Well, I always figured I'd be back before this.* Many competed to be chosen by human sept for this life, subsidized by a race of farmers and gleaners whose one great sinful pride lay in their books.

Tacked to the far wall lay a chart showing the "devolution" of various dialects spoken on the Slope. Like branches splitting off from parent roots, there were multiple downward shoots for each Galactic language in current use. This older depiction showed the bias of scholars over in Linguistics, and was colored by one unassailable fact—the billion-year-old Galactic languages had once been perfect, efficient codes for communication. Deviation was seen as part of a foretold spiral toward the innocence of animal-like grunts—the *Path of Redemption* already blazed by glavers—a fate variously dreaded or prayed for by folk of the Slope, depending on one's religious fervor.

Human tongues were also traced backward, not over a billion years but ten thousand. Earthling authorities like Childe, Schrader, and Renfrew had carefully rebuilt ancestral languages and many of those grammars were more primly structured, better at error-correction, than the "bastard" jargons that followed. What better evidence that human devolution began long before the landing on Jijo? Did not all Earth cultures have legends of a lost Golden Age?

One conclusion—the missing Patrons of Earth must have been interrupted in their work, forced to leave humanity half finished. True, the ensuing fall was masked by some flashy tricks of precocious technology. Still, many scholars believed Earthlings had much to gain from any road leading toward re-adoption and a second chance, especially since they appeared to be heading that way anyway.

That's the orthodox view. My model takes the same data, but projects a different outcome.

Her most recent chart resembled this one—*turned upside down,* with lightless roots transformed into trees, showing the Six heading in a new direction.

In many *directions.*

If no one interferes.

Yesterday, she had shown her latest work to Sage

Bonner, whose enthusiasm reignited the pleasure of a colleague's praise.

"Well, my dear," said Jijo's oldest mathematician, stroking his bald pate, "you do seem to have a case. So let's schedule a seminar! Interdisciplinary, of course."

He punctuated his enthusiasm with a sloppy GalTwo emotion trill of anticipation.

"We'll invite those stuffy pedants from Linguistics. See if they can bear to hear a bold new idea for a change. Heh. Heh-cubed!"

Bonner probably hadn't much followed her discussion of "redundancy coding" and chaos in information theory. The elderly topologist just relished the prospect of a brisk debate, one that might knock down some ensconced point of view.

If only you knew how good an example you are of my thesis, she had thought affectionately. Sara hated to disappoint him.

"We can have it when I get back from Gathering, with luck."

Alas, there might be no return from her coming journey. Or else, it might be to find that the explosers had done their duty at last, bringing down the stony roof, and with it a prophesied age of darkness and purity. She was turning to go, when a low *thunk* announced a message ball, landing on her desk. Above the in-box, a fleshy tube bounced in recoil, having spit the ball from a maze of pipes lacing the Biblos complex.

Oh no. Sara backed away, hoping to leave before the furry sphere unrolled. If the messenger found no one home, it would simply reenter the tube and report the fact to whoever sent it.

But the ball uncoiled swiftly and a tiny mouselike form scrambled up the box to see her, squeaking delight over achieving the purpose bred into it by the ancient Buyur—to deliver brief messages via a network of cross-linked tunnels and vines. With a sigh, Sara put out her hand, and the courier spat a warm *pellet* into her palm. The pill squirmed.

Suppressing distaste, she raised the little symbiont—a

larger cousin of a parrot tick—and let it writhe inside her ear.

Soon, as she feared, it began speaking with the voice of Sage Taine.

"Sara, if this reaches you, I'd like to talk before you go. . . . It is essential to clear up our misunderstanding."

There came a long pause, then the voice hurried on.

"I've thought about it and have lately come to believe that this situation is largely my fau—"

The message stopped there. The record bug had reached its limit. It began repeating the message over again, from the beginning.

Fault? Was "fault" the word you were about to say?

Sara tipped her head until the bug realized it wasn't wanted anymore and crawled out of her ear. Taine's voice grew distant, plaintive, as she tossed the bug back to the furry little messenger, who snatched it, tweaking it between sharp jaws, making the bug receptive for Sara's reply.

I'm sorry, she almost said aloud.

I should have made allowances. You were tactless, but meant well, in your haughty way.

I should have been honored by your proposal, even if you first made it out of a sense of duty.

I reacted badly when you renewed the offer at Joshu's funeral.

A month ago, I was thinking about finally saying yes. There are worse lives on the Slope than the one you offered.

But now everything had changed. The aliens had seen to that. *Dwer* had what it would take in the new era to come. He'd thrive and sire generations of fine hunter-gatherers, if an age of innocence really was at hand.

And if it's death the aliens have in mind for us? Well, Dwer will fool them, too, and survive.

That thought made Sara poignantly glad.

Either way, what use will Jijo have for intellectuals like us, Taine?

The two of them would soon be more equal than ever, alike in useless obsolescence, before the end.

Sara said nothing aloud. The messenger ball gave a stymied squeak. It popped the bug into one cheek, then reentered the tube, vanishing into the maze-work of conduits that laced Biblos like a system of arteries and veins.

You're not the only one. Sara cast a thought after the frustrated creature. *There's more than enough disappointment to go around.*

The *gopher* was already putting on steam when Sara hurried to the dock. Ariana Foo waited nearby, the twilight shrouding her wheelchair so that she resembled some human–g'Kek hybrid.

"I wish I could have a few more days with him," she said, taking Sara's hand.

"You've done wonders, but there's no time to spare."

"The next kayak pilot may bring vital news—"

"I know. And I'd give anything to hear from Lark. But that reasoning will only take us in circles. If something urgent happens, you can send a galloper after us. Meanwhile I have . . . a feeling that we'd better hurry."

"More dreams?"

Sara nodded. For several nights her sleep had been disturbed by ill-defined impressions of alpine fire, then watery suffocation. It might just be a return of the claustrophobia she felt years ago, as a youthful newcomer under the overhanging roof-of-stone. Or else maybe her nightmares echoed something real. An approaching culmination.

Mother believed in dreams, she recalled. *Even as she drilled into Lark and me a love of books and science, it was* Dwer *whom she heeded, whenever he woke with those powerful visions, back when he was little—and then the week before she died.*

The steam packet hissed, its boilers straining. Two dozen donkeys thumped and whinnied, tethered at the stern alongside sealed crates of books.

Contrasting strangely, a different sound came from the ship's bow. Delicate, melodic *music* consisting of parallel chains of halting notes, somewhat twangy. Sara tilted her head.

"He's getting better fast."

"He has motivation," the sage replied. "I expected him to choose a simpler instrument, like a flute or violus. But he pulled the dulcimer off the museum shelf and seemed to draw some deep satisfaction out of counting its strings. It's simple to learn, and he can sing along, when a tune spills out of memory. Anyway, he's fit for a journey, so"—she took a deep breath, looking weary and old—"give Lester and the other High Mucketies my regards, will you? Tell them to behave."

Sara bent to kiss Ariana's cheek. "I'll do that."

The retired sage gripped her arm with unexpected strength. "Safe journey, child. Ifni roll you sixes."

"Safe house," Sara returned the blessing. "May she roll you long life."

Ariana's chimp aide pushed her upslope, toward the comfort of an evening fire. It was becoming a habit for Sara to doubt she would ever see someone again.

The captain gave the order to cast off, guiding his precious boat gingerly away from the camouflage shelter. Jop and Ulgor joined Sara at the rail, along with several morose-faced librarians, appointed to carry precious volumes to uncertain safety in the wilderness. Soon the churning shove of the paddle wheels settled to a reassuring rhythm, working with the Bibur's current to turn them downstream.

The spaceman played along with focused monomania. Hunched over a small, wedgelike instrument, he hammered its strings with two small curved mallets, faltering often but radiating passion. The music laced through bittersweet memory as Sara watched the mighty fortress slip by, with its many-windowed halls. The stone canopy seemed to hover like a patient fist of God.

I wonder if I'll ever be back.

Soon they passed the westernmost edge of laser-cut stone—the mulching grounds. There were no banners today, or mourners, or busy little subtraekis consuming flesh, preparing white bones for the sea. But then, amid the dusky gloom, she did spy a solitary figure overlooking the river. Tall and straight-backed, with a sleek mane of silver-gray, the human leaned slightly on a cane, though he seemed far from frail. Sara's breath caught as the *gopher* swept by.

Sage Taine nodded—a friendly, even ardent display for such a diffident person. Then, to Sara's surprise, he lifted an arm, in a gesture of unadorned goodwill.

At the last moment she gave in, raising her own hand. *Peace,* she thought.

Biblos fell behind the chugging steamboat, swallowed by gathering night. Nearby, the Stranger's voice broke in, singing words to a song about a voyage of no return. And while she knew the lyrics expressed his own sense of loss and poignant transition, they also rubbed, both sweetly and painfully, against conflicts in her own heart.

> *For I am bound beyond the dark horizon,*
> *And ne'er again will I know your name . . .*

XXIII. THE BOOK OF THE SEA

g'Kek roller, can you stand and
gallop
across the heavy ground?
Traeki stack, can you weave a
tapestry,
or master the art of fire?
Royal qheuen, will you farm the
forest heights? Can you heal with
your touch?
Hoonish sailor, will you endure the
plains, or spin along a cable,
stretched up high?
Urrish plainsman, would you sail to
sea, or sift fine pages out of slurried
cloth?
Human newcomer, do you know this
world?
Can you weave, or spin, or track
Jijo's song?
Will all or any of you follow in the
trail blazed by glavers?

The Trail of Forgiveness through
oblivion?
If you do, save room to remember
this one thing—
You were one part of a union greater
than its parts.

—The Scroll of the Egg
—(unofficial)

Alvin's Tale

I DIDN'T BEGRUDGE MY POSITION CRAMMED WAY back, far from the window. At least not during the long descent down the cliff face with the sea looming ever-closer, closer. After all, I'd seen this part before and the others hadn't. But once we hit water, and my friends started cooing and oohing over what they saw through the bubble up front, I started getting a little resentful. It also put me in a bind as a *writer*, faced with having to describe the descent later, to my readers. At best I could see a bare patch of blue over the backs of my compeers.

Looking back on it, I suppose I could solve the problem, in several ways.

First, I could *lie*. I mean, I haven't decided whether to turn this story into a novel, and according to Mister Heinz, fiction is a kind of lying. In a later draft I might just write in a window aft. That way my character could describe all sorts of things I only heard about from the others. Or else I could pretend I was up front all along. In fiction, you can be captain if you want to be.

Or maybe I should rewrite it from *Pincer*'s point of view. After all, it was his boat, more than any of ours. And he had the best view of what happened next. That would mean having to write believably from a *qheuen*'s perspective. Not as alien as a traeki's, I suppose. Still, maybe I'm not ready to take on that kind of a challenge, just yet.

All of this assumes I live to do a rewrite, or that anyone else survives who I'd care to have read my tale.

Anyway, for now, this semitruthful journal style will

have to do, and that means telling what I really saw, felt, and heard.

The deploying drums transmitted a steady vibration down the hawser. The fresh air inlet hissed and gurgled by my left ear, so it was hardly what I had pictured as a serene descent into the silent deep. Now and then, Ur-ronn would gasp—"What was that?"—and Pincer identified some fish, piscoid, or skimmer—creatures a hoon usually saw dead in a net-catch, and an urs likely never glimpsed at all. Still, there were no monsters of fantasy. No faery minarets of undersea cities, either. Not so far.

It got dark pretty fast as we dropped. Soon all I made out were little streaks of phosphor that Tyug had smeared in vital spots around the cabin, such as the tips of my motor cranks, the depth gauge, and the ballast release levers. With nothing to do, I catalogued the odors assailing me from my friends. Familiar aromas, but never quite so pungent as now. And this was just the beginning.

A reason to be glad no human came along, I thought. One of many problems contributing to friction between urs and Earthlings had been how each race *smelled* to the other. Even today, and despite the Great Peace, I don't figure either sept would much enjoy being cooped up in an oversized coffin with the other for very long.

Ur-ronn started calling out depths from the pressure-bladder gauge. At seven cables she turned a switch, and the eik light came on, casting twin beams into cool, dark waters. I expected those in front to resume their excited exclamations, but apparently there was less to see at this depth. Pincer identified something only every few duras, in a voice that seemed disappointed.

We all tensed at nine cables, since trouble had struck there the first time. But the milestone passed uneventfully. It should, since Uriel had inspected every hoof of the hawser personally.

At eleven and a half cables, a sudden chill swept the cabin, causing fog briefly to form. Every hard surface abruptly went damp and Huck cranked up the dehumidifier. I reached out to touch the garuwood hull, which seemed markedly cooler. *Wuphon's Dream* turned and tilted slightly, facing a new tug, no longer the same languid downward drift. From soundings, we had known to expect a transition to a deep frigid current. Still, it was unnerving.

"Adjusting ballast for trim," Huck announced. Closest to dead center, she used Uriel's clever pumps to shift water among three tanks till the spirit levels showed an even keel. That would be vital on reaching bottom, lest we topple over at the very moment of making history.

I thought about what we were doing. In Galactic terms, it was consummately primitive, of course. Earth history makes for much more flattering comparisons—which may be one reason we four find it so attractive. For instance, when Jules Verne was writing *Twenty Thousand Leagues Under the Sea*, no human had ever gone as far down into the oceans of Terra as we were heading today. We savages of Jijo.

Huck shouted—"Look! Is that something down below?"

Those eyes of hers. Even peering past Pincer and Ur-ronn, she had glimpsed bottom first. Ur-ronn turned the eik beams and soon the three of them were back at it again, driving me crazy with oohs, ahs, and k-k-k-k wonderment clicks. In frustration I turned the crank, making the rear wheels thrash till they yelled at me to quit, and agreed to describe what they saw.

"There's a wavy kind of plant," Pincer said, his voice no longer stuttering. "And another kind that's all thin and skinny. Don't know how they live, with no light getting down here. There's lots of that kind, sort of waving about. And there are snaky trails in the mud, and some kind of weird fishes dodging in and out of the skinny plants. . . ."

After a bit more of that, I would've gladly gone back to wonderment clicks. But I kept quiet.

". . . And there are some kurtle crabs—bright red and bigger than any I ever seen before! And what's that, Ur-ronn, a mudworm? You think so? What a mudworm! . . . Hey, what's that thing? Is that a dro—"

Ur-ronn interrupted, "Half a cavle to bottom. Signaling the surface crew to slow descent."

Sharp electric sparks broke the cabin's darkness as she touched a contact key, sending coded impulses from our battery up an insulated strand, woven through the hawser. It took a few duras for the rumbling grumble of the deploying drums to change pitch as the brakes dug in. *Wuphon's Dream* jerked, giving us all a start. Huphu's claws raked my shoulder.

The descent slowed. It was specially agonizing for me, not knowing how much farther bottom lay, when we'd make contact, or with how much force. Naturally, nobody was confiding in good old Alvin!

"Hey, fellas," Pincer resumed, "I think I just saw—"

"Adjusting trim!" Huck announced, peering with one eye at each of the spirit levels.

"Refocusing the lights," Ur-ronn added. "Ziz shows one yellow tentacle to starvoard. Current flowing that direction, five knots."

Pincer murmured—"Fellas? I *thought* I just saw . . . oh, never mind. Bottom appears to slope left, maybe twenty degrees."

"Turning forward wheels to compensate," Huck responded. "Alvin, we may want a slow rearward crank on the driver wheels."

That jerked me out of any resentful mood. "Aye-aye," I said, turning the zigzag bar in front of me, causing the rear set of wheels to rotate. At least I *hoped* they were responding. We wouldn't know for sure till we hit the ground.

"Here it comes," Huck announced. And then, apparently recollecting her missed estimates during the trial run, she added—"This time for sure. Brace yourselves!"

When I write about all this someday from these notes, perhaps I'll describe sudden billows of mud as we plowed into the ocean floor, gouging a long furrow, sending vegetation tumbling and blind subsea creatures fleeing in panic. Maybe I'll throw in fierce saltwater spray from a blown seal or two, tightened frantically by the heroic crew, in the nick of time.

What I probably *won't* admit in print is that I couldn't even tell the exact moment when our wheels touched down. The event was, well, more than a bit *murky*. Like sinking a probe fork into the rind of a shuro fruit and not being quite sure whether you've speared the core nut yet.

"Murky" also described the scene around us as slime-swirls spiraled, slowly settling to reveal a dead-black world, except down twin corridors of dazzling blue cast by the eiks. What I could see of those narrow tunnels showed a slanting plain of mud, broken here and there by pale slim-stemmed "plants" that needed no sunlight to thrive, though I couldn't begin to guess what else they lived on. Their leaves or fronds seemed to wave back and forth, as if in a breeze. No animal life moved in our beams, which wasn't that surprising. Wouldn't we top-dwellers hide if some weird vessel plunged into our midst from above, casting forth both noise and a searing gaze?

Forcing the comparison, I wondered if any suboceanic locals thought *their* judgment day had just come.

With her telegraph key, Ur-ronn pulsed the message everyone above waited to hear. *We are down,* she sent. *All is well.*

Yes, it lacks the poetic imagery of flags planted, eagles landed, or infinitives boldly split. I shouldn't complain. Not all urs are born to recite epic sagas on demand. Still, I think I'll change it in rewrite—if I ever get the chance, which right now seems pretty unlikely.

Again, sparks jumped the tiny gap, this time without Ur-ronn touching it. A reply from above.

Welcome news. Proceed.

"Ready, Alvin?" Pincer called back. "All ahead, one quarter."

I responded—"Ahead one quarter, aye, Captain."

My back and arm muscles flexed. The crank seemed reluctant at first. Then I felt the magnetic clutch take hold—a strange sense of attachment to once-living g'Kek parts that I tried not thinking about. The special mud treads worked as I felt resistance. *Wuphon's Dream* shuddered forward.

I concentrated on maintaining a steady pace. Pincer shouted steering instructions at Huck while holding Uriel's map for reference. Ur-ronn correlated our bearing with her compass. The hawser and air hose resumed transmitting the distant rumble of deployer drums, unreeling more tether so we might wander ever farther from safety. The confined space resonated with my deep work umble, but no one complained. The sound wrapped itself around me till I felt encircled by hoonish shipmates, making the cramped confinement more bearable. Like a ship far at sea, we were all alone, dependent on Ifni's luck and our own resourcefulness to make it home again.

Time passed. We fell into a rhythmic routine. I pushed, Huck steered, Ur-ronn aimed the headlights, and Pincer was pilot. Pretty soon, it began to feel like we were old hands at this.

Huck asked—"What were you saying, Pincer, just before we landed? Something you saw?"

"Sonething with lots of *teeth,* I vet!" Ur-ronn teased. "Isn't this just avout when we're suffosed to see nonsters?"

Monsters, I thought. My umble annexed a laughquaver.

Pincer took the teasing well. "Give it time, chums. You never can tell when . . . there! Over to the left; that's what I saw before!"

The *Dream* listed a bit as Huck and Ur-ronn leaned forward to look, causing the rear wheels to lose half their traction. "Hey!" I complained.

"Well, I be despoked—" Huck murmured.

"And I vee drenched," Ur-ronn added.

All right, so I whined a bit—"Come *on,* you grass-fed bunch of sour-mulching—"

Just then the ground slanted a bit more, and my narrow tunnel view finally swept across the scene they'd all been staring at.

"Hr-rm-rm!" I exclaimed. "So *that's* what got you all stirred up? A bunch of *dross coffins?*"

They lay scattered across the ocean floor, canted at all angles, many half buried in the mud. Scores of them. Mostly oblong and rectangular, though a few were barrel-shaped. Naturally, all traces had vanished of the ribbons that once bedecked them, honoring the bones or spindles or worn-out tools cast off by some earlier generation of sooners.

"But dross ships never come into the Rift," Huck complained, pushing two stalks toward my face. "Ain't that right, Alvin?"

I twisted to peer past her damn floating eyes.

"They don't. Still, the Rift is officially *part* of the Midden. Another section of the same down-sucking what-sit."

"A tectonic suvduction zone," Ur-ronn put in.

"Yeah, thanks. So it's a perfectly legal place to dump dross."

"But if no ships come, how did it get here?"

I was trying to make out which kinds of coffins were present and which were missing. That could help pin down when the spill had been made. There were no human-style chests or urrish reed baskets, which wasn't surprising. So far I'd only seen g'Kek and qheuenish work, which could make the site pretty darn old.

"The cartons arrived the same way we did, Huck," I explained. "Somebody dumped them off the cliff at Terminus Rock."

Huck gasped. She started to speak, then paused, and I could almost hear wheels turning in her head. Dumping from land just isn't done. But she must have already reasoned that this place was an acceptable exception. If a portion of the Midden really did pass right underneath Terminus Rock, and assuming there must have once been settlements nearby, this would have been a cheaper way of burying Grandpa than sending his coffin out to sea by boat.

"But then how did the boxes get so far from land? We've come cables and cables by now."

"Tides, mudslides," Pincer answered. But I rumbled negation.

"You forget how the Midden's supposed to work. It *sucks* stuff *in*, isn't that right, Ur-ronn?"

Ur-ronn whistled despair over my insistent oversimplifying. She motioned with two hands. "One tectonic flate slides under the other, you see, creating a trench and drawing old sea floor along with it."

"To be dragged underground, melted, and renewed, pushing underneath the Slope and making volcanoes. Yeah, I get it." Huck turned all four stalks forward, pensively. "Hundreds of years since these were dumped, and the dross has only come this far from where it fell?"

Only few seconds ago, she had been amazed by how *great* a distance the crates had come from the cliff! I guess it goes to show how different time can seem, when you shift from the perspective of a person's lifetime to the life cycles of a world. In comparison, I don't suppose humans have much to brag about, living twice as long as urs. We're all bound for Jijo's slow digestion soon enough, whether or not alien invaders leave us alone.

Pincer and Ur-ronn consulted their maps, and shortly we were under way again, leaving that boneyard where another generation of sinners made their slow way toward pardon in melted stone.

About half a midura later, with a sense of great relief, we found Uriel's "jack."

By that time my arms and legs ached from rowboating the crank handle at least a couple of thousand times, responding to Pincer's insistent commands of *"speed up!"* or *"slow down!"* or *"can't you go any faster?"* Of the four of us, he alone seemed to be enjoying himself, without any qualms or physical ague.

We hoon elect our captains, then obey without question while any sort of emergency is going on—and this whole voyage qualified in my mind as a screaming emergency—so I tucked away any resentment for later, when I pictured getting even with Pincer in many colorful ways. Maybe the gang's next project *should* be a hot-air balloon. Make him the first qheuen to fly since they gave up starships. It'd serve him right.

By the time Huck finally yelled "Eureka!" my poor muscles and pivots felt as if we'd covered the entire width of the Rift, and then some. My first relieved thought was—*No wonder Uriel provided so much hawser and hose!*

Only after that did I wonder—*How did she know where to tell us to look for this jeekee thing?*

It stood half buried in the mud, about twelve cables south of where we first touched down. Judging from the portion that was visible from my "vantage point" way in back, it consisted of long spikes, each pointed outward in a different direction, as if aimed toward the six faces of a cube. Each spike had a big knob at the end, hollow I guessed, to prevent sinking in the muck. It was obviously meant to be found, being colored a garish swirl of reds and blues. Red to really stand out at short range, since the color's almost totally absent underwater, and blue to be visible from farther away, if your beam happened to sweep across it in the deep darkness. Even so, you had to be within less than a cable to see the thing, so we'd never have come across it without Uriel's instructions. Still, it took two search spirals before we stumbled on the jack.

It was the strangest thing any of us had ever encountered. And don't forget, I've heard a g'Kek umble and witnessed a traeki vlen.

"Is it Buyur-uyur?" Pincer asked, superstitious awe invading his voice vents, along with a returned stammer.

"I bet a pile of donkey mulch *that's* not Buyur-made," Huck said. "What do you think, Ur-ronn?"

Our urs pal stretched her neck past Pincer, her muzzle drying a patch of the bubble window. "No way the Vuyur would've vuilt anything so frightful-ghastly," she agreed. "It's not their style."

"Of *course* it's not their style," Huck continued. "But I know whose it is."

We all stared at her. Naturally, she milked the moment, pausing till we were on the verge of pummeling her.

"It's *urrish*," she concluded with a tone of smug conviction.

"Urrish!" Pincer hissed. "How can you be so—"

"Exflain," Ur-ronn demanded, snaking her head to peer at Huck. "This ovject is sophisticated. Uriel could forge nothing like it. Not even Earthlings have such craft."

"Exactly! It's not Buyur, and no one currently living on the Slope could make it. That leaves just one possibility. It must have been left here by an original sooner starship, when one of the Six Races—seven if you include glavers—first arrived on Jijo, before the settlers scuttled their craft and joined the rest of us as primitives. But *which* one left it? I'd eliminate us g'Keks on account of we've been here so long that I'll bet the jack would've moved a lot farther into the Rift by now. The same probably holds for glavers, qheuens, and traeki.

"Anyway, the clincher is that Uriel knew exactly where to find it!"

Fur riffled around the rim of Ur-ronn's nostril. Her voice turned colder than the surrounding ocean. "You suggest a conspiracy."

g'Kek stalks twined, a shrug.

"Not a horribly vile one," Huck assured. "Maybe just a sensible precaution.

"Think about it, mates. Say you've come to plant a sooner colony on a forbidden world. You must get rid of anything that'd show on a casual scan by some Institute surveyor, so your ship and complex gear have to go. Nearby space is no good. That's the first place cops'd check. So you sink it amid all the stuff the Buyur dumped when they left Jijo. Sounds good so far.

"But then you ask yourself—what if an unforeseen emergency crops up? What if someday your descendants need something high-tech to help 'em survive?"

Ur-ronn lowered her conical head. In the dimness I

could not tell if it denoted worry or rising anger. I hurried to cut in.

"Hr-rm. You imply a long view of things. A secret kept for generations."

"For centuries," Huck agreed. "Uriel no doubt was told by her master, and so on back to the first urrish ancestors. And before Ur-ronn snaps one of my heads off, let me rush to add that the urs sages showed great restraint over the years, never seeking to use this cache during their wars with qheuens, then humans, even when they were getting their tails whipped."

That was meant to calm Ur-ronn? I rushed to save Huck from mutilation. "Perhaps—hrm—humans and qheuens had their own caches, so there was a standoff." Then my own words sank in. "Maybe those caches are being sought now, while we serve as Uriel's dipping claw, in search of this one."

There was a long silence.

Then Pincer spoke.

"Sheesh-eesh-eesh. Those aliens up at the Glade must really have the grown-ups spooked."

Another pause, then Huck resumed. "That's what I'm *hoping* all of this is about. The aliens. A mutual effort of the Six, pooling resources, and not something else."

Ur-ronn's neck twisted nervously. "What do you mean?"

"I mean, I'd have liked Uriel's word of honor that we're down here seeking powers for the defense of *all* the Commons."

Not simply to arm urrish militia, in some of the grudge fights we've heard rumors about, I thought, finishing Huck's implication. There was a tense moment when I could not predict what would happen next. Had tension, worry, and Tyug's drugs strung our urrish friend to the point where Huck's baiting would make her snap?

Ur-ronn's neck slowly untwisted. An effort of will, I saw by the dim light of the phosphors. "You have . . ." she began, breathing heavily. "You have the oath of *this* urs, that it will ve so."

And she repeated the vow in Galactic Two, following

it with a laborious effort to *spit* on the floor, not an easy act for one of her kind. A sign of sincerity.

"Hr-rm, well, that's great," I said, umbling for peace. "Not that any of us ever thought any different. Right, Huck? Pincer?"

Both of them hurried to agree, and some of the tension passed. Underneath, however, seeds of worry had been laid. *Huck,* I thought, *you'd bring a jar full of scorpions in a lifeboat, then drop it just to see who swims the best.*

We got under way again and soon were near enough to see how big the jack really was. Each of the bulbous balloonlike things at its spiky tips was larger than *Wuphon's Dream.* "There's one of the cables Uriel talked about," Pincer announced, waving a claw toward one spike, from which a glossy black strand made a relatively straight line, though buried in places, aimed north, in the direction we had come.

"I bet anything that line's broken somewhere tween here and the cliffs," Huck ventured. "Prob'ly used to go all the way to some secret cleft or cave near Terminus Rock. From there the cache might've been hauled in without an urs ever having to get her hooves wet. That end point may've gotten cut in an avalanche or quake, like the one that killed my folks. This jack thing is a backup, so the cord can be picked up again, even if the first end point is lost."

"Good thinking. It does explain one thing that had me puzzled—why Uriel had so much equipment on hand. Stuff that proved so useful for diving. In fact, it makes me wonder why she needed us at all. Why didn't she have a hidden bathy of her own in the first place?"

Ur-ronn was getting over her funk. "A g'Kek accountant inventories the forge warehouse regularly. He'd notice anything as un-urrish as a *suvnarine,* just lying around, ready to ve used."

Her voice was sarcastic. Yet Huck agreed.

"The difficult parts were there, the pumps and valves and gaskets. I'm sure Uriel and her predecessors figured they could whip up a hull and the rest in a matter of months. Who ever expected an emergency to strike so quick? Besides, we bunch of crazy kids offered a perfect cover story. No one will associate us with god-caches from the Galactic past."

"I prefer to think," Pincer interjected, with a dramatically miffed tone of voice, "that the real reason Uriel begged pretty-please to be allowed to join our team was the superior design and craftsmanship of our ship-hip."

We quit bickering to stare at him for a moment —then laughter filled the tiny cabin, making the hull vibrate and waking Huphu from her nap.

The four of us felt better then, ready to get on with the mission. The hard part was over, it appeared. All we had to do now was order Ziz to attach a clamp to the cord on the jack's other side and signal Uriel to haul away. There would then be a long wait while we slowly rose up toward the surface, since g'Keks and urs are even more likely than humans to get the bends if air pressure changes too rapidly. From books we knew it's an awful way to die, so a tedious ascent was an accepted necessity. We had all packed snacks, as well as personal articles to help pass the time.

Still, I was anxious to get on with it. Claustrophobia was nothing compared with the ordeal that would commence when everyone onboard—each in his or her unique way—started feeling the need to go, as some Earthling books politely put it, "to the bathroom."

There would be, it seemed, one slight difficulty in clamping on to the second cord.

We saw the problem at once, upon rolling around to look at the jack's other side.

The second cord was missing.

Or rather, it had been *cut*. Fresh-looking metal fibers waved gently in the subsea currents, hanging like an unbraided urrish tail from one of the jack's spiky ends.

Nor was that all. When Ur-ronn cast our beams across the ocean floor, we saw a wavy trail in the mud, meandering south, in which direction the cord apparently had been dragged. None of us knew how to tell if this was done days, or jaduras, or years ago. But the word *recent* came to mind. No one had to say it aloud.

Electric sparks flashed as Ur-ronn reported the situation to those waiting in the world of air and light. Surprise was evident in a long delay. Then an answer came back down, crackling pulses across the tiny spark gap. *If in good health, follow trail for two cables, then report.*

Huck muttered. "As if we've got any choice, with Uriel controlling the winch. Like a little case of narcosis or the cramp-jitters would make a difference to her?"

This time, Ur-ronn didn't turn around, but both tails switched Huck's torso sharply, just below the neckline.

"Ahead one half, Alvin," Pincer commanded. With a sigh, I bent over to begin again.

So we set forth, keeping one beam focused on the snake-trail through the mud, while Ur-ronn cast the other searchlight left and right, up and down. Not that seeing a threat in advance would give us any kind of useful warning. There was never a vessel as unarmed, slow, and helpless as *Wuphon's Dream*. That severed cord we had seen—it had been made by beings using Galactic technology, intended to survive millennia underwater and still retain immense strength. Whatever had sliced it apart wasn't anything I wanted to make angry.

A deeper, more solemn mood filled the cabin as we crept onward. After cranking for more than a midura against the ever-changing traction of slippery muck, my arms and back were starting to feel the stinging tingle of second-stage fatigue. I was too tired to umble. Behind me, Huphu expressed her boredom by rummaging through my backpack, tearing open a package of pish fish sandwiches, nibbling part of it and scattering the rest through the bilge. Splashing noises and a wet tickling on my toe-pads told of water accumulating down there— whether from excess humidity, or some slow leak, or our own disgusting wastes, I didn't care to guess. The aroma inside was starting to get both complex and pretty damn ripe. I was fighting another onset of confinement dread when Pincer let out a shrill yell.

"Alvin, stop! Back up! I mean engines back full!"

I wish I could report that I saw what caused this outburst, but my view was blocked by frenzied silhouettes. Besides, I had my hands full fighting the momentum of the crank, which seemed determined to keep turning in the same direction despite me, driving the wheels ever forward. I held the wooden rods in a strangle grip and heaved with all my might, feeling something pop in my spine. Finally, I managed to slow the axles, then at last bring them to a stop. But for all my grunting effort, I could not make them turn the other way.

"I'm getting a list!" Huck announced. "Tilting forward and to port."

"I didn't see it coming!" Pincer cried out. "We were climbing a little hill, then it just came out of nowhere, I swear!"

Now I could feel the tilt. The *Dream* was definitely tipping forward even as Huck frantically pumped ballast aft. The eik beams seemed to flail around the darkness up ahead, offering an unsettling view of yawning emptiness where before there had been a gently sloping plain.

I finally managed to get the crank turning backward, but any sense of victory was short-lived. One of the magnetic clutches—attached to a wheel salvaged from Huck's aunt, I believe—gave way. The remaining roller bit hard into the mud, with the effect of abruptly slewing us sideways.

The beams now swung *along* the lip of the precipice we were poised upon. Apparently, what we had thought was the main floor of the Rift had been but a shelf along the outskirts of the *actual* trench. The true gash now gaped, ready to receive us, as it had received so many other things that would never again partake in affairs up where stars glittered bright.

So many dead things, and we were about to join them.

"Shall I cut ballast?" Huck asked, frantically. "I can cut ballast. Pull the signal cord to have Ziz inflate. I can do it! Shall I do it?"

I reached out and took two eyestalks, gently stroking them in the calming way I had learned over the years. She wasn't making any sense. The weight of all the steel hawser we trailed was greater than a few bricks slung under the belly of *Wuphon's Dream*. If we cut the hawser too, we might rise all right. But then what would keep the air hose from tangling and snapping as we spun and tumbled? Even if it miraculously survived, unsnarled, we would shoot up like the bullet-ship in Verne's *First Men in the Moon*. Even Pincer would probably die of the bends.

More practical with death looming before us, Ur-ronn fired off rapid spark-pulses, telling Uriel to yank us home without delay. Good idea. But how long would it take, I wondered, for the crew above to haul in all the slack? How fast could they do it without risking a crimp in the air hose? How far might we fall before two opposite pulls met in a sudden jerk? That moment of truth would be when we discovered just how well we'd built the *Dream*.

Helplessly, I felt the wheels lose contact with the muddy shelf as our brave little bathy slid over the edge, starting a long languid fall into darkness.

That, I guess, would be a nice, dramatic place to end a chapter, with our heroes tumbling into the black depths. A true-to-life cliff-hanger.

Will the crew ever make it home again?

Will they survive?

Yeah, that'd make a good stopping point. What's more, I'm tired and hurting. I need to call for help, so I can make it to the bucket in the corner of this dank place and get some relief.

But I won't stop there. I know a better place, just a bit farther down the stream of time, as *Wuphon's Dream* slowly fell, rotating round and round, and we watched the eik beams sweep a cliff face that rose beside us like the wall of an endless tomb. Our tomb.

We dropped half of our ballast, which helped slow the plunge—till a current yanked ahold of the *Dream,* dragging us faster. We dropped the remainder but knew our sole chance lay in Uriel reacting perfectly, and then a hundred other things working better than there was any hope of them working.

Each of us was coming to terms with death in our own way, alone, facing the approaching end of our personal drama.

I missed my parents. I mourned along with them, for my loss was in many ways as bitter to me as it would be to them, though I wouldn't have to endure for years the sorrow they'd carry, on account of my foolish need for adventure. I stroked and umbled Huphu, while Ur-ronn whistled a plains lament and Huck drew all four eyes together, looking inward, I supposed, at her life.

Then, out of nowhere, Pincer shouted a single word that overrode the keening of our fears. A word we had heard from his vents before, too many times, but never quite like this. Never with such tones of awe and wonder.

"Monsters-ers-ers!" he yelled.

Then, with rising terror and joy, he cried it out again. *"Monsters!"*

No one has come to answer my call. I'm stuck lying here with a back that won't bend and a terrible need for that bucket. My pencil is worn down and I'm almost out of paper . . . so while I'm waiting I might as well push on to the *real* dramatic moment of our fall.

All was confusion inside *Wuphon's Dream* as we plunged toward our doom. We tumbled left and right, banging against the inner hull, against cranks, handles, levers, and each other. The view outside, when I could see past my wildly gesturing comrades, was a jumbled confusion of phosphorescent dots caught in the eik beams, plus occasional glimpses of a rising cliff face, and then quick flashes of something else.

Something—or *some things*—lustrous and gray. Agile, flitting movements. Then curious strokings, rubbing our vessel's hull, followed by sharp raps and bangs all along the flanks of our doomed boat.

Pincer kept babbling about monsters. I honestly thought he'd gone crazy, but Ur-ronn and Huck had changed their wailing cries and were leaning toward the glass, as if transfixed by what they saw. It was all so noisy, and Huphu was clawing my aching backside between frenzied attacks on the walls.

I felt sure I made out Huck saying something like—
"What—or who—could they possibly be?"

That's when the whirling shapes divided, vanishing to both sides as a *new* entity arrived, causing us all to gasp.

It was huge, many times the size of our bathy, and it swam with easy grace, emitting a growl as it came. From my agonizing prison at the back, I could not make out much except two great eyes that seemed to shine far brighter than our failing eik beams.

And its mouth. I recall seeing *that* all too well, as it spread wide, rushing to meet us.

The hull groaned, and there were more sharp bangs. Ur-ronn yelped as a needle spray of water jetted inward, ricocheting back at me.

Numb with fear, I could not stop my whirling brain long enough to have a single clear thought, only a storm of notions.

These were *Buyur ghosts,* I guessed, come to punish living fools who dared invade their realm.

They were *machines,* cobbled together from relics and remnants that had tumbled into the Rift since long before the Buyur, in epochs so old, even the Galactics no longer recalled.

They were home-grown sea monsters. Jijo's own. Products of the world's most private place.

These and other fancies flashed through my muddled brain as I watched, unable to look away from those terrible onrushing jaws. The *Dream* buffeted and bucked—in sea currents, I now suppose, but at the time it felt she was struggling to get away.

The jaws swept around us. A sudden surge brought us hurtling to one side. We hit the interior of the great beast's mouth, crashing with such force that the beautiful glass bubble *cracked.* Frosted patterns spread from the point of impact. Ur-ronn wailed, and Huck rolled her eyestalks tight, like socks going in a drawer.

I grabbed Huphu, ignoring her tearing claws, and took a deep breath of stale air. It was awful stuff, but I figured it would be my last chance.

The window gave up at the same moment the air hose snapped.

The dark waters of the Rift found their rapid way into our shattered ship.

XXIV. THE BOOK OF THE SLOPE

Legends

It took twenty years to recover the first human band of sooners—a sizeable group who fled to the scrublands south of the Vale, rejecting the Covenant of Exile that their leaders had signed, just before the Tabernacle went tumbling to the depths. They risked both desolation and the law in order to get away, and had to be dragged back, shuddering in dread, all because they could not bring themselves to trust hoon or traeki.

In retrospect this seems so ironic, since it was qheuens and urs who caused human settlers grief during two subsequent centuries of war. Why then did so many Earthlings fear the peaceful ringed ones, or our cheerful friends with the broad shoulders and booming voices? The star-cousins of both traeki and hoon must have seemed quite different when our ancestors' first starships emerged onto the lanes of Galaxy Four.

Unfortunately, most galactology records burned in the Great Fire. But other accounts tell of relentless hostility by mighty, enigmatic star-lords calling themselves Jophur, who took a leading role in the Sequestration of Mudaun. That fearsome atrocity led directly to the Tabernacle exodus—an outrage executed with single-minded precision and utter resoluteness. Traits not often observed in traeki here on the Slope.

It is also said that hoon were at Mudaun, portrayed in the accounts as dour, officious, unhappy beings. A race of stern accountants, dedicated to population control and tabulating the breeding rates of other races, unswayed by appeals to mercy or forbearance.

Could anyone recognize, in these descriptions, the two most easy-going members of the Six?

No wonder hoon and traeki seem the least prone to nostalgia about "good old days," back when they flew about as gods of space.

—Annals of the Jijoan Commons

Sara

WITH DAWN BLEACHING THE EASTERN SKY, weary travelers trudged into Uryutta's Oasis after a long night march across the parched Warril Plain—a teeming, thirsty crowd of donkeys and simlas, humans and hoon. Even urrish pilgrims stepped daintily to the muddy shore and dipped their narrow heads, wincing at the bitter, unmasked taste of plain water.

Full summer had broken over the high steppe, when hot winds ignited rings of circle grass, sending herds stampeding amid clouds of dust. Even before the present crisis, wayfarers avoided the summer sun, preferring the cool moonlight for travel. Urrish guides bragged they would know the plain blindfolded.

That's fine for them, Sara thought, swishing her aching feet in the oasis spring. *An urs doesn't fall on her face when a chance stone turns underfoot. Me, I like to see where I'm going.*

Predawn light revealed mighty outlines to the east. *The Rimmers,* Sara thought. The mixed-race expedition was making good time, hurrying to reach the Glade before events there reached a climax. On the plus side, she was anxious to see her brothers, and to learn how well Bloor was implementing her idea. There might also be medical help for her ward, the Stranger, if it seemed safe to reveal him to the aliens. A big if. Nor had she quite given up on getting to see one of the fabled library consoles of the Great Galactics.

Yet there was also much to fear. If the star-gods did plan on wiping out all witnesses, it would surely start at the Glade. Above all, Sara worried that she might be taking the Stranger into the hands of his enemies. The dark, ever-cheerful man seemed eager to go, but did he really understand what was involved?

A whistling sigh fluted from Pzora's corrugated cone, as the traeki siphoned water from the pond, fatigued despite having ridden all the way in a donkey-drawn chariot. A new rewq draped across Pzora's sensor ring, one of two Sara had bought from the fresh supply at Kandu Landing, to help the traeki pharmacist treat the wounded alien, even though she wasn't keen on the symbionts herself.

A chain of bubbles broke the surface near Sara's foot. By Loocen's silver light, she made out *Blade,* from Dolo Village, resting underwater. The hasty trek had been hard on red qheuens, and blues like Blade, as well as those humans too big to burden a donkey. Sara had been allowed to mount every even-numbered midura. Even so, her body ached. *Serves me right for leading a bookish, cloistered life,* she thought.

A raucous cheer rose up where urrish donkey-drivers piled grass and dung to make a campfire. Simla blood was drained into a tureen, followed by chopped meat, and soon they were slurping tepid sanguinary stew, lifting their long necks to swallow, then bending for more—sinuous silhouettes whose rise and fall was eerily accompanied by the Stranger's plinking dulcimer. Meanwhile a hoon cook, proud of her multirace cuisine, banged pots and sprinkled powders until spicy aromas finally overcame the stench of roast simla, restoring even Sara's queasy appetite.

A little while later, full dawn revealed stunning tan-and-green mountains towering across the eastern horizon. The Stranger laughed as he worked shirtless, helping Sara and the other humans do a typical camp-chore assigned to Earthlings—erecting shelters of g'Kek blur cloth, to shade travelers and beasts through the blazing day. The star-man's muteness seemed no handi-cap at working with others. His pleasure at being alive affected all those around him, as he taught the others a wordless song to help pass the time.

Two more days, Sara thought, glancing up toward the pass. *We're almost there.*

The oasis was named for a nomad warrior who had lived soon after urrish settlement on Jijo, when their numbers were still small, and their planet-bound crafts pitifully crude. In those olden times, Uryutta fled east from the rich grazing lands of Znunir, where her tribal chiefs had vowed fealty to mighty Gray Queens. Uryutta led her fellow rebels to this wadi in the vast dry plain, to nurse their wounds and plot a struggle for freedom from qheuen dominance.

Or so went the legend Sara heard that afternoon, after sleeping through the hottest part of the day—a slumber during which she had dreamed vaguely of water, cool and clear, raising a terrible thirst. She slaked it at the spring, then rejoined the other travelers under the big tent for another meal.

With a few hours still to go before dusk, and a leaden heat still pressing outside, tinkers and pack-handlers gathered around a storyteller, accompanying her recital with foot-stamps and switched braided tails. Even after gaining books and printing, urs still loved the oral tradition, its extravagance and impromptu variations. When the bard's chant reached the Battle of Znunir Trading Post, elongated heads swayed together. Triplet eyes stared past the poet toward times gone by.

So the traitor cavalry scattered
Willing slaves, the cowards were driven
Into the trap Uryutta had fashioned
Tumbling screaming through Deep Stink Crevasse
There to mix sulfurous death smells
With their own dry-pouch, death-fearing rankness.

Listeners hissed contempt for gutless renegades. Sara pulled out her notebook and took notes on the anti-

quated storytelling dialect, already devolved from
GalTwo, long before humans came.

> *Then wheeled Uryutta, ready to confront*
> *The dread footmen of gray qheuen matrons*
> *Males in armor, males with weapons*
> *Of sharp-edged hardwood, flashing so brightly*
> *And clattering claws, keen to tear hide,*
> *Poised now to flay us in shreds for their mothers.*

This time the urs listeners vented repeated low grunts,
marking respect for a tough foe, a sound humans first
heard the third generation after arriving, when Earthlings
won their own place in the pre-Commons chaos.

> *Now is the time! Our chief gives the signal.*
> *Bring forth the weapons, tools newly fashioned.*
> *Bring forth the longsticks, come forth you strongbacks.*
> *Stab now to miss, but stab hard below!*
> *Bear now the burden. Bear it, you strongbacks!*
> *Heave! Claws a-flashing, over they go!*

At first Sara had trouble following the action. Then she
understood Uryutta's combat innovation—using "long-
sticks," or rods of boo, to tip over the invincible qheuen
infantry. Urrish volunteers served as living fulcrums,
braving snapping claws and crushing weight while their
fellows heaved, toppling one qheuen after another.

Despite the ecstatic song of vengeful slaughter, Sara
knew the historical Uryutta's victories had been short-
lived, as qheuens adjusted their tactics. It took a later
breed of heroes—the warrior smiths of Blaze Mountain—to finally drive gray tyrants off the high plains. And
still the queens thwarted the rising Commons, until humans brought new-old skills to the art of war.

Not all the urs were celebrating past glories. The caravan chief and her aides knelt on a peko-skin rug, planning the next trek. From their gestures over a map, they
clearly meant to skip the next oasis and make a hard
dash for the foothills by sunrise.

Oh, my aching feet, Sara thought.

The chief raised her conical head, hissing as one human pilgrim neared a tent flap.

"Got to go," explained Jop, the Dolo tree farmer.

"What, leaking again? Are you ill?"

Jop had spent most of the journey immersed in a copy of the Scroll of Exile, but now he seemed affable. He laughed. "Oh, no. I jest drank too much lovely spring water. Time to give it back to Jijo. That's all."

While the flap was briefly up, Sara glimpsed bubbles in the pond again. Blade was back under, soaking for the next hard march. Was he also blocking out the storyteller's victory paean over defeated qheuens?

The flap fell, and Sara looked around the pavilion shelter.

Kurt the Exploser used a compass to draw loopy arcs on sheets of graph paper, growling over his labors, making a papermaker's daughter wince as he crumpled one sheet after another in frustration. Nearer to Sara, *Prity* also drew abstract figures, more economically, in a patch of sand. Pulling at her furry chin, she consulted a topology text Sara had brought from Biblos.

My, what an intellectual caravan, Sara observed sardonically. *A would-be priest, a designer of things that go bang, a geometrical chimpanzee, and a fallen mathematician, all hurrying toward possible destruction. And that just begins our list of oddities.*

Over to the left, the Stranger had set aside his dulcimer to watch Kurt's nephew, young Jomah, play a game of *Tower of Haiphong* with a red-qheuen salt peddler, a pair of Biblos librarians, and three hoonish pilgrims. The contest involved moving colored rings over a hexagonal array of posts, stuck in the sand. The goal was to pile a stack of rings on your Home Post in the right order, largest at the bottom, smallest on top. In the advanced game, where ring colors and patterns signified *traeki* attributes, one must wed various traits to form an ideal traeki.

Pzora seemed more entranced by the storyteller than the game. Sara had never heard of a traeki taking offense at *Tower of Haiphong,* even though it mimicked their unique mode of reproduction.

"See here?" the boy explained the game to the Stranger. "So far I got swamp flippers, a mulching core, two memory rings, a Sniffer, a Thinker, and a Looker."

The star-human showed no sign of frustration by Jomah's rapid speech. He watched the apprentice exploser with an expression of intelligent interest—perhaps he heard Jomah's warbling voice as something like musical notes.

"I'm hoping for a better base, to let my traeki move around on land. But Horm-tuwoa snatched a walker torus I had my eye on, so it looks like I'm stuck with flippers." `

The hoon to the boy's left crooned a low umble of gratification. You had to think fast, playing *Tower of Haiphong.*

> *"Build me a dream house, oh my dear,*
> > *fourteen stories high.*
> *Basement, kitchen, bedroom, bath,*
> > *I'll love you till I die."*

Jomah and the others all stopped what they were doing to stare at the Stranger, who rocked back and laughed.

He's getting better at this, Sara thought. Still, it seemed eerie whenever the star-man came up with the verse to some song, perfectly apropos to what was going on at the time.

With a glitter in his eye, the Stranger waited till the other players were engrossed once more in their own stacks. Then he nudged Jomah, covertly pointing out a game piece ready to draw from the reserve box. The boy stared at the rare torus called *Runner,* trying so hard to stifle a yelp of joy that he coughed, while the dark alien patted him on the back.

Now how did he know that? Do they play Tower of Haiphong, *among the stars?* She had pictured space-gods doing—well, *godlike* things. It was encouraging to think they might use games with simple pieces—hard, durable symbols of life.

Of course, most games are based on there being winners . . . and losers.

The audience hissed appreciatively as the bard finished her epic and left the low platform to accept her reward, a steaming cup of blood. *Too bad I missed the end,* Sara thought. But she would likely hear it again, if the world lasted beyond this year.

When no one else seemed about to take the stage, several urs stretched and started drifting toward the nearest tent flap, to go outside and check their animals, preparing for tonight's trek. But they stopped when a fresh volunteer abruptly leaped up, clattering hooves on the dais. The new storyteller was *Ulgor,* the tinker who had accompanied Sara ever since the night the aliens passed above Dolo Village. Listeners regathered around as Ulgor commenced reciting her tale in a dialect even older than the one before.

> *Ships fill your thoughts*   *right now,*
> *Fierce, roaming*   *silently.*
> *Ships fill your dreams*   *right now,*
> *Far from all*   *watery seas.*

> *Ships cloud your*   *mind-scape now,*
> *Numberless*   *hordes of them.*
> *Ships dwarf your*   *mind-scape now,*
> *Than mountains,*   *vaster far.*

A mutter of consternation. The caravan chief corkscrewed her long neck. This was a rare topic, widely thought in poor taste, among mixed-races. Several hoonish pilgrims turned to watch.

> *Ships of the*   *Urrish-ka*
> *Clan of strong*   *reverence.*
> *Ships of the*   *Urrish host.*
> *Clan bound for*   *vengeance!*

Bad taste or no, a tale under way was sacrosanct till complete. The commander flared her nostril to show she had no part in this breach, while Ulgor went on evoking an era long before urs colonists ever set hoof on Jijo. To a time of space armadas, when god-fleets fought over incomprehensible doctrines, using weapons of unthinkable power.

> *Stars fill your thoughts*   *right now.*
> *Ships large as*   *mountain peaks,*
> *Setting stars*   *quivering,*
> *With planet-sized*   *lightings.*

Sara wondered—*why is she doing this?* Ulgor had always been tactful, for a young urs. Now she seemed out to *provoke* a reaction.

Hoon sauntered closer, air sacs puffing, still more curious than angry. It wasn't yet clear that Ulgor meant to dredge up archaic vendettas—grudges so old they made later, Jijo-based quarrels with qheuens and men seem like tiffs over this morning's breakfast.

On Jijo, urs and hoon share no habitats and few desires. No basis for conflict. It's hard to picture their ancestors slaughtering each other in space.

Even the *Tower of Haiphong* game was abandoned. The Stranger watched Ulgor's undulating neck movements, keeping tempo with his right hand.

> *Oh ye, native*   *listeners*
> *So-smugly*   *ignorant,*
> *Planet-bound minds,*   *dare you*
> *Try to*   *conceive?*
>
> *Of planet-like*   *holes in space,*
> *In which dwell*   *entities,*
> *That planet-bound*   *minds like yours*
> *Cannot*   *perceive?*

Several hoon umbled relief. Perhaps this *wasn't* about archaic struggles between their forebears and the urs.

Some space-epics told of awesome vistas, or sights baffling to modern listeners, reminders of what the Six had lost, but might regain someday—ironically, by forgetting.

> *Cast back your*   *dread-filled thoughts,*
> *To those ships,*   *frigidly,*
> *Cruising toward*   *glory's gate,*
> *Knowing not*   *destiny.*

If the first bard had been ardent, chanting bloody glory, Ulgor was coolly charismatic, entrancing listeners with her bobbing head and singsong whistle, evoking pure essences of color, frost, and fear. Sara put her notebook down, spellbound by vistas of glare and shadow, by vast reaches of spacetime, and shining vessels more numerous than stars. No doubt the yarn had grown in retelling, countless times. Even so, it filled Sara's heart with sudden jealousy.

We humans never climbed so high before our fall. Even at our greatest, we never possessed fleets of mighty starships. We were wolflings. Crude by comparison.

But that thought slipped away as Ulgor spun her rhythmic chant, drawing out glimpses of infinity. A portrait took shape, of a great armada bound for glorious war, which fate lured near a dark region of space. A niche, mysterious and deadly, like the bitter hollows of a mulc-spider's lair. A place wise travelers skirted, but not the admiral of this fleet. Steeped in her own invincibility, she plotted a course to fall on her foes, dismissing all thought of detour.

> *Now from one*   *black kernel,*
> *Spirals out*   *fortune's bane,*
> *Casting its*   *trap across,*
> *Throngs of*   *uneasy stars. . . .*

With a sudden jerk, Sara's attention was yanked back to the present by a hard tug on her right arm. She blinked.

Prity gripped her elbow, tight enough to grow painful—until Sara asked—"What is it?"

Letting go, her chim consort signed.

Listen. Now!

Sara was about to complain—*That's what I was doing, listening*—then realized Prity did not mean the story. So she tried to sift past Ulgor's mesmerizing drone . . . and finally picked up a low mutter coming from *outside* the pavilion.

The animals. Something's upsetting them.

The simlas and donkeys had their own camouflaged shelter, a short distance away. Judging from a slowly rising murmur, the beasts weren't exactly frightened, but they weren't happy, either.

The Stranger also noticed, along with a couple of librarians and a red qheuen, all of them backing away, looking around nervously.

By now the caravan chief had joined the crowd of rising-falling urrish heads, lost in a distant place and time. Sara moved forward to nudge the expedition leader—carefully, since startled urs were known to snap—but all at once the chief's neck went rigid of its own accord, anxious tremors rippling her tawny mane. With a hiss, the urs matron roused two assistants, yanking a third back to reality with a sharp nip to the flank. All four stood and began trotting toward the tent flap—

—then skittered to a halt as phantom *shapes* began rising along the shelter's western edge—shadowy centauroid outlines, creeping stealthily, bearing spiky tools. A dismayed screech escaped one of the caravan-lieutenants, just before chaos exploded on all sides.

The audience burst into confusion. Grunts and whistling cries spilled from stunned pilgrims as the tent was ripped in a dozen places by flashing blades. War-painted fighters stepped through the gaps, leveling swords, pikes, and arbalests, all tipped with bronze-colored Buyur metal, driving the churned mass of frightened travelers back toward the ash pit at the center.

Prity's arms clasped Sara's waist while young Jomah

clung to her other side. She wrapped an arm around the boy, for whatever comfort it might offer.

Urrish militia? she wondered. These warriors looked nothing like the dun-colored cavalry that performed showy maneuvers for Landing Day festivals. Slashes of sooty color streaked their flanks and withers. Their weaving, nodding heads conveyed crazed resolve.

A caravan-lieutenant bolted toward the stand where weapons were kept, mostly to ward off liggers, khoobras, or the occasional small band of thieves. The trail boss shouted in vain as the young urs dove for a loaded arbalest—and kept going, toppling through the stand and skidding along a trail of sizzling blood. She tumbled to a stop, riddled with darts, at the feet of a painted raider.

The expedition leader cursed the intruders, deriding their courage, their ancestry, and especially her own complacency. Despite rumors about trouble in far corners of the plains, peacetime habits were hard to break, especially along the main trail. Now her brave young colleague had paid the price.

"What do you want?" she demanded in GalTwo. *"Do you have a leader? Show her (criminal) muzzle, if she dares to speak!"*

The tent flap nearest the oasis lifted, and a burly urrish warrior entered, painted in jagged patterns that made it hard to grasp her outline. The raider chieftain highstepped delicately over the lieutenant's bloody trail, cantering to a halt just before the caravan commander. Surprisingly, both of her brood-pouches were full, one with a husband whose slim head peered under the fighter's arm. The other pouch was blue and milkveined, bulging with unfledged offspring.

A full matron was not usually prone to violence, unless driven by duty or need.

"You are not one to judge our (praiseworthy) daring," the raider captain hissed in an old-fashioned, stilted dialect. *"You, who serve (unworthy) client/masters with toomany or too-few legs, you are not fit to valuate this band*

of sisters. Your sole choice is to submit (obsequiously), according to the (much revered) Code of the Plains."

The caravan chief stared with all three eyes. *"Code? Surely you do not mean the (archaic, irrelevant) rituals that old-time (barbaric) tribes used, back when—"*

"The code of war and faith among (noble, true-to-their-nature) tribes. Confirmed! The way of our (much revered) aunts, going back generations before (recent, despicable) corruption set in. Confirmed! Once again, I ask/demand—do you submit?"

Confused and alarmed, the caravan chief shook her head, human style, blowing air uncertainly like a hoon. With a low aspiration, she muttered in Anglic,

"Hr-r-r. Such jeekee nonsense for a grownuf adult to kill over—"

The raider sprang upon the merchant trader, wrapping their necks, shoving and twining forelegs till the caravan chief toppled with a groan of agony, wheezing in shock. Any Earthly vertebrate might have had her spine snapped.

The raider turned to the pilgrims with her head stretched far forward, as if to snap anyone in reach. Frightened prisoners pressed close together. Sara tightened her grip on Jomah, pushing the boy behind her.

"Again I ask/demand—who will (unreservedly) submit, in the name of this (miserable excuse for a) tribe?"

A dura passed. Then out of the circle staggered a surviving lieutenant—perhaps pushed from behind. Her neck coiled tightly, and her single nostril flared with dread as she stumbled toward the painted harlequin. Trembling, the young urs crouched and slowly pushed her head along the ground till it rested between the raider's forehooves.

"Well done," the corsair commented. *"We shall make a (barely acceptable) plainsman of you.*

"As for the rest, I am called UrKachu. In recent (foolish) days I was known as Lord High Aunt of Salty Hoof Clan, a useless, honorary title, bereft of (real) power or glory. Now banished from that (ungrateful) band, I co-lead this new company of cousin-comrades. United, we

resurrect one of the (great, lamented) warrior societies—the Urunthai!"

The other raiders raised their weapons, bellowing a piercing cry.

Sara blinked surprise. Few humans grew up ignorant of that name, fearsome from bygone days.

"This we have done because (so-called) aunts and sages have betrayed our glory race, falling into a (reviled) human trap. A scheme of extermination, planned by alien criminals."

From an abstract corner of her mind, Sara noted that the raider was losing control over her tailored, old-fashioned GalTwo phrasing, giving way to more modern tones, even allowing bits of hated Anglic to slip in.

The other raiders hissed supportive counterpoint to their leader's singsong phrasings. UrKachu leveled her head toward the pilgrims, twisting and searching, then stopped before a tall, dark human male—the Stranger.

"Is this he? The star-demon?"

The spaceman smiled back, as if not even bloody murder could break his good humor. This, in turn, seemed to set the painted urs back momentarily.

"Is this the (selected, sought-after) one?" UrKachu went on. *"Sky-cousin to those two-legged devils we have lived among for (long-suffering) generations?"*

As if trying to perceive a new form of life, the crippled star-alien flipped the veil of his new rewq over his eyes, then off again, comparing perspectives on the urrish marauder. Perhaps, with meaning robbed from words, he found some in the riot of emotion-laden colors.

A new voice spoke up, as smooth and coolly magnetic as the warrior chief was fiery-fierce, answering from *behind* the mass of huddled pilgrims.

"This is the one," Ulgor assured, emerging from the tight-packed, sweaty crowd, stepping toward UrKachu. Like the Stranger, she showed no trace of fear.

"It is the (promised) prize, recovered from far-off Dolo Town. Recently confirmed by a human sage to be one of the star-demons, not Jijo born."

While the pilgrims muttered dismay at Ulgor's betrayal, UrKachu's hooves clattered joy. *"Those from space will pay (dearly) for his return. For this they may offer one thing valuable above all else—survival for some (though not all) urs on Jijo."*

Many things suddenly made sense. The motive for this raid, as well as Ulgor's spellbinding performance on the storytelling platform, designed to keep the caravan crew inside while the *Urunthai* moved stealthily into position.

A slim shadow fell between the two urrish leaders. A new voice cut in, speaking Anglic.

"Don't forget friends, we'll be demandin' a bit more'n just that."

A human form stood in the torn entry. Moving away from the late-afternoon glare, it resolved as *Jop*, the Dolo Village tree farmer. "There's a whole list o' things we'll be needin' if they're to get their boy back, hale and whole"—Jop glanced at the Stranger's scarred scalp—"or as whole as the poor veg will ever be."

Sara realized. *He went outside to signal the raiders while Ulgor kept us distracted.*

A strange alliance. A human purist helping urrish fanatics who named their group after the ancient Earthling-hating Urunthai Society.

A *frail* alliance, if Sara overheard rightly when UrKachu muttered sideways to Ulgor—

"Would things not prove simpler without this one?"

Tellingly, the painted warrior winced and shut up when Ulgor gave her leg a sharp kick, out of view of the other urs.

Sara detached Jomah and Prity, sheltering them in the crowd before taking a step forward.

"You can't do this," she said.

Jop's smile was grim. "And why not, little book-worm?"

It was a victory to keep a tremor out of her voice.

"Because he may not be one of the gene-thieves at all! I have reason to believe he may actually be an enemy of theirs."

Ulgor looked the Stranger up and down, nodding. "A

fossivility that natters not at all. What counts is—we have goods to sell and can set a frice."

That price Sara could envision. For UrKachu, a return to glory days of wild warriors roaming free—not incompatible with *Jop's* goal to have all the dams, machines, and books cast down, speeding humanity along the Path of Redemption.

Neither seemed to fear the chance of renewed war, so clear was the contempt each held for the other. At the moment, it hardly mattered.

We are in the hands of maniacs, Sara thought. *Fools who will ruin us all.*

Asx

AND NOW RETURNS THE ROTHEN SHIP. BACK from its cryptic mission probing nearby space for some unknown god-purpose.

Back to collect the station it left behind, and its crew of biological prospectors.

Back to gather up a treasure-hold of purloined genes.

Back to cover up their crime.

Only now, that erstwhile-buried station gapes before us, a twisted ruin. One Rothen and a sky-human lie on makeshift biers, robbed of life, while the surviving visitor-invaders rage choleric, vowing retribution. If any doubted their intent before, my rings, can it be ambiguous anymore? We are bound to be punished. Only means and extent remain in doubt.

This is what the rebel zealots desired. No more confusion. An end to hints and sweet, lying promises. Only the cleanliness of righteous opposition, however uneven our powers against those we must resist. Let us be judged, the zealots demand, by our courage and faith, not our hesitation.

The hot, unwinking star moves across our pre-dawn sky, orbiting slowly closer, an angel—or demon—of vengeance. Do those aboard already know what has happened? Are they even now plotting the storm to come?

The zealots argue we must seize the survivors—Rokenn, Ling, and Rann—as hostages for the protection of every member of the Commons. And the remaining starman, Kunn, when his aircraft returns to its shattered base.

Horrified, our qheuenish High Sage, Knife-Bright Insight, skewers the zealot logic.

"You would pile one crime on another? Did they harm us, these aliens? Did they strike the first blow, with their *clinics* and high-paying *jobs*? You have slain two of them based on mere speculation of ill intent! Now you would kidnap the rest? Let us imagine that those on the ship *agree* to your demands, promising not to attack the Six. What is to stop them changing their minds, once the hostages go free?"

The zealot chief replies—

"Who says they will go free? Let them dwell among us for the rest of their natural spans, living as deterrents to alien vileness."

"And after that? How foolish to think in terms of mere lifespans! Star-gods ponder long thoughts. They plan long plans. To slay us now or in fifty years, what difference will that make, in the grand scheme of things?"

Some onlookers murmur agreement. To others, however, it is as if the sage has made a fine joke. They laugh in various ways and shout, "It makes a big difference to those now alive!"

"Anyway," the urrish leader of the zealots adds— *"You are wrong to say they had not yet attacked us, or attempted (villainous) harm. To the contrary, our (justified) explosive feat stopped their (vile) scheme just in time!"*

Soot-stained and fatigued, Lester Cambel sits on a nearby boulder. Now he lifts his head from his hands, and asks—

"What do you mean by that?"

"I mean their (foul) intent was to begin a program of

annihilation by igniting (fratricidal) war among the Six!"

The gathered onlookers absorb this silently.

Knife-Bright Insight demands—"Can you prove this?"

"Solid (irrefutable) evidence is on the way. But first, should you not hear (supportive) testimony from your own (highly revered) fellow sage?"

Confusion reigns, until Phwhoon-dau steps forward to speak. Our hoonish colleague has been strangely silent, taking little part in events, save to carry Vubben downhill from the ill-starred pilgrimage. Now his long, scaly spine unbends, as if glad to pass a heavy burden.

"It is too short a time that I have had to ruminate upon these matters," he demurs.

"You would ruminate a geologic age, dear friend," Lester Cambel jests in a gentle way. "Even your most tentative wisdom is greater than any other, except the Egg's. Please share it with us."

A deep, rolling sound emanates from Phwhoon-dau's pendulous, vibrating sac.

"Hr-r-rm. . . . For almost two jaduras, I have kept careful records of statements made by our guests from space, especially those spoken formally, as if written by someone else for the sky-humans to say aloud. I had several linguistic reference works from Biblos, which I sometimes consult when judging disputes between individuals of different races, speaking different tongues. Despite our local dialect devolution, these works contain useful charts regarding syntax and variable meaning. I do not claim great expertise—just a backwoods practicality—in scrutinizing the aliens' statements."

"But you reached conclusions?"

"Hr-r. Not conclusions. Correlations perhaps. Indicating a possible pattern of intent."

"Intent?"

"Intent . . . r-r-rm . . . to incite divisiveness."

Ur-Jah comments from the wallow where she curls in exhaustion from the futile rescue effort, scratching for survivors amid the smoky ruin of the aliens' station.

"This is not the first tine such a susficion has veen

raised. We all have anecdotes to tell, of innocent-sounding renarks which sting gently at first, like a shaedo-fly, laying eggs that fester a wound that never heals. Now you say there is a consistent fattern? That this was vart of a deliverate flan? Why did you not sfeak of this vefore?"

Phwhoon-dau sighs. "A good scholar does not publish provisional data. Also, the aliens seemed unaware that we have retained this skill, charting the meaning in phrases. Or rather, that we recovered it with the Great Printing. I saw no reason to leak the fact too soon."

He shrugs like a traeki, with a left-right twist. "I finally became convinced when Ro-kenn spoke to us all, during the pilgrimage. Surely it occurred to some of you that his aim was to strike sparks of dissension with his words?"

"It sure did!" Lester Cambel growls. Assent echoes loudly from many humans present, as if to convince others of their sincerity. Hoofed urs stamp uncertainly, their hot tempers clearly frayed from the long enervating night. Only hard-won habits of the recent Peace have kept things calm till now.

Phwhoon-dau continues. "The formal dialect of Galactic Six used by the Rothen star-god allows little room for ambiguity. Ro-kenn's disconcerting words can have but two possible interpretations. Either he is tactless to a degree beyond all stupidity, or else the objective was to incite a campaign of genocide against human-sept."

"Against their own veloved clients?" Ur-Jah asks, incredulous.

"That is irrelevant. Even if the Rothen claim of patronhood is true, why should they care about one small, isolated band of feral humans, long cut off from the race as a whole, genetically inbred and several hundred years out of date, perchance even defective, psychologically backward, polluted by—"

"You've made your point," Lester interrupts testily. "But in that case, why *pick* on us?"

Phwhoon-dau turns to our human peer, umbling apologetically. "Because among the Six, man-sept is greatest in its technic lore, in its imperfect-but-useful recollection of Galactic ways, and in its well-remembered skill at the art of war."

There rises a muttering from some qheuenish and urrish listeners, yet no actual disagreement. Not from anyone who knows the tale of Battle Canyon, or Townsend's Ambush, or the siege of Tarek Town.

"All of these factors make your kind the obvious first target. Moreover, there is another reason. The effect your race has had upon the rest of us. As newcomers, when your rank was lowest, still you opened your sole treasure, your library, to all. After your great victories, when your status towered highest, you refused many privileges of dominance, instead bowing to the sages, accepting limits called for by the Great Peace.

"It is this record of *restraint* that makes you dangerous to Rothen plans. For what good is it to incite war, if your intended victims choose *not* to fight?"

Yes, my rings, we observe/note the crowd's reaction. A hush as Phwhoon-dau evokes images of reconciliation, gently dousing still-simmering sparks of resentment. It is a masterwork of mediation.

"Once men-sept is gone," Phwhoon-dau goes on, "it would prove simple to goad disaffection among the rest, pretending secret friendships, offering assistance. Handing over tailored plagues, for instance, letting each race come up with clever ways to deliver death bugs to their foes. Within less than a generation the job would be complete. The sparse record left in Jijo's soil would show only that six sooner races once sank low here, never reaching redemption."

Uneasy silence greets this scenario painted by our hoonish sage.

"Of course, none of this is proven," Phwhoon-dau concludes, rounding to stab a finger toward the zealot chieftain. "Nor does it justify the horrors we have seen this night, perpetrated rashly, without consulting the sages or the Commons."

The urrish rebel lifts her head high, in order to peer over the crowd toward the east. With a glad snort, she turns back to Phwhoon-dau.

"Now arrives your proof!" She whistles jubilantly, helping shove an opening through the ranks of spectators, as dawn reveals dusty figures galloping down the trail from the Holy Glade.

"Here, also, is your justification."

Lark

HARULLEN CALLED DOWN FROM THE CRATER'S edge. "You two had better come up now!" the heretic shouted. "Someone's going to catch you and it'll mean trouble. Besides—I think something's happening!"

Physical and emotional exhaustion had taken their toll of the gray aristocrat's polished accent. He sounded frantic, as if serving as reluctant lookout were as risky as poking through perilous wreckage.

"What's happening?" Uthen shouted back. Though a cousin to the qheuen above, Lark's fellow biologist looked like a different species, with his scarred carapace streaked by gummy ash. "Are they sending a robot this way?"

Harullen's leg-vents fluted overtones of worry. "No, the machines still hover protectively over Ro-kenn, and the two servant-humans, and the cadavers, all surrounded by a crowd of local sycophants. I refer to a commotion over where the sages have been holding court. More zealots have arrived, it seems. There is ferment. I'm certain we are missing important news!"

Harullen may be right, Lark thought. Yet he was reluctant to leave. Despite the stench, heat, and jagged stubs of metal—all made more dangerous by his own fatigue—dawn was making it easier to prowl the ruins of the buried station in search of anything to help make sense of it all.

How many times had he seen Ling vanish down a

ramp into these secret precincts, wondering what lay inside? Now it was a blackened hell.

I aided the zealots, he recalled. *I gave them copies of my reports. I knew they were going to do something.*

But I never figured anything as brutal as this.

Neither had the star-gods, who clearly never guessed that angry primitives might still know how to make things go boom.

They never asked the right questions.

"I tell you something's happening!" Harullen shouted again, making no effort at originality. "The sages are in motion—toward the aliens!"

Lark glanced over at Uthen and sighed. "I guess he means it, this time."

His friend had been silent for some time, standing over the same spot. When Uthen replied, it was in a low voice that barely disturbed the ash beneath his feet.

"Lark, would you please come look at this?"

Lark knew that tone from past field trips, exploring for evidence of Jijo's complex living past. He picked his way toward the qheuen, slipping gingerly between torn metal braces and seared, buckled plating, lifting his feet to kick up as little of the nasty dust-ash as possible.

"What is it? Did you find something?"

"I—am not sure." Uthen lapsed into GalSix. *"It seems I have seen this before. This symbol. This representation. Perhaps you can confirm?"*

Lark bent alongside his friend, peering into a recess where the rising sun had yet to shine. There he saw a jumble of rectangular lozenges, each thick as his hand and twice as long. Uthen had scraped aside some half-melted machinery in order to reveal the pile. One slab lay near enough to make out a symbol, etched across its dark brown surface.

A double spiral with a bar through it. Now where have I seen—

Lark's hand reached where Uthen could not, stroked the rectangle, then picked it up. It felt incredibly light, though now it dawned on him that it could be the weightiest thing he had ever touched.

"Are you thinking what I'm thinking?" he asked, turning it in the light.

Uthen plucked the slab from his hand, holding it in a trembling claw.

"How can I not be?" the qheuenish scholar replied. "Even half-animal, reverted primitives should recognize the glyph of the Great Galactic Library."

The "evidence" lay strewn across the trampled grass. Ro-kenn's piercing eyes surveyed a tangle of wires and glossy spheroids that the zealots had recently brought down from the Valley of the Egg. Clogs of dirt still clung to a necklace of strange objects, from where it had till lately been buried, next to the holiest site on Jijo.

Two clusters of onlookers formed semicircles, one backing the assembled sages, the other reverently standing behind the star-god. Many in the second group had been patients at the forayers' clinic or believed their claims of righteousness above all law. Among the humans on that side, faith in their rediscovered patrons seemed to glow, depicted by Lark's new rewq as intense red fire, surrounding their faces.

Gone was the Rothen's prior mien of furious wrath. Ro-kenn's humanoid features once more conveyed charismatic poise, even serene indulgence. He spent another dura looking over the jumble of parts, then spoke in prim Galactic Seven.

"I see nothing here of interest. Why do you show me these things?"

Lark expected the young urrish radical—leader of the rebel zealots—to answer, as both plaintiff and defendant, justifying her group's violence by diverting blame to the aliens. But the young dissenter kept well back, huddling with a crowd of humans and urs, consulting texts.

The hoonish sage, Phwhoon-dau, stepped forward to confront the Rothen emissary.

"We seek to ascertain whether these tools of high acumen are yours. Tools which some of our children found, within the last turning of Jijo's axis. Tools which *some-one* buried surreptitiously, in close contact with our beloved Egg."

Lark watched Ling's reaction. Since he already knew her pretty well, no rewq was needed to translate her shock of recognition. Nor the embarrassment that followed as she worked things out in her own head. *That's all I needed to know,* Lark thought.

Ro-kenn seemed nonchalant. "I can only guess that some among you natives placed it there—as your foolish rebels placed explosives under our station."

Now Ling's reaction was to blink in surprise. *She didn't expect to hear him lie. At least not so baldly, with no time to prepare a smooth performance.*

Glancing to one side, the star-woman noticed Lark's scrutiny and quickly looked away. Lark wasn't proud of the satisfaction he felt, over the reversal of their moral positions. Now it was *her* turn to feel ashamed.

"Use your instrumentalities," Phwhoon-dau urged the tall Rothen. "Analyze these implements. You will find the technology far beyond anything we Six can now produce."

Ro-kenn shrugged with an elegant roll of his shoulders. *"Perhaps they were left by the Buyur."*

"In that place?" Phwhoon-dau boomed amusement, as if Ro-kenn had made a good-natured jest. "Only a century ago, that entire valley glowed white-hot from the Egg's passage to the upper world. These tendrils would not have survived."

The crowd murmured.

Lark felt a tug on his sleeve. He glanced around to see that a short blond figure—Bloor the Portraitist—had slinked up behind, bearing a box camera and tripod.

"Let me shoot under your arm!" the photographer whispered urgently.

Lark felt a frisson of panic. Was Bloor mad? Trying this in the open, with the robots at their wariest? Even if Lark's body shielded *that* angle, people on both sides would see. Despite Phwhoon-dau's masterful performance, could they count on loyalty from *everyone* in the milling throng?

With a helpless sigh, he lifted his left arm enough for Bloor to aim at the confrontation on the Glade.

"Then I have no other explanation for these items," Ro-kenn answered, referring to the snarled mass of gear. *"You are welcome to speculate to the extent that you are able, until our ship arrives."*

Ignoring the implied threat, the hoonish sage went on with an air of calm reason that made the Rothen seem edgy by comparison.

"Is speculation required? It's been asserted that several sets of eyes *observed* your robots, on a recent foggy night, deliberately implanting these devices underneath our sacred stone—"

"Impossible!" Ro-kenn burst forth, temper once more flaring. *"No life-forms were in any position to witness on that night. Careful scans beforehand showed no sentient beings within range when—"*

The Rothen emissary trailed off midsentence, while onlookers stared, awed and amazed that an urbane star-god could be suckered by so obvious a ploy.

He must be awfully accustomed to getting his way, Lark thought, *to fall for such a simple trap.*

Then a strange notion occurred to him. *Many Earthly cultures, from ancient Greece and India to High-California, depicted their gods as spoiled, temperamental adolescents.*

Could that be racial memory? Maybe these guys really are our long-lost patrons, after all.

"Thank you for the correction," Phwhoon-dau answered, with a graceful bow. "I only said it was so *asserted*. I shall rebuke those who suggested it. We will take your word that there were no witnesses on the night that you *now admit* your robots planted these strange, alien devices next to our Egg. Shall we leave that aspect now and proceed to *why* they were planted in the first place?"

Ro-kenn appeared to be chewing on his mistake, working his jaw like a human grinding his teeth. Lark's rewq showed a discolored swath that seemed to ripple across the upper part of the Rothen's face. Meanwhile Bloor whispered contentment as he took another picture, pushing a cover slide over the exposed plate. *Go away,* Lark silently urged the little man, to no avail.

"I see no further purpose to be served by this session," the alien finally announced. He turned and began to move away, only to stop when confronted by the gaping crater where his station once lay, recalling that he had no place to go.

Of course Ro-kenn *could* climb aboard a robot and simply fly off. But till either Kunn's aircraft or the starship arrived, there was only wilderness to flee to. No shelter beyond this glade filled with inconvenient questions.

A shout rose up from the cluster of urs and men over to the left. The huddle broke, revealing a beaming Lester Cambel, burdened by several large-format volumes as he hurried forward. "I think we found it!" he announced, kneeling with several assistants beside one of the spheroidal knobs that ran along the tangled mass of cable. While an aide pried at the box, Lester explained.

"Naturally, none of us has the slightest idea *how* this device works, but Galactic tech is so refined and simplified, after a billion years, that most machines are supposed to be pretty easy to use. After all, if *humans* could pilot a creaky, fifth-hand starship all the way to Jijo, the things must be darn near idiot-proof!"

The self-deprecating jest drew laughter from both sides of the crowd. Pressing close to watch, the throng left no easy or dignified avenue for Ro-kenn or his servants to escape.

"In this case," Cambel continued, "we assume the gadget was meant to go off when all the pilgrims were in place near the Egg, at our most impressionable, perhaps as we finished the invocation. A good guess would be either a timer or some remote control trigger, possibly a radio signal."

An aide succeeded in getting the cover off, with an audible pop. "Now let's see if we can find something

like the standard manual override switch they show on
page fifteen-twelve," Lester said, crouching closer, consulting one of the open volumes.

Ro-kenn stared at the book, filled with crisp diagrams,
as if he had just seen something deadly creep out of his
own bedsheets. Lark noticed that Ling was looking at
him once again. This time, her expression seemed to
say, *What have you been hiding from me?*

Although she lacked a rewq, Lark figured a wry smile
would convey his reply.

*You assume too much, my dear. It blinded you,
preventing you from asking sound questions. It also
made you patronizing, when we might have been
friends.*

All right, maybe that was too complex to transmit by
facial expression alone. Perhaps what his smirk actually
said was—Such nerve! *You* accuse *me* of hiding things?

"I protest!" interjected the male sky-human, Rann,
towering over all but the hoon and a few traeki as he
stepped forward. "You have no right to meddle with the
property of others!"

Phwhoon-dau crooned softly, "Hr-r—then you avow
ownership of this invasive thing, placed without permission in our most sacred site?"

Rann blinked. Clearly he hated the present weakness
of the aliens' position, having to fence words with savages. Confused, the tall sky-human turned to Ro-kenn
for guidance. While they conferred, heads close together, Lester Cambel continued.

"The *purpose* of this contraption was what had us stymied for a while. Fortunately, I'd already been doing
some research on Galactic technologies, so the texts
were somewhat familiar. Finally, I found it listed under
psi emitters!"

"Here's the switch, sir," an aide declared. "Ready
when you are."

Lester Cambel stood up, raising both hands.

"People! This is a first and final warning. We've no
idea what we're about to set off. I assume nothing fatal,
since our guests aren't flying out of here at top speed.

However, since we've no time for careful experiments, I advise you to at least step back. The cautious among you may retreat some greater distance, perhaps twice the diameter of the Egg. I'll count down from ten."

Uthen wanted to stay and watch, Lark thought. *But I made him go hide those library disk-things we found.*

Did I actually do him a favor?

Cambel drew a deep breath.

"Ten!"

"Nine!"

"Eight!"

Lark had never seen a g'Kek outrace an urs before. But as the crowd dissolved, some of the Six showed surprising haste to depart. Others remained, tethered by curiosity.

Courage is one trait that binds any true union, he thought with some pride.

"Seven!"

"Six!"

Now Ro-kenn himself glided forward. *"I avow ownership of this device, which—"*

"Five!"

"Four!"

Ro-kenn hurried, speaking louder to be heard past the tumult. *"—which consists merely of instrumentation, innocently emplaced—"*

"Three!"

"Two!"

Faster, in frantic tones. *"—to study patterns cast by your revered and sacred—"*

"One!"

"Now!"

Some humans instinctively brought their hands up to their ears, crouching and squinting as if to protect their eyes against an expected flash. Urs pressed arms over pouches. g'Keks drew in their eyes, while qheuens and traeki squat-hugged the ground. Rewq cringed, fleeing the intense emotions pouring from their hosts. Whatever a "psi emitter" might be, everyone was about to find out.

Lark tried to ignore instinct, taking his cue instead

from Ling. Her response to the countdown seemed a queer mix of anger and curiosity. She clasped both hands together, turning to meet his eyes at the very moment Cambel's aide stroked a hidden switch.

Asx

CONFUSION BRIMS OUR CENTRAL CORE, OOZING through the joint-seals that bind us/we/i/me, seeping bewilderment down our outer curves, like sap from a wounded tree.

This voice, this rhythmic recitation, can it be what we know it not to be?

The Egg's patternings have stroked us so many ways. *This* ruction has familiar elements, like the Sacred One's way of singing. . . .

Yet—there is also a metallic *tang,* simplistic, lacking the Egg's sonorous pitch and timbre.

One sub-cadence draws us toward it, clattering like a hasty quintet of claws, pulling our attention, as if down a dark underground funnel.

Suddenly, i/we coalesce, submerging into strange existence as a *unified* being. One encased in a *hard shell.*

Pentagonal resentment surges. This "me" is filled with rage.

How dare they tell me I am free!

What unnatural law is this Code of the Commons? This rule that "liberates" my kind from the sweet discipline we once knew, imposed by our gracious queens?

We who are blue—we who are red—surely we yearn to serve, deep in our throbbing bile nodes! To work and fight selflessly, assisting gray dynastic ambitions! Was that not our way among the stars, and before?

The native way of all qheuens?

Who dared bring an end to those fine days, forcing

alien notions of liberty into carapaces too stiff for a deadly drug called freedom?

Humans dared impose these thoughts, breaking up the union of our well-ordered hives! Theirs is the fault, the shell-bound debt to pay.

And pay they shall!

After that, there will be other scores to settle. . . .

i/we writhe, experiencing what it feels like to crouch and run on five strong legs. Legs meant for *service*. Not to a mere nest, crouched behind some puny dam, or to some vast abstraction like the Commons, but to grand gray matrons, noble, gorgeous, and strong.

Why does this vivid perception flood through our dazzled core?

It must be the Rothen artifice—their psi-device—part of their scheme to influence each race of the Six. Tricking us into doing their will.

Quivers of surprise shake our/my rings. Even after so many years of friendship, i/we had never realized—the qheuen point of view is *so weird*!

Yet no weirder than the *next* sensation that comes barging into our shared consciousness.

The feel of galloping hooves.

A hot breath of the dry steppes.

The burning flare of a psyche at least as egocentric as any human being.

Now I am urrish-ka! Solitary, proud as the day I emerged from the grass, little more than a beast. Nervous, but self-reliant.

I may join the tribe or clan that adopts me off the plain.

I may obey a leader—for life has hierarchies that one must endure.

Yet inside I serve one mistress. Me!

Can humans ever know how their gross smell scrapes my nostril membranes? They make good warriors and

*smiths, it's true. They brought fine music to Jijo. These
are valid things.*

*Yet one conceives how much better the world would be
without them.*

*We had fought our way up high before they came.
From the plains to fiery mountaintops, we stretched our
necks over all others on Jijo—till these bipeds dragged us
down, to be just another race among Six.*

*Worse, their lore reminds us—(me!)—how much we
have lost. How much is forgotten.*

*Each day they make me recall how low and brief my
life is doomed to be, here on this spinning ball of mud,
with bitter oceans all around. . . .*

The indignant narration gallops past our ability to follow. Its resentful thread is lost, but another takes its
place, imposed from the outside by a force that throbs
through the little mountain vale.

This beat is much easier to follow. A cadence that is
heavy, slow to anger—and yet, once roused, its ire
seems hopeless to arrest short of death.

It is not a rhythm to be rushed. Still, it beckons us . . .
*Beckons us to ponder how often the quicker races
tease we poor, patient hoon,*
    how they swirl around us,
    how often they seem to talk fast on purpose,
    how they set us to the most dangerous tasks,
    *to face the sea alone, although each lost ship
wrenches a hundred loved ones, tearing our small families apart with wrenching pain.*

*Humans and their stinking steamboats, they have kept
the skills, pretending to share, but not really. Someday
they will leave us rotting here, while they go off on ships
made of pure white light.*

*Should this be allowed? Are there ways they can be
made to pay?*
    •   •   •

Confusion reigns.

If these pernicious messages were meant for each separate race—to sway it toward aggression—then why are we/i receiving *all* of them? Should the Rothen not have targeted each sept to hear *one* theme, alone?

Perhaps their machine is damaged, or weak.

Perhaps *we* are stronger than they thought.

Breaking free of the hoonish rhythm, we sense that two layers of bitter song remain. One is clearly meant for *Earthlings*. Reverence is its theme. Reverence and pride.

We are superior. Others specialize but we can do anything! Chosen and raised by mighty Rothen, it is proper that we be greatest, even as castaways on this slope of savages.

If taught their place, the others might learn roles of worthy service. . . .

we/i recall a phrase. *Direct empathic transmission*—a technique used by Galactic science for the better part of half a billion years.

Knowing makes the manipart stream of voice seem more artificial, tinny, even self-satirical. Of course this message was to have been amplified somehow through our Holy Egg, at a time when we would be most receptive. Even so, it is hard to imagine such prattle winning many believers.

Did they actually think we would fall for this?

Another fact penetrates our attention: *There is no layer for the wheeled ones!* Why is that? Why are the g'Kek left out? Is it because of their apparent uselessness in a program of genocidal war?

Or because they were already extinct, out there among the stars?

One resonance remains. A drumbeat, like hammers pounding on stacks of stiff round tubes. A reverberation that howls in a manner this composite self finds eerily familiar.

Yet, in some ways it is the most alien of all.

<MACRO-ENTITY PRIESTLY DECLARATION, DIRECT FROM ORATION PEAK OF KNOWING-iD IRATE HOSTIL-ITY.

<RESPONSE=VOWED END TO PERSONAL INSULT! LET PERPETRATORS (EARTHLING) FACE ANNIHILA-TION . . . >

We shrivel back, dismayed. *This* egomania is far greater than any of the other broadcasts, even those aimed at urs and men! And yet—it is aimed at *traeki*!

Do you see what is happening, my rings? Is *this* a taste of the proud willfulness that used to flow from coercive despot-toruses? Those tyrant psyches that once domi-nated our cognition rings? Overlord-collars that were abandoned on purpose by the traeki founders, when they fled to Jijo?

Is this is how resentment tasted to those haughty *Jophur*? (Yes, shudder at the name!)

Mighty beings who still prowl the stars, in our image. Ring cousins whose waxy cores are ruled by monomani-acal ravings.

If so, why do these rantings mean so little to our mani-colored segments? Knowing them for what they are, why do they seem so banal? So uncompelling?

The demonstration ends. All the scraping emissions fade as power runs out of the alien device. No matter. We now know the purpose of this tangle of cables and balls. To cast poison, amplified and lent credibility by passage through the Egg.

All around the meadow, anger seethes at this blas-phemy, at this puerile appeal to our basest animosities. Passions that were obsolete even before the Egg ap-peared.

Is this how poorly you think of us, star-lords? That we might be fooled into doing your dirty work?

We perceive the crowd regathering, a muttering fuming throng, contemptuous of the bobbing hissing robots. Humans, urs, and others mix more freely now, sharing a heady kind of elation, as if we Six have passed an awful test. Passed it stronger and more unified than ever.

Is this the worst they can do to us?

That is a question i overhear several times.

Yes, my rings, it occurs to us that the Glade is but a small part of the Slope, and we present here make up only a fragment of the Commons.

Is this the worst they can do to us?

Alas, if only it were so.

Sara

THE URUNTHAI LIKED TO TRAVEL FAST AND LIGHT, not burdening their donkeys any more than necessary. The Urunthai also believed in the Path of Redemption—they did not much approve of books.

The librarians never had a chance.

Still, the trio of gray-robed archivists protested desperately when they saw the late afternoon bonfire. Two humans and their chimp assistant tore frantically at their bonds, pleading, entreating, trying to throw themselves across the wax-sealed crates they had been escorting to safety.

The ropes saved their lives. Watching with arbalests cocked, the painted Urunthai guards would not have flinched at shooting a clutch of pasty-skinned text tenders.

"You like fire?" one warrior taunted in thickly accented Anglic. "Fire *cleanses*. It vurns away dross. It can do the sane thing with *flesh*. Hoo-nan flesh, vurns so nice."

The librarians were reduced to silent weeping as flames licked the wax, then split the wooden chests, tumbling cascades of volumes that fluttered like dying birds. Paper pages flared as brief meteors, yielding whatever ink-scribed wisdom they had preserved for centuries.

Sara was glad Lark and Nelo couldn't see this.

Many texts were copied, during the Great Printing or after. The loss may not be as bad as it looks.

Yet how much longer would those duplicates endure this kind of age, filled with self-righteous sects and crusades, each convinced of their own lock on truth?

Even if the star-gods never wreck Biblos, or force the explosers to do it for them, fanatics like Jop and UrKachu will only grow more numerous and bold as the social fabric unravels.

As if to illustrate the point, a squadron of Jop's comrades entered camp before sundown—a dozen hard-looking men equipped with bows and swords, who slaked their parched throats at the oasis without turning their backs on UrKachu's clansmen, but glanced with satisfaction at the pyre of dying books.

The two groups have a common goal. An end to literary "vanities." Replacing the current sages. Hewing closer to the dictates of the Scrolls.

Later, when we're all firmly on the Path, we can return to slaughtering and ambushing each other, deciding who's top predator on a sinking pyramid of redeemed animals.

The blaze collapsed, spewing sparks and curled paper scraps that seemed to swoop in whirling air currents. Standing next to Sara, the Stranger caught one in his hand and peered, as if trying to read what it once said. Perhaps he recognized something that was much like him, in a poignant way. Once eloquent, it had now lost the magic of speech.

The librarians weren't alone watching with horrified, soot-streaked faces. A young mated pair of hoonish pilgrims clutched each other, umbling a funeral dirge, as if a loved one's heart spine lay in the filthy coals. Several qheuens stared in apparent dismay, along with—*lest we forget*—a handful of sorrowful urrish traders.

The smoke-stench made her think of darkness. The kind that does not end with dawn.

"All right, everybody! Your attention, please. Here is the plan."

It was Jop, breaking the somber silence, approaching as part of a foursome, with UrKachu, Ulgor, and a grim, sunburned man whose rugged face and flinty hardness made him seem almost a different species from the soft, bookish librarians. Even the Urunthai treated this human with grudging deference. Painted warriors stepped quickly out of his way. Sara found him *familiar* somehow.

"We'll be leaving in two groups," Jop went on. "The larger will proceed to Salty Hoof Marsh. If any militia platoons hear o' this raid and care to give chase, that's the first place they'll look, so some of you may be 'rescued' in a week or so. That's fine by us.

"The smaller group's gonna go faster. Humans will ride, switchin' to fresh donkeys every half midura. Don't cause trouble or even *think* of sneakin' off in the dark. The Urunthai are expert trackers, and you won't get far. Any questions?"

When no one spoke, Jop shoved a finger at the Stranger. "You. Over there." He gestured where the biggest, strongest-looking beasts were tethered single file, beside the oasis pond. The Stranger hesitated, glancing at Sara.

"It's all right. She can go along. Can't have our hostage goin' sick on us, eh?" Jop turned to Sara. "I expect you'll be willin' to take care of him awhile longer."

"If I can take my bags. And Prity, of course."

The four leaders muttered among themselves. UrKachu hissed objections, but Ulgor sided with the humans, even if it meant sacrificing some of the booty robbed from the caravan merchants. Two donkeys had their trade goods dumped on the ground, to make room.

Another argument erupted when the Stranger straddled the animal he had been assigned, with his feet almost dragging on both sides. He refused to surrender the dulcimer, keeping the instrument clutched under one arm. With ill temper, UrKachu snorted disgust but gave in.

From her own perch on a sturdy donkey, Sara watched the hard-faced man gesture toward Kurt the Exploser, sitting with his nephew, silently watching events unfold.

"And you, Lord Exploser," Jop told Kurt with a respectful bow, "I'm afraid there are questions my friends want to ask, and this is no place to persuade you to answer 'em."

Ignoring the implied threat, the gray-bearded man from Tarek Town carried his satchel over to the donkey train, with Jomah close behind. When a pair of Urunthai reached for the valise, Kurt spoke in a soft, gravelly voice.

"The contents are . . . delicate."

They backed away. No one interfered as he chose a pack beast, dumped its load of plunder on the ground, and tied the valise in place.

Equal numbers of human radicals and Urunthai warriors made up the rest of the "fast group." The men looked almost as ungainly on their donkeys as the tall Stranger, and more uncomfortable. For many, it must be their first experience riding.

"You aren't coming?" Sara asked Jop.

"I've been away from my farm too long," he answered. "Also, there's unfinished business in Dolo. A certain *dam* needs tendin' to, the sooner the better."

Sara's head jerked, but it wasn't Jop's statement of destructive intent that made her blink suddenly. Rather, she had glimpsed something over his shoulder: a stream of bubbles, rising to the surface of the pond.

Blade. He's still underwater, listening to everything!

"Don't worry, lass," Jop assured, misconstruing her briefly dazed look. "I'll make sure your dad gets out, before the cursed thing blows."

Before Sara could reply, UrKachu cut in.

"Now it is (well past) time to end delays and perform actions! Let us be off!"

One of her tails switched the lead donkey's rump, and the queue jostled forward.

Abruptly, Sara slid off her saddle and planted her feet, causing her mount to stutter in confusion, sending a ripple of jerks down the chain in both directions. One of the rough men tumbled to the ground, raising amused snorts from some Urunthai.

"No!" Sara said, with grim determination. "First I want to know where we are going."

Jop urged in a low voice, "Miss Sara, please. I don't even know myself—"

He cut off, glancing past her nervously as the flinty-eyed hunter approached.

"What seems to be the problem?" His deep voice seemed strangely cultured for his rough appearance. Sara met his steady gray eyes.

"I won't mount till you tell me where we're going."

The hunter lifted an eyebrow. "We could tie you aboard."

Sara laughed. "These little donkeys have enough trouble carrying a willing rider, let alone one who's throwing her weight around, trying to trip the poor beast. And if you truss me like a bag o' spuds, the bouncing will break my ribs."

"Perhaps we're willing to take that chance," he began—then frowned as the Stranger, Kurt, and Prity slid off their beasts as well, crossing their arms.

The warrior sighed. "What difference can it possibly make to you, knowing in advance?"

The more he spoke, the more familiar he sounded. Sara felt *sure* she had met him before!

"My ward needs medical attention. So far, we've held off infection with special unguents provided by our traeki pharmacist. Since you don't plan to bring ers chariot along with your 'fast group,' we had better ask Pzora for a supply to take with us."

The man nodded. "That can be arranged." He motioned for the Stranger to go join Pzora.

Unwrapping the rewq that had lately replaced his gauze bandages, the spaceman exposed the gaping wound in the side of his head. On seeing it, several desert-men hissed and made superstitious gestures against bad luck. While his symbiont joined Pzora's rewq in a tangled ball, exchanging enzymes, the Stranger made a flutter of rapid hand motions to the traeki—Sara thought she caught a brief snatch of *song*—before he bowed to present his injury for cleaning and treatment.

She spoke again.

"Furthermore, any stock Pzora provides will stay good for just a few days, so you better figure on taking us someplace with *another* expert pharmacist, or you may have a useless hostage on your hands. The star-gods won't pay much for a dead man, whether he's their friend or foe."

The renegade looked at her for a long, appraising moment, then turned to confer with UrKachu and Ulgor. When he returned, he wore a thin smile.

"It means a slight detour, but there is a town so equipped, not far from our destination. You were right to point this out. Next time, however, please consider simply voicing the problem, without starting out quite so confrontationally."

Sara stared at him, then burst out with a guffaw. It seemed to cut some of the tension when he joined with a booming chuckle—one that took Sara back to her earliest days as a student, underneath the overhanging fist-of-stone.

"Dedinger," she said, breathing the name without voice.

The smile was still thin, disdainfully bitter.

"I wondered if you'd recognize me. We labored in different departments, though I've followed your work since I was expelled from paradise."

"A paradise you sought to destroy, as I recall."

He shrugged. "I should have acted, without trying for consensus first. But collegial habits were hard to break. By the time I was ready, too many people knew my beliefs. I was watched night and day until the banishment."

"Aw, too bad. Is *this* your way of getting another chance?" She motioned toward the bonfire.

"Indeed. After years in the wilderness, ministering to a flock of the fallen—humans who have progressed furthest along the Path—I've learned enough—"

UrKachu's shrill whistle of impatience was not in any known language, yet its short-tempered insistence was plain. Again, Dedinger lifted an eyebrow.

"Shall we go, now?"

Sara weighed trying again to get him to name a destination, out loud. But Dedinger was insane, not stupid. Her insistence might rouse suspicions and maybe even give Blade away.

With an acquiescent shrug, she clambered back aboard the patient donkey. Watching with narrowed eyes, the Stranger remounted, too, followed by Kurt and Prity.

The remaining survivors of the ill-starred caravan seemed both pitying and relieved to be less important to the Urunthai. As the fast group rode out of the Oasis, heading south, the fading bonfire wafted bitter odors, along with dust and pungent animal smells.

Sara glanced back toward the moonlit pool.

Did you hear any of that, Blade? Were you asleep? Was it a garbled blur of uncertain noise?

Anyway, what good could a lone blue qheuen do, in the middle of a parched plain? His best bet was to stay by the pond till help came.

A mutter of beasts lifted behind Sara as the second party got under way, more slowly, following the same path.

Makes sense. The larger bunch will trample the trail of the smaller. At some point, UrKachu will veer us off, letting any pursuers keep following the main party.

Soon they were alone on the high steppe. Urunthai trotted alongside, agile and contemptuous of the awkward humans, who winced, dragging their toes as they rode. In reaction, the men began taking turns sliding off their mounts to run at a steady lope for several arrow-flights before swinging back aboard. This shut up the derisive urs and also seemed a good way to avoid saddle sores.

Alas, Sara knew she was in no physical condition to try it. *If I live through this, I'm definitely getting into shape,* she thought, not for the first time.

The man with slate eyes ran next to Sara for a few duras, sparing her a wry, eloquent smile. He was so wiry and strong, it amazed Sara that she recognized him. The last time she had seen Savant Dedinger, he was a pale intellectual with a middle-aged paunch, an expert on the most ancient scrolls, and author of a text Sara carried in her own slim luggage. A man once honored with status and trust, till his orthodox fanaticism grew too extreme for even the broad-minded High Council.

These days, the sages preached a complex faith of divided loyalty, split evenly between *Jijo,* on the one hand, and the ancestors' outlaw plan, on the other. It was a tense trade-off. Some solved it by choosing one allegiance over the other.

Sara's brother gave his full devotion to the *planet.* Lark saw wisdom and justice in the billion-year-old Galactic ecological codes. To him, no fancied "path of redemption" could ever make up for flouting those rules.

Dedinger took the opposite extreme. He cared little about ecology or species preservation, only the racial deliverance promised by the Scrolls. Seeking pure innocence as a way to better days. Perhaps he also saw in this crisis a way to regain lost honors.

By moonlight, Sara watched the banished sage move with wiry grace—alert, focused, powerful—living testimony for the simpler style that he preached.

Deceptively simple, she thought. *The world has countless ways of not being quite as it seems.*

The Urunthai slowed after a while, then stopped to rest and eat. Those with pouched husbands or larvae needed warm simla blood every midura or so, although the human raiders chafed and complained, preferring a steady pace over the urrish fashion of hurry-and-relax.

Soon after the second of these breaks, UrKachu veered the party onto a stony ledge that extended roughly southeast like the backbone of some fossilized behemoth. Rougher terrain slowed the pace, and Sara took advantage to dismount, giving respite to the donkey and her own bottom. Exercise might also take some chill stiffness out of her joints. She kept her right arm on the saddle though, in case some unseen stone made her stumble in the dark.

The going went a little easier with second moonrise. Backlit by silvery Torgen, the mountains seemed to loom larger than ever. North-side glaciers drank the satellite's angled light, giving back a peculiar blue luminance.

The Stranger sang for a while, a sweet, soft melody that made Sara think of loneliness.

> *I am a bar'n island,*
> *apart in the desult sea,*
> *and the nearest skein of land*
> *is my stark thought o' thee.*

> *O' say I were a chondrite,*
> *tumblin' sool an' free,*
> *would you be my garner-boat?*
> *An' come to amass me?*

It was Anglic, though of a dialect Sara had never heard, with many strange words. It was problematical how much the star-man still grasped. Still, the unrolling verses doubtless roused strong feelings in his mind.

> *Am I the ice that slakes your thirst,*
> *that twinkles your bright rings?*
> *You are the fantoom angel-kin,*
> *whose kiss gives planets wings. . . .*

The recital ended when UrKachu trotted back, nostril flaring, to complain about *unbearable Earthling caterwauling*. A purely personal opinion, Sara felt, since none of the other urs seemed to mind. Music was on the short list of things the two races tended to agree about. Some urs even said that, for bringing the violus to Jijo, they could almost overlook human stench.

For an auntie, UrKachu seemed a particularly irritable sort.

The man from space fell silent, and the group traveled in a moody hush, punctuated by the clip-clop of the animals' hooves on bare stone.

The next blood-stop took place on the wind-sheltered lee side of some towering slabs that might be natural rock forms but in the dimness seemed like ruins of an ancient fortress, toppled in a long-ago calamity. One of the weathered desert-men gave Sara a chunk of gritty bread, plus a slab of bushcow cheese that was stale, but tasty enough to one who found herself ravenously hungry. The water ration was disappointing, though. The urs saw little point in carrying much.

Around midnight, the party had to ford a wide, shallow stream that flowed through a desert wadi. Always prepared, Ulgor slipped on sealed booties, crossing with dry feet. The other urrish rebels slogged alongside the humans and animals, then dried each other's legs with rags. After that, the Urunthai seemed eager to run for a while, till the moisture wicked out of their fibrous ankle fur.

When the pace slackened again, Sara slid off her mount to walk. Soon a low voice spoke from her right.

"I meant to tell you—I've read your paper on linguistic devolution from Indo-European."

It was the scholar-turned-hunter, Dedinger, striding beyond her donkey's other flank. She watched him for a long moment before answering.

"I'm surprised. At fifty pages, I could afford to get only five photocopies cranked, and I kept one."

Dedinger smiled. "I still have friends in Biblos who send me engaging items, now and then. As for your thesis, while I enjoyed your ideas about grammatical reinforcement in pre-literate trading clans, I'm afraid I can't bring myself to accept your general theory."

Sara didn't find it surprising. Her conclusions ran counter to everything the man believed in.

"That's the way of science—a cycle of give-and-take. No dogmatic truth. No rigid, received word."

"As opposed to my own slavish devotion to a few ancient scrolls that no human had a hand in writing?" The flinty man laughed. "I guess what it comes down to is which direction you think people are heading. Even among conservative Galactics, *science* is about slowly improving your models of the world. It's future-oriented. Your children will know more than you do, so the truth you already have can never be called 'perfect.'

"That's fine when your destiny lies *upward,* Sara. But tradition and a firm creed are preferable if you're embarked on the narrow, sacred road downhill, to salvation. In that case, argument and uncertainty will only confuse your flock."

"Your flock doesn't seem confused," she acknowledged.

He smiled. "I've had some success winning these hard men over to true orthodoxy. They dwell much of each year on the Plain of Sharp Sand, trapping the wild spike-sloths that lurk in caves, under the dunes. Most don't read or write, and their few tools are handmade, so they were already far down the Path. It may prove harder convincing some other groups."

"Like the Explosers Guild?"

The former scholar nodded.

"An enigmatic clan. Their hesitation to do their duty, during this crisis, is disturbing."

Sara raised her eyes toward Kurt and Jomah. While the senior exploser snored atop an ambling donkey, his nephew held another one-sided conversation with the Stranger, who smiled and nodded as Jomah chattered. The star-man made an ideal, uncritical audience for a shy boy, just beginning to express himself.

"Maybe they figure they can blow it all up just once," Sara commented. "Then they'll have to scratch for a living, like everyone else."

Dedinger grunted. "If so, it's time someone reminded them, respectfully, of their obligations."

She recalled Jop's talk of taking Kurt somewhere to be "persuaded." In more violent times, the expression carried chilling implications.

We may be headed back to such times.

The flinty insurgent shook his head.

"But never mind all that. I *really* want to discuss your fascinating paper. Do you mind?"

When Sara shrugged, Dedinger continued in an amiable tone, as if they sat in a Biblos faculty lounge.

"You admit that proto-Indo-European, and many other human mother tongues, were more rigorous and rational than the dialects that evolved out of them. Right so far?"

"According to books carried here by the *Tabernacle*. All we have is inherited data."

"And yet you *don't* see this trend as an obvious sign of decay from perfection? From original grammars designed for our use by a patron race?"

She sighed. There might be weirder things in the universe than holding an abstract chat with her kidnapper under a desert sky, but none came to mind.

"The structure of those early tongues could have risen out of selective pressure, operating over generations. Primitive people *need* rigid grammars, because they lack writing or other means to correct error and linguistic drift."

"Ah yes. Your analogy to the game of Telephone, in which the language with the highest level of shaman coding—"

"That's *Shannon* coding. Claude Shannon showed that any message can carry within itself the means to correct errors that creep in during transit. In a *spoken* language, this redundancy often comes embedded in grammatical rules—the cases, declensions, modifiers, and such. It's all quite basic information theory."

"Hm. Maybe for you. I confess that I failed to follow your mathematics." Dedinger chuckled dryly. "But let's assume you're right about that. Does not such clever, self-correcting structure *prove* those early human languages were shrewdly designed?"

"Not at all. The same argument was raised against biological evolution—and later against the notion of self-bootstrapped intelligence. Some folks have a hard time accepting that complexity can emerge out of Darwinian selection, but it does."

"So you believe—"

"That the same thing happened to preliterate languages on Earth. Cultures with stronger grammars could hang together over greater distances and times. According to some of the old-timer linguists, Indo-European may have ranged all the way from Europe to Central Asia. Its rigid perfection maintained culture and trade links over distances far beyond what any person might traverse in a lifetime. News, gossip, or a good story could travel slowly, by word of mouth, all the way across a continent, arriving centuries later, barely changed."

"Like in the game of Telephone."

"That's the general idea."

Sara found herself leaning on the donkey as fatigue prickled her calves and thighs. Still, it seemed a toss-up—aching muscles if she stayed afoot versus shivering on a bruised coccyx if she remounted. For the little donkey's sake, she chose to keep walking.

Dedinger had his teeth in the argument.

"If all you say is true, how can you deny those early grammars were superior to the shabby, disorganized dialects that followed?"

"What do you mean, 'superior'? Whether you're talking about proto-Indo-European, proto-Bantu or proto-Semitic, each language served the needs of a conservative, largely changeless culture of nomads and herders, for hundreds or thousands of years. But those needs *shifted* when our ancestors acquired agriculture, metals, and writing. Progress changed the very notion of what language was for."

An expression of earnest confusion briefly softened the man's etched features.

"Pray, what could language *be* for, if not to maintain a culture's cohesion and foster communication?"

That was the question posed by members of Dedinger's former department, who spurned Sara's theory at its first hearing, embarrassing her in front of Sages Bonner, Taine, and Purofsky. Had not the majestic civilization of the Five Galaxies been refining its twenty or so standard codes since the days of the fabled Progenitors, with a single goal—to promote clear exchange of meaning among myriad citizen races?

"There is another desirable thing," Sara replied. "Another product of language, just as important, in the long run, as cohesion."

"And that is?"

"*Creativity*. If I'm right, it calls for a different kind of grammar. A completely different way of looking at error."

"One that *welcomes* error. Embraces it." Dedinger nodded. "This part of your paper I had trouble following. You say Anglic is better because it *lacks* redundancy coding. Because errors and ambiguity creep into every phrase or paragraph. But how can *chaos* engender inventiveness?"

"By shattering preconceptions. By allowing illogical, preposterous, even obviously *wrong* statements to parse in reasonable-sounding expressions. Like the paradox—'This sentence is a lie'—which can't be spoken grammatically in any formal Galactic tongue. By putting manifest contradictions on an equal footing with the most time-honored and widely held assumptions, we are tantalized, confused. Our thoughts stumble out of step."

"This is good?"

"It's how creativity works, especially in humans. For every good idea, ten thousand idiotic ones must first be posed, sifted, tried out, and discarded. A mind that's afraid to toy with the ridiculous will never come up with the brilliantly original—some absurd concept that future generations will assume to have been 'obvious' all along.

"One result has been a profusion of new words—a vocabulary vastly greater than ancient languages. Words for new things, new ideas, new ways of comparing and reasoning."

Dedinger muttered, "And new disasters. New misunderstandings."

Sara nodded, conceding the point.

"It's a dangerous process. Earth's bloody past shows how imagination and belief turn into curses unless they're accompanied by critical judgment. Writing, logic, and experimentation help replace some of the error-correction that used to come embedded in grammar. Above all, mature people must consider that most unpleasant of all possibilities—that their own favorite doctrines *might* prove wrong."

She watched Dedinger. Would the man catch on that she had aimed that barb at *him*?

The exiled pedagogue gave Sara a wry smile.

"Has it occurred to you, Miss Sara, that your last statement could apply to *you* and your own beloved hypothesis?"

Now it was Sara's turn to wince, then laugh aloud.

"Human nature. Each of us thinks *we* know what we're talking about and those disagreeing are fools. Creative people see Prometheus in a mirror, never Pandora."

Dedinger spoke with an ironic edge. "Sometimes the torch I carry scorches my fingers."

Sara could not tell how much he meant the remark in jest. Often she found it easier to read the feelings of a hoon, or g'Kek, than some members of her own enigmatic race. Still, she found herself enjoying the conversation, the first of its kind in quite some time.

"As for trends here on Jijo, just look at the new rhythmic novels being published by some of the northern urrish tribes. Or the recent burst of hoonish romantic poetry. Or the GalTwo haiku imagery coming out of the Vale—"

A sharp whistle cut her short—a guttural, stop-command piped by UrKachu's upstretched throat. The queue of tired animals jostled to a halt, as the Urunthai leader pointed north of a stone spire, decreeing that a camouflaged shelter be raised in its long, tapered shadow.

In its shadow . . .

Blinking, Sara looked around to see that the night was over. Dawn-light filtered over the peaks, sifting through an early-morning haze. They had climbed *among* the mountains, or at least the rocky foothills, leaving behind the parched Warril Plain. Alas, they were by now far south of the well-worn trail leading to the Glade of Gathering.

Dedinger's courtliness clashed with his rough appearance, as he excused himself to organize his men. "I've enjoyed matching wits," he told her with a bow. "Perhaps we can resume later."

"Perhaps."

Although the discussion had been a pleasant diversion, she had no doubt the man would sacrifice her, along with all of her ideas, on the altar of his faith. Sara vowed to be ready for any occasion to sneak her friends away from these fanatics.

Right. An old man, a boy, a chimpanzee, a wounded alien, and an out-of-shape intellectual—even if we got a huge head start, these urs and desert-men would catch us faster than you can transform a sine wave.

Still, she gazed north toward high peaks where momentous events were taking place in hidden valleys, and thought—*We'd better move fast, or else Ifni, God, and the universe will surely move on without us.*

A<small>sx</small>

NOW COMES *OUR* TURN TO THREATEN.

Proctors fight to hold back a furious throng, hemming our erstwhile guests inside a circle of rage. The remaining alien-lovers, mostly humans, form a protective ring around the star-beings, while the twin robots swoop and dive, enforcing a buffer zone with bolts of stinging lightning.

Lester Cambel steps forward, raising both hands for calm. The raucous noise ebbs, as members of the mob ease their pressure on the harried proctors. Soon silence reigns. No one wants to miss the next move in this game, wherein all of us on Jijo are tokens being gambled, to be won or lost, counting on our skill and luck.

Lester bows to the Rothen emissary. In one hand he bears a stack of metal plates.

"Now let's drop all pretense," he tells the star-god. "We know you for what you are. Nor can you trick us into genocidal suicide, doing your dirty work.

"Furthermore, should you try to do the job yourselves, annihilating all witnesses to your illegal visit, you will fail. All you'll accomplish is to increase your list of crimes.

"We recommend that you be satisfied. Take what you will from this world, and go."

The male star-human bursts forth, outraged. "How dare you speak so to a patron of your race!" Rann chastises, red-faced. "Apologize for your insolence!"

But Lester ignores Rann, whose status has diminished in the eyes of the Six. A toady/servant does not dictate to a sage, no matter what godlike powers he wields.

Instead, our human envoy offers one of the metal plates to Ro-kenn.

"We are not proud of this art form. It uses materials that won't age or degrade back into Mother Jijo's soil. Rather, it is adamant. Resistant to time. Properly stored, its images will last until this world again teems with legal sapient life.

"Normally, we would send such dross to where Jijo can recycle it in fire. But in this case, we'll make an exception."

The Rothen emissary turns the plate in the morning light. Unlike a paper photograph, this kind of image is best viewed from certain angles. we/i know what it depicts, do we not, my rings? The plate shows Ro-kenn and his comrades just before that ill-starred pilgrimage—a journey whose horrors still drip vexingly down our waxy core. Bloor the Portraitist developed the picture to serve as an instrument of blackmail.

"Other images depict your party in various poses, performing surveys, testing candidate species, often with backgrounds that clearly portray this place, this world. The shape of glaciers and eroding cliffs will set the date within a hundred years. Perhaps less."

The rewq covering our/my torus-of-vision reveals ripples crisscrossing Ro-kenn's face, again a dissonance of clashing emotions—but which ones? Are we getting better at reading this alien life-form? The second of our cognition rings seems deeply curious about the clashing colors.

The Rothen holds out an elegant hand.

"May I see the others?"

Lester hands them over. "This is but a sampling. Naturally, a detailed record of our encounter with your ship and crew has also been etched on durable metal, to accompany these pictures into hiding."

"Naturally," Ro-kenn answers smoothly, perusing one plate after another, turning them in the sunshine. "You have retained unusual arts, for self-accursed sooners. Indeed, I have never seen the like, even in civilized space."

This flattery draws some murmurs from the crowd. Ro-kenn is once more being charming.

Lester continues, "Any acts of vengeance or genocide against the Six will also be chronicled this way. It is doubtful you can wipe us out before hidden scribes complete such a record."

"Doubtful indeed." Ro-kenn pauses, as if considering his options. Given his earlier arrogance, we had expected outrage over being blackmailed in this way, plus indignation over the implied disrespect. It would not surprise us to see open contempt for an effort by half-beasts to threaten a deity.

Instead, do we now perceive something like *cautious calculation* cross his features? Does he realize we have him cornered? Ro-kenn shrugs in a manner not unlike a human. "What shall be done, then? If we agree to your demands, how can we be certain these will not reappear anyway, to plague our descendants someday? Will you sell these records to us now, in return for our promise to go in peace?"

Now it is Lester who laughs. Turning half toward the crowd, he gestures with one hand. "Had you come after the Commons experienced another century or two of peace, we might have trustingly accepted. But who among us has not heard stories told by old-timers who were *there* when Broken-Tooth deceived Ur-xouna near False Bridge, at the end of the old wars? What human has not read moving accounts of some great-grandfather who escaped the slaughter at Truce Gorge, during the Year of Lies?"

He turned back to Ro-kenn. "Our knowledge of deceit comes self-taught. Peace was hard-won—its lessons not forgotten.

"No, mighty Rothen. With apologies, we decline simply to take you at your word."

This time a mere flick of one slender hand holds back the outraged Rann, checking another outburst. Ro-kenn himself seems amused, although the strange dissonance once more cuts his visage.

"Then what guarantee have *we* that you will destroy these items, and not leave them in a place where they may be found by future tenants of this world? Or worse, by Galactic Institutes, as little as a thousand years from now?"

Lester is prepared with an answer.

"There is irony here, Oh mighty Rothen. If we, as a people, remember you, then we are still witnesses who can testify against your crime. Thus, if we retain memory, you have reason to act against us.

"If, on the other hand, we successfully follow the path of redemption and forgetfulness, in a thousand years we may already be like glavers, innocuous to you. No longer credible to testify. If so, you will have no cause to harm us. To do so would be senseless, even risky."

"True, but if you have by that time forgotten our visit, would you not also forget the hiding places where you cached these images?" Ro-kenn holds up a plate. "They will lie in ambush, like lurker missiles, patiently awaiting some future time to home in on our race."

Lester nodded. "That is the irony. Perhaps it can be solved by making a vow of our own—to teach our descendants a song—a riddle, as it were—something simple, that will resonate even when our descendants have much simpler minds."

"And what function will this puzzle serve?"

"We will tell our children that if ever beings come from the sky who know the riddle's answer, they must retrieve these items from sacred sites, handing them over to the star-lords—your own successors, Oh mighty Rothen. Naturally, if we Six retain *detailed* memory of your crime, we sages will *prevent* the hand-over, for it will be too soon. But *that* memory will not be taught to children, nor passed on with the same care as we teach the riddle. For to remember your crime is to hold on to a poison, one that can kill.

"We would rather forget how and why you ever came. Only then will we be safe from your wrath."

It is an ornately elaborate bargain that Lester offers. In council he had been forced to explain its logic three times. Now the crowd mutters, parsing the idea element by element, sharing bits of understanding until a murmur of admiration flows like molten clarity around the circle of close-pressed beings. Indeed, the bargain contains inherent elegance.

"How shall we know that all the items will be accounted for in this way?" Ro-kenn asks.

"To some extent, you must trust to luck. You were gamblers coming on this mission in the first place, were you not, mighty Rothen? I can tell you this. We have no grand desire to have these images arrive across the ages for Institute lawyers to pore over, looking for reasons to punish our own species-cousins, still roaming the stars. In their hardness and durability, these plates are an insult to our own goal on this world, to be shriven down to innocence. To earn a second chance."

Ro-kenn ponders this.

"It seems we may have come to Jijo a few thousand years too soon. If you succeed in following your Path, this world will be a treasure trove."

His meaning is not clear at first, then a mutter passes through the crowd, from urrish snorts to qheuenish hisses and finally booming hoonish laughter. Some are impressed by Ro-kenn's wit, others by the implied compliment—that the Rothen would wish to adopt any presentient races that we Six might become. But that reaction is not universal. Some of those assembled seethe angrily, rejecting any notion of adoption by Ro-kenn's folk.

Don't we/i find this anger silly, my rings? Have client races any control over who becomes their patron? Not according to lore we've read.

But those books will be dust long before any of this comes to pass.

"Shall we swear oaths?" Ro-kenn asks. "This time based on the most pragmatic assurance of all—mutual deterrence?

"By this new arrangement, we shall depart in our ship, waiting only till our scout craft returns from its final mission, choking back whatever bitterness we feel over the foul murder of our comrades. In return, you all vow to forget our intrusion and our foolish effort to speak through the voice of your Holy Egg."

"It is agreed," replies Knife-Bright Insight, clicking two claws. "Tonight we'll confer and choose a riddle whose secret key will be told to you. When next your kind comes to Jijo, may it be to find a world of innocents. That key will guide you to the hiding place. You may then remove the dross images. Our deal will be done."

Hope washes over the crowd, striking our rewq as a wave of soft green tremors.

Can we credit the possibility, my rings? That the Six might live to see a happy ending? To the zealots this seems all that they desired. Their young leader dances jubilation. Now there will be no punishment for their violent acts. Rather, they will be known as heroes of the Commons.

What do you say, my ring?

Our second cognition-torus reminds us that some *heretics* might *prefer* that angry fire and plagues rid Jijo of this infestation called the Six. And yes, there is yet another, even smaller heretical fringe. Eccentrics who foresee our destiny lying in a different direction—scarcely hinted by sacred scrolls. Why do you bring this up, my ring? What possible relevance can such nonsense have, at this time and place?

Scribes write down details of the pact. Soon High Sages will be called to witness and assent. (Prepare, my lower rings!) Meanwhile, we ponder again the anomaly brought to our waxy notice by the rewq, which still conveys vexing colors from Ro-kenn. Could they be shades of *deceit*? Deceit and *amusement*? Eager gladness to accept our offer, but only in appearance, buying time until—

Stop it, we command our second ring, which gets carried away all too easily. It has read too many novels. We do not know the Rothen well enough to read subtle, complex meanings in his alien visage.

Besides, don't we have Ro-kenn trapped? Has he not reason to fear the images on those plates of hard metal? Logically, he dare not risk them being passed on to incriminate his race, his line.

Or does he know something we do not?

Ah—what a silly question to ask, when pondering a star-god!

While hope courses the crowd, i/we grow more nervous by the dura. *What if they care nothing about the photographs? Then Ro-kenn might agree to anything, for it would not matter what vows were signed, once his almighty ship arrives. From that point on, with his personal safety assured* . . .

. . .

we never get a chance to complete that dripping contemplation. For suddenly, something new happens! Far too quickly for wax to ooze.

. . .

It begins with a shrill human cry—

One of the sycophants, a devoted Rothen-follower, points *behind* the star-beings, toward the raised bier where their two dead comrades lie—

Silky cloths had been draped across the two who were slain in the explosion. But now we see those coverings are *pulled back,* exposing the late Rothen and the late sky-human—

Do we now perceive *Bloor* the Portraitist, poised with his recording device, *attempting to photograph the faces of the dead*?

Bloor ignores growls of anger rising from those-who-follow-the-Rothen-as-patrons. Calmly, he slides out one exposed plate and inserts another. He appears entranced, focused on his art, even as attention turns his way from Rann, then an outraged Ro-kenn, who screams in terse Galactic Six—

Bloor glimpses the swooping robot and has time to perform one last act of professionalism. With his fragile body, the portraitist shields his precious camera and dies.

Have patience, you lesser rings that lie farthest from the senses. You must wait to caress these memories with our inner breath. For those who squat higher up our tapered cone, events come as a flurry of muddled images.

Behold—the livid anger of the star-gods, apoplectic with affronted rage!

Observe—the futile cries of Lester, Vubben, and Phwhoon-dau, beseeching restraint!

Witness—Bloor's crumpled ruin, a smoldering heap!

Note—how the crowd backs away from the violence, even as other dark-clad figures rush inward from the forest rim!

Quail—from the roaring robots, charging up to strike, ready to slay at command!

Above all, *stare*—at the scene right before us, the one Bloor was photographing when he died. . . .

An image to preserve as long as this tower of rings stands.

Two beings lie side by side.

One, a human female, seems composed in death, her newly washed face serene, apparently at peace.

The other figure *had* seemed equally tranquil when we saw it last, before dawn. Ro-pol's visage was like an idealized human, impressive in height and breadth of brow, in strong cheekbones and the set of her woman-like chin, which in life had sustained a winning smile.

That is not what we see now!

Rather, a quivering *thing*, suffering its own death tremors, creeps *off* of Ro-pol's face . . . taking much of that face with it! The very same brow and cheek and chin we had been pondering—these make up the *body* of the creature, which must have ridden the Rothen as a rewq rides one of the Six, nestled so smoothly in place that no join or seam was visible before.

Does this explain the dissonance? The clashing colors conveyed by our veteran rewq? When some parts of Ro-kenn's face relayed tart emotions, others always seemed cool, unperturbed, and friendly.

It crawls aside, and onlookers gasp at what remains— a sharply narrower face, chinless and spiny, with cranial edges totally unlike a human being's.

Gone is the mirage of heavenly comeliness in Earth-ling terms. Oh, the basic shape remains humanoid, but in a tapered, *predatory* caricature of our youngest sept.

"Hr-rm . . . I have seen this face before," croons Phwhoon-dau, stroking his white beard. "In my readings at Biblos. An obscure race, with a reputation for—"

Rann whips the coverings back over the corpses, while Ro-kenn shrilly interrupts, *"This is the final outrage!"*

Our rewq now clearly show Ro-kenn as *two* beings, one a living mask. Gone is the patient amusement, the pretense at giving in to blackmail. Until now, we had nothing to blackmail *with*.

Until now.

The Rothen points to Rann, commanding— *"Break radio silence and recall Kunn, now!"*

"The prey will be warned," Rann objects, clearly shaken. "And the hunters. Dare we risk—"

"We'll take that chance. Obey now! Recall Kunn, then clear all of these away."

Ro-kenn motions at the crowd, the sycophants, and all six sages

"No one leaves to speak of this."

The robots start to rise, crackling with dire strength. A moan of dread escapes the crowd.

Then—as is sometimes said in Earthling tales—All Hell Breaks Loose.

The Stranger

He strums the dulcimer slowly, plucking one low note at a time, feeling nervous over what he plans to attempt, yet also pleased by how much he is remembering.

About urs, for instance. Ever since first regaining consciousness aboard the little riverboat, he had tried to pin down why he felt so friendly toward the four-footed beings, despite their prickly, short-tempered natures. Back at the desert oasis, before the bloody ambush, he had listened to the ballad recited by the traitor Ulgor, without understanding more than a few click-phrases, here and there. Yet the rhythmic chant had seemed strangely familiar, tugging at associations within his battered brain.

Then, all at once, he recalled where he heard the tale before. In a bar, on faraway—

—on faraway—

Names are still hard to come by. But now at least he has an image, rescued from imprisoned memory. A scene in a tavern catering to low-class sapient races like his own, frequented by star travelers sharing certain tastes in food, music, and entertainment. Often, songs were accepted as currency in such places. You could buy rounds of drinks with a good one, and he seldom had to pay cash, so desired were the tunes warbled by his talented crewmates.

. . . crewmates . . .

Now he confronts another barrier. The tallest, harshest wall across his mind. He tries once more but fails to come up with a melody to break it down.

Back to the bar, then. With that recollection had come

things he once knew about urs. Especially a trick he used to pull on urrish companions when they dozed off, after a hard evening's revelry. Sometimes he would take a peanut, aim carefully, and—

The Stranger's train of thought breaks as he realizes he is being watched. UrKachu *glares at him, clearly irritated by the increasing loudness of the thrumming dulcimer. He quickly mollifies the leader of the urrish ambushers by plucking at the string more softly. Still, he does not quite stop. At a lower, quieter level, the rhythm is mildly hypnotic, just as he intended it to be.*

The other raiders—both urs and men—lie down or snooze through the broiling middle of the day. So does Sara, *along with* Prity *and the other captives. The Stranger knows he should rest, too, but he feels too keyed up.*

He misses Pzora, *though it does seem strange to long for the healing touch of a Jophur—*

No, that is the wrong word. Pzora is not one of those fearsome, cruel beings, but a traeki—*something quite different. As he grows a little better at names, he is going to have to remember that.*

Anyway, he has work to do. In the time remaining, he must learn to use the rewq *that Sara bought for him—a strange creature whose filmy body covers his eyes, causing soft colors to waft around every urs and human, turning the shabby tent into a pavilion of revealing hues. He finds unnerving the way the rewq quivers over his flesh, using a sucker to feed from veins near the gaping wound in his head. Yet he cannot turn down a chance to explore yet another kind of communication. Sometimes the confusing colors coalesce to remind him of the last time he communed with Pzora, back at the oasis. There had been a moment of strange clarity when their cojoined rewqs seemed to help convey exactly what he wanted.*

Pzora's answering gift lies inside *the hole in his head—the one place the raiders would never think to search.*

He resists an urge to slip his hand inside, to check if it's still there.

All in good time.

While he sits and strums, the oppressive heat slowly mounts. Urrish and human heads sink lower to the ground, where night's lingering coolness can still be dimly felt. He waits and tries to remember a little more.

His biggest blank zone—other than the loss of language—covers the recent past. If ten fingers represent the span of his life up to now, most of the final two digits are missing. All he has are the shreds that cling when ever he wakes from a dream. Enough to know he once roamed the linked galaxies and witnessed things none of his kind ever saw before. The seals holding back those memories have resisted everything he's tried so far— drawing sketches, playing math games with Prity, wallowing in Pzora's library of smells. He remains fairly certain the key will be found in music. But what music?

Sara snores softly nearby, and he feels a swelling of grateful fondness in his heart . . . combined with a nagging sense that there is someone else he should be thinking about. Another who had his devotion before searing fate swatted him out of the sky. A woman's face flickers at a sharp angle to his thoughts, passing too swiftly to recognize—except for the wave of strong feelings it evokes.

He misses her . . . though he can't imagine that she feels the same, wherever she may be.

Whoever she may be.

More than anything else, he wishes he could put his feelings into words, as he never did during all the dangerous times they spent together . . . times when she was pining for another . . . for a better man than he.

This thought thread is leading somewhere, he realizes, feeling some excitement. Avidly, he follows it. The woman in his dreams . . . she longs for a man . . . a hero who was lost long ago . . . a year or two ago . . .

lost along with crewmates . . . and also along with . . .

. . . along with the Captain . . .

Yes, of course! The commander they all missed so terribly, gone ever since a daring escape from that wretched water world. A world of disaster and triumph.

He tries conjuring an image of the Captain. A face. But all that comes to mind is a gray flash, a whirl of bubbles, and finally a glint of white, needlelike teeth. A smile unlike any other. Wise and serene.

Not human.

And then, out of nowhere, a soft warbling emerges. A sound never before heard on the Slope.

* My good silent friend . . .
        Lost in winter's dread stormcloud . . .
            Lonely . . . just like me . . . *

The whistles, creaks, and pops roll out of his mouth before he even knows he's speaking them. His head rocks back as a dam seems to shatter in his mind, releasing a flood of memories.

The music he'd been looking for was of no human making, but the modern tongue of Earth's third sapient race. A language painfully hard for humans to learn, but that rewarded those who tried. Trinary was nothing like Galactic Two or any other speech, except perhaps the groaning ballads sung by great whales who still plumbed the homeworld's timeless depths.

Trinary.

He blinks in surprise and even loses his rhythm on the plucked dulcimer. A few urs lift their heads, staring at him blankly till he resumes the steady cadence, continuing reflexively while he ponders his amazing rediscovery. The familiar/uncanny fact that had eluded him till now.

His crewmates—perhaps they still await him in that dark, dreary place where he left them.

His crewmates were dolphins.

XXV. THE BOOK OF THE SEA

*Beware, ye damned who seek
redemption.
Time is your friend, but also your
great foe.*

*Like the fires of Izmunuti,
It can fade before you are ready.
Letting in, once more,
The things from which you fled.*

—The Scroll of Danger

Alvin's Tale

I TRIED READING *FINNEGANS WAKE* ONCE UPON A time.

Last year.

A lifetime ago.

It's said that no non-Earthling has ever grokked that book. In fact, the few *humans* who managed the feat spent whole chunks of their lifespans going over Joyce's masterpiece, word by obscure word, with help from texts written by *other* obsessed scholars. Mister Heinz says no one on the Slope has any hope at all of fathoming it.

Naturally, I took that as a challenge, and so the next time our schoolteacher headed off to Gathering, I nagged him to bring a copy back with him.

No, I'm not about to say I succeeded. Just one page into it, I knew this was a whole different venture from *Ulysses*. Though it looks like it's written in prespace English, the *Wake* uses Joyce's own language, created for a single work of art. Hoonish patience would not solve this. To even begin to understand, you have to share much of the author's *context*.

What hope had I? Not a native speaker of Irish-English. Not a citizen of early twentieth-century Dublin. Not human. I've never been inside a "pub" or seen a "quark" close up, so I can only guess what goes on in each.

I recall thinking—maybe a little arrogantly—*If I can't read this thing, I doubt anyone else on Jijo ever will.*

The crisp volume didn't look as if anyone had tried,

since the Great Printing. So why did the human founders waste space in Biblos with this bizarre intellectual experiment from a bygone age?

That was when I felt I had a clue to the *Tabernacle* crew's purpose, in coming to this world. It couldn't be for the reasons we're told on holy days, when sages and priests read from the sacred Scrolls. Not to find a dark corner of the universe to engage in criminally selfish breeding, or to resign from the cosmos, seeking the roads of innocence. In either of those cases, I could see printing how-to manuals, or simple tales to help light the way. In time, the books would turn brittle and go to dust, when humans and the rest of us are ready to give them up. Kind of like the Eloi folk in H. G. Wells's *The Time Machine*.

In neither case did it make any sense to print copies of *Finnegans Wake*.

Realizing this, I picked up the book once more. And while I did not understand the story or allusions any better than before, I *was* able to enjoy the flow of words, their rhythms and sounds, for their own extravagant sake. It wasn't important anymore that I be the only person to grok it.

In fact, there came a warm feeling as I turned the pages and thought—*someday, someone else is going to get more out of this than I did*.

On Jijo, things get stored away that seem dead, but that only sleep.

I've been pondering that very thought while lying here in constant pain, trying to bear it stoically whenever strange, silent beings barge into my cell to poke me with heat, cold, and prickly sharpness. I mean, should I feel *hope* as metal fingers probe my wounds? Or sour gloom that my blank-faced tenders refuse to answer any questions, or even to speak? Shall I dwell on my awful homesickness? Or on the contrary *thrill* over having discovered something wonderfully strange that no one on the Slope ever suspected, not since the g'Keks first sent their sneakship tumbling into the deep?

Above all, I wondered—am I prisoner, patient, or *specimen*?

Finally I realized—I just don't have any framework to decide. Like the phrases in Joyce's book, these beings seem at once both strangely familiar and completely unfathomable.

Are they machines?

Are they denizens of some ancient submarine civilization?

Are they invaders? Do they see *us* as invaders?

Are they *Buyur*?

I've been avoiding thinking about what's really eating away at me, inside.

Come on, Alvin. Face up to it.

I recall those final duras, when our beautiful *Wuphon's Dream* shattered to bits. When her hull slammed against my spine. When my friends spilled into the metal monster's mouth, immersed in cold, cold, cold, cruel water.

They were alive then. Injured, dazed, but alive.

Still alive when a hurricane of air forced out the horrid dark sea, leaving us to flop, wounded and half dead, down to a hard deck. And when sun-bright lights half-blinded us, and creepy spider-things stepped into the chamber to look over their catch.

But memory blurs at that point, fading into a hazy muddle of images—until I awoke here, alone.

Alone, and worried about my friends.

XXVI. THE BOOK OF THE SLOPE

Legends

We know that in the Five Galaxies, every star-faring race got its start through the process of uplift, receiving a boost to sapience from the patrons that adopted them. And those patrons were bestowed the same boon by earlier patrons, and so on, a chain of beneficence stretching all the way back to misty times when there were more than five linked galaxies—back to the fabled *Progenitors,* who began the chain, so very long ago.

Where did the Progenitors *themselves* come from?

To some of the religious alliances that wrangle testily across the space lanes, that very question is anathema, or even likely to provoke a fight.

Others deal with the issue by

claiming that the ancient ones must have come from "somewhere else," or that the Progenitors were transcendent beings who descended graciously from a higher plane in order to help sapient life get its start.

Of course one might suggest that such facile answers simply beg the question, but it's unwise to suggest it too loudly. Some august Galactics do not take it kindly when you point out their inconsistencies.

Finally, there is one cult—the Affirmers—who hold the view that the Progenitors must have *self-evolved* on some planet, boot-strapping to full sapiency all by themselves—a prodigious, nigh-impossible feat. One might imagine that the Affirmers would be more friendly to Earthlings than most of the more fanatical alliances. After all, many Terrans still believe our race did the very same thing, uplifting ourselves in isolation, without help from anyone.

Alas, don't expect much sympathy from the Affirmers, who see it as arrogant hubris *for mere wolflings to make such a claim. Self-uplift, they maintain, is a phenomenon of the highest and most sacred order—not for the likes of creatures like us.*

—*A Pragmatist's Introduction to Galactology*, by Jacob Demwa, reprinted from the original by Tarek Printers' Guild, Year-of-Exile 1892.

Dwer

IT DID NO GOOD TO SHOUT OR THROW STONES AT the glavers. The pair just retreated to watch from a distance with blank, globelike eyes, then resumed following when the human party moved on. Dwer soon realized there would be no getting rid of them. He'd have to shoot the beasts or ignore them.

"You have other things to keep you busy, son," Danel Ozawa ruled.

It was an understatement.

The clearing near the waterfall still reeked of urs, donkey, and simla when Dwer warily guided Danel's group across the shallow ford. From then on, he borrowed a tactic from the old wars, reconnoitering each day's march the night before, counting on urrish diurnal habits to keep him safe from ambush—though urs were adaptable beings. They *could* be deadly even at night, as human fighters used to find out the hard way.

Dwer hoped this group had lazy habits, after generations of peace.

Rising at midnight, he would scout by the light of two smaller moons, sniffing warily each time the trail of hoofprints neared some plausible ambuscade. Then, at dawn, he would hurry back to help Danel's donkey train plod ahead by day.

Ozawa thought it urgent to catch up with the urrish band and negotiate an arrangement. But Dwer worried. *How does he expect they'll react? Embracing us like brothers? These are criminals. Like Rety's band. Like us.*

The spoor grew fresher. Now the urs were just a week ahead of them, maybe just a few days.

He began noting *other* traces. Soft outlines in the sand. Broken stone flakes. Fragments of a moccasin lace. Smudged campfires more than a month old.

Rety's band. The urs are heading straight for the heart of their territory.

Danel took the news calmly. "They must figure as we did. The human sooners know a lot about life in these hills. That's valuable experience, whether it can be bought, borrowed—"

"Or tortured out of 'em," Lena Strong finished, whetting one of her knives by the evening's low red coals. "Some urrish clans used to keep human prisoners as drudges, before we broke 'em of the habit."

"A habit *they* learned from the queens. There's no call to assume slavery is a natural urs behavior. For that matter, back on Old Earth *humans* used to—"

"Yeah, well, we still have a problem," Dwer interrupted. "What to do when we catch up."

"Right!" Lena inspected the knife-edge. "Do we pounce fast, taking the urs all bunched together? Or do it hoon-style—picking them off one at a time."

Jenin sighed unhappily. "Oh, Lena. Please stop." She had been cheerful throughout the journey, until hearing all this talk of fighting. Jenin had joined this trek in order to be a founding mother of a new race, not to hunt down beings who had once been her neighbors.

Dwer's heart felt the same pain as Jenin, though his pragmatic side agreed with Lena.

"If we have to, I'd rather do it fast," he muttered, glancing at the donkey carrying their most secret, unspeakable "tools."

"It shouldn't come to that," Danel insisted. "First let's ascertain who they are and what they want. Perhaps we can make common cause."

Lena snorted. "Send an emissary? Give away our presence? You heard Dwer. There's over a dozen of 'em!"

"Don't you think we should wait for the second

group, then?" Jenin asked. "They were supposed to be right behind us."

Lena shrugged. "Who knows how long they'll take? Or if they got lost? The urs could find us first. And there's the human tribe to consider."

"Rety's old band."

"Right. Want to let them get killed or enslaved? Just on account of we're too scared to—"

"Lena!" Danel cut her off. "That will do for now. We'll see what's to be done when the time comes. Meanwhile, poor Dwer should get some sleep. We owe him whatever rest he can get."

"That ain't half what he's owed." Lena muttered, causing Dwer to glance her way, but in the pre-moonrise dimness, he could make out only shadows.

"G'night all," he said, and slipped away to seek his bedroll.

Mudfoot looked up from the blanket, chuttering testily over having to move. The creature *did* help warm things up at night, which partly made up for its vexing way of licking Dwer's face while he slept, harvesting perspiration from his forehead and lip.

Dwer lay down, turned over—and blinked in surprise at two pairs of giant round eyes, staring back at him from just three meters away.

Jeekee glavers.

Normally, one simply ignored the placid creatures. But he still couldn't shake the memory of that pack of them, clustered greedily around a dead gallaiter.

He tossed a dirt clod vaguely their way. "Go on! Get!"

Just as vaguely, the pair turned and sauntered off. Dwer glanced at Mudfoot.

"Why not make yourself a *bit* useful and keep those pests away?"

The noor just grinned back at him.

Dwer pulled the blanket over his chin, trying to settle down. He was tired and ached from sore muscles and bruises. But slumber came slowly, freighted with troubling dreams.

·   ·   ·   ·   ·

He woke to a soft touch, stroking his face. Irritably, he tried to push the noor away.

"Quit it, furball! Lick a donkey turd, if you want salt so bad."

After a surprised pause, a hushed voice answered.

"Reckon I never been welcomed to a man's bed half so sweetly."

Dwer rolled onto an elbow, rubbing one eye to make out a blurred silhouette. A woman.

"Jenin?"

"Would you prefer her? I won the toss, but I'll fetch her if you like."

"Lena! What—can I do for you?"

Dwer made out a white glint—her rare smile.

"Well, you *could* invite me in from the cold." Her voice sounded soft, almost shy.

Lena was buxom and sanguinely female, yet *soft* and *shy* were two words Dwer had never linked with her before. "Uh—sure. . . ." *Am I still dreaming?* he wondered as she slid alongside, strong hands working to loosen his clothes. Her smooth skin seemed to blaze with ardent heat.

I must be. The Lena I know never smelled this good.

"You're all knotted up," she commented, kneading his neck and back with uncanny, forceful accuracy. At first, Dwer's gasps came from released muscle strain. But Lena somehow also made each jab or digging twist of her calloused fingers seem feminine, erotic.

She got halfway through the massage before Dwer passed his limit of self-control and turned over to gently but resolutely reverse their positions, taking her beneath him, repaying her vitality with a vigor that welled from weeks of pent-up tension. Hoarded worry and fatigue seemed to explode into the air, into the forest, into her as she clutched and sighed, pulling him closer.

After she slipped away, he pondered muzzily—*Lena thinks I may die, since my job is to be up front in any fight. This might be the last . . . the only chance. . . .*

Dwer drifted into a tranquil, dreamless repose—a slumber so blank and relaxing that he actually felt rested by the time *another* warm body slid into the bedroll next to him. By then, his unconscious had worked it out, crediting the women with ultimate pragmatism.

Danel will probably be around later, so it makes sense to use whatever I have to give, before it's gone.

It wasn't his place to judge the women. Theirs was the harder job, here in the wilderness. His tasks were simple—to hunt, fight, and if need be, to die. Theirs was to go on, whatever it took.

Dwer did not even have to rouse all the way. Nor did Jenin seem offended that his body performed but half awake. There were all sorts of duties to fulfill these days. If he was going to keep up, he would simply have to catch what rest he could.

Dwer woke to find it already a midura past midnight. Though he felt much better now, he had to fight a languid lethargy to get dressed and check his gear—the bow and quiver, a compass, sketch pad, and hip canteen—then stop by the dim coals to pluck the leaf-wrapped package Jenin left for him each night, the one decent meal he would eat while away.

For most of his adult life he had traveled alone, relishing peace and solitude. Yet, he had to admit the attractions of being part of a team, a community. Perhaps, under Ozawa's guidance, they might come to feel like *family.*

Would that take some of the bitter sting out of recalling the life and loved ones they had left behind, in the graceful forests of the Slope?

Dwer was about to head off, following the urrish track farther in the direction of the rising moons, when a soft sound made him pause. Someone was awake and talking. Yet he had passed both women, snoring quietly and (he liked to imagine) happily. Dwer slipped the bow off his shoulder, moving toward the low speech sounds, more curious than edgy. Soon he recognized the murmured whisper.

Of course it was Danel. But who was the sage talking to?

Beyond the bole of a large tree, Dwer peered into a small clearing where satiny moonlight spilled over an unlikely pair. Danel was kneeling low to face the little black creature called Mudfoot. Dwer couldn't make out words, but judging from tone and inflection, Ozawa was trying to ask it *questions,* in one language after another.

The noor responded by licking itself, then glancing briefly toward Dwer, standing in the shadows. When Ozawa switched to GalTwo, Mudfoot grinned—then twisted to bite an itch on one shoulder. When the beast turned back, it was to answer the sage with a gaping yawn.

Danel let out a soft sigh, as if he had expected to fail but felt it worth an effort.

What effort? Dwer wondered. Was the sage seeking magical aid, as ignorant lowlanders sometimes tried to do, treating noor like sprites in some fairy tale? Did Ozawa hope to *tame* Mudfoot, the way hoon sailors did, as agile helpers on the river? Few nonhoon had ever managed that feat. But even if it worked, what use was *one* noor assistant? Or would Dwer's next assignment—after dealing with urrish sooners and then Rety's band—be to run back and collect more of Mudfoot's kind?

That made no sense. If by some miracle the Commons survived, word would be sent calling them all home. If the worst happened, they were to stay as far from the Slope as possible.

Well, Danel will tell me what he wants me to know. I just hope this doesn't mean he's gone crazy.

Dwer crept away and found the urrish trail. He set off at a lope that soon strained forward, pulling him with unwilled eagerness to see what lay beyond the next shadowy rise. For the first time in days, Dwer felt whole and strong. It wasn't that all worries had vanished. Existence was still a frail, perilous thing, all too easily lost. Still, for this narrow stretch of time he pounded onward, feeling vibrantly alive.

Rety

THE DREAM ALWAYS ENDED THE SAME WAY, JUST *before she woke shivering, clutching a soft blanket to her breast.*

She dreamed about the bird.

Not as it appeared the last time she had seen it— headless, spread across Kann's laboratory bench in the buried station—but as she recalled first glimpsing the strange thing. Vivid in motion, with plumage like glossy forest leaves, alert and lustrous in a way that seemed to stroke her soul.

As a child she had loved to watch native birds, staring for hours at their swooping dives, envying their freedom of the air, their liberty to take wing, leaving their troubles far behind. Then one day Jass returned from a long journey to the south, bragging about all the beasts he had shot. One had been a fantastic flying thing that they took by surprise as it emerged from a tidal marsh. It barely got away after an arrow tore one wing, flapping off toward the northwest, leaving behind a feather harder than stone.

That very night, risking awful punishment, she stole the stiff metal fragment from the tent where the hunters snored, and with a pack of stolen food she ran off, seeking this fabled wonder for herself. As luck had it, she guessed right and crossed its path, spotting the fluttering creature as it labored onward with short, gliding bounds. In a throat-catching instant of recognition, Rety knew the bird was like her—wounded by the same man's taste for senseless violence.

Watching it hop-glide ever westward, never resting, she knew they shared one more trait. Persistence.

She wanted to catch up with it, to heal it, talk to it. To learn its source of power. To help it reach its goal. To help find its home. But even disabled, the bird soon outdistanced her. For a heart-aching time, she thought she had lost it forever. . . .

At that point of harsh emotion, without transition, the dream shifted to another scene. Suddenly, the bird was right in front of her, closer than ever, fluttering inside a jeweled cage, dodging a mist of golden, cloying drops . . . then cowering away from searing knives of flame!

Frustration choked Rety, unable to give aid. Unable to save it.

Finally, when all seemed lost, the bird did as Rety herself would have done. It lashed out with desperate strength, dying to bring down its oppressor, the agent of its torment.

For several nights in a row the dream ended the same way, with someone's insistent arms holding her back in shameful safety while the bird fired its own head upward toward a hovering, shadowy form. A dark rival with dangling, lethal limbs.

It seemed revenge was going to be another of those things that didn't turn out quite the same in real life as she'd imagined.

For one thing, in her heart, Rety never reckoned on Jass taking pain so well.

The hunter lay strapped to a couch inside the scout aircraft, his ruggedly handsome features twisting as Kunn kept the promise he had made. A promise Rety regretted a bit more each time Jass clamped back another moan, choking it behind gritted teeth.

Who would've thought he'd turn out to be brave, she pondered, recalling all the times Jass used to brag, bluster, and harass other members of the tribe. Bullies were supposed to be cowards, or so one of the tribe's aged grandfathers used to mutter when he was sure the young hunters wouldn't hear. Too bad the old geep would never know how wrong he'd been. That battered patriarch had died during the months since Rety left these hills.

She tried steeling her heart during the contest of wills between Kunn and Jass, one Jass was bound to lose. *You want to find out where the bird came from, don't you?* she asked herself. *Anyway, don't Jass deserve everything he's getting? Ain't his own stubborn-headedness bringing this on himself?*

Well, in truth, Rety had played a role in stiffening the hunter's resistance, thus extending his torment. Kunn's patient, insistent questions alternated with grunts of pure glaverlike obstinacy from Jass, sweating and contorting under jolts applied by Kunn's robot partner.

When she could take no more without getting sick, Rety silently slipped out the hatch. If anything changed, the pilot could call her on the tiny comm button the sky-humans had installed under the skin near her right ear.

She set off toward the campsite, trying to appear casual in case any sooners watched from the shrubby undergrowth.

That was how she thought of them. *Sooners.* Savages. No different in kind from those puffed-up barbarians on the Slope, who thought themselves *so* civilized with their fancy books but who were still little more than half-animals, trapped on a dirty world they could never leave. To a sky-being like herself, they were all the same, whichever side of the Rimmers they led their dirt-scratching lives.

She smelled the camp before reaching it. A familiar musty blend of wood smoke, excrement, and poorly tanned hides, all mixed with a sulfury pungence rising from the steam pools that always drew the tribe here this time of year—a fact that had made it easy to guide Kunn to this pocket canyon, high in the Gray Hills. Rety paused halfway to the campsite, smoothing down the sleek jumpsuit Ling had given her, soon after she became the first Jijoan to enter the underground station, that wonderland of luxuries and bright marvels. Ling had also bathed Rety, treated her scalp, and applied potions and rays to leave her feeling cleaner, stronger, even *taller* than before. Only the livid scar on one side of her face still marred the mirror's transformed image, and that would be tended, she was assured, when they all went "home."

My home too, Rety mused, resuming a brisk pace until all moaning traces of the hunter's torment faded behind her. She drove out memory of Jass's squirming agony by calling to mind those images the sky-foursome had shown her—of a splendid, jewellike city, tucked inside a steep-walled valley. A city of fairy towers and floating castles, where one lucky branch of humanity lived with their beloved patrons, the wise, benevolent Rothen.

That part didn't quite appeal to her—this business of having *masters* who told you what to do. Nor did the Rothen themselves, when she met the two living aboard the station, who seemed too pretty and prim, too smugly happy, by far. But then, if Ling and Besh loved them, she supposed she could get used to that idea too. Anyway, Rety was willing to do or put up with anything to reach that city of lights.

I always knew I belonged someplace else, she thought, rounding a bend in the forest. *Not here. Not in a place like this.*

Before her stretched a debris-strewn clearing dotted by half a dozen ragged shelters—animal hides thrown over rows of bent saplings—all clustered round a cook fire where soot-smudged figures hunched over a carcass. Tonight's meal. A donkey with a neat hole burned through its heart. A gift, courtesy of Kunn's handy hunter-killer robot.

People dressed in poorly tanned skins moved about at chores or simply slouched through the middle of the day. Their complexions were filthy. Most had matted hair, and they stank. After meeting the Slopies—and then Ling and Besh—it was hard to picture these savages as the same *race* as herself, let alone her own tribe.

Several male figures loafed near a makeshift pen where the new prisoners huddled, having barely moved since they were herded into camp a couple of nights back. Some of the men chopped at tree stumps with machetes swiped from the newcomers' supplies, marveling at the keen blades of Buyur metal. But the men kept well away from the pile of crates Kunn had forbidden them to touch, awaiting his decision which to destroy.

A handful of boys straddled a new fence of laser-split logs, passing the time by spitting, then laughing as angry complaints rose from the captives.

Shouldn't let 'em do that, Rety thought. *Even if the outlanders are nosy fools who oughtn't have come.*

Kunn had assigned her the task of finding out what brought the prisoners to these parts, violating their own sacred law. But Rety felt reluctant, even disgusted.

Dawdling, she turned to survey a way of life she once thought she'd never escape.

Despite the tumult of the last few days, tribal life went on. Kallish, the old clubfoot, still labored by the stream bed, hammering stone cores into flake arrowheads and other tools, convinced the recent influx of iron implements would be a passing fad. He was probably right.

Upstream, women waded through shallows, seeking the trishelled juice oysters that ripened in volcanic heat this time of year, while farther upslope, beyond the steamy pools, a cluster of girls used poles to beat Illoes trees, gathering the tart fallen berries in woven baskets. As usual, females were doing most of the hard work. Nowhere was this more evident than near the cook fire, where grouchy old Binni, her arms bloody past the elbows, took charge of preparing the donkey for roasting. The headwoman's hair was even grayer than before. Her latest baby had died, leaving Binni irritable with swollen, tender breasts, hissing at her two young helpers through wide gaps between yellow-brown teeth.

Despite such signs of normality, most tribe-folk moved in a state of sluggish distraction. Whenever anyone glanced Rety's way, they *flinched,* as if she were the last thing on Jijo they ever expected to see. More shocking than a glaver standing upright.

Rety, the god.

She held her head high. *Tell your stinky brats about it by the campfire, till the end of time. Tell 'em about the girl who talked back to big mean hunters, no matter what they did to her. A girl who wouldn't take it anymore. Who dared to do what you never imagined. Who found a way to leave this stinking hell and go live on a star.*

Rety felt a thrill each time someone briefly met her gaze and quickly looked away.

I'm not one of you. Never was. And now you know it too.

Only Binni showed no trace of being overwhelmed by the deity Rety had become. The same old disdain and disappointment lay in those metal-gray eyes. At age twenty-eight, Binni was younger than any of the forayers, even Ling. Still, it seemed nothing on Jijo, or in heaven, would ever surprise her.

It had been years since Rety last called the old woman "Mama." She wasn't tempted to resume now.

With her back straight, she walked past the chefs and their grisly work. Inside, though, she wavered.

Maybe it wasn't such a good idea to come back here. Why mix with these ghosts when she could be in the aircraft, relishing victory over her lifelong enemy? The punishment being executed on Jass seemed rightful and good, now that she didn't have to face his agony up close. That contradiction made Rety nervous, as if something were missing. Like trying to use moccasins without laces.

"wife! there you are, wife! bad wife, to leave yee alone so long!"

Several clansmen scurried out of the way, making room for a four-legged creature, galloping past their ankles like some untouchable, all-powerful being. Which the little urrish male *was,* in a sense, since Rety had loudly promised horrors to anyone laying a hand on her "husband."

yee leaped into her arms, squirming with pleasure even as he scolded.

"wife leave yee alone too long with female foes! they offer yee soft, warm pouch. temptresses!"

Rety flared jealousy. "Who offered you a pouch! If any of those hussies—"

Then she saw he was teasing. Some of the tension in her shoulders let go as she laughed. The little critter was definitely good for her.

"relax, wife," he assured her. "just one pouch for yee. go in now?"

"In now," she replied, unzipping the plush hip bag Ling had provided. yee dove inside, wriggled around, then stuck out his head and long neck to peer at her.

"come now, wife. visit Ul-Tahni. that sage ready talk now."

"Ah, is she? Well now, isn't that awfully nice of her."

Rety didn't relish going to see the leader of the outlanders. But Kunn had given her a job, and now was as good a time as any.

"All right," she said. "Let's hear what the hinney has to say."

Dwer

THE URS, IT APPEARED, HAD DONE THE SMALL HUman expedition a favor. In receiving death and devastation, they had left a warning.

A tale of callous murder was clear to read through the dawn light—in seared and shattered trees, blackened craters, and scattered debris, pushed by a gusty, dry wind. The violence that took place here—just a few days ago by Dwer's estimate—must have been brief but horrible.

The plateau's terraced outlines were still visible after ages of softening by erosion and vegetation. It was a former Buyur site, going back to the last race licensed to use this world—legal residents dwelling in heavenlike towers, who went through their daily lives unafraid of the open sky.

Dwer traced the terror that recently fell upon this place. All too vividly he pictured the panicked urrish settlers, rearing and coughing with dread, coiling their long necks, with slim arms crossed to shield their precious pouches as the ground around them exploded. He could almost hear their screams as they fled the burning encampment, down a steep trail leading into a narrow defile—where *human* footprints swarmed in abruptly from both sides, tracked by crude moccasins, mingling with urrish hooves chaotically.

He picked up shreds of home-twisted twine and leather cord. From countless signs, Dwer pictured ropes and nets falling to trap the urs, taking them prisoner.

Couldn't they tell they were being herded? The aircraft aimed off to the sides and all around, to drive them. So why didn't the urs scatter instead of clumping in a mass to be caught?

Several patches of sticky sand gave him an answer. The overall intent might have been capture, but the flying gunner had few qualms about enforcing the round-up with a corpse or two.

Don't judge the urs too harshly. Do you know how you'll *react when lightning bolts start falling all around? War is messy, and we're all out of practice. Even Drake never had to cope with anything like this.*

"So, we're facing an alliance between the human sooners and the aliens," Lena concluded. "Kind of changes things, don't it?"

Danel Ozawa wore a bleak expression. "This entire region is compromised. Whatever fate befalls the Slope will now surely happen here, as well. Whether by plague, or by fire, or hunting their victims one at a time with machines—they'll scourge the area as thoroughly as back home."

Danel's task had been to carry a legacy into the wilderness—both knowledge and fresh genes to invigorate the human tribe already living here—to preserve something of Earthling life in case the worst came to pass. It was never a joyous enterprise, more like the mission of a lifeboat captain in some ancient tale about a shipwreck. But at least that endeavor had been based on a slim hope. Now his eyes lacked all trace of that emotion.

Jenin protested, "Well, didn't you just say the sooners and aliens were allies against the urs? The star-gods wouldn't turn on the tribe now, would they?"

She stopped as the others looked at her, their expressions answering better than words.

Jenin paled. "Oh."

Moments later, she lifted her chin once more.

"Well, they still don't know we exist, right? So why don't we just *leave*, right now? The four of us. What about *north*, Dwer? You've been up that way before. Let's go!"

Danel kicked some debris left by the urs' riotous flight and the looting that followed. He pointed to a narrow cleft in the rocks. "We can build a pyre over there."

"What are you doing?" Jenin asked, as Dwer led the donkeys where the sage indicated and began unloading their packs.

"I'll set the grenades," Lena said, prying open a container. "We'd best add some wood. I'll gather these broken crates."

"Hey! I asked you guys—what's going *on*?"

Danel took Jenin's arm while Dwer hauled a portion of their supplies to one side—food and clothing plus a few basic implements, none containing any metal. Left behind in a stack were all the books and sophisticated tools they had taken from the Slope.

The sage explained.

"We brought this legacy in order to maintain some minimal semblance of human culture in exile. But four people can't establish a civilization, no matter how many books they have. We must prepare for the likelihood that all of this must be destroyed."

Clearly the prospect gnawed at Ozawa. His face, already haggard, now seemed sliced by pain. Dwer averted his gaze, concentrating on the work at hand, separating only supplies helpful to a small party of fugitives on the run.

Jenin chewed on the news and nodded. "Well, if we must live and raise families without books, I guess that just puts us ahead of schedule, no? A bit farther along the Path of—"

She stopped. Danel was shaking his head.

"No, Jenin. That is not the way things will be.

"Oh, we four might as well try to survive. But even if we *did* make it to some far-off valley, beyond reach of whatever demise the aliens have planned, it's unlikely we'd adapt to a strange ecosystem in time. Rety told us that her band lost half its first generation to accidents and allergic reactions. That's typical for sooner groups, till they learn what's safe to eat or touch. It's a deadly, trial-and-error process. Four just isn't enough."

"I thought—"

"And that leaves out the problem of inbreeding—"

"You can't mean—"

"But even if we could solve all of those dilemmas, it still wouldn't work, because we *aren't* going to start a band of fallen savages, spiraling into ignorance, even if the scrolls give that fate all sorts of fancy names. Human beings never came to Jijo for the Path of Redemption."

Dwer looked up from his work. Lena halted as well, holding a thick tube with a clockwork fuse at one end. Up to that point, Ozawa had been explaining what Dwer already knew. But now silence reigned. No one was going to move or speak until the sage explained.

For a second time, Danel Ozawa sighed deeply.

"The secret is passed on to a few, each generation. But I see no point in concealing it from you three, whom I now think of as kin, as family.

"Some of the other five races were appalled when we built Biblos. The Great Printing seemed to imply we had no intention of ever forgetting. Our founders did some smooth talking to explain the flood of books. A *temporary measure,* they called it. A way to help all races live in enough comfort to concentrate on developing their souls, till we're spiritually ready to move on down the Path.

"Officially, it's the long-term goal of each of the Six. But the *Tabernacle* founders never meant their descendants to devolve down to speechless proto-humans, ready for some race of star-gods to adopt and uplift."

The sage paused until Dwer finally broke in. "Then why *are* we here?"

Danel shrugged. "Everyone knows that each race had ulterior motives. Those forbidden to breed at home sought a place where they can have offspring as they please. Or take the g'Keks, who tell of persecutors, hounding them throughout the star lanes."

"So humans came to Jijo because folks on Earth weren't sure they'd survive?"

Ozawa nodded. "Oh, we'd made a few friends, who helped Earth get a Library branch. And having uplifted two client races, we won low-level patron status. Still, Galactic history doesn't offer much hope for a wolfling race like ours. We already had enemies. The Terragens Council knew Earth would be vulnerable for a long time to come."

"So the *Tabernacle* crew *weren't* outcasts?"

Danel ticked a thin smile. "A cover story, in case the colonists were caught, so the Council could disavow them as renegades. In fact, our ancestors were sent to find a hidden refuge for humankind." The sage raised his hands. "But where? Despite rumors, no route is known *beyond* the Five Galaxies. *Within* them, every star is catalogued, many with lease-holders to watch over 'em. So the Terragens searched the Great Library to see what other races did in our position.

"Despite flaws, the 'sooner' phenomenon showed promise."

Lena shook her head. "There's a lot you're leavin' out. Like what we're supposed to be *doing* here, while hiding, if our mission isn't to go down the Path."

"If Lester or the others know, they haven't told me," Danel answered. "Maybe we're to sit tight and wait for the universe to change. Anyway, that hardly matters now. If our culture's finished, I won't have any part in going on as wretched fragments, whelping kids who will be no more than savage brutes."

Jenin started to speak, but then pressed her lips.

"At least we know Earth *has* survived a few hundred years," Dwer said.

"Though the forayers say there's a crisis," Lena noted. "With Earth in the middle of it."

Danel looked away, his jaw set.

"Hey," Dwer said, "aren't the *sky-humans* exactly what that Terra Council wanted? To have a branch of humans off somewhere safe from whatever happens to Earth? Those guys you met back at the Glade have these Rothen characters to protect them."

Danel exhaled. "Perhaps, though who knows if they'll *remain* human under that influence? The irony of being murdered by cousins seems too much to bear."

The sage shook himself, as if shedding cobwebs.

"Let's prepare that pyre. If these items cannot serve a civilized tribe of exiled Earthlings, then we can at least do our duty by this world and leave no dross. Lena, set the timer to go off one day from now, if we don't return."

"Return?" Lena looked up from her preparations. "I thought we were giving up—"

She rocked back as the sage whirled, with some of the old fire in his eyes.

"Who said anything about giving up! What's the matter with you three? Look at your faces. Are you going to let one little setback get you down?"

A little setback? Dwer wondered, glancing at the blast scars and shattered trees surrounding the urrish encampment. "I don't get it. You said we can't finish our mission."

"So?" Danel Ozawa demanded. "We're adaptable. We'll *switch missions*! We're not colonists anymore—so what?

"We can still be warriors."

Rety

THE PRISONERS LAY DEJECTED IN MUDDY WAL-
lows, necks drooping, already stinking after two days'
confinement in the dank pen. Thirteen urs who would
have preferred the arid plateau where they had settled,
till a warcraft screeched over their camp without warning, casting lightning, driving the survivors toward Jass
and the other hunters, waiting with rough ropes.

Thus Kunn had fulfilled his side of a bargain, ridding
the hills of a recent, hated urrish infestation. In return,
Jass was to guide Kunn to the site where he and Bom
first saw the flying bird-thing. No one knew why the deal
later broke down—why Jass abruptly changed his mind,
preferring the robot's caresses over giving the pilot what
he wanted.

No one except Rety.

*Binni used to say—why defy men, who can beat you
if you make them mad? Use words to nudge and guide
the brutes. Make 'em think it was their idea all along.*

But I kept talking back, didn't I?

*Well, I finally tried it your way, Binni, and know
what? You were right. Nothing I could do to Jass could
ever hurt him like he's hurting himself, right now.*

Bom was guarding the gate to the prisoners' pen. The
burly hunter hurriedly obeyed her command to open
up, not once meeting Rety's eyes. He knew where his
pal was now. Just two things kept Bom from sharing the
same fate. First was his notoriously poor sense of direction. Alone, he could never find the place where he and
Jass had spotted the metal bird.

The other thing was Rety's whim. Bom's abject cringing pleased her more than screams. *This* bully was
scared half out of his breech-clout.

When she glared at the boys spitting at the prisoners,
they jumped off the wall and ran. She cast curt laughter

after them. The tribe-kids never used to speak to her in
the old days, either.

She entered the pen.

Ul-Tahni, leader of the unlucky urs, greeted Rety with
a fluid bow of her long neck. From a gray-fringed snout,
she launched into a series of whistles and clicks, till Rety
broke in.

"None o' that now!" she admonished. "I don't follow
that jabber."

Wincing, Ul-Tahni switched to Anglic.

"I afologize. Your attire deceives the eye into seeing a
Galactic-level entity."

Rety lifted her head. "You weren't dee-seeved. That's
exactly what I am."

I hope, she added inside. Rann and the others could
change their minds before the ship returned, especially
once she gave them all she had in trade. Even if the
forayers kept their word, she *would,* in time, have to
learn all those crazy languages they used among the
stars.

"Again, regret for having offended. Is it true, then? You
have veen adofted off Jijo's forlorn desert into the
running-clan of star creatures? What a fortunate young-
ling you are."

"Yeah," Rety agreed, wondering if the urs was being
sarcastic. "So, yee says you're ready to tell us what your
bunch was doing out here, beyond the Rimmers."

A long sigh blew the gray fringe.

"We arrived, disgracefully, to set uf a colony, freserv-
ing our kind in a secret sanctuary."

Rety grunted. "That much is obvious. But why here?
Why now?"

"It is a site already ascertained to ve havitavle . . .
suitavle for sustaining Earthlings, and therefore the donkeys we rely on. You yourself testified to that fact."

"Ah." Ul-Tahni must have been one of the junior sages
in the pavilion when Rety told her story to the High
Council. "Go on."

"As to our haste—we sought to elude the fate soon to
fall on the Slofe, annihilation at the hands of star-felons."

Rety reacted angrily. "I've heard that damned lie before. They'd *never* do a thing like that!"

Ul-Tahni rocked her head. "I stand corrected. Clearly such fine entities would not slay folk who had done them no hurt, nor cast death without warning from a cloudy sky."

This time the sarcasm was thick. Rety glanced at a young middling urs with a nasty burn along one flank, from the flying robot's heat beam.

"Well, I guess it's just your tough luck we had reason to come visit, asking directions, and found you already at war with my old family."

"Not war. A transient discord. One we did not initiate. Naturally, your cousins were shocked to see us. Our idea was to vanquish their reflex hostility with resolute friendliness. To induce cordiality with gifts and offers of assistance."

"Yeah, right." Rety knew how early human settlers had been treated by urrish clans of yore. "I bet you also counted on having better weapons than any they had here."

Again, a snorted sigh. "As *your* associates crushed *us*, using fower far greater than our own? It kindles wonder—could this chain of uneven strength ve extrafolated?"

Rety didn't like the bemused look in those beady urrish eyes. "What do you mean?"

"A conjecture. Could there exist forces as far suferior to your new lords as they are over us? In all the wide galaxies, can one *ever* be sure one has chosen the right side?"

The words sent twinges up Rety's spine, reminding her of recent disturbing dreams.

"You don't know *nothin'* about galaxies an' such, so don't you pretend—"

At that moment a sudden yelp cut her short, as yee popped his head out of the pouch, mewling with unease. A ripple of reaction spread among the prisoners' husbands, who emerged howling, swinging their heads to face south. Soon the larger females followed suit, clambering to their feet.

Rety worried—was it a revolt? But no, clearly something was unnerving them.

"What d'you hear?" she demanded of yee.

"engine!" the little urs answered, corkscrewing his agile neck.

A moment later Rety sensed it too. A distant whine. She brought a hand to the bump near her ear and pressed.

"Hey, Kunn! What's going on?"

There followed a long pause, during which the open line relayed cabin sounds—switches being thrown, motors revving. Finally, the pilot's voice buzzed near her skull.

"Jass chose to cooperate, so we're off now in search of the source of your metal bird."

"But I want to go too!"

Kunn's reply was cool.

"Jass told me everything, including the reason *he resisted so hard. It seems you convinced him I'd finish him off the moment he told what he knew. That he would live only until then. Now why did you tell the poor bastard such a thing, Rety? It caused inconvenience and unnecessary pain."*

Rety thought—*Unnecessary for you, but darn important to me!* Revenge was only half of her rationale for manipulating Jass. But it would have been enough all by itself.

"Kunn, don't leave me. I'm one of you now. Rann an' Besh, an' even Ro-pol said so!"

Suddenly she felt small and very vulnerable, with urs in front of her and Bom behind at the gate, surrounded by others who would surely love to bring her down. She covered her mouth and lowered her voice, whispering urgently for the little transmitter, "The sooners'll turn on me, Kunn. I know it!"

"Perhaps you should have thought of that before." Another long pause followed. Then—*"If Rann hadn't*

insisted on long-range radio silence, I could talk it over with the others before deciding."

"Deciding what?"

"Whether to bring you back, or to leave you where you began."

Rety fought down a trembling that coursed her body, in response to Kunn's harsh words. Her hopes were a bright tower that seemed about to crash.

"I'll tell you what, I'll leave the robot to protect you, Rety. It will do what you say till I get back. Do not abuse the privilege."

Her heart leaped at the phrase—*till I get back.*

"I promise!" she whispered urgently.

"Treat this as a second chance. Question the urs. Destroy their weapons. Don't let anyone leave the valley. Do a good job and we may wipe the slate clean when I return—providing my hunt flushes out the prey at last.

"Kunn out."

The line clicked, cutting off the cabin sounds. Rety quelled an urge to press the button and choke out another plea to be taken along. Instead she set her teeth grimly and climbed the fence rails to stare as a silvery dart lifted out of the narrow canyon, turned in the morning light, then streaked southward, leaving her with a heart as cold and barren as a glacier.

Dwer

THE SOONER VILLAGE WAS A SIMMERING PLACE that squatted at the base of a canyon filled with dense, sulfurous, listless air.

A hellish place, from an urrish point of view.

Dwer's high vantage point looked down at the captives, in their cramped pen. Long necks drooped, and they lay like the atmosphere, barely moving.

"I count about a dozen, not including dead ones, just as you said," Lena noted, peering through her compact telescope. "I guess you'll do as a tracker, fella-me-boy."

"Thanks, Oh Mistress of Forbidden Devices," Dwer answered. He was getting used to Lena's ways. She always had to get a little *bite* in, even when making a compliment. It was like a noor, purring on your lap, who repays your petting by dipping its claws briefly into your thigh. The funny thing was—he'd actually been getting used to the idea of making a life with this woman, along with Jenin, Danel, and the lost tribe of human exiles. Even discovering the urrish invasion hadn't made the notion absurd. Danel had been right. There *might* have been room for common cause.

But now all such ideas were obsolete. Over to the left lay the reason why—a silver-gray machine, shaped like a hoonish cigar with stubby wings. It was the first alien thing Dwer had seen, since almost being killed with Rety by a floating robot that evening in a mulc-spider's lair.

The sky-car should not be here in the badlands.

It meant the demolishment of all their plans.

It also had no business being so beautiful.

Dwer was proud of this overlook, high on the canyon wall, which surveyed from the village, past the steam pools, all the way to the flying machine, sitting in a nest of crushed vegetation.

"I wish the yokels would stop movin' around. It's hard gettin' a good count," Lena complained. "At least the kid said the local bully-boys won't let women use weapons, so they aren't combatants to worry about."

She sniffed disdain over such a stupid waste of resources.

Dwer would prefer not to fight Jijoan humans, as well as the alien kind. Anyway, their only real chance lay in achieving complete surprise.

Sharing the cramped ledge, Dwer felt Lena's breast pressing against his arm, yet it provoked no arousal. Their bodies seemed to grasp that a change had occurred. There would be no more passionate episodes. No life-affirming gestures. Sex and gender were important to colonists planning to raise families, not to a raiding party bent on destruction. All that mattered now were skills. And an ability to count on one another.

"It looks like a standard atmospheric scout," Danel Ozawa said. "Definitely a fighter. I wish we brought along just *one* text on Galactic technology. Give me the glass, will you?"

Like Dwer's and Lena's, Danel's face now bore jagged, charcoal slashes that were supposed to muddle the pattern-recognizing optics of alien killer machines. Dwer preferred thinking of it as war paint.

"Well, I'll be—" Danel muttered. "Here, take a look. I guess now we know how the star-gods found this place."

When Dwer got the telescope, the first thing he noticed was that the flyer's hatch now lay ajar, revealing part of the interior, including banks of control panels. *If only we were close right now,* he thought. *With the door open and no guard robot in sight . . .*

"Look to the right, up the trail a ways," Danel urged.

Dwer shifted the spyglass, sweeping till he glimpsed a small figure dressed in one of the aliens' one-piece garments, moving toward the sooner encampment.

"Great Ifni's Egg!" he yelped.

"What is it?" Lena demanded, grabbing the scope as Dwer rolled on his back, staring past tangled branches at a murky sky.

"Well, well," Lena muttered. "Looks like she caught up with us, after all."

"I should've strangled her when she stole my bow. I should've left her to the damn spider."

"You don't mean that, son," Danel chided.

Dwer knew the sage was right. Still, he grumbled. "Oh, don't I? She was a pain from the start. Now she's ruined everything."

"Perhaps Rety was coerced." But the sage sounded unconvinced as they took turns with the telescope. Each of them had seen the girl's clothes, her freshly coifed hair, and her confident stride, swaggering into camp like she owned the place.

"She's gone to see the prisoners," Lena reported, a little later. "Talking to one of 'em now. . . . Those urs sure look ragged, poor things." Lena tsked, and her sympathy was clearly more than sarcastic. "I wish I could make out—"

She stopped as Dwer suddenly gripped her arm, reacting to a faint, high keening that seemed to scrape the inside of his skull. The noor beast chuttered irritably, shaking its head and sneezing. Soon the noise deepened and grew loud enough for the rest of them to hear. Even Jenin, who was on lookout duty upslope, hissed a worried query.

The clamor came from the *aircraft*. It made Dwer's teeth feel as if they were loosening in their moorings.

"Something's coming out!" Lena exclaimed, turning the telescope. "It's the robot!"

Dwer saw a hovering black dot with dangling tendrils separate from the ship, whose hatch then closed. The air shimmered from expelled dust as humming motors lifted the scout off the ground. The gray arrowhead was larger than the house Dwer grew up in, yet it *wafted* upward and turned lightly, stopping when its nose pointed almost due south. Then the heavens echoed its fierce growl as it plunged away, receding faster than anything he had ever seen.

"Damn," Danel cursed. "We missed our best opportunity."

Lena wasn't watching the departing scout. Instead, her eyes followed the black robot, now cruising toward the tribal village.

"Don't worry," she assured. "I expect we'll get another chance."

The glavers were back. Of all irksome times for the stupid things to tag along!

They must have followed, at their own lazy pace, all the way from last night's campsite. Now they mewled unhappily at the sights and smells of the fetid ravine, but that did not keep them from following Dwer as he left the shelter of the forest, heading toward the cluster of rude huts.

Dwer glanced back at Lena Strong, crouched at the

edge of the last line of trees. With raised eyebrows, she asked if he wanted her to shoot the idiotic beasts. He said no with a terse headshake. They were dangerous only to a man who was trying to hide. And he did not mind being conspicuous at this point. In fact, that was the general idea.

Still, when he passed a rotting log, he gave it several swift kicks, exposing a rich trove of grubs swarming the interior. The distracted glavers crooned delight and dove in for the kill.

Which left just one irritation, the scampering noor beast, who darted through the meadow grass and between his legs.

Trying to ignore Mudfoot and carrying his bow slung over one shoulder, Dwer walked with feigned nonchalance past a devastation of jagged tree stumps toward the bustling sooner tribe. The prisoners' pen lay a quarter of an arrowflight to the left, the huts to the right. Straight ahead, a cook fire fumed smoke that hovered lazily, as if reluctant to depart.

Come on, people, Dwer mused when he was over halfway across the pocket meadow and still unnoticed. *Don't you have any sort of sentry system?*

He pursed his lips and whistled a tune—"Yankee Doodle," the first thing to come to mind.

Finally, one of the kids peering at the urrish captives glanced his way, did a gaping double take, and began screaming, pointing at Dwer.

Well, whatever works.

Their reaction might have been different as recently as a week ago. For generations these people had seen no outsiders at all. Now, after making contact with an urrish band, then flying aliens and a lost cousin transformed into a goddess, they took his arrival pretty well. Only three out of four ran away, howling in terror. Hesitantly, with goggle-eyes that showed white around the rims, the remainder gathered to stare at him, edging forward in a clump when he showed no sign of aggression.

Dwer motioned for one boy to come forward.

"Yeah, that's right, you! Don't worry, I won't bite."

He squatted down in order to seem less imposing. The boy, a filthy urchin, looked like one for whom *bravado* was as important as life. Dwer knew the type. With others watching, the lad would rather die than let himself show fear. Puffing his chest out, the kid took several steps toward Dwer, glancing back to make sure his courage was being noted.

"What a fine young man," Dwer commented. "And what would your name be?"

The boy looked nonplussed, as if no one had ever asked him that before. Didn't everybody in the world grow up knowing each other's names?

"Well, never mind," Dwer said, aware the throng was growing larger as curiosity overcame dread. "I want you to run an errand for me. If you do, I'll give you something special, understand? Good. Please go to *Rety*. Tell her someone she knows is waiting for her—" Dwer turned and pointed the way he came. "—over there. By the trees. Can you remember that?"

The boy nodded. Already, calculating avarice had replaced fear. "What'll I get?"

Dwer pulled a single arrow from his quiver. It was made by the best fletchers of Ovoom Town, perfectly straight, with a tip of razor-sharp Buyur metal that gleamed in the sunshine. The boy reached out, but Dwer snatched it back.

"*After* you bring Rety."

Their eyes met in brief understanding. With a blasé shrug, the boy swiveled and was gone, squeezing past the crowd, shouting for all he was worth. Dwer stood up, winked at the staring tribesmen, and began sauntering back toward the forest, whistling casually. Glancing back, he saw a good part of the clan following at a distance. So far, so good.

Oh, hell, he cursed when he saw the glavers. *Get out of the way, will you?*

They had finished browsing at the rotten log and now sauntered toward him. Dwer worried—when they saw the villagers, might they panic and bolt toward the prisoners' pen? The female glaver turned one globelike eye toward the approaching crowd. The other eye then followed, a sure sign of concern. She snorted, and her mate reared backward in surprised dismay. They whirled—and fled in exactly the direction Dwer feared!

With a tracker's sense of light and shadow, he noted Jenin Worley crouching by a tree, where the forest came nearest the prison-corral. One of Dwer's objectives had been to attract notice *away* from there.

He had the bow off his shoulder and an arrow drawn when *Mudfoot* suddenly reared out of the tall grass, waving its forepaws in front of the glavers, hissing. The glavers skidded to a halt and reversed course with astonishing spryness, cantering away with the noor yipping close behind.

For some reason the locals found all of this terrifically funny. It didn't seem to matter that they had never seen a noor before. They guffawed, pointing and laughing uproariously at the glavers' distress, clapping as if Dwer had put on a show for their benefit. He turned around, grinning as he reslung the bow. Anything to keep their regard riveted this way.

Abruptly, the crowd fell silent as a shadow fell across Dwer. A low, eerily familiar whine raised shivers up his spine. Shading his eyes against the sun, he looked up toward a hovering black shape, all jutting angles and hanging tendrils, like a certain demon that still haunted his dreams—the fire-spitting monster that had finished off the old mulc-spider of the mountains. Despite a penumbral glare surrounding it like a fierce halo, he made out the same octagonal symmetry. Only this one wore a rounded silhouette, perched on one jutting shoulder.

"So. You made it all the way here, after all," the silhouette commented. "Not bad for a Slopie. You're no fluff-baby, I guess—though the trip seems to've wore you down to a rag man. I seen you look better, Dwer."

"Thanks, Rety," he said, edging aside so the sun would not blind him. He also wanted to get closer to the forest. "You, on the other hand, never looked so good. Been taking it easy?"

She answered with a curt chuckle that sounded husky,

as if she hadn't laughed a lot lately. "I turned down the offer your sages made—to have me hike all the way back here afoot, guiding a bunch o' geeps. Why walk, I figured, when I can ride?"

Now he could make her out clearly. Except for the old scar, she seemed quite *made over,* as they said in certain parts of Tarek Town. Yet the same sullen wariness lay in her eyes.

It was also his first chance to have a good look at an alien machine. Eight even rectangles made up its sides, black without highlights, as if sunshine had trouble glancing off it. Below, a pair of tendril-arms dangled menacingly on either side of a globe that was studded with glass facets and metal tubes. Danel had warned him to watch out for that globe. On top, where Rety sat in a lashed-on saddle, the robot's surface looked flat, except for a spire rising from the center. An "antenna," Danel had identified it.

Dwer nodded toward the hovering machine.

"Seems you've been making new friends, Rety."

The girl laughed again—a sharp bark. "Friends who'll take me places *you* never saw."

He shrugged. "I'm not talking about star-gods, Rety. I mean the friend giving you a ride, right now. Last time I saw one of these things, it was trying to kill us both—"

She cut in. "A lot's changed since, Dwer."

"—and oh, yeah, it was burning the hell out of that *bird* thing you cared so much about. Ah, well. I guess sometimes it just pays better to join those who—"

"Shut up!"

The robot reacted to its rider's anger by bobbing toward him. Retreating, he noted movement by the spherical cluster of lenses and tubes under the machine's blocky torso, turning fluidly to track him. On a hunch, Ozawa had called it a weapons pod, and Dwer's every clawing instinct confirmed the guess.

A crowd gathered beyond Rety, most of the human tribe, watching this confrontation between a ragged stranger and one of their own who had harnessed a flying devil. It must seem a pretty uneven matchup.

Some things are exactly as they seem.

Dwer caught a flash of movement toward the prison-pen. Jenin, making her move.

"Well?" Rety demanded, glaring down at him.

"Well what?"

"*You* sent for me, idiot! Did you hike halfway round the world just to try and make me feel guilty? Why didn't you stay away, once you saw what's going on here?"

"I could ask you the same question, Rety. What are you doing? Showing off for the folks? Getting some payback? Did the star-gods have some special reason to need a guide to this armpit of Jijo?"

Complex emotions crossed her face. What finally won was curt laughter.

"—*armpit?* Heh. That just about tells it all." She chuckled again, then leaned closer. "As for what Kunn is lookin' for, I can't tell ya. It's a secret."

Rety was a lousy bluffer. *You don't have the slightest idea*, Dwer pondered, *and it galls you.*

"So, where's that pack of Slopies you were gonna lead out here?" she demanded.

"In hiding. I came ahead to make sure it's safe."

"Why shouldn't it be? Nothin' dangerous here, except maybe my nasty ol' cousins . . . an' a bunch of smelly hinneys—"

When she said that, a piping whistle, like faint, piccolo laughter, vented from a padded pouch at her waist.

"And killers from outer space?" Dwer added. "Planning to wipe out every thinking being on the planet?"

Rety frowned. "That's a damn lie! They ain't gonna do it. They promised."

"And what if I showed you *proof*?"

Her eyes darted nervously. "More lies. They just wouldn't do nothing like that!"

"Like they wouldn't shoot a poor, unsuspecting bird-thing, I suppose. Or attack those urs without warning."

Rety turned red as Dwer hurried on.

"Come along. I'll show you what I'm talking about."

Before she could refuse, he turned to walk back

toward the forest. "I left it over there, behind that stump."

The girl grumbled but followed on her robot steed. Dwer worried that the machine might be more sophisticated than Ozawa guessed. The reference works the sage had studied were three hundred years out of date and sparse on details. What if the robot both understood speech and could tell he was lying? What if it could read his *thoughts*!

The tree stump was thicker than most. The sooners must have worked hard with their primitive tools to hack it down, when they made this clearing. Dwer bent to pick up two things he had stashed on the far side. One, a slender tube, he slid up his tunic sleeve. The other was a leather-bound book.

"What is it?" Rety demanded, nudging the robot to drop closer. Atop the machine's flat upper surface there protruded short tentacle-things with glossy ends. Three swiveled toward Dwer, while the fourth watched for danger from the rear. So far, Danel Ozawa had been right about the robot's mechanical organs. If these were "eyes," then that narrow spindle jutting up from the robot's center—

"Show me!" Rety demanded, dropping closer still, peering at the small volume, containing about a hundred paper pages, a treasure from Danel's Legacy.

"Oh, it's a book," she muttered with contempt. "You think you can prove anything with *this*? The Rothen-kin have pictures that move, an' talk, an' tell you anythin' you want to know!"

Exactly, Dwer thought. *They can create images to show exactly what you want to see.*

But he answered with a friendly nod. "Oh, sorry, Rety. I forgot, you can't read. Well, open it up, and you'll find this book has pictures, too. I'll explain them, if you like."

This part had been Danel's idea. Back at Gathering, the lesser sage had seen Rety flip through dozens of picture books in apparent fascination—when she felt no one was watching. Dwer was trying to mix insult with encouragement, shame with curiosity, so the girl would have no choice but to look at this one.

Wearing an unhappy grimace, Rety reached down further and accepted the book. She sat up and riffled the paper leaves, clearly puzzled. "I don't get it. What page should I look at?"

The robot's hover-fields brushed Dwer's leg, making all the hairs stand on end. His mouth felt dry, and his heart pounded. He fought a wave of anticipation-weakness by pure force of will.

"Oh, didn't I open it to the right picture? Here, let me show it to you."

As Rety turned toward him, the robot dropped lower. Dwer raised his arms, reaching toward the book, but staggered when he bumped the robot's side.

It was fiery death if the thing thought it was being attacked. Would the machine recognize normal human clumsiness and make allowances?

Nothing happened. The robot didn't fear his touch.

"Hey, watch it," he complained. "Tell your pal here to take it easy, will you?"

"What? It's not any o' *my* doin'." She kicked the machine. "Leave him be, you stupid thing!"

Dwer nodded. "All right, let's try again."

Both hands went up. His legs were like coiled springs—and Dwer's life seemed to float above him like a sound, ready to flee on the wind.

He leaped.

The robot's brief hesitation ended in a sudden yowl, joined instantly by a series of sharp detonations, coming from the nearby forest. *Heat* flared between Dwer's legs as he yanked two of the sensor-heads, using them as hand-holds to swarm desperately up the machine's flank, away from the deadly ball. Pain erupted along one thigh the split instant before he hauled his torso atop the gyrating machine. He clutched the bucking thing with his left hand while his right brought forth the slender tube.

The world was a blur of trees and clouds and whirling sky. More explosions pealed, accompanied by horrible *sizzling* sounds. Desperately, Dwer shoved the tube at the robot's central spindle and squeezed.

Traeki enzymes combined and emerged in an acrid, fizzing stream, vanishing down openings at the spindle's base. Dwer kept squirting despite the robot's wild pirou- ettes, until his aim was spoiled by *Rety,* shoving his arm away. Only then did Dwer note her screams amid the general tumult. When her *teeth* clamped on his wrist, Dwer's own howl joined in. The half-empty tube es- caped his convulsing hand, tumbling away.

Purple steam rose from the robot's center. The spindle began to slump. Dwer shook Rety off and with a reck- less cry threw himself on the drooping antenna, taking it in both hands, heaving with all his might. He shouted an ululation of triumph when the whole thing tore free at the base, though it left him rolling across the flat surface, clutching futilely for a hold.

Flailing, he tumbled off the edge, falling toward the meadow floor.

Dwer never worried, during that brief interval, about striking some rock or jagged tree stump. The machine would likely dice him to bits before he ever hit the ground.

But he was *not* sliced. Nor did he strike the rough meadow. Blinking in surprise, he found that a pair of *arms* had caught him!

Relief was tempered when he saw the arms belonged to the robot.

Oh, great. Out of the frying pan and into the—

There came another series of detonations, and the hovering machine rocked as if slammed along one side. Hanging below the octagonal body, Dwer saw part of the globe underneath explode in a spray of steel and glass. The weapons-ball was already a smoking ruin. Not a single lens or tube appeared intact.

Great work, Lena, Dwer thought, proud of how well she used the terrible devices that only she and a few others on the Slope were trained to use. Firearms that did not use a bit of metal. He turned his head in time to see more brief flares as Lena or Danel fired again from the forest edge. The machine rocked as another exploding shell impacted. This time one of the dangling tentacles holding Dwer shuddered and went limp.

That was definitely Lena's work. *What a clever girl,* he thought, half-dazed from pain. *The sages chose well. I would've been a lucky boy, if things had gone according to—*

He got no chance to finish the thought, as the robot whirled around to flee, zigzagging across the meadow, using his body as a shield between it and danger. Dwer saw Lena rise and take aim with her launcher, then lower it, shaking her head.

"No! Shoot, dammit!" he screamed. "Don't worry about me!"

But the rushing wind of flight carried off his words. Lena dropped her weapon and hurried to a figure lying on the ground nearby, slumped beside a second missile tube. She turned Danel Ozawa over, revealing a red river pouring from his chest.

The robot's next zigging turn spun that poignant scene away. Now Dwer spied terrified villagers cowering beyond a low hill of garbage near the prisoners' pen. So dismayed were they by the battle that they seemed unaware of the group now circling around *behind* them—Jenin Worley and a dozen newly released urs. The former captives held ropes and arbalests. Dwer prayed this part of Danel's plan would turn out all right.

"All or nothing," Ozawa had said. *"Either we live together as civilized beings, or let's end it. End it now—bringing as much harm to our enemy as we can."*

Dwer had time for one benedictory thought, as Rety's cousins grew aware of the reversal taking place behind their backs.

Learn to be wise. . . .

Then the village vanished as the fleeing machine streaked around a bend, whipped through a forest aisle, and plunged almost straight downhill, accelerating.

Rety was still shrieking from her perch, wailing for it to stop. From Dwer's point of view, dangling underneath, the ground seemed to sweep by in a blur. Fighting the buffeting wind, he brought up both arms to grab the base of the tendril wrapped around his torso, holding him horizontal to the rushing terrain. If he tore it loose, the fall might kill him, but anything would be better than this torment.

He tugged with all his might, but the tentacle would not budge. It *flexed* occasionally, yanking him up in time to miss being smashed against some boulder or shrub. Soon they were swooping beside the canyon's central stream, an obstacle course of sudden turns and bitter, stinging spray. Disorientation forced Dwer to close his eyes, moaning.

Faintness took hold, threatening to haul him the rest of the way to unconsciousness.

Come on, he chided. *Now's not the time to give up. If you can't escape, at least check and see if you're bleeding to death!*

Pain helped him concentrate, ignoring the looming vertigo. It came in a nagging medley, from a searing ache in his left thigh, to Rety's teeth-marks that still oozed blood from his right hand, to the chafing rub of the robot's arm, all the way to a series of awful, biting scratches that clawed into his hip, then his abdomen, and finally his chest—as if someone were stabbing him with clusters of sharp needles, working their way up along his battered body.

He opened his eyes—and shrieked at the sight of a gaping mouth, filled with horrible, glistening fangs!

"Oh, Ifni . . ." he moaned. "Oh, God oh God oh God . . ."

Even when he knew the truth about the specter that loomed inches from his face, it didn't help much. At this point, and for a while longer, all Dwer could manage was a frail, thready whimper.

Mudfoot, the noor, yawned a second time, then settled into the narrow space between Dwer's chest and the robot's hard shell. The beast watched the boy—jibbering from one shock over his limit. With a sigh of affectionate scorn, it started chuttering, less to comfort Dwer than for its own simple pleasure, making a sound somewhat like that of a hoon sailor, umbling a song about the joys of travel.

Asx

IF THE COMMONS SURVIVES—IF WE SIX ENDURE into times to come—no doubt it will be called the Battle of the Glade.

It was brief, bloody, and tactically decisive, was it not, my rings?

And strategically futile. An interval of flame and terror that made my/our manicolored bands so very glad/sorrowful that we are traeki.

Sorrowful because these stacks of rings seemed so useless, so helpless to match the frantic pace of other beings whose antic warlike fury drives them so quickly in a crisis. With such speed that waxy imprints cannot form within our core, except duras behind actual events.

Sorrowful that we could not help, except to serve as chroniclers-after-the-fact, bearing testimony to what already took place.

And yet we are also *glad,* are we not, my rings? Glad because the full impact of violence never quite fills our central cavity with a searing steam of dread. Not until the action is already over, leaving the dead like smoky embers, scattered on the ground. That is a blessing, is it not, my rings? To us, horror is seldom an "experience," only a memory.

It was not always so. Not for the beings we once were, when our kind roamed the stars and were a terror on the Five Galaxies. In those days, creatures like us wore bright shining rings. Not only the ones given to us by our patrons, the Poa, but *special* collars, donated by the meddlesome Oailie.

Rings of power. Rings of rapid decisiveness and monumental ego. Had we possessed such rings but moments ago, they might have spurred us to move swiftly, in time to help our friends during the struggle.

But then, if the old tales are true, those same rings might have kept us from having friends in the first place.

Stroke the wax. Trace the images, frozen in fatty drippings.

Images of atrocity and dread.

There lies Bloor, the portraitist, a smoldering ruin, draped over his precious camera.

Nearby, can we trace the slithering path of a dying creature? A symbiont crawling off the face and brow of the dead Rothen named Ro-pol? Revealing in its wake a sharp, angular visage, humanoid, but much *less* so than we had thought. Less charismatic. Less winsomely womanlike than we were led to believe.

If Bloor died for seeing this, are all eyes now accursed?

There, screams Ro-kenn, ordering Rann, the star-human servant, to call back the fierce sky-car from its distant errand, even if it means "breaking" something called "radio silence."

There, screams Ro-kenn once more, ordering his slave-demons, his robots, aloft to—"clear all of these away."

Meaning us. All witnesses to this abrupt revelation. All who know the secret of Bloor's Bane.

Up, up rise the awful instrumentalities, meting out slashing doom. From their bellies lash spears of cold flame, slicing through the stunned host, turning it into a roiling, screaming mob. Four-legged urs bound high into the air, screeching panic. Qheuens cower low, trying to burrow away from rays that carve chitin as easily as flesh. Humans and hoon throw themselves flat on the ground, while poor g'Keks spin their wheels, trying to back away.

We traeki—those left at Gathering after weeks of silent departures—mostly stand where we were, venting multi-fragranced fumes of woe, erupting wet fear-stench as cutting beams slice through popping toruses, spilling rich liquor, setting our stacks afire.

But *look*! Stroke the image layers one more time, my rings. See the darkly clad ones? Those who rush forward *toward* the terror, not away? Our vision spots scry little, even by daylight, for their clothing blurs them in uncanny ways. Nonetheless, we/i trace squat qheuen shapes, running with humans crouched on their backs, and urrish troops sweeping alongside. There comes, as well, a booming noise, a rarely heard sound, that of lethal *hoonish* ire. From their midst, these dim shapes raise strange tubes, even as the soaring demons turn their killing rage upon the newcomers, slashing at them mercilessly.

There is a place . . .

It is here, in our core, where the wax depicts only a *roar*—a flash—an overload of searing afterimages—and then . . .

What followed now lies before us.

Cinders—where the robots fell to sully Jijo's holy soil, shattered and reduced to dross.

Three sky-lords—stunned to find themselves held captive, taken prisoner, stripped of their godlike tools.

A poignant field—strewn with lamented dead. So many dead.

A makeshift infirmary—where even more wounded writhe and grimace, crying diverse plaints of pain.

Here, at last, is something we can do in real time. Perhaps they can use the assistance of an old retired pharmacist.

Is it agreed, my rings?

Wonderful unanimity. It makes easier the unaccustomed haste as i hurry forth to help.

Sara

THE HARD MARCH HAD TAKEN NOTHING FROM the tension between the two rebel groups. UrKachu's painted warriors and Dedinger's dun-clothed hunters eyed each other warily while eating separate meals under an aged canopy of patched and weathered blurcloth, never wandering far from their weapons. Members of each group took turns sleeping after supper, no more than six at a time, while the rest kept watch. Sara found it hard to imagine this alliance lasting a dura longer than it was in both sides' perceived self-interest.

What if fighting broke out? In these close quarters it would be no artful exercise in maneuver and strategy but a roiling tumble of slashing, grappling forms.

She recalled the frontispiece illustration in volume one of *The Urrish-Earthling Wars,* by Hauph-hutau, one of the most popular titles published since the Great Printing. In small type, the great historian acknowledged copying the scene from a *Tabernacle*-era art book, showing the sculpture frieze that once surrounded the Parthenon, in ancient Greece. That famous relief depicted a long row of mighty figures, clenched in mortal combat—naked men brawling with furious monsters, half human and half horse, who reared, kicked, and slashed at their foes in a bitter fight to the death. According to myth, the feud broke out during a festival of peace and concluded with extinction for the centaur race.

Of course, an urs had almost nothing in common with a centaur, beyond having four legs and two arms. Yet the symbolism of the frieze was so eerie, so unnerving, that it became notorious during the age of struggle, helping steel the resolve of both sides. Sara had no wish to see such a bloody scene enacted in front of her.

Of the others taken captive at Uryutta's Oasis, young Jomah was already out like a snuffed candle, curled in his bedroll, fast asleep. The Stranger picked away at his meal of corn mush, frequently putting down his spoon to pluck a series of soft notes from his dulcimer, or else performing the ritual of counting its strings. Numbers, it seemed, were like music to him—a window to what he once had been, more faithful than the knack at sentences, that he had lost.

Kurt, the exploser, doodled on his notepad, occasionally picking up one of the little books he kept so secretively, either in his valise or the inner pocket of his gown. He covered his work whenever any human or urs passed close but seemed not to mind that *Prity* lingered nearby, after bringing his meal. Putting on her best I'm-just-a-dumb-critter act, Prity spent some time pretending to inspect her leg for lice. But soon the little chimp was peering over the exploser's shoulder, rubbing her chin, drawing her lips past her gums, exposing a grin of silent, delighted interest.

Sara had to squelch an urge to laugh out loud. At the same time, she worried.

The Urunthai and desert-men are politely leaving Kurt alone, for now. The habit of deference to explosers runs deep and is hard to break. But they also promised "persuasion" when we reach our destination. Does Kurt really imagine he can keep his work secret then?

He'd be better off throwing his notebooks into the fire.

Sara restrained her own curiosity. Explosers were a mysterious, formidable sect. Frankly, she doubted the wisdom of the Urunthai in messing with them.

"We won't wait till nightfall, vfore setting forth," Ulgor told Sara, passing near her bedroll. "I'd catch uf on sleef, if I were you."

The urrish tinker's unpainted pelt, well-kept mane, and piercing black true-eyes set her apart from her wild cousins. There was no air of antagonism, no anti-human hostility. After all, Ulgor had visited Dolo Village dozens of times, always on friendly terms.

Sara shook her head. "I can see what drives the others. Religion can be a strong motive when you think your descendants' salvation is at stake. But what do *you* get out of all this, Ulgor? I know it can't be profit."

The narrow, conical head split in a triangular grin.

Sara did not need a rewq to know the expression was sardonic.

"Why exclude the overt reason? Earnings. Fersonal gain."

Sara quoted scripture: " 'What use will be all your wealth and goods, two leagues down Redemption's Road?' "

Ulgor breathed a soft whistle of laughter. "Little good at all. On the other hoof, hero status can ve useful in a clan of savages. Ferhafs I will ve one of the great chiefs of the plains, higher in renown than Ur-Chown!"

Ulgor's self-mocking tone dismissed that idea, while encouraging Sara to keep guessing.

Sara suddenly felt tired. "You're right, Ulgor."

"You think so?"

"Indeed I do. It *would* be a good idea to catch up on sleep, while I can."

The tinker stared, twisting her neck a half spiral. "I thought you wanted to know—"

Sara covered a yawn. "Please be assured, Ulgor, that I am very sorry I asked."

With that she turned away to lie down on her bedroll. Prity hurried over to tuck the blanket around Sara, then chuffed at Ulgor, shooing her away. Sara listened to the urbane traitor's hooves pound a nervous retreat, as if burdened by Sara's contempt.

She really was exhausted. Her muscles throbbed from several days' unaccustomed exertion, and her tailbone from jarring contact with the hard leather saddle. And there was an emotional element.

I was given a job to do. Several of them. Now it looks like I won't complete even one.

A low, repetitive thrum pervaded the pavilion, like the synchronous, pulselike snoring of the urs. It was the Stranger, plucking his dulcimer's lowest string, so softly and regularly that no one, not even UrKachu, might find any cause for complaint, creating a lulling rhythm, resembling less a heartbeat than the rise-and-fall cadence of ribcages—both urrish and human—as members of both parties slept.

Ariana figured he'd develop new skills, to compensate for those he lost, she thought. *I guess this musical sensitivity is part of that.*

Just after dawn, while the two radical groups worked to set up camp, the spaceman had played for the urrish males, briefly released from the close confines of their wives' pouches, taking advantage of the break to stretch their legs in the fresh air. A few males kept close watch on maturing larvae, with six short legs and no arms, almost ready to be spilled onto the plains and fend for themselves.

Using two curved mallets to strike the dulcimer strings, the Stranger had accompanied himself as he sang a chain of children's melodies, familiar enough to flow smoothly from undamaged memory. Sara even recognized a few. Among the rest, one seemed especially apropos.

"I had a little husband, no bigger than my thumb,
I put him in a pint pot, and there I bid him drum;
I bought a little handkerchief, to wipe his little nose,
And a pair of little garters, to tie his little hose."

He repeated the verse several times, and soon, under his encouragement, the males were beating time to the song, crooning along. Sara recalled thinking, if he wound up stranded on Jijo and had no future in any other profession, the fellow could certainly find employment in one of those modern Tarek Town day-care centers.

If we still have such luxuries when all this is done.

Prity plopped herself in front of Sara. Sniggering softly, the little chimp flattened a patch of sand and began drawing figures with a stick—mostly convex, parabolalike shapes that climbed, turned over, and fell once more to zero. Prity chuffed and pointed, as if eager to share a joke. But Sara could not concentrate. Fatigue overcame the throbbing of her abused body, drawing her down to helpless slumber.

·   ·   ·

She dreamed of Urchachka—world of grass—its plains whipped endlessly by hot winds, seared by frequent fires, or else swept by scorching rains of glittering volcanic dust. After each scalding episode, the plains seemed strewn with ashy death—yet bright stems always burst forth in prolific flashes, pushing skyward fast enough to be tracked by a patient eye.

On busy Urchachka, water seldom stayed long on the ground. *Life* sucked it up, caching it in buried tuber reservoirs that meshed across whole continents, or else in bulbous, multihued spore-pods, or in the lush grass stems themselves. These, in turn, were browsed by herds of grazing beasts—nervous brutes whose three-pronged horns used to wave threateningly toward danger, till they found themselves tended in great herds, protected by creatures more formidable than any past predator.

In the manner of dreams, Sara dwelled concurrently both within and outside the images. At one level, her mind's eye peered through a forest of waving fronds, feeling wary and fearful, alert to dodge being trampled by the great beasts, or worse, being gobbled by accident in their ever-crunching maws.

Holes in the fecund loam led down to underground warrens—a lightless, crowded realm of sweet roots and frequent violent encounters—a domain that had lately begun to seem all too cramped, confining. The world of light above now appeared paradise by comparison—for those large enough to snake their necks above the tips of wafting grass.

With a slim, detached portion of her mind—the fragment that *knew* she was dreaming—Sara marveled at the power of imagination. A gift allowing her to inflate what little anyone on Jijo knew about Urchachka—from terse entries in a prelanding encyclopedia, plus a few fables passed by urrish storytellers. Tales about days before their fallow breed was discovered on its torrid home world, by a patron race who dropped from the sky to claim that strain of clever herders, guiding them upon the Rising Path. The road of uplift, toward the stars.

The detached part could observe but had no other power over a fantasy like this one. A *color* dream, potent, forceful, and emotional. A fey fantasm, with momentum all its own. A vision of clouded, insentient paranoia.

Darting between bulbous stems, evading the big dumb herbivores, she followed a smell of drifting smoke and came upon the trampled circle surrounding a smoldering pit of ashes, with a crowd of lanky four-legged figures lounging around its rim. She peered cautiously at the Big Ones. Only lately had she recognized them as larger versions of herself, older cousins and aunts, instead of dangerous horrors with flashing hooves and alarming tempers. Now she spied on them, creeping closer, fighting an ever-growing temptation.

An urge to step forward, out of the grass, and announce herself.

She had seen others do so, from time to time. Other small ones like herself, shaking off the dust of their burrows and stretching out their necks. Boldly moving to assert their claim, their birthright to a place by the fire. About a third of those who did so were ignored, then tolerated, accepted, and finally welcomed into the tight web of intermeshing loyalties. The rest did not meet happy ends. There seemed to be a trick of timing involved. A ritual of twisting necks and groveling abasement that varied from group to group.

Then there was *smell*. It was best to approach a band that had a good aroma. One like your own.

Stealing closer, she watched the party of adults, some with pouches that squirmed with lucky males who had found safe refuge from the dangerous world. Dimly, she recalled having once lived in such a place. But now she was much too big.

The adults lay sheltered by tall stems from the beating sun, resting with their long necks curled round upon their backs. Now and then, one of them snorted when her breathing fell briefly out of phase with the others. The third eye—the simple one without lids—kept watch.

Overhead, a swarm of tiny flying things hovered in parasitic avarice, wary for any chance to dive and briefly suck at an exposed lip, or pouch flap, or even a blood-rich eyelid, and get away again before quick hands or jaws snapped. Sara watched as one unlucky bug was snatched before landing. In a fluid motion, the adult popped the buzzing bloodsucker into her mouth, crunching away without bothering to rouse from her slumber.

I don't recall diving insects when I read about the urs homeworld, pondered the detached part of Sara's drowsy mind, *or in any tale of Urchachka.*

Gradually, it dawned on her that she wasn't making it all up. Rather, her unconscious was borrowing from events in the real world. Her eyes were open just a crack, and through the dreamlike diffraction of her inter-laced lashes, she was watching *actual* urs do what she had thought she imagined.

As before, half of the *Urunthai* lay curled on sandy wallows, breathing with uncanny unison under the blur-cloth canopy. Nothing seemed much changed from when she had last gazed at her captors. But then some-thing happened that correlated eerily with her dream—a low, buzzing sound, accompanied by whizzing motion through the air. A small, insectlike object darted from left to right, toward one of the dozing urs. In a flash, the sleeper snatched the hurtling speck out of the air with her gaping, three-jawed mouth, chewing contentedly with both main eyes still closed. The central one, unlid-ded and faceted, retained the glassy dullness of full sleep as the warrior settled back down, snoring heavily.

I've never seen that happen before, Sara pondered. *Are there bugs here in the foothills that attack urs like those on their homeworld?*

Taut, bowstring tension ran up Prity's spine as the little chimp edged backward, pressing against Sara with an elbow. Sara slowly lifted her head to scan the Urunthai. Those awake fondled their arbalests and switched their tails nervously, as if beginning to suspect that something was wrong. Their long necks stretched, waving left all at the same time, then at Dedinger's desert men, and onward to the right. When they turned away again, there came another low twanging buzz, so familiar it almost seemed unnoticeable. Once more, a small shape sped toward a dozing urs. Again, it was snatched from the air and consumed without rousing the sleeper.

Sara followed the arc of that brief flight, backward across the tent to where the *Stranger* sat at his dulcimer, still plucking at the lowest note, creating a steady hypnotic rhythm. The rewq draped over his eyes only partly masked an enigmatic smile.

Sara realized two others were watching the starman—Dedinger and Kurt the Exploser.

Sniffing at the humid air, UrKachu motioned for Ulgor to join her outside. The four painted warriors on duty went back to tending their weapons.

The Stranger bided his time, softly plucking the string. He kept up a slow, soothing cadence until the wary Urunthai guards settled back down. Then, with his left hand, the Stranger touched the side of his head and slipped two fingers under the filmy covering provided by the rewq—reaching *into* the hole in his head, Sara realized, with a touch of nausea. When the fingers emerged, they held a tiny object, a pellet, about the size of one of the message balls used in the Biblos Library. While his right hand plucked the string another time, his left brought the pellet forth, poising it for the next stroke.

He's using the dulcimer as a launcher! Sara realized, watching in fascination.

She noted a slight difference in the sound, a buzzing dissonance as the tiny pill spun through the air toward another sleeping urrish rebel. It missed this time, dropping half a body length short of the target.

Dedinger was in motion, surreptitiously nudging his comrades, using furtive hand signs, telling them quietly to prepare. *He doesn't know what's going on, but he wants to be ready when the pulp hits the screen.*

The tent flap opened, and UrKachu reentered, without Ulgor. The chieftain sauntered over to one of the sleeping Urunthai and prodded her—an action that normally would have a wiry urs on her feet in an instant. But there was no response. The raider kept on snoring.

Alarmed, UrKachu began jabbing, then kicking the sleeping warrior. Others hurried over to help. In moments it grew clear—of eight who had gone down to sleep, all but two were lost in a soporific stupor.

The dulcimer twanged again, and several things happened at once.

UrKachu swiveled angrily and shouted in Anglic—"Stof that infernal racket, now!"

Meanwhile, a tiny object sailed over the dying coals, toward the confused warriors. One of them snapped reflexively, taking it with her jaws. Almost instantly, her nostril flared and her neck stretched to full extension, trembling along its length. The urs began to wobble at the knees.

Sara would not have thought she could react so fast, scrambling backward with Prity, gathering up the blanket-swathed Jomah, hauling the sleeping boy to the rear of the tent. Swift as ghosts, Dedinger's men were already deploying in a crescent, surrounding the Urunthai, with arrows nocked and drawn.

"What's going on?" Jomah asked, rubbing his eyes.

The wobbly urs drifted to one side, fell against another, and collapsed, ribcage heaving slowly, heavily.

"Remain calm," Dedinger announced. "I urge you to lay down your weapons. You are in no condition to fight."

UrKachu stared blankly, dismayed by the sudden reversal of power. Her group *had* outnumbered the humans. But now her remaining followers stood in a cluster, unready, at the Earthlings' mercy. The Urunthai leader growled.

"So, in this (perfidious) treason, the nature of human (so-called) friendship is revealed."

"Yeah." Dedinger laughed, a little smugly. "As if *you* planned things any different, when the chance came. Anyway, there is no cause for panic over this. We'll still keep our side of the bargain, only as *senior* partners, with a few slight changes, such as the destination for tonight's march. Once there, we'll let you send a message—"

He might have meant to sound soothing, but the words only infuriated UrKachu, who cut in with a shrill battle cry, hurling herself toward Dedinger, unsheathed knives flashing.

"No!" screamed the Stranger in an outburst of reflex horror as feathered shafts sprouted from the thorax of the Urunthai leader. "No dammit! dammit! dammit!"

UrKachu's remaining followers followed her example, charging into a hail of arrows. Half were riddled during the first half dura. The survivors leaped among their bipedal foes, slashing and drawing some blood before being dragged down by weight of human numbers.

Finally, with no living Urunthai left on their feet, the panting, wild-eyed desert men began turning their knives on the unconscious ones, those whose drugged stupor never let them take part or defend themselves.

To the Stranger, this was the final straw. Screaming curses, he threw himself on the nearest human, throttling his neck ganglia. The hunter struggled briefly, then sagged with a moan. The star-man leaped at another, hurling streams of epithets.

Sara pushed Jomah toward the tent flap and cried—"Prity, take him to the rocks!"

In the blurry muddle of split instants, she saw three of Dedinger's hunters turn and assail the Stranger. One tumbled away, tossed by some tricky twist of the alien's body, while another found himself suddenly burdened with a new problem—*Sara*—hammering at his ribcage from behind.

If only I listened, when Dwer tried to teach me how to fight.

For a moment things went well. Sara's short-but-burly adversary groaned and turned around, only to catch her knee in the gut. That didn't stop the hard-muscled hunter, but it slowed him, letting Sara get in two more blows. Meanwhile, the Stranger threw his remaining foe aside in a dazed heap and started to turn, coming to her aid—

The avalanche hit then. A tide of male-human wrath that dragged both of them down. Sara struck ground with enough force to knock the breath from her lungs. Someone yanked her arms back and sharp agony made her gasp, wondering if the limbs were about to tear off.

"Don't harm them, boys," Dedinger commanded. "I said ease off!"

Distantly, through a muzzy fog of pain, she heard blows landing as the former sage slapped and hauled his men back from the brink of murderous revenge. Desperately, Sara managed to swing her head around to see the Stranger, pinned down, red-faced, and bleeding from the nose, but well enough to keep up a faint, hoarse stream of inventive profanity. The outpouring was as eloquently expressive, though not quite as fluent as song. Sara worried that shouting and straining so hard might reopen his injuries.

The leader of the human rebels knelt by the Stranger, taking his face in both hands.

"It's too bad you can't understand me, fella. I don't know what you did to the urs, but I truly am grateful. Made a complicated situation simple, is what it did. For that reason, and because your living carcass is still valuable to us, I'll hold back my guys. But if you don't settle down, I may be forced to get unpleasant with your friend here."

With that he nodded pointedly at Sara.

The Stranger glanced at her, too, and somehow seemed to grasp the threat. His stream of scatological curses tapered, and he ceased heaving against the men holding him down. Sara felt relieved that he stopped straining so hard—and strangely moved to be the reason.

"That's better," Dedinger said in the same smooth, reasonable voice he had used before UrKachu's fatal charge. "Now, let's take a look at what you've got hidden in that handy little hole in your head."

The ex-sage began to peel back the Stranger's rewq, revealing the wound from which he had taken the mysterious pellets.

"No!" Sara shouted, despite sharp pain when two men yanked her arms. "You'll give him an infection!"

"Which his star-friends will cure, if they so choose, once we make our exchange," Dedinger answered. "Meanwhile, this stuff he was feeding the urs seems worth looking into. It could prove powerfully handy during the years ahead."

Dedinger had finished pulling back the rewq and was about to insert his hand, when a new voice broke in, whistling a trill-stream of rapid Galactic Two.

"Sara, I (earnestly) urge you to (swiftly) close your eyes!"

She turned her head and glimpsed *Kurt*, the Tarek Town exploser, holding a small brown tube. A burning string dangled from one end, giving off sparks at a furious pace. The exploser cranked his arm back and threw the tube in a high arc, at which point Kurt dove for cover.

Sara squeezed her eyes shut tight as Dedinger began to shout a warning to his men—

A flash like a thousand lightning bolts filled all reality, stabbing through her eyelids. At the same instant, roaring noise shook her like a bird in a ligger's jaws, rolling the mass of sweaty men off, releasing her twisted arms, so that waves of *relief* clashed with agonizing sensory overload.

It was over almost the moment that it happened— except for howling reverberations, rebounding off the stony pillars that now could be seen towering over the shredded tent . . . or perhaps they were shock waves hammering inside her own head. Hurriedly she fled the tangle of screaming men, who clutched their useless eyes. Blinking past purple spots, she made out one other human who could stand and see: Dedinger, who would also have understood Kurt's brief warning. The desert prophet peered ahead while holding forth a gleaming blade of Buyur metal.

He yelled past the bedlam in her ears and charged at Kurt, knocking the old man down before the exploser

could bring a new weapon to bear. Sara recognized a
pistol from pictures in ancient texts.

"So much for exploser neutrality!" Dedinger shouted,
twisting Kurt's arm until the old man groaned and the
weapon fell. "We should have searched you, and tradition be damned."

Overriding pain, Sara tried to spring at the ex-sage,
but he lashed out with savage backhand, knocking her
down amid a swirl of spinning stars. Consciousness wavered. Only gritty resolution let her rise again, turning
on her knees to try one more time.

There came another flash-and-roar, as Dedinger fired
the pistol just past her and then tried awkwardly to cock
for a second shot—before being bowled over by two
hairy forms, hitting him from both sides. Sara somehow
managed to fling herself into the fray, joining Ulgor and
Prity in subduing the former scholar, whose wiry
strength was astonishing for his age.

Fanaticism has rewards, she thought, as they finally
managed to tie Dedinger's hands and feet.

Recovering his weapon, Kurt backed away, taking a
rocky perch where he could watch the moaning remnants of the desert gang, as well as the surviving urs.
Especially Ulgor. The tinker's sudden return might have
been fortuitous, but that would not make him trust her.

A sticky sensation made Sara stare at her hands, trying
to separate red stains from vision-blotches left by Kurt's
stun bomb. The stains had the color and scent of *blood.*

It isn't me—and Ulgor wouldn't bleed this shade of—

It was *Prity* stanching a crimson flow from a deep
gash in her side. Sara took the trembling little chimp into
her arms and fought a sudden fit of weary sobs.

The wrecked tent was a horror scene of dead or deliri-
ous Urunthai and flash-blinded men. The Stranger
seemed in better shape than most, when he finally staggered to his feet. At least he could see well enough to
help Ulgor bind the arms of Dedinger's crew, while
young Jomah returned to hobble the legs of sedated urs.
Still, it soon grew clear that the battered man from the
stars could not hear a blessed sound.

Against every instinct that urged her to be thorough, Sara forced herself to make do with a pressure compress over Prity's wound. It did not seem immediately life-threatening, and someone else might yet be saved by quick action. So with the chimp's grunt of approval, she hurried over to one wheezing quadruped, a young urs thrashing feebly with an arrow through her neck, whose labored breathing made noisy, purple bubbles—

—and who died with a shuddering gasp of despair, before Sara could do a thing to help her.

A_{sx}

BATTLE-ECHOES GOUGED THE LAND, ONLY A FEW short duras ago.

Firebolts lashed from heaven, scourging the Six, laying open flesh, chitin, and bone.

Traekis gushed molten wax across the tortured valley, or else burst aflame, ignited by searing beams.

Oh my rings, what images lay seared throughout our trembling core!

The dead.

The dying.

The prudent ones, who fled.

The rash heroes, who came.

Their blur-cloth tunics are now grimy with mud and grue, no longer quite as slippery to the eye. Young tree farmers and donkey-drivers. Simple keepers of lobster pens. Junior hands on the humblest fishing coracles. Volunteers who never imagined their weekend training might come to this.

Our brave militia, who charged into that maelstrom, that cauldron of slicing rays. Amateurs, soft and unready after generations of peace, who now wince silently, clenching their limbs while horrid wounds are dressed or while life slips away. Bearing agony with the gritty resolve of veterans, their suffering eased by the only balm that soothes.

Victory.

Was it only yesterday, my rings, that we feared for the Commons? Feared that it might fly apart in jealous hatreds fostered by crafty star-devils?

That dread fate may yet come to pass, along with a thousand other terrors. But not today. Right now the arrogant aliens stand captive, staring about in surprise, stripped of their godlike tools, their hellish robots destroyed by the crude fire-tubes of our brave militia.

A day of reckoning may not be far off. It could swoop at any moment from an unforgiving sky.

Yet there is exhilaration. A sense of relief. The time of ambiguity is over. No more subtle games of misdirection and innuendo. No more pretense or intrigue. Ifni's dice have been shaken and cast. Even now they tumble across Jijo's holy ground. When they stop rolling, we will know.

Yes, my second ring. You are right to point this out. Not *everyone* shares a sense of grim elation. Some see in recent events cause for nihilism. A chance to settle old grudges, or to spread lawlessness across the land.

One vocal minority—"Friends of the Rothen"—demands the release of Ro-kenn. They advise throwing ourselves prostrate before his godlike mercy.

Others call for the hostages to be done away with at once.

"The starship may have means to track its lost members," they claim, *"perhaps by brain emanations, or body implants. The sole way to be sure is to grind their bones and sift the dust into a lava pool!"*

These and other testy groups might think differently, if the full truth were told. If only we sages could divulge the plans already set in motion. But secrets are innately unfair. So we hold our peace.

To the folk of the Six, we say only this—

"Go to your homes. See to your lattice screens and blur-webs. Prepare to fight if you can. To hide if you must.

"Be ready to die.

"Above all, keep faith with your neighbors—with the Scrolls—with Jijo.

"And wait."

Now our survivors hurry to pull down pavilions, to pack up valuables, to bear the wounded off on litters. Children of all races spend one sacred midura scouring the Glade for every scrap of dross they can find. Alas, that midura is all we can spare for tradition. There will be no festive mulching ceremony. No gaudy caravan, bearing ribboned crates down to the sea and ships—the most joyous part of any Gathering.

Such a pity.

Anyway, the aliens' ruined station will take generations to haul away, one donkey-back at a time. That task must wait for after the crisis. If any of us remain alive.

The hostages are spirited off. Caravans depart toward plains, forest and sea, like streams of sentient wax, creeping in liquid haste to flee a fire.

The sun retreats, as well. Bitter-bright stars now span that vast domain called The Universe. A realm denied the Six, but where our foes roam at will.

A few of us remain, rooted to this sacred vale, awaiting the starship.

Are we/i in agreement, my rings? To linger near the Holy Egg, resting our base on hard stone, sensing complex patterns vibrate up our fatty core?

Yes, it is far better to rest here than to go twisting up some steep, rocky trail, hauling this old stack toward an illusion of safety.

We shall stay and speak for the Commons, when the great ship lands.

It comes now, roaring out of the west, where the sun lately fled.

A fitting replacement, the ship hovers angrily, erupting a brilliance that puts daylight to shame, scanning the valley floor with rays that sear and scrutinize. Scanning first the ruined station, then the surrounding countryside.

Searching for those it left behind.

XXVII. THE BOOK OF THE SEA

Animals exist in a world of struggle, in which all that matters is one result—continuity of self and the genetic line.

Sapient beings dwell in nests of obligations, to their colleagues, patrons, clients, and ideals. They may choose fealty to a cause, to a godhead or philosophy, or to the civilization that enabled them to avoid living animal lives.

Knots of allegiance cling to us all, even after treading down the Path of Redemption.

Still, children of exile, remember this—

—in the long run, the Universe as a whole owes you nothing.

—The Scroll of Hope

Alvin's Tale

PERHAPS THE SPIDER-THINGS FIND ME AS EERIE AS I find them. Maybe they are trying their best to help. Given the little that I know, it seems best to take an attitude of wait-and-see.

We hoon are good at that. But I can only imagine what poor Huck is going through, if they put her in a cell like this one. A steel room with barely enough room to spin her wheels before hitting a wall, with the ceaseless drone of some weird kind of engine humming in the background. She's got no patience and may have gone quite loco by now.

If Huck's still alive.

She seemed to be, when last I saw her, after our plummet into the Midden's icy depths was stopped by crashing into a sea monster's gaping mouth. I recall seeing Huck sprawled on a metal surface, wheels spinning, kicking feebly with her pusher legs, while the floor and walls shook under a roaring wind that scraped my ears with incredible screeching pressure.

That pressure saved us, driving out the crushing mass of water before we drowned. But at the time, all I could do was scream, wrapping my arms around my head while my back convulsed from the blow I'd taken, escaping from our broken *Wuphon's Dream*.

Vaguely, I was aware of someone else howling. Ur-ronn huddled in a far corner, sliced and torn by slivers of her precious shattered window and further panicked by the drenching wetness.

Looking back, it seemed a miracle she was breathing

at all, after the *Dream* broke up and harsh sea pounded in from all sides. The force of that blow slammed me against the garuwood hull, while my friends spun away, heads over hooves and rims.

I had never before seen an urs try to swim. It's not a pretty sight.

I remember thinking it would be my *last* sight, until that explosive cloud of bubbles poured in from a hundred wall slits, splitting the water with a foaming roar. The bubbles frothed together, merging into that screeching wind, and we survivors flopped onto the splintered wreckage of our beautiful bathy, gasping and gagging into dark, oily puddles.

Of the four of us, only Pincer seemed to come through with any power of movement. I seem to recall him clumsily trying to tend Ur-ronn's wounds, pinning her against a wall with his scarred carapace while fumbling with two claws, pulling shards of glass out of her hide. Ur-ronn wasn't cooperating much. She didn't seem coherent. I couldn't blame her.

Then a door opened, opposite the clamshell mouth that bit through the *Dream.* It was a smaller portal, barely offering clearance for two *demons* to emerge, one at a time.

They were horrible-looking, six-legged beasts, with horizontal bodies longer than a hoon is tall, flaring wide in back and bulging up front with huge, glassy bubble-eyes, black and mysterious. They stamped into the chamber, awkwardly crushing both Uriel's depth gauge and Ur-ronn's compass underfoot, looking like waterbugs, whose spindly appendages met along a tubelike body that glistened and flexed with fleshy suppleness. Smaller limbs, dangling in front, looked like mechanical tools.

All right, I'm describing a lot of stuff I couldn't have seen all that well at the time. It was dark until the spider-things entered, except in the sharp glare of two beams cast from opposite walls. Also, I was half conscious and in shock, so nothing I write can be taken as reliable testimony.

Especially my impressions of what came next.

Waving their own dazzling lanterns, the two shadowy forms began inspecting their catch, first pausing to illuminate and stare at Pincer and Ur-ronn, then poor Huck, wheeling vainly on her side, and finally me. I tried to move and nearly fainted. When I fought to speak or umble, I found my bruised throat sac would not take air.

Funny thing, I could swear the monsters talked to one another while they looked us over, something they never do now, when they enter my cell in teams to tend me. It was an eerie, trilling, and ratcheting kind of speech, totally unlike GalTwo or any other Galactic language that I know. And yet something about it felt familiar. Each time their lights fell on another of us for the fiist time, I swear the beasts sounded *surprised*.

When they reached me, part of my terror was eased by the sudden appearance of *Huphu*. Somewhere in my addled mind, I'd been worried about our mascot. Abruptly, there she was, rearing in front of me, chattering defiance at the towering spider-things.

The creatures rocked back, amazement now so evident that I might have been watching them with perfectly tuned rewq. One of the things crouched down and murmured hurriedly, excitedly, either talking excitedly *about* the little noor or right *at* her. I couldn't tell which.

Can I trust that dreamlike impression? At this point, as they say in some Earthling books, I was fading to vacuum, fast. In retrospect, it seems an illusion.

One thing I *know* I fantasized. Something that comes back now more as notion than memory. Yet the image clings, flickering the same way consciousness flickered, just before dimming out.

Without warning, a final figure crept into view, crawling from under a slab of our poor shattered bathy. Half-flattened and deformed, *Ziz* regathered its conical shape while the two monsters staggered backward, as if they had seen something deadlier than a poison-skenk. One of them swung a gleaming tube at the battered traeki partial and fired a searing bolt that blew a hole in the poor stack's middle ring, flinging it against the wall near Huck.

My overtaxed brain shut down about then. (Or had it done so already?) Yet there *is* just one more vague, dreamlike impression that clings to me right now, like a shadow of a phantom of a ghost of stunned astonishment.

Somebody spoke, while the midget traeki oozed sap across the sodden floor. Not in the trilling whistles the creatures used before. Not in GalSeven or any other civilized tongue—but in Anglic.

"My God—" it said, in tones of disbelief, and it struck me as a human female's voice, with a strange accent I never heard before.

"My God—all these—and a Jophur too!"

XXVIII. THE BOOK OF THE SLOPE

Legends

It is said that we are all descended from unlucky races.

According to many of the tales told by the Six, there is endless war, persecution, suffering, and fanaticism amid the Five Galaxies. But if this really were typical, that civilization could not have lasted even a million years, let alone a billion or more.

If it were typical, places like Jijo would be teeming with countless sooner infestations, not just half a dozen.

If it were typical, worlds like Jijo would have been used up long ago.

Other accounts tell that the vast majority of star-faring races are relatively *calm*. That they manage their interests, raise their clients, and tend their leased worlds with serene attentiveness to good manners and the ancient codes, while trodding the Upward Path toward whatever transcendence awaits them. They see the abrasive antics of zealous, fanatical alliances as tasteless, immature—but why intervene when it is simpler and safer just to keep your head (or heads) down and mind your own business?

Clients lucky enough to be adopted into such moderate clans grow up peaceful and secure, except during those intervals—legendary *Times of Change*—when upheaval overwhelms even the cautious and discreet.

Then it is the hardy that tend to thrive. Those toughened by scrappy interactions in the back alleys of space.

Those alleys claim victims, though. It is said that we Six count among the bleeding refugees who slunk away from lost causes and broken dreams, seeking a place to hide. To heal. To seek another path.

To search in quest of one last chance.

Sara

IT WAS A MUDDLE, ANY WAY YOU LOOKED AT IT.
The stun-bomb had driven the pack animals into
hysterical flight, yanking free of their tethers to run wild
through the maze of stony spires. Someone would have
to go search for them, but only after the wounded were
tended with what skill Sara possessed.

Those humans who were blinded—perhaps tempo-
rarily—needed to be calmed, then fed by hand. Later,
the dead must be dragged to a flat spot where a pyre
could be raised, to sear their corpses down to ineluct-
ble dross—a neat, transportable pile to be gathered and
sent to sea.

There was an added complication. Several dead
Urunthai had been carrying husbands or larvae. Sara
herded together the strongest that crawled out of
pouches—those with any chance of surviving—into a
makeshift pen where the diminutive males took charge
of their offspring, chewing and regurgitating small bits of
meat for the pasty, caterpillarlike, pre-infant urs.

*In tales praising the glory of war, they never talk about
the hard stuff that comes after a battle. Maybe people
wouldn't fight as much if they knew they'd have to clean
up the awful mess.*

Kurt and Jomah finally got her to sit down around
sunset, to eat and rest for a while. By then the day had
dimmed, and the campfire's glow flickered across two
ranks of sullen captives—human and urrish—who
stared at each other, sulky, half-blind, and petulant.
None seemed more melancholy than the former sage,

the scholar-turned-prophet who had argued with Sara so confidently half a day before. Dedinger glared calculatingly at Kurt, who cradled the pistol carefully, never letting any of the prisoners out of his sight.

Before sitting down, Sara first checked Prity's stitches, which still oozed enough to worry her. It had been difficult sewing the wound, with the chimp understandably twitching and with Sara's eyes blurry from the stunbomb. After she had done all she could for her little assistant and friend, Sara looked around for the Stranger. He had been a great help all afternoon, but she had not seen him in over an hour, and it was past time for his medicine.

Kurt said, "He went off thataway"—indicating southward, into the rocks—"to try catching some donkeys. Don't worry. That fellow seems to know how to take care of himself."

Sara quashed her initial reaction—to berate the exploser for letting the star-man head into an unfamiliar wilderness all alone. The alien was a cripple, after all, and might get hurt or lost.

But then, she recalled, he was a strangely *competent* cripple. Clever and skilled in ways that had little to do with words. And for a man with such a peaceful demeanor, he fought very well.

With a shrug, Sara accepted what could not be changed and sat down to partake of the desert warriors' wafer bread and a jug of leathery-tasting water.

"In the morning we must gather wood for a pyre, since we haven't any scavenger toruses for 'proper mulching," she said between mouthfuls, speaking more loudly than normal, because everyone was still rather hard of hearing. At best, it took a shout to carry over the steady ringing in her own ears. "And we should send someone for help."

"I'll go," Jomah volunteered. "I'm the only one who wasn't banged up in the battle. I'm strong an' I've got a compass. Uncle Kurt knows I won't get lost. And I can move real fast."

The senior exploser looked uncomfortable. His

nephew was very young. Still, after a moment's reflection, Kurt nodded. "It makes sense. He can head—"

"Of course *I* an the one to send," Ulgor interrupted, turning from tending the campfire. "I can run faster and farther than the child, and I know these hills well."

Sara choked. "Not a chance! I can't believe we haven't tied you up yet with the others! Let you *go*? So you can hurry off and collect more of your fanatic friends?"

Ulgor turned her narrow head to peer at Sara sideways. "As if those friends are not *already* on their way, dear daughter of Nelo? UrKachu sent envoys ahead, don't forget. Let us suffose that Kurt's nephew could reach the Glade without encountering a ligger, or a fack ot khoovrahs. If he heads north, I guarantee the first folks he encounters will ve UrKachu's allies, hurrying to join us."

Now it was Kurt's turn to interrupt, with a short, hard laugh.

"And who says we're headin' north?"

Both Ulgor and Sara looked at him. "What do you mean? Obviously we have to . . ."

Her voice trailed off as she saw the exploser smile. *Come to think of it, Kurt never explicitly said the Glade was his destination.* She had assumed, quite naturally, that his urgent business lay there. *But he might have planned to leave our group at Crossroads, where the rest of us would turn uphill toward the Egg.*

"Others of my guild have already gone to help the High Sages. But the boy and I have interests in another direction. And while we're on the subject, I suggest you should consider coming along, Sara. For one thing, it's the last direction the Urunthai are likely to look."

It was the longest speech she had ever heard Kurt make, and her mind churned with implications. For instance, why was he saying this *in front* of Ulgor?

Because any determined urs could track a bunch of humans and donkeys over a fresh trail. Obviously, Ulgor has to come along, or else be eliminated.

But then, didn't the same logic require that they murder all the other survivors, too? Kurt surely knew that

Sara would never permit that. Anyway, the problem would not go away simply because they got a couple of days' head start. A good tracker, like Dwer, could hunt them even over a trail that had gone cold.

She started to raise these matters, then stopped, realizing that Kurt could not give a satisfactory answer with the seething outlaws listening nearby.

"You know I can't go," she said at last, shaking her head. "These men and urs will die if left here like this, all trussed up, and we clearly can't release them."

If she had any doubts about that, one look into Dedinger's wrath-filled eyes settled the matter. That cold fury was a problem only a great deal of time and distance would solve. The more the better. "I'll stay and take care of them till their friends arrive," she added. "The Urunthai will probably protect me, since I fought to help save some of them—though they may still keep me prisoner. I may even be able to stop 'em from slaughtering Dedinger's gang.

"But you and Jomah ought to go ahead. Assuming we get some of the donkeys back, you can take Prity and the Stranger along. With tons of luck you might get them somewhere with a pharmacist and a strong militia outfit. I'll follow for several arrowflights and brush away your trail, then I'll use more donkeys to trample a mess of false paths leading out of here."

A soft whistle of grudging respect escaped Ulgor. "You are, indeed, your vrother's sister."

Sara turned and pointed at the elegant tinker. "Of course this means *you* have used up the free time you earned by helping us at the battle's end." She bent to pick up a length of tent rope. "It's time for you to join the others by the fire, neighbor."

Ulgor backed away. *"You and who else plan on enforcing that ruling?"* she asked in defiant GalSix.

Kurt cocked the pistol. "Me and my magic wand, Ulgor. You just stop right there."

Ulgor's long neck slumped in defeat. "Oh, all right," she murmured, disconsolately. "If you're going to ve so insistent. I suffose I can stand it for a little while."

Amid Ulgor's stream of placating words, it took a dura or two for Sara to realize—*she's still backing up!*

Confused by mixed signals, Kurt wavered until Dedinger cried out. "She's *faking,* you fools!"

In a blur, Ulgor whipped around and plunged into the twilight dimness. Kurt fired once—and missed—as the urrish rump vanished amid the rocks. Their last sight of Ulgor was a flourish of twin braided tails. The captive urs lifted their heads from drug-hangover misery to chortle with amused glee. Several *human* captives laughed at the exploser's discomfiture.

"You need more practice with that thing, grandpa," Dedinger observed. "Or else hand it to a guy who *hit* something the one time he tried."

Prity bared her teeth and snarled at the ex-sage, who sarcastically feigned terror, then laughed again.

He spent time around chimps in Biblos, Sara thought, laying a hand on Prity's knee to restrain her. *He should know better.*

Then again, there's no fool like a bright fool.

"Well, that tears it," Kurt muttered to Sara. "It's my fault. I should've listened to you. Tied her up, even though she helped save my life. Now she can lurk out there watching us. Or run and bring her gang before we get far enough away."

Sara shook her head. *Far enough away for what?* Surely Ulgor's escape only hastened the inevitable.

The exploser motioned for her to come closer. When she sat down, Kurt's lips pressed together hard before he finally decided to speak, so softly that her battered ears could barely hear.

"I've been thinkin' lately, Sara . . . it seemed a gift from the Egg to find you traveling with us. A fluke-blessing of Ifni. Your skills could prove quite useful to something . . . a project I'm involved with. I was going to ask you at Crossroads."

"Ask me what?"

"To come south with us"—his voice lowered further still—"to Mount Guenn."

"To Mount—" Sara blurted, standing up.

At Kurt's panicked expression, she sat back down and dropped her voice. "You're kidding, right? You know I have business at the Glade. *Important* business. If the radicals think the Stranger is important enough to kill over, don't you think the *sages* ought to have a chance to look him over and decide what to do? Besides, if the aliens *are* his friends, it's our duty to help him get modern medical—"

Kurt waved a hand. "All quite true. Still, with the path from here to the Glade blocked, and with another task waiting that could be more important—"

Sara stared at the man. Was he crazy as Dedinger? What could possibly be more important?

"—a task one of your colleagues has been working on, down at the place I mentioned, for several weeks now—"

One of my colleagues? Sara blinked. She had seen Bonner and Taine, a few days ago, at Biblos. Plovov was at Gathering. Then who . . . ?

One name came to mind.

Purofsky the astronomer? Down at Mount Guenn? Doing what, in the Egg's name?

"—a task which seems to cry out for your expertise, if I might be so bold."

She shook her head. "That—place—is all the way beyond the Great Swamp, past the desert and the Spectral Flow! Or else you must take the long way around by river and then by sea—"

"We know a shortcut," Kurt put in, absurdly.

"—and just a while ago we were plotting a mad dash just to reach the nearest *village,* as if it were as hopeless as a journey to a moon!"

"I never said it would be easy." Kurt sighed. "Look, all I want to know right now is this. If I *could* convince you it was possible, would you come?"

Sara bit back her initial reply. Kurt had already pulled miracle powers and god-machines out of that satchel of his. Did he also have a magic carpet in there? Or a fabled antigravity sled? Or a gossamer-winged glider to catch the offshore wind and loft them to a distant mountain of fire?

"I can't waste time talking nonsense." She stood up, worried about the Stranger. It was getting dark fast, and though Ulgor had fled to the northwest, there was no guarantee she would not circle around to seek and surprise the man from space. "I'm going to go look—"

A scream interrupted, making her jump. A shrill ululation of surprise and outrage that warbled melodically, almost like a snatch of frantic song, rebounding off the rocks so many times that their bruised ears could not pin down where it came from. Sara's back shivered with empathic terror at the awful sound.

Prity snatched up one of the long urrish knives and stepped closer to the nervous prisoners. Jomah fondled the smallest of the desert hunters' bows, nocking an arrow against the string. Sara flexed her hands, knowing that a weapon should be in them, but the thought of holding one felt obscene. She could not bring herself to do it.

A character flaw, she admitted, a bit dazedly. *One I shouldn't pass on to kids. Not if we're headed into an age of violence and "heroes."*

Tension built as the wail intensified. An eerie howl that seemed one part pain, one part despair, and eight parts humiliation, as if death would be preferable to whatever the screamer was going through. It grew louder and more frenzied with each passing dura, causing the prisoners to crowd together, peering anxiously into the gloom.

Then another sound joined, in basso counterpoint. A rapid, unrhythmic thumping that made the ground tremble like an approaching machine.

Kurt cocked the pistol, holding it in front of him.

Suddenly, a shadow took form at the western fringe of firelight. A monstrous shape, slanted and heavy, protruding forward at a rising angle, leading with an appendage that flailed and thrashed like a cluster of waving arms and legs. Sara gasped and stepped back.

A moment later it resolved itself, and she let out a

shuddering sigh, recognizing *Ulgor* as the protrusion, moaning in distress and shame, held up in the air by the adamant embrace of two armored, pincer-equipped, chitinous arms.

Qheuenish arms. The remaining three out of five stumbled forward clumsily, fighting for balance as the writhing urs fought to break free.

"Resistance is useless," a scratchy but familiar voice whistled from two leg-vents, a voice dry with the same caked dust that fooled Sara at first, into thinking the armor was slate gray. Only near the fire did a hint of the true shade of blue glimmer through.

"Hello f-f-folks," croaked Blade, son of Log Biter of Dolo Dam. "Could anybody s-s-spare a drink of water?"

The night was clear, windy, and extremely cold for this time of year. They nursed their fuel supply for the fire and draped fragments of the shredded tent over huddled groups of captives, to help them retain body heat. Darkness hauled the urs—including a tightly bound Ulgor—down toward sleep, but the human insurgents muttered together under their makeshift shelter, making Sara ponder glumly what they must be scheming. Clearly they had less desire than the surviving members of UrKachu's band to see more Urunthai arrive over the hilltops, tomorrow or the next day. If they sawed or chewed through their bindings in the darkness, what deterrence value would Kurt's pistol hold in the event of a sudden charge?

Granted, many of the men were flash-blinded. And *Blade* was a comfort to have around. Even wheezing dust, and with the softer chitin of a blue, he was an intimidating figure. With him present, Sara and the others might even risk taking turns trying to get some sleep.

If only we knew what's happened to the star-man, she worried.

He'd been gone for several miduras. Even with Loocen now up to shed a wan glow across the countryside, it was all too easy to imagine the poor fellow getting lost out there.

"The gunshot helped lead me to your camp," Blade explained once Sara and Jomah had sponged out his vents and eye circle, using up much of their precious water. "I was becoming rather desperate, unable to follow your trail in the fading light, when I heard the bang. A bit later, there was the reflection of your fire off yonder spire."

Sara looked up. A flicker did seem to dance across the tall stone tower. Perhaps it would guide the Stranger home.

"Imagine my surprise, though, when someone came running forth to greet me!" Blade chuckled out three vents. "Of course, my shock was nothing like *Ulgor*'s when she saw me!"

The qheuen's tale was simple, if valiant. He had waited underwater, back at Uryutta's Oasis, until UrKachu's fast group departed, followed by the slower expedition of captives and booty. Blade spent the time contemplating his options. Should he strike out for Crossroads or some other settlement? Or else try to follow and give help when help might do the most good? Either decision would mean dehydration and pain—not to mention danger. Sara noticed that Blade never mentioned a third option: to wait at the oasis until someone came along. Perhaps it never occurred to him.

"One thing I didn't expect—to find you four *in charge,* having overcome both groups all by yourselves! It appears you never needed rescue, after all."

Jomah laughed from atop Blade's carapace, where he was sponging off the qheuen's scent-slits. The boy hugged his blue cupola. "You saved the day!"

Sara nodded. "You're the biggest hero of all, dear, dear friend."

There seemed no more to say after that. Or else, everyone was too tired for more words. They watched the flames in silence for a while. At one point Sara stared at Loocen, observing the bright, reflected-sunlight twinkle of abandoned Buyur cities, those enduring reminders of the might and glory that once filled this solar system and that would again, someday.

We sooners are like Jijo's dreams, she thought. *Ghost-like wraiths who leave no trace when we are gone. Passing fantasies, while this patch of creation rests and makes ready for the next phase of achievement by some godlike race.*

It was not a comforting contemplation. Sara did not *wish* to be a dream. She wanted what she did and thought in life to matter, if only as contributions to something that grew better with time, through her works, her children, her civilization. Perhaps this desire was rooted in the irreverent upbringing provided by her mother, whose offspring included a famous heretic, a legendary hunter, and a believer in crazy theories about a different kind of redemption for all of the races of the Six.

She thought back to her conversation with Dedinger.

We'll probably never know which of us would have been right, if the Commons had been left alone to go its own way. Too bad. Each of us believes in something that's beautiful, in its own way. At least, a whole lot more beautiful than extinction.

Silence allowed some of the world's natural sounds to grow familiar once again, as residual tintinnations in her ears slowly ebbed.

I should be glad not to be completely deaf or blind at this point—let alone dead. If there's any permanent damage, I'll manage to live with it.

The Stranger set a good example, ever cheerful despite horrific loss of much that had made him who he was. She decided, at times like these, any attitude but gritty stoicism simply made no sense at all.

Of the sounds brought forth by the night, some were recognizable. A floating cadence of sighs that was wind, stroking the nearby prairie and then funneling through the columns of twisted stone. A distant, lowing moan told of a herd of gallaiters. Then came the grumbling rattle of a ligger, warning all others to stay out of its territory, and the keening of some strange bird.

While she listened, the keening changed in pitch,

waxing steadily in volume. Soon she realized, *That's no bird*.

It wasn't long before the sound acquired a throaty power, steadily increasing until it took over possession of the night, pushing all competitors aside. Sara stood up and the bulging tent fragments rippled as others reacted to the rising clamor—a din that soon climaxed as a bawling roar, forcing her hands over her tender ears. Blade's cupola shrank inward, and the captive urs bayed unhappy counterpoint, rocking their long necks back and forth. Pebbles fell from the nearby rocky spires, worrying Sara that the towers might topple under the howling shove of disturbed air.

That sound—I heard it once before.

The sky grew radiant as something *bright* passed into view—decelerating with a series of titanic booms—a glowing, many-studded tube whose heat was palpable, even at a distance of—

Of what? Sara had glimpsed a starship only once before, a far-off glitter from her treehouse window. Beyond that, she had pictures, sketches, and dry, abstract measurements to go on—all useless for comparison, as her mind went numb.

It *must* still be high up in the atmosphere, she realized. Yet it seemed so *big*. . . .

The god-ship passed from roughly southwest to northeast, clearly descending, slowing down for a landing. It took no great ingenuity to guess its destination.

For all its awesome beauty, Sara did not feel anything this time but a sour churn of dread.

Lark

IT WAS HARD TO MAKE OUT MUCH FROM A DIStance. The blaze of light coming from the Glade was so intense, it cast long shadows, even down the forested lanes of a mountainside, many leagues away.

"Now you see what you're up against," Ling told him, standing nearby, watched by a half-dozen wary militiamen. "This won't be anything like taking down a couple of little bodyguard robots."

"Of that I have no doubt," Lark answered, shading his eyes to peer against the glare, as searchlights roved across the crater where the alien station lay in ruins. After two days without sleep, the far-off engines reminded him of a growl of a she-ligger, just returned from a hunt to find her pup mauled and now nursing a killing rage.

"It's still not too late, you know," Ling went on. "If you hand over your zealot rebels—and your High Sages—the Rothen *may* accept individual rather than collective guilt. Punishment doesn't have to be universal."

Lark knew he should get angry. He ought to whirl and decry the hypocrisy of her offer—reminding her of the evidence everyone had seen and felt earlier, proving that her masters planned genocide all along.

Two things stopped him.

First, while everyone now knew the Rothen planned inciting bloody civil war, aimed foremost at the *human* population of Jijo, the details were still unclear.

And the devil lies in the details.

Anyway, Lark was too tired to endure another mental tussle with the young Danik biologist. He turned his head in a neck-twist that mimicked an urrish shrug, and hiss-clicked in GalTwo—

"Have we not (much) better things to do, than to discuss (intensely) absurd notions?"

This brought approving snickers from the guards, accompanying the two of them into hiding. Other groups were escorting Rann and Ro-kenn to separate concealed places, dispersing the hostages as far apart as possible.

Yes, but why did they put me in charge of Ling?

Maybe they figure she'll be too busy constantly fighting with me to plan any escape.

For all he knew, the two of them might be stuck together for a long time to come.

Silence reigned as they watched the mighty starship cruise back and forth, shining its fierce beam onto every corner of the Glade, every place where a pavilion had stood, only miduras before. From a remote mountainside, it was transfixing, hypnotic.

"Sage, we must be going now, it's still not safe."

That was the militia sergeant, a small wiry woman named Shen, with glossy black hair, delicate features, and a deadly compound bow slung over one shoulder. Lark blinked, at first wondering who she was talking to.

Sage—ah, yes.

It would take some getting used to. Lark had always figured his heresy would disqualify him, despite his training and accomplishments.

But only a sage can rule in matters of life or death.

As the group resumed their trek, he could not help glancing at Ling. Though half the time he "wanted to strangle her," that was only a figure of speech. Lark doubted he could ever carry out his duty, if it came to that. Even now, smudged and gaunt from exhaustion, her face was too lovely by far.

A midura or so later, a blaring cry of dismay filled the mountain range, echoing round frosted peaks to assail them from all sides, setting trees quivering. A militia soldier pointed back along the trail to where the starship's artificial glow had just grown impossibly brighter. They all ran to the nearest switchback offering a view southwest and raised their hands to shield their eyes.

"Ifni!" Lark gasped, while guards clutched their crude weapons, or each other's arms, or made futile hand gestures to ward off evil. Every face was white with reflected radiance.

"It . . . can't . . . be . . ." Ling exhaled heavily, sighing each word.

The great Rothen ship still hovered over the Glade—as before, bathed in light.

Only *now* the light blazed down upon it from *above*—cast by a new entity.

Another ship.

A much, much bigger ship, like a grown urs towering over one of her larvae.

Uh . . . went Lark's mind as he stared, struggling to adjust to the change in scale. But all he could come up with was a blaspheming thought.

The new monster was huge enough to have *laid* the Holy Egg and still have room inside for more.

Trapped underneath the behemoth, the Rothen craft gave a grinding noise and trembled, as if straining to escape, or even to move. But the light pouring down on it now seemed to take on qualities of physical substance, like a solid shaft, pressing it ever lower toward the ground. A *golden* color flowed around the smaller starcraft as it scraped hard against Jijo's soil. The dense lambency coated and surrounded it, congealing like a glowing cone, hardening as it cooled.

Like wax, Lark thought, numbly. Then he turned with the others and ran through the forest night for as long and as hard as his body could bear it.

Asx

WHAT IS THIS, MY RINGS? THIS SHIVERING SENSATION, coursing through our stack?

It feels like dread familiarity.

Or a familiar dread.

Amid this horrible glare, we stand rooted in the festival glade with the Rothen ship grounded nearby, encased in a bubble of frozen time, with leaves and twigs caught motionless, mid-whirl, next to its gold-sealed hull.

And above, this new power. This new titan.

The searing lights dim. Humming an overpowering song, the monstrous vessel descends, crushing every remaining tree on the south side of the valley, shoving a new bed for the river, filling the sky like a mountain.

Can you feel it, my rings?

Can you feel the premonition that throbs our core with acid vapors?

Along the vast flank of the starship, a hatch opens, large enough to swallow a small village.

Against the lighted interior, silhouettes enter view.

Tapered cones. Stacks of rings.

Frightful kinfolk we had hoped never to see again.

Sara

THE STRANGER HURRIED INTO CAMP A WHILE AF-ter the second ship passed overhead. By then, Sara had recovered enough to bring her mind back down to matters close at hand.

Matters she could do something about.

The star-man came from the south, herding a half-dozen weary donkeys. He seemed excited, feverish with need to tell of something. His mouth opened and closed, gabbling incoherently, as if trying to force words by sheer will.

Sara felt his forehead and checked his eyes.

"I know," she said, trying to calm his overwrought nerves. "We saw it too. A huge damn thing, bigger than Dolo Lake. I wish you could tell us whether it was *your* ship, or someone you don't like much."

In fact, she wasn't even sure the man could hear her voice, let alone follow her meaning. He had been closer to the stun-grenade and less prepared.

Nevertheless, something seemed strange about his excitement. He did not point at the sky, as she would have expected, nor to the north, where the two ships were last seen descending, one after the other. Instead, he gestured *southward,* in the direction he had just come.

The Stranger's gaze met hers, and he shuddered. His brow furrowed in concentration as he took several deep breaths. Then, with a light suddenly in his eyes, he sang,

> *"Blacks and bays, dapples and grays,*
> *Coach and six white horses,*
> *Hush-a-bye, don't you cry,*
> *Go to sleepy, little baby."*

His voice was raspy and Sara saw tears. Still, he went on, triggering verses that he knew by heart—that lay ready, even after many decades, creased in undamaged folds of his brain.

> *"When you wake,*
> *you shall have cake,*
> *and all the pretty*
> *little horses."*

Sara nodded, trying to sift meaning out of the lullaby. "All the pretty litt—oh, Ifni!"

She whirled to face the explosers.

"He's seen more urs! They're here already, swinging south to take us from behind!"

Kurt blinked a couple of times, then began to open his mouth—but was cut off by a fluting whistle of jubilation from the prisoners.

Ulgor stretched her neck toward them. "I *told* you our allies would not take long arriving. Now cut these cords so I can intercede, and fersuade our Urunthai friends not to treat you too badly."

"Sara," Kurt said, taking her elbow. But she shrugged him off. There was no time to spare.

"Kurt, you take Jomah, Prity, and the Stranger into the rocks. The Urunthai can't follow well in rough terrain. You might reach high ground if Blade and I stall them. Try to find a cave or something. Go!"

She swiveled to face the blue qheuen. "Are you ready, Blade?"

"I am, Sara!" The blue clacked two fierce pincers and stepped forward, as if prepared to fight the Battle of Znunir Trading Post all over again.

More laughter made her turn around. This time it was *Dedinger*. The former sage chortled amusement.

"Oh, don't mind me, sister. Your plan sounds delightful. It'll save my life and those of my men. So by all means, Kurt, do as she says! Head for the rocks. Go!"

Sara quickly saw what Dedinger meant. If Urunthai reinforcements found they could not follow the fugitives through a boulder field, or down some narrow grotto, or up a garu tree, that could force them to renew their broken alliance with the band of human radicals, forgoing vengeance—at least for as long as it took the desert trappers to hunt Kurt and the others down.

She sagged, seeing the futility of it all.

We've been through so much, only to come right back where we started.

"Sara—" Kurt said again. Then the old man stopped what he had been about to say and cocked his head. "Listen."

The clearing went silent. Moments later, she heard it too—the approaching clatter of rushing hooves. A great many of them. She could feel their rumbling haste through the soles of her feet.

Too late to come up with another plan. Too late for anything but dignity.

She took the Stranger's arm. "Sorry I didn't catch on when you first tried to warn us," she said, brushing the worst streaks of dust off of his clothes and straightening his collar. If he was to be their prize, he should at least look the part of a valuable hostage, not some ragamuffin drifter. He repaid her with a tentative smile. Together, they turned south, to face the onrushing cavalry.

The newcomers swelled out of the darkness, from between giant pillars of stone. *They're urs, all right,* she thought. Burly, powerful and well-armed they spilled into the clearing in a disciplined skirmish pattern, taking positions on all sides, brandishing their arbalests, scanning for danger signs. Sara was startled, and a bit insulted, when the vanguard simply ignored the standing humans and Blade, finding them no threat at all.

More surprisingly, they paid little more heed to the trussed-up prisoners, leaving them right where they were.

Sara noticed that the war paint of the new arrivals was unlike that of UrKachu's band—more restrained, dabbed in smoother, more flowing lines. Could that mean they weren't Urunthai, after all?

From the dismayed look on Ulgor's face, Sara realized this was not the band of "friends" the tinker was expecting. She nursed a slim reed of hope. Could they be militia? They wore no formal brassards or tunics, nor did they *act* like the typical urrish militia unit—local herdsmen who drilled for fun every eighth day, when the weather was good.

Who are *these guys?*

Skirmishers whistled that the area was clear. Then a senior matron with a gray-fringed muzzle sauntered into the firelight. She approached the Dolo Villagers and lowered her neck, respectfully.

"We regret our tardiness, friends. It is sad you were inconvenienced, vut we are glad to see you overcane your trouvles, without helf."

Sara stared as Kurt touched noses with the aged urs. "You're not late if you arrive in the nick of time, Ulashtu. I knew you'd scent our affliction and come for us. . . ."

At that point, Sara lost track of the conversation. For the Stranger pulled her about, squeezing her arm tight while a nervous, excited quaver throbbed along his skin.

More figures were approaching out of the darkness.

Perplexing shapes.

At first she thought it was another party of urs, outfitted for war. Very *large* urs, with strange, stiff necks and an odd way of moving. For an instant she recalled the ancient illustration that once rimmed the Parthenon—the one depicting savage, mythical *centaurs*.

A moment later, she sighed.

Silly thing. It's only men riding donkeys. Ifni! This darkness would make anything ordinary seem mysterious, especially after all we've been thr—

She blinked and stared again.

They were *big* donkeys. The human riders' feet did not drag but perched high off the ground, astride great torsos that seemed to pulsate with raw animal power.

"It's them!" Jomah cried. "They're real! They weren't all killed off, after all!"

To Sara it felt like witnessing dragons, or dinosaurs, or stag-griffins come alive off the pages of a storybook. A dream made real—or a nightmare to some. The Urunthai prisoners let out a howl of anger and despair when they realized what was stepping into the firelight. This meant their one great achievement—their league's sole claim to fame—was in fact a failure. A farce.

The riders dismounted, and Sara realized they were all women. She also saw that several more of the great beasts followed behind, bearing saddles but otherwise unburdened.

No, she thought, realizing what was about to be asked of her. *They can't seriously expect me to climb onto one of those things!*

The nearest beast snorted as the Stranger reached up to stroke its mammoth head. The creature easily outmassed four or five urs, with jaws big enough to swallow a person's arm, whole. Yet, the man from space pressed his cheek against its great neck.

With tears in his eyes, he sang again.

> *"When you wake,*
> *you shall have cake,*
> *and all the pretty*
> *little horses."*

Epilogue

It is a strange universe.

He ponders this without putting it in words. It's easier that way.

Lately, he has found quite a few means to express ideas without the swarm of busy, smacking, humming, clattering noises that used to run through all his thoughts.

Music and song. Numbers. Pencil sketches. Feelings. And the strange colors cast by those funny living-visors people sometimes wear on this world.

Rewq.

He can think the name of the beasts and is proud of the accomplishment.

As he slowly gets better, he finds he can contemplate important names more clearly.

Sara, Jomah, Prity . . .

And some other words, occasionally two or three at a time.

Memory, too, is becoming more clarified. He can recall the scoutship, for instance, blasted as he tried a futile diversion, attempting to draw a hunter ship away from its prey.

He failed, taking a jolting series of blows, and there had followed a period that was still a blur to him, a vague impression of rapid movement and change . . . after which he found himself plummeting, on fire, crashing—

No, no. Think of something else.

Riding. That was a much nicer thing to muse upon.

Riding a saddled animal. A spirited *horse*. The heady, surprising joy of it, with cool wind in his face, bringing a thousand amazing smells.

How strange to find so many things to like about this new world! About a life robbed of the one thing that makes most humans *human*. A command of words.

And now he remembers. Something very much like this injury of his happened *before*. To a friend.

To his captain.

An image swirls through his mind. A handsome, sleek-gray figure. Flukes thrashing through water filled with tiny bubbles. A narrow, bottle-shaped jaw, filled with pointy, grinning teeth. A brain, wounded, but still profoundly wise.

Silently, he mouths three syllables.

Crei . . . dei . . . ki . . .

And all at once this triggers *more* memories. More friends. A ship. A mission. A need.

An image of watery depths. So deep and black that no light could ever penetrate—a hiding place, but no sanctuary. In all the vast cosmos, there is no sanctuary.

But now, as if released from the prison of his illness, one more thing swarms through his mind, surprising him with sudden recognition.

A name.

My . . . name.

Slippery from pent-up frustration, it shoots out from wherever it had lain, dammed up for so long. Caroming back and forth, it finally settles down within reach.

It ought never have gone away. It should be the most familiar word in a person's life, yet only now does it return, as if to say "welcome back."

Riding through a night washed with exotic moonlight, surrounded by curious beings and a culture unlike any he had ever known, he now laughs aloud, ecstatic to be able to do this simple thing. This one, cherished act.

My . . . name . . . is . . . Emerson.

The End of Part One

Acknowledgments

For those familiar with my other work, this volume may seem a departure from my normal custom of trying to write novels that stand on their own. That was my intention this time, but the story kept growing, evolving beyond even the length of huge tomes like *Earth* and *Glory Season,* leaving me no alternative but to "go the trilogy route." There is no shame in the practice—trilogies have their own lavish, wide-screen, Technicolor attraction. But in future I trust that I'll plan better.

I hope to bring out volumes two and three promptly.

I'd like to thank the following people for helping with their comments and criticism to make this complicated story work, among them Gregory Benford, Anita Everson, Joy Crisp, Mark James, Dr. Bruce Miller, Jim Richards, Prof. Jim Moore, and Dr. Steinn Sigurdsson. Also, my gratitude to members of SPECTRE, the Caltech science fiction club: Aaron Petty, Teresa Moore, Dustin Laurence, Damien Sullivan, Micah Altman, John Langford, Eric Schell, Robin Hanson, Grant Swenson, Ruben Krasnopolsky, and Anita Gould. Special thanks are due Stefan Jones and Kevin Lenagh for helping enhance and embellish my poor efforts. My deep appreciation also goes to Jennifer Hershey, Ralph Vicinanza, and Cheryl Brigham, for their dedication and wisdom.

David Brin, March 1995

In Memory of Dr. James Neale,
Kiwi third-baseman,
healer and friend.

KEVIN LENAGH

Turn the page for a special preview of
INFINITY'S SHORE
by David Brin

David Brin's magnificent new Uplift trilogy continues in his latest hardcover novel, *Infinity's Shore*. Brin masterfully returns us to Jijo, where multiple sapient species share the same planetary home. But Jijo faces a dire threat to the existing order, glimpsed in this early scene from the novel—which also displays the vaulting imagination that has earned David Brin the highest accolades of the science fiction field. **Don't miss *INFINITY'S SHORE,* on sale in hardcover in November 1996 from Bantam Spectra Books.**

STREAKERS

Kaa

Gleaming missiles struck the water all around him, especially whenever he surfaced to breathe. The spears were crude weapons—hollow wooden shafts tipped with slivers of volcanic glass—but when one of the keen-edged harpoons grazed his flank, Kaa lost half his air in a reflexive cry of agony. The harbor—now a cramped, exitless trap—reverberated with echoes of his sonar moan.

The hoonish sailors seemed to have no trouble moving around by torchlight, rowing their coracles back and forth, executing their captains' orders. Each shout from a bulging throat sac made the water's tense skin hum like a beaten drum as the snare tightened around Kaa. Already, a barrier of porous netting blocked the narrow harbor mouth.

Worse, the natives had reinforcements. Skittering sounds announced the arrival of clawed feet, scampering down the rocky shore south of town. Chitinous forms plunged underwater, reminding Kaa of some horror movie about giant crabs. *Red qheuens,* he realized, as these new allies helped the hoon sailors close off another haven, the water's depths.

Ifni! What did Kuki and Mopol do to make the locals so mad at the mere sight of a dolphin in their bay? How did they get these people so angry they want to kill me on sight?

Kaa still had some tricks. Time and again he misled the hoons, making feints, pretending sluggishness, drawing the noose together prematurely, then slipping beneath a gap in their lines, dodging a hail of javelins.

My ancestors had practice doing this. Humans taught us lessons, long before they switched from spears to scalpels.

Yet, he could not help but note, this was a contest the

cetacean could not win. The best he could hope for was a drawn-out tie.

Diving under one hoonish coracle, Kaa impulsively spread his jaws and snatched the rower's oar in his teeth, yanking it like the tentacle of some demon-octopus. The impact jarred his mouth and tender gums, but he added force with a powerful thrust of his tail flukes.

The oarsman made a mistake by holding on—even a hoon could not match Kaa strength to strength. A bellow of surprise met a resounding splash as the mariner struck saltwater far from the boat. Kaa released the oar and kicked away rapidly. That act would not endear him to the hoon. On the other hand, what was there left to lose? Kaa had quite given up on his mission—to make contact with the Commons of Six Races. All that remained was fighting for survival.

I should have listened to my heart.

I should have gone after Peepoe, instead.

The decision still bothered Kaa with nagging pangs of guilt. How could he obey Gillian Baskin's orders—no matter how urgent—instead of striking off across the dark sea, chasing after the thugs who had kidnapped his mate and love?

What did duty matter—or even his oath to Terra—compared to that?

After Gillian signed off, Kaa had listened as the sun set, picking out distant echoes of the fast-receding speed sled, still faintly audible to the northwest. Sound carried far in Jijo's ocean, without the myriad engine sounds that made Earth's seas a cacophony.

The sled was already so far away—at least a hundred klicks by now—it would seem forlorn to follow.

But so what? So the odds were impossible? That never mattered to the heroes one found in storybooks and holosims! No audience ever cheered a champion who let mere impossibility stand in the way.

Maybe that was what had swayed Kaa, in an agonized moment. The fact that it was such a cliché. *All* the movie heroes—whether human or dolphin—would routinely forsake comrades, country, and honor for the sake of love . . . every romantic tale urged him to do it.

But even if I succeeded, against all the odds, what would Peepoe say after I rescued her?

She'd call me a fool and a traitor, and never respect me again.

So it was that Kaa found himself entering Port Wuphon as ordered, long after nightfall, with all the wooden sailboats shrouded beneath camouflage webbing that blurred their outlines into cryptic hummocks. Still hating himself for his decision, he had approached the nearest wharf, where two watchmen lounged on what looked like walking staffs, beside a pair of yawning noor. By starlight, Kaa had reared up on his churning flukes to begin reciting his memorized speech of greeting . . . and barely escaped being skewered for his trouble. Whirling back into the bay, he dodged razor-tipped staves that missed by centimeters.

"Wait-t-t!" he had cried, emerging on the other side of the wharf. *"You're make-king a terrible mistake! I bring news from your own lossssst ch-ch-children! F-from Alvi—"*

He barely escaped a second time. The hoon guards weren't listening. Darkness barely saved Kaa as growing numbers of missiles were hurled his way.

His big mistake was trying a third time to communicate. When that final effort failed, Kaa tried to depart . . . only to realize belatedly that the door was shut. The harbor mouth was closed, trapping him in a tightening noose.

So much for my skill at diplomacy, he pondered, while skirting silently across the bottom muck . . . only to swerve when his sonar brushed armored forms ahead, approaching with scalloped claws spread wide.

Add that to my other failures . . . as a spy, as an officer . . . Mopol and Kuki would never have antagonized the locals so, with senseless pranks and mischief, if he had led them properly.

. . . and as a lover . . .

In fact, Kaa knew just one thing he was good at. And at this rate, he'd never get another chance to ply his trade.

A strange thrashing sound came from just ahead, toward the bottom of the bay. He nearly swung around again, dodging it to seek some other place, dreading the time when bursting lungs would force him back to the surface. . . .

But there was something peculiar about the sound. A softness. A resigned, *melodious* sadness that seemed to fill the water. Curiosity overcame Kaa as he zigzagged, casting sonar clicks through the murk to perceive—

A hoon!

But what was one of them doing down here?

Kaa nosed forward, ignoring the growing staleness of his air supply, until he made out a tall biped amid clouds of churned-up mud. Diffracted echoes confirmed his unbelieving eyes. The creature was *undressing*, carefully removing articles of clothing, tying them together in a string.

Kaa guessed it was a female, from the fact that it was a bit smaller and had only a modest throat sac.

Is it the one I pulled overboard? But why doesn't she swim back to the boat? I assumed . . .

Kaa was struck by a wave of image-rupture alienation—a sensation all too familiar to Earthlings since contact—when some concept that had seemed familiar abruptly made no sense anymore.

Hoons can't swim!

The journal of Alvin Hph-wayuo never mentioned this. In fact, Alvin had implied that his people passionately loved their boats and the sea. Nor were they cavalier about their lives, but mourned the loss of loved ones even more deeply than a human or a dolphin would. Kaa suddenly knew he'd been fooled by Alvin's writings, sounding so much like an Earth kid, never mentioning things that he simply assumed.

Aliens. Who can figure?

He stared as the hoon tied the string of clothes around her left wrist and held the other end to her mouth, calmly exhaling her last air, inflating a balloonlike fold of cloth. It floated upward, no more than two meters, stopping far short of the surface.

She's not signaling for help, he fathomed as the hoon sat down in the mud, humming a dirge. *She's making sure they can drag the bottom and retrieve her body.* Kaa had read Alvin's account of death rituals the locals took quite seriously.

By now his own lungs burned fiercely. Kaa deeply regretted that the breather unit on his harness unit had burned out after Kuki shot him.

He heard the qheuens approaching from behind, clacking their claws, but Kaa sensed a hole in their line, confident he could streak past, just out of reach. He tried to turn . . . to seize the brief opportunity.

Oh hell, he sighed, and kicked the other way, aiming for the dying hoon.

It took some time to get her to the surface, where her entire body shook with harsh, quivering gasps. Water jetted from nostril-orifices at same time as air poured in through her mouth, a neat trick that Kaa kind of envied.

He pushed her close enough to throw one arm over a drifting oar for support, then he whirled around to peer across the bay, ready to duck the sudden rush of a horrid spear.

None came. In fact, there seemed a curious absence of boats nearby. Kaa dropped his head down to cast suspicious sonar beams through his arched brow—and confirmed that all the coracles had backed off some distance.

A moon had risen. The big one. Loocen. He could make out silhouettes now . . . hoons standing up in their row-boats, all of them turned to face toward the north . . . or maybe northwest. The males had their sacs distended, and a steady thrumming filled the air. They seemed oblivious to the sudden reappearance of one of their kind from a brush with drowning.

I'd have thought they'd be all over this area, dropping weighted ropes, trying to rescue her. It was another example of alien thinking, despite all the Terran books these hoons had read.

Kaa was left with the task of shoving her with the tip of his rostrum, a creepy feeling coursing his spine as he pushed the bedraggled survivor toward one of the docks.

More villagers stood along the wharf, their torches flickering under gusts of stiffening wind. They seemed to be watching . . . or listening . . . to something.

A dolphin can both see and hear things happening above the water's surface, but not as well as those who live exclusively in that dry realm. With his senses still in an uproar, Kaa could discern little in the direction they faced. Just the hulking outline of a mountain . . . wearing a flickering star near its highest point. A star that *throbbed,* flashing on and off to a staccato rhythm.

Kaa could not make anything of it at first . . . though the cadence seemed reminiscent of Galactic Two.

"Ex-x-xcuse me—" he began, trying to take advantage of the inactivity. Whatever else was happening, this seemed a good chance to get a word in edgewise. "I'm a dolphin . . . cousin to humansss. . . . I've been sssent with-th a message for Uriel the—"

The crowd suddenly erupted in a moan of emotion that made Kaa's sound-sensitive jaw throb. He made out snatches of individual speech.

"Rockets!" One onlooker sighed in Anglic. "The sages created rockets!"

Another spoke GalSeven in tones of wonder. *"One small enemy spaceship destroyed . . . and now the big one is targeted!"*

Kaa blinked, transfixed by the villagers' tension.

Rockets? Did I hear right? But—

Another cry escaped the crowd.

"They plummet!" someone cried. "They strike!"

Abruptly, the mountain-perched star paused in its twinkling bulletin. All sound seemed to vanish with it. The hoons stood in dead silence. Even the oily water of the bay was hushed, lapping softly against the wharf.

The flashing resumed, and there came from the crowd a moan of shaken disappointment.

"It survives, exists, the mother-battleship continues," went the mutter of a traeki somewhere in the crowd, reciting in GalTwo.

"Our best effort has failed.

"And now comes punishment."

SOONERS

Blade

". . . the most effective warheads were the ones tipped with toporgic capsules, filled with traeki formula type sixteen an' powdered Buyur metal. Kindle beetles were useful in settin' off the solid rocket cores. A lot of the ones that didn't use beetles either fizzled or blew up on their launch pads. . . ."

Blade listened to the young human recite her report to an urrish telegraph operator, whose rapid key strokes became fast-departing beams of light. Jeni Shen winced as a pharmacist applied unguents to her singed skin. Her face was soot-covered and the left side of her jerkin still gave off smoldering fumes. Jeni's voice was dry as slate and it must have been painful for her to speak, but the recitation continued, nonstop, as if she feared this mountaintop semaphore station might be the first target of any Jophur retaliation.

". . . Observers report that the best targeting happened in rockets that had message ball critters aboard. Usin' 'em that was just a whim of Phwhoon-dau's, so there weren't many. But it seemed to work. Before he was killed, Lester said we should all re-examine all the Buyur critters we know about, in case they have other uses . . ."

The stone hut was crowded. The missile assault, and the subsequent fires, had sent refugees pouring through the passes. A wave of sophonts Blade had to wade through in order to reach the militia outpost where he might make a report of his adventure.

Only the semaphore was already tied up with frenzied news—about the successful downing of the last Jophur corvette, for instance . . . and then the failure of a single rocket to dent the mother ship, even slightly. The night of soaring hopes crashed even further when casualties became known, including at least one of the High Sages of the Six. Yet, a low level of elation continued. Bad news, after all, was only to be expected. Even a taste of victory, however, came amplified by a resonance of sheer surprise.

Blade recalled vividly the fiery plummet of both burning halves of the ruined starship, setting off firestorms. *I'm glad it only landed in boo,* he thought. According to the Scrolls, all of Jijo's varied ecosystems weren't equal. Greatboo was a trashy alien invader—like the Six themselves. The planet was not badly wounded by tonight's conflagration.

Me neither, Blade added, wincing as a g'Kek medico tried to set one of his broken legs.

"Just cut it off," he told the doctor. "The other one too."

"But that will leave you with just three," the g'Kek complained. "How will you walk?"

"I'll manage. Anyway, new ones'll grow back faster if you cut all the way back to the bud. Just get it over with, will you?"

Fortunately, he had managed to land on two legs spread apart at opposite sides of his body. That left a tripod of functioning legs to use, dragging himself from the fluttering tangle of fabric and gondola parts. The moonlit mountainside had been rocky and steep, a horrid place for a blue qheuen to find himself stranded on a chill night. But the beckoning glimmer of flashed messages, darting from peak to peak, encouraged him to limp onward until he reached this sanctuary.

So, I'll be able to tell Log Biter and the others my tale, after all. Maybe I'll even write about it. Nelo should provide backing for a small print run, since half of my story involves his daughter. . . .

He knew his mind was drifting from starvation, thirst, pain, and lack of sleep. But he could not rest now. If he did, he would lose his place in line, right after Jeni Shen. The station commander, hearing of his balloon adventure, had given Blade a priority just below the official report on the rocket attack.

I should be flattered, Blade thought. *But in fact, the rockets are used up. Even if there are some left, the element of surprise is gone. They'll never succeed against the Jophur again.*

But my idea's not been tried yet. And it'd work! I'm living proof of it.

The smiths of Blaze Mountain have got to be told.

So he sat and fumed, half-listening to Jeni's lengthy, jargon-filled report, trying to be patient.

When the amputation began, Blade's cupola withdrew instinctively, shielding his eye-strip under thick chitin, preventing him from looking around for something distracting. He tried pulling his mind back to the time when he briefly flew through the sky . . . the first of his kind to do so since the sneakship came, so long ago.

But a qheuen's memories are not often strong enough to use as a bulwark against pain.

It took three strong hoons to keep the leg stretched out straight enough for the medic to do it clean.

Lark

A second stench greeted him when he waked.

The first one had smothered cloyingly. When it filled the little room, the world erased under a blanket of sweet pungency.

The new smell was bitter, tangy, repellent. It cleaved the insensate swaddling of unconsciouness, like a sharp light spearing through darkness. Lark jerked upright while his body convulsed through a series of sharp sneezes. There was no transitory muziness of confusion. All at once he knew the cell, its metal floor and walls, the cramped despair of this place.

A greasy doughnut shape—purple and still covered with fatty mucous—sent a final stream of misty liquid jetting toward his face. Lark gagged, hurriedly backing away.

"I'm up! Cut it out, dung-eater!"

The room wavered briefly as he turned, searching . . . and found Ling close behind, wheezing at the effort of sitting up. Livid marks showed where Rann had throttled her, nearly taking her life.

That reminds me . . . where's Rann?

In moments he spied the Danik agent's bare feet, jutting from beyond the rotund bulk of Ewasx.

Ewasx? Or is it still Asx?

The ring stack shivered. Trails of waxy pus trickled down

from twin wounds on either side, where the vlenned rings had made their escape.

I could try to find out . . . try talking to—

But Lark saw an *orderliness* to the trembling toruses—a systematic rhythm, almost regimented. Warbling sounds escaped the speaking vents on top.

"H-h-h-alt. humans . . . I/WE COMMAND . . . obedience . . ."

The voice wavered unevenly, but gained strength with each passing dura.

Ling met his eyes. There was instant rapport.

Asx had gone to a lot of trouble to provide gifts.

Time to give them a try.

"STOP THAT!" Ewasx adjured. "You are required to . . . desist . . ."

Fortunately, the Jophur's limbs were still locked in rigor. The lowermost shivered with resistance when the Master Ring tried to make them move.

Asx is still fighting for us, Lark realized, knowing it could not last.

"Use the purple one," he told Ling, who cradled the larger of the newborn toruses. "Asx said it opens locks."

She lifted her eyes doubtfully, but presented the ring to a flat plate beside the door. They had seen Ewasx touch it whenever the Jophur wanted to leave the cell. Meanwhile, Lark used his shirt as a sling to carry the smaller, crimson torus. The one so cruelly injured by Rann. The one Lark was supposed to deliver to the High Sages—an impossible task, even if the mangled thing survived.

A moan echoed from behind Ewasx. It was the Danik warrior, rousing at last. *Come on!* Lark urged silently, though Ling almost surely had never used such a key to force a lock.

The purple ring ooze a clear fluid from pores near the plate. Clickety sounds followed, as the door mechanism seemed to consider. . . .

Then, with a faint hiss, it opened!

He hurried through with Ling, ignoring bitter Jophur curses that followed them until the portal shut again.

"Where now?" Ling asked.

"You're asking me?" He laughed. "You said Galactic ships are standardized!"

She frowned. "The Rothen don't have any battlecruisers like this. Neither does Earth. We'd be lucky to glimpse one from afar . . . and even luckier to escape after seeing it."

Lark felt creepy standing half naked in a metal alien passageway filled with weird aromas. Any moment, a Jophur might enter this stretch of corridor, or else a war robot might come hunting them down.

The floor plates began vibrating, lowly at first, but with a rising mechanical urgency.

"Just guess," he urged, and tried to offer an encouraging smile.

Ling answered with a shrug. "Well, if we keep going in one direction, sooner or later we're bound to reach hull. Come on, then. Standing still is the worst thing we can do."

The hallways were deserted.

Occasionally, they hurried past some large chamber where Jophur forms stood before oddly-curved instrument stations, or mingled in swaying groups, communing amid clouds of vapor. But they rarely moved. As a biologist, Lark could not help speculating.

They're descended from sedentary creatures, almost sessile. Even with the introduction of Master Rings, they'd retain some traeki ways, preferring to work in one place, relatively still.

Lark found it weird, striding past closed doors for more than an arrowflight—then another, and a third—using their pass-key ring to open armored hatches along the way, and meeting no one. *Asx must have taken this into account, giving us even odds of reaching an airlock and . . .*

Lark wondered.

And then what? If there are skyboats or hover plates, Ling might understand their principles, but how will she operate controls made for Jophur tentacles?

Maybe we should just head for the engine room. Try to break some machinery. Cause some inconvenience before they finally shoot us down.

Ling picked up the pace, a growing eagerness in her steps. Perhaps she sensed something in the thickness of the armored doors, or the subtly curved wall-joins, indicating they were close.

The next hatch slid aside—and without warning they faced their first Jophur.

Lark felt an overpowering impulse to spin around and run away. The thing was bigger then Ewasx, with component rings that shimmered a glossy, extravagant health he had never seen on a Jijoan traeki. *The way Rann compares to me,* Lark thought numbly.

During that brief instant, his companion lifted the purple ring, aiming it like a gun at the big Jophur. A stream of scent-vapor jetted toward the stack, which hesitated for a moment . . . then raised up on a dozen insectoid legs and sidled past the two humans, proceeding down the hall.

What was that? A recognition signal? A forged safe conduct pass?

He could imagine that Asx—wherever the traeki sage had concealed a sliver of self—might have observed all the chemical codes a Jophur used to get around the ship. What Lark could not begin to picture was what kind of consciousness that implied. How did one deliberately hide a personality within a personality, when the new Master Ring pulled all the strings?

The Jophur rounded a corner, moving on about its business. Ling met his eyes and together they both let out a hard sigh.

The airlock was filled with machinery, though no boats or hoverplates. It seemed too soon to worry about that yet, as they closed the inner door and hurried to the other side, applying the trusty pass-key ring, eager to see blue sky and smell Jijo's fresh wind. If they were lucky, and this portal faced the lake, it might even be possible to leap down to the water. Surviving that, their escape might be cut off at any point, once they passed into the Jophur defense perimeter. But none of that seemed to matter right now. The two of them felt eager, indomitable.

Lark still cradled the injured red ring, wondering what the sages were supposed to do with it.

Perhaps Asx expects us to recruit commandos and return with exploser-bombs, using these rings to gain entry . . .

His thoughts arrested as the big metal hatch started rolling aside. Their first glimpse was not of daylight, but stars.

An instant's shivering worry passed through his mind before he realized—this was not outer space, but night time in the Rimmers. A flood of bracing, cool air made Lark instantly ebullient. *I could never leave Jijo,* he knew. *It's my home.*

A pale glow washed out the constellations where a serrated border crossed the sky—the outline of eastern mountains. It would be dawn soon. A time of hopeful beginnings?

Ling held out her free hand for Lark to take as they strode to the edge and looked down.

"So far, so good," she said, and he shared her gladness at the sight of glinting moonlight, sparkling on water. "It's still dim outside. The lake will mask our heat sign. And this time there will be no computer cognizance to give us away."

Nor convenient breathing tubes, to let us stay safe underwater, he almost added, but Lark didn't want to dampen her enthusiasm.

"Let's see if there's anything we can use to get down to the lake, without having to jump," Ling added. Together they inspected the equipment shelves, lining one wall of the airlock. She cried out excitedly, a few duras later. "I found a standard cable reel! Now if only I can figure out the altered controls . . ."

While Ling examined the metal spool, Lark felt a change in the low vibration that had been growling in the background ever since they escaped their prison cell. The resonance began to rise in pitch and force, until it soon filled the air with a harsh keening.

"Something's happening," he said. "I think—"

Just then the battleship took a sudden jerk, almost knocking them both to the floor. Ling dropped the cable reel, barely missing her foot.

A second noise burst in through the open door of the

airlock. An awful *grinding* din, as if Jijo herself were complaining. Lark recognized the scraping of metal against rock.

"Ifni!" Ling cried. "They're taking off!"

Helping each other fight the shaking, they reached the outer hatch and looked down again, staring aghast at a spectacle of pent-up nature, suddenly unleashed.

Well, so much for jumping in the lake, he thought. The Jophur ship was rising glacially at first, but the first few dozen meters made all the difference, removing the dam that had drowned the valley under a transient reservoir. The Festival Glade was transformed into a roiling tempest. Submerged trees tore loose from their sodden roots. Stones fell crashing into the maelstrom as mud banks were undermined. While the battlecruiser climbed complacently, a vast flood of murky water and debris rushed downstream, stripping everything in its path, free to pour toward distant, unsuspecting plains.

Too late, Lark realized. *We were too late making our escape. Now we're trapped inside.*

As if to seal the fact, a light flashed near the open hatch, which began to close. An automatic safety measure, he figured, for a starship taking off. Lark barely suppressed an overpowering temptation to dive through the narrowing gap, despite the deadly chaos waiting below.

Ling squeezed his hand fiercely as they caught a fleeting glimpse of something shiny and round-shouldered—a slick, elongated dome, uncovered by retreating waters. Even by dawn's pale light, they recognized the Rothen-Danik ship, still shut away within a prison of quantum time.

Then the armored portal sealed with a loud boom and hiss, cutting off the all-too fleeting breeze. Trapped inside, they stared at the cruel hatch, sharing the dismay of shattered hopes.

"We're heading north," Lark said. It was the one last thing he had noticed, watching the ravaged valley pass below.

"Come on," Ling answered pragmatically. "There must be some place to hide aboard this bloated ship."